POLO
Players Only Live Once

Mehmet Ali

Cadmus Publishing
www.cadmuspublishing.com

Published by Cadmus Publishing
www.cadmuspublishing.com
Port Angeles, WA

ISBN: 978-1-63751-408-5

Table of Contents

I saw you in the sun.
I fell backwards into your universa, in your inertia and vice
versa.
Possibilities and probabilities and viabilities,
Taking my abilities to try and really be that isle of flattery so you
believe that I'm not just who I seem to be.
Believe in me.
Or be free of me.

PROLOGUE

They say if you smoke too much it'll make you stupid and if you drink too much you'll get soggy and drown. But I drank and I learned how to swim in profound waters and I smoked and then flew up from the desert to a wide oasis overlooking the heavens. So to all the warnings I say, if. Days in prison are full of what ifs, a little curious magic that brings the players inside something to talk about so we can keep our heads held high. All the times I missed, those days I never saw, I spotted them in the universe of unknowns where fantasy murders reality.

Now here we go again.

What if this girl named Bandy and my old lady changed places? What if my woman was really that pretty thing with the milky white spot on her mouth? How would it be if me and her were the ones shacking up trying to get by? How would all of Bandy's cognac skin feel in the bedroom?

This fantasy is so forbidden that I might have just left it alone if my best friend never started asking questions. He had a needle in his arm. His baby cousin working behind the tattoo gun stopped drilling long enough to look over at me for an answer.

"What are you doing to these girls brother? How does it work, Cerrio? Tell me what you're selling them so I go out and play cards every night like you do."

I took a hard pull on a long menthol and said, "nobody's selling anything. I just make it do what it do. They give me a little bit of their money from the club and I invest it. They take care of me on the back end. Nobody's selling anything. At least not me."

"Do y'all go dancing?"

"Why would we go dancing?"

"I mean do you take them out? Movies, dinner, stuff like that?"

"No, we don't anywhere. Besides a little grocery shopping that's the most that we get out."

"Interesting," he replied. "Very interesting."

Desirée pressed down the foot pedal again. "Sounds just like something a pimp would say."

"I don't know why you guys are talking like this. I really don't. I told you I'm trying to help the girl."

"How? By selling her the lie that she actually needs you for something?"

"Desirée, that's what you think? That I'm running down a lie to steal money from my woman?" I pointed at Socks sitting in the chair. "Ask this man what he knows about me. I bet he tells you I get my own paper. I don't need to cheat her."

She sucked her teeth. "Your fucking woman. I'm sure. You got no job, no car, no place to live. But she has all of that."

"Calm down," muttered Socks

"No, let her finish. I want to hear how this ends."

"She doesn't need you," said Desirée. "But without her you're ass'd be out in the street. It's men like you, Cerrio. Deadbeat bastards always keeping a good woman down. You're using that girl. The other one too. You got out of prison and found two sweethearts to sell themselves so you don't have to work for a living. I bet all you do is sit up in that hot ass apartment and get high every day."

I jabbed my cigarette at her. "Watch your mouth. I don't have to use anyone and that girl will give me whatever it is I want. Problem is you're just not listening. Because if you were you'd see that this ain't about me it's about her. She said she wants to start a business and I'm just out trying to help her build something for the cause."

Desirée scoffed. "Socks, where did you find this boy?"

"Please, Dez. Just do the tattoo," he mumbled.

"Who's the boy?" I asked.

"Is he serious cuz? Trying to build something for the cause? Trying to help her out? Are those the lines he's serving that poor girl?"

"Fuck off, Desirée."

"No, fuck you coward! A real man would have at least had it in him to admit he's taking her money all for himself. Give her a chance to fight for it at least!"

"That's funny because I know you wouldn't fight me for it."

She jumped out of her chair. "Wanna find out? I ain't one of those dizzy little bitches working hard to keep you all warm and fed! No man in this world will ever take anything from me! That's facts!"

I smiled. "Sounds like you got daddy issues."

She was raging, a hundred degrees coming straight towards me like a magic carpet on ball bearings. Socks got in the way and snatched his cousin off her feet before the fireworks could start. He held her by the waist while she screamed about killing me from the very bottom of her lungs. Even if walls could talk they still wouldn't repeat all the things that got said. All of which I'd heard before, although some I forgot a long time ago.

She was digging deep, taking it all the way back to prison. Talking about how my girl must be desperate or slow or both for trying to buy a future from someone who will never be anything but a number. Socks held on tight. His chest leaking ink and blood while he did his best to keep her from unleashing havoc. "Get out of my house!" she screamed. "If you ever come back I swear to Jah I'll kill you!"

"Calm down," said Socks. "Nobody's winning right now."

And I said, "it's all good brother. That's the best thing she's said all day."

I walked to the refrigerator. Dez, yelled louder. She was spraying spit from her full lips and peeling Socks skin away like he was an orange. I knocked over the milk on the top shelf and took a beer. My best friend just shook his head. "Come on dawg, you're just making things worse." I nodded to him. "Amen to that, brother."

I don't want to put a hand on Desirée. That's not my style, never has been really. I'm not a pimp either. But the insinuations were tickling a sense of rage inside me that had been building up long before this girl ever turned around and started going nuts. Because it seems like no matter how far I go or how many dues I pay there's always more punishment waiting right up ahead. And right now I'm just dying to punish something back.

She kept clawing at Sock's arm until little streams of red made trails down his elbow. My partner knows I hate beer but he watched me drink deep from a bottle simply because the spite felt delicious. It was good enough to crawl underneath his cousin's skin the same way she did such a good job of getting down under mine. I wiped my mouth with the back of a hand, she stomped her feet deep into the carpet. I took the whole six pack out the front door with me, she swore a list of death threats on her father's grave. All of her fury spilled out on the sidewalk and scared the little birds off of her neighbor's mailbox. Some days I pray for a rage like that, the kind people spill blood just trying to hold back.

I think somebody is going have to tell truth about judgement one day. It is not off limits on this earth, it is not reserved for the great Creator and the everlasting hereafter. Judgement is right here and now in the present. There are no rules to it either, all anyone needs is a belief about you. Sock's baby cousin judged me in the harshest light and hit me in a spot where it hurt the most. While I held fast on the surface reality was I hadn't felt good about me and my girl's relationship in a real long time, for most of the time, maybe more often than not. I knew what type of responsibility I carried, the damage I had done. I knew I was part of her unraveling. Other people might circle the drain but not my baby, she circled around me.

The other five beers grew warm in the front seat of her car as I drove them across town. Seeing them sweat reminded me of the first time me and my baby got drunk together. I was flying blind and the day was hot as inferno just like it is now. I dropped ice cubes in our Michelobs because they spent all day baking in the trunk of my aunt's car where I had stashed them the night before. She watched me do it and then laughed herself into a fit of tears. After we got tipsy then she promised not to tell everyone at school that I was such a square.

Out in front of her apartment I passed Desirée's beer out to a crew of sun beaten men in long sleeved jumpsuits. They were Mexican workers, olive skin, dark hair, immune to the scorch of a thick, Carolina summer just like me. Biggest difference is they pressure washed siding in the heat of the day while I scrambled for a living. They all wanted to know my name. "No names," I said. The oldest of the crew looked at me strange and asked if I was from "the company."

All the amigos started talking at once. Don't ask me what they said. In high school there was a Spanish class I had to take for my diploma except I don't have diploma. From inside the car I watched them figure it out, one by one they gave up caution. Gave up on suspicions of me being from "the company," whatever that means, and started drinking. The oldest told a story through broken teeth while the rest adjusted their sweat stained hats. When the yarn was all spun then each one broke out in a smile. When the beers were finished the empty bottles were left in the back of the work truck and while the fellas got right back to pressure washing. It must be amazing to find happiness in such small things like an honest day's labor. I know a little bit about it, not the work but the small things. Staring at the water running down the wall in glassy, tainted rivers took me straight back to the land of taboo.

I see Bandy cuddling and soft touching. She's that type of girl. One who sometimes shows her claws on the outside but is always warm in the middle. Maybe we get on each other's last nerve for sport and fight with the same energy just like two people who hate each other. Then, she might cook up dinner to make amends or maybe to lightly poison me and I'd go out and buy her sparkling gold jewelry to drape all over that fine, black body. She could wear the drip with no clothes on, pile her hair up high and ride hard on top of me until her body sang out like Billie Holiday.

She could be my Queen of Sheba, I could be like King Solomon. We could have dripping wet sex in the temple and take offerings like the church. She might go tell all her girlfriend's that I'm no good and of course I would agree because that's the common consensus. The fast lane could be our permanent home, only time we might want to slow down is to plot our own excellence.

I turned on the radio and thought about my woman upstairs. My real woman. The one in my life today. She was up there right now, always upstairs, always waiting. Except right now I needed something else. I needed another lady in the moment like real change needs a whole lot of time to take effect. And no matter how long it took my girl would be there waiting for me in the exact same place. So, I put her car in reverse and backed away slow and then pulled away faster and then I was gone before she even had a chance to catch me.

Chapter 1

CHEVY JAMES

My first time in a strip club and it's a slow night. Slow enough to remind me that I want everything right fucking now which has always been the case ever since the beginning and which will probably be my fast track straight to the end. The girls still dance, though. They dance no matter what because no matter what someone is always there to throw a few dollars around in the air. Except that's not me. I just came here to celebrate and been told in no uncertain terms to keep my money far out of it. My best friend didn't give me permission to spend a dollar on anything tonight, not a lap dance, not a shot of liquor, not even twenty dollars to throw in on the hotel room later when we leave here with something nice on our arms.

I don't plan on breaking any of his rules either. It's perfectly okay for me to just sit here and watch these dancers for free all night or from now until the last part of forever if life is really good. Permission though, I mean what is that? I never asked for any before because if I had then we wouldn't be here. That's what this celebration is all about. Breaking rules, suffering consequences, coming back for more.

Socks brought me to this little club called Sugar Bares tonight as a way to say welcome home. He's my brother in a way that brotherhood goes deeper than family and he knows I don't need permission for anything. We go back to a junior high school classroom throwing paper balls to the front at a teacher just wishing to retire. Back before we were delinquents and back then I thought we made ruckus but now I know better. The ruckus is in us, on us, sometimes against us. It's all over our names like sand on a long, white, stretch of beach.

My brother promised to pay for everything tonight per his word. His word is good too but the girls are working hard in here and I'm a firm believer in hard work. So, while nobody's looking I slip a fistful of ones from my pocket and throw some on stage. The pretty redbone in gold platforms rewards me with a slow backslide down the pole and then I let go of the rest.

I like this little place called Sugar Bares. The play on words in the name is amusing. I like the bar where drinks are poured underneath dim lights without a lot of questions asked. I like the dimes on stage doing the most with their bodies with zero clothes on. I like that they don't close shop until the last person in here is ready to call it a night.

An exquisite beauty in tall heels notices that I don't spend enough. She's built for dancing, lithe with strong calves and a flat stomach that makes her body glitter twinkle like shooting stars when she steps through between tables. She's the darkest thing in the club. A plush, chocolate, vixen. A wizard on the pole. The type who never leaves home without a plan either. I watch her come over flashing a smile lit up by gorgeous white teeth. She puts both hands on my shoulders and throws a velvet, black, thigh north over my waist just to give me a peek up the middle. When she lowers down in my lap I instantly feel a fever striking up.

That's another thing I like about this place. A club like Sugar Bares in the middle of North Carolina is about the only place you can touch a dancer. Try this anywhere else and you're eighty-sixed and maybe not on your feet either.

When I grabbed Chocolate's waist that big smile went up two shades brighter and she cocked her head to the side. She starts out calling on a holy name. "Jesus, and here I was worried you weren't enjoying yourself." A curtain of silver hair slid out from behind an ear and brushed across her shoulder.

"Shy much?" she asked.

"Not really. Why?"

"Because all these pretty girls in here are just begging for your attention. Like that one you been watching on stage. I guarantee she won't turn you down."

"Good to know," I replied. "But I'm content. You ever heard of that before?"

"Huh-unh, I never tell what I hear." She winked. "That's my rule. Maybe my only rule."

"I get it."

"But?"

"But you're pretty ambitious for the silent type."

She threw her head back and laughed a little too loud. "Baby, you know it. 'Cause I'm here for a reason. But enough about little ol' me. What do you like?"

"Me, I'm simple. Just don't think too hard about what you're going to do next."

Chocolate liked the banter. It was refreshing like that first drink of cold milk right when you wake up in the morning. At least that's what I thought when she took me back to the back to a room set up with two leather couches the color of fire and a bottle of champagne. The couch on the left against the wall was completely empty. The other one had a big surprise in it. Her name was Seville.

I know Seville. We went to school together, me, her, and Socks. But we don't call her that and that's how you know we really know her. A long time ago in way that seems like only yesterday we started calling her Chevy because Seville is too long and cutting it down to Sevy wasn't sexy enough. Anyway, freshman year somebody yelled Chevy down the hallway one day and she turned her head and that's about all I remember from high school. That and that back then we had a childish love jones lasting all the way past her graduation before it crashed to a stop when I rode off in chains three years ago.

At some point I realized the obvious. This isn't a two for one, its a set up. Chocolate isn't hanging around to watch the ball drop either. She's a ghost. Gone right back out on the floor before the tension in the room can reach its apex. I thought about following her because I know this could get ugly. The door is right there, just put one foot in front of the other and get lost before my cake gets baked in this red leather oven.

Except I couldn't run away. After Seville watched me walk in we locked eyes and right then it was over. She crossed her legs and put on a face that wasn't sweet at all. We weren't sharing a moment right then, we were matching glares like two sworn enemies. She's looking for something and I know what it is. She wants to see the glint in my eye that says I still love her. Right now I want a lot of things. Among them a place to call home, a trip to paradise, a chance to make up for a lot of lost time. All that is right in front of me, all that and more and all I have to do is ask. But I'm a man and I have this pride, the type that swells up whenever it sees a challenge coming over the horizon. So for a while we just sit there and stare.

I was still thinking about following Chocolate out the door when Seville hopped off the couch. She moved from one side of the room to the other fast like a sprinter and right into my lap before I could even blink. Those soft lips pressed so hard against mine it hurt and our tongues found each other like a compass always finds north. She worked her mouth over mine until she knew every part of me was all hers for the taking. It was like the girl had been waiting her whole life for our kiss on that couch. Through her barely there underwear she felt me pushing up against her more and more and when she knew I was hard as I was ever going to get then she pulled back and slapped me straight across the face.

The sting of pins and needles was hot on my cheek before I even noticed her hand following through. This woman, just as passionate about hitting as she is as about kissing and twice as fast. I rubbed the red mark on my face and asked what it was for. "Because you're an idiot," she said. "Because you didn't come see me when you came home." Then, her voice goes soft. "Because I missed you, Cerrio."

"Hey, I was going to come see you."

"Uh-huh, but you didn't. You came here instead so you could see some ass."

"This was Socks idea. He wanted to celebrate me coming home."

"So I guess you didn't want to celebrate anything with me then."

"I told you. I was going to come see you."

"Yeah, like when?"

In one smooth motion I pushed her out of my lap and stood up. "We're not doing this. Three years ago you made a decision to sign off and that outfit you got on right now tells me there's really no regrets about it."

She looked up at me from her place on the VIP couch. Two honey brown eyes pleading, aching, seething, all at the same time. Those eyes are two dripping wet pieces of candy shining like gold money in the light. On some lucky nights I see them looking to me in a dream and when I wake up I can't remember anything else.

"So that's it then? You're just gonna come in here and throw me away, right? No hug. No, hey Chevy how ya been? Just judge me and hurt me and hurry back out the door to go find something to take home tonight."

I shook my head. "Nice try, but you're the one who threw me away. In prison when I needed you the most you just up and disappeared."

"Is that how you see it?"

"I see it the way it happened."

There's a long moment of silence and then a great, big, sigh. She said, "I just wanted to see you and say, hey. Maybe that wasn't such a good idea. I don't know. I got to go, though. They're going to be calling me up to the stage any minute."

She rose off the couch and flipped some hair back. I sniffed and the air in here wasn't like the rest of the club. It was thick with cheap perfume and heavy with something more passive, aggressive. A part of me really likes making her upset. It tickles my dark side to think about getting even with the woman who left me on a whim. Revenge isn't coming though. Chevy swept it under the rug when she reached in her top and pulled out a thick roll of cash. The money was new, dark green with a little bit of shine and dead president's face staring away into nothing. She handed it over with a strained smile spread across her lips.

"It's good to see you, boo. Have a good time out there tonight."

I took the gift, turned it over in my hand. A half inch roll of fifty dollar bills curled in a hair tie is more than a surprise. It's proof that even though I was gone I was definitely not forgotten.

It's coming home money. Getting started money. I never stopped loving you money. While I studied it she slipped past me on her way out the door. She never lied about being due up any minute. When I stepped out right behind her the DJ was warming up the crowd with a practiced intro read straight off an index card. He gave the house a rundown, called my baby a homegrown, homegirl with plenty to offer and it was hard for me to tell deep down inside whether to laugh or be livid.

Everything is different on the other side of the room with the couches. Its like a whole different world out here. The lights are dim again, drinks are pouring, hands are clapping, music blaring. We were so much safer alone by ourselves with that bottle of champagne. Now that we're back in the thick of things all the hype of revenge is gone. Some part of me that isn't fit for getting even just wants to grab her, hold her, find out what's wrong and rub all the tender spots that hurt. The very last thing I want to do is let this reunion go. In fact I don't ever want to let anything go again.

I catch up to her in the small corridor and grab her by the wrist right where the arm bone makes that hard knot under the skin. Chevy spun that guitar shaped body all the way around like a top so we were face to face breathing on one another.

"What?"

I balked. "So that's all I get is a pissed off what?"

"Look, I don't have time for games Cerrio. Just tell me what you want."

"I want to know what you're doing here."

"I'm working. Now, let me go."

She tried to snatch her wrist away but I kept holding on tight.

"I'm not letting you go until you answer my question. This ain't you. Why you doing this?"

She put on a face that looked a lot like trouble. "Do you really want to know?"

Shit. I knew I had waived the right to be mad no matter what came out of her mouth for an answer. Chevy didn't let the pause last long before she said, "I'll tell you at two o' clock." I said, "What happens at two o' clock?"

"That's when I get off and I'm all yours. For as long as you'll have me."

I brought the Cutlass. She loves the Cutlass. Chevy tells me the blue-gray paint brings back old memories, I told her the peanut butter leather in the backseat is a good place to make new ones. The car belonged to my Aunt Denise ever since I can remember. Monday mornings she used to drive it to work and on Friday nights I snuck it out of the driveway to go play grown-ups with a long legged girl named Seville James. She remembers those times, back when we were kids and they called a family ride. Now we're all grown up and the Cutlass is a classic.

Those days were fun. Once upon a time when we were hot and clumsy, making messes but somehow always keeping the upholstery clean. But these days are fast.

At two in the morning she still had me waiting. Forty extra minutes died on the clock before I saw her come out of Sugar Bares side door in a black on black tracksuit and the same heels she wore up on stage. I heard them clack, clacking on the damp parking lot asphalt like pony hooves trotting all the way home.

We drove out to her apartment complex by the YMCA. The Cutlass was barely off before her clothes got lost. Seville's body is just like an hourglass, curvy in the middle and ready every time. She unbuttoned my pants but left the underwear alone. Classic Chevy, always wants to make me work for it. The rest went little by little. First I rubbed my hand down over the softness between her thighs. She purred until my palm was wet and then a light moan escaped her lips when she watched me touch my tongue to a tip of a finger. "Oh, you're nasty," she said. I shrugged to it. "Some things just never change."

She smiled and kissed me like I was going off to battle. The woman smelled like Christmas, like cinnamon and spice cake with a fat splash of vodka. When her mouth came off mine she had a breast in each hand. I watched close, my hardness pushing against her fire as she worked from the bottom of both C-cups up the stiff bronze nipples in the middle. She pinched them hard between her French tipped nails and then tugged a little and bit her bottom lip.

My shaft flexed. It hurt to be him, all cooped up just begging for a dance. I finally freed your highness and touched him against the luscious, dark, spot deep between her thighs. She watched it swell until I ached and then ran one of those French nails up the backside. I grabbed her wrists and pinned them to the steering wheel. She followed my lead, gripping the grain and pushing her chest all the way out just so those heaving breasts could brush right against my lips. I gave each side its own attention. A little left and a little right, licking, kissing, sucking until goose bumps rose up on her collarbone and she shivered in the heat.

Pretty soon the Cutlass was a steam kettle. Our bodies grew stickier under the warm tones of tall streetlights fighting to illuminate this long awaited revival. All the fog growing up the windows made the sex deliciously dirty, vulgar as porn, beautiful as a carol. When she didn't want to play anymore then she slid me inside. She was naked but the heels stayed on, knocking against the dashboard and the door handle in an up tempo that started slow and worked its way into a incessant throb.

She rode hard on top and I kept her hands on the wheel thrusting back with every inch. Every time our bodies crashed together something glowed in her eyes, a helpless, pouty, shaken look that drives every man crazy when his woman is splashing down on top of him with unkempt aggression. When we collided together those brown sugar, nipples danced in tight, little, circles right in my face. Winding like bike wheels until she came and then a lifetime of pent up fury flooded all over my lap. She was a goddess on fire. Spreading her legs to the brink, arching her back to the wheel just so I could feel everything she had to bring. And she brought and she brought and then I brought and I had my hands on her waist gripping harder and harder until she made a little squealing noise like an alarm that told me to lighten up.

When it's over she stays on top and stirs me around inside of her.

"You're ain't going home yet are you?"

"No. Not until you answer all my questions."

But Chevy knew she didn't have to answer anything. In fact she didn't even try for any explanation until the sun came up the next morning in its place in the east.

Not that I was pressuring. We went up to her apartment and she did all the things I liked to keep me occupied. We sexed, drank Hennessey. Did it again and drank some more. She did the womanly thing and worked me over nice and slow until dawn with the baby making music playing the entire time. The sandman came and got us while we were somewhere between half drunk and listening to Marvin Gaye talk about sexual healing. Before the cozy heat of slumber took me down into its bosom I heard Chevy James whisper three little words up against my chest.

"Welcome home LaDecerrio."

CHAPTER 2

43-DIMES

"Do you ever wear clothes?" I asked

The smell of breakfast opened my eyes. When I actually got out of bed she was gone, off in the kitchen whipping up grits just like her mother used to with cheese and a pound of sausage. When I came in Seville was standing over the stove topless, long wooden spoon in one hand, green bottle of Tabasco in the other. I watched her fix a plate, listened to her hum a tune, stared unabashedly at the amble backside as it flexed underneath a pair of arctic, white panties when she reached up for a glass from the very top shelf.

She loaded me up a wide Correll dish and set down hard on the table. "Do you want me to go put a shirt on Cerrio? Is all this bothering you right now?"

"Not even. I'm just curious."

"That's funny. I thought I worked all the curiosity out of you last night."

"That's not what I mean. I mean I'm curious about this new you. I never knew a Chevy like this before."

You know that moment right after you realize you just fucked up? That's what came over me next. She gave me a stare between mad and hurt and said, "I see."

"See what?"

"Tell me something, Cerrio. Do you still love me?"

I put my arm on the chair, elbow hanging over the back a little bit. "Now, how come you get to ask me that?"

"Because I want to know. People change. You just said it yourself, I'm not the same Chevy you're used to. So let's find out. Does my heart really beat in your chest?"

"Hold on, you never answered my question from last night. What are you doing dancing around at Sugar Bares?"

She ignored me, sucked hot grits off a fingertip and turned away. "I'll be back," she announced. Then, I had to watch her switch down the apartment's narrow hallway until she disappeared all the way out of sight behind the bedroom door where we knew each other last night.

After she was gone there was nothing. I knew this sort of nothing, it was familiar to me, so very cold and absolute. No noises, no scents, no shadows doubling back across the wall. Seeing Seville depart reminded me of that day I had to go away. It was hard in that place made of concrete and steel but it was a lot easier than dealing with these emotions.

The woman should have known better, of course I loved her. The fact that she went to work at a place so far beneath her and how it burned up my patience like a book of matches didn't matter at all. Or at least not too much. At least not enough to forget about all that we used to have before.

Because even though I hated the way she made a living I'd still rather have her in my face railing with anger about making it by any means necessary than have to think about her somewhere brokenhearted and lonely. See, because nobody can love Seville the way I can. Others can try and I'm sure they all did during my time away. They probably came bringing flowers and cards and they were probably all dappered down like a villain in a movie. She might have ate their fancy chocolates and saved their roses in a vase but that was all a pittance. They didn't pass notes to her in the hallway during ninth grade and a little bit of tenth. They didn't drive her to cheerleading practice even after dropping out of school or listen to her body fears when her arms started getting longer and thinner and she thought her figure was starting to turn into Gumby's. No, they didn't, but I did, and I've been sincere to the woman since before she ever was one. Since the genesis of Chevy James.

Before my feelings made me get up she came back from the bedroom. A blue shirt covering her up with a little, green, gator riding high on the chest holding his mouth wide open. I squinted hard at the logo. "Is my tennis shirt?" I asked it like I actually played the game. Like I really knew the sport instead of just recognized the clothes.

She said, "no. This is the shirt you left behind when you went away. I packed it up with all our other stuff after the landlord evicted me from our apartment because I wouldn't sleep with him. Of course I could have paid the rent but that wasn't an option either." She pulled on the collar. "This is the only thing I had left because someone stole everything out of my car when I was at a job interview trying to get $7.25 an hour at your favorite restaurant."

"What's my favorite restaurant?"

"Wherever I'm serving."

"Fair enough. But why didn't you just move back home, though?"

She poured herself some orange juice and sat down at the table. "Home he says! Jesus, is he for real? My daddy hated you. I mean haaated. When I walked out of his house to go live in yours it was with the full understanding that I could never come back."

"And he told you that?"

She flapped her hand. "Please, you know he was never that nice. He told me I was a prostitute and it was against his religion to live under the same roof with something so heathen. He called me the spawn of the devil. Or maybe it was the pawn of the devil. I don't know. Either way the man never went to church but he was always sold out on his own holiness."

She took a small sip of juice and kept on going.

"Anyway, the shirt is mine. You might have bought it but I earned it. When Wendy's gave me that first paycheck I cried. Then, I went over to Sugar Bares with this on and got hired on the spot. I couldn't do the nine to five thing, Cerrio. Not if I wanted to make it. So, after the club owner put me on the stage that first night I just never looked back."

The truth hurt bad. A thousand years in jail couldn't make me feel as defeated as she did in just under a minute. Another part of our history is that before going to prison and after dropping out of high school I moved from home to a place where I could peddle my dope bags much better. I told Seville to join me in the fray. She came obediently on a whim and a promise that I'd take good care of her. Now here we were, up in her apartment looking at each other for a new place to start.

"Alright your turn."

I blinked my eyes. "What? My turn on what?"

"I answered your question about why I strip now you answer mine. Do you still love me? Or am I the bitch my daddy always said I was?"

I jabbed my fork at her face so hard Chevy almost fell out of the chair trying to avoid getting stabbed. "Don't ever say that. Matter of fact you're not even allowed to think like that. Not even when you're alone all by yourself. I don't care what you did or what your goddamn daddy said we're not entertaining that. You understand?"

She gave me a face, a turned on look that almost brought us straight back to what we did in front of the YMCA last night.

"Are you hearing me Seville?"

"Of course, baby. I hear you. And there won't be no more of that, I promise."

She lived by her word but I swear to God if she hadn't then we never would have moved back in together. We didn't plan on it, the eloping just sort of happened while neither of us was paying attention. I started coming over in the afternoons to hang out, spending the night to have fun, then one day I just forgot to leave. Next thing is we're grocery shopping together on Saturdays, me pushing the cart while she navigates the store with a list of items scrawled out on yellow paper. Even with all that it still didn't hit me until we took a trip down the pasta isle. Chevy pulled two boxes of Ben's rice off the shelf and held them up for me to see like on The Price Is Right. "White or yellow?" she asked. I pointed to the yellow and somehow that made our thing official.

We were happy and that stands out above everything because besides our botched history we were chronically poor. It was easy enough, though. She just wanted me to drop her off and pick her up again on the nights she worked and stay at home with her on the nights she had off.

All that was in the beginning, when there was nothing but stars in our eyes, before little things snuck up on us like shades of distrust. I was quietly selling dope again and she was clipping coupons from the Sunday paper. Even though she danced five nights a week somehow we were always still hanging by a thread. Not that I could say much with a box of baking soda stashed in her kitchen cabinets. Common sense said "keep it simple." She never said a thing about the white residue on her silverware so why get messy? Rich or poor this life was still good. Just keep picking her up and dropping her off at the club every night and things would be okay and then fate came to ridicule us in the dead heat of July.

One night I left Socks in the middle of a dice game on Booker street and pulled into the club parking lot right before the big hand on my watch reached the top of the dial. Chevy always popped out of the side door of Sugar Bares at two fifteen sharp. No more heels clacking asphalt with the sweatpants on. That was only for special occasions when she wanted me to see her toes. Now it was a two minute walk through the parking lot in low top

Filas and by seventeen after she was buckled up next to me and we were gone like yesterday's sunset.

But that night two fifteen turned into two twenty-five and then ten minutes later there was still no Chevy coming around the building. I sat in her little, yellow, Passat with all the windows down. Evenings don't mean cool air in North Carolina but it was more than bald heat that was making me sweat. Seville running late felt strange because we operated so much like clockwork. Two fifteen side door opens, two seventeen we're gone. I can admit that I was worried sitting there in her car. Preachers say it's a sin to worry but they also say life is a sin. They say you wake up the morning and you're already wrong before you can even wipe the sleep out of our eyes.

The closer my watch got to three the more I sinned. Other girls came out and stayed in pairs, only stepping to the shadows to spark an after work special. Then they came right back to the light through a cloud of smoke.

Tiny pearls of sweat blossomed on my upper lip. I wiped them away with one hand and white knuckled the steering wheel with the other. All the bad things that could happen to a girl and all the inherent, ugly risks that came with being a fine dancer shook around in my head like chickpeas in a beanbag. They grew louder than the sirens racing through the city's front streets. The only thing making more noise than my fears were the minutes still ticking down to nothing on my watch.

Ten seconds before I lost my mind Sugar Bares side door swung wide open like a yawning mouth and she came out, looked around, spotted the car and beelined towards it in her soft soled balling shoes. Chevy walked alone even though I told her a thousand times that she needed to get a buddy like all the other girls. "You never know," I said. "People are crazy out here." Saying things like that you never think how you might be talking about yourself.

She didn't talk when she got in the car, just stuffed both hands in her hoodie pockets and looked straight out the window. My baby is a moody thing, been that way ever since the start of ninth grade. She might ice me out all the way home and then we'll make love in the shower. But when I put the Passat in gear all the sudden Chevy had something to say.

"Wait. Hold on a minute."

I frowned with my face half hidden in the dark. "Why? What are we doing?"

"Nothing. I just need to get something."

A second later the side door popped open again. The metal pushbar went back with a sound like a janky gun being cocked. Those sparkling eyes right beside me went straight to the woman coming out and I stared too. Sometimes a man just came help it, worst part is there were no features to see from the spot where we were sitting. Just a silhouette gliding towards us underneath the club sign's flickering neon light. The walk teased me, those hips twisting like a cat on a fence were a preview to paradise. She swung them east to west runway style while I tried my hardest not to blink. I knew that strut from somewhere, I just couldn't tell the place until she came around the Passat's left side and looked down in the passenger window.

"That guy wants to know if he can pay you with a sack," said Chocolate.

Seville's voice came out in a whisper coated with thistles. "Half and half," she replied. "I need the money. Rent's due."

Chocolate nodded and I said not a word as the girl who offered me a bogus two for one once upon a time stepped off to go collect. She walked back through the parking lot, into the club's front entrance and came back out the side again before the song on the radio even changed. The fast rotation might have been amazing except I wasn't in the mood for surprises. She did her signature strut one more time over to passenger's side of the car, reached a manicured hand in her pants pocket and came back out with it clutching a bag of white powder and a few crinkled bills. The dark girl put everything in Chevy's open palm right through the window and when she pulled back, I reached over and snatched it all away.

"What are you doing!"

"You better turn that question around." I looked dead into those honey brown eyes reflecting desperation. "What are you doing?"

Chocolate slinked away. Seville fired back.

"Come on Cerrio, don't play games. You know what's going on up in there. You know the city. This ain't nothing new."

I put a finger to my chest. "I know what's going on? Is that what you just said?" I held up her night's payment. "Here's a hundred dollars in cocaine that I know is definitely cut to shit. And fifty more in cash. You're out here every night spreading your legs for peanuts and you think I know all about it? You think I give this shit my approval?"

"How do you know it's cut?" she asked.

"What?"

"The powder. How do you know it's cut to shit?"

"For real? That's the thing you're most worried about?"

"Well, you're supposed to be the expert."

"Shut up!"

"Fuck you, Cerrio! You think you got it all figured out. You think this is all so goddamn easy? You can't do what I do. You don't even have a life!"

"Look at you, out here every night working for scraps. Ridiculous. Why don't you just get a job bagging groceries at Food Lion?!"

"It's not like this every night Cerrio."

"Whatever. You'll say anything."

I threw the drugs and money at her, she scrambled to scoop the bag up first while I put the Passat in drive. Chevy was bent down trying to pluck her cash off the floor when I mashed the gas pedal hard with my foot and her head thumped against the dashboard like somebody threw a book at our side fender. We screeched out of the club parking lot in a thin cloud of burnt rubber. She let out a whimper when the bottom scraped the sidewalk and sparks kicked up but she held her peace and we made it home in record time. Racing through the city at three thirty in the morning I don't know how we didn't get pulled over by the cops.

Looking back it seemed so miraculous but I wish miracles could be more flexible from time to time.

Back at the apartment there was no sleep. I was too angry to lay down and Seville was high as a kite five minutes after walking in and throwing her bookbag on the kitchen table. I stayed away from her, sat alone in the dark in front of the TV with the remote in my hand. She left me there to be upset with no interference. A good call because I had lots of ugly regrets that I had no business taking out on her. Personal debts buried deep inside that couldn't be repaid in money, only actions, strictly change. It's just that I wasn't ready. Or if I was ready to change then I just didn't know how.

I thought about her pitiful payment over and over again just to kill myself a little more inside. Seville with the golden eyes didn't deserve to live like this, she should be away at some university graduating with a degree or in a magazine posing for a spread. Chevy could be anything. She had the body, the brains, the face, but she also had an addiction poisoning her soul and his name was LaDecerrio Lloyd.

When she told me that story in the kitchen about the blue shirt I secretly thought about how she should have listened to her daddy. He had it right from the beginning. His daughter should have been running in the opposite direction back when we were kids, far away from me and into her dreams and then things would have been so much different. Maybe not for me but definitely for her. She could have been anything but instead she was right here with me. Regrets don't pay the bills though, and so here we are, shouldn't be together but we can't stay apart. So what do we do?

What do we do?

After a while the silence gets to her. Chevy comes in the living room and stands next to the TV with a hand on her hip waiting for me to acknowledge her presence. When that fails then she tries at being nice.

"Hey, you want me to fix you something to eat?"

I ignored her, just kept staring at the television, didn't say a word and I didn't know she had a wooden mixing spoon in her hand until she flung it at my face. Naturally, I jumped off the couch.

"What are you gonna do Cerrio? Huh?"

"Throw one more thing in here and see what happens."

"Oh really? Let me tell you something I'll throw whatever the hell I want whenever I want because this is my house. And you're not just gonna sit around here and ignore me. You're mad. I get that. But that ain't no reason to be mean. 'Cause I been nothing but good to you, Cerrio. So if you want to have an attitude then you can just leave."

"You know what? That sounds like a good idea."

So, I started towards the door. After the first two steps she was right on my heels.

"Where you going?"

"I'm leaving. Taking the option you gave me to get out and dodge. Right now."

A smart man would never turn his back on his enemy. I unlocked the apartment, turned the knob on the entrance and pushed open. In the smallest hours of what was left of the night the sky was pitch black. It was the darkest part, the hour just before dawn when the birds are pulling sleepy worms out of the dirt for breakfast. I took one step out into it and immediately felt two fists crashing on the back of my skull.

I turned around and she swung again. Chevy's hands are little but fast and viciously strong from gripping the pole every night which made her bony knuckles against my jaw feel like a bag of rocks being hurled off a roof right at my face. I weaved the next one and she threw a right cross but I caught her wrist and held on tight.

"Stop it!" I yelled.

"No, you stop it. I can't believe this! First sign of trouble and you want to run away from me!"

"You're high. That bad coke is messing you up."

"You're an asshole. Prison messed you up."

"We went on like that for a while. Screaming like fiends do in a back alley with better and better insults that cut closer to the bone. She broke free a few times and threw some hands. I never hit back but every second or two I'd have to push Chevy into the wall before she could plant both feet and get in her southpaw stance. At some point I caught both of those delicate wrists again and shook her up like a Magic 8 Ball.

"Quit it! Calm down!"

She whipped her head back and forth like she had a demon inside and screamed fuck you like it was the chorus of her favorite song. From the next apartment over a little Asian lady stalked us from her doorway. When my baby and I finally got tired of warring with each other we noticed her staring in stunned silence at the melee going down. She pulled her head back into the apartment like a scared turtle going back in it's shell. When the door shut I heard the deadbolt slide in place decisively.

"You know that lady?"

Chevy shook her head. "I never even knew anybody lived there."

"Maybe she just moved in. Shit, I got to go. She probably went to call the cops on us. You know soon as they find out I'm on parole it's straight to jail."

"I'm coming with you."

I let go of her. The fistfight immediately became thing of the past, water under the bridge. Now we were partners in crime trying to get away from the scene before the police could respond to a sure thing. She grabbed the keys off the table and we fled down the stairs two at a time to hit the road all over again.

True enough this thing of ours seems strange. Truth be told sometimes it feels strange to me too, otherworldly almost how we relish so much in the drama. At least we're not bored, though. Maybe crazy but not docile and when the dust settles we're actually a little better than we were before. Because something about the crucible of adversity never fails to take a strong thing and make it twice as solid.

I drove Chevy's yellow Passat all the way out to the interstate headed west towards Tennessee. She didn't say a word. No questions about where we were going or minor complaints about driving too fast. We drove with nothing but the nonstop sound of the engine humming in our ears. This wasn't uncomfortable silence, more like a dull quiet to think about something or anything or maybe nothing at all.

I glanced over at the passenger's side and saw her gazing up towards the pink and purple hues painted across the sky.

"That's us," I said.

She whipped her head around fast like her neck was broken. "What are you talking about? What's us?"

"The sunrise. See those different colors mixing around up there to make the perfect picture? That's how you and me are."

Chevy shifted in her seat. "Say whaaat? Is Cerrio getting sentimental on me right now?"

I put up a hand in surrender. "You know, we were all good when it was quiet. I'll just say you're right and I ain't gonna say nothing else. Promise."

"Ah, come on, I like the poetry side of you. All lovey dovey and stuff. It's cute. Except we're the same color though."

"What?"

"Mm-hmm." She held her arm up right next to mine. "See."

I took my eyes off the road to check and sure enough our skin tones matched exactly. It was crazy, I could have been looking at one arm. Uncanny but it then again it made perfect sense.

She laughed. "Uh-huh, told you."

"Alright, so if we had a baby how would it come out? Three of us can't all be exact same color."

"There's no rule against it."

I tipped my head back and forth. "Maybe. Maybe not. It just don't seem right, though."

"Well, in that case I guess it depends on who's genes he gets more of."

"Wait, how do you know it's a boy?"

"Please, you think I want to raise a baby girl just like me?"

"I don't know. It might not be that bad. You were pretty good growing up."

"Is that why you were trying to run away from me just now?"

A mail truck crawled in front of us. I got in the left lane to get around it but then my foot stayed stuck on the gas. We rode faster and faster, blazing through the sparse early bird traffic like a jet headed for takeoff. I wasn't even thinking about it until she put a hand on my thigh. "You know you can't just speed down the road every time you get mad at me."

I sighed, pumped the brakes. She was right. I looked at her for a half mile, no makeup on like she wore in the club just the tones of her natural flesh in the day's first light. I said, "Seville, tell me you got a plan B, because if you don't then I'ma have to go. We're close as baseboards are to the floor but I can't just stand by and watch you pop it at Sugar Bares from now until forever. You got to understand that. You got to see how it's too much for me to carry around. It's not all a pride thing either."

We rode in silence again, went deep into the quiet. A mile, then two, on the third she responded. "I always dreamed about having my own salon. That's something me and my mother used to talk about all the time. She liked the idea because I said I'd do her hair for free."

"I remember your mother. Beautiful lady. How's she been?"

"She passed last year. Some new strain of flu put her in the hospital and she was gone in a week."

"God, I'm sorry. I should have asked you about her a long time ago. I feel like shit now. We been together for weeks, I should have realized you weren't calling her or anything. Shit, I'm sorry, Chevy. You're mama really was a gem too. But it's all the more reason for you to put the dream together. In her memory."

She scoffed. "There's no money to put together anything for anyone's memory."

We passed a billboard that caught my attention. I looked at it until it got too close to see.

"You know something, that just don't seem right. How much you make at Sugar Bares every night? On average."

"A little more than two hundred fifty. Some goes to the owner, though. It's like you gotta rent the stage."

"Uh-huh, and how much goes to powder?"

She paused. "I don't know."

"Bullshit, you know. Come on, be honest. How much?"

"Maybe half."

I nodded like I understood and then made a decision. "You're done working there."

Chevy looked at me like I just bit her arm. "And what are you going to do, Cerrio? Sell crack out of my apartment until we can afford to buy a studio?"

"Get for real. I'm going to take you down to 43-Dimes and you're going to get a gig on stage there."

"What do you know about strip clubs? What makes you think 43-Dimes is any better than the place I work now?"

"Because they put up billboards on the fucking interstate. You ever seen a billboard for Sugar Bares out on the road? You ever seen one anywhere?"

Chevy James the high school graduate sat back and searched her head for an answer that wasn't coming. I waited on mute with my hands on the wheel at 5 and 7 because there wasn't anything else to say after that. After a quarter mile she reaches across the gap between the seats to rub away tension in my shoulder that I didn't even know was there. That's her way of saying we're okay, that she agrees with me even if she only concedes. That's progress. Our progress. And we kept on riding straight into the new dawn.

CHAPTER 3

LESBIAN HOUSEGUEST

I heard about a place on the Southside, far back in a cul de sac with tall weeds growing where you can go missing real easy without too much notice. Because winning is simple, it's getting away that's the hard part. At the casino security guards walk you out to your car and wish you a good night. In the city of Winston-Salem, North Carolina a good night is a new winner coming home from the gambling house all on his own under broken street lights. There's a .40 caliber under my shirt, he's always with me in case somebody just can't stand to lose. I never shot anyone with it, or if I did then I don't remember, or if I remembered then I just can't tell you. One thing you learn pretty quick is that nothing in this city is actually for certain.

Socks told me the poker games in the basement always have legs. He said you could play all night if your money is long enough. The place was easy to find. The Caprice on the lawn had wheels shined up like a brand new penny and the ship gray paint on the porch was peeling off like a weekend sunburn. Me and four other men sat around a small table in the bottom of the house. There were no other games tonight, just us staring at our cards trying to add something up while a blue nose pit named Psycho wandered around the basement clicking four, fat toenails on the cement floor.

Poor dog. They must have been feeding that thing dynamite and Ritalin ever since it was a puppy. Psycho had muscles all over even in his forehead and every time someone reached in their pocket for anything his ears went back flat against his skull. I hate cages because I've been in a few myself but it was hard to focus with a panting animal like that moving around freely. In my hand were two jacks and down my pants was the loaded Llama in case the pit bull went bananas.

The players on my left were greener than that spit of grass growing in the front yard. They called every single bet each and every time. The guy on my left had pure luck on his side, the type who couldn't be beat. He should have been a stick of gum so he could never lose flavor just like he refused to lose a hand. The one in the middle kept looking at me more and more as the game went on. The looking wasn't lost on me, it meant somebody at the table couldn't afford to lose. You know what they say, there's always got to be one.

Except here there was two because I couldn't afford to lose either. I got up. Stretched out. Told the fellas I had to take a piss. Nobody protested my exit but the constant staring never stopped. In the bathroom I counted out my winnings. Four hundred and ten dollars spread out on top of the toilet tank. Not a fortune. Chevy could slay that at the mall in a cool three minutes, but luck can't be pressed, so four hundred and ten was going to have to be good for tonight.

I splashed water on my face from the faucet and tucked the cash. Flushed the toilet for good measure in case somebody was listening and used the loud noise as cover to check the slide on my pistol. Before leaving I had to give the house his cut, fifteen dollars for every hundred won downstairs. If I don't pay he'll never know but Psycho had sharp eyes and his long, doggy nails were already clicking up the basement steps.

I paid what I owed and told the houseman to invest in real canine food. You know, some kibble, steak, maybe whatever's leftover on the kid's plates after dinner. Anything besides pills and gunpowder. But they don't take good advice on the Southside and I guess they don't give none either because halfway across the street I heard trouble talking at my back.

"Man, where you going?"

"Catch me next time," I said and kept right on pushing up the cul-de-sac.

"Motherfucker, just gonna run off like that? Ain't gonna let me win my money back?"

"You're not listening. I said 'catch me next time'."

"Where you going, though?"

"Got to go pick up my girl."

"Where she at?"

"Working, she's getting off right now. Catch me next time!"

"So, you ain't gonna let me win my money back?"

I pulled the Llama off my waist, whipped around and let off a rocket. I knew the voice at my back belonged to whoever was staring a hole through me down in the basement but even if I was wrong you still can't let anybody follow you alone at night in a city like this. Especially when they ain't taking no for an answer.

The .40 bullet went into a mailbox post spraying fat, wooden splinters all over the gambling house lawn. The player who couldn't win scrambled behind an SUV on rims and sent me two back. Both his shots smashed into an old Thunderbird resting by the curb. The big Ford rocked side to side on its springs like a tiny sailboat lost at sea.

My pistol doesn't shoot peas but what I had still couldn't move a 5.0 cloaked in steel. The shooter aiming from across the street was playing with a cannon, maybe it was something I had never seen before since coming home from prison. I don't know. All I know is he kept on drilling. Three shots rang out after I ducked behind the rust eaten fender of the ruined sports car. He squeezed another one into the heavy Thunderbird in a spot dangerously close to the gas cap and the sturdy springs beneath all four wheel wells creaked back like loose floorboards. I didn't see the second bullet but I heard the third as it buzzed right past my ear into somebody's flowerpot and clay shrapnel exploded across a weather beaten porch covered with roaches in heat.

This isn't the first time something like this has happened. Coming home with someone else's money is always like coming up the wrong side of the mountain from the shallowest part of town. I let off my response at the truck where the poker loser was trying to take cover. He pointed around the back of it and tried to fire another burst from whatever he had when my first shot caught him up high in the shoulder. Fresh blood splatter reached all the way across the Lincoln Navigator's back window and the shooter went down clutching his right arm.

I raised up and moved down a row of houses that were caught in different stages of alright condition and boarded up for destruction. The .40 roaring the whole time as I tried my best to get off the street before someone spread my thoughts all over the sidewalk. It was imperative to fade away fast, a matter of life and death. But before I could get far someone came out on the gambling house porch looking to end it all. The shadow upped a gun longer than my arm and then I heard paws scuffing the street like brass tacks on a marble floor. That's when I knew I was in over my head. A poker loser with a hurt shoulder, that I can handle. But me versus two shooters and a wild animal on the other side of town named Psycho, that was plain suicide.

I aimed for the new gunman's head, missed and shattered the porch light instead. Broken glass tinkled everywhere and when he ducked low then I took off running. All around me rounds skipped off the street, sparks lighting up the night as they crashed to a stop on the unforgiving road. Psycho was three steps back and moving like a race horse, barking and slobbering without any fear of getting shot in the face or the ass from either side.

I raced to the car. Dove in the front seat and prayed to God it didn't end up suffering the same fate as the old Thunderbird all riddled with holes. If I get shot that's one thing, call it occupational hazard. Shit like that comes with the territory. But if my

Chevy's ride takes a slug in a shootout by the gambling house there will be hell to pay. A hot one sailed past the window while I was jamming the keys in the ignition and burrowed itself deep into a telephone pole. I saw the next one take Psycho's head away while he was on the driver's side glass smacking his heavy paws in a mindless frenzy.

Dead dog in the street and it could have been me. Instead I turned the Volkswagen on and left a strip of rubber by the pit bull's twitching tail. The gun was too hot to go back on my waist so I slid it under the seat on a thru street right as a cop car flew by going in the opposite direction. I said a silent prayer of relief when he didn't turn around in my rearview mirror.

When the Llama cooled down then I realized he was empty. Seville is going to be ill when I tell her that I need more bullets. She knows I have to have them, though. Because a gun without ammunition is just a liability. Out of the two of us she's the only one who can go buy them without risking a brand-new prison sentence. She doesn't like it because there's something about a stripper in heels with a box full of shells at the checkout counter that makes eyebrows go up every single time. But even if she hates making the run she won't ever say no. Chevy is reliable, she'll get them no matter what because at the end of the day, at the end of it all, when the dust finally settles, we always want to see each other again.

First she has to warm up, though. She needs to melt down a little so she can slide around in my hand like a wet ice cube. A pharmacy three blocks up from her apartment stays open all night. They sell top shelf orange juice for bougie dancers and white roses and cards with glitter on them for when a man needs a woman to do a little something extra for him. I take all that plus a bottle of peach nail polish up to the counter where the white kid behind the register stands frozen like he's trying to play freeze tag.

I don't understand these people, they see a dark face in the middle of the night and right away think its a robbery. When he asked if I was alright of course I said "yes." What he should have asked me is if I wanted paper or plastic.

Out in the car I dug around for a pen. When one turned up I put the card on the dashboard to write out a message for that flower of a woman in my life throwing shade under her petals. Sitting in the pharmacy parking lot in the middle of the night with one leg hanging out the door I tried thinking up a master-piece. Except there was nothing to say. The words, they never came, creativity didn't blow in on the breeze. Instead hot wind whipped through the car and stung me high in the arm. The pain made me angry but it was the mental block that made me furious. I threw Chevy's writing pen as far as I could across the parking lot and watched it skip to abandonment right in front of the store. Looking at the white shopping bag in the passenger's seat I realized a candle probably would have been better. Candles don't need words but cards need a message and right now I didn't have one to save my life.

For all my little tantrums there's comfort back at the apart-ment. A big dose of it on the living room couch with two smooth legs folded to the side. She was all into a movie about an old photograph that makes two people fall in love in the bayou of Louisiana. A southern coast romance story. It's a perfect fit for her. I don't know how but it just is.

Bandy doesn't turn around when I come in. I haven't got that type of regal influence for so much focused attention. Instead she keeps her eyes on the movie and talks over her shoulder like a bus driver calling out the next stop on his route.

"Is that you, Chevy?"

"No, it's me," I said, "the other half."

"Oh."

"Damn, don't sound so depressed about it."

She waved a hand. "My bad. I thought maybe she came home early. How was your night?"

"Exciting."

Bandy is a bronze skinned girl with a thin body and soft cheek bones. She's got curious features like a cat, sharp eyes with knife point corners at the ends and a small nose that curves out so gently it doesn't even cast a shadow. She started showing up around the apartment one day maybe two weeks ago. When we first met she was sitting in that same place on the couch putting gold polish on her toenails. It was in middle of the day and I had just woken up and there she was, this woman built like a reed with a quarter sized white spot right next to her mouth where the pigment was blank. She had a knee under her chin and her foot on a piece of newspaper gently putting coats of color on her feet and when I approached I swear to God it took all of me not to lean down and press my lips against that pretty pale spot on her face.

Kissing that girl would have sent us one of two ways, to heaven or the hospital. Chevy keeps a cute .32 up on the top shelf of her bedroom closet, a girl gun, and she would have gladly put Barbie bullets in both of us had we been caught liplocking on her sofa. Around town I had a little freedom. She couldn't say much by virtue of how she made a living, but the home front was strictly off limits. We had a pact, she didn't bring home any tricks and neither did I.

Anyway, Bandy was too good for all that doggedness. She stripped and smoked a little a reefer but that was mostly to get her through college. The stripping and the smoking. Plus, she worked out an hour a day and spent most of her time over here at the apartment doing homework. Not that school makes you a good person, not that exercise does either. Thing is Chevy trusted her. Sometimes Bandy would be all alone around here by herself and sometimes she'd be with my girl in the back bedroom sipping liquor and giggling while me and Socks watched ESPN out on the living room couch. She never abused the trust granted to her, never tried bringing any johns from the club over here for a good time like the place was all her own. She knew about loyalty which is so, so much more than I can say about most people no matter what it is they do for a living.

Bandy didn't say anything else to me. Her attention went right back to the movie where an old woman was looking at the black and white photo through the screen door on a porch. On the other side was her young granddaughter standing there waiting for the memories to wash over both of them. I watched for a second, thinking about how something like a picture can become its own character in a movie. Sort of like how guns and cards have their own theater roles in my life.

Tonight's action meant south Winston was off limits. It meant I had to find another spot on Mondays which wouldn't be so bad if there weren't so many ducks coming through that run down house laid back in the cul-de-sac. Take the good with the bad, though. At least I didn't come out like Psycho. As long as the paramedics weren't scraping me off the sidewalk with a shovel everything else could be figured out after a while. I just had to think about it which is exactly what I did as I sorted through the junk in the pharmacy shopping bag.

The orange juice went on the bottom shelf of the refrigerator. Flowers and card went on the counter. Nail polish went with me to the living room.

The peach acrylic wasn't for Seville. It was for Bandy because that gold stuff she kept slapping on didn't do her toes any justice. She had this special look, something classy with a thrill that usually only comes from pictures in a magazine. The type of thing that makes old people say, "they don't make them like that anymore." That metallic gold was killing it, though. The color was all vengeance, too much edge ruining the vanity. I know they say if it ain't broke don't fix it but this girl's vogue needed some real mending.

"Don't look now but I got you something."

Bandy tore her eyes off the television and sat up. "My God, what is that?"

I held out bottle of peach like an offering. "This is your color. Trust me just try it."

"No, fool. That."

She pointed up to my left shoulder and I followed her finger to the end of my sleeve. Bandy was frozen just like the boy at the pharmacy. I guess dark colors are a hell of a thing no matter who you are, especially the shade of wet crimson running down the side of my T-shirt.

"Shit, I got shot. Look at that. It didn't even hurt until right now."

Bandy stood up to examine. She touched my sleeve. "It looks like they grazed you. It's still pretty bad. You're going to need stitches."

I cleared my throat. "Stitches huh?"

"Yeah, probably no less than ten. Maybe fifteen. And let me guess, you can't go to the hospital with this."

"I mean...yeah, I can go. But I'm probably not coming back after the uh, procedure is done."

"Procedure huh? Sounds ominous. Where does Chevy keep the first aid around here?"

"First aid?" I blew out a sigh. "First aid. First aid. First...aid."

I thought about the question too long. We didn't keep nothing like that around here. Closest thing we had to first aid was hot water, cotton balls and a bottle of vodka.

Bandy shook her head like we should know better, then she left. Went out to her car and brought back a box with a red cross silk screened across the top. She popped it open and the works were in there, gauze, scissors, tape, bandages, little packs of alcohol wipes. Ten minutes later I was sitting at the kitchen table shirtless taking shots and getting put back together again.

She was good for an amateur. Every time the thread went down and in through my skin I watched the muscles underneath that white spot on her face ripple softly. The cream circle was so easy to get lost in, it was sexy and roguish all at once. It called for attention even if you didn't want to give any and even if you knew it was rude to stare you still had to keep your eyes right there anyway. Like a drop of milk in a sea of coffee it demanded focus, maybe undeserved, maybe even inappropriate. Until you realized the darkness all around is what made the light part beautiful.

Bandy caught me looking but she didn't make a big deal about it. The stares weren't anything new to her, she was used to reckless eyeballs. I just hoped mine said something much, much different than all the rest.

"So what happened?" she asked.

I took a drink of vodka. "Told you. I got shot."

"And what were you doing before you got shot?"

She saw me looking again, this time it was a sideways glance from the corner of my eye. When it registered Bandy immediately quit working the needle.

"I'm not the police, Cerrio."

"I know you're good people Bandy. It's just we never talked like this before. Thing is I'm always at the gambling houses winning. And tonight somebody just couldn't take losing."

She went back to mending me. "So you always win, huh?"

"Always."

"Sounds like a lot of luck."

I thought about about the blue nose laid out in the street. "Lucky enough I guess. Where did you learn how to sew people up?"

"My girlfriend's a nurse."

"You said 'your girlfriend'?"

She looked up. "Yes, I did. Does that bother you?"

"I don't think so. Should it?"

"Don't know why it would. Just like I don't know why it bothers some other people. I just wanted to make sure we weren't judging each other around here."

"Mama, look around. Does all this you see paint a picture of judgement?"

"You don't have to live better than anyone just to look down on them. It's not like it all has to make perfect sense."

"I guess when you put it like that then it does make sense."

The bottle went up to my lips again, then I thought twice and it came back down. "Bandy, I like you. I mean, I like that you go to school. I know you're going to do something major after you graduate. Just don't forget about us when the money starts rolling in."

She's not the type you get a second chance with, there's no do over's. So, when she put the last stitch in, tied the string off and said, "thank you" I almost spit my liquor back out.

"Thanks for what?"

She snapped off her latex gloves over the kitchen garbage. "Men usually only do things for me when I'm pulling my pants down. Then there's you out there getting shot just to bring me back a little, bottle of nail polish. I don't even like peach but I guess I got use it now." She smiled. "There's a million of them out there, Cerrio. But there's only one you."

"Hey, stop it. You're making me sound like a hero."

"Hell no, you're no hero. Just different that's all."

"Is that what Chevy says?"

She gave me a sneaky look and shrugged her shoulders. Bandy wasn't going to break any girl code. So, I let it go and she went back to the couch. In the middle of her walk is when creativity popped a flare. In the parking lot with the card on the dashboard it was bleeding out of the cut in my arm. Now the leak was full of thread and the message was caught at the seam. I took a pen from Bandy's school bag and she came back over to the table just to watch me put it all down letter by letter.

CHAPTER 4

HEAVEN'S CASH

I find you alive, glowing and cleverly gorgeous. You're so complete just like a masterpiece and just like a masterpiece nothing even comes close. You are a work of art only art is never absolute so there's a small place for imperfections but you are always, forever, and everyday flawless.

You find me alone, in straits and a little bit bewildered. Trying to figure out this thing called life in a sideways world that keeps steady tabs on every mistake. Except I can't blame the world for any troubles with me, the same way I can't give anyone else credit for us growing closer together. Am I too much for saying its my efforts that put a smile on your pretty, brown, face? Who knows? All I know is that making you smile is my greatest joy, and someone once told me true happiness is being good at what you love.

Chevy read the card two times, next morning we were out buying bullets. I parked her Volkswagen in the fire lane so she wouldn't have to go all the way across the store parking lot like the boy collecting carts for seven fifty an hour. Everybody watched her leave. Hips swinging, heels clacking, toting a double layered shopping bag with something inside that might save my life. It was just like high school, eight a.m. on the dot she would show up to class and we all took a moment of silence just to think about her.

Late afternoon found me and Socks leaned against her yellow Passat enjoying the last of the last part of the day. It was the best time of year in North Carolina, almost nine o' clock and the sun was still burning orange in the wide open sky. The days were longer now and the nights were twice as wild. Walk outside and you might see your shadow stretched out six feet long on the pavement. That meant pretty soon the heat would be unbearable around town and then there promised to be gunplay everywhere.

We draped all over her car watching the orange ball of flame slide down and out. I was smoking purple reefer, my partner stared away with both ears perked up waiting for a rewind about last night's shootout.

"Who had the long gun?" he asked.

I blew a cloud out in front of the sun. "I don't know."

"Who hit you in the shoulder?"

"Man, I don't know."

I passed the reefer. Socks took a long pull on the blunt that made a red streak run up the side and kept on going.

"Did you see the Caprice on the lawn?"

Yeah, it was the same place you told me about. They had a dog too. Big motherfucker, like a lion. Dead now, though. Someone sicced him on me and he got shot in the head."

"You killed a dog?"

I sucked my teeth. "Come on now you know better. I'd never do anything like that. They killed him trying to get to me."

"I can't wait to see those boys on the town." Socks made his hand like a pistol and took an air sight across the apartment complex. "Bam, straight to the face."

"No, no, don't start that shit. Because you shoot at them and then they shoot at you." I rolled my hands. "Then I shoot back at them and next thing you know we're all in a war."

My partner had heart, he kept a pistol on him just like me, just like Chevy. Chalk it up to a city thing. Anyway, the point is he could take care of himself. He was a shooter and a fighter, always had been since he could swing a punch and carry iron. I just didn't want to see him get cut short on account of me. I wasn't ready for my best friend's funeral just yet.

I looked at my watch and told him I had to get ready for the card sharks tonight. He was high and the more we kept standing around the more we were going to talk about making trouble until eventually we would talk ourselves right into a murder. Whoever grazed me probably robbed somebody this morning and had already moved on by now. Socks told me he wanted to go check out a girl he met living in Cleveland projects anyway. I told him to be careful. Cleveland projects ain't no place to be messing around late at night when the temperature is up.

After he was gone I closed my eyes. It was hard to know what felt better, this quick gasp of calm or the last rays of Carolina sun kissing down on my face. Maybe I was just high, dreaming purple sensations like the kind that make good ideas and bad decisions. When the reefer was gone then bass started knocking over by the complex stop sign. I opened my eyes as a Jeep with no doors moved around all the parked cars cooling in the dusk to fill the spot where Socks' Pontiac was just dripping oil. The driver took extra time getting out. She primped her hair, pushed up her breasts, added on another layer of lip gloss. A moment after those long legs swung out the driver's side then here came that signature strut in a tall pair of heels.

Chocolate walked up to me wearing a big, fat smile. Through her white tank top I could see a pair of Hershey D-cups rising up in the heat like oven baked biscuits.

She sniffed the air. "Mmm, smells good out here."

"Really? 'Cause all I smell is Clive Christian and cocoa butter."

"Oh, well I guess that's just me then."

"Perfect," I said. "So, what's up? What you got going tonight?"

"Nothing special. Just came to see your girl. She around?"

"Upstairs, getting ready for the club."

"Uh-huh, and what about you? Where you going to play cards at tonight?"

I rubbed my arm. "You know these jokers out here are really getting fed up with my luck. Might be time for me to spread out. I'm thinking about High Point."

"Go where you need to go, Cerrio. Just don't let none of these suckers put you down into early retirement."

"Never."

"Good, because I'm not coming to your funeral if you get killed by some loser."

"Goddamnit, is that how it is?"

"I'm just being honest," she said.

Chocolate is cool and severe and a little bit august, which means high class, and I'm wound up and high enough to see the rings around Venus. Chevy is upstairs in the apartment probably dipping into her coke stash getting ready for work. I know she thought she had it hidden real good in a lipstick tube. Only thing is the lipstick never got used but the tube was always getting moved around in different spots on the medicine cabinet shelves. I was going to take a little dip in it myself and Chocolate was right in front of me making that ass twist up every single step.

They stayed in touch after Sugar Bares, seems like my baby's relationships are always complicated. Each one comes with a touch of sin like a slow trip to the bottom. But if hell is underneath and the club is in between then heaven is this, two black girls in the kitchen with a roll of cash. When we walked in through the apartment's front door neither of them held back, they came together like magnets, hugged each other and talked about hair. At least I think it was about hair, every word from their conversation came out faster than I could even listen.

Chocolate thought Seville would go back to Sugar Bares, thought she'd see Chevy James return on hands and knees begging for her spot back on the pole. When that didn't happen then she started getting curious and asking questions like how is the money over at the other place? "Good," said Chevy. Of course it was, I'd never take my woman to any poor man's establishment looking for a job. Her tips paid rent and kept the pantry stocked and she even had a little left over to invest.

That last part peaked the dark girl's interest. Both perfectly arched eyebrows went up like gas prices always do on a holiday weekend. Chocolate wanted to know what Chevy had, she wanted opportunity. In the end that meant I took her money and worked the same magic for her at the card house just like I did for baby.

Out of all the money given to me I promise I never spent a dime of it on myself. If I asked Chevy would have handed it over. She would have given me the world on a soft, cashmere pillow if I desired but taking from her felt a lot like stealing, and I couldn't steal from my girl's dream. See, I knew her mother once upon a time too and her memory meant something real to me. She was a tall woman with deep mocha skin and ink black hair that stayed in a long braid down her back. It was hard to believe she was gone now. Chitara James understood that I was misunderstood even before I knew what any of that meant. Plenty of times when I came over to the house looking for her daughter she would sit me down and just talk to me like a mother talks to her son. She would fix me dinner even if I had already eaten. Then, when her old man pulled up the driveway she'd wrap my plate and shuffle me right out the back before Seville's daddy came storming in through the front.

A shop in Mrs. James's name was a worth getting behind. Such a solid aspiration that I almost wished I'd thought of it first. But it was good enough just to participate. I never pocketed anything meant for the cause, but I did take Chevy's money with me to the gambling houses every night. Now, if I lost then it would have been stealing but I don't steal and I don't lose. Not at cards anyway.

I asked if Chocolate was going to quit Sugar Bares and get a job dancing at 43-Dimes. Chevy told me she didn't know. All she knew was the other stripper showed up on Tuesdays with a crisp wad of hundreds for me to do magic tricks with at night. She never lied. I hung around long enough to watch a rubber banded roll of hundreds change hands from darkest to lightest before sliding off to the bathroom where things just got better.

There was no reason to open the medicine cabinet, her Maybelline tube was right there on the counter. I started realizing the benefits of cocaine after Seville became a hit at the new club. I was out in the streets more than ever now. You could catch me all over town hustling with my heart on my sleeve. Because me and these girls, we had an agreement never to let each other down. They loved me and soothed me and cooked my food and heard my problems and then put me back together again when all the streets wanted to do was tear me apart. My using drugs was for them because they kept me rigid in the face of the good, bad and the deadly. I can't say it was all business, admittedly sometimes it was recreational. But more likely it was a tune up. Just a line or three to get sharp before a long night on somebody's card table.

I looked for a straw. I looked for a hand mirror. I was looking so hard I tipped the lipstick tube over and enough powder spilled out by the sink to make up two good lines. The first one went up my nose through a rolled twenty-dollar bill. I waited for a minute before taking the other the exact same way.

The shit worked fast. One minute I was wiping my nose and the next a marathon was running inside my head. In the poor excuse for a vanity mirror right above the sink I saw myself and maybe someone else. We were together, both in the shower dripping wet with no clothes on. I blinked the vision away but my eyes were still bloodshot, my thoughts still dangerous.

From nowhere Chevy started banging on the bathroom door. "Cerrio, you in there?"

I snatched up her lipstick tube, capped it and threw it in the cabinet.

"I'm using the fucking bathroom!"

"When you coming out?"

"Right now."

I slammed the medicine cabinet shut but not before the tube rolled back out. I chased it around as it surfed the sides of the sink circling the drain.

"Hurry up!"

"Kill your noise! I'm zipping my pants!"

I caught the tube and got it back on a shelf, pulled the door open and there she was standing with hands on hips. "Cerrio, you been in here like, thirty minutes. What are you doing?"

"I'm pissing in the bathroom. Why you rushing me? Do I rush you?"

"I didn't hear the toilet flush."

"Jesus, you're worse than a detective."

She pushed on me playfully. "Shut up."

"I'm serious. Banging on the door like it's a raid. Asking me what I'm doing."

"Whatever. Look, me and Chocolate are getting ready to leave. She's taking me to the club tonight. So, uh, you can stay here."

I sniffed and touched my nose. "Is she coming to pick you up later too?"

"Nope, just dropping me off. She's driving to Greensboro anyway to see somebody. I'ma ride with her to save gas."

"I don't get it."

She crossed her arms. "Get what? What don't you get, Cerrio?"

"I'm the one who always puts gas in the car."

Chevy rolled her eyes and told me I was smoking too much. That might be true but I told her that getting high was the only natural way to put up with her because she didn't have it all. Incidentally she didn't take me seriously. She said, "I got everything you need and a whole lot more." Then, she smacked her ass and I smiled by a window painted shut because life is so strange. One night you're dodging bullets right in front of a dog, the next you're in heaven with God's glowing angels. Chocolate heard my girl's jazz and gave her a high five, then they both hip bumped in the kitchen and broke out laughing.

And I said amen.

CHAPTER 5

ZOO TRAINER

I liked Sugar Bares but I love 43-Dimes. Seville does too, she never says so out loud but she never has to either. The club owner was flamboyant but knew what was good for business. He took one good look at that tight body and almond complexion she was wrapped up in and gave her locker number one in the dressing room. From there things just got better, the money, the drugs, the clientele. The old Chevy reinvented herself, started dying her hair red and getting her nails done with little rhinestones in them. Her new look was cold seduction speedballing into merciless lust. I liked it and I worried about who else might like it too.

When she found more than one ride to work I kissed her round face for making my life that much easier. Bandy said I just wanted to use the car all night, but she didn't know how those shadows around the side of Sugar Bares were still a part of my nightmares. Ever since I caught my baby working for peanuts those smoky silhouettes scratched down my spine like icicles. In a deep sleep I saw the door of the old club yawning open like a demon's mouth, heard panicked footsteps falling on damp asphalt faster and faster until something made them quit. A lighter flicked to let a tiny, pathetic flame try for the world to cut through that tight fist of darkness. Then, the fire went out and I waited for the girl to come but she never made it. I see her running towards the light, a little piece even gets on her, just a touch of pale glow on the curve of a cheekbone before a hand snatches her back into the black well of fear.

So when I woke up to different divas around the apartment calling on Chevy for the carpool I felt relieved. They dressed in stilettos, popped gum to keep their lips moist because good coke always dried them out. When they came inside I watched carefully, of course they were too good at what they did to not notice. They caught me looking and asked my opinion. "Do these shoes look nice? Are my legs long enough? What do you think about this tattoo?" I approved more than I should have but whenever I was wrong my baby would tell them the truth one way or the other on the way to the club.

After the women were gone I took the Passat to the Circle K across the street. It was Tuesday again, Chocolate just dropped off a new roll of cash and I needed plenty of Aces to go to work with tonight, a few kings. Maybe even a joker if it was dealer's choice. Posted by the curb was Doorman. A vintage junkie I gave the name to because he always held the door for everybody when they went in and always asked for change when they came back out. Sometimes he had a girlfriend who hung around for a while when he had enough heroin to share.

I gave Doorman a job pumping gas. While he filled the tank I went in and bought decks of cards, red and blue, a Maverick, a Bicycle, and a cold malt liquor. Out in the car I opened up each box, pulled out every ace, king and queen and put them off to the side. The pump clicked. Doorman hung it up and came around to my window hopping foot to foot in anticipation of getting paid. It was hard to know what moved him more, strong dope or the fabulous touch of a woman. I never asked him, it wasn't my business to know. I just tipped the usual ten so he could go cop and get down to whatever made him feel better.

He rubbed the bill between his fingers savoring the feel of real paper money. "Thanks Magic."

"Who's Magic?"

"Man, that's you. Every time I see you in and out of here it's always with a bunch of cards like you're going to do a magic show." He squinted at the boxes on my lap. "Say, what do you do with all them cards anyway?"

"Now Doorman, I know you haven't lived this long being nosy, am I right?"

"Hey, no problem man." He threw his hands up in surrender. "Never seen a thing."

To show we were good I handed him the cold malt liquor in a brown bag and said, "thanks." Doorman took his drink and skipped back to the the store in time to catch a fat woman going in with two swollen ankles. And I went back to the apartment to get ready for anything. I spread the face cards out on the counter, threw the rest in the garbage. The losers laid on top of the trash like souls of the dead crying out for revenge. Justice is fickle though, especially because anything was possible now, a straight, a flush, maybe even half on a down payment for a condo in the city if my hands were smooth enough tonight.

If I lost it would have to be a reckoning but if Chevy saw all those number cards in her kitchen garbage there would be a rift through the stars. I took every one out of the trash and grinded them all down the disposal so she would never know the truth. After the last nine of clubs spun to shreds in the sink drain then the air in the room bent like a sail. There was a transfer of energy so soft and controlled it took all five senses too genuinely witness. It settled quietly on my shoulders like the weight of a hand. When I turned to brush it off there was Chocolate standing right beside me in the kitchen.

She wore a smile half crossed between tickled and heinous. I flicked a switch on the wall to make the disposal die slow. When the drain gargled for the last time then she finally parted her lips to say, "I just came back to get my phone."

"You scared the shit out of me. How did you even get in here?"

"The door was open. Your honey should probably tell the landlord about that latch."

"What's the matter with the latch?"

"It don't stick."

She walked back to the door and pushed it closed. A half second later I watched it creak open again.

"See? Anybody could just drop right in. Especially when you're in here grinding all types of evidence down the sink."

"I'll tell Chevy to call the Super. She'll get him on it tomorrow."

"I hope so. It's important to stay secure." Chocolate winked. "So, where you going tonight? Got any special places in mind?"

"I'm still running them ragged up in High Point. There's a hot streak up there for me that just won't quit."

"Oh, High Point's kind of far for me. But, um, the way you make it sound I just might have to take the trip."

"It's twenty three miles from here. Get on the highway you can be there in fifteen minutes."

"Well, it minus well be on Jupiter. I never had any good reason to go. Is it a nice town?"

"Depends. If you like furniture then it's right up your alley. They put a big wooden dresser out every year and try to sell it."

"My place needs new furniture. How big is it?"

"Bigger than that crazy looking Jeep you got."

She wiggled a finger side to side. "Don't make fun of my Jeep. My Jeep turns heads."

"You're making me wonder now. Is the truck really that bad?"

"I don't know. Want to drive it out to High Point and see?"

I narrowed my eyes. "You want to go to gambling with me?"

"All the sudden you're worried. It's only twenty three miles you said."

"I thought you just came by here to get your phone."

She pointed around me. "Right over there."

I turned around. Right there on the microwave a thin Samsung with a pair of lips on the case like someone was kissing ass.

"Are you going to hand it to me or what?"

Normally when a woman finds her phone she starts looking for missed messages, calls, all that, but not here. I passed the device to her a little less than arm's length away and Chocolate shoved it in her pocket without even saying thank you.

"So, we going?"

I shook my head. "That ain't happening. No way can I take you out with me on the road."

"Don't act like that, Cerrio."

My whole face frowned. "How am I acting?"

"Like a bitch can't handle herself."

"See, you say that now but something bad happens and then what? I can't stitch you up like Bandy did me and I'm not making any midnight runs to the ER for a woman who don't want to listen."

She took a long second to smooth out her wrinkle free shirt and then spoke slowly in a voice meant for wayward, little children.

"Let me ask you something, Cerrio. Where were you all of last year?"

"Ah, that's easy. Prison."

"And, what about the year before that?"

"Prison."

"And, the one before that?"

"Same place. What's your point?"

"All that time you've been gone I've been out here on my own. See, I'm not going anywhere. Because I been doing this forever. Before you or Chevy ever came around I had already been in the club every night and seen it all. In fact you might go somewhere before I do."

When I took my back off the counter that Clive Christian perfume I joked about before stood before me in a cloud.

"You're tough, huh? Let me guess. That stripper life made you hard and you got no fear anymore."

"All I fear is being broke."

"Good answer. I like it."

"Does that mean you're going to take me up to High Point so I can see how my money flips?"

"You want to watch me work, Chocolate? Is that what this is really all about? Do you just want to see me cook?"

"Your cooking is in the sink. And I ain't got nothing to do tonight. No appointments. No Sugar Bares. Nothing. That's why my phone ain't rang. Since you're getting ready to go to another city where I've never been maybe you might need somebody to watch your back out there."

I looked away at the refrigerator, at the calendar Chevy used to mark off her work nights. "You got a gun?"

"Is church on Sunday?" she asked.

Her Jeep had four-wheel drive, no doors and when it got up close to the light little, gold, flecks gleamed in the purple paint. Heads turned exactly like she promised. An Arabian gambler riding next to an Ebony dancer was a wild burst of neon that made the streets go blind as soon as they saw us. Everything they knew head dived off a cliff with no parachute when I steered that truck around the block. Chocolate relished in it, we were exotic together in a way that posing eccentrics only wish to be and she purely loved the feeling. I could tell by the little things she did. The way she had her hair swept all to one side showing off that long neck. How she kept checking the mirrors to find out who was watching us as we flew down the road.

For me this was normal. Just another day in the life. I've always been different, never been the same. Chevy James showed me how to embrace that anomaly. This isn't some sort of victory for me. I didn't choose the fate of being one in a million. But whether people love it, or hate it, or just plain don't understand means nothing. Just so long as they don't get in my way.

Pulling up in the hood outside Chucky's house in High Point earned us a lot of different stares. The crowd standing out front ogled openly with all kinds of looks from interested to bitter and of course fresh, fat, lust. She hopped out of the Jeep popping her gum and turned it on, then up. The crowd split apart like a fault line to let that signature strut get its swag on through. It was extra nasty, the hips didn't twist so much as they glided around in circle like warm butter in a sautée pan.

I've seen some women with a dynamic measured in bananas and their energy is nuts. A few of them were on Chucky's porch holding red, plastic cups but right now they didn't count. This wasn't fruit and grains, this was pure sugar melting right down into syrup. Every eye moved side to side following that body. A wife slapped her husband's face, somebody else whistled. The men were gone before Chocolate even made it up the steps, the women saw me and just wanted to know how we met.

I lied to her in the beginning but back then it was hard to know how that could be the start to so many things sinister. Truth is High Point hadn't seen me in a real, long time. I hadn't gambled here in years. It was on my to do list up near the top but tonight the dancer out front had made it number one.

Chucky didn't recognize me at all. He hadn't seen my face in years just like the city. That wasn't unfair, I hardly remembered him either. Three calendars in prison makes a man forget friends and towns but enemies and debts don't fade away so easily. I never owed Chucky a dime which is why he didn't say hello right away when he answered the door. The old man glared at me with two suspicious eyes peeking out from under a blue-black fedora. He touched his hat and chewed on a cigar. I could see him itching for the pistol on his hip as he squinted at me through one, long, lazy loop of smoke.

"Really, old man?" I shook my head in fake disappointment. "Is that how you treat a good friend?"

He squinted even harder. "Cerrio, is that you? What the hell?"

"The one and only. Did you miss me, old man?"

He pushed the screen door wide open to give me a hug. "Miss you? Shit, I almost shot you!"

"Shoot me? Man, that's cold. And here I thought this whole time we was like favorites, Chuck."

"Don't take it personal." We backslapped some. "You know you're like family to me. Shit, I like you better than some of my own cousins hanging 'round here. It's just I ain't seen ya in a while. My memory's bad" He lowered his voice. "And things been happening."

"What kinda things?" I asked.

"Jackers. Niggas looking for a come up. All these cards and dice make people think I'm rich."

"Probably got something to do with all these cats hanging out around here on your porch. Who are all these motherfuckers anyway?"

"Ah, nobodies. Just some of my nephew's friends. They drink out here but nothing else happens so why not let'em stay." Chucky's eyes slid over to Chocolate. "But who's this?"

I presented Sugar Bares finest like a game show prize. "This spicy, thing right here is a friend of Chevy's. You remember my old lady Chevy, right?"

"How could I ever forget?" Chucky stepped back. "Come inside and introduce us."

It was scorching in the house just the way I like it. Warm bodies and big clouds made up a mafia of relentless, pounding heat. Sweat percolated in my moustache and in a minute I knew I'd be wearing it on my back just like a jersey. Chucky's place was bought with city money so whatever it lacked in cool air was made up for with wide spaces. The old man got hit by a transit bus, High Point paid him out of court and he used his whole settlement to buy the biggest house on the same block right where he grew up.

Uncle Chucky showed me how anything is possible even for people like us. He went from a kitchenette apartment to four bedrooms, two baths, and a screened in back porch with a long living room to watch Sunday afternoon football. The walls were clean, the windows were sticky, and everything inside was white as an Iowa state jury all the way down to the holiday lights strewn up by the ceiling on ghost skinned wire.

He led us through a thin sea of underground gamblers. As we weaved through the crowd Chucky got ever sweeter on Chocolate. She did a good job of making him feel like a young stud all over again minus that shitty kitchenette apartment he lived in once before. The sex oozed between them down the hallway and rolled along through the smoke while he gave us the short tour. Their energy spilled out all over the cream carpet and touched every picture on the wall. They wanted each other like saints want peace but for all the wrong reasons.

In a minute all three of us came out the back door and landed on his screen porch. I think this little amenity is the real reason Chucky had to have the house in the first place. It was basically an eight yard long deck that served as a mosquitoes paradise until he built a screen around it and put in furniture and vases. Chocolate hung alone in the corner looking coy as I've ever seen her while Chucky guided me over to a poker table where he knew I'd stay long enough for them to get properly acquainted. When the players saw him coming chairs scraped the floor for a spot to open up. Chucky clutched my shoulder with that rigid, old man grip that's strong for no reason.

"Everybody, this is Cerrio. Now, I know he's ugly and he's a lowdown dog. But he's still family so let's treat him real good tonight."

Scattered talk came over the table. Another old man twisted around in his seat. "Does that mean we take his money?"

"You goddamn right you take his money. Wouldn't have it any other way. And don't nobody think about leaving here without paying the house either."

The table roared with laughter. Chucky's players liked the jokes but they knew he was dead serious about money. Someone passed me a fresh deck to deal. Before I picked up the cards off the table Chocolate tugged hard on my sleeve.

"Bet big."

I gave her the stone face and flat eyes. "I thought you just came to watch. Now you're here coaching too?"

"Trust me, Cerrio. You want to hold back, hold it back in the bedroom. Right now play your cards and bet like a man."

No free looks in the spot. The old man who twisted around in his seat let me know it before I finished shuffling the deck. He like to smirk after he talked, before he talked too, and then he would touch on his starched shirt collar which was highly annoying.

"The ante is ten dollars, son. Or you can fold without seeing anything."

I put a wadded ten down in the center of the table with a ton of disrespect. He grunted disapprovingly and I dealt. After cards were down a big man down the line bet twenty dollars on the first round. He was a fat brute, the type who might eat a whole Christmas turkey just to shorten up your holiday. I looked at my hand and saw another fat, fucking loser. Eight of hearts, three of clubs. A complete disgrace. But Chocolate's words kept ringing in my head. "Bet big."

So, I stayed in the hand. Even worse than that I bet on it, throwing twenty more in the pot just to see three cards flipped over. Jack of clubs, nine of diamonds, four of diamonds. So much for the deck having its rhythm in the stars. This really couldn't get any more random.

The old man pulled on his collar. "Forty dollars to anybody who wants see more," he announced. I saw his lip twitch after he talked. Maybe a tell, maybe a medical condition. The mulatto kid next to me with a money sign on his face raised another fifty and everybody folded except the old dog and me clinging on to a final gasp of hope.

Though it was still my deal someone else flipped over another card and then my heart dropped down in my lap. A lonely queen of spades frowned up like her best days were all behind her. Fifty more got thrown in the pot and someone raised again but nobody truly cared anymore. I threw my losers away like I should have from the very start and the old man swept the table clean with a smile on his face. That was the tone, one happy better and the rest of us grim and salty. Cold part is I could tell he was cheating. But really what could I say?

Still I never stopped. Because Chocolate came to work tonight and you already know how I feel about hard work. I imagined her back arched, heels down, dripping sweat on Chucky's creaking mattress just to make the rent. Thinking like that kept me betting big for her. For her and my baby, Chevy. But forty minutes later no win after no win had me hemorrhaging money all over the white house's eight yard porch. And then pretty soon it was almost over.

My rubber banded knot was lower than the valley of the dead when out of nowhere she came around gliding those curvy hips all over again. The mulatto looked up first, let go of his cards like all five fingers on his right hand simply forgot about the game and his jaw went with them. His pair of threes fluttered down to the floor in slow motion then all at once the porch got quiet. Ragged breathing came out from twenty slacked jaws in a toxic cloud of mouth while Chocolate stepped through the heat. I was starting to notice a constant pattern. This woman had a special way with entrances. First Sugar Bares and now this, lesser girls could take some notes.

She went back to the truck and tore that tight white T-shirt in all the right places. Where once it was glued to her frame now you could see the pole muscles flex every time she so much as breathed. The collar was stretched down to her cleavage and the tail was ripped at an angle just so the boys get a peek at that sexy stomach where a belly ring swung wild every time she put one foot in front of the other.

If there was any confusion here's where it died. Chocolate definitely came to work tonight. She saw the lucky old man looking hungry just as much as she looked thirsty and leaned in on his side.

"Who's winning?" she purred.

He pulled on his collar. "That'd be me, Sugar."

"Mmm, well it looks fun. Wish I knew how to play."

"Aw, it ain't too hard, baby. Pull up a chair right here and I'll teach you."

She bit her bottom lip and did as she was told. The fellas on both sides of me looked strange but I just shrugged my shoulders up to my ears and slid my ass on over. Shit, what else could I do? When Chocolate squeezed in we almost choked on her fragrance. She watched calmly as the cards got dealt out all across the table in a circle. When no one else was looking she caught my eye and mouthed two words. "Bet big."

I did just what she said like a trained animal and the old man won more of Chevy's money. Every time it got swept off the table he chuckled too hard until his gut shook like a tickled pig's. Chocolate kept egging him on. She would giggle and rub his leg and coo out a bunch of saccharin "oh my gods" just to stroke his limp ego.

In another twenty minutes the game was finished. All that flirty bullshit burned my ears and I could have strangled them both with the stiff shirt collar he couldn't quit fingering. My only fun was imagining the old man wheezing out one last breath while Chocolate kept up her I-need-a-daddy act. But in the end the old man swept the table and me and the mulatto kid wiped off our foreheads and went looking for drinks. This was my own fault. Why in the world did I listen to a ho on the road? In Chocolate's life this was just a party, in mine it's a living. I was down five hundred dollars, my back was against the ropes and the only way out was through. Because going home defeated meant being comfortable with so many other uncomfortable things. Broken promises and burnt bridges, weak hopes too frail to support a future and fallen expectations worn thin and threadbare like a tired washrag.

I found a way back right inside the house of all places. A blackjack game going slow in the den with simple rules and a rube dealing. Every time he looked away I slipped a card from the Circle K gas station in my palm and put it on the table. In five hands I got back everything I lost outside. On the sixth I bet back half and doubled up. If Chucky would have seen me cheating no doubt it would have been gunplay. So, thank God for the small things. The dealer just scratched the short hairs on his chin and blamed the freestyles of fortune for what had to be once in a lifetime chances.

"Must be your lucky night," he muttered.

I shrugged. "Even a garbage can gets a steak every once in a while."

He laughed. "That's a good one. Mind if I use it?"

"Be my guest. Long as you're not ashamed to steal."

Quietly, I slipped back outside to the Jeep, left him chuckling like an idiot by the table. There's so many cards in a house twenty-one deck that Chucky won't even know what hit him until tomorrow comes. Maybe not even then. But I should leave Chocolate, just take off back to Winston-Salem and let her hang out here all night with that old man drunk off lust. I don't know why I risked my perfect record trying to do exactly what she wanted. What am I a fucking zoo animal? One thing is for sure, though. It won't ever happen again. I'm not snorting cocaine in a bathroom and getting shot at in cul-de-sacs just to make old men rich in the next town over.

Her keys are in my pocket. If I left right now it would teach the girl something real important about me real fast. Then she would tell Chevy and they would both give me hell in that same hot apartment where I had somehow moved in. That meant a whole lot of neck popping and finger snapping and hands on hips would all be going down at the same time. Thinking about that whole chorus of attitude almost made me want to peel out in her truck right now. Because honestly I like when these girls get a little riled up and go in authentically. It's a secret aphrodisiac I keep to myself, a little fetish that might be slightly twisted but never let's me down.

The sweet smell of weed floated to me through the air. A big lady across the street had on a flowing pink house dress and a matching scarf on her head. I walked over, asked about a soda, a cigarette, a bag. She pulled all three from her dress, took my money and gave me a light. I was high before I even made it back to the truck where Chocolate was sitting in the front putting touch ups on her face in the mirror.

"You ready to go?"

"Been ready."

"Uh-oh, he's trippin'. What's the matter, boo?"

"You almost cost me tonight. You and that goddamn old man. I don't know if he's your type or what but-"

"You serious?" She snapped her make-up compact shut. "Are you flashing on me right now on the side of the road?"

"Fucking right I'm serious. This is the last time you do anything with me. That's a promise."

"No, I mean are you seriously that stupid?"

I blew hot smoke through my nose. "The keys to your truck are in my pocket. You wanna walk home tonight?"

"Shut up, nobody's leaving me." She dug deep in her bra and pulled out a loaf of cash. "See this? That old man had trick written all over him. Shit, I saw a hundred tricks in there. This place is filled with them. It's a goldmine and the bigger you bet the more money goes around the table and when the game is over then I can tax the winner as much as I want."

Chocolate turned her lean body in the bucket seat so we could look right in each other's eyes. Instead, I stared straight down at the money. She licked her finger and peeled off a few bills, enough to cover my losses if I actually had any. She held them out to me and then snatched it all back in one quick motion.

"Listen close because I won't repeat myself. We keep this thing strictly between us. Call it a side job. Matter of fact call it whatever you want, I don't much care. But don't ever tell Chevy. Far as she knows I work alone."

She held out the money one more time and smiled that long, wicked, fishhook smile. "Deal?"

Chapter 6

GREENWAY AVENUE

Great cities are like beautiful women, they both come with a lot of history. There are still a few places in this town that are almost what we used to be when tobacco was king. Small glimpses of a time past when cigarette companies used to have enough crisp, corporate money to fly menthols to Egypt. Greenway avenue is a street in the middle of Winston-Salem with just a little bit of polish left over from those good old days. My Aunt Denise has a house right there, her place is one of those pieces of the bygone era with more history in it than just what's in the 60's architecture and more smoke caught in the walls then you can find in a Camel filter.

It's a rugged, brick symbol of an ugly struggle.

They didn't like Aunt Denise and they means everybody. See, we were foreigners and she was a woman and not a white one. People were angry about us having a home. I don't where we should have lived, where they wanted us to go. But in the face of it all she never moved. Her and my Uncle Daya, my real blood uncle, worked hard for that house.

When I walked in the living room spearmint hit me in the face. It was a strong scent that immediately faded, one of those where you keep on inhaling first to get the aroma and then to make sure your nose isn't playing a game. I sniffed and sniffed like a hustler smelling his mark right next to him on the train and Aunt Denise came out from the den asking if I was "sick or something." I pulled my shirt sleeve a little lower to make sure she couldn't see the stitches. She asked again. "Are you sick? Need a tissue?"

"No, I'm okay. I feel fine. Great really."

"Don't sound like it to me. I heard sniffling like you were crying."

"I'm just smelling those new candles you got. They're nice."

"Yeah, that's air fresheners, Cerrio. I plug them in the wall so the house won't smell like Mistys all the time."

"You still smoke them things?"

"Mm-hmm. Filtered. Ultra lights. Two packs for the price of one because I had a coupon." She folded her arms. "You sure you ain't sick?"

"Told you I wasn't"

"Well, you're acting contagious, standing six feet away and everything. How come I haven't even got a hug yet?"

I stepped forward, leaned down, wrapped my arms around the woman and embraced her and one of those itchy shawls old women grow close to when they get on in years. She smelled like the house and a little bit like baked bread. When I let go she asked if I was hungry. Not a good question. Everybody's hungry when they come to the house on Greenway avenue.

"I got porkchops thawing in the sink. Help me in the bathroom and you can have one."

That's another thing about this house, nothing's free. Showing up here always turns me into a volunteer. The only job I ever had in life is the to-do list hanging inside the kitchen cabinet that never gets done. I clean the gutters and dust the lamps and mow the lawn and rake the grass. I do it for the obvious reason, Aunt Denise is the mother I never had. I don't know where my real mother went, apparently nobody else does either because they never, ever told me. Even if they did I never asked because Aunt Denise was more than enough. She raised a boy into a man with my uncle helping out in the middle and after he died she kept his belt hung in the closet to finish the job.

Back then I tried cutting corners, that's why there's no sticks left in the backyard. Because picking switches leaves little trees naked and stubborn asses raw. Aunt Denise had her ways and means. She always found out when I got lazy and didn't wipe the top shelf or reach up and wax the roof of her car. I swear I thought I had a chance because I could walk on my own but she's had my number down even from a wheelchair since fifteen years ago.

She rolled in the bathroom. Got her hair wet and made me the shampooer. There's worse things than cleaning hair I guess. My fingers were rubbing, massaging, lathering. Little white bubbles spun around sticking to the mirror and popping to death over the sink. I broke a sweat working in circles and Aunt Denise hummed contently with her eyes closed.

"Put a little more in there."

"I don't think your head can take no more."

"You want to eat you'll put some more in there."

My stomach roiled. I doused her head again and a new team of suds blew up on her roots.

"What's all this about anyway? Why you dying your hair? Is it a mid-life crisis."

"Only men have those." She said it with a matter-of-fact insinuation. "Women go through something else and I'm past that already. This is for my date tonight."

I quit the shampooing. "No shit?!"

"What did you say?"

"I said, 'that's beautiful'. Good to see you getting your groove back. Turn your head some. There you go, right there. So, who is he?"

"Some man from my church. He plays the organ and his daughters sing in the choir."

"A music man. I like it. What his daughters look like?"

"Ugly as burnt matches. Trust me you're not missing a thing. They can sing like you wouldn't believe, though. Voices like a river." She spread her hands out. "Voices like a harp."

I laughed. "Maybe I'll go one Sunday and see for myself."

"So, what you been up to? Got a job this summer?"

"Yeah, I, uh, work at Costco sometimes. Just a few hours a week. It's a part time thing but the boss said it might turn into more. Come on, let's rinse this out."

She turned her chair around and leaned back in the sink. "Sounds good but I know when you're lying. Where you been staying?"

"With a friend."The sink water started burning my hand

"What's her name?"

"Hold on, how do you know it's a her? I could be staying with Socks. Did you ever think about that?"

"Maybe, but I know you LaDecerrio Lloyd. And if I had to guess I'd say you're shacking up with that same girl you used to be in love with. The same one who stayed with you after you left here and went to jail for drugs." She popped one eye open. "Tell me."

"Alright, you're right."

"Good." She sighed with content. "That makes me feel way better. You know I pray a lot about that girl. She really loves you, Cerrio. Reminds me of how I was when I first met your Uncle Daya."

I quit rinsing and looked in the mirror. "That's all good. But who's praying for me?"

She wasted no time pulling her head out of the sink. Aunt Denise looked me up and down then pointed to some towels folded up on a caddy. I grabbed the plushest one, cocaine white and fluffy as a marshmallow. She took it to wrap her wet hair up in a turban. Once the thing was tucked down in every right place a pack of Misty lights came out. She fit the filter between her lips.

"See, I knew you were sick." She struck a match. "Twenty-two years old, fresh out of prison. Trying to get it right with your old lady. Yeah boy you got problems. Sit down, right there on the tub, and tell me all about them."

I perched myself on the edge of the tub and almost ran down the whole story. About Flossy and the pressure washing Mexicans. About Chevy on the pole and how I think I got her there. She almost heard my feelings, every one of them, right there in her smoky bathroom beside the peeling pink wallpaper Uncle Daya put up just before he died. But when I tried talking nothing came out.

Because what do I know about problems? Compared to a wheelchaired widow what I knew could fit loose in a thimble. Aunt Denise hasn't been out with a man since 1999. The year before we all thought the world was going to end. The same year she stopped feeling anything from the waist down. We didn't have Christmas that year or any year after that. Things have changed I guess. Winters and summers have passed again and again. Now here we are in different places. She's back out mingling, I'm charting dark clubs. Maybe she'll even put up a tree on the first week of December like we used to do before.

So, I said nothing, just stared. She pulled on that long cigarette and nodded like I had said it all anyway.

"Remember that one story your uncle used to tell?"

"I don't know."

"About the man who lost everything?"

"Is this some fable about me?"

"Surprisingly Cerrio, everything is not about you."

I rubbed my head. "I was just trying to see if you wanted to get on my case. You been riding me pretty hard since I walked in the door, auntie."

"Well, that's how you know I love you."

She took one last pull off the ridiculously long square and threw half of it in the toilet. I swear she just smokes to be doing it.

"I told your uncle this story. It's really my mother's. I wish she could have told you because she tells it better than me but she just ran out of time.

One man had everything and another man came and stole it all. The man who gets stole from looks for his stuff everywhere but never finds it. So, he goes around town asking everyone have you seen my car? Have you seen my money? Have you seen my wife? Have you seen my kids?"

"His kids got taken too?"

"I told you. Everything."

"Shit."

"Watch your mouth. That's two times already."

"My bad"

She went on. "So, he's asking. Did you see anyone come around my house? And everybody tells him no because they hadn't seen thing. After a while he can't find any clues so he hits a wall. And then he sits down and figures out a way to get all his precious things back."

"How'd he do it?"

"Old fashioned way. He works for it. Goes in everyday and sweats for a boss who promises to give it all back. But the boss trickles it in. He gives the man back everything in little, tiny pieces like feeding a bird in a cage."

"I get it. The man learns to appreciate everything like he never did before, right?"

"Wrong. The big boss feeds him like a bird so the man will keep on laboring up until the day somebody comes and steals his stuff all over again. And then the cycle starts over."

"No, I don't remember that story." I looked around the bathroom. "But I'll never forget where it was when you told me."

"You ain't even heard the best part."

"What?"

"The man who lost everything, the thief and the big boss are all the same person."

I blinked. "Wait. Who is he?"

Aunt Denise, the old woman who smelled like spearmint and baked bread, held her peace. She shook her towel wrapped head east to west. "No, now that part I can't tell you." She looked at me a little sadly. "I just can't, Cerrio. Some things you got to figure out all on your own. Now come on and dye my hair."

+ 68 +

CHAPTER 7

CRIMINAL ECSTASY

Behind the dryer in the house on Greenway avenue there's a loaded shoebox. After Aunt Denise left with her church boyfriend I took it out and closed the blinds. Inside was the future of me and Chevy. I dumped it all over the floor like a man who lost interest then sat down to count. In a while there was a number, eight thousand, three hundred and twelve dollars. Not a bad start but that's all it was, just a start. Ten more shoeboxes then maybe we could be at the foot of realizing our dreams, which are actually Chevy's dreams, which are mine to make come true. Ten more shoeboxes. That's a lot of gambling and shooting, stripping and tricking, a whole lot of opportunities for things to go wrong and plenty of chances for our second chance to fly south.

At dusk I pulled up to the apartment. I was late and she was posted at the bottom of the steps dead set on a fight. She had her rings off, tapping her foot like Thumper on the sidewalk. I told her to calm down. She said, "don't tell me to calm down." And then we got down to it.

In the car she sucked her teeth just to catch a breath between complaints about how I was going to get her fired. I told her to relax, one time being late isn't so bad. Everybody gets a pass on that first one. By the time we hit the third stop light there was name calling, the serious kind that people drag in to therapy. We had good material, an arsenal of put downs to shoot back and forth at one another. It was a verbal trench war that Dr. Phil could of made a mini series out of. On the highway it was a full blown argument. Between shouts I changed lanes, the drive to 43-Dimes was long and there were plenty of chances to take a break but neither of us would dare back off.

Assassinating each others character is one of the things me and Chevy do best. After being together so long we knew how to emphasize sad points and tear each other apart. We took turns doing it, slinging hate at each other across the front seat until a motorcycle blew by smashing down the broken white line in the middle of the road. Blue lights flashed in the mirror and I felt my stomach curl into a tight little ball. Chevy didn't miss a beat. She held her palm out and I passed the pistol from my waist right to her straight over the middle console. I eased the Volkswagen to the shoulder, watching the bright lights strobe across the dashboard to get a last vision of freedom. When the cop car raced past us on eight angry cylinders we both blinked at the windshield like two idiots waiting to get slapped back to reality.

Chevy caught her breath. "You good, baby?"

"Shit, it don't get no closer than that."

"Definitely don't." Chevy looked in the mirror on her side. "I don't see no more. Think he was chasing that bike?"

"Police car can't catch a motorcycle unless it crashes into something. Then he's got real problems."

Chevy nodded and then the car was still. A semi rumbled past just inches away and the draft must have been the only thing moving between us for what felt like a year.

"I'ma call the club." She fished in her bag for the phone.

I raised an eyebrow. "For what? To tell them you're going to be late? We still got time."

She shook her head. "To tell'em I'm feeling sick. I'm sneezing and coughing and if I go on stage tonight all the other girls touching that pole behind me are all going to come down with something too."

"You serious? It's Friday. All those businessmen are going to come drop a load to start off the weekend. There might be fifty bands on the floor tonight. You don't want to miss that."

"True." Chevy touched one of her earrings. "There's always a lot of money on the floor every Friday but I think I'm needed somewhere else right now."

"Where?"

"We both been working hard every night. Maybe we need to have one to ourselves."

"Oh, I see. And this the part where I'm supposed to say I'm sorry?"

"Not even. I don't ever want any man of mine to be sorry. I just want him to be in love with me."

It was took much poetry to argue with. To much sentiment to defend against. Money be damned, at least for tonight I guess. I sat back and listened to more semis blowing by on the long haul while Chevy dialed the club. The call went fast because nothing is less sexy than a sick dancer sneezing all over half naked girls in a tightly packed dressing room. It's tough to get more anti-sex than that.

After she put the phone away I felt two fingers walking up the side of my arm. "Here we are, playing hooky again just like the old days. Now all we need is the Cutlass to make it come together." She paused. "Actually, I don't think we need the Cutlass. I'm blushing already."

I looked her up and down. "Where?"

"Boy, you know where. Come on, let's go get something to drink."

I slapped the car in drive. "What are you thirsty for?"

Chevy said she wanted vodka but she really wanted to browse. Because every woman is a shopper at heart. The lady behind the counter at the ABC store stared us down. She gave Chevy that special look old biddies reserve for the younger, faster generation that's coming right behind them. It wasn't the polyester skirt hugging those smooth thighs or the bleach white top screaming for a sneaky look when the headlights came on. It was all the skin in between. The toned legs and the open toe heels and those plump breasts aching to escape like a midnight jail break. Too much of a good thing, that's what made the old bag bitter. The misery lines in her face told me she had been this way for a long time, forever even. The spite might have even been contagious but ever since that cop car sailed past me in traffic nothing could make me ill at all.

We sauntered down the aisle with the expensive liquors. Chevy likes to run her fingers over the embossed labels to feel their texture. She was reaching for a bottle of bourbon when I pulled back and slapped her ass maybe just a little too hard. That giant peach sounded off like a firecracker in a mailbox. She jumped six inches to the ceiling, kneed a fifth off the shelf and the bottle crashed to the floor sending bourbon and glass spread out everywhere in the shape of a dirty star. The old lady behind the counter couldn't wait to yell at us. She wanted me to pay for it. When I told her fuck off then her husband exploded out from a door in the back wall.

If it was just me I think I could have apologized my way out. But Chevy had a big problem and he was coming down the aisle looking high strung. He had on boots way too thick for the summer and the moisture of gin twinkling in his moustache. Chevy grabbed me, I grabbed a bottle of Hennessey. We were falling all over each other just trying get away. She almost lost a heel rushing for the exit but I pulled her up with a hard grip on that too overwhelmed halter top. The fabric strained and crackled in my hand like embers in a brush fire and then when the cotton couldn't take anymore her chest finally broke free.

Boots and moustache stopped cold in his tracks, his wife screamed so hard her cheeks turned pink, blue, purple, then plum. Suddenly the burglar alarm exploded with panic noise calling us robbers and fair game for anybody trying to be a hero. The old bag pointed a long, accusing finger and a good Samaritan tried to answer the call. He put a hand on my shoulder, the one with the chopper scar Bandy sewed up like she was shutting a mouth. Then, Chevy upped her .32 and he crossed his eyes when she cocked the hammer right in his face. The hero let go of me, swallowed spit, tried hard to keep his focus on something, anything besides those two big titties bouncing backwards out the door.

I put an arm around her waist and we pushed outside with spilt liquor on our shoes. She kept the gun level and the devil constant in her eyes. I would have been proud, very proud like a parent at the spelling bee, but there wasn't any time. We were out of there, scraping the curb in her Passat while husband and wife stood in front of the ABC store with hands on hips. Second getaway in just under two months, for a couple trying to work on something special it felt like maybe we were on our way.

The stolen Hennessey tried rolling behind the gas pedal. I kicked it back underneath the seat and took us through a red light without any interference. Chevy glanced back over a shoulder, she threw her head back and screamed like she was trying to call the coast. When I hit the corner skidding she was stomping her heels on the passenger's side with the pistol pointed up raging about how she was the greatest that ever, ever, ever lived and of course there was no one around to dispute it.

I checked the mirrors to make sure there weren't anymore lights dancing behind us. After none split my vision I saw my baby put herself away one side at a time, never letting go of the gun.

"Hey, put that thing down." I laughed to show her I was feigning the fear. "I don't know if I can trust you with a pistol right now. Even if it is just a Barbie gun."

"Shut up, you're the nut anyway. Why'd you slap my ass so hard back there?"

"I don't know. Guess I thought you'd like it."

She giggled. "And I did. I liked the whole thing. God, it was such a rush. I needed a good rush. That was the most fun I had since my mama died. And you got a free fifth too. Maybe we should try that at the shoe store so I can get some new boots."

"Nope, next time we rob something it's going to be for cash."

She tsked and put her pistol in her purse right next to mine. "See, you're no fun."

"That's okay, somebody has to be the responsible one. Hey, you know what?"

"No, but I think you're going to tell me."

"I was just going to say you look pretty damn good pointing that gun."

"Thought you said you didn't like me with a gun in my hand."

"See, you don't listen. What I said is, 'I can't trust you with it'."

Chevy smiled. Then, she licked a finger and pressed it on my cheek. "That's one for you tonight, baby. But don't worry. Mama's gonna catch up later."

The moon was full. A big, cream sphere hanging in the sky inviting all kinds of wildness. I wanted to dress it up like a clock, put numbers and hands on it to tell the time because time validates everything. We weren't in Winston-Salem anymore. We ran away from home to the west where the city of Greensboro held her arms wide open. Chevy knew this place better than me, all I knew is that the cops out here had way bigger problems on a Friday night than two liquor store crooks hopped up on a rush.

Coming off the highway I turned down Flag street, flew past the Bellflower Inn and the Lady of Christ Mission and sailed straight to the track where the real ladies were strolling under the lunar milkshine. The market was open for business, every type held a corner, all the gorgeous ones and the wannabes too. Even though the town was different business was still the same.

It's the same no matter where you go, Chevy was the same too. She's a hood baby, the two pistols buried in her purse told you so. She knew the lost neighborhoods of Greensboro like the back of her hand. She gave me directions to the corner store where smokers out front flashed her gap toothed smiles. They had names like Doorman, Cola, and Nickels. Handles made up just to fit the traits they held close as their pipes.

She bought a dark colored soda, a cup of ice, a five pack of gum and chips. The soda went with my stolen cognac over cubes of ice. When she poured Chevy didn't get a drop on her purse or the guns inside. Cola bubbles hissed to the top as we drank down the road, passing the cup back and forth, sipping easy over potholes, holding it down low at every intersection. One mile in she was lit and begging me to let her shoot both our pistols at a stop sign where a hard working girl paced by the road. The alcohol was talking to her in a voice full of bass. Before she got us both in trouble, again, I took us to a spot overlooking the city and parked her Passat in the trees.

Shrouded in darkness there was no more reason to hide. We drank like man was originally supposed to, out in the open doing whatever felt right. I took the bottle, Chevy topped off her cup. We hung like berries right in front of her car sipping Hennessey with the radio turned up and the doors wide open. It was Jodeci singing about a woman with a body you just had to see from behind. On that I could relate. Chevy looked like a little lunatic swaying with the beat. She hummed all the words because she didn't know the lyrics. I laid on my side of the hood, back against the windshield, watching, admiring, picking at the Hennessey label until she looked over.

"Are you spying on me now?" She frowned. "Real sneaky, Cerrio."

I laughed. "Nobody's spying. I'm just checking you out."

"Well, that's a point for me."

"Hell no you don't get any points for that."

"Uh, I'm the bitch who saved your ass tonight. So, yes, I do."

"Incredible. You should have been my lawyer, I'd have been home a long time ago." I sat up. "What's this game you're always cheating at anyway?"

"I'm not cheating you just got caught looking. Didn't you hear me when I said I'd catch up later?"

I swished the liquor around in the bottle. "Fucking incredible."

She hopped off the car. "Come on, let's dance."

"Hunh-unh, you know I can't dance."

"Can't, or won't?"

Chevy rubbed on me until I put the fifth down just to get a hand around her waist. I had palm flat against her skin and my balance was a little off on the edge of the hood when she jerked my wrist hard. "Dance!"

So, we did a slow number on top of crunchy grass in nature's ballroom. Chevy twisted in the dark with her eyes closed and smile on her face that showed something more than teeth. The liquor made her feet light, fingers numb, her head a little warm. In the pale moonlight her skin glistened with a sweet sheen of sweat that looked too delicious to simply leave alone. I French kissed her flesh just to steal a taste and the nectar tingling on my tongue made the rest of me jealous. Before the song changed on the radio I had my whole mouth on her neck drinking up a boutique of flavors, salt and cinnamon, sugar and caramel, wild and intoxicating. She tilted her head back to give me more of that throat to devour. When I traced my tongue up the curve of her jaw she purred like a kitten.

"One for me," I whispered.

No, I don't know how this game works but as always I found a way to win. I know Chevy doesn't like her skirt hiked up, been that way since tenth grade. I tugged on the fabric while she wriggled her hips and together we got her half naked on the hood of the Passat. Soon as the polyester was down by her ankles naturally the panties came next. They were the ones she picked out at the mall. Limited Edition Vickie's Secret with the only solid spot of fabric right in the middle where she had the most flavor.

This time there was no help. I didn't need it when I pushed her smooth legs high and slid that special underwear off all by myself. She was already wet before they ever came away. I made her spread wide, so far apart a light breeze dried sticky juices spread up on the inside of both thighs. Chevy stirred around begging in anticipation with her mouth closed. I teased first, flicking my tongue like a snake over her button, listening to her groan with impatience as I grazed a thumb down the center.

When I plunged my face in the middle her legs shuddered like thunder had struck. Five slender fingers pushed me down deeper and deeper into the cush as my tongue whipped up a hurricane all over her clit. When the levy broke Seville thrusted forward and held her brown thighs close to my cheeks as the waves rolled over me like cleansing water.

After the flood passed she was grinning from ear to ear. I didn't ask for a return, never had to in my life. We may fight dirty but we always play fair. She bit her lip and reached for the liquor cup. Chevy sipped long with mischief in her eyes until her mouth was full and when that hot throat was cool all over again then she unbuckled my pants and kissed the print.

The woman had power. She took me in a little at a time, sucking slow beneath the trees, swallowing inch by inch until my whole length was deep in a cold ice bath. When I found the back of her throat a rope of drool touched down on her ruined halter top then I sprung in her mouth and tapped the pallette. She looked up to me and moaned like a desperate virgin. All the time keeping the same rhythm, down easy and back fast so I grew another inch between her lips. A hot bead of precum slid out of the tip, Chevy giggled and rubbed it around until her mouth glowed in the dark. After that she went gently so I wouldn't erupt too soon before she was ready. Every so often she took a tour to the top, went around and came back down again. I tugged at the cotton barely holding her breasts together. When the girls broke free again then she tossed her hair back and worked even harder. Making lollipop noises, using hands, twisting in a fever until I almost finished all over her silk tongue.

She brought me right to the edge then stopped on a dime. Just got up in front of me wiping the corners of her mouth like she had something to say. But we didn't talk. I mean what was there to discuss? Instead, she took my hands and pushed them up on her chest. I could feel her heart beating fast through my fingertips as she worked my palms in circles, using the perspiration to lubricate tiny spins that went closer and closer towards her hard nipples until I caught them between two digits. I tugged gently pulling all the way to the tips and letting them snap back one by one on their own.

"Fuck me," she growled. It's what we both wanted. At the apartment we make love sometimes but the drinking and the robbing and the hot breezes blowing through our Greensboro hideout had made us greedy. Let the love making stay home with the dishes tonight. Right now we wanted criminal ecstasy.

Caramel painted an extra coat of gloss on the Volkswagen's hood when I set her up there again. She leaned back, arms locked behind her, legs wide open so I could crash right into the perfect curve of her pelvis. I gave her all my best strokes, every merciless thrust drowning out the radio while I punished her tenderness. The hold of her womanhood felt like a drug, like the warmth of a velvet high trying to build up into the fire of addiction. If bad habits had birthdays this is how they would celebrate. "Fuck me," she said again, insistent on the point she wanted me to break her like a dish. I sunk my fingers deep, deep into the flesh to get a good grip because everything was so hot and slick that it might all just slide off and melt into the earth.

I was smashing so hard I could feel bruises coming in on my thighs and Chevy was still begging for more. We reached the top of the mountain together, her first just like always. She clutched my arms until she broke a nail and arched her back to an impossible curve. My air came out in ragged breaths like bedsheets tearing apart while she screamed my name out to the constellations. All the birds woke up in their sycamore nests. They flew circles in the air and then a pounding sweet orgasm soaked me down to the bone. I told her to keep going, bring the rain, be a good girl and wet me down. And Chevy gave up everything because good lovers never hold back from one another. Every drop her body left for me sent a flying, electric rush out into the night.

I got out right on time. Not too late and not so soon that I that I was standing there holding myself in the dark. Chevy took every hot splash purring like a kitten and laughed at the map I painted all over her stomach.

She said, "I don't think I've ever have this much fun in Greensboro."

"Me neither. Never."

"Feel better?" she asked.

I rubbed myself against her just to be a fool. "Much better."

"Well, when you're done tickling the south can you find me something to clean up with?"

"Don't know. Maybe I just should just let you suffer."

"Maybe." She closed her legs. "But you won't. Go ahead and grab that blanket out of the backseat too."

It was all very simple, sex and a blanket, but the simple things are what I missed most in the years we were separated. All the elements came together that night to give us the gift of laying naked in each other's arms against the cool car windshield. The weather and the liquor and even the mistakes came together in alignment with the universe. Simple things are the driveway to life.

Chevy wanted this moment, maybe she had a right to it and even though I played tough all the time like I could go on without her I think she knew I wanted it just as bad as she did. Why? Why did she let me play this game? Because somehow she knew I wasn't as bad as everyone always made me out to be. She knew I had desires, as many as the demons scrambling for first place in the kingdom of darkness. But even if I had everything I wanted it would all mean nothing if her heart wasn't still beating inside my chest.

CHAPTER 8

LITTLE SINGER

I had a dream about the man who lost everything. He showed up just before morning looking rich and happy, singing for the first time since the day he went out to work for it all back. His hard lesson must have been over. The boss who promised to give him all the things that he held dear must have lived up to his word and he was finally free to go live the good life. I sang in tune with him for as long as I could. When the music ended then his tragedy started all over again.

Me and Chevy woke up on the hood still smelling like sex. We left the car doors open and the radio turned up to ten. There was no more music left for the dawn, every song got played for five straight hours until Saturday morning came blazing in our faces like Haley's comet. Her skirt was wrinkled and the halter was so out of shape she had to double knot it in the front just to keep it up. A big cocoa colored woman found us in the woods putting our clothes back on. She was a lady cop with three stripes on her shoulder and a tangled pair of jumper cables she didn't know how to use. When she talked a little I found out she came up on our spot by following fresh Pirelli tracks pressed down in the dirt.

After a little more chatter Chevy snatched her pink panties off the windshield and jammed them down in her purse right on top of our pistols. "Hurry up," she muttered.

I had the battery jumped on the third try and we drove home on a prayer with no seatbelts and a headache. Then, in the next few days everything that went up came crashing back down. We chased the feeling that we found out in the woods. Somewhere Chevy read that cayenne peppers can give a man more stamina. Afternoons she was whipping up big pots of yellow grits with double doses of hot sauce and everyday when I woke up at the stroke of twelve she served them up hot and greasy with pork sausage on the side and steam still rolling off a thick coat of cheddar painted right on top.

She caught a few different rides to work and Chocolate drove me to the gambling houses after dark. When I told her that Socks was the one taking me out to play cards at night my girl just put on smile like she was a dumb. That was a weekend of lies but by Monday she couldn't take anymore.

Chevy came in the bedroom while I slept late and shook me up like a can of spray paint. I tried to tell her it was too early. She hit me hard with a soft pillow and said, "get up and put your fucking pants on. I need a new battery."

Uncle Daya told me you got to pick your battles. We argue a lot but this time I could see it was no use. I ran her errand in Bandy's Honda, just me and the college girl rolling like bandits through high noon traffic while Chevy stayed home to watch Wendy Williams talk Hollywood gossip from a chair. The ride was quiet. Our battle to be mute fought with no hands and baited breath. The only noise came when my teeth clacked over a pothole and she reached over and snapped the radio on.

We fell out before the shopping trip, if that's what you want to call it, right in there kitchen where only good things are supposed to happen. Bandy loves pictures, that's how it started. Maybe it's petty but pettiness is like beauty, it's all in the eye of the beholder. Anyway, the woman loves photos, loves taking them. Tries taking some of me too but I hate the camera. So what? She wasn't going to quit. That afternoon she left her books on the counter and brought her phone over to the kitchen table while I was poking sausage with a fork and said, "look at these."

I stretched my neck to see her phone. "What am I looking at, mama?"

"Pictures my girlfriend took at the car show."

I stared at the screen while she stole a little orange juice from my glass. Bandy was draped all over a mean Maserati in a pair of Greek heels. The whip, thin, leather straps wrapped all the way up to her knees like vines. She smacked her soggy, fruity lips and scrolled down. Four other pictures followed the first one, every shot showing a different side of the same girl like a brand-new version of an untold thrill. Seeing her dolled up I could feel the cayenne kick in. By a souped up Toyota she looked risky, legs crossed sitting on Mercedes hood that was fancy. Showing off a thigh tattoo in teeny shorts on the back of a truck rugged and fierce.

I talked around a mouth full of grits. "I like these."

"Say that then."

"You know I'd never lie. I love'em. Looks like you two had a good time out there."

"Oh, but that ain't nothing." She winked like a smooth criminal. "I heard you had a reeeal good time with someone, somewhere out in the woods. Maybe, three or four nights ago."

"Yeah, but there's no pictures of that."

She tsked. "Too bad. That's why you should let me make you a Facebook page."

I pushed her phone back against her chest. "That ain't going to work."

"Come on, Cerrio."

"No Bandy, I'm just not one of those people."

"What people?"

"The kind who take good pictures." I snapped my fingers. "What's the word?"

"Photogenic?"

"Yeah, I'm not like that. You can tell I'm not because I don't even know the word."

"Well, let me fix you up then. I can make you look real good for the camera. I mean, you're halfway there already."

"Just let it go, Bandy."

She paused. "What's the matter with you?"

"Nothing's the matter. I just don't have time for that shit. On the phone all day tapping a screen. That's what you do, fine. But don't twist your little brain into a knot thinking I want to join the team."

The one who said words don't hurt must have never used the sharp ends. Bandy blushed with fury. She wanted a gut shot. Something to make me feel the same shame that was stabbing through her stomach right now. Revenge was just one tidy sentence away to make me curl up in a ball. She could have said it, she could have said I was institutionalized. That I'd been in prison for too long and now I didn't know anything about the real world that had thrown me away like a broken racehorse. She built up to it. I could almost hear the curses tingling on her tongue but she wouldn't spit it out. The woman was too golden to fight fire with fire. Not like me and Chevy who were ready to kill each other if the chicken got burnt. It wasn't a matter of passion, that was all there. It's just that the lady inside Bandy was much bigger than the man sitting at the table.

If war is clear then ours must have been crystal. Me and Bandy had a quiet feud, very uncomfortable but not invisible. When Chevy came through the kitchen wearing hers and my Lacoste shirt she could smell the tension cooking. The air between us was thick with drama. Bandy opened her mouth like she had something to say. I looked at her and she looked at me and then raised her eyebrows to say who won.

Those pouty lips went back together again without ever saying one word.

The college girl came to the apartment that day just to take me on an errand. And even though we successfully kept our ugliness private it still didn't do a thing to ease the bruises. Winding through traffic on the way to the store for Chevy's battery our silence stayed firmly in place, we didn't say one word to each other. Bandy played the radio wide open in her Honda and I counted out of state license plates. The one's north of Virginia counted for a point, south from the last Carolina was two points. West was zero. All the time I tallied she plotted revenge.

Shopping always reminds me of family. Aunt Denise likes showing me off at the store to normal, working class people almost like I'm successful. I guess it's a parent thing. I shake some hands and smile like a fool and flirt with a few older women who keep it just as jazzy as you like, if you like. And if the place is really one of her favorites I might even take an application. Then, I throw it in the trash soon as her wheelchair is turned around.

One of the grown women I hit on just for fun was beeping a price gun down an aisle full of headache pills. I saw her from behind in a blue vest bouncing to the rhythm spilling from her headphones. When I came up she gave me a hug and an invite to her church. I hugged her back, got perfume on my shirt that smelled too much like old lady for Chevy get seriously worried about and made up fake plans for Sunday that she didn't believe. It might have been a struggle except this old church girl was way past dogging us young'uns about our weak excuses. I wriggled off the hook and then showed her the short shopping list Bandy gave me out in the car.

The only item scrawled on the paper made her smile change into something more curious. Then, the headphones came down and her mouth twisted up the way people's mouths do every time the gas bill comes in too high.

"Christ, all this for one person?"

I said, "yeah." She said, "damn" and the rest of it is a lesson in revenge.

I read Bandy's list just one time before hopping out of the Honda. It was a single item that I didn't recognize with the number six wrote down next to it for the amount she wanted. In hindsight I should have bent my ego and broken our silence to ask a few questions because now I was at the checkout counter with a half dozen tubes of yeast infection cream.

My cheeks blushed fire and I felt karma bite me like a wild dog while the clerk called for a price check. At the same time a sneaky grin touched my lips. In life women playing games is just business as usual, that's my account anyway. This is one of those moments I'll reach for in the back of my mind every day of a brand-new sentence. I felt the memory build it's own fort, a safe space to live and thrive while the checkout girl bagged all six tubes with reckless eyeballs. But next time I think about this trip it will be the day after forever because I don't plan on going back behind bars.

Out in the parking lot I wanted to give Bandanna a piece of my mind. She was clutching the Honda steering wheel. Up above helicopter blades beat the clear, blue sky. I had it all figured out. No severe name calling like me and Chevy James did, slinging swords like that was way too much for the kittenish college girl. I had my aggression tuned up just right for her though, not too hot and not too cold. Call me Goldilocks. The fastballs were loaded and ready to go until the chopping waned and a voice full of flowers reached to me from the Honda.

She wasn't loud, wasn't supposed to be, she wasn't built for that. She was just strong. Her sound built up into a big, rising, wave and then crashed into my ears until I was happily deaf to everything else. It should have been from the radio because greatness always seems like that, like it's being telephoned in from far away. Except this time it was right here, four feet away living and breathing like the natural born truth. Eyes closed, head back, stringing notes together in a harmony sweet enough to make angels fall down and weep in the golden streets of heaven. It was a song I never heard before. Probably something buried deep in one of those composition books she always brought over to Chevy's apartment to study out of. Such a wonderful hiding place too, right under my nose because all those notebooks were supposed to be full of schoolwork. But what did school matter? Bandy had all the class anyway.

Her voice and the vision didn't have a thing to do with a love interest, not a man or a woman or even a dollar. She spun lyrics more powerful than anything about rising from the ashes like a blazing Phoenix. The last notes were so beautiful that it made me fear for the end. I tried willing the music to stay a little longer but while I was busy begging she slow walked her tune right down to the finish.

I craved more so I waited. Isn't that real music, though? A true artist giving away just enough to breathe fresh air on your soul so you'll come back for more. Plus, jumping in the front seat too soon would have let Bandy know she had been spied on anyway. I counted out a slow sixty second buffer before sliding in the car with the plastic shopping bag.

Bandy did a good job of hiding her amusement when I got in the Honda. "Did you get the stuff?" I threw the half dozen tubes of cream in her lap and she broke out in a full fit of laughter. "See, that's what you get for all that mouth earlier. Bet you think twice before being mean to me again."

I balled up the bag and threw it out the window. "You win. Let's go, take me home."

She frowned until the white spot was close to her chin. "What's wrong, Cerrio? Ah shit, is it Chevy? Y'all fighting again?"

"Why do you keep asking me questions? The prank is over. You got me. Let's get the fuck outta here already."

"So that's how you treat me? Thought we was friends."

"Don't worry about it. We're friends. Just drive."

"Then talk to me," she whined. "This ain't the person who buys me nail polish and asks questions about my classes. You know, friends talk Cerrio."

I stared out the window at a man carrying bags like the one blowing in the wind across the parking lot. In my time I learned a lot about the word friend. A friend is anyone you meet who's willing to talk. Anyone you do business with, anybody who buys you a drink. Friends come, friends go and then they stab you back. Don't trust friends because friendship and loyalty don't mix too well.

Bandy was waiting for me with a wide open expression. I looked at her hands wrapped around the steering wheel, eight slender fingers extended out, a pinky with a small gold band on it, thumbs underneath. At the end of each digit I saw peach acrylic painted on her nails.

"The thing with the cream. That was good" I said. "You should have seen how those people were looking at me when I dropped all those tubes on the counter."

She smiled. "My sister taught me that. I'll call her and tell her how much you liked it."

"I never heard you talk about a sister. What is she, like you?"

"No."

"Different parents?"

"Different lives."

"Sounds like me and Chevy. Different lives. Except now our lives are more or less the same."

"You say that like it's a bad thing."

"I say what's real. I came home bleeding after a midnight shootout. You had to patch me up like a ripped jacket. Either that or it was a trip to the hospital and then to jail. Maybe not even in that order. Think I want that for Chevy?"

"But she loves you, Cerrio and you can't help who you love. Look at me and Neesha. You think it's easy for us? No way, this shit is hard. I'm a Christian born and raised but I can't go to church anymore because I have a woman in my life who makes me happy. Churches don't like that sort of thing. If we just split up then I could go back but that's like giving in. And you ain't giving are you, Cerrio?"

"Never that."

"So, then we got to stick to the plan."

"What plan?"

"What plan do you think? Chevy's hair salon."

"Chevy's salon," I repeated. "That's got a good ring to it. I'd love to see it on a sign. Who told you about it?"

"She did. I told you, Cerrio, friends talk to each other."

"Uh-huh, and what else do y'all talk about around the house?"

"No sir, that's just between us girls."

"Do you sing to Chevy when I'm not there?"

Bandy was about to turn the Honda over, she froze with the car keys caught between her painted fingers. "You're tripping. I never sing. I-I-I don't even like music."

"That's a bad lie. I heard you in the shower once and when I walked up to the car just now. And everybody likes music."

"Cerrio don't."

"What are you running from? Your voice is amazing. You know it. I know it. Maybe it's time everybody else did too."

"I said, 'don't goddamnit!'"

"Really Bandy? Friends talk to each other. Isn't that what you just said? Or maybe I got it all wrong. Maybe you just use friendship as a means to get what you want."

She sniffed. "Don't say that!"

"Tell the truth. Friendship is something you use to work secrets out of people. Secrets and maybe money. It's a tool like a screwdriver and I'm the fucking paint can you're trying to pry open. It's all tactics with you."

"That's not it!"

"Sing then, bitch!"

She balled up a petite fist and punched me in the shoulder. "Shut up, don't call me that! You don't ever call me that!"

"What are you so scared of?"

"Nothing, I'm not scared of anything."

"So, if I find you a nice stage to go on will you sing your heart out to the crowd like you just did to this windshield?"

"Don't try it."

For a moment I forgot that Bandy didn't belong to me. And for the first time ever I could hardly blame myself because it was just something that was so easy to forget. Sometimes, not having her made me jealous but right now was not one of those times. Right now I wanted to drive fast for miles and miles because right now Bandy had me fucking livid.

We weren't getting anywhere and I don't even know where we were supposed go so I opened the car door and just never closed it. All this mindless anger and loud arguing was pointless. At least Bandy was smart enough not to call me back. She knew a lot better than to waste her breath on the wind. She was going to save her air to tell Chevy everything that got said in the Honda and then they would hold court in her apartment and a landslide of questions would be coming to arrest your boy later on.

I walked a mile and a half to University avenue. Socks picked me up from a gas station at the edge of a shopping center with a shoe store and a Sally's beauty supply and together we thought about answers. He said, "maybe if I stayed away all day Chevy would just go to work and forget about the whole thing. I love Socks but I was starting to figure out that he didn't know a lot about women. That, "she'll forget about it" theory didn't even make it up to the apartment. Chevy met me at the top of the stairs in her bunny slippers. The door was wide open, jazz noise spilling out over the rail because she does all her best thinking to Miles Davis's saxophone. That's when her top floor connections come together like jigsaw pieces. When I stepped back a little I could see the whole picture staring me down with vengeance. Butter smooth music and piano keys, Socks is going to love hearing about how this goes. Just thinking his reaction made me break out in a stupid smile.

My baby crossed her arms and threw a hip out to the side. "Oh, he thinks it's funny? I know what you did, Cerrio. Bandy is sensitive and you're screaming at her and calling her a bitch and trying to make her sing. Like, who the fuck are you supposed to be?"

"Relax, we're even. She left me on foot at the store."

"Don't try that. I know you walked off. She said, 'you didn't even close the car door'."

"So, you're on her side."

"This isn't about taking sides. And if you had any chance of being right, I mean just a little bit, this much." She held her fingers up a breath apart. "Then we wouldn't be outside talking for the whole world to here."

"Please, the neighbors know you live for this type of shit. Who told you to come out here anyway?"

I brushed by her to get inside. Chevy stayed on me, furry slippers slapping off the carpet during a break between songs.

"You know what! You're sick picking on Bandy like that! You're a fucking monster! And where's my battery?"

"Guess what, I don't have it."

"So, how am I going to work tonight?"

"Call one of them street rats you get high with, maybe they'll give you a ride."

"Watch your step," she warned. "Bandy's feelings get hurt she might cry but I'm the one who cooks your food."

I whipped around in her face and she stepped back into the coffee table. "Me and your friend had a little falling out. So what? I was just trying to explore her gift and she got brittle. She caught feelings. It was nothing. Tomorrow it'll all be over."

"Liar," she snapped. "I know you pressed her."

"Yeah, who wouldn't? The girl's a natural. I just thought she needed a little push. I mean, what's the point of having talent if she's never going to use it?"

"I don't know, Cerrio. What's the point of having a man around if he doesn't act right?"

I came for the argument, stayed for the mind games. Miles hit a long note on his saxophone and after that we didn't speak again. The other night in Greensboro Chevy talked about getting a bigger place. I thought it was just the Hennessey talking but now it made all the sense in the world. Because for a day and a half we walked around with a silence so big that it was hard to squeeze down the hallway. She didn't have any words for me and every time I came in the kitchen Bandy had her face down in a textbook. Even the other dancers from the 43-Dimes didn't give me the time of day anymore. When they came over I shot lingering stares on purpose and they sent back a lot of concentrated nothing.

After forty eight hours of cooking my anger came back pure and everything that wouldn't concede with it burned off in the sleep I just could not catch. The back bedroom was too hot for all the wrong reasons, Bandy had laid claim to the couch to watch TV long before we ever had our issues, and I wasn't taking the floor so instead I took the bus all the way back to Greenway avenue.

When Aunt Denise saw the pain written in my eyes she said two words, "woman problems." Implied and correct and then she whispered a prayer up to God's ear. Not for me but for all the women who were cutting my mind up into little tiny ribbons.

CHAPTER 9

MISPLACED RELIGION

I'll tell you a secret so soft in your ear and when no one else wants to listen I tell it to the Cutlass. It's my temple on wheels, a sort of sanctuary. Aunt Denise bought a new car so these days the blue-gray girl spends her golden years hanging around in the garage sparkling like a gem. She didn't need any wax because the last coat I put on still shined like glass but I brought a rag anyway just to dust off the dashboard. She already knew about the stash behind the dryer so I talked about the junkie who held open doors and the cul-de-sac shootout. Then I told her about a brand-new sort of mess where every woman was angry with me all under the same roof. How they came in the living room just to breath up all the hate and then sneezed it back in my face on their way out the door.

She listened good until I fell asleep on her soft backseat leather. Chevy's mama came to me in a dream, stepping through a haze that drifted upwards like heat waves rolling off a hot tin roof. We came face to face. I saw the diamonds in her hair, tasted the apples on her breath every time she exhaled. Strange but not strange that even in this other universe nothing much had really changed. Chitara James was upset with me just like every single woman on the other side. Before we got to talk about it I felt the earth open up it's jaws and swallow me whole. The flowers rooted in shifting soil spun like pinwheels until the petals flew off in a hurricane of floral blades and then the hands of my sins pulled me down deeper and deeper until the dirt closed up again.

When just a needle hole of light shined through I woke up. My senses were in a fog and cigarette smoke filled the garage touching every corner where the mouse traps Aunt Denise laid down ate like kings. Her church boyfriend was there looking at me upside down through the glass, pulling on one of her effeminate Mistys snagged from the box. I went for my waist but there was nothing to grab. This is the only place in the world where I don't have to walk around with protection.

"What'chu reaching for?" he croaked.

I looked at my palm, empty. The sweat on it made me remember shoving the heat under those rose bushes next to the house. "Nothing," I replied. "Just twitching. Bad dreams I guess."

"Looks to me like you got a demon. Looks like he's on your back pretty hard too. Maybe you oughta come down to church and let the Lord work it out."

I sat up. "Take it easy with the God stuff, alright. I just barely woke up."

"Just saying. Invitation's open. I know your aunt would love to see you come and sit in the pews."

He blew a cloud adding another layer to the smoke. Walked to the wall and brushed a hand across a row of tools hanging up making wrenches tapped together with a sound like wind chimes.

"Nice stuff here. Must have cost a fortune."

"It belonged to my uncle. He was a carpenter. And a plumber. He was everything."

"I heard a lot about him. Sounds like he was quite a man."

"That's funny I ain't heard much about you. What do you do?"

"I make sweet, sweet music for the congregation. Songs to worship by."

"You're an organ player?"

He snapped his fingers. "That's right."

I stood up, smoothed my shirt, slammed the Cutlass door shut harder than I meant to. "And you got two daughters in the choir. Man, I bet it's like a little gospel concert in your house all the time. How much does your family act get paid?"

"Everythin' ain't about money," he drawled. "I'm a saved man. My soul has no price."

"That's so beautiful. Here you are just helping my aunt around the house. I mean her soul belongs to the Lord too and you're his helper. So where do you plan on starting? Dishes? Windows? Floors? The bathroom needs cleaned."

"Me and your aunt got a thing going on."

"Yeah, that's interesting."

"How's that?"

"Don't you think you're a little young? Somebody once told me you can't help who you love but this is different. I mean, she's got twenty years on you. And in case you ain't noticed she can't walk."

"God don't see age. Denise Lloyd is a lovely woman. And when a thing feels right there's just no holding back."

"How can it feel right when she's dead below the waist?"

That made him rock back on his heels in dirty sneakers. He blew another cloud of smoke that hung low just above his hair and tried another angle, intimidation.

"Listen, here's a fact. I saw that gun in the front yard tucked up in the pine needles. That thing is big enough to stop an elephant. You're lucky because anybody else probably would have called the police soon as they saw it."

"If you find a gun around me don't call the police. Call the Lord. That's what you do right?" I leaned on the car. "What kind of church you got to anyway?"

He blinked. "Same one as your aunt. Baptist."

"Baptists know you're over here trying to fuck an old lady in a wheelchair?"

His face went flush, for all that grand church boy talk he was just an undercover sinner living a lie. Pretending to be redeemed from regular evil everybody suffers under. Couldn't take exposure because God really hates a fake. I saw his hand slide up towards a pipe wrench on the wall, before he could clutch the handle I snatched his shirt collar and twisted it in a tight ligature. Every vein in his scrawny neck jammed with blood until his throat looked like a map of angry cords. He wheezed for mercy but the fingers still groped for the hammer on Uncle Daya's sawhorse. I slapped him hard and a palm print cooked hot on his cheek while he strained for a ripe gulp of air.

The church pretender gave up on weapons and gripped my shirt. His hold was weak. This whole religious game was weak, not just phony but sad and stale and bearded with rot. I pushed him backwards and he put out his arms out like an airplane trying to fight turbulence but he just wanted a little balance. That was the key to everything, a little bit of balance. Instead he went all one way and banged into the Cutlass's front fender before falling sideways to the floor. When his head bounced off the concrete that's about the time Aunt Denise came sailing down the garage ramp.

"Stop it!" she screamed. "Stop that right now!"

I picked up church boy's cigarette from where it rolled under a car tire. "Look at this. Dirty clothes and thrift shop shoes. In here smoking your Mistys and touching Uncle Daya's tools. Don't you see it? This man is here for your checks. Your his mark, Aunt Denise. He's looking at you like a scam."

She pointed to the door. "Out. I want you out of here right now."

My mouth hung open like a trapdoor. "Me, what the hell did I do?"

"Two words, Cerrio. My house. This is my house and this is my company and you are not going harass whoever I want to bring over here to spend time around me!"

"Are you serious?!" I pulled the fraud up to his feet by his shit brown dyed hair. "First of the month this clown is going to be elbows deep in your money. Your money! And I'm the only one who's going to be be over here to stop him. I'm the one who's going to have to save your crippled ass!"

She shook her head. "Cerrio, you got a long, long way to go. You are not an angel and I do not need saving. Now leave before I call the police."

I looked at her boyfriend, if he could really be called that, before thrusting him forward into a pile of cardboard boxes. They slid away from each other as his weight came through slicing down like a cake knife. When his head thumped the wall a cracking sound echoed up to the ceiling and then dropped on our ears. Aunt Denise threw a hand up to her mouth and I leaned far down enough so my voice was hot on her temple. "One little afternoon date and this is what happens? All of the sudden I'm the bad guy?"

Her nostrils flared and then she wheeled her chair back just a bit to get the right range and punched me in the mouth.

A little while ago someone told me that if I can't hurt others I'll only hurt myself. That talk came from a psychiatrist in prison. He was living the dream, getting paid to find flaws in society's dark side is easier than playing target practice on the side of a mountain. I told him that and he scribbled it down on his pad. He had funny handwriting but he never lied. When there's no one left worthy to destroy then it was just me self destructing. That's why when I pulled the dryer up with a bare hand the sharp, steel edge slicing down in my gun palm hurt just perfect.

Lint blew up in fat, gritty storm to wage war with the breathable air. Aunt Denise coughed and yelled at my back while I ripped apart the shoebox and stuffed street cash in any pocket where it would fit. She wanted me out and she wanted to know what else I had hidden in her house. Her boyfriend came limping right behind her snitching about the pistol in the bushes. Before I walked out the door I turned around and told her that I hoped, above all things, that she had really found true happiness.

Outside in the heat the day wasn't fading. There was plenty of sunlight left to unravel my problems or maybe make more. Anything could happen but it would all go a lot smoother with eight bands in my pants. I had a few bills clutched tight in my gun hand to stop the bleeding from that gash the Maytag left behind. All the rest was balled up and jammed down deep and I could feel it scratching against both thighs like steel wool.

It didn't take long before the money in my grip became soaked with droplets that left a red, trail on the sidewalk. A stray dog sniffed behind me, some bitch who enjoyed the scent of something sinister all dressed up as a man. We walked like pet and master across a bunch of city blocks until downtown where she turned over a trash can and chased rats into the street.

I bought the bandages to fix my hand up at the pharmacy. Inside where the air conditioning called all loiterers exhausted from the heat there were a ton of questions about my bloody money. The clerks asked them silently with big, alarming eyes but over at the bus station no one even bothered to look twice.

Bums and diesel engines spewed fumes up to the shelter's sprawling metal ceiling, AKA the biggest plot of shade known to the city. People moved everywhere, only place they didn't scramble was inside on benches waiting for their chariot to arrive. I didn't come for a ride in a stretched out coach. I just wanted to sit here and observe until the swirling dirt made a brown seam on the cut below my fingers. A lot of people do the same thing even when they don't have any wounds you can actually see. Business men and filthy no accounts come down to watch this vibrant place in the center of the Winston with deep affection. By the laws of common sense it should be full of rot, but that's cliché, very expected but not quite true. Instead, there's a march of life going on down here all day made up by so many things romantically flawed moving in a flow. Socks said, "it's like sitting behind the front gates of the fallen garden while the locks get changed." Maybe he's no good with relationship advice but I got to give the man credit. My brother is as profound as a ghetto Jesus.

I left before the middle of the day turned into a stale afternoon and found a place to hide out. There were bikers and rednecks and stay at home moms way out from the trailer park just here to get tipsy in their cowboy hats at a bar called Sally's laid back by the old courthouse. A certain feeling moved through the air and country music twanged from a jukebox in the corner. The flag above the liquor bottles told me this was the perfect place to escape. No one familiar with me would be sniffing around a watering hole full of mysteries where the dogma set the tone.

Sally was a man wearing a hat with a brim trying to run a bar for the city's good old boys. I saw a lot of potential for tensions to become phenomenal but I wasn't worried. Whatever happened in here could never come close to the drama that had been riding up and down Chevy's hallway for the last couple of days. He looked me over with some of that same dogma in the air speaking through his eyes. I put a ten in the tip jar and watched his iron face melt into a half grin. I half grinned back and ordered a double shot of Grand Marnier with a spring water chaser.

Sally poured me up under the Confederate stars and stripes just like I was an old friend. We had a conversation I'll never remember about all the tattoos covering his arms. He had a story for each one, it was a timeline that started in his late teens and by twenty-one I faded out and was thinking about Chevy again. She still didn't have battery for her car. How would she get to work tonight? Maybe she would have to go by herself on the bus which was a depressing thought. Except I don't get sad, I get angry, which is exactly why Aunt Denise's boyfriend was picking up her dryer off the floor right now.

I thought about calling Socks to come down and play pool. I know he's not doing anything because we're the same like that. We could get drunk and leave out of here with a couple of housewives on our arm. Sally and his friends would be seething about it, maybe somebody would even say something way out of line. I sort of hoped so because deep down inside I was looking for a fight. And since I couldn't lay hands on any of the women drilling down on me lately and the fucking church boy was such a disappointment he minus well have not even tried at least I could get a run for my money right here, and I could at least respect some of these rednecks for wanting action before me and the mountain of muscle I call my brother wiped this place up like a runny nose.

Me and Socks, just like the old days. He likes fighting just as much as the best of them except he's more skilled at it. He'll ride with me on anything but only if I let him and goddamnit I know better. Taking myself to ruin, now that's one thing, but taking a brother over the edge is a sin too much. Even a midnight shooter slapping choir boys in his crippled aunt's garage has to know when a thing is way over the limit.

So, I drank alone in the strange bar letting the day fade away all around me. Sally cleaned glasses and rapped on about himself until the clock's short hand reached down to the six. Hours passed. The crowd thickened a little and my hand felt better but just like in the dream with Chevy's mother nothing really changed. I was still the darkest person in the room both inside and out. Then, someone else took the stool beside me and Sally's face went hard all over again.

CHAPTER 10

SHAME PUDDLE

I blinked like the sun was in my eyes and Chocolate slapped a twenty on the bar so hard I'm pretty sure she jammed a finger. "I'm looking for my partner. He's light-skinned. Got good hair." She touched the spot between her eyebrows. "And a big nose. Have you seen him?"

The good old boy stared at us with all the love of a cottonmouth. I expected that but I didn't expect Chocolate to grin back at him and push her luck with a wink. "Don't worry," I said. "She's with me." Sally didn't like it but he fixed us a pair of new drinks anyway. When his back was turned I pointed up to the Confederate banner hung high above the liquor bottles.

"See that? How much you want to bet that ain't the Georgia state flag up there?"

Chocolate scoffed. "Please, none of these white boys scare me. You know how many will meet me anywhere I tell them just to have a chance with a black queen? I'll give you a hint, it's one hundred percent. That's my kill rate, baby. I'm everybody's type no matter where I go."

"Adorable. But right now we look like the bottom of an oil pan in here. So before we have to shoot our way out of this one, let me ask. What are you doing here?"

Shots landed on the bar, Chocolate ignored hers and ordered us more. Sally twisted up his face like he was ready to spit on us. I thought the woman beside me just came to be reckless. Didn't think she ever had a plan. Stupid me.

"Well," she began. "I went by the apartment but you weren't there. Then, I saw that yellow car that belongs to your girl parked out front in the same spot since Saturday."

"Chevy told you we were fighting?"

"No, but you just did. Don't feel bad, though. It was plain as day. Believe me, I know when a home is broken. One side of the bed is all neat, car ain't running right, no dishes in the sink because there's none to wash because she eats off paper plates. Plus, she had that look and Bandy was right there sharing it. So I thought, he's not out buying anything and its too early for gambling so that means LaDecerrio must be hiding somewhere trying to get numb."

"How do you know my whole name?"

Chocolate ignored the question and hummed. "Now if I went missing where is the last place anybody would look for me?"

"What a waste. You could have had a long, career as an investigator."

I plucked my drink off the bar but before a drop touched my lips Chocolate snatched the whole glass away. "Cut the shit," she hissed. "I hunted you down to see if you wanted to hustle tonight. 'Cause that's what you do, Cerrio. That's what makes you happy. Because this, this is just low." She narrowed her eyes. "Look at my shoes. Do you see them?"

"I see them."

"Watch."

She poured the liquor out with a noise like a horse pissing on grass.

"That's you right now. Down there at the bottom."

Before I could snap her head off for talking down to me she dumped the next shot and the next until all the drinks she bought were pooled up on Sally's sticky, nicked, floor. The good old boy stood there slack jawed behind the bar. Mouth wide open catching flies while his temple throbbed. Chocolate has that sort of effect on men. She slid off her stool ever-so-gently so as not as to splash one of her pumps in the puddle and gave me an invitation.

She said, "Cerrio."

I said, "that's me."

"You coming?"

I answered with my feet. One in front of the other until we were back out there in the day and in her purple Jeep that was fast becoming night and our getaway machine. In all righteousness what else could I do? Chocolate was a brazen, lady, savior come to pull me back from an all white no man's land in a time of distress. She came in head first to clash skulls with the best of them. Her and that wild truck with no doors and there I was a little bit infatuated. Me and my big nose with an eye on each side watching that two liter bottle figure sashay in no hurry.

CHAPTER 11

MAGIC TRICK

"Can you believe that shit? Someone tried to sell me a wallet. A fucking wallet. Now, what am I gonna do with that? My money don't fold!"

Chocolate nodded while she listened to the old man pontificate, then she heard the faint rustle of a long, brittle fingernail reach underneath his fedora to scratch against a sand, dry, scalp. He thought he was a player talking all that shit about wallets and money and Chocolate let him believe it with all of his heart because Chucky was such an excellent trick.

"Having a good time?" he asked.

She smiled adoringly at him over the rim of a red, plastic cup. "Sure daddy. Having a ball."

"You're awfully quiet tonight. Something wrong, Sugar? It ain't me is it?"

"No, it ain't you. I'm just thinking that's all."

"About what?"

"Several things. Well, no that's a lie. Right now I'm thinking about one thing and one thing only."

"Damn it, Sugar you drive me crazy. That's okay, though. 'Cause you know I like it."

He winked his eye. Most girls would call Chucky a jackpot. He paid top dollar for what he wanted, came fast as a rocket, and never hinted about any free action like those penny pinching johns trying to save a nickel on a fuck. But most girls were thots or afterthoughts and this one didn't plan on giving him anything tonight. No, tonight she had her eyes on another man.

Chucky wanted to ask something else but instead went right back to scratching his head while they both stood at the top of the stairs. Chocolate swished a swallow of vodka around in her cheeks and watched the crowd down below in the big, white, house. The weather outside was no good for cards. Heavy mist and the tepid threat of rain had the inside jam-packed even more than usual. Everybody slithered around each other in Cerrio's favorite spot like vipers in a pit. She watched the Arab closely, time was on her side, and right now she had him right where she wanted him.

There's two types of dark women, the kind you inevitability fall for and the ones who become trouble not long after that. Chocolate is both, mysterious and sophisticated and maybe even a little bit grimy. Ever since that first night out in High Point we had been rolling together. We were a team, a duo, two action stars straight from the street. The traditional pair they might have seen coming but not us, not at all. They weren't ready for us. Not at all. And while they wondered all about us we always left them a little bit broker than they were before. Pulling off in that glittery Jeep at the end of the night snapping rubber bands around their hard earned money.

She always picked the spot, that was the unspoken rule. She knew every place to bet on something big in the city of Winston-Salem, who ran them and what they liked. Most of the time she even knew what kind of car the houseman drove. Chocolate was everything in the streets except for a rookie. That's why I never fought against the rule.

Some nights she took us to places I never knew existed, little hole in the wall joints with cards in the back, liquor in the basement, and everybody just praying the front door didn't get kicked in. All of that was fun and dangerous and right up my alley but none of it held a thing to the fast times at Chucky's.

This uncle always had free drinks whenever we came around. Chucky liked Chocolate just as much as any man and that's about all it takes. Somehow he still thought I was in charge of her and something told me she never really made a big deal about it. Anyway, it wasn't my fault what he thought and long as I didn't let it get to my head she was happy to play along. There was nothing to lose when we acted natural. Every dog has his day, every pawn has a play. And whichever character I fit best came alive when we pulled up to the big, white house to a small fanfare right before the old man led us to the kitchen and put drinks in our hands.

"How y'all been?" he asked.

"I don't know." I shot a look at Chocolate. "What do you think?"

"Never better," she replied.

"That's good. Yeah man, that's real good. You know there's a big dice game going on upstairs. Everybody famous in High Point is up there shooting right now."

"How many of your nephews are up there with them, Chucky?"

He looked into his cup. "Just Marshal. I keep him around for security reasons."

"So, if I go upstairs and it's a family reunion do I get free plays all night?"

"Hell no!" Chucky snapped back to his gentleman manners for the lady's sake. "Sorry, nephew. I meant, no that's not happening."

"Didn't think so. I love you unc' but I'm not going upstairs to make your boys any fatter. Think I'll just stay down here and stick to what I know."

"Poker?"

I nodded. "Exactly. Poker."

Chucky didn't have to guide me around anymore. I wasn't that much of guest. He stuck his elbow out and Chocolate put her hand through the crook and I watched the couple float away like a pair of bubbles on their way to go find a quiet spot while the rest of the house boiled down like a tea kettle. It was packed. Slick bodies pressing in close on every side and every piece of glass dripping condensation like candle wax. The spot was a sauna tonight, I mean it was so hot the fucking chandeliers were foggy.

In the den sweat and gunmetal mingled in the air to make up the ripe scent of risk. If I died here tonight they would bury me in the yard like a stash of dirty money. I could play soft, keep the hazards down to a minimum, but there's no fear in this house.

A chair had opened up for me right in time for a fresh deal. As the cards went down around the table everyone tossed their cash right in the middle. I don't know who started betting first but the two red queens in my hand begged me to raise. Calls went all the way around before the first three on the board got shown. I hit quietly, no one saw it in the push. Them not paying attention was the error that could make me rich. They bet into my queens like swimmers paddling straight towards the mouth of a great white. I had precision in my bite, every raise slow and easy until we came all the way down to the last card. That's when I pushed it all in the center like Chucky taught me years ago. Sour faces creased up all around, the boys clutching losers knew their wives were going to be ill when they came home with those pockets touching. Feelings didn't matter much though, not so long as my .40 was part of that faint scent of sweat and pistols rising up in the heat.

Winning felt good, better than sex but not better than making love. Then came the woman, Chocolate in my line of vision clutching the straps of her tan Fendi pumps between two, long fingers. We had a code, part of the beauty is we never practiced it. Me and Sugar Bares finest didn't prepare signals in her Jeep on the way to the spot. We just made up our own language of scandal right there across whatever game we happened to come around.

Any other night Chocolate would always go on the opposite side of the table so our eyes could lock. If I got a bad hand then I'd do a thing where I checked my watch and she'd lean forward to show a little bit of cleavage. While everybody else worked hard breaking their necks trying get a peek down her shirt I'd hurry up and make a quick change of cards. If she licked her teeth that meant watch for the bluff. If she crossed her legs that meant fold and get out of there. When she took off her shoes then it was time to go.

Except we hadn't even been here an hour yet and that just wasn't enough time to get any money. She sucked her teeth loud enough for the whole house to hear. When I ignored the noise then she got anxious like one of those puppies you can't leave alone on vacation because they'll tear up your furniture and chew on the rug. She watched as the cards got dealt out again. I checked my two down on the table which were mediocre as any butter face skank drinking down at Sally's right now. Still, I bet a hundred in the blind like it was standard procedure. A stupid thing to do. The wager was ugly but I just needed to make the point that we weren't going anywhere yet.

The rest was streamlined gambling. All the cards on table got flipped over in seconds without any more cash coming out. Everybody folded in the beginning except an old lady in a sequin jacket. She looked like somebody's grandmother, like she should have been somewhere singing hymns in a church pew on Sunday morning. Instead, she was right here with me at the neighborhood card game. Chocolate didn't cross her legs, she just flipped her hair back like she was trying to show off her good side. I wasn't worried, figured that was just her being her usual arrogant self. I dropped my cards and sequin Jackie had a straight flush. Before anyone blinked a hundred dollars and my entire fan club that had gathered to watch my winning streak were all gone. The old woman took the cash and the fly girls who were her nieces went upstairs to find Chucky's nephews.

When I got off the table the dancer came right to my side. Chocolate was unapologetically black, hoop earrings hanging, thick braids swinging, gold bangles clanging down next to her lemon, lime finger nails. Before I took too much of her in and got lost she popped off. "See that? You shoulda listened. If you'd left when I came in holding my shoes you would have saved your money."

"I didn't know that lady had a good hand back there. Why didn't you cross your legs like you were supposed to?"

"Forget it. I got something better anyway. Something I know you're really going to like."

I watched her pull a key from deep out of her bra. Sort of like watching a magician pull flowers out of his sleeve except the props were a lot better. She flashed the metal in the light with a smirk on her lips.

"What is that?"

"It's a house key. The one who gave it to me just called. He wants to see me."

"You mean right now?"

She sucked her teeth. "Of course I mean right now. Aren't you listening?"

"I always listen."

"No you don't. Otherwise you'd still have a hundred dollars."

I spun away. "Get lost. I'm going back to the table."

She tsk, tsked at my back. "And here I was thinking you wanted to get some real money. Guess you must like playing tug of war for a little bit of change in your fake uncle's house."

I turned around at the sound of bread just like she knew I would right into that cold, smooth face wearing a calculated smile. From only a foot away it was easy to smell trouble but that's what I liked about her, the essence of risk spilling from her pores like strange noises leaking from a locked closet. Well, that and just about every goddamn thing else.

"What do you got?" I asked. And Chocolate started talking about a trick out in High Point close to Chucky's house but far enough away that we still had to drive there. He was a tax lawyer. Married and paid in full and she was putting her best everything on him. The sex and the head and the dressed up facade like it was more than just the money that kept her coming back every week. I didn't catch his name, that part wasn't important. What was important is how Chocolate had him so ready to leave his wife. There was going be a quickie divorce and then her and him were going to run off to a land far, far away to live happily ever after.

The more she explained it the harder I laughed. We were outside when the story ended and I was wiping tears out of my eyes. This woman has a tight philosophy on starry eyed marks sucked up in a scandal, all of them go down. That's city girl reasoning, don't argue with it or you'll be next. I could see her favorite trick in a pressed down shirt, creased khakis, answering the door of her motel room late at night with a box of candies in his hand. The way she had this lawyer spiraling off even had me a little bit dizzy. She said he said, "he already had a diamond ring picked out for her ring finger." Chocolate would take the rock, no shame in that, but she wasn't going anywhere. Playing mind games had earned her a key to the front door of the tax lawyer's house and she wanted to pull a late-night burglary right now.

She asked if we were riding and I climbed in her Jeep with no definite answer. Looking through the space where the door was supposed to be I saw the big lady across the street with her pink scarf on. She smoked on the porch in a rocking chair, lighters in her dress, a switchblade by the ashtray.

"Is he home right now?" I asked.

Chocolate shook her head. "No, he's downtown working extra late in his office."

"You were going to meet him in his office?"

"Yeah, it's big enough to do it."

"And what happens when you don't show up to fuck him?"

"Then he'll call me back and I'll say I'm stuck in traffic."

"He's gonna believe you're stuck in traffic in the middle of the night?"

"I'll tell him a semi flipped over on the road. Believe me, a horny man will believe anything I want him to."

"What about the wife?"

"Gone on a girl's trip in Myrtle Beach with her sister."

"Alright, let me drop you off to him and I'll go take care of it. Just call me when you're done."

"What, and let you take all that money home to your little girlfriend? Huh-unh, no way. I didn't come this far to get skipped."

"How do you know there's even anything in the house? It could all be bullshit, costume jewelry and silverware."

"Because he's got a safe. And it's healthy."

Then Chocolate did something I never saw her do before, she took a bump of powder right there in the Jeep. That's when I should have known there was more than meets the eye but like I said before, I was infatuated.

She checked her nose in the mirror and turned the radio down to one.

"So, what are you going to do, Cerrio? You want the safe or you want to go back in and fight Della Reese all night to get your hundred dollars back?"

My stare went back to the reefer lady again. She had her skinny, orange cat out in the front yard with his nose in the air sniffing for more pussy. This was a tax lawyer's safe and there was no good reason not to go in. If I had an excuse then maybe somebody should have written it down for future use. Here is why I can't help Chocolate get paid tonight, here is why I cannot help you. She was the girl in school with the keys to the cafeteria and I was the boy on the playground with crumbs around his mouth. Just a little runt fed up with scraps and hungry for more.

The orange cat looked at me from the front yard and that settled it. We were going to see how the other side ate tonight.

Chocolate gave me directions to a nice neighborhood, the kind of place where neither of us fit in. I knew exactly where we were even if I'd never been here before. This was the long rainbow sagging with riches, a pot of gold hung off the end of every silver spoon like a seashell necklace around a beach girl's tanned neck. People out here knew the sort of Christmases and birthdays and everything else that came with no limits. In fact they probably didn't know what limits were besides the ones posted out by the highway telling them to check their speed. If that was my only worry in life then I could die today happy as a boy duck in a pond full of female swans. While me and Chevy fought hard to manage the rent these elites were planning vacations somewhere at another house with another car, maybe even with another family.

We passed twenty colonial style homes, federal style homes, plantation style homes. I knew the differences in architecture because I used to read real estate magazines in prison. I knew the difference between an open floor plan and a bay window but I didn't need all that semi education to notice luxury. It was all in the neatly trimmed front lawns and the driveways filled with Europeans.

"Shit, you sure you know somebody out here?"

Chocolate touched her titties, so self-obsessed. "You think I'd ride out here for no reason? You should know me better than that by now."

"Don't get mad. I never doubted you for a second."

"Cerrio, you had to be drug out here for this. I had to save you from sweating it out all night in that hot house like a slut in a free clinic."

I cut the headlights off. "Thing is I just can't make it easy. Four fifths of life is all about balance. Everybody else spoils you so I have to go the other way with it."

"Wow, that is the sexiest bullshit I've heard in a real long time. But you still talk too damn much. Turn up here."

We went left at the stop sign. I eased off the gas and the Jeep crept to the end of the block mostly it's own.

"Right here," said Chocolate. "Stop."

I pushed the brakes in front of a brick house with a black Panamera out front. "I thought you said he wasn't home."

"Relax, he's gone. Just stay here a minute and keep the Jeep running."

"If he's gone who's Porsche is that?"

"That's just his toy. The man is in a mid-life crisis. He drives a Range Rover most of the time but a Porsche to the golf course and his wife has a Chrysler."

"No shit." I didn't know whether to be impressed or disgusted. "He has all that and his wife just drives a Chrysler?"

"Yep, but he always takes the Range to work."

I looked over at the piece of German engineering like it had better answers. "This guy must be a real asshole."

"Most men are," she sighed. "Let me check out the house. Wait two minutes after I cut the porch light out and then come in."

"Wait. What if his wife came home already?"

Chocolate was halfway out of the truck already. "Then we leave. That's why you keep the Jeep running."

She jumped out like a hooker but stepped off like a society girl. Medusa in a pair of jeans with long legs slicing up the driveway. I looked around for something to cover my face with. The search didn't go far. She left her button down on the passenger's seat right there beside me. I wrapped the shirt around my face, pulled it tight and tied the sleeves behind my neck. The striped Polo smelled just like lavender. With essence of Chocolate all in my nose it got hard to focus on the new crime. I tried to concentrate on the porch light, tried to wait with my hand on my gun for whenever it died and I had to spring into action. But the shirt was invading my senses, making me drunk and all at once those dangerous thoughts I fought so hard to tamp down came streaking through my brain with a full head of steam.

Chevy I loved, Bandy I thought the world of, but Chocolate had academics. She was the one I saw behind me in the shower when I was raiding Chevy's Maybelline tube. Now I knew. She was the vision coming to me in bathroom right before my baby almost caught me in her coke. Now I knew. The licorice dancer was picture perfect and if I ever needed someone with talent for the cause this made perfect sense. Now I knew.

Chocolate was for real, a shameless pedigree blindfolded to the haters. She sold sex like a chef whips dinner, like a baker bakes cake, like a dog buries bones, like a whale drinks water. I doubted she used the bathroom because when that woman pulled down her pants it was for business only and business was good. Push to come to shove she would give this trick one on the house just to keep the con going, or she might even show his wife a good time and have them both racing against each other to see who was first to run away with her. She was talented and could break a trick out of anything. She did it for the Gucci shoes and the Chanel purse and the Dolce glasses and of course for the money. Always for the money.

The porch light went dark and a lamp came on inside the house like the illumination was switching places. For the first time it occurred to me that we probably should have planned this thing a little better. I didn't know if I was supposed to rush in right away or bring it slow. Chocolate hadn't done a good job of filling in the blanks. No fumbles, though. We didn't need a complete set of rules to know that true art of crime is about never getting caught.

I took it easy creeping up the narrow stone walk with the Llama held down low. Sugar Bares best dancer should have been right there at the door waiting to hustle me inside. Except I knew better, the energy changed as soon as I put my first foot up on the stoop. I paused, tightened the shirt around my face and checked the pistol one last time. Cracked the front entrance open just a barely, a little and a little more and then the wind put out a hand and pushed it six inches wider. Inside the lights were the type that can be turned up bright or dimmed down low. Chocolate had them up just high enough to see into all four corners of the living room without straining my retinas.

She never lied. Her lawyer friend was in the money up to his elbows. I wonder how many people he cheated just to live like this. Stepping in I thought I felt a little Alex Murdaugh vibe coming through. The place was laid out like a tiny museum. Oil paintings on the wall, Persian rug on the floor, a statue of Atlas in the corner holding the world on his shoulders. I thought if I could have just one thing it would be that statue, the man under the globe looked like the only one who truly understood where I was at right now.

I saw Chocolate's shadow on the wall taking the steps two at a time to the second floor. I followed her up to the landing and froze. Voices drifted down the hall, her and a man talking all about a back massage. "Make sure the oil is nice and warm, Tina. You know I like it when you touch me baby but goddamn your hands are always so cold."

Chocolate cooed to him extra sweet. "Sorry daddy, but these hands will be warm once we move to Guam."

"Fuck Guam. We're going to the Caymans where Lillian can't catch me. I checked on it and her lawyers can't take a thing from me long as I'm out there. I can keep all my money and every dime is tax free, baby."

"Ooh, I like the way you think."

The bedroom door stood open only an inch. I shut one eye, used the other to focus through the gap. Chocolate loomed over the bed as fully dressed as she was in the truck while the fat trick laid face down naked as a newborn. She looked at me standing there, held her shiny, oiled hand up in the shape of a gun and pointed it right at the back of the heavy lawyer's head. This was a new sign, one we never used before at the gambling spot. It meant take him.

Now, I saw the plan except it only took shape on presentation. I sucked up two sharp breaths. This girl had ice in her veins. Cold as a winter breeze blowing over a concrete coffin in a penguin's den and this trick was going to have the aftertaste of her chilliness living in his mouth from now on. I crossed the threshold. The whale on the mattress was calling out for Tina to hurry up and rub him down when I grabbed a clump of his thin gray hair and pressed the .40 to his skull. That bloated face went down deep into the sheets until both flabby cheeks were swimming in linen. A hard muffled scream shook the fat around his neck like a tambourine, it left his mouth and went into the pillow top with spit and drool and a few curses that meant less than nothing.

"Don't kill him," said Chocolate.

"Alright lover boy change of plans. The date is over. Now, all I want is what's in the safe and you can see tomorrow. And I know you want to see tomorrow, right?"

I pulled his head back by the hair in my grip and the whale gasped for air like a drowning sailor. "Tina, who is this?! Who are you!?"

I leaned down real close so be could feel the sting of Chucky's cheap, house vodka steaming on my breath. "Tina's not here right now and if you don't quit screaming and give me what I want pretty soon you won't be either. Now, where is safe? Tell me quick before I get angry."

"You should listen to him," said Chocolate.

"Fuck you!" He thrashed on the mattress. "You break into my house! Do you know I am?!"

I drug him off the bed by his salt and pepper whisps and the dancer hopped sideways as that huge body crashed on the floor like a bomb hitting concrete. He laid there wheezing, manhood pathetic, body crooked. I kicked him and my foot got lost deep in a roll of fat.

"Show me the safe!"

"Don't kill him," said Chocolate. "You're not ready for that."

"And who are you to tell me what it is I'm not ready for?"

She put her hands up chest high. "You got the gun, boo. You got the power."

It wasn't long before I found out how much I was loving this power, it wasn't long after that before I found out how to abuse it. That man on the floor looked like the judge and the prosecutor and the man who killed my uncle and put my aunt in a wheelchair for the rest of her life because he didn't like us living better than he ever would. I kicked him eight more times, the last one caught him straight in the mouth and he spit out a tooth.

"Alright," he gasped. "I'll show you. Take whatever you want. Just, quit kicking me already."

For some sick reason I was loving this, like Chocolate I had the power and control. The best, worst trick took me down to the bottom of his house to a beautiful basement looking like something right out of a fancy home television show. It was upscale bar designer, leather couch, big screen television, souvenir beer mugs from different pubs up on a high wall shelf. A pool table set off the spread. A heavy wood and marble piece with thick, black felt that begged to be petted. A stick rack blended in nicely with the furniture and right behind that was the safe.

The rack hung on three hinges like the screen door at my aunt's house. With his good hand the whale eased it open. With the other he held on tight to his bruised side. I didn't let him get dressed while we were upstairs or even fix his mouth. Humiliation had to come with this. I told myself it was for the wife who had to drive an American brand while he whipped true luxury and schmoozed strippers on their bed but all that was a lie. It was just me working out a vendetta built up big enough for a champion.

I could tell his rib was broken by how those swollen jowls tightened up in agony every time he took a breath. The man was suffering and it was wonderful and when he put the right combination into the safe and the door popped open a much more wonderful thing flashed before my eyes.

I had Chocolate hanging around upstairs watching the windows close for any unexpected cars that might pull up and yell out if she saw one. I told her to cut the lights out so nobody could see her move around in the living room and she gave me the finger, her way of telling me she knows what she's doing. A little reminder that even though I have gun she has control because she's the one who brought me to this lick, not the other way around.

I pistol whipped her trick to sleep and then called her down to the basement. The woman didn't even make past the third step before panic started falling out of her mouth. "Didn't I say you were doing too much? All that cowboy shit and look what happened. He's fucking dead. Goddamnit, now what we gonna do? How are we going to get this body out of here?"

I waved a hand. "Calm down he just sleeping. I had to knock him out so I could call you down here. Otherwise I would have been screaming that other name he kept saying in the bedroom."

She clicked her tongue and sassed it out. "Tina?"

"Yeah." I tipped my head to the side. "You know you're really more like a Raquel."

"Raquel, huh?" She crossed her arms. "So, he's not dead then?"

"Come on, I just told you he's sleeping. Now, take off your shirt."

"What?"

"Take off your shirt, I said."

"Cerrio, I don't care about what you're into but even if I was now is not the time."

"Tina, Raquel, whoever the hell you are. Cut the stubborn shit and listen. You see all this right here?" I moved so she could get an eye full. "I need something to put all this in. I can only carry so much in my hands."

"Then, use the shirt around your face."

"It's not big enough. Look."

I moved over some more, the lithe dancer peeked around me at her fat trick's stash and after that there were no more protests. It was a four foot tall steel fortress packed with lavish treasure, jewelry, guns, shiny rare coins, and money. Always the money. Chocolate hovered over me bouncing around in her emerald green bra from foot to foot. Tits jumping and mouth moving with the same words on her lips. "Hurry up. Hurry up. Hurry up."

We got everything we came for and then some. For the first time ever I listened good, tied her shirt off at the top end in a double knot and took it all. Shit, I think I even got the house note. Chocolate was just as keyed up as I was and after I had the last gold dollar stuffed down in her cotton top she she lost her heels again, skipped over the body sprawled on the floor and raced me back to the glittering Jeep.

CHAPTER 12

HOOD THERAPY

Isailed down I-40, fast lane only, ninety-two miles an hour with a whole lot of double, triple checks in the mirror. Red tail lights on the road glowed all over Chocolate's supple flesh. Her mouth was smoldering and those moist lips shimmered like a thousand little embers giving birth to a new fire.

The view from the driver's side made my foot heavy. I sped through the night faster and faster until the needle on the dash touched triple digits. Cold wind whipped through the doors that weren't there and goose bumps drew up on both of us. Mine on my arms, hers traveled from the throat all the way down to her emerald bra. They looked like seeds of braille rising up on the skin to tell a story and I almost made a wish to be blind just so I could feel the tale come into fruition. Traffic slowed, brake lights ignited and all those braille seeds lit up like flares. Like her whole body was going to burst into a ball of flames and turn me, her, and the Jeep into an asteroid racing straight towards the hood with the worst kind of violence.

Fifteen miles away we found a roach motel sitting right off the highway. It wasn't clean, the night manager gave me fair warning before I even took the room key from him. There were no sheets on the mattress and a tired air conditioner tried banging its last bit of freon through rusted vent slots. Chocolate cut it off and pulled the curtains, little cigarette burns dotted the floral pattern so the fabric looked like it had been hit with birdshot in a gunfight.

None of that mattered because right now we were too raw for details. She yanked a white towel off the bathroom rack and spread it out on the bed. I turned her shirt over on top, cash coins, and jewelry fell out together in a heap of sexy contraband. We separated everything, then we counted the money and split the jewelry. She got all the necklaces, I took a few rings. There was a four carat garnet set in a gold brooch that must have belonged to the fat trick's wife, and if it didn't then I felt even more sorry for her than I did before. Smaller princess cut diamonds bordered the main stone and slightly bigger ones were patterned all the way up the chain like an icy crust. Every rock was clear as water in a room the color of bread crusts. On the bed it looked purely ridiculous, just as out of place as we were in the bar that afternoon. Then, Chocolate scooped it up in her hand and the thing became instantly perfect.

That brooch must have been the only thing she ever loved. I could see the affection written all over her face, a genuine fondness thawing the cold in her heart. She didn't want the guns. I kept those and gave her most of the coin collection. She didn't even watch me split it up, just turned the piece of jewelry over and over in her hand countless times with stars in her eyes. Not that I minded, not that I would rip her off either. Perverse as he was Denise Lloyd's nephew would not burn up his last shred of morality trying to cheat a working girl out of her just due in an indigent motel.

She posed in the mirror. Turned left then right with the gold resting heavy on her collarbone. "How do I look?"

I took careful notice of her, silent except for the sound of my own breathing in my ears and then said, "just a little bit like royalty I guess."

"I know what you're thinking." She stayed glued to her own reflection. "And don't worry. I'll have this sold by the end of the week. Whatever I get for it we'll split."

"Don't make promises we both know you can't keep."

She whipped around all full of vinegar with the claws out. "You think I'm a liar?"

"No mama, I don't think anything. I just know who you are."

"And who am I, Cerrio? Go on and tell me."

"You're a woman. I mean look at you. Acting like a queen with the crown jewels on. Think I want to get in the way of that?" I shook my head. "No way, just let me keep the coin collection and we can call it even."

She put a fist on her hip. "Ah, I see what this is. You trying to fuck me ain't you?"

"Not at all." I ran my hand through the piles of loot on the bed. "See all this right here? This will hold me for a while."

But she didn't believe me and really neither one of us thought she would because a true sex symbol has to be paranoid about her looks, the same way a really rich man has to hold on to his wallet for dear life. She's accustomed to it and I guess it's only right, natural even. But it felt intriguingly wrong when she came to sit down beside me on that dirty, naked mattress.

She smiled and not with that man eating grin again like she worked with back at Chucky's palace. This time it was something very different when those lips curved into a look that seemed so much more invitational. All that stood between us were mere material things, guns and money and flashy jewels. Replaceable stuff we never even knew we never even knew about right up until the moment we had it. And she was still shirtless in that posh, green bra when I realized that even thought we were inside and it was the middle of the night it was still 400 degrees in the shade and hot as hell.

No doubt about it things were warm, no doubt things were changing. For the very first time I noticed the denim of Chocolate's jeans clinging to her thighs like a wet leaf on a windshield. There's a hole on inner part close to the knee that no one would even get a chance to see unless they were sitting down right beside her just like this. I wanted to put my finger down in there just to find out what it would have felt like. Such a stupid fantasy I know, but stupid things always wind up in the most impossibly dangerous outcomes.

Even if this room is filthy it's still paid up until ten o' clock tomorrow and Chocolate is still smiling right at me when I tore my stare away from her pants. She's been holding that face for so long it's starting to feel like a sign of delirium. Or maybe it's just me because now I'm noticing everything else about her too. The swell of her breasts and the curve of her neck arching out to those strong shoulders and the dark abyss of her belly button looking tantalizing in this pitiful, muddy light.

She was right not to believe it when I said everything else on the bed would hold me. The tension living under my skin is turning into pure damnation right now. I don't know how or when we slipped into this place of being so comfortable. All the adrenaline from earlier is gone, replaced by a more intoxicating chemical that feels cozy as a fleece down. She crossed her legs and put her hands behind her flat down on the bed in the perfect shape of an A. She starts talking about something, I couldn't tell you what the conversation was but every word falling from her mouth sounded impossibly romantic. Voice dripping slow with smoky affection, all cigars and bourbon like heaven had given the gift of speech to a velvet lounge in the heydays of saxophone jazz.

I leaned my back on the weak excuse for a headboard and asked Chocolate her name, first or last it didn't matter. I even would have settled for a pair of initials. But she is a professional and she knows this business is nasty, very nasty, so she doesn't give any names. Ever.

In the end she didn't stay and I didn't leave. The dancer hung around for a while and we snorted lines off the sink to celebrate. Before riding off with her new riches she left a little cocaine in a bag on the bedside table for me to start my engine up in the morning.

Come eight a.m. those cigarette burns in the curtains beamed through like laser pointers. Chevy called me while I was in the shower. I ignored her and the first text message she sent said just a few plain words. She wanted to know where I'd gone, she said Bandy was worried too. Her mind was on me but all my thoughts were on avoiding the tendrils of mold growing up the shower tiles like wild grape vines. Aunt Denise called while I was drying off, I didn't answer her either because all I cared about was last night's heist. I tallied up the lick with the hustling money that came out of the shoebox and romanced the numbers in my head. All together I counted a nice seventy thousand. The coins were worth something too, I know because they looked just like the ones used Uncle Daya used to collect.

All in all it was a fucking good night, good enough to fall back from the sweaty scene of gambling for at least a while. I didn't have to bet on anything for a week. Not professionally and definitely not in anyone's house. Not unless I really wanted to. Now was my time but for what I didn't know. Maybe for anything, hopefully for something. Maybe a chain, a car, or some new boots for Chevy like she was hinting about before. That's the problem with never having anything. When you finally do get something you don't even know where to start.

Chevy called again and my mind was everywhere. Her next text came through in all caps, no emojis. She put everything off the top of her wounded heart down in a nice collection of four letter words and then called to give me some more. I ignored her, again, and took the last line up the nostril. All my attention was on the motel television where me and Chocolate had made the news. A local reporter caked in drug store makeup stood in front of the brick house we violated talking straight into the camera about the work we did last night. She called it a crime of heinousness, a serious breach of the community's peace of mind and I wondered if anybody asked the fat trick's wife how she felt when she woke up this morning and realized her marriage had collapsed.

I really wanted to hear the rest, dying to find out if we'd killed that white whale but my phone would not shut up. This time the ring tone was like an ambulance siren screaming through traffic sending panic down the road. Socks number lit up on the screen. Strange because he never woke up before me, not even back in the day when we had to catch the bus together to school. I picked up and pressed the lime green button, drowsy breathing growled at me from the other end of the line.

"What the fuck is going on?" He asked the question the long way, trying to show he was serious.

"Probably the same thing that was going on before you called."

"Don't be an asshole."

I dabbed white grains off the table with a finger. "Why not? If I was anything else you wouldn't believe me."

I heard rustling while Socks switched phone hands. "Listen, Seville is calling me because she thinks you're over here hiding. What do you want me to tell her?"

"Tell her I'm on Jupiter, I don't give a shit. She's the one that ran me out. Her and that goddamn fan club she runs kept side eyeing me up in the apartment. I can't live like that. I mean, you know how it is. We fight a little-"

"Y'all fight lot."

"Whatever, we fight all the time. I make a mistake and we get mad for a while but this was different. This was war."

"What was the fight about?"

"This one was about her little friend with the white spot on her mouth."

"You fucked her?"

"Not at all. I'm proud to say I never touched the woman. And that's me being honest."

"Then, I don't understand. If you didn't sleep with the woman then why aren't you waking up at home right now?"

"You ask a lot of questions for eight in the morning."

"Answer smartass."

I sighed. "Thing is the girl can really sing. I never knew before because she hides her voice so well. It's like...it's like she's ashamed of it or something."

"Does she sing like Whitney?"

"Whitney, Brittany, all of 'em. Her voice is moving." I licked my finger. "I mean you gotta hear it. She's amazing. And, uh, I just wanted to hear her some and then we fell out and I had to leave."

I heard more rustling on the line. "So, you want me to tell Chevy you're out on Greenway?"

I had to think about it hard. Chevy wouldn't harass me at all if she thought I was at Aunt Denise's house. She respects the old woman way too much to be a nuisance. That would buy me a week to let the whole thing cool off but I said, "no, don't lie to her."

"Well then where the fuck are you?"

"I'm at the Village Inn. West 40 by the Waffle House."

"With?"

"With nobody. I'm here by myself."

"Something ain't right. Motherfuckers don't just go out of town to the Village Inn on hiatus. What room you in?"

I checked the motel keyring. "My key says twenty-three."

"Alright, I'm coming. Don't do anything stupid."

After I hung up I thought about our conversation some more, don't do anything stupid, he says. Seems like everybody was putting more pressure on me to behave. Only one that let me purge was Chocolate. She skipped through my mind while I ripped the wet shower curtain down and used it to wrap up my half of the treasure we got away with. Maybe that was her form of generosity, some trick of the darkness telling her to do me a simple favor with no strings attached by just letting me run up the chaos. My brain snacked on different sides of that same theory until both sides eventually hated each other. In my head the arguments went rounds in a sparring match, part of it was the powder. Rick James said, "cocaine is a helluva drug." But some of it was my morals evaporating like merengue in the rain.

When Socks showed up tapping on the door he had questions about the clear curtain folded in at all corners and suspicions about everything in the middle. I killed them all with guns and money. A nickel plated Ruger from the fat trick's safe and a couple hundred handed over to him bought me a nice, long, moment of silence.

I left the housekeeper a good tip by the alarm clock and then Socks started talking about the Waffle House across the highway because he skipped breakfast just to come get me. That's where the peace ended, over fried potatoes and a black cup of coffee. Between every bite he clinked the steel fork off his hard diner plate louder and louder until it rang in my ears like a bell over the door of an Italian butcher shop.

He look at me, full sunlight glaring in his face through the window. "Do you know Chevy is still the best thing to ever happen to you? I don't care if you sleep with other women. That's natural. But I want to make sure you always know where home is"

I touched my nose. "Come on man not right now."

He squinted. "Man, give me some."

"It's gone already," I barked. "I did it all in the room. The same place where I thought I paid you to be quiet."

"That wasn't a settlement," he snapped. "You got money in a shower curtain, gold rings on my floorboards and your girlfriend's calling me all about it but she doesn't even know yet." He mopped up some gravy with a big biscuit. "What you been up to, Player?"

I sipped a little coffee and thought about just how much to tell him when it came to last night. It was too much to handle all at once so I decided to ease him down into it slow.

"Do you remember when we were twelve years old and you thought that girl in gym class really liked you?"

"She did like me."

I made a buzzer noise. "No, she liked the bags of candy and Marlboros we used to steal everyday from the Asian store by the bus stop. And you stole more and more until that last time when we both got caught. Actually, you got caught and then Aunt Denise gave me the belt because she knew I was in on it."

He frowned. "I still can't go to that store."

"That Asian lady is still alive?"

"Yeah, but the girl I gave the suckers to ain't. She overdosed in a Wendy's bathroom last year. That's the reason they started making people get a key for the door."

A strong smell of bacon wafted through the air as we tried to squeeze out a better memory of the girl who used to use Socks for treats. When none came then I had to move on.

"There's this dancer from Sugar Bares. One that Chevy is real close to."

"A tall broad?"

"Yeah."

"Smells like heaven?"

"Same one."

"Is she the one with the long legs?"

"Good, you know her. Now listen and don't say shit because I'm only telling you this once, and it's only between us. I've been taking that girl gambling with me every night when I go out. We got a little scheme. She does her thing in the bedroom while I play cards."

Socks set his fork down. "So, Dez was right huh? You are pimping these girls."

"Give me a break."

"You can change the label but the box looks the same. Don't get me wrong. I don't knock your style. It's not like you're making them do anything they don't want to do. They're using their own free will and they got a right to make a living."

"And if one of them ends up in the gutter? Then what?"

"You mean if Chevy ends up in the gutter then what are you going to do." He shrugged. "I don't know, brother. Then, I guess I'm with you on the road to revenge."

Socks wiped his mouth and the waitress came around to pour fresh coffee. When she asked about the bill my brother just smiled at her. He still had that last sentence on his mind, participation in some kind of close up war might have been a daydream for him. Before stepping off she pulled two mints out of her apron and put them down on the table. Socks unwrapped his impatiently and popped it like an aspirin.

"Man, I don't know why you quit talking. We're not leaving here until you tell me every detail. So, what's the broad's name?"

I paused for a beat. "Chocolate. That's the only thing I ever call her."

"Yeah, makes sense." He sucked on the mint and nodded.

"You remember Uncle Chucky from High Point?"

"Old man who got hit by a bus? I remember him. He runs a dice game now up in that big white house."

"Last night I was up there playing cards. Chocolate loves hitting his spot."

"Bet Chucky likes hitting her's too."

"Jesus, you should see him. Poor girl can't last five minutes. As soon as she walks in the door he's got her by the arm and they're going upstairs."

"What about you? You ever hit it?"

"That's not what I said."

"Listen brother, I don't blame you. I've seen that woman from behind and I woulda done the same thing."

"I already told you. No."

Socks stared at me for a long second. "Alright, calm down. I believe you. Whenever you lie your mouth always twitches."

"Huh? For real?"

"Yep, always. Every single time. Don't worry about it, though. Nobody else ever notices."

I checked my reflection in the napkin holder. "How do you see it?"

Socks sighed a long, needlessly exasperated sigh and said, "because I been around you fifteen fucking years, I see everything. Now come on with the rest of the story, man."

I put the napkin holder back and fought off a urge to look at myself just one more time. "Uncle runs a lot more than dice now. There's usually a poker game somewhere in the house. Blackjack too. While he's playing leapfrog with the girl upstairs I'm down there getting to it. I mean business. And they couldn't stop me last night. I had a hot hand and things were going smooth and then all the sudden-" I snapped my fingers. "She pops up and a hundred dollars is gone just like that. You know that never happens. Not to me. So, after I lose of course I'm ill and then she starts flashing this key around saying she has something better."

I leaned in and lowered my voice. "She had a mark out there in High Point. This high dollar trick living on the rich side of town. Fat spread like a museum. And the guy is married but he's infatuated with her. He was ready to leave his wife and run away. Chocolate had him thinking he could change her life. Make her into an honest woman and all that."

"I know the game, Cerrio."

"Uh-huh, then you know what comes next."

"She sets him up."

I nodded. "Sets him up proper. Made the poor bastard think he was getting a massage and a blowjob. Then I came in there and beat him stupid. After that we took everything."

"Man, you make it sound easy."

I sat back and looked around, eyeing everybody in the diner for little uncomfortable shifts.

"Chill," said Socks. "Nobody heard anything."

"Ain't no telling."

"Trust me, brother. I wouldn't be in here if I thought these people were worried about us. So, what are you going to do now?"

I dropped my own piece of candy in hot coffee and stirred it until the steam smelled like winter blend machiatto. "I'm gonna do whatever I want. But first thing's first."

Socks crunched the last shard of mint between his back teeth. "What does that mean? First thing's first?"

"It means we need to go find a car parts store so I can do some gift shopping before the club opens."

We left the Waffle House, another healthy tip on the table under my plate for the stumpy girl who gave us mints. First thing's first means I went and bought a battery because even if Chevy and I weren't loving each other very much right now there were still responsibilities to take care of. We could fight for a month or maybe even a few years like last time but I'll be goddamned if I let her walk around with a dead car double parked out front while the other dancers laughed about it. I put my first purchase right in the driver's seat where she would have had to sit on it to miss it and Socks gave me a towel to cover it up so the neighborhood smokers wouldn't pull a smash and grab to take it to the store for a refund. Then, I moved on before her or that Asian lady could peek through the blinds and come outside.

My brother told me to just give up and apologize. I thought about it while we rode around smoking grapes. This standoff with Chevy felt good, but to who really? In the end we were just fighting against ourselves. Me and the man driving with the reefer between his lips have been through a few scrapes ourselves, not lover spats, more like sibling rivalries. But it doesn't matter how far apart we go because when the dust settles the outsiders always clench us back together like a boa wrapped tight around his lunch.

Because these glittered down dancers have been driving me crazy. Even in my dreams they take me on a ride and right now I'm just one short night's sleep away from using my pistol. I mean, not on them. Never that. But definitely on purpose. That's for sure.

Maybe you don't see it but I'm slowly losing my mind, getting dizzy racing from situations that start out mostly bad and then get worse. Now, I can't even trust a good thing when it happens. That's my new reflex, it just emerged one day last week out of nowhere. Then again it could be some old paranoia mixed back stronger. I don't know, but either way I swear to God if one more hot blooded stripper starts orbiting around me I'm going to lose my mind.

Socks listened to me rant like that in a spasm while pungent clouds gathered up around the Pontiac's ceiling. "Balance brother, that's what you're missing."

"Balance, he says. Aren't you even listening? I'm walking a tight rope everyday. What do you call that?"

Socks fired up another blunt and I watched a bunch of kids ride their bikes up the sidewalk, two boys chasing three girls. It was the same game we used to play in the summer when bicycles and swimming pools gathered all of our attention, before the rigors of manhood demanded all of our focus in every season.

"Goddamnit, I need a break."

He smoked. "Now you're making sense. Let's go to The Rose Petal tonight They say it all goes down in there."

Now, he had my full attention. "They say it goes down?"

"In a good way."

"Does the joint have strippers?"

"No, no naked women. It's not that sort of place. It's a uh," he rolled his hands while searching for the right words, "upscale sort of establishment."

"Alright. But what are we going to wear? I been in these same clothes almost two days."

"Man, you are full of problems. Ten seconds ago you were talking like one of those people who's about to walk into work and start shooting everybody. But, I ain't going to let that happen."

I punched him in the shoulder. "Why? 'Cause you love me? Come on Socks your supposed to be hard out here. Blowing a few grapes got you soft all the sudden?"

"Shit, you're dreaming fool. I just don't want have to explain to Chevy why I let you lose it."

"How you going to stop me?"

"Retail therapy. That girl from Cleveland projects showed me the way to do it with her student loan check last week. Trust me brother, I feel way better."

CHAPTER 13

ROSE PETALS

Dressing up always makes me want to go out on the town. Now what's more natural than that? And even though new spots usually make me anxious The Rose Petal had a special quality about it that made old inhibitions easy to break. A lit up stage with voices big enough fill Broadway bellowing soul, sorrow, and salvation held me down in a seat while the sweet smell of grass took the edge off. Socks wanted to come here, unlike me he never feels anxious no matter where he went. This place is new for him too. The Rose Petal is fresh to the whole city because the club hadn't been open barely a month yet.

On the drive over I asked him again if this place had strippers and again Socks said "no," and I said, "hallelujah." Actually it came out like "hal-e-fucking-lujah" and he just shook his head because it was easy to tell that I really needed to lay off the dancers for a while.

But I digress.

How did we end up here? Not in this club I mean in these clothes, in pinstripes and slacks. How did we go from pant and shirt hoodlums to suit and tie niggas before the sun even went down? The short answer is Socks again. The long answer is this.

We left Chevy's apartment complex with the windows up. There was a bus stop close to the Circle K where the kids on bikes stopped to drink cold, generic sodas and put the cans over their back tires so they could sound like motors. Socks took a left at the light, cut through a back road that paralleled Cleveland park and came out at a stop sign on twenty fifth street. From there the road took us straight downtown. He drove out around the edges to avoid block to block red lights and swung in close right where the skyscrapers tapered down low and became simple and forgettable brick and mortar squares.

A mile from the railroad tracks somebody got turned up on nostalgia and made the old tobacco warehouses into leaf lofts, fancy places for business types to live in. Nestled in between them in a hidden spot next to a coffee store and a pet groomer was a tailor shop.

This was a family business far removed from silly mall gimmicks. A family establishment where the owners, a Russian father and his two sons, stared me down right inside the door like I might steal something. Now, some Arabs don't like Mother Russia and some of Russia's son's don't do well with my kind either but when I pulled out a green knot they saw I had just what it takes to get along. Holding all that cash I could have been from Moscow but when I opened my mouth and spoke with a Piedmont accent they knew I was just a local passing in from the east side.

It was everything you thought a Russian suit store would be and I loved it. That old world masculinity was the reprieve I needed, the break I desperately craved. I know my own masculinity is as toxic as a misogynistic oil spill but that has nothing to do with the cherry wood shelves holding fine, shiny fabrics that bathed your skin in luxury, or the mannequins frozen in imposing poses with dark colors and waxy leather belts with almost no slack at the end. It has nothing to do with the shined up shoes set on the wall next to round tins of black polish and brushes meant to keep them that way. You can hate me all you like, despise me to death even, but it's much harder to hate the swag.

Socks knew the two brothers, he stood around up at the counter talking broken Russian while their dad hunted down my sizes in the back. A black man with dreadlocks speaking Siberian in a small city in western North Carolina. Shocker. Jaws should be dropping to the floor right now but only if we live inside predictions.

Vladimir, that's the dad's name, took care of us like we were family. He put style together the same way a sous chef puts down his own signature dish. At the end of all his work I came out dappered down in a white Givenchy shirt with a burgundy sport coat. Socks got a paisley embossed blazer with a charcoal vest, a choice of two black shirts and twin rose gold figaro chains that draped on his chest right above the third button so they wouldn't get tangled like too much thread pulled off a spool. As for drip I got a yellow Cuban link. When it kissed the little bit of light stuffing itself inside the store Socks whistled low. "Color me impressed, brother."

No man is perfect but the Russians got us close. I looked vintage but not old, like savvy met her soulmate coming back from history and they had a baby born just for dressing up to kill.

I know this much, we ain't ever going back to the mall again. After being fitted around the shoulders and waist all those cramped dressing rooms and ugly ink packs set to go off by the automatic doors seemed like a bad joke, like somebody wanted you to feel tortured when you just wanted to spend money.

I spent so much on outfits that the Russians hugged us like we were visiting cousins before bagging up our stuff. Ask me and I'll tell you there's never been so many colors embracing under one roof. Black, brown and white. Capitalism and Communism. Then, Socks and I came here looking presidential, took up a pair of couches facing one another on the mezzanine where the vocalists down below could be admired from a higher point of view and let a baby faced waitress who reminded me of the tennis player Coco Guaff take our drink order on a tablet while the women sitting downstairs at the bar eyed us coolly.

I told her, "I like Ace of Spades."

Socks shrugged. "I'm a straight up Hennessey man myself."

"Better get some sparkling Rosé over here too. I see a lot of ladies out stretching their legs tonight. Some of them might be thirsty."

"All of them are thirsty," responded the waitress. "Anything else?"

"Yeah," I replied. "What is your name?"

"Around here they call me Leila, but all my friends call me Secret."

Secret moved on to another group deliberating about vodkas and I kept on soaking up the atmosphere. Something wild held my focus down below, she was sliding up on a bar stool with a perfect round peach held tight in cheetah print leggings. Her nails were longer than three of Secret's put together and the braids down her back, blue as a lake. I liked her style, so loud I could feel the bass thumping in my chest just watching her order. Me and Chevy were not getting along right now and the loud girl looked like she could handle a lot of pent up frustration.

I guess Secret knew a few good tippers when she saw them, a quick eight minutes went by and she brought the bottles out ice cold. She popped the Ace of Spades with five painted fingernails. The four that weren't the thumb said "WSSU." I pointed. "Is that your school, Winston-Salem State?" She nodded, said "go Rams," filled our glasses until tiny bubbles threatened spillage over the top. Socks told her she couldn't leave without showing school spirit. He's a nut and I thought Secret, who's real name was Leila, who had a face like Coco Guaff, would just laugh it off. Her being an employee and all. But instead, she put a third glass on the table and in a strange twist of roles I poured her up just as much as she did us so we could all drink to the home town University.

"I'm proud of you brother. You done real good for your first rodeo."

"It was just a good day. Make no mistake, I ain't planning a career out of going in people's homes."

The waitress took her cue. She plucked the glass she drank from off our table then disappeared quietly.

"Shit, I understand," my brother said. I'm probably moving on myself."

I raised the gold bottle high for a toast. "To quitting."

"Quitting what?" he asked.

"You just said you were moving on."

Moving on is never easy. That was the bait and this was supposed to be the part right before Socks jerked the line and snagged a big one. I was supposed to pine over what quitting really meant because after all I had just gotten started. But like that song drifting up from down on stage I had heard this one before. There was something on the horizon and I thought that I could have absolutely left this world without ever knowing what it was but my brother just hated to see a good hook left alone.

He took a long drink and wiped his mouth with the back of a hand. "How do you lose so many fucking arguments with Chevy? Good as you are at twisting words she shouldn't even stand a chance."

I put my hands out. "I'm not twisting up your words, brother. It sounded to me like you wanted to celebrate retirement. Now, from what I don't know. I figured we get to that part later."

"You know what?" Socks put down the Rosé. "This shit hurts my stomach. Listen Cerrio, there's something big coming up. A nice lick. Shitload of money. Supposed to be me and a couple of dudes going in but if I'm being honest I don't much trust'em." He paused to let it sink in then leaned forward to be dramatic. "This is a big job and I need somebody I know is down. Loyal."

"Makes no sense. Why work with people you don't trust?"

"Because they're good at what they do. And it's a shitload of money."

"You said that already." I took a swallow of Hennessey. "But I guess it really must be if you need three people. Who's the mark?"

"The Pinnacle bank in Kernersville."

I whistled low. "Man, you are something else. Is it the clothes or the bottles that got you trippin' right now?"

The big man clenched his jaw. Every muscle underneath the brunette cheek skin rippled like a rock thrown in a pond. Just one fluid motion beginning and ending over and over again.

I shook my head before he got startd. "Look man, my thing was good. No doubt. But it was also blood and luck. The broad put it together and the mark just wasn't in any shape to fight back. Perfect scenario, the type of thing real jackers dream about and I fell ass backwards into. But man, a bank? Shit, that's a whole different animal. Whole 'nother criteria. Banks got alarms and guards. For fuck's sake Socks they got shit we don't even know about."

The jaw froze, he talked slow. "Hey, I'll give it to you, brother. You are one very lucky son of a bitch. Even more than you say you are. Because anybody, and I mean anybody else would be on the floor right now apologizing for that ignorant shit you spewed just now."

"Don't get in your feelings, man. A bank is not especially easy to take down. And all I am is an amateur who had a little good fortune. It's not in my skill set."

He smacked his hand off the table so hard the bottles rattled. "Are you serious? Some blowjob bitch you been knowing a month put something together and now you don't think I can do the same thing? You think this is something I came up with taking a shit this morning?"

"Calm down. We're here to have a good time, remember?"

"Fuck you," he growled. "I thought you knew this but I'll tell you anyway. I ain't some clown hanging around on the fringes waiting for my shot. All these one and done crooks, I don't mess with them. This right here," he tapped his finger hard on the table, "this been in the makin's since before you came home."

"All I'm saying, man, is that one piece of work gone right doesn't make me a professional. I told you I'm not making a career out of this."

Socks snapped his thick fingers signaling for the waitress. Shift change must have happened during our talk because Leila with the baby fat on her cheeks didn't come back. She'd been replaced by a tall mulatto girl with a gold stud in her nose and when she talked I saw more gold on her bottom four fronts that matched the carats in my chain. He asked her for a napkin and a pen. I would have made a request too, but the waitress smelled tension and spun off before Socks even got down to writing.

"That thing you did in High Point," he said, "isn't going to last forever, brother. I don't know what you're going to do when you run out of cash and coins to sell but here's an idea."

He folded the napkin over, slid it across the table. I went to open it until he put his giant mitt over mine. "Don't look right now. Wait until later on when the fun is over, then check it out. Think about all the things you really want and then get back to me. Soon."

I looked at the pale, pink napkin like it might explode. "What's on here?"

"A number, maybe a dream. I don't know. Call it whatever you want. Just hook up with me on this and promise it will all come true."

I been knowing this man a long time. Long enough to know his word means everything, and that's all a man has anyway. His worldly promises. The bond he speaks.

I put the napkin in my pocket and fought the whole night just to keep my mind off the number folded inside. We didn't talk about it, we didn't talk about Chocolate or robbing anything else either. No more shop talk whatsoever. More conversation was just going to lead to more conversation when everything that needed to be said was all in one word. Either yes or no.

He didn't press me, no more pricking holes in the good time we were having. Socks just wanted to look expensive as he felt and do something with all the energy charging through his bones. Brown liquor makes my brother move around the same way earthquakes make tsunamis rearrange a beach front. When the women who glimpsed us from below took their places on our couch he put the Hennessey bottle to his lips and went bottoms up. Before he could drown himself a freckled Creole with syrup dripping from her voice came up with a better idea.

"Let's play pool." She clutched the Rosé tight. "Me and my sisters against you two misters. Rules of the game are every ball you miss costs a shot and scratch is double."

One thing about life, when a Creole woman makes rules you don't dispute them. Her friends already knew as much and they broke up in teams. One pair shot balls while the others stood around trash talking with filthy mouths that couldn't kiss a mother. We kept the Hennessey on our side. They took doses of pink Rosé after Socks knocked off the seven, the four, then the nine, but he banked the twelve ball too easy and it lost steam in a crowd of solids.

The girls went crazy like Summer Jam. We took our drinks per the rules but Socks took double since it was his error. After whistles were wet the Creole took the long stick between her slim, musical fingers and called her shot, three ball, left corner. A little crowd gathered around to feed off the suspense and we were all on edge until she broke our hearts just like I knew she would.

The three clacked in the hole and the crowd went wild. Drinks spilled, hands clapped, women danced. Pure pandemonium erupted all across the felt table and spread through the club reaching into every corner to call out more onlookers. People chose sides. Team suits, that was us, verses team Creole, that was them. And the next opponent gave us quick redemption. She stepped up awkward like she never shot pool a day in her life and charged the cue ball straight through a cluster of stripes. It sailed to the side pocket, teetered gently on the edge like gravity wasn't sure what to do. She winced and leaned to the side and the whole crowd leaned the other way until Socks blew hard and just like that it was over.

Team Creole's fans booed but there were smiles all around. I clapped my hands together while the women called us cheaters like they were blowing crooked kisses. Socks lifted the Hennessey, held it high for the crowd to see. "We're good sports, though."

"Always," I added

And then women and men drank together until all our throats were on fire. When the bottles finally came down again then I felt tiny taps on my shoulder. It was the loud girl from down by the bar with the leggings and the lake blue hair. "Next game is mine," she said.

Her name was Henna. Born and raised in Chicago, came down to North Carolina just for a job in analytics. I don't know what that is but I know she talked a lot and kept the conversation interesting. She said she was living in Burlington right now but thinking about moving to Winston-Salem to get closer to work. Said she came out to here tonight to see what the city was like. I asked her what grade did she give the town. She asked, what town? I said, "this town. My town." She took a minute and said, "a low B plus." I said "a low B plus is just a B" and then she wanted to know what I was going to do improve the score. Like I said, "interesting conversation."

I let her win the pool game and drink up my champagne. Then, we found a hotel room and made a mess in all four corners. We had a good time doing it, a damn good time making the mattress cry. Henna had a tattoo on her lower back that said Heart Breaker in long, loopy calligraphy that rippled on impact. When the fun was done she fell asleep and then it was just me and midnight television taking turns watching each other.

That's when I remembered the napkin. It took nerve to unfold, the kind that comes when something you know you shouldn't really like probably won't be so easy to reject. I sat on my side of the bed, feet on the carpet, Henna snoring softly beside me, little hotel lamp burning on the table right next to the phone. Socks memo paper had the club's name printed in a circle around a white rose and below it was the numbers he had scrawled out in pen. I saw five digits lined up in a row. I stared at the figure while Henna rolled over in the sheets and thought about how many chairs would fit in Chevy's salon.

CHAPTER 14

SORE EYES

Henna made me feel good, like a strong drug she took me to the top of the mountain, when the high wore off I landed deep in the ocean. But morning came around with sudden emptiness. Just a bunched up sheet on the other side of the bed and loud makeup stains smeared all over her pillow case. Anybody else probably wouldn't mind so much if the day after looked just like business as usual. I almost didn't mind either, my ego felt good but there was a wound going a lot deeper. Henna's curvaceous body had been the bandage covering it up, then daylight came and ripped it away.

This wasn't her first escapade. I could tell by how she left the "do not disturb" sign hanging outside on the door handle. Housekeeping puttered through the hall rattling a dingy cart that sputtered on plastic wheels. When they stopped I saw the light underneath the door eclipse. A comment card slid through, management wanting to know how my stay was going. On a scale of one to five it was hard to say, the pool is green and the maids steal anything laying around shiny like wild raccoons. The survey went in the toilet. I pissed on it until the water looked like Gatorade then flushed the soup away. Maybe they can get better answers through the mail.

Look, I was done flirting with misery. The lights went out on that party a whole day ago. Now, I was feeling my way straight up the backside of sadness. Part of me was trying to convince the rest of myself that there was no more place left for the one woman who saw me into manhood. Let Chevy go, I thought. Close the door and bury that piece of history and walk away. Finally.

It sounded so easy. I started working on the plan alone in a cell all by myself, first day out it died right in my face. The woman wasn't disposable. She was a faction of me, her passion lived inside my bones, her gold eyes winked towards me in the dark and her lilting voice called out my long name even when we were too far apart to hear one other. I admit that more than anything I wanted her warm love, perhaps because I knew it was all that could save me. Yet, here I was settling for tepid affections and fast situations that left me laying cold right before dawn.

Living lies, holding back the truth with a stiff arm because there were too many blemishes waiting to turn into jagged scars that itched every time I got nervous. Deception was my best company and his fingers were pushed deep into the face of honesty with a far reach. And so I tried filling in the gaps between what was really real to me and what must kill the pain with all the other sort of things people usually embraced, clothes and chains, liquor and sex. Apart they sounded so good and but all mixed together it stunk like garbage and that's how I felt, like fucking trash.

Wednesdays me and Chevy go grocery shopping. I still act like I hate it even thought by now she knows better. At night we hang alone. After Bandy leaves we drink white wine straight from the bottle and then kick it with no clothes on. She calls it lovers in the middle and I like the name. It's exactly where we are, in the middle of the week, in the middle of summer, in the middle of always trying to pull something together Whatever other night she gets off from the 43-Dimes club is completely random but Wednesdays are for King and Queen.

Before that last bit of sentiment dried up and blew away I had to get over to the other side of town. Today was Wednesday and my watch told me Chevy hadn't left yet. It was still early and she was probably sitting around in her scarf on the floor clipping coupons with Bandy helping between glances at her phone. I had on fresh clothes and new cologne, dark sunglasses to block out the sun. Despite all the fashion suspicions of inadequacy still loomed heavy like bullies on the corner taunting choir boys on their way to sing at church.

I took the bus to Greenway again. It was a short walk to the house and a quick hop over the fence. If the someone saw me they wouldn't even think twice about it. After twenty-two years every neighbor on the street knew my face. I'm the nephew. The same one who's been in and out of the side bedroom window breaking curfew and hiding dope sacks by the fence since '92.

Landing on the other side I felt the backyard grass brushing against my ankles. It was far too thick for a thin set of wheelchair tires, if Aunt Denise came out here she'd get bogged down in a second. That was good for my plan but bad for the conscience. I wanted to change pants and mow the lawn, then trim the front hedges but time was ticking. By now Chevy probably had her shopping list ready and her hair already teased up.

Aunt Denise doesn't know about the butter knife I keep buried in her flower bed. I dug it up with a hand, a few pulls of dirt and the handle shined up at me like it was saying hello. The lip of the garage doorframe that covers the crack between the edge and seal has a space just big enough to slip the tip of the blade between. I wedged it through careful so the wood wouldn't scar. When the end touched the latch I pulled down, then backward, and suddenly the door clicked open. It swung back and little dust motes flew around wildly in a gust of fresh air. I saw her sitting there, the wheel turned hard left so I knew she got used at least once by that piece of shit boyfriend trying to milk my aunt for checks. He put the keys back in the visor and when I pulled it down they fell right inside my hand like they were finally coming home.

I drove the Cutlass through town in midday traffic with my thoughts tied up in a knot. What if Chevy was really done? Maybe her mama came to her in a dream like the man who lost everything came to me and said, "use your common sense. The boy's no good, leave him alone." Now, now could I argue with a case like that? A sentimental Wednesday wasn't going to fade those type of orders.

I stopped at the Circle K to pull myself together. Doorman's girlfriend was out front, a shot of heroin had her caught between nodding off and scratching white, ashy lines on a bare arm that already needed a lot of lotion. Another dude hung with her. Seemed like these days every woman had a new man to love on. It was something like a fever, like a deadly contagion just traveling through the air on an invisible wave. Looking up at the apartment I wondered if Chevy had caught it too. She could have any man she wants and that means any man could be up there replacing me right now just the same way a new stranger was down here replacing the old Doorman.

That happens sometimes, once in a while a buzz sweeps through the town swishing women up like a broom clearing shattered glass off a sidewalk. The other doorman begged for change without even holding open the store's entrance and scouted the parking lot looking for tossed cigarette butts. I didn't like him but I watched until words merged together in my mind to make up a conversation with Chevy that would go somewhere past hello.

Bandy was up in the apartment, sitting at the kitchen table where a plate of grits used to get parked in front of me when I woke up every afternoon. But the adventuress I called Bandanna wasn't in the room at all. Only the student sat there surrounded by books packed with all the knowledge, not a bad thing. I guess a girl can't expect to get far in school without doing her assignments. Except this all the sudden student left me outside banging on the door like the census man and that put a lot of salt in my making up plans.

Instead of a butter knife I had a flat key, Chevy got it cut for me the very first week I officially came home. She had left the house already but I made up excuses to keep her there. The Passat was gone from its spot out front, maybe she got it hauled to a garage so a real mechanic could install the new battery or maybe she was just finishing up her hair in the bathroom. That could have made sense except the frying pan wasn't on the stove and her shoes weren't by the door. If I needed more proof that she'd fled before I got there Bandy had CNN playing low on the television when it was almost time for Wendy to start.

"You didn't hear me knocking?"

Bandy kept her eyes on the printed words in her economics book. "This isn't my place. I don't answer the door."

"Quit acting like you're a guest. You're here enough to see who it is."

"Well, I don't live here, okay?!"

"Fine, fuck it, I got a key anyway."

She didn't say a word. Strange, somehow it felt more like we had broken up more than just fallen out. She patted her fishbone braids with a tiny hand and kept her face pointed to the book.

"Who did your hair?" I asked it quietly trying to cultivate a conversation.

"Me," she muttered.

"Looks nice."

She tapped her pencil hard off a page. "Look Cerrio, Chevy ain't here right now. She went out."

I put my hands up in a quick surrender. "Alright, shit, don't bite my head off. You know when she's coming back?"

"I dunno. She didn't say."

I looked at the television. A news anchor in Atlanta was giving tips on how to beat the heat. He suggested doing all your hard work in the cool of the day and taking a long break from noon to four.

"Hey, you hungry? Want to go get some chicken?"

"No thanks, I got a lot of work to do."

"Okay Bandy, I get it. You're mad, Chevy's mad. Everybody's pissed at me and that's all fair. But I wasn't just trying to make you sing. I wanted to see your gift. And I'm not sorry for that. You have rare talent. The type people will pay well to get a taste of and anybody who hears you will say the same thing."

For a second neither of us said a thing and then her cheek blushed, it went down to her neck and eventually made it all the way to her hands. And a tiny shimmer was in her eye, just a glint in the light that threatened to become a tear sliding down over her delicate cheekbone. She hurried up and swiped it away, a careless move, not intentional. I knew because the wetness wasn't even a streak yet before she had the hand back over her other eye. Too late though, I had already seen the black and blue bruise. It was just a small flash of ugly but still more than enough.

I cupped her face by the chin and tilted it up towards the window. "Who did that to you?"

She pushed my hand off. "Quit, it's not a big deal. I gave some woman's husband a dance and she found out. That's all."

"That's all? A woman did this to you over a dance?"

"Her and some friends. They jumped me in the alley."

"What did they look like?"

"Stop asking questions, Cerrio. I'll heal up. It's not a big deal."

"You look like a fucking cage fighter. You tellin' me that's not a big deal?"

She slammed her fist down on the table. "Fine, you want the truth! A trick punched me in the face. Hard. He got drunk. Wanted to do some nasty shit. The things he asked me to do-." She cut herself off. "I told him no. He pushed me, I slapped him, he blacked my eye. And, I'm not a singer. So, let it go already.

I thought this is what good parents must feel when their kids wind up lost. Maybe this is it, the screaming, the tantrum, the razor-sharp sense of disbelief dropping inside my stomach like a navy anchor. I didn't think about feeling sorry for Bandy the same way she didn't get all emotional when I came in bleeding and holding out nail polish. Sometimes women save my life and sometimes I get to save theirs too, but that germ of pity decomposed in the back of our minds a long time ago because any trait of weakness leads to certain death in this small world of ours.

She brushed something imaginary off her pants. "Don't worry. I'll tell Chevy you came by."

"We'll catch up later. In the end we always do. Now, back to you. What's really going on out there?"

"Is it that hard to figure out? School ain't free. These books cost a fortune. I need money, Cerrio. That's what's going on."

Three mismatch chairs sat around the kitchen table. One had a bookbag in it with a smiley face button on the strap, the other still had Bandy trying to keep her face turned away. I eased in the last seat slowly and spoke slow in my bedtime voice.

"You know what I think? I think you think that all I know about is cards and dice and how to get high. But look around Bandanna, everybody you're mixing it up with is just like you. We're all trying to put something together out here. Everyday just trying to make ends meet and free ourselves from this mess of the streets. But that doesn't mean people get to abuse us. No one, and I mean no one gets a pass to beat on you when you're out there doing the best you can."

"What was I supposed to do? Shoot him?"

"That's an option. Or you could have called me. Because I'm your friend. Not like your phone buddies you never see taking pictures of their breakfast in the morning but a real partner. Somebody who'll come pull you out the fire before you melt down like wax."

She looked up at me, one eye rheumy, the other bloodshot and swollen. "You sure you don't want me to tell Chevy you stopped by?"

I sighed the sigh of sprawling defeat. What did I expect coming here? My old lady's forgiveness, a happy ending to whatever we were butting heads about? Maybe just no more long afternoons in a weird downtown bar and maybe something like regular chat at the table. But I got none of that. Instead, I got a clear message that I wasn't any sort of habit a girl had trouble giving up.

After a bout of disappointment there was a long seven steps back out the door and a return trip to Circle K where the irregulars out front were still busy checking ashtrays. That's why I stayed inside the apartment, because outside was just a whole world full of catastrophes and venom waiting to chew someone up. I went in the bedroom and left Bandy alone to take up her usual space on the couch. We kept away from each other like this sweltering apartment was a big spread instead of just a one bedroom barely a step above the projects on Cleveland avenue.

The queen mattress called me like it knew how to use first names. Lying down I felt so old, my back was sore, my knees ached like tired joints do before a winter storm comes in and Henna's third or fourth joyride still had my hips sore. In a second I was gone, back to Sally's all over again. The only warning before arriving is when I closed my eyes. On the wall his jukebox changed records, after a moment of pause Aretha Franklin's "Chain of Fools" song drifted through my dream. I spun around quick to see who changed the record but they were already gone, blown out of there like candle in a windstorm.

The whole place was different now, no more valley of the shadow of morons, no customers and no tattooed bigot pouring up reluctant shots either. Now it was a hallway to Mount Zion blanketed in something sacred that smelled like fresh cut strawberries and antique wood. The walls were walnut paneling, amber lights washed over pearl topped tables just big enough for two. There were no edges because every straight line in the new Sally's ended in a curve from the dark slab where shots got served to the bottom of all four legs on every stool. The only thing that had points were the quadruple tips on the flag still hanging high above the mirror behind the liquor bottles.

The Confederate colors were gone just like Sally was. Now, it was something with a female shadow on a yellow background. Even in silhouette the woman looked iconic, regal, important. I felt like I should have known her and I felt lost because I didn't. I tried hard to place her but the placement eluded me like that familiar name resting right on the tip of your tongue. She had full lips, a feline face. A hoop earring hung down close to her cheek below hair that was swept up and back in a style that cloaked strength in seduction like it was swearing bold revolution on a platform you could forever trust.

I was still looking, drinking her in because I knew I'd see her again when I felt something brush at my side. A touch of breath kissing the hair on my arm like tiny lady bug feet. I turned to wipe it off and there she was, Chevy's mother in a dress whiter than cream holding a long stemmed glass full of deep, red wine.

I blinked. "Mrs. Chitara?"

She nodded a hello. "Cerrio."

"What is this? Is-is this the place you go when you die?"

"Not even, this hole in the wall is familiar to you. That's the only reason I'm here. Now, forgive me because I know it's something different from before but no one told me how long I would be here waiting for you. It could have been a year or maybe ten minutes. In the meantime, all those sharp edges were making me anxious."

"How long has it been?"

She drank a little. "Oh, I don't know. Time doesn't worry me anymore."

"But you just told me a year or ten minutes."

"Again, that was for you. Something familiar to express my patience."

I glanced back up at the flag. "So, who's that?"

"Who knows?" She looked at me slyly. "Who do you think she is?"

"Is it...is it God?"

"You think I know God?"

"Yeah. If anybody knows it'd have to be you."

"Flattering. But if I knew God then my daughter wouldn't be working in a strip club."

Suddenly the record stopped. Aretha faded away to go find another sleeper in a dream while I found my own words.

"Mrs. Tara, forgive me but I'm not understanding. Aren't you supposed to be in a better place now? How can you be mad?"

"Because you're the problem, Cerrio."

I shook my head. "No, now that ain't true. Anybody looking can see I'm just down here trying to make it."

Mrs. Chitara James twisted her wine glass between two fingers. "I remember yesterday when I was feeding you my strength. Now look. My daughter dances in dark clubs just to put food in her mouth. That's how you have repaid my kindness and all I can do is be livid. That is until now. Now, I have power and I've been waiting to show it to you."

This wasn't good, I leaned back from her. "What power?"

She nodded to the bar, when I looked a figure in light stopped wiping the wood to lift a scale and set in front of me. A triple beam with one side way down and the other lifted high up like an offering. Chitara James pointed to the high side. "Your good deeds." Then she gestured the low end. "Your bad deeds."

I swallowed hard but held my cool. "So what? You've judged me and now you're going to send me to hell?"

"You like playing games." She set the wine down and spread a deck of 52 across the bar. "High card for your destiny."

"Serious?"

"Unless you want me to serve you your destiny now."

She looked at the scale and I quit asking questions. Choosing took a second, I tried to see through the cards but here ain't like Chucky's place. You can't cheat the house.

I pulled a two with no suit. Definite loser. Chitara James picked her card out, shimmied it from the others and looked at it in silence.

She jutted her chin at me. "What do you have?"

I couldn't believe I was playing this game for my soul. I flipped the two over so she could see it. "Nothing, am I going to hell yet?"

"Put it on the left side of the scale."

I listened and added my loser two on the weight of good deeds. Nothing. The scale didn't budge. Mrs. Chitara layered her own card on top of mine and then the high side gently, softly, barely came down. She stuck a fingernail in between the plate and the base where it had just lifted off and said, "a little room."

"Why did you do that? You had me."

"You mistake me, I never had you. This isn't about revenge. It's about Seville. If the bad deeds touch down again then she will be out of your life for good."

"That's my destiny?"

"A part of it."

"What's the rest?"

"You'll know it when you get there."

"How many bad deeds do I have left before everything goes south? Before I wind up at the point of no return?"

"The scale doesn't know how to count. Only how to weigh. A few little mistakes, a few good ones, they can all even out. Or one big one error can bring you down."

"What about your power? You said you wanted to show it to me."

"I did," she replied. "I just used it to save you."

CHAPTER 15

BRAIN STRIPES

Mrs. Chitara James drank the last swallow of red wine and let her cup drop, as soon as the glass shattered all over the new Sally's floor my eyes came open.

I woke up at dusk. The rest of the day was sliding down the wall through the blinds in pink and orange hues. Bandy had slipped away during my nap and Chevy never came home. A deep sense of loneliness kept me pinned down on the bed for what could have been eternity or just another chance to doze off. I laid there still as the cemetery listening for anything like the slightest sound would magically put me on my feet. When the refrigerator started humming then I sat up blinking in the fading twilight.

I thought about the dream. I've had ones much stranger but none more vivid. The hair on my arms stood at attention and a small paper cut on my finger where I flipped the dead card of destiny over leaked a single drop of wet blood.

My stomach growled, nothing had touched down in it since me and Henna went through a drive thru last night. That was eighteen long hours ago, after the club but before Bandy showed me the mixed tones in her eye.

My phone rang, Aunt Denise calling for her car back. I pressed the red button to decline and rubbed my own eyes so I could see my way into the kitchen. Chevy knows how pots and pans have been my friend since high school but that's a different story. Right now my plans were all about a recipe. I was thinking noodles whipped in garlic butter and cheese melted down on top, a thin flaky crust sticking to the sides of a lasagna dish and red velvet cake for dessert. Food is magic, it does what words can't and if it's made right, with love and care, then the talking can begin.

It might not be a conversation wet with praise but it will definitely be a whole lot better than that silence still trying to run me down from the back bedroom. The same people who say something is better than nothing are the ones who can't come home to an oven making smells and still act like they don't care. So, either Chevy is going to see dinner and turn up and fight or she'll take me back and love me all over again. Any way it goes I bet my whole life to fifteen minutes she won't just turn around and walk away.

Standing between counters it was easy to see how much Chocolate had been right, anyone with eyes could tell that a man hadn't been up in here at all. The sink was spotless, stovetop burners wiped clean underneath, all the dishes put back in their right places. I switched the oven on and then up three hundred and fifty degrees. Five minutes later I opened the door and fresh heat scudded through the room making a coat of sweat grease the palm of my hands. I washed them slow under a faucet with water hot as I could take it. Chevy had just enough lemon dish soap to be insignificant, use a little or use none at all it didn't matter. The difference was nothing but a final rinse around the bottom of the bottle.

That's exactly what I did, filled the plastic container up with a half inch of steaming tap and shook it until fat bubbles lined up on all sides. When I twisted it back open again the top slipped between my fingers. It hopped across the linoleum like a rabbit in the grass, bounced off the dishwasher Chevy never used because her mother never believed they did any good anyway and spun dead in front of the trash can packed with random garbage.

Aunt Denise calls back, I ignore her again to focus on the can swelled with parts of Chevy's life she has no use for anymore. Without touching anything I could tell the bag inside won't just pull out. Someone needs to hold the bottom of the plastic bin while the other person works it free and hopes there isn't a violent explosion of trash waiting at the end. No telling what would blow out of there, a smorgasbord of paper and female products mixed with soggy fruit peels via Bandy's vegan diet. It stunk a little and crumpled baggies with cocaine residue sat on top of the pile like props in a setup. I look closer and see that they all have clean lines running up the sides like a fingernail has been raked across to scrape the dust.

Maybe Chevy was starting to use more shit and hide it less but I was never concerned. It was a phase, she'd either get over the drugs or grow out of them or the connection would vanish when the time was right. When the salon was open and we were done bringing home money from the streets she would put all that away, and I would too. A good theory but it was all dope around here and no food. The cupboards were bare, besides sparkling plates there was only decorative butterfly print paper lining the bottom of each shelf. And that humming refrigerator was cooling down nothing but an open two liter soda standing beside a day old casserole in the same lasagna pan I had big plans for.

I saw the signs and knew I couldn't stay. I tried taking the trash with me but the bottom of the bag really did bust open and a riot of loose garbage went everywhere. More little baggies with scrape marks up the side lept out on the floor and then I heard that goddamn Maybelline tube laughing at me from inside the medicine cabinet. A second later the Asian lady living next door saw me flying down the steps two at a time like the building was on fire. She yelled at my back in her language, every syllable chopping out in pieces that fell down without any pause for a breath. I cleared the rest of the metal stairs at full sprint and thought about what it's like to lose your mind.

At the light in front of the Circle K I pulled my shirt off, let the windows down, turned the music up. My belly was still empty but I could starve better then I could take it up in that apartment. Across the street on the other side of the intersection a white Ford Taurus tried hard to look harmless. In the evening it was impossible to see the undercover waiting inside at this distance, all I could do is smell him. The brass on his badge, the steel on his waist, a mix of soulless, lethal metal cloaked in plainclothes just waiting for a takedown.

I dropped my .40 on the floor and tried to kick it deep underneath the seat. It wouldn't go. Every time my heel hit the Llama's barrel gunmetal knocked loud against the bolted down seat track. What a fucking problem to have. The same thing that might save my life wouldn't even get out of the way long enough to let me live freely.

I couldn't see the pistol fall down at an angle that put the handle right against the iron bracket underneath the driver's side seat. In that position it would never go back. But still I kept kicking because I didn't dare didn't dare look down. Posted at the stoplight the top half of my body struggled to look calm while the bottom half fought it's own close quarters war. I must have kicked that pistol a hundred times. Then, I switched feet and put my left down on the Cutlass brake pedal so I could give it my all with the right. Kicking and watching the intersection I had to believe that if the police started sting operations right under my nose on the east side then things must be much worse than I ever imagined. Between Chevy's coke habit secretly growing out of control and the sheriffs hitting home runs straight out of my ballpark this was pretty much the end of the world.

But the simple solution is usually the right one. I looked down, and then I reached down, and it was so easy just to put a hand in between my legs, pull the gun out and slide it backwards again. Simple but risky as shit because cops look for little things like that.

Anyway, I should know better. Blaring cocaine rap in a classic car two months out of prison with a tank top on is filthy rich thuggery but that's the fundamentals of who I am whether for better or worse. Worse is that I run away, best is that I can be myself, worse is when I have to look in the mirror and see the man who's hurting the ones I really love. Best is when I get a little money to cover up my own pain. Thinking about it now made me glad that I didn't have a little girl to call my own. Then, I sat up straight and saw somebody's real daughter leaning in through my window.

"Wanna have some fun?" she asked unashamedly.

I stared for a second before remembering the cops. My eyes flicked to the Taurus, I expected the jump out boys to do what their handle implied, jump out to come and get me.

The light turned green. The girl at the window saw her last chance going up in smoke. Once upon a time someone told me never to punish a good effort, so I didn't protest when she opened up the door and hopped in like I was an Uber. Plus, there wasn't any time to say no between swinging the Cutlass left into the Circle K parking lot and watching the Taurus in every mirror. The white Ford went away on a broken muffler that was too loud to ever be a cop car. It was music to my ears. Things were going to be all right I thought and I thought fate was finally going to give me a break but that was before I turned to see who was with me.

The gas station lights shined bright all over a baby. She couldn't have been more than sixteen, maybe fourteen looking at her straight on. The skin on her face was too fresh for the game, no blemishes or stress lines digging in yet. All that makeup made it hard for her to sweat. She was a school kid painted up like a China doll and out of the two of us she seemed the least nervous. I was shaking, still checking the mirrors for signs of police while she was asking if we were going to do it right there by the curb.

I cut her off. "What the fu..." I breathed deep, trying to re-member this wasn't Chevy who dealt with me on a regular basis. "Where are your parents?"

She sucked her teeth. "I'm a grown woman, okay? Now, we doing it or what? 'Cause I ain't got all night to be talking to you."

I swallowed hard and realized that this is how you lose your mind. This is how it starts. Running down a flight of metal steps straight into a kid at the red light trying to sell herself in a low cut shirt. An old man rode a bike right past us, chain clicking on sprockets like pearls against clean teeth. He coasted to the side of the store, leaned it up against the brick wall stained with spray paint. I wanted that bike because I knew I couldn't run anymore. The circle of madness had closed in on me faster than I could get out. Spiraling around full speed until there was nothing but a tiny dot left in the middle with my name written all over it.

The real Doorman came to my window on tilt. He was already drunk, a lit cigarette hung loose between his lips while he said something about me having a brand new, fresh, date. Then he looked in the car and saw the girl who should have been bottled up in her parent's house doing homework and made a rude, panic, noise.

When I got out of the Cutlass silently swearing in my mind Doorman stepped back to give me some room. He looked me up and down, adjusted his hat. All his body language told me he wanted action. I raised my head waiting for his next move but the junkie had nothing to give. All those years snorting heroin had taken the fight out of his soul.

I offered him a beer, he shrugged. Thinking I was a pervert apparently wasn't enough to make him to turn down a free drink "Why not?" he said. "I'll take a cold one."

I turned to the girl checking her face in the visor mirror. "Hey, you hungry?" She thought about it and told me to bring her back some cigarettes.

It really could not be any worse than this, I thought. The kid was playing the part and doing such a good job that it made me wonder what Chevy was like at the very beginning of her own career.

Doorman stayed right beside me on the way to the front of the store, he didn't hold the door open. Nearby a fleet of sirens screamed, the first of what would be many tonight. When they faded he reached out and put a hand on my chest.

"Magic, man what are you doing? That's a baby."

I glared at him. "I didn't ask her to ride with me. She jumped in at the fucking light."

"So, how come you're buying her cigarettes then?"

"That's not what's happening. In fact nothing's happening. I'm just gon' buy her a soda and some chips and then send her ass on her way."

"That's Ahmet's girl."

Me and Doorman looked at each other before we both turned to look at Brenda. In all the times I'd been up to the Circle K this was the first time I had ever heard her speak. Her lips were more parched than they had been earlier in the afternoon. When she ran her tongue over them they drank up the spit immediately.

"Give me some of that square, Melvin," she demanded.

Doorman obediently passed his girlfriend the cigarette, I watched the sharing without a word. I just didn't have the heart to tell him that his part time lady had a stranger out on this same spot barely three hours ago.

He snorted and spit on the ground. "How do you know who she belongs to?"

"Because, she got that Alabama A tattooed on her neck. Ahmet always brands his girls like that." Brenda took a drag. "The ink was fresh last week, all red and everything. Bet it's healed up by now."

I scratched my head, always the last to know everything. "Who's Ahmet?"

Doorman touched his hat again. "Shit, he's a pimp Magic. Just like you is, man."

I popped. "Quit saying that shit. I'm not a pimp!"

He shrugged. "Well, he is and he's cold with it. Takes girls who don't want to live at home no more and then turns them out."

"You mean runaways?"

A nod from the junkie. "Got Nessa's nice like that. Had her stayin' with him up at the Motel 8 before she dropped out of school. She said 'he was all nice in the beginning.' Bought her new clothes and a Mickey Mouse watch. Then he started slapping her around. Turned her out on dope and made her turn tricks uptown for him."

"Whoa. Back up, back up. Who the hell is Nessa?"

"That's my girlfriend," said Brenda. "She's in jail doing fifty years."

"Fifteen years!" yelled Doorman.

"That's what I said!" she screamed back.

Doorman snatched the burning Kool out of his girlfriend's mouth, a piece of her lip skin almost came with it. Brenda wrinkled up her face and I thought she was going to spit on him but she didn't have any left to waste.

"How old was her niece?"

Doorman frowned. "To tell you the truth I ain't sure. She was in high school, I know that much."

In the Cutlass the little girl up front was putting lip gloss on in the visor mirror like this was just any Friday night in her boyfriend's car. That was the same thing Chevy used to do when we used to cruise around back in the day. Looking on didn't make me reminisce, it was just more ill on an ill night in a week of raging sickness.

"She was fourteen," chimed Brenda.

I turned back to her. "Who was?"

"Nessa's daughter, fourteen when she ran away. Almost fifteen when they found her."

This was sad and even though I hadn't done anything I felt all eyes judging me guilty beyond a reasonable doubt inside the store. Of course no one was looking. Down the aisle the man on the bike pulled a case of Heineken's out of a cooler while a shadier character behind him slipped two tall cans inside his shirt. At the front counter another woman from Chevy's complex picked a cigar to split open while her friend worked a nickel across a scratch off ticket. No one cared about the little street girl sitting outside waiting for the box of Newports I was never going to buy. She could lose her life tonight, no reason behind it, just a kid in a bad way and everybody here would easily move on because they never stopped in the first place.

I tried to fight the feelings of sympathy by focusing on Doorman's beer. A little voice inside my head said, "pity is not the program." Maybe I could get drunk too, get rid of the girl and piss the tonight away just like I did last night and pretty soon that would be my new routine until I wound up in the corner like those two fighting over a menthol out front.

Whatever her circumstances that wasn't my problem, all I needed to do was tell her to leave. Demand it. I'm not Ahmet out here making a living feeding kids to the street. I'm a gambler, a robber, by popular belief maybe a pimp. Although the jury's still out on that. Still, whatever I'm guilty of peddling babies is not on my résumé, not today, not even close.

But will the baby make it to see tomorrow? The same way I made it to all those next days that should have never been seen. In front of the beer cooler I had a long argument with myself. Tomorrow when the little girl shows up on the news or on the back of a milk carton next week would she be my problem then? What would another damaged female look like in my nightmares? How can I suck up a dead girl and live with myself when I was running away from garbage on the floor and ghosts in medicine cabinets? The answer is I couldn't. I fought against it because anything close to a yes meant that she was my problem right here and now.

They say it takes a village and I'm just one man. Why me? Where's all the so called villagers? These other people around me were here every single day and they didn't even care. I envied them so much, their ignorance was saving them from the Amber alert going off in my head. Black female, brown skinned, gap in her teeth, between fourteen and sixteen last seen wearing jean shorts in a Cutlass driving west through town.

Fuck me. How do I get into these things? "Why?" I asked out loud. "Why me? Why goddamnit?!"

The woman beside me at the coolers gave the best look of shock, best I'd seen in a real long time when the argument moved from my head to my lips. Then, she grabbed her son and drug him away before I could hurt his ears anymore. I laughed. That kid didn't give a shit about my rant. He was on a mission with his chubby hand reaching out trying to snag any piece of candy hanging loose down the aisle.

His mama must have thought I was crazy but somehow crazy works. It's the most natural stripe of brain that pulls fine work out of madness and solves riddles and builds monuments. After crazy is genius and after that is perfection. It was crazy when astronauts went to the moon, crazy when people started flying planes into hurricanes to measure windspeed. I ain't an astronaut but if I didn't have crazy I might just not have anything at all. Mine lived in little fragments separated by things like stress and expectations, cards and violence, sex and drugs. But when the kid snatched a Tootsie Roll off the shelf somehow it all came together like an outfit and then I realized exactly who I needed to call.

CHAPTER 16

CHRONIC MYTH

She never stopped to think about the next generation. Since tomorrow is never promised what sense was there in taking careful care of the future? Just another philosophy coming from the belly of the beast. Chocolate had plenty of them, twenty-five to be exact, one for each year she had been alive and her next birthday was coming up soon. She already had the twenty sixth written down in a secret place.

Cerrio called while she was pressing the Jeep's gas pedal to the floor in a pair of slick, new heels courtesy of the fat trick who once knew her as Tina. They were tight around the toes but that was good, tight meant new, not stretched out or cheap. She had a lot of work tonight, perhaps too much, although that was pretty unlikely. Chocolate never had a day of work she couldn't handle. Her phone was going crazy in a handbag that came straight off the rack at a quaint boutique in downtown Charlotte. After a quick lane switch she fished it out and tapped ignore. By the time her left turn signal cut off the screen lit up again.

Just another trick begging for a little of her time. Chocolate pressed the green button but tossed the device over on the passenger's seat. When the fool on the other end finally got tired of hearing wind whistle in his ear then he could hang up, if not then Chocolate would have to turn off her phone to save the battery.

Who invented men anyway? Morons. Chocolate never met one she couldn't turn into a mark. Although, Chevy's boyfriend seemed to be a fairly slight difference. He was a creature with two faces, one sensitive and energetic, the other just like a wild animal. Chocolate liked animals which is why she had a dog.

Cerrio called back, she could see his number flashing on call waiting while the trick still trying to buy some of her time desperately waited for the relentless wind to give up. Chocolate knew that with her brains and the Arab's insanity they could become fabulously rich. Paid beyond their wildest dreams. In fact the man listening to the crisp road air whip through her Jeep was the next mark being groomed for another robbery. So, whatever Cerrio was blowing her up for had better be a serious emergency.

I guess in a strange way it made perfect sense that the girl in my car almost lost her mind when that loud purple Jeep pulled up beside us. Chocolate was the first person I thought of, the only one still talking to me, at least treating me like I was still alive. It took four tries to reach her and when she finally showed up at the Circle K the kid in the Cutlass started to cry. Her levy burst and the tears poured out darkening the front of her shirt. Through the sobs I could hear her saying she wasn't ready for this. That must have been the purest thing I heard come out of anybody's mouth in almost a week.

I looked at her stepping down, six foot tall in platform heels, pouty lips creased in a frown, skin blending in seamlessly with the night. This kid had a right to be scared. Here came the keeper of the keys to the game she was knocking hard on the door of.

She wasn't fazed seeing a grown man with a young girl. She looked at me stone faced with that cop-in-a-movie demeanor. She was like the serious detective with all the experience who comes in on a murder and smokes a cigar over the body. She never flinched. The more incredible and outrageous the crime the less emotion the detective showed.

But it wasn't all stoic. Her nostrils flared a little and it looked like she wanted to slap me when I came around the side of the car. Somewhere someone once said the blacker the berry the sweeter the juice, but the kick is strong too. That's the reason I slowed my approach a little when we came in arm's reach.

"Don't go spinning out on me," I said. "It ain't what it looks like."

"So, you called me out here to say it ain't what it looks like." She shot a look at the girl with the cheap mascara running down her cheeks. "If you need an alibi it's going to cost you, Cerrio. Six hundred dollars and that's not a one time fee."

"Did you not just hear me? I said, 'nothing's going on here'."

"Must be if she's crying like that."

I looked at the kid trying to wipe her snotty nose with a too small shirt.

"Man, she was just fine before you came."

Chocolate strutted back to the Jeep. "Robbing that trick got your mind fucked up, Cerrio. Call me a little when later you want to get some more money."

Watching her go I realized for the first time why she took the doors off her truck. Because without them she didn't have pause to let anyone make their last plea.

"You ain't listening," I said.

"That's because I don't care," she half shouted back. "Whatever this little game is I don't have time for it. I'm still giving Chevy money for you to go work with and you're out here in your new car." She gestured towards the whip. "Doing whatever this is. And that's your business. Just make you sure you pay the girl, okay? Because nothing's worse than a cheap pervert."

I grabbed her by the arm, the skin was so smooth my fingers almost slid back off. A lesser woman would have twisted an ankle in those tall platforms but Chocolate just turned around and gave me those ready for anything eyes. She wasn't strong enough to break free but the muscles tensing under my palm made me talk a little bit faster.

"She caught me a the light. Asked if I wanted to have some fun. Swear on me I didn't answer. She just got in. I swear to God, Chocolate, the girl just opened the door and hopped right in."

She replied in a tone dripping with sarcasm. "Well, that's a real shame. It is. But it still don't explain why I'm here."

"Stop standing there popping your fucking gum and listen! I called you because I don't know what to do with her. If I kick her out the car and she winds up on the news tomorrow I'll never forgive myself." I gripped her arm tighter, talked a little lower. "I been having a lot of bad dreams lately. I don't need another one, know what I'm saying? Now, either help me out with this or I don't want to see you around these projects no more."

Chocolate didn't respond to all my outbursts the way Chevy did, by hurling insults and throwing hands. She stayed calm and tilted her chin high to look down in my face. We stood there letting the enigma of the night pick up out on the street. Cars went by making noises in an ocean of traffic. Somebody yelled, Brenda cackled, shards of human presence bombarded the air all around us while she stared at something deep beneath my skin.

"Give me your keys."

I dug the whole ring out of my pocket and dropped them in her hand. "Now what?"

"Now you go take a walk. Stay gone for twenty minutes. Don't come back no sooner."

"What are you going to do?"

She closed her hand around Aunt Denise's keyring. "I'm going to handle business. That is unless you want to stay?"

"Fuck it, I'll go. But I ain't walking."

Twenty minutes was a low ball. It took at least that long for Chocolate to call me back in the road and say "stay gone a little longer." I had her purple Jeep doing eighty miles an hour down State Route 311 where no cops hide out, watching trees go by in a blur with the high beams washing over cracked yellow lines painted on the blacktop. Right before every intersection I cooled it but when the light turned green or the stop sign seemed point-less then I turned up and smashed again.

Twelve miles later the bluster of the highway faded into a scattered blend of mud streaked work trucks. By the woods the sky grew thicker and darker, owls hooted in the forest canopy papered over with fine mist. When there were no more cars then I heard a train horn float one, long, note from miles off in the distance. The air is so pure here that a low noise like that could travel on forever. After the sound faded it was just the crickets and the frogs calling in the blind.

I drove easier like time was on my side. The lust for speed evaporated when there was nothing left to leave behind. I thought of my Uncle Daya. Why did he have to go so soon? All that life they stole from him made me want to live mine twice as hard. He loved these long, back stretches by the traintracks. He used driving as therapy, a brain exercise. The essence of travel was his chance to unravel because the open road was the only place big enough for him to iron out his thoughts.

He had this thing, my uncle, where he believed one day wom-en would take over the whole world. He knew females were the future before people started wearing it on their t-shirts. He thought everything here would belong to the ladies and men and our ideas were doomed to become history. I don't know if every swinging dick on the planet was going to wind up in ashes and get condemned to the past but his theory must have been truth. After telling so many lies I can tell you that falsehood is never very hard to sell on people.

All his friends, they laughed, called him crazy and told him to go home. I did too, not the going home part but I made fun of Uncle Daya at least for while. Then I came upon manhood and realized it's true, females are the future. But the future is now, no more phoning it in from a place full of guesses. Uncle is gone, Aunt Denise has a new man, and the veteran from Sugar Bares was behind the wheel of the family Cutlass.

Chocolate called back before I got too far from the city. She told me come back and park the Jeep up in the apartments so we could take a ride with the kid. I sat in the back seat staring at the streets while the females up front toyed with the radio. The girl felt more comfortable with a woman driving. They talked for an hour while I was gone, bonding over a chat I could die happy without ever hearing. When we got to twenty-fifth street Chocolate buzzed the window down and instantly the smell of rain permeated the Oldsmobile. No drops on the windshield yet but it was definitely coming.

"Anybody hungry?" I asked.

The dancer eyed me up in the mirror, then she looked over at the girl who nodded slowly like the quiet in the car was a mandate never be broken.

"There's a Church's up there," I said.

"What's that?" the girl asked.

"A chicken shack," replied Chocolate. "But I don't ever eat there."

"Why? Is it 'cause of the name?"

"No, because its too cheap. Come on now you think I can look this good eating off a dollar menu?"

They both laughed and it was music to my ears, the kind of song I hope plays loud from the jukebox the next time a dream about a bar comes banging through my skull. I sat in the backseat feeling my pockets because I already knew I was paying for dinner the same way monkeys are born just knowing how to peel bananas.

It didn't hurt to spend on them. The girl ate like she hadn't been fed in a week, pizza with pineapples, bread sticks, cinnamon rolls and root beer. Watching her I made up a story in my head. She was a good kid, studied hard and made the honor roll. Then, one week some girls invited her to a party where she tried alcohol for the first time. Some Mad Dog 20/20 stolen from the Texaco station when the clerk wasn't looking. She took a few sips until it caught up with her and by that time it was too late. A boy she thought looked handsome and cared about her took her in a closet and that was the night. A day and a half later she went to school vomiting. Couldn't figure out was wrong and told the nurse who gave her a pregnancy test that came back positive.

The nurse called her parents to give them the news. Her mama and daddy were waiting in the living room at four o' clock to confront her but four turned into five and then five went to six and by seven they got the picture. Their daughter had run away, too ashamed to face them with a baby she hopped a bus and ducked down low in the back until the very last stop. Got off and walked until her feet hurt and that's where she met Ahmet, right at the end of the line where she would be most vulnerable. Where dreams always sell the best.

On the other side of the table Chocolate sat next to me. Shoulder to shoulder in a tiny booth sporting vinyl seats I could feel her warm body pressed gently against mine starting at the arms and running down my left side all the way to my hip. She pilfered hot wings from a paper boat loaded up with a greasy twenty piece while our rescue project murdered a meal for three.

While we loitered around inside the rain started. It came down in a sprinkle, pitter pattering on the ground making puddles hardly deep enough to get your shoes wet. By the time Chocolate took us home to her floor level spread the clouds broke open for real and water started coming down in sheets. The girls ran in covering their heads, it was funny watching them sprint like fawns. They cleared the sidewalk trying to stay dry and rushed into the building before I even slid out of the backseat. Judy was nice enough to hold the door open for me. That was the baby's name, I learned it in a guessing game after she fell asleep all by herself in Chocolate's den.

Her home is cozy and cool, the exact sort of place you want to be in the middle of a Carolina summer. It was hard to know whether to go or stay, I was leaning towards escape. Hanging around at this place I felt like I was hiding out right in plain sight, like an alligator waiting to spring on housecats from the shallow end of the neighborhood pool. A lamp with Chinese writing tossed a little bit of light across the room to brighten up a whole Asian theme. Tiny geisha figures were lined up on a small piano by the wall, the ceramic girls were frozen in poses with one arm above their head and the other on a hip. To make it even a rug on the floor showed a red sun hanging over a coyfish pond and the sleek swimmers going upstream.

There was a simple neatness in the clutter. When she came out of the back bedroom wearing sweats and a T-shirt stretched tight across her breasts I saw a little dog rush out in front. The mixed breed terrier got a thousand whiffs of my shoes and he was working his way up to the pants before Chocolate finally called him off.

"Don't worry," she reassured. "Franky's not a biter. He's just simple. Aren't you Franky?"

The dog disobeyed, smelled me a little longer until I stood up and smoothed my shirt. "You uh, want to run back out to Chevy's crib and get your Jeep?"

"Did you cover it up?"

"Yeah, you told me to."

She flapped a hand. "Relax, just let it sit. Long as she's covered up we straight. I can't drive it anyway with the sky falling down outside. Now, what do you want to drink?"

"Nothing, I'm good."

The phone rang. Chocolate pulled it out of her pocket and I heard the voice on the other end murmur a question. She answered back in a voice so silky smooth it was like listening to another person talk. At a break in conversation she held the phone against her chest.

"Where you fixin' to go?"

"North side," I replied. "I heard about a new place up on Cherry Street where they're paying like royals."

She put the phone to her ear again. "What's that baby? You got to say it again, I know but I could barely hear you out here in this storm."

The guy on the line repeated himself while she picked her nails and Franky sat back shifting his black dog eyes between us like he was judging which one to believe.

"Sorry boo, not tonight." She took the phone down one more time. "What do you want, Cerrio? I got Absolut and iced tea and a jug of lemonade. Pick one."

"Did you hear me? I got to go, it's important."

"And I got three or four horny tricks out there using their hands tonight, So, do you like vodka or Lipton?"

I sighed. Why fight it? "I'm good on the vodka," I told her. "Not in the mood. Just pour me some of that tea."

Chocolate ignored my order and brought us both liquor anyway. She spiked my drink and then made her own with ice. After mixing them both with a spoon she carried my tea over to the couch, dragging the heels of her naked feet on the rug until she took a heavy load off. I smell the odor in our cups when she passed mine over. It didn't turn my stomach but I knew too much would get me in trouble.

"I would offer you some powder but the girl might come out and see us getting tuned. I ain't trying to explain that."

"Fine by me. Last thing I need right now is drugs anyway." I raised the glass. "You're a damn good host, though."

"It's hostess."

I sipped liquor laced Lipton and smacked my lips. "What?"

"You called me a host but I'm a woman. So, I'm your host-ess."

"Alright excuse me, hostess, you're very good at this. Especially since I didn't have anywhere to go tonight."

"Oh, I know."

"Quit lying. You didn't know shit."

"Cerrio, I'm all over. I know everything that's going on in this town."

"You're good, I admit. But I think you're pushing it." I nodded to the den. "You didn't know about her"

"No, but I didn't have to. That's where you came in. The lucky man out on the street was playing superhero."

"I've never been lucky. You know I cheat every night."

Chocolate scratched her dog behind the ear. Franky wagged his tail and stretched his neck so her polished nails could dig a little deeper.

"Guess what her name is?"

"Gimme a clue. Does it start with an A?"

No, it starts with a letter between H and N."

I took a swallow of vodka and tea while the letters swam around in my head. "Is it Lacey?"

She shook her head. "Not even close."

Another drink. "Hilda?"

"There's no black girls named Hilda."

"Ah-ha, see that's where you're wrong. I went to school with an African girl named Hilda. She used to braid my hair so tight I couldn't even blink."

"Regardless, you're zero for two."

I shrugged. "Fuck it, I give up."

"The girl's name is Judy. She wants to be an actress."

"And there's the scheme."

"What are you mumbling about?"

"Street games," I said. "The gimmicks we live everyday. Dealers cut the dope. I cheat at cards. You trick the tricks. It's all a ruse. Another form reality, except it's our reality. I bet Ahmet told Judy he was a movie producer. She probably thought she was on the way to something big. Some starring role. That's the best part of being a kid, though. Everything's real."

Chocolate made a noise and I thought she was choking before she exploded in wild laughter. All poise was lost. The coolness was gone as the suave, playgirl cracked up on the couch holding her elbows while the rest of her lithe body shook in a spasm of chuckles.

"What the hell is so funny?"

"You are. Oh my God, I needed that."

"Me?"

"Yes, all that talking about the boogeyman." She wiped away a tear. "Ahmet is an old myth women in the group home used to make up stories about to keep young girls off the stroll. I used to hear about him all the time when I was fourteen. I wanted to kill him so bad until I found out he's just a figment of some broken ho's imagination."

"That's fucked up. So, where did Judy come from?"

A foster home in Charlotte. She ran away a month ago because she didn't like the parents. Shady little thing stole some clothes from the mall and sold them to buy a bus ticket out here."

I stared at a geisha, the laughs were over now and serious Chocolate was back. "Sure this ain't another one of those things you only think you know about?" I asked. The last bit of jokiness fell off her face. She set her drink down, leaned away from me and pulled her shirt up. The skin on her hip was scarred with a thin four inch line hooked at the end like a cane.

"Westside Mikey gave me this the last time we talked."

I took a long examination and a short sip. "You used to work for him?"

"No, he did this because I wouldn't work for him. You want to touch it?"

I resisted the urge to brush her blemish, to feel the raised, pink line and reflect on her pain. Mercifully, she rolled her shirt down.

"Trust me sweetie, there isn't a pimp or a player in this city I ain't came across. If the boogeyman was out there I'd be at his door right now getting even about that little one in my den."

"Shit, that's the best news I heard all week. For a whole two hours I've been imagining an Arab who looks like me peddling young girls around town like Turkish cigarettes."

"He thinks his people can do no wrong. Delusional much?"

"Delusional, no. I know my people are just as bad as anybody else. I see the news. I just didn't want there to be a case of mistaken identity. Say, why did Judy choose this place anyway?"

"She didn't, Winston chose her. Her grandma lives in Memphis in a house with a big backyard. But she ran out of money on the way and had to get off at the Greyhound downtown. Girl's been out here working the streets. Living off candy bars and fast food. She showers up at year round high school in the boy's locker room while they're out at soccer practice."

"You mean the girl's locker room."

"No, the girls don't have showers. They don't have a soccer team either."

"I can't believe she told you that."

"Mm-hm, and she also told me you were pure as the driven snow."

"Come again?"

"I asked and Judy told me nothing happened between you two. She said she pushed and you wouldn't do it. A real gentleman."

"And I told you from the fucking start nothing happened."

"Don't get brittle. I can't take anyone's word at face value. Only a fool would do that."

"Why? I trust Chevy."

A sneaky grin touched Chocolate's cheeks. "And she trusts you too. That's why y'all are just so cute together."

I knew she was feeling herself, feeling the vodka and the upper hand that came naturally from me being on her turf. She shifted on the couch making a little creaking noise when her soft behind sunk deeper into the leather.

"Is this why you wanted me to stay and hang around? Because you need some entertainment to unwind?"

"Yes, Cerrio you got me all figured out. I'm just an around the way girl bored to death on a weeknight. Please sir, have mercy on me."

"Shut up, quit begging it looks bad on you." I sipped and swished the drink around in my cup. "You know, I could have left. But I guess making you laugh is a lot cheaper than driving around in the rain."

"Safer too," she said. "But I was never worried. You couldn't have left here anyway."

"The door is right there. Ten steps and I could be dancing backwards through mud puddles. Unless you think you got enough strength to hold me back."

"Uh, you called me to come be front and center of everything. Now I'm supposed to be the bossy bitch holding you back? All I did was offer you a drink. Albeit aggressively," she added. "But the ghosts, now see that's who you need to blame. Those same ones from the nightmares you talked about earlier walked in here right behind you and closed the door. They're the ones ain't letting you out. And they're holding down a fort inside your mind something serious."

Just like that day I was grinding decks of cards down Chevy's garbage disposal the air in the room changed ever so slightly. Something came and something went and Franky stood up twitching his wet nose trying to sniff it out while I held my breath. Chocolate drank deep from her cup. She let the liquor swim around in her mouth and then put the glass down beside her to reach out and touch my hair.

"I'd love to see what they built up there. How the fort looks. Who's in charge. How many men are there? How many women?"

"All women," I said.

"Only spirits?" she pressed.

"I don't know."

She felt her way through to my scalp and then took her hands away and crossed her legs. "Don't worry, Cerrio. Those kind of spirits, they tend to move on after a while and I got a good feeling I'll be right here when they do. When the ghosts disappear and the fort is abandoned and you are too," she winked, "I'll still be around. Just as long as there's money to made I'll be right here waiting."

CHAPTER 17

TRAP TALK

The hotel maids stole what they could from my room, change off the dresser, a quarter bottle of Patron kicked behind a chair. Minor things to laugh about when I saw them downstairs vacuuming the lobby because all the good stuff was put away.

Whatever I got from Chocolate's trick stayed locked up in the room safe and sometimes when my mind ticked incessantly I took the gold coins out just to make them spin around on the bedside table. They danced three in a row like a stage act but every time I tried dancing a fourth the first two would go down like gunshot victims. Suddenly, I hated those coins, laying down on the carpet they made me sick. Two hundred dollars a piece and they were so fragile they couldn't even stand up on their own. It reminded me of a baby, helpless and weak on the floor crying out for attention. But the baby was getting old, and helpless wasn't cute anymore.

Out in the street a war was brewing. A Corolla with six kilos in the trunk had gone missing from a trailer park right beside the same pizza place where I bought Judy dinner. Besides that the story was fragmented, woven together with pieces of rumors to make up a quilt of traphouse gossip. I don't know who could be dumb enough to leave a car like that unattended but now the Southside Mexicans were riding around looking for clean head-shots in our neighborhood seven nights a week.

Socks had already been in a firefight and came out clean. All the bullets buzzed into his mama's house ripping away chunks of wooden porch beams and shattering the plant pots in front of her kitchen windows. This was my war too, even though I didn't start it and I didn't have the drugs or the Toyota I was still here in the city and under the street code that was enough. Since I look a little Mexican anyway I had it coming from both sides. Angry glares from neighborhood boys on the corner by the stop sign and confused expressions from brown faced shooters leaning against a store that sold phone cards with directions all written in Spanish.

Who's funeral came first depended on who had better aim. I couldn't stop the shells if they came but I definitely had to reply. That was the second reason I scooped all the Indian head coins into a bag made for hotel ice and drove them to the other side of town, to the back of a store with a hand painted sign out front that said "no refunds" in three different languages. Beside the sign was a curtain hanging in a doorframe that led to the space where the rest of the store's inventory absorbed the smell of nonstop incense.

A few people mingled around picking up merchandise. Care-fully examining the items with barely an expression just to put them back down again gently like raw eggs. This is as busy as it gets. There was never going to be any rush of shoppers like a black Friday sale at Target. This shop was too calm and serene for that type of full scale customer invasion.

I knew the little Afghan woman who ran this place, she could be pressured into a deal about as much as broken glass can be pressed into a baseball. Together, we went to her morgue of for-gotten valuables. She swished the thick fabric of the curtain back with a small hand and we stepped into the storage space like the last act in a musical. Twangy middle east music drifted through the medium sized space made much bigger with wide aisles and sparsely stocked, metal shelves that stayed forever spotless. In her office I poured the coins out on a desk crowded with yellow, sticky notes and printed receipts.

Immediately Bibi was turned off, she had a nasty face on even before the gold stopped clattering. Her husband Sam stood by a water cooler wrapping an extension over his arm and under his elbow. They talked to each other in Farsi mixed with Arabic. The conversation sounded like a machine gun, her asking questions and him firing back rat-a-tat-tat.

I stood by and listened like a language student, hearing everything, gathering only the basics. Enough to know Chocolate's trick must have been important. He was a known attorney, the type of guy who's abuse made waves not ripples that splashed across the interstate into the next town over like the aftershock of an earthquake.

Bibi and Sam had heard about it. They knew about the robbery but the white whale's plans to skip out with a stripper and leave his wife hanging like a porch swing never quite made it through the grapevine. After his money and teeth were gone I guess the women were just a footnote in the story.

The brassy Afghan woman tapped a finger on the desk. "Did you hear about that lawyer who got robbed?" She nodded to her husband with the orange loops of cord on his shoulder. "Sam says he has a lot of friends who work in the fifth street building downtown."

"You mean the federal building?" I asked.

"Yes, that's the one." She clasped her hands on the desk in front of her. "I don't know where you got these, Cerrio and I'm not asking. But I wish you hadn't brought them here. There's no way I can take them and my advice is that no one else should be selling them either."

"And if I sold a few already?"

"Then, you're either very lucky or very foolish. Sitting here it's not so easy to tell."

I smiled bright but no one was laughing with me.

"Look, Bibi you don't have to give me what these are worth. Shit, you don't even have to give me half but I gotta have something. Because I want to keep seeing tomorrow. You already know what's going on out there."

She said, "all I know is my store. Past that I am blissfully stupid."

"Bullshit." I leaned in and put both palms flat on the desk. "You know my big brother, Socks? He already got shot at in front of his mama's house. They blew the poor old woman's flower pots all over her front stoop."

She ignored my dramatics, leaned back and lit up a cigarette. "If he's your brother then wouldn't she be your mother too?"

"That's not the point."

"No, you're very right. The only point is that there's nothing I can do for you. Nothing. If you like flirting with a long time in prison then that's okay. Like they say, 'to each their own'. But me, I would never trust anyone who wants to buy these."

"So don't sell them. Melt them."

She took pull on her square. "Melt them?"

"Why not? Then, there's no evidence. I'll even pay you."

I had her attention. Bibi furrowed those Arabian thick eyebrows until they came together like mating caterpillars. "But, what would I melt them into?" she asked.

The idea was in my head where it had been since Chevy's mother sat right beside me at the new Sally's bar. That flag above the bottles stayed stamped in my brain because that feline woman from the silhouette was even more of anomaly than me. I saw her at night when I couldn't sleep. She was the curiously familiar unknown, a part of the past, all of the future and a little bit of right now.

Bibi told Sam to get me a pencil so I could let her out and the pair watched close while I put the contours down perfectly on an ivory piece of paper. From the cat eyes to the curve of her jaw every line drew her closer to this world and when I was done I thought I saw the revolution looking back up at me.

Bibi held the cigarette between her lips, took the picture and tilted it to the lights. "Who is this, Cerrio?"

"Shit if I know. She came around the other night when things got quiet. And don't ask about her name either. That part hasn't hit me yet." I took my drawing back. "So, what'chu think? Can you make it work?"

Bibi switched her brown eyes from my art to me to her husband to the gold coins still spread out on her desk. "Alright," she said. "I think there should be enough here to make a medallion."

"That's a lot more than what it takes for a medallion. I need a chain too." I knocked hard on the wood desktop. "And, what about that protection?"

In her language they call her Maman. Around the way they call her Bibi. I just call her for help. Bibi believed in options too. She had another husband before Sam which made her a disgrace to the imams back home so she switched her religion to Buddhism and told them not expect any more donations. Standing side by side people always mistook us for family. From the long oval cuticles on her fingertips to the beauty marks on her and my left eyelids we're one in the same. This little Afghan is hard on a deal but we look too much alike for her to flat out refuse me.

She laid out my decisions in the back of the store. In the break room way away from the thick curtain separating us from the clean world an AR-15 and a 10.22 assault rifle rested on a oak table. Sam saw us looming over the hot guns and didn't make a sound. Just slid past to the mini-fridge for a cold yogurt and a bottle of fig and honey syrup for his lemon tea lunch break. He filed back out silently to go snack somewhere in peace until the bell over the front door chimed him back to attention.

In the end it was the AR, it felt like a righteous reward for living long enough to change some young girl named Judy's life. Riding with it I wondered what the clever runaway would grow up to be. A nurse or a scientist, maybe an activist or a doctor working in some third world country like where I was from.

I laid the gun on the back floorboard of the car underneath a knockoff blanket Bibi was going to trick somebody into buying as a real Persian rug. She told me the chain would be ready in a week. That was plenty of time for cocaine in the city to get crazy expensive. The prices went from high to ridiculous to making everybody think that maybe rehab was a cheaper option. I cut my dope twice with a double dose of Arm and Hammer then cruised around for three days smoking Black and Mild cigars to cover the smell of fresh gun oil permeating Aunt Denise's Cutlass.

Riding around with a pocketful of rocks, a chopper and two loaded clips I was the living definition of stupid. If the cops stopped me it was a quick trip to the penitentiary but nowadays in the city I'd rather be caught with it then without it.

All I had on my mind was a question. Am I my brothers keeper? It tied right in with what Bibi said. Her pawn shop logic about if my brother got shot at in front of his mother's house didn't that mean my family got hit too wasn't just some idea she cooked up to piss me off. It was a real question of virtue that ate at me until Friday afternoon when me and Socks were high on the last good, white lines in town shooting up the south side trailer park on behalf of his mama's flowerpots.

Someone called my phone but I couldn't hear the ring over artillery busting. My brother had the whole AR-15 hanging out the window of a brown sedan we rented for two stones. His finger stayed down on the trigger while he tried cutting an aluminum sided, single wide in half like a peanut butter sandwich.

Through the rearview I spotted some slick haired gangsters sporting out of season Starter coats. They ran around the corner of a mobile home on bricks, one slid in the dirt falling sideways and letting his pistol skitter uselessly into a patch of weeds. The other two stood tall, pointed their weapons and squeezed. A plethora of bullets shredded the sedan's back window, hollow points whizzing by my cheek through the interior like a swarm of mad hornets. I ducked. Socks didn't. Instead, he aimed for the jackets in the middle of the road but the assault rifle clicked on empty.

We don't have a system for times like this, like me and Chocolate at the gambling house we just know how to communicate better in hot situations without any words. Some people call it chemistry but I ain't a chemist. When I took the Llama off my lap and turned the car sideways Socks leaned his seat back to let me aim right past his face. Five .40 rounds went out the window on his side in a fast burst, bam, bam, bam, bam, bam.

Hot smoking shells jumped out like a salmon run going upstream. One of the slick gangsters folded, a crimson stain spread across his Starter coat turning the royal blue fabric a grotesque plum purple. He screamed on his way down to the dust but his partners didn't give a shit, they scattered while more brass casings bounced around in the car. I dumped so many shots that my hand cramped inside the rubber glove I had on. When the gun finally clicked then I noticed Socks comically slapping away shells before any of them had a chance to burn his skin.

I pulled the smoker's shot up Nissan behind an abandoned check cashing place boarded up with plywood. Long, wailing sirens like the type that go around on top of an ambulance were already cutting through the air followed by the much more striking roar of police cars speeding faster in a fleet. Socks took the AR-15 and ran up the hill to the Cutlass with me on his heels losing ground fast.

I ran out of breath, sweating up the blacktop with one hand clutching the .40 like I was born with asthma. Soon as we got to the car Socks tossed the automatic in the backseat while I bent over gasping for air on the cracked sidewalk. It took precious seconds for me to get my wind back, by the time we were in the car riding back down the hill of a band of brand new Dodge Chargers with police decals on their sides were burning up asphalt looking for the emergency. We hit a stoplight and I drove straight through, tires screeching and a car horn called out angrily as I swerved through the intersection. Socks swore then reached back to cover everything up with Bibi's fake Persian rug.

"Goddamn, you're losing it, fool!"

"I flicked him a look across the seat. " The fuck are you talking about? It was just a red light."

I weaved around a van and took a sharp turn right out in front of it. Socks gripped his seat and dug his nails into the dashboard.

"Slow down!"

"Shutup, I know how to drive!"

"Man, what happened? You used to be calm. Always cool unless it was something about..."

"Something about what?" I asked.

"Nothing brother, just keep on driving."

I slammed the Cutlass's brakes in the middle of the road. A big box truck almost folded into our back bumper.

"We've never had any secrets Socks. What is it?"

He breathed hard, his ropy arm still braced against the dash. "I been knowing you a long time brother, and you always been calm unless it's something about Chevy. Maybe you just need to apologize to her. Just suck it up and take the blame this once."

"Take the fucking blame?" I repeated incredulously.

"That's not something I'd usually say but, yeah. You gotta fix this shit between you and her or you're going to get yourself killed out here."

I thought about the coke bags in the trash and Bandy's bruised up face at the kitchen table. Thought about the silhouette in my dreams and which way my scales were tipping. "You don't know what I been going through. The shit I been seeing lately."

"What does that mean?"

"It means it's rough being me. But I been trying my ass off."

Socks made a noise like a steam pipe springing a leak. "You're not trying, you running. Buying suits and smashing sluts from the The Rose Petal. How's that trying? If Chevy was sleeping with another man right now you wouldn't even know it because you're out here in the streets trying to kill the pain."

I cocked back and hit him. It wasn't a plan, just a reflex caused by too much truth raining down extremely fast. I've never been a better fighter than my brother. Ever since we were kids he could hold his own and little bit of mine too. After we got out of the car it was no time before I ended up bent backwards over the hood dodging his lefts and his rights.

He put four knuckles on the sheet metal three times before a glancing fist caught the corner of my right eye. That's how the fight ended, just as quick as it began with one, flush, hit. He could have went on longer but every face on the sidewalk was pointing towards us. People froze in their tracks, cars stopped, a metro bus downshifted to get a last impression of us going at it.

"Fuck this," he said. "I'm going to my mama's."

I got off the hood with a phone bell ringing in my head. "Run! Run, you fucking rabbit! And don't think about calling me when they come back and shoot up the house again either!"

Socks ignored me and hustled to the sidewalk then to the brush that barely covered a chain link fence guarding the backside of Cherry Street housing projects. He never once looked back. Just deserted me over the rusty fence and I watched the soles of his shoes as he trotted through the tall grass on the other side.

Out in the street things were moving again, when I looked around everybody diverted their eyes pretending like they never saw any contentions in the first place. The bus was gone, full of town gossips with a fresh story to tell and a stream of cars carefully eased around me and the Oldsmobile's doors hanging wide open.

My eye throbbed. Before I moved the Oldsmobile from the middle of the road a blue spot in the shape of a scorpion blossomed from the end of my eyebrow to the top of my cheekbone. Every two minutes I was in the rearview checking to see how much it grew. I was happy when no swelling came until I realized Socks had taken it easy. He could have split my head up the middle with his scarred knuckles then left me half dead in the street with a couple of kicks.

By the time I reached the hotel I was fighting hard to hold off the wooziness. I wanted sleep because anything in my dreams would be nicer than this tightly wound, spiraling, out of control madness. In the lobby little ibuprofens held the promise of relief behind vending machine glass. They were paper two packs. I paid for six and swallowed them all dry while the maids wiped windows with blue bottles of spray.

Out of the elevator I treaded down the carpeted hallway, past decorative lights in the shape of half moons mounted up on both sides of the wall to the fifth room from the end. The whole walk I thought about the noise of the guns and the fighting and the relentless sun and how this throbbing in my head was trying to race past the blooming soreness in my face to take first place in today's hurt.

No Chevy, no Socks, no Aunt Denise to be the voice of reason.

I slid the key card down in the door fast like a guillotine blade. I could almost feel the mattress springs underneath my back while the sandman sprinkled his dust like a pinch of seasoning. Then I opened the door and all the dizziness hit me right under the chin. I blinked twice to make it go away but then the room went fuzzy like I was looking at it through a coat of wax.

The last thing I remember is two's. Two beds, two dressers, two lamps. Whatever used to be alone in the hotel room suddenly gained a twin and then I fell face first on the carpet in a swirl of darkness.

CHAPTER 18

PAPER BADGES

I think it's a concussion. Hold his head straight. No, straight. Like this."

Firm hands at both of my temples while a woman above talked down with a lot of measured certainty. She was blurry. A soft vision of sandy blond hair haloed by a halogen light glaring right above us. In a second another face partnered right beside her, a bald man with a groomed moustache that hardly moved when he talked.

"His eyes are open. Yeah, he just blinked."

"Can you hear me?"

Fingers snapped in my face and then they stuck up in what looked like a peace sign. I winked my eye to get the best count. "How many?" asked the woman.

"Six?"

"Yep, concussion. Probably got it somewhere else and then made it worse when his head hit the floor."

"Where we at?" I asked.

The woman snapped off her gloves. "You're in the back of the ambulance. Housekeepers at the hotel found you on the floor of your room and called 911."

The buggy hit a pothole making the gurney and everything else not bolted to the floor jump high in the air. When it all crashed back down again my head slammed hard on the thin mat and the two medics in front of me went fuzzy all over again. The girl banged hard on the slab of metal separating us from the driver's cab. "Watch the road!" She looked at me with a hint of sympathy. "Sorry, fucking new drivers."

"Don't worry," I said. "You can make it up at the hospital with some painkillers."

They laughed out loud but I was so serious. The front of my skull felt like somebody was going through it with a jackhammer.

"Hey, you guys got the top lights on?"

The moustache medic looked at me like I asked if he had a daughter I could date. "Of course. Nothing but the best when you're with us. You must've been took ride with those guys from Reynolds Clinic."

"Assholes," chimed the big girl. "This is an equal opportunity ride. Earlier we had a guy back here shot in the chest. Almost died. Bullet missed his heart by this much." She held her fingers apart by a centimeter. "But that don't matter. Whether you got a nosebleed or a hole in your heart everybody in this bucket gets the champagne treatment."

At the ER the doctor said she was right, I did have a concussion. Socks knocked the shit out of me which makes plenty of sense considering how well he always solved problems with his hands. They called him Socks because that's how he took care of business, socking people, and fresh off a shootout this afternoon his business was me.

The hospital wasn't so bad, though. It wound up being the calmest place I had touched down in maybe a week. Because it was the middle of the day it was way too early for the nurses to be swamped like they would be later on tonight. The doctor came to see me in twenty minutes and left quick like I was taking up her lunch hour. I got no drugs because I asked one more than once and the thin Indian lady in the long, white coat didn't believe in my pain anyway. She thought I just wanted to get high, of course she was right. I wanted to go to cloud nine or nine hundred and fifteen, whichever step was first on the staircase to heaven. But pills were secondary, I was going to be lucky to leave the hospital with my freedom.

I smelled the cops around the corner coming off the elevator. It was easy to tell they were investigators because they weren't weighed down with all those accessories like street pigs. No belt with a taser and mace and a radio that could call out to Saturn. Instead, they came in wearing Izod shirts creased at the sleeves, department issued iron holstered on a clever clip at their waists. They started out casual because they knew confrontation wasn't going to get them anywhere. In fact the best way to talk them- selves into nothing was to come on hard and strong. Either way it really didn't matter, I wasn't going to give them a thing. The shorter one tried hard to put up a genuine smile but his face got pinched and it looked like he had side pains.

"How you feeling?"

"Been a lot better," I replied.

"Yeah, I bet. Anyway, I'm Detective Banks." He tipped his head towards the other half. "That's Edwards. We just wanted to ask you some questions."

I watched the tallest one, Edwards, reach in his back pocket and pull out a piece of paper all typed up with my rights. The ones that say you have the right to remain silent with a line at the bottom waiting for someone to sign them away. I was shaking my head before he even had it unfolded.

"I got nothing to say."

"Take it easy," said Banks. "You don't even know what we want to talk to you about."

"I know it ain't baseball and fishing."

"True, but what if I told you somebody shot up the mobile home park on the south side and there's a witness saying they saw a car out there that looks just like yours? Wouldn't you want to straighten out that little misunderstanding."

"That's easy. I wasn't there."

Edwards rocked back on his heels and played bad cop. "So, when we test your hands for gunpowder residue the results are going to be negative?"

I almost said, "fuck if I know." But then I remembered how that big paramedic lady doused my hands in sanitizer while we were in the back of ambulance bouncing around like tennis balls with the rookie driver whipping up front. It wasn't standard issue hospital stuff either. She brought own brand that had a scent of something clean and fresh that made me think of a waterfall.

In the end the badges came up empty. The test on my hands showed nothing conclusive, nothing to go on, but they can do those on site now which means I need to be more careful. Especially since the detectives already had my record in their back pocket right next to that piece of paper that they couldn't get me to sign. They knew even before I face planted in the doorway I was up to absolutely up to no good. A peek under the blanket on the Cutlass floorboard or a suspect line up would have brought it home. They just didn't have that magic paper with the word warrant printed across the top. Instead they brought the one that got them nowhere. Dumbasses.

Give it time, though. Something better than intuition told me the investigators weren't giving up just yet.

CHAPTER 19

ITALIAN GIRLS

I walked away from the hospital with a handful of low grade pills and strict orders not to do anything rough. No tackle football and no more fistfights for at least two weeks. When I walked through the lobby I saw the same sandy blond lady who doused my hands in alcohol and unwittingly saved me from a cell. I took her face in my hands and put a kiss on her cheek that grazed her lips so close she could taste my moustache. Then, she held her fingers out and wiggled them so the little diamond on her hand could sparkle in the ER lights.

"Sorry baby, I'm married."

"Dammit, what a shame. And here I was planning to sweep you off to Hawaii this weekend. Show you my beach house out in Oahu and a whole collection of surfboards."

"My husband loves the beach." She flashed a smile and looked over my shoulder where the cops were still hanging around trying to pick up a clue.

"You should go home," she said. "Lay low. Spend some time with your lover."

Her last word came out like, "lovah." And it made me wonder if it showed to the whole world how bad I really needed Chevy James.

After the detectives came I dropped back and fell away like a sunken island. I was hotter than hot which means I was a walking furnace and the only thing that could cool me off was a little seclusion out in the open. The King's Inn was the perfect place. Sitting right on University Parkway bumped up next to the baseball field where a few hundred fans walked by every minute of the summer it was the best place to hide in plain sight. The owners took cash, housekeeping didn't bang down your door before nine o' clock, and nobody stole your shit while you hung by the pool. In other words it was decent.

That peace of mind felt good but it ended after just three days when Bibi called me deep in the afternoon. I was outside in the sun smoking while my room door hung open like the entrance on every corner store in town without air conditioning so it was easy to hear the phone shrilling like a banshee. I answered and kept watching the local barflies get an early start on their evening routine as old maman told me in low tones that my piece was ready.

She must have felt a little dark magic coming through on it because she kept the store open way past five o' clock just so I could come down and get it ASAP.

Of course I wouldn't want it any other way. I'm impatient just like the rest and that gold medallion felt like my way back to something that was halfway normal. Fuck a breath of fresh air, I needed the same thing that I'd always had. So, I drove the Cutlass slow watching over my shoulder to see if any unmarked sedans were following close behind and the scene in my head went like this; I show up at Chevy's apartment with the lady head that I saw on the flag all trimmed in gold. Maybe with flowers and candy but not a box of chocolates because that's not creative enough so it'll have to be something with yogurt and nuts and fancy shit like that. Chevy looks through the peephole, sees me, flings open the door all teary eyed and we fall into each other's wide open arms like we've both been through hell because the girl missed me just as much as I missed her.

I floated down to the pawn shop on seventeenth avenue thinking about what kind of love that must be. It was distracting, calming, bigger than life. For the last mile and a half it kept my eyes out of the rearview mirror looking for detective's creeping in the long, afternoon shadows. It must have been the same thing Adam felt for Eve. Then the light changed to green and I thought that it couldn't be, Adam must have felt something much, much purer because back then life was still undefeated.

I double parked out in front and left the Cutlass sitting sideways. Any other time Bibi would have thrown a fit but right at the door I could tell we were in a rush. She ignored the reckless parking and frowned up at the bell ringing over top of us like it was calling her names. I could barely pause to wipe my feet on the mat before she was poking me in the side with three hard fingers trying to usher me to the back behind the thick curtain. For a moment I thought there would be another gun show in the break room, a few oiled AK's or something laid out on the lunch table ready for the choosing. But that was just wishful thinking. Bibi didn't want to feed into any more of the violence running rampant through the streets and I couldn't have blamed her. That wasn't her cause.

We went past boxes and wood pallets and a mop bucket full of gray water that Sam forgot to empty on the way to her cluttered office. All this rushing felt wrong, like we were creeping around in a kind of forbidden love affair. Except Bibi would never do that, she wouldn't turn her husband into a fool which is another reason I love her. Another reason she commands my respect.

She was rummaging in a drawer and paused to look me in the eye. When she forgets good grammar and talks that broken, sand nigga English I know things are getting serious.

"Police been here twice this week. And they call me three times." She pulled out two business cards and threw them both on the desk. Upside down I read one. It said, "lead investigator, WSPD."

"They keep ask about that lawyer."

"What did you say?"

"I say no, like always. But the man who owned this gold is one of them. They all like brothers and they not going to give up until someone found out who took it. Then, they hang that person."

I didn't bother to remind her they don't hang people in the States anymore. Bibi had a sad look on her face when she set the medallion down hard on top of the business cards. My piece was all wrapped up in a ruby red velvet cloth with frayed edges like sleeves torn off a sweater. The color and the look and the two of us together made it all feel very Aladdinish. Now, all we needed was a flying carpet and a little monkey that steals fruit.

I wrapped five fingers around the cloth, even before lifting it up I knew the thing was heavy. When I peeled a red corner back my heart jumped like a farm girl on her very first hayride. The jewelry was everything I thought it would be except it was more. It was like Bibi had gone in my head and come back with a glittering, gold replica of everything I envisioned in the bar with Chevy's mother. Like she was the one there at the jukebox changing Aretha Franklin songs and then ghosted me before I had a chance to turn around.

Before I could say thank you she was back on her feet telling me to leave. Telling me not to come back anymore. Banishing me into exile.

"You're banning me from here?"

"I have to, Cerrio. Things are out of hand now. You are too dangerous. Don't try cozying up to Sam either. He's already got instructions to show you the door if you ever come by."

I swallowed hard. And somehow without even knowing it I was already backing away. "Maybe I'll call you sometime. When all this blows over."

She shook her head. "I'll never answer."

I bought another outfit. Seems like all I did these days was change clothes. A lanky Italian girl on an extended spring break helped me pick out a pair of red suede shoes and new Gucci pants. I swear I'd never shop at the mall again but the retail therapy made me feel better at least. I found a Lacoste shirt that matched and tried everything on with a belt in the dressing room, never once looking in the mirror. For some reason my uncle came to mind again. You got to be kidding, I thought. Twice in a week. I remembered how he used to say clothes don't make a man. Then, he'd turn around and tell me and Socks to dress comfortable.

I pulled the medallion out and set it beside me on the small dressing room bench. Bibi's solid gold lady head was a masterpiece in a purple velvet box with a spade on top. When the light hit her eyes the clustered diamonds sparkled with affection. I still didn't know what to call her, I guess Chevy could pick out a name later.

Clothes don't make a man and jewelry can't make a woman. But maybe it's the other way around. Just to find out I bought a sundress. The same slim Italian girl took me to a lady with all the same sizes as Chevy, 33-23-32. Her acetate name tag had a glare on it like it was hot in the sun. "Madeleine," it said. She smiled at me and I smiled back and fought off a wild temptation to hold my arm up against hers so we could measure tones. Maddy was Italian too, she looked like the lanky girl's more curvy Sicilian cousin and her skin was two shades darker than mine which made her three more than Chevy but pasty next to Chocolate. Fucking Chevy, no matter how much my world turned the compass always landed back on her.

"All men think about is what's good for them. What they want. What they need. Even when it seems like they're being nice it's just because they want something."

Chevy pressed down hard on the gas pedal and sped out of the Mercedes dealership with Taneesha in her ear on Bluetooth. It almost made her feel silly to stake a case against men to a bona fide lesbian. Bandy's girlfriend wasn't really man hater in the traditional sense, or any sense, but she could definitely side with Chevy in the debate.

Tonight was a school night and the Thursday afternoon before the North Carolina Aggies had their annual Friday night homecoming fest felt like a good time to buy a new car off the lot. A month and half at 43-Dimes and the coke drought in the city, and voila, Chevy had enough saved up to put a down payment on a new-used, Benz. Bandy showed her how to do the finance paperwork and gave her $300 for the tags, she called it an early birthday present.

Chevy quit taking rolls of cash from Chocolate so there wouldn't be any hard feelings when a shiny Mercedes started showing up everywhere she did. But when LaDecerrio found out it wouldn't be that easy. Thinking about him made her drive even faster.

Neesha baked a cake and listened close to the tea. She found out Chevy James was sensationally devilish. She had two bank accounts and Cerrio didn't know a damn thing about either one of them. Apparently, he thought his girlfriend just danced all night and then handed over the money to him first thing in the morning. And even though she felt like he was cut from a different cloth Taneesha still didn't interrupt Chevy's rant. She knew it was better to be quiet, people said she listened so well it was like talking to a tape recorder.

When her platonic girlfriend was done she planned on asking if the club was still hiring. She thought about how much it would cost to buy a Jaguar. Taneesha liked the X types, she wanted one in teal green with straw colored leather and polished walnut on the steering wheel.

Suddenly Chevy halted her rave, the words jammed in her throat and she went another direction. "Wait, wait," she said. "Someone's calling me on the other line."

The phone went flat in Neesha's ear long enough to whip cold butter and cream cheese into thick, rich frosting. She licked the spoon thinking about how good she was getting at this baking thing. Thick streaks of sugar stuck around the sides of the bowl didn't lie. She was almost already to marry it to the layers of red velvet standing on the cake plate before Chevy's voice came back in her ear clear as day against six o' clock traffic. When she talked the glass dish fell out of Taneesha's mixing hand and then the phone followed. Down, down, down to the floor in an instantly forgotten sideways heap.

I'm not so much a planner but last time I went up to the apartment unprepared I learned things the hard way. I couldn't avoid seeing a black eye in the kitchen or a trash can loaded with paraphernalia if it happens to be there but I at least had a sketch of a strategy when I got behind the wheel of the car. The rest came to me on the drive over.

Just tell Chevy I'm sorry like Socks was talking about before he knocked my head off and then give her the gifts starting with the sundress first. Chevy will eat up what's inside the shopping bag but try to act nonchalant. She's good at that casual, so what, nothing-really-gets-to-me type of attitude. She showed it the best that very first night at Sugar Bares, played cool until we were all alone and then kissed me and popped me and brought me home like a rottweiler rescued from the animal shelter.

But I promised myself that I wouldn't call bullshit when she downplays the dress. I'll just give her the medallion Bibi made and let the face looking back at her in solid gold bring out all of her true emotions.

I pulled up to the apartments and hopped out thinking I could already feel two smooth arms wrapping around me in an embrace of happy forgiveness. I could almost hear a big, fat, gasp leaving those pouty lips. She was going to love draping that chunky thing around her throat, and she was going to wear that designer sun dress with the plunging neckline until the seasons changed.

Chevy quit pacing the kitchen floor and took the phone away from her ear to listen a little harder. She was good with sounds, good at figuring out who was coming according to the noises that arrived before them. When she was little she could close her eyes and call out which one of her cousins were coming down the hallway by the way their heels drug the carpet. And she knew that motor outside anywhere. It was one of a kind and when it pulled up she heard the low, throaty, growl of a well oiled engine prowling around downstairs like a cheetah stalking its prey. She raced to the window and split the blinds wide enough to peek through even though she never even had to look. The way the transmission dropped, the way the exhaust pipes rattled, the way the brakes whined a little on an easy stop threw her back to the days of another age. She forgot all about the phone and left it laying on the counter to kick her slippers off. Chevy wanted to have her running shoes tied tight before Cerrio even knocked on the door.

Now here's what happens to all the best laid plans. They dropped off the stairwell and splattered dead on the sidewalk just to make room for something much bigger. I fell awake on the tenth step going up before she came out in a pair of Air Max with no socks, T-shirt and cut off shorts that had white pocket squares hanging down below the fray line.

She snatched me by the wrist talking fast like usual. I couldn't make out all she said but I got the most important part. Bandy was in trouble. Again.

CHAPTER 20

PSYCHO'S GRAVE

"Where's she at?"

Chevy tugged me down the steps with a firm grip and talked faster than she could even breathe.

"She's hiding in a bathtub somewhere. It's bad, Cerrio. She's scared. Probably hurt. Girl called me crying. We got to go get her."

"Get her from where, Chevy? I need a destination. A place to go."

"I don't know but I know who does."

"Who?"

"Chocolate."

"Chocolate?"

"Yeah, Bandy kept saying she introduced her to a new guy from Sugar Bares. He was supposed to be different."

We jumped in the Cutlass and slammed the doors.

"Different as in what? Was it a good different or a bad different?"

"Doesn't matter. We just got to find Chocolate."

But the dark dancer was in Mrytle Beach. After our pizza dinner she took Judy home to her grandmother's in Tennessee and then beelined straight for the last Carolina just in time for Black Bike Week. Between shopping sprees and shootouts I was checking on her little dog, Franky. I even kidnapped him for a while to live with me at the King's Inn. Of course Chevy knew none of that and I couldn't tell her without things going nuclear so I said, "we ain't gonna find Chocolate."

Chevy whipped her neck around so fast I thought she separated it. "We go to. We can't find Bandy without her."

"Call her again."

"Who?"

"Bandy, who else?"

"I did. Her phone's off."

Chevy looked at me with the same harrow shimmering in her eyes I saw when I slapped the dirty powder out of her hands in a parking lot, late night in east Winston. Back then the desperation was a sprout, a bud growing in the ground that you had to look hard at not to step on, now it was a full grown tree swaying in the hurricane winds of fear.

Our stupid adversity died right there in the car. The split between us instantly closed by the exact same thing that made it. That colorful, little Bandanna.

I drove out of the apartments and whipped the Cutlass up into the Circle K parking lot. I had the door open before the wheels were even stopped. "Stay here," I said. Chevy leaned all the way across the seats until her ass was halfway up in the air "Where you going?"

"I'm just going in the store for a minute. I'll be right back."

Doorman rose up off the cement curb and I stiff armed back into a Pepsi machine. He looked stunned but who gives a fuck. I slipped deep in the store, threw a look over my shoulder just to make sure Chevy hadn't jumped out to follow me inside and walked back to the corner where the beer coolers met the magazine rack. I pulled my phone from the pocket of my new Gucci slacks and found the number I needed. I dialed but before hitting send I double checked behind me again. Chevy was standing in the sun talking to Doorman, probably apologizing and explaining my brutal shove.

No answer so I tried again. She picked up on the last ring. I could hear motorcycles rumbling in the background.

"How's my baby?" she yelled over the motor noise.

"Franky's fine. I fed him this morning. I need your help."

I could hear the pain in Chocolate's voice that this wasn't going to be about her. "What is it, Cerrio? What's the matter now?"

"It's Bandy. She's in trouble. Chevy is saying something about a new trick you turned her on to. Who is he?"

"We been through this before. I don't give any names."

"Fine, where does he live?"

"That's like giving you a name."

"You think this is a fucking game? Listen, you dizzy bitch tell me where your friend lives so I can go in. Or don't ever come back to town again."

There was a pause and I thought she might hang up. A crotch rocket whizzed by sounding like a giant hornet. Then she said "south side, yellow house close to the one with the Thursday night spades game. Look for the black truck out front."

"That's better, thanks."

"I'll see you when I get back. Keep feeding Franky And Cerrio?"

"Yeah?"

"Don't ever talk to me like that again in your life."

After that the line went dead and I ran out of the store and almost crashed straight through the door like a cartoon character. When Chevy saw me coming she climbed back in the Cutlass and Doorman jumped to the side while we peeled rubber.

Winston-Salem isn't that sort of sprawling, spread out city like Chicago or Atlanta or even Charlotte, North Carolina. That means the south side isn't big either because really no side of town can be that big. Neighborhoods just sort of run into each other so that once you're deep in one you're already coming out the other. That was the good news. Bad news is I don't play spades. I mean, I know how but it's not my speed and so Chocolate's tip about a Thursday night game meant nothing to me.

Chevy turned the radio down to a hum and talked incessantly. She didn't know what I knew, didn't know what to look for as I drove recklessly through the hood blowing red lights and fishtailing around tight corners. Even though there wasn't time to enjoy it I still missed this part of us. When she gets anxious she pours herself out to me on a back-to-back binge of nerves until the heat in her soul dies down to a low simmer. I rode the curbs like I was always supposed to be there and fed her on energy. "Don't worry. I got this, okay. We're gonna find her."

And I don't know if she believed me because the driving didn't match the calm in my voice. Any cop riding behind me would have been flush with good cause to run us down like rabbits but I listened hard and the sirens weren't there, looked and the top lights weren't either. So, I sailed through the back streets with the sidewalk dwellers coughing up my dust and the mall shopping bags sliding across the backseat until gravity pulled them down and hit a cut and then there it was standing just one lot up from the cul-de-sac where Psycho got killed.

Precision in signals, that's the only way to really explain how we found that house with the sad, sagging roof and the banana colored window shutters. Is Bandy really in there? It seemed so surreal to be at the right place this easy, a no way moment out of the pages of true life. I mean, the fucking FBI couldn't have figured it out as fast as I did. But I had one thing that the feds didn't and she had a teeny dog named Franky.

I pressed the brakes hard. They didn't squeal this time and Aunt Denise's Cutlass didn't even come to a full stop before I was out with the hot sun licking yellowish, heat rays off the back of my pressed shirt. I had the .40 in the same spot as always, the fitted Gucci slacks pressed the gun metal deep into my flesh so me and the strap moved as one up the unkempt lawn.

Chevy slid in the driver's seat quiet as a whisper while I approached the house. The closer I got the more I hated this place. The overgrown grass, the faded black utility truck with wind beaten paint, the rusted mailbox leaning left like it had been smacked by a bat last Halloween. I been down my whole life, been in prison, been in the PJ's, been in the trap, but all that was hopscotch and this made my skin crawl. This was the picture of bad news, a run down house of pain painted with rejected brushes that could only form a nightmare.

The door was unlocked but I kicked it loose anyway because that's just how I felt. There was my foot causing an explosion and then the rotting wood ruptured apart around the dented knob. Inside I saw thick strips of tape criss-crossing over each other on the windows like the city was bracing for a hell of a storm. Except this wasn't hurricane season and that duct tape looked old like the sticky side had melted into a hard glaze the same as cane sugar does in a hot frying pan.

I never figured out the puzzle of the taped up windows. It became less important when a figure emerged from the shadows wearing a stained wife beater with what had to be blood on the front. He had dark features, raccoon eyes, a wild moustache tinged with gray close to the lip. The barrel on the ten gauge in his hands looked used. He pointed it and I ducked.

Before my eyes adjusted to the dimness there was a flash like a shooting star and fast flying bird shot sprayed the wall behind me. I rolled behind a blue sofa powdered with fresh dust just as another explosion fired through living room ripping my eardrums. Fresh pellets emptied couch stuffing into the air. In a minute my eyes were working fine and my ears were ringing bells. Through the chaos of noise I could hear Chevy screaming at me to shoot back.

Four shots from my .40 cal destroyed a flat screen TV and a lamp. The fifth skimmed a chunk of thigh meat from the shadow with the shotgun. I heard a yell and blood splattered from the hallway light switch all the way down the wall, it looked like somebody had gutted a rat by the baseboards. But he wasn't done, not at all. The gauge went off again lighting up every corner of the dark living room, shredding the taped up window so the sticky strips flapped in the outside breeze.

I didn't really want to kill him, for Bandy absolutely, just not in the middle of the day with the family car parked right out front because that didn't seem like a smart moment for a homicide. The shotgun went off again and the ceiling fan came down right next to me. Instead of wasting more precious shells tearing up the house I needed a plan. When the gauge click-clacked again I pushed the sofa all the way across the living room right into shotty boy's knees. He flipped over the ruined back cushion, got up a foot in the air and crashed back down right beside me on the floor.

I saw him clear now, dark skin, not black though, olive complexioned like me with jet black hair. Looking down I could see the evil twisting beneath his flesh. I thought about Mrs. Chitara. If I killed him right now how would that weigh on the scales she showed to me? Would I be a hero in the house of God or just a monster killing another monster? Good or bad, heaven or hell, it didn't much matter. All that really meant something was the girl with the white spot on her mouth. Where was she?

A hard, bulging, gut hung out from shotty boy's filthy, ribbed tank top that was a size too small. I jumped on his belly and smacked him with the pistol. Face bones cracked and a second later his nose leaked wet, glossy crimson all over that caterpillar moustache while I tried forcing answers.

"What did you do with Bandy?"

Shotty boy spit high in the air. "Go fuck yourself."

I wiped sticky, red droplets off my brow and smiled at him. His warm breath in my mouth was like a rancid fish swimming in a pond of blood. And I smiled and I smiled until my face was just a jacket of teeth looking down on him with unfettered lunacy and I said, "you must really fucking hate yourself."

Chevy was sitting there not doing anything, just letting the sun bake her face through the crystal clear windshield while the noise of war echoed out into the street. Her bony knuckles were white, half from gripping the steering wheel like a bar on a roller coaster seat and the rest from nerves. Her throat was raw from yelling at Cerrio to do what he was going to do anyway but what was she going to do?

Across the street a neighbor peered through her blinds before letting them snap back into place again. Being spied on made things just a little bit worse, but just a little is a ton in a situation like this. Chevy felt herself heating up even more and she gripped the wheel so hard her hand cracked like a pigeon's wishbone.

Is this how she was going to tell the story? From the perspective of a nervous girl watching out window with her foot held down on the brake pedal? And of course there would be a story because you don't sit curbside in a car while the man you've been fighting with all week goes after a slug in some shitty traphouse all over a college girl who just wanted to make ends meet and never, ever talk about it.

Really how could you not talk about it? Only what would she be able to say when someone pointed her way over a bottle of vodka or a tray of white lines and asked Chevy about her role in things. Was she going to look all sheepish and admit to doing nothing? Tell how she sat there waiting and being optimistic? Just thinking about that sort of confession seared her soul with a certain condemnation. She wanted to grip the wheel harder but it was impossible to clamp down anymore. Chevy hated the sitting, this dumb and pathetic idleness. And she felt like she was going to have to die a little each time she breathed tale about today because the fact of the matter is she hadn't done a goddamn thing.

There was reefer stink in the car, buried deep in the seat cushions from LaDecerrio's smoking, a little cigar smell too that would never escape even with all the windows down. When Chevy breathed in she could taste them both through her nose. Why did that man have to ruin everything, she thought. From his life, to her life, to their love and now this beautiful car where it had all started everything he touched turned into a funeral. She looked behind her half expecting the odor of smoke to be sitting up waving back at her. Shopping bags were thrown around in every direction and the new clothes Cerrio splurged on were spilled out in a heap like a pile of dirty laundry.

Underneath everything a small rug was laid out on the floorboard ever so neatly. Or maybe it was really a blanket. Hard to tell without picking it up. Regardless, it was too nice to be here. Too good for this place like daddy always said his daughter was too good for that trashy boy from Greenway avenue. Chevy knew the rug-blanket thing was never meant to be a prop in some shootout at the end of a neighborhood with a twisted stop sign. Someone had taken extra care to make it special and yet here it was, a fluent, paramount of elegance in the heart of destruction.

She heard a childhood song play on a loop while she slowly pulled a corner back. "One of these things is not like the other." Then, she saw the long, black barrel peaking out at her and it all made sense. "One of these things does not belong."

CHAPTER 21

CLUTCH BITCH

She kicked off her shoes in the car. Any other day she would have been in her heels, only right now she had come prepared for something besides dancing. Somehow, she knew that was going to be the best part of the story when she told it, how she arrived with no strategy but ripped through the place like Haley's comet shooting through the clear night sky.

High school gymnastics taught her a long time ago how to balance on her own two feet much better than in anybody's man-made sneakers. That was just a little bit before she met Cerrio, many moons ago but sometimes she felt like she was still just getting to know him.

The biggest thing she ever shot was her daddy's nine millimeter at a tree in the backyard and that was easy but when the long gun she found in the back of the Cutlass woke up Chevy wanted to be absolutely sure about her footwork. The nosy neighbors across the road parted their blinds again and this time they didn't snap back. Fuck them, she thought. This time she was really going to give the peepers something to look at so when they told their own story she would be written in as the most ferocious female shooter in south Winston. They would be the spectators, the frightened ones looking from a safe place as the car tires peeled off the blacktop in a last, blast of smoke and they would remember Chevy James as that clutch, bitch on fire.

I pistol whipped him again, harder and harder until the Llama was heavy and his face turned into raspberry pie. When my arm got tired I knew I was doing too much. Each time I hit him with the gun I was one step closer to murder in the first but really wasn't it all his fault? He could have kept things simple. All I wanted to know is what happened to Bandy. Where had he hid my singing girl with the white spot riding high in her lips?

I found her alive but the pretty girl was gone. How anyone can mess up a thing so delicate I'll never figure out but shotty boy did it and he did a damn good job. In the hallway bathroom in a bathtub soaked with fear and sweat I saw a monument of pain. Legs writhing, hands twitching, one eye open and the one that used to be black before now completely swollen shut. Bandy wouldn't ever be the same after today, I knew because I knew I wouldn't be either. Whether we walked out of this sad house on ten toes or crawled away through glass on hands and knees the ugliness would always be with us.

On one end of the tub her phone was smashed to pieces and at the other her wrist was handcuffed tight to the hot water knob. She couldn't see me from the eye swollen closed. When I moved a little closer she kicked her bare feet and tried to slide up the tile wall. All the struggling twisted her cuffs and made the metal dig in spitefully and bright blood streamed down in a hurry towards her torn shirt sleeve.

She was crying, trying to scrape her toes and dig her heels into the slippery, plastic tub to get away from the person she thought had come again to finish this horror that he had started. When she slid back my eyes caught sight of a pink stained tooth on top of the drain. I grabbed her face between two hands so we could look at each other.

"Bandy, it's me, baby. It's Cerrio."

She stopped squirming long enough to focus with the one good eye. "Cerrio. You...you here?"

"Of course I am, mama. I told you I would be if you ever needed me."

She blinked and tried to talk a little more through trembling, split lips. Since she had already screamed her throat raw every single word came out like animal paws scratching on a chalk board. "Sorry," she rasped. "So, so sorry."

"Don't worry. You're okay now."

"Sorry."

"Bandy, don't be sorry. Be strong. We got to get out of here."

I leaned down and stroked her cheek. Only a simple touch made her flinch like my hand was a whip.

She kept trying to talk, trying to say sorry. Fumbling for apologies. I told her forget about sorry and she gave me a weak nod and a strained grin that evaporated just as soon as I stood up and kicked the hot water spigot off where her cuffs were looped.

She found the voice to scream again when the scalding liquid stung all the fresh cuts on her body. The noise was like someone dying in a fire. I reached down through the billowing steam quick as I could and scooped her out of the tub like a newborn fawn. I couldn't look at her face, not because of the wounds but because she was crying and if I started crying too then neither of us would be able to see the way back to daylight.

Out in the hallway we were greeted with the sound of thunder breaking through the dimness. It was the ten gauge again. My eardrums almost blew out and for a second I saw nothing but white. I don't know how but shotty boy was back on his feet again, active and angry. I felt his evil in my bones and smelled the gun smoke running towards the ceiling.

Me and Bandy ducked back in the bathroom. She couldn't scream again so now she just whimpered in my arms. I tried my best to concentrate next to the sink in case some part of me had been hit with copper BB's that I had yet noticed. Bandy looked at me with a face full of fear supposed to be disguised like strength. Her one good eye pleading for a chance to live but for a moment I wondered if it was just better for us to die.

Shotty boy cocked his gun, another round sounded out tearing away a circle chunk of plaster just two feet from us. I turned my back to the noise still holding Bandy close. She hung on to my neck while a little bit of bird shot hit the bathroom door latch and ricocheted into the cheap pressboard frame.

If we perished right now our spirits could go high above this place where the images of sweat and blood and mangled teeth didn't exist. We could be free as birds but my idea of freedom was selfish, the same as I am selfish, just like we all are sometimes. She had worked too hard clinging on to this life for me to simply wish us away like yesterday's news. I wasn't really looking to die today anyway. Chevy's mother was waiting for me on me other side and if I showed up there holding on to another pretty girl that wasn't her daughter there would be a lot of explaining to do. Like an eternity of it.

Heaven wasn't an option, neither was hell or a place in a dream in between. I put Bandy down with her back against the wall and she covered both ears while I upped the .40 to let loose in the blind. Four or five shots went around the scarred doorframe hitting both sides of the hallway. Something glass shattered apart and then there was silence. I stood up, broke the bathroom mirror, sat back down again and used a shard to look down the hall towards the living room. In the reflection clouds of smoke illuminated by the sunlight swirled in a funnel.

Everything was suddenly quiet but I knew that was illusion, real smoke and mirrors in the very truest sense. Shotty boy was still out there bleeding into his moustache, I could hear him breathing and a fresh shell going into the ten gauge chamber and Bandy letting out a squeak from her spot under the towel rack. I turned to her with a finger over my lips. She nodded and cupped a hand over her swollen mouth. Looking back in the triangle of mirror I was just in time to see the shotgun being leveled and I jumped back before a ball of fire blinded me and then the roar came next.

His aim was getting better, a few more inches would have taken my roof off. Instead, the rest of the door latch that wasn't nicked disappeared in a blizzard of sawdust. I pointed the Llama, squeezed again, the gun clicked on empty and my heart dropped. I tried a second time, bracing my wrist for the violent kickback that never came. Bandy squealed behind her palm. Now, it was my turn to say sorry. After shooting up the trailer park with Socks I had less than half a clip. Last time I saw Bibi I got a new batch of shells for the AR but Chevy hadn't been around to go shopping for the one thing I never left home without.

Shotty boy moved closer, a floorboard creaked so gently underneath his weight the noise was almost cozy. In the jagged shard of mirror I watched him inch one step towards the bathroom door like an elephant tiptoeing on eggshells. As my fingers dug deeper into the sharp glass edges biting my skin I thought, this is it. I was going to die by way of revenge looking at the man I should have killed because he did the same thing to me. I turned the light out. In the darkness Bandy slipped under me. Her voice was long gone now but words were worthless anyway. She took my hand and simply held it. I knew what she was saying, that it was all okay. At least I had held to my word and came for her like I said.

In the mirror I saw our last moments drawing closer and closer. I kissed Bandy's forehead and held my breath and focused on the feeling. Not fear. Just hate. I hated the whole world because there were so many people in it and none of them were coming to save this woman or the one outside. We were all just Judy's. Little lost girls and boys ate up by the streets and nothing more than dust in the wind.

Bandy clutched my hand tighter. I turned to kiss her goodbye. "I love you Bandanna. Never think twice about that." She smiled as best as she could in the dark just before the final shots rang out.

Chevy took in no air. She just squeezed the trigger like her daddy taught her out on the back lawn when she was just a little girl. Hot shells ate up what was left of the furniture, chewing off a loveseat armrest and cutting a table in half before she even blink. There was a scurrying out of sight in the hallway like someone was trying to move fast but didn't know where to go. That's all she needed, just that pinch of uncertainty.

She pressed her back against the wall and moved towards the sound on the bare soles of her gymnast feet. Pieces of glass crunched under her toe but she swallowed down the pain. She was light as air, deadly as cancer and when she swung around the corner there was no hesitation. A man with a gleam in his eye was trying to shove shells into a shotgun with a smoking barrel. Chevy leveled the long gun and let the it go. From this close aiming didn't matter.

Bandy was clutching my hand like a woman in labor when a thud echoed up the hall. Then, the shots died and we both looked at each other in the shadows. I picked up the mirror and pointed it carefully down to where the shotgun was last aimed. Squinting at the reflection I saw a shape towering through wafting smoke. I knew it anywhere, on a pole, in a bedroom, at the end of the earth or on top of the world. The she called to me like a dove cooing down from heaven.

"Cerrio, where are you?"

"We in here," I whispered. "In the bathroom."

Her naked feet slapped the hallway floor as she rushed to find me and Bandy gulping deep breaths of relief. Chevy appeared in the broken doorway, looked down, her face just a shadow in the dark with no features but I could tell she was riding high on adrenaline. When she reached for the light switch I told her no. She paused thinking what right question to ask but we had no time for that because sirens were already going up in the background.

Down the driveway the searing afternoon daylight blinded us. Walking out of that dark house was like walking out of a cave straight into the flare of a white, hot explosion. I carried Bandy in my arms like a fireman and in the shining one o' clock sun that's when Chevy really saw what had happened. One look and she froze, a hand flew to her mouth and a river of tears welled up in her golden eyes. The rest of her face was colored with murder, now more than me she wanted to go back in and make sure the job was finished. But the sirens were getting closer and I doubted shotty boy would be walking this side of life again anyway. He was face down on the hardwood in a pool of crimson with his body twisted in that careless way that shows a fast, disrespectful demise.

I told her to stay focused. Chevy sniffed, fought off her feelings and nodded, wiped her eyes and jumped in the driver's seat of the car, popped the transmission and a second later I filled up the backseat with Bandy in my lap.

The tires were screaming before I even had the door shut. Same way in, same way out. We were gone just as fast as we had arrived, peeling out and blowing a stop sign on the way to the highway on the way straight to the hospital.

CHAPTER 22

GOLD LADYSMITH

A few nights after Bandy went to the emergency room Mrs. Chitara came back. She was in that same white dress on a boat made of glass. I got on board and we sailed away like the navy. Two novice mariners in a see through ship on a journey with no map. I turned the wheel, she navigated from a chair holding a glass of wine steady in her hand. We went around the moon and docked in a pearl city set in front of the lost planet. It was a beautiful place, something like paradise and I almost asked if this was the place people go when they die but somehow I already knew better.

I confess I had been waiting for her. It was selfish because I expected gratitude, a thank you at least for saving her daughter's friend's life. But there was none of that, no credit for doing what I did. Turns out I can't even get credit in my wildest dreams.

Chevy's mother wasn't happy about me almost killing a stranger. I turned and asked her why pulling Bandy out of that house with a shotgun on me didn't count for something, anything, maybe just a head nod and a smile. Then, the boat left and I woke up in a place where I actually felt like a hero.

Taneesha let me stay at her apartment. Shotty boy might be dead or worse maybe he woke up on the floor with investigators all around him and decided to talk about what happened. Anyway, since I saved her girlfriend and the King's Inn was like a rat trap to police she gave me a place to lay my head in safety. She also ran my baths, cooked dinner, called me chivalrous and folded my clothes into neat, sharp cornered squares like we were in the military.

She was a wife without the sex. Depending on who you ask some people say that's exactly what a life is like anyway. We even took a little time in the evening to talk just like married people do. Taneesha would be over the stove, one hand on a hip stirring a steaming pot and spilling the town gossip while I sat at the table listening. I heard her as if I was a real husband, call it practice for when I do the actual thing with Chevy, and every once in a while she would turn around with her spoon dripping in sauce and say, "try this."

I told her my problems, she ran down the neighborhood's who's, who. She was a glitter bomb. All dramatic and zany and smart enough to mix recipes and then disguise the leftovers in different colored plastic tubs in the refrigerator so I couldn't tell which container they were in. Staying at Taneesha's house I was more than just a hustler married to the streets. I was a real star. All the labels, whatever problems me and Bandanna had seen before found a black hole to fall down in underneath her girlfriend's roof.

In fact, every single thing that brought me to Taneesha seemed to vanish, you could say it all just ran away. Except someone called someone and then on Tuesday afternoon I came back from the store there was every single thing that brought us together sitting right there on the couch.

Chevy and Taneesha were side by side, both of them staring at me with sharp looks that meant business. When I was three steps outside the door they we're deep in a talk about Bandy, maybe about me, maybe about something much simpler than that. Maybe it was girl chatter about hair and nails but since they clipped it off midsentence soon as I walked in I guess it wasn't too much of my business anyway, or maybe if it was they would have kept right on going.

A soap opera played on television, two actors profess a secret love for one another. When the scene ended dramatic music made just for the show lifted out in a light, cold, harmony. Taneesha got up on the first commercial and said something about having to go iron clothes before fading away into her bedroom.

After the door clicked shut Chevy pointed to the white plastic bag hanging down from my fingers.

"What'chu got?" she asked.

"Soda and hot fries." I responded.

"What kind of soda?"

"Just regular."

She shifted her weight on the couch, put an elbow on the cushion and her head in her hand. "Neesha says you been hiding out over here."

I said, "yeah, it's probably better for me to lay low for a little while. She understands that."

"I understand too, Cerrio. Remember, I was there? But I don't know why the hell you went out and risked being seen just for soda and some chips."

"Guess that don't make a lot of sense. You think it's because I lied?"

"Well shit, that's exactly what I'm thinking."

"Then, what if I told you this wasn't soda? What if I said this was two beers and I was fixin' to get drunk right now?"

"Heeey, now, that's the Cerrio I know! There's clean glasses in the kitchen. Go ahead and get me one too."

She never lied, clean glasses in the kitchen and beer in one just for Seville. I took it straight out of the dishwasher, leaned it to the side and poured from the can until a little bit of foam slid off on the counter. She took her drink on the couch and gave me back a thank you. I sat by her in the place that was still warm from Taneesha's booty and popped a tall boy for myself. When I leaned back she raised hers up in the air for a toast.

"Here's to you kicking ass," she said.

I looked at Chevy sideways. "And what about you? Gunning him down like fucking Rambo?"

"Okay, what about it?"

"Are we just going act like that never happened?"

She shrugged. "Fine then. Cheers to me too."

We touched cup against can over the middle cushion and drank. Me more than her but not by much and when the beers were back down again then I asked how the girl was doing.

"She's good," said Chevy. "This is her last day in the hospital."

"Right on, tell her I said 'hello'."

"I'm not your secretary, Cerrio. You want to tell Bandy something be a man and go tell her yourself."

"Can't right now. The cops are on me."

"Don't give me those weak ass excuses."

"Don't try me, then. For two days you and her treated me like I had the flu. Both of you walking around in that apartment staying far apart all the time. I couldn't take it, so I left."

"And?"

"And that shit is awkward. Did she tell you I came by to talk? It was your day off but you were gone somewhere."

Chevy said, "If you wanted to talk then we would have had a discussion like two adults."

"Oh, you mean like this one?"

"Stop it, Cerrio."

"You're right," I said. "My bad. I ain't trying to fight. I fought a lot these last few days and I'm wore out."

"Then why don't you listen? You weren't trying to talk to me at all for those two days and then you just left. And what happened last time you left? How long was it before we saw each other again after that?"

My baby hates being ignored. I guess we're the same that way. If it came down to a choice of walking over hot coals and taking the cold shoulder Chevy would be over the coals every time. Crazy part is ignoring her is the best the way to get her undivided attention.

I rose up off the couch and she went off. "There you go, running away again just like always." Her words clipped off like that in real short sentences to tell me all about myself. They went up like water on a windshield, rolled straight off me and flew harmlessly in the air. On my way over to the closet behind Taneesha's front door she talked a little louder. While she was working up to full strength I reached for something inside. By the time I pulled out the bookbag her lips were glistening wet for an argument. Her shoulders were loose and that neck was rolling just about as good as those curvy hips do every night on the stage.

I dug down in the bag through clothes and the rest of my cash all the way to the bottom until my hand touched a brand new pistol. I had to throw the Llama away, too much heat on that thing for me to keep him anymore. Taneesha bought me a Remington .45 from a sports store by the mall as a thank you gift for saving the love of her young life.

Fat rolls of fifty dollar bills scratched the skin on the back of my hand as I pulled it back out. Chevy's smart, bright as the rim of a solar eclipse. Smart enough to take a moment to turn down the noise when she saw what I had. All her hair was up in a bun and I could see her neck stretching to get a better look. I held Bibi's purple box close to me to keep the suspense alive as long as possible.

She pointed. "What is that?"

"This, this is what I came to see you with the other day. Something I got made special."

"Well, what the hell is it?"

"Shit Chevy, is that how you talk to somebody who's about to hand you something?"

"Give it here."

I forgot how fast she was, just in arms reach she snatched it right out of my hand. Coming from another that might have been rude and I might have been ready to make war but not here and now. No more fighting, instead I couldn't help but smile as she handled the velvet box carefully trying to find the top.

The lid went back slow at first, then it popped all the way open and the gold face inside shot white stars of light dancing all over her cheeks. Chevy gasped because she couldn't hold on to that too cool demeanor she had perfected over her whole life.

"What do you think, girl? You like it?"

"It's...goddamn it's gorgeous. Is this real gold? I mean solid all the way through?"

"Yeah, through and through."

"Oh my God," she breathed.

I sat beside her on couch again, closer than before. Chevy took the necklace out of its box for the very first time and put it around her throat. I helped her with the clasp and all that cold, gold sent a shiver running down her spine. After we got it on she touched the lady head in the middle like she was connecting to its spirit.

"I talked to your mama," I said. It seemed out of nowhere but she didn't balk at the randomness. Instead, Chevy looked back at me. "What did she say?"

"A lot of things." I pointed to where her hand was still touching the jewelry. "That woman is part of the dream I had when we met. I was supposed to give it to you the other day when we had to go get Bandy but we were... you know, doing stuff. And while we were in that house she was in my pocket the whole time. Maybe it sounds crazy but I think she's what got us all out of there."

"So, she's our protection."

"I don't know. I think she represents a redefinition. Something new and different. Real potential really realized."

"Well shit, boo. Sounds like you put a lot of thought into this."

"I had some time. I got you a sundress too. It's still in the closet."

Chevy touched my face. She cupped my chin in her hand and held it so we were looking right into each other's eyes.

"Don't think this gets you off the hook, boy."

"You ain't seen the dress yet."

"I'm serious, Cerrio. Diamonds and gold don't buy you a moment with me."

"Then, what's it going to take?"

"You. I chose you. But if you just up and leave every time we have an argument then we got a real long road ahead of us."

"I didn't leave, I went away and counted."

She dropped her hand. "What?"

"I did a lot of math, Chevy. Counted up every single dollar we put away for your salon. When I finished then I counted it all up again and realized we're still going to be grinding in the streets a long time before we scrape up enough to make a serious move. And, that's if everything goes right. And you know it won't."

"I know it won't. But that's why we got a team."

I paused, scratched my head, squinted at her. "Come again?"

"A team." Chevy ticked the players off on her fingers. "You, me, and Bandy."

"Hell no, not Bandy."

"Look, I know what you mean. I do. But just calm down and listen."

"No you listen to me. I'm not pulling any more half dead bodies out of a strange trap house. Now push come to shove I'll come get any one of you out of a jam. You know that. But Bandy is a no go. No way."

I got up and went to stand in front of the sliding glass door. Bright, red cardinals pecked at the dirt and cars rode by. A good moment to be alive by any standard and I wasn't going to let this girl die turning tricks in the street while I went on to see more sunny days. Chevy got up and walked over to me, she took my hand in hers. "Come on baby, time for us to go. Bandy will be out of the hospital soon and we got something to tell you."

"Tell me now," I muttered.

She leaned in close until I felt the medallion put a cold kiss on my arm. "You didn't hear me. I said, 'we have something to tell you'. That means she gets to speak too."

All that afternoon the Cutlass smelled like azaleas. Not a bad thing. I like flowers. I like black women. I like it when black women make my car smell like flowers.

The hospital made me jumpy, though. Real ambulances wailed out of sight while people in uniform moved with purpose or smoked outside on the sidewalk. In the car I kept watching out for the big paramedic lady who didn't know how she helped me beat an arrest. It was a good game. I mean, I knew I'd never see her just like she knew how I was trouble at the very first sight but it was still a hell of a distraction. Something to kill time and hold me down so I wouldn't peel out of there in a bad episode of anxiety.

Between that and the radio I kept it together in my head until they rolled the skinny girl out the sliding doors in a royal blue wheelchair. This was before I knew anything about hospital policy and nothing made me angrier than the thought that Bandy was going to be like Aunt Denise until the chair stopped and she rose up like it was all some sort of act in a play. A nurse took the chair away and then just that fast she was part of the people again. Someone completely normal on the outside. I even saw the doctors checking her out from a picnic table where they were sitting down eating sandwiches on a lunch break.

The girls all crammed in the backseat side by side like skiers on a lift. They were handsy with her, oohing and aahing like girls do, they even buckled her in. But when she reached up to tap me on the shoulder everything got quiet.

I looked in the mirror, six brown eyes looked back in anticipation. The girl had a hand up to her mouth almost like she was covering a cough. I saw a team of bruises still fading on her face, a long scar ran from her hairline all the way down to her temple. It would never go away but she wore it so well it was hard to be mad about. That thin line was a quiet mark of strength. When the bruises heal, when college is over, when the lights come on in her bright future it would still be there to remind everybody of where she came from.

"Mama, you good?"

"I'm good," she replied.

"You look good too. Don't let nobody tell you different."

She smiled but forgot to put her hand up and I saw the big gap where her front tooth used to be last week. In a second I was snared in a run of bad memories. Her bleeding in the bathtub, a ten gauge blasting through paper thin walls in a smoky house, me fighting back tears so we could get somewhere before the police showed up.

I put the car in drive so I wouldn't break down. "So, where we going?"

No answers from the crowd. Then, Bandy took her seatbelt off and before it zipped all the way back in it's place she was squeezing through the front seats and plopping down next to me trying to cover up a wince. I knew that look when she touched her side below the spot where her bra should have been, a broken rib. I had the same thing in prison once. Hurts like a bitch and every time I breathed a bolt of pain shot through me like I had my finger stuck in a socket. But Bandy just smiled. Then, she hugged me hard around the neck even though it made her teeth clench and someone in the back took a picture, I heard a camera shutter clicking and Taneesha waved her Samsung around in the air.

She smiled. "I don't care what you say, Cerrio. Like it or not this one's going on Facebook."

CHAPTER 23

PILL DOG

We were out on the town. Again. Shopping. Again. We hit the stores real hard in the day to look good for when we went out later on at night. All the time I was waiting for Bandy to walk up to me and explain what her role was in team Chevy, at the boutiques, at the wig store, at the jewelers. I might have gone up and just asked her, faced the woman like a man the way I was leaned on to do back at Neesha's place. But every hot summer minute she was steeped in two fiery girls so there was hardly a moment for me.

They wanted to celebrate her homecoming at The Rose Petal on open mic night, and even though the real plot was swirling all around me like honeybees I never caught on until it was way too late. The place was packed wall to wall and I was starting to feel like that's not unusual. Not unusual either that there were larcenous hearts everywhere in the building all beating to the same decadent rhythm while everyone with actual talent made a show of sticking to their lines on stage. Being around so many body's had me on a cold, razor's edge. I was sweating, perspiring through my palms and wiping the slickness off on a pair of designer pants the color of cream.

Chevy clung to my arm like static in the laundry. She let go to dig a pill deep out of her bra. "Here, take this."

I examined the white oval she dropped in my palm. "Where'd you get a pill?"

"From Bandy. She's got a whole bottle the doctor gave her for pain."

"These things strong?"

"Strong enough. I took two at the nail shop earlier and I can't feel my face."

I chuckled. "Goddamn, and you're in here drinking?"

She kissed me on the cheek. "Relax baby, you're all nerves. Take that and calm down already."

I took the little oval down dry while she watched. "Don't worry," she said. "You'll feel better in a minute."

"We'll see. You know, I knew a light skinned girl from the eastside who used to pop these things from time to time."

Her face tightened. "Did she talk you into trying one straight out of her bra too?"

"No, but she always got the drinks whenever we went out."

"Uh-huh and what kind of girls do you like, Cerrio?"

"I just told you. Go get the drinks."

I knew she understood me when she stepped off to the bar. Chevy is just as savvy as she is jealous. High or sober you got to be quick on your feet around here. That's all a part of winning.

In the club a round of applause went up for the new talent coming on stage. A thick woman in a ballroom dress adjusted the microphone to sing us a song about a man who left her alone and broken hearted. Her tune was sad, moist with depression. Still there was elation in the air, still smiles on faces. When she got the bluesiest part of the number then that's when the painkiller kicked in.

Going up I thought about Henna, maybe she was in here tonight choking a barstool with that big behind. No doubt that could wind up in an awkward moment but suddenly Your Highness, Mr. Cool pulled up and I was too collected to care. When the song ended Her Majesty, the singer, bowed a little while the crowd gave her more applause. I joined in. Her name made me smile for no reason, so did the sash she was wearing that made her character complete.

I confess I've never done pills before, never swallowed anything harder than an aspirin. Maybe that's why my feet felt light like I could run across water and it might have been why everything slowed down like a plane coasting to a stop right before a voice beside me said, "I knew she was your type."

CHAPTER 24

NO JOB

My hands were numb, the edge was off, the king was on and the whole world was fuzzy. The spotlight was acting kind to Her Majesty soaking it up on stage. It traced nicely along the lines of her curves and made the dress hanging off her shoulders look green in some places and blue in others. The dark spot under her breasts looked like the color of a midnight frost on a winter lake while the sleeves on her arms sparkled like a shimmering mermaid's tail.

I looked up and there was Socks towering over me like Moses on the mountain. He slid up while I was lost in the high and gone with the music. The applause tapered away, replaced by the soft chime of silverware tinkling.

"What are you doing here?" I asked.

He raised a vodka and shook the ice in his glass. "Had to get some of these half price drinks, brother. This is the last week of the grand opening. I see you're out tonight enjoying the show."

I rubbed my face. "Look, whatever you're off of-"

"Relax brother, it ain't like that. This isn't the place where people come to settle disputes. I see you brought Chevy. Y'all made up?"

"Yeah, everything's good. She brought me here, actually."

"Doesn't matter just as long as you're back home."

"Trust me, it wasn't easy."

"It never is. That's how you know it's really worth it, though."

"Who you here with? That girl from Cleveland?"

"Nah, some boys from Happy Hill."

"That's an odd date."

Socks drank his vodka. "They're good guys." Took another drink to kill the rest and added, "they did a little shooting in that same trailer park we scorched the other day."

"Shooting don't make a man. And it damn sure don't make a good one."

"Hey, you're right. Why don't you meet'em and make your own judgement?"

Happy Hill is a housing project the city demolished years ago. It was the type of PJ's where you wanted to be with slip and slides for the kids and weekend barbecues where the chicken wings were big as baby legs. Once in a while, about every year, some nightclub in town throws a major party and all the people who used to live there come together and mingle like a high school reunion.

It's been a while since the bulldozers ran through those apartments and turned the place into a parking lot. Some of the kids who used to skip around Happy Hill spraying water guns in the summer have come of age now and I saw two of them sitting at Socks' table looking hungry as hyenas.

When he introduced me no one gave any real names and the names they did give didn't ring any bells. But names or handles I wouldn't remember. My brother knew as much, so he made it real easy for me. "This is my crew," he said.

I tapped four unfeeling fingers on the lily, white tablecloth and checked the faces around the table. Two dark skinned cats, one skinny, one husky, both killers. A waitress with a peach straining the back pockets of her jeans sauntered by in a spotless apron. The husky one leaned back to enjoy the view.

My brother wanted to know one thing. "Did you check that number on the napkin I gave you?"

"Uh-huh, I checked it."

"And what do you think? Is a hundred bands good enough to count you in?"

At the sound of money Husky snapped his attention back to the table, his skinny partner never flinched. I didn't like either of them but for the right price maybe we could all be friends.

Over at the bar Chevy was mingling, high on me and whatever pills were hidden in that bra I would take off later. I watched her talk it up with a middle-aged woman on a stool wearing a blue camisole. She had to be forty, from this far away I was compelled to see how she measured up against the older crowd. Women envied her, men wanted to be in her. She was a black Kardashian, a basketball wife, or something close who was well to do with sparkly tennis bracelets on both wrists and a body that didn't betray anything a day over twenty-nine. She showed my girl a string of pearls that looked like enamel and Chevy one upped her with the gold lady head that watched over us from my pocket in that crumbling yellow house.

I breathed in and felt a rush of good sense wash over me. "You know what?"

"What?" asked Socks.

I said, "I been getting shot at a lot lately, like a fucking lot. That shit's stressful. I live on the edge and I even like it. But I ain't ready for a bank job. Especially after the week I just had. I think I'm gonna have to pass on this one."

His face showed no disappointment but Husky and Skinny exchanged glances of flagrant disbelief. I don't know how he thought to find me here tonight but I bet Socks had told them I was a sure thing on the way over. But there was no angst, no anger, he just shrugged like the waitress told him the kitchen ran out of oysters and said, "there's still time to think about it."

He could have applied a little more pressure and won. Socks knew all the soft points, he knew I only knew success in small doses like someone who only knows the grocery store for it's snack aisle. A month ago I was broke, now I was riding around in a new Mercedes weighed down with stripper bodies. That was a hell of a change. That was the magic of money and it was just the tip of the iceberg. He knew that too and he knew what it was worth to exploit my incessant greed, but he still let it go just like that fight we had on the side of the road. Only brothers know that type of mercy.

Chevy came around switching hard, margarita in one hand, double shot of Hennessey in the other. She was high as gas and acting a little shitty to keep the boys in the club from getting too comfortable. Our whole table saw her glide like a swan on a lake through a sea of people and plop down in my lap like I was a piece of furniture.

She spoke to Socks first. "Hey you, long time no see."

"Sister, you look just as gorgeous as you did yesterday."

She popped her collar. "Shit, I could agree."

"What's going on these days?"

"My business keeps me hopping. You know it's a full time job staying above ground out here."

"Amen," said Husky. "I'll drink to that."

She touched her margarita glass against his beer bottle dripping sweat on the table cloth. There was a line of salt on the rim like a heavy frost, she licked a few grains off before tilting it back against her lips. Husky cleared his throat. I let the noise go and killed the Hennessey without thinking too much about what it would do when a pill was already in me. When the glasses came back down again then a few people started putting their hands together. I didn't notice the clapping winding up until Chevy licked juice off her lips and looked down on me.

"You ready, baby?"

Socks made a I-know-what-you-guys-are-talking-about kind of grunt and Chevy took no time to set him straight. "That's not what I mean. I mean, are you ready to hear what Bandy has to say?"

"Oh, is she finally ready to get off the fence and come talk to me?"

"Nope, there's not going to be any talking."

I opened my mouth to argue but Chevy put a finger on my lips and went, "shh." The lights came down. Behind a microphone bathed in a circle of white spotlight on stage stood a thin woman lonely and stoic. I hardly recognized her with all the changes that had come and gone over the week but in a breath she made the whole club understand.

The Rose Petal hushed before her and Bandy sang, and we listened and when she was done I clapped until I could feel my palms again with Chevy still in my lap. Then, we all applauded for the girl who left all her fear behind in a stranger's bathtub at the end of town just eight long days ago.

C H A P T E R 25

CRUSHED MEDICINE

Everyday the Cutlass was becoming more and more of a legend. Each mile a brand-new story Chevy unraveled sitting on Taneesha's sofa earlier that afternoon while I was out getting the beer. I don't know how much ground she covered, how many story's she told on my walk back and forth to the store. She talks faster than I can think sometimes but I know no one ever mentioned the blood on the door.

Right below the window a stripe of dark red talked about the time when Bandy's split head bumped up against the upholstery while we raced to the hospital. I tried to get it out the best I could. In the heat of the day and the cool of the evening I scrubbed with carpet cleaner and floor brushes. The stain faded but it would never disappear. It was something to look at in case the legend started waning, a memorial to that day when Aunt Denise's Cutlass became a hood ambulance.

"I called Chevy because that was like my one shot. She was the last chance. And I ain't gonna lie, I never thought you would really come. Then, he broke down the door and smashed my phone so I couldn't call anybody else and I thought, well, this is it."

Taneesha looked at me, I looked at Chevy, Bandy cast her eyes straight down to the floor. The Rose Petal closed at two and after that the hands on the clock meant nothing. By then we were all high on pain killers up in Chevy's apartment with a fan moving back and forth behind us stirring up a fresh sensation every time it passed. Cash was on the coffee table, seven hundred dollars that all belonged to the second place winner of The Rose Petal's very first annual open mic night. Bandy finished in a dead heat right behind the curvy blues woman in the mermaid dress and they put up a picture of her by the front door.

That was the moment she graduated from top amateur to pro. All her money was going to a gold tooth but not before we celebrated with some of those hundreds getting rolled perfectly to fit up our nose. Chevy crushed the pills and I sniffed. She touched her face even though she couldn't feel it and after that the only thing moving in the apartment were three fan blades chopping thin air.

It didn't start out this way, all somber and difficult. After the club our new shooting star was so high on fame she floated like a bubble. We came home to finish getting drunk, started sliding a bottle of Hennessey back and forth across the coffee table taking shots, laughing about how she jumped off stage right after her song, ran straight into my arms and wrapped both legs around me so I was wearing her around my waist like a championship belt. Then the seventh or eight shot of liquor kicked in, we were swimming in it when the subject changed. It went another way around an unseen corner where maybe none of us were really ready to go.

Bandy still had the floor. The way she was filling her new role in fame was like she had always been there. She used the attention like a producer uses the light to give his picture that specific mood. She loaded the emptiness blowing through the air with the wisdom of a teacher. I watched her hit the bottle again and set it down. "Once," she said. "That's all I'm gonna live is this once. And if you hadn't came Cerrio it would all be over by now. You were there just like you said you'd be."

She took another moment and used the quiet like an exclamation mark. "I owe you Mister LaDecerrio Lloyd."

"My first name ain't mister. And you don't owe me nothing. That's not how any of this works."

Bandy ignored me. "I shouldn't have gotten mad that day we went out. Truth is I was really happy you liked my singing. I wanted to talk to you, to tell you how I really felt. It was just so hard to believe somebody could think I was good. But before I found a way to reach you, you just up and left."

"I told him," Chevy said. "About that running."

"Again with this?"

"If everyone's telling you the same thing, Cerrio maybe you should listen."

"Look, I was going through some things."

"He really was," chimed Taneesha. "Going through some stuff, I mean."

Bandy looked at me with flat eyes. "Nobody heard my voice like that since fifth grade. Not even Neesha. Back in elementary me and my friends had a little group. We sang in school talent shows like TLC. I was supposed to be Left Eye but behind my back they called me Michael Jackson."

When she pointed to her face heads nodded in understanding. "Kids can be mean as hell," I said. "Trust me I know. Being foreign and having this nose, it was tough."

"They used to call him Jafar in homeroom," added Chevy.

"It wasn't just the kids, Cerrio. I could have dealt with that. It was my mama's boyfriend. He never worked, just stayed home all day drinking Wild Irish Rose. He was a ridicule artist. The gold standard too. He would always find me playing with my Barbie dolls or doing a puzzle in my room and barge in waving around a bottle and point at my cheek and say, 'what's the matter with you, are you sick little girl?' I'd say 'no sir'. Then he'd say, 'well how come you got spots all on your face? Are you a goddamn cow? A cheetah? A leopard?' Then, I'd cry and he'd laugh himself into a fit of hiccups while I ran away to go hide under the porch."

Taneesha made a whimpering noise. She clasped her hands together and put them against her mouth while Chevy dried her eyes. The fan blades were solo again, whirring in circles hunting down heat in every corner. I said nothing, my job right now was to be appreciative with no words.

Bandy said, "I remember trying to color in my light spots with mama's makeup. She spanked me for it and he laughed about that too. That was the last straw. I swore I was going to sing something beautiful at the spring talent show to make my mama proud. Then, I thought I could convince her to kick his sorry ass out in the street.

He heard me practicing in my room. I was singing in the mirror with my hairbrush like a microphone. Singing loud as I could. Doing my dance moves with the music turned all the way up like I was the only one in the whole world. Rello, that was his name, stumbled in wearing his white drawers and ripped the stereo cord out of the wall. He whipped me with it until my legs bled. After that mama dumped him but I always did my singing in the shower or somewhere secret so nobody would hear me."

"I'm sorry Bandanna."

She shook her head. "Don't say that. There's nothing to be sorry for. You reversed it, Cerrio. I never did win that talent show. The stereo plug put criss cross welts on my legs that made it hurt too bad to dance. I could barely even sit down. After that I was all alone, my friends quit talking to me. My little TLC gang and my mother's boyfriend killed my confidence and it was like that for a long, long time."

"Fuck'em," said Chevy.

"Yeah, I guess. None of them are around anymore anyway." Bandy pointed at me. "But you are, Cerrio. And you brought it back. That's why I killed it on stage tonight. Because I love singing and I love my voice. And after that demon smashed my teeth and my phone, I swore to God that if I lived to get out of that house I'd never forget how to love myself again."

My move was sudden. I got up off the loveseat like it just bit me in the ass and sidestepped towards the door. Chevy turns and looks at me without a gesture of premonition like she had seen this type of thing before.

"Cerrio, what are you doing?"

"Nothing, you got any weed in here? Around the house I mean?"

"No, I don't know what you mean. You been waiting all day for this girl to talk to you, now sit down and listen."

"No."

She took her hand away from her face. "What?"

"I been waiting a long time for somebody to talk to me but not like this."

"Like what?"

"I don't know. Now, we're all here and I don't even know what's going on anymore."

"I wish you could see yourself right now. You're acting nutty. What the fuck is wrong with you?"

"It's the pills," said Taneesha. "He just needs some water."

She got up to get me a glass like this was her house and I was her guest and Chevy was just there dropping by for a casual after hours visit. But when she turned away I fled. Gone again before I even realized I was moving or how it even looked.

This time Chevy didn't chase me, she didn't put her little fists against the back of my skull on the way out the door. She sat there still like nothing even happened. Maybe she wasn't trying to show off her bad side in front of company, maybe she was just too high or too tired.

Those were all the things I told myself as I put one foot in front of the other on the way to escape. But the truth was much simpler, I was just scared. Chevy knew it, she hated when I left abruptly because it showed I was too frail to be something else. Because after running the streets and all this filthy rich thuggery really what was left? I was no hero, no sensation, nobody's role model or inspiration. I was Cerrio Lloyd a tenth grade dropout, a screwbaby from the east side of Winston-Salem, a simple felon with complicated demons and that's what always kept me charging towards the nearest exit into the arms of whatever was most ruthless.

Bandy caught me on the stairs. She stood two steps up stretching her reedy arm out far as it would go to seize me in the dark. There was no light except whatever came from the sky, every place a bulb should have been was just an empty socket because every time management puts up new ones around Chevy's projects the dope boys break them out so no one can see their faces clearly on camera.

On the stairwell me and the new star were just a couple of shadows looking like we were on our way out to join the rest of the city. In the dark little noises took on a deeper tone, lonely sounds with nothing for them to blend into like there usually was all through the day. A baby cried, someone yelled when they dropped a hot skillet on their foot, a screen door eased open creaking on three hinges like a ghost stepping on a wood pier and then it banged shut hard like a trash can lid got thrown off a roof.

I watched the twinkle in Bandy's eye as she searched fruitlessly in the dark. A little fear was in her, a little flash of nerves like a little bit of what happened before was trying to come back and clear up the rest of her strength.

"It's just the old lady upstairs," I said. "Her door's fucked up. Been that way for months."

Her grip on my arm eases. "When's the last time somebody told you that you were a good man, Cerrio?"

"Not lately."

"I'm smarter than that."

"Well, that's why you go to school."

"Why don't we got in the car and I'll ask you again?"

In the parking lot there was more to see thanks to light poles shining too high above us for rocks to reach. A half hour before sunrise I couldn't see any purple hues teasing on the horizon yet but that didn't mean much, around here dawn can sneak up on wheels. Right now the old men who sold newspapers at the intersection were out making rounds to every Winston-Salem Gazette box so they could show up by the stoplight with a stack of current events after sunrise. It's a living I guess. Until then me and Bandy got honest over a bottle that rolled under the seat. She likes the way gin looks like crystal going down her throat. Through the blue label I could see her clearing enough for a triple shot.

"Tell me this, what are you going to say when they ask you about your very first performance at The Rose Petal?"

She licked her lips. "That I loved it."

"Everybody will say that. Plus, you got the second place cash to prove it. I mean, what else?"

"I'll tell them I love my city."

"Don't tell Neesha that."

"Why not? She's part of the city too." Bandy pointed at me with the bottle. "But what are you going to say when they ask you about my second act?"

"You mean on stage?"

"No, on the moon. Yeah, on stage."

"At The Rose Petal?"

"Huh-unh, I'm going someplace where I can sing my heart out and you can really gamble like a champ."

I rubbed my chin and a little strip of bruised velvet cut the sky while I watched it close for an answer. Bandy lifted the bottle and let the gin slosh against her lips.

"Can I tell you something?" she asked.

"Tell me something I been waiting a whole day to hear."

"I can do better than that. I'll tell you something you been waiting your whole life to hear."

That was a helluva buildup. "Okay, I'm listening."

"Chevy doesn't blame you for her life."

She's drunk, I thought. But drunk or not Bandy had still leased a big piece of headspace in my mind where her words were all alone so there weren't many places to check for equity.

"What are you doing to me right now, Bandy?"

"Stop worrying, this isn't a bad thing." She passed the gin and shifted in her seat. "Seville loves you Cerrio. She came to see me in the hospital and we talked about you every single day. For hours. Seriously, I almost told her to leave."

"That bad, huh?"

"Like you wouldn't even believe. I kept sending her down to the cafeteria to go get Jello just to get a break from it."

"I'm flattered. And I don't say that often. Although, I have been saying it a lot since me and her got back together."

"And I'm not mad. But when you love someone what do you do? You make them proud of you, right?"

"Makes sense I guess."

"And you help them when you can."

"Okay," I said.

"And me and Chevy came up with a way to do both. We found a place. Not some basement establishment but a real casino where you can win some good money."

"There's no casinos around here."

"You need to listen more. Did I say anything about it being around here?"

"We're going to travel? I mean, what about my job?"

"Nigga, you ain't got no job."

I laughed. "Why I got to be a nigga?"

"Because I love you. Now listen." Bandy leered at me. "You listening?"

"I'm all ears, mama."

She pointed to the gap in her mouth. "Tomorrow, I'm getting this fixed. Then we're going shopping."

"Please, I can't handle another day of shopping."

"Well, what are you going to wear to Savannah?"

I had the bottle up and tipped back before it froze. "Savannah, Georgia?"

"I don't know of another. And when you walk on that casino boat out on the wide, blue, river it's going to be in a crisp, white suit with two girls on your arm. Me, of course, I'ma be one and there goes the other."

I followed her finger pointing up to the balcony where Chevy leaned over the rail. That gold necklace dangling off her neck like a bunch of grapes hanging off the vine and I could see the diamonds in the first official light of the day. Neesha was right beside her, they all knew I wasn't leaving for real. I think the only one who didn't know it was me. This was part of their plan. A plan born in the hospital like a baby and raised on love like a child. Not just any love, but the wild, pure, tonic that's just a little bit imposing and justifiably envious.

Black love.

CHAPTER 26

TRICK BAG

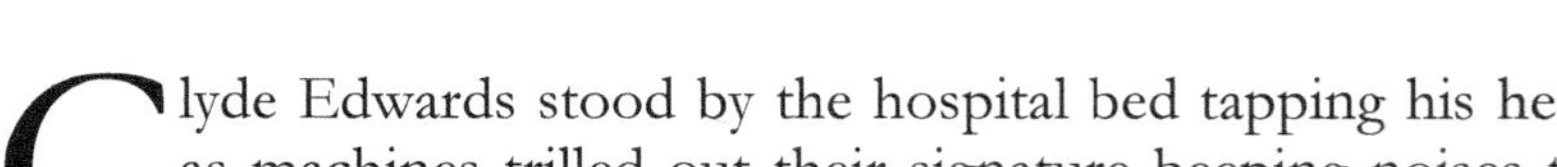

Clyde Edwards stood by the hospital bed tapping his heel as machines trilled out their signature beeping noises to let everyone know Mr. Dominguez wasn't dead just yet. Unfortunately. He looked down a the man's puffy, lacerated face and felt no pity. Instead, a hint of a thrill touched his heart.

According to the file Patrick Dominguez went by the handle Barney. Nobody knew the reason why he chose that over something easier like say, Pat or Domino. His choice was a mystery but whatever. Barney was still a true scumbag, a lowlife, a real piece of shit even by the standards of the underbelly and Edwards guessed his change of name was just a tactic to keep people from knowing about his real M.O.

Patrick Dominguez, the violent rapist from Vogler street, had already served twelve years on state for sexual assault against a teenage hooker he found in Wilmington beach a dozen calendars ago. It wasn't a regular rape, if there even is such a thing. The girl was bitten and burned between the legs with a piece of met-al, doctor thought it was a hot clothes hanger. From everything the police reports said Edwards believed Dominguez seriously

✦ 240 ✦

thought he had killed the girl and then left her for dead in a beachside motel room. Investigators said it was the type of place where you could get three stones of crack and a happy ending for less than what a tank of gas costs in the city.

If it had happened in his town Edwards would have rolled up his own sleeves and rearranged Barney's face himself a long time ago. None of that mattered now, though. Because whoever got to him had done a real good job. Back in the day old timers on the force would have called this a thorough ass stomping, the sort of foul play city cops took their badge off to get a piece of while the brass kept busy looking the other way. But every scumbag has something to offer, even a broken down one numb on Deloden laid up in a hospital gown.

Dominguez had paper a mile long with eleven parole violations and counting. Some were for minor things like not showing up to an appointment with his P.O. or speeding tickets. Others were more serious, soliciting prostitutes stuck out the most. Edwards cited it as a true failure of the system. Here was this bad guy walking around free and still up to the same old shit, probably got away with it a few times already too.

If Clyde Edwards was worth the gold shield around his neck then he had to know Barney's name change didn't mean a thing. He was still Patrick Dominguez at heart, still up to the same audacious atrocities that cost him a decade plus behind bars. Only this time someone went apeshit. Barney had crossed the wrong street hooker or her pimp and then they came back to show him who could play sick games better. Not often do you see a guy beat up and shot in his own house, a vicious stabbing is much more common than that, plus these touches were personal. An automatic weapon and a heavy hand to the face is a good way to send an ominous message to Barney's buddies in case they were into the same things he was.

The detective sat down on the edge of the bed. Dominguez drug his legs but his banged up body wouldn't let him go far.

"I'm going to give you one chance to level with me Barney." Edwards pointed to the hamburgered face and wound his finger in a tight circle. "Why did this happen?"

The rapist tried sucking his teeth, since most of them were broken it came out like a wet hiss. "I told you. It was a robbery. Some kids came in the house and beat me good."

"Did they tell you what they wanted?"

"Fuck if I know. Robbery's a robbery, man. Nobody handed me a wish list."

Edwards nodded like it all made sense. "I see. So these robbers, did they take you into the bathroom? Because we found a lot of blood in there. I mean, a fuckton. Your tub was red as a tampon, Barney. Almost looked like you were making strawberry preserves in there."

"No," said Dominguez. He thought again. "I mean, I don't remember everything. They beat me pretty bad so some of the details are kinda fuzzy."

The detective liked this part of the game. When he knew he had something but it wasn't quite clear yet. The way the crook kept trying to slither told him the truth was still hidden. That's the part he liked best, watching them squirm and rattle off stupid nonsense answers like the one Patrick just came off the hip with.

"I've been to your house Patrick. I walked around in the bedroom to get a good feel for the place. Personally, I think it's a shithole. There's not one goddamn thing in there that would make anyone want to shatter your face about. But that doesn't make much sense, does it?" Because here you are, laying around in bed like somebody's bitch taking blood transfusions while the people who really need them are still held up on a waiting list. So, I'll ask again, and this is really the last time. Why did this happen? Who did you piss off, Barney?"

"How should I know?" he spat. "They were fucking kids. Probably high on PCP or something. Shit like this happens all the time. Don't you ever watch the news?"

Edwards turned away to pull something out of his pocket. When he whipped back around suddenly Dominguez had a different look on his face.

"You see this?" The detective leaned forward and dangled a clear plastic bag with bold red letters across the top that said "EVIDENCE." Dominguez shook his head energetically rubbing a clumps of stringy dark hairs off all over the faded hospital pillow.

"Look a little closer," the detective growled. "Do you see it?"

"I don't know. Wh-what is that supposed to be?"

"What does it look like, stupid? It's a bunch of bloody hair forensics found stuck to the side of your tub like wet chewing gum."

Dominguez reached for the call button to bring in a nurse. Edwards caught his wrist, pushed it down hard on the bedspread to keep his prey in check and put the bloody hair right up to his cheek so the plastic bag stuck to his bandages.

"Who was she Patrick? What little nickel and dime bitch did you beat up this time?"

"Hey man, what the fuck is wrong with you? Look at me, I'm the victim! There's no beat up girl nowhere!"

Edwards wiped his mouth. "You like fucking with me, Patrick? Fine, tell you what I'll do. I'm going to call up your parole officer. He'll be down here in ten minutes to gaff you up on a new violation. I might have to get creative but don't worry. Me and him together, we'll think of something." He snapped his fingers. "Hey, I got it. I'll just tell him you threatened me. Then, when you get downtown I'll be right there front and center to hand the magistrate a brand new sex charge against you."

Edwards shook the evidence bag. "And this is all I need to do it with. Who cares if the case sticks? The courts are so backed up right now you'll be sitting in county at least a year waiting for a trial if you really want one. Except you're going to take a plea deal because your record is too fucked up for a jury to hear. So, while you're waiting to sign papers and take a chain bus back to the joint guess what I'm going to do? Pay attention because this is the best part. I'm gonna show up at the jail two times a week just for you. Probably after lights out so all the fellas can see you leave for a special visit with Winston PD's finest. Won't that be nice, Pat? Then, you can go to prison as a rapist and a snitch."

From the hospital bed Barney could see his future, it wasn't bright. He looked at the detective and then flicked his eyes to the bag in his hand.

"There was a girl," he finally said.

"Okay." Edwards nodded. "Now we're getting somewhere. Where is she?"

"I don't know. For real. She left."

"Is she dead, Patrick? Did you kill her once you were done?"

"No, I told you. She left. She was the one who shot me."

Edwards stood up straight. "A woman shot you with an AR-15?"

Dominguez nodded. "She was a hooker. I called her to come hang out for a good time and she showed up with some coke and beers."

"Who's blood is in the tub?"

"Probably hers. I clipped her with the shotgun and she ran in the bathroom."

"When did all of this happen?"

"I don't know. It must have been after four o' clock because the mail already came. We had a couple of beers, smoked a rock to loosen up. Then right before we were gonna get down to business she went back out to her car."

"Do you always pay whores and let'em leave without giving you any action?"

"She said 'she needed to get her pill'. I thought she meant birth control so I let her go. I ain't trying to get some street bitch pregnant. But then she came back with a gun and tried to rob me."

"Rob you for what? The money you were supposed to give her?"

"No, for drugs. She thought I was somebody big, like a cartel guy or something."

Before Edwards could ask what kind of idiot broad would ever be dumb enough to believe Barney was part of the cartel the room door opened. He turned around to see his other half leaning in with a hand holding the knob. Banks stood there for a second, the sweat beading on Dominguez's forehead told him the interrogation was going full throttle. God, he hated to interrupt this but for the last ten minutes their captain had been blowing up the phone in his right front pocket.

"Hey Clyde we got to roll. They want us downtown for a briefing."

Edwards shoved the plastic bag back in his pocket. "Yeah, coming right now."

He shot one last glance at the pathetic thing on the hospital bed just to keep fear alive. Maybe he had it all wrong, maybe this right here was really his favorite part, seeing pure panic in a criminal's face right before walking away.

Banks stayed beside his partner all the way down the hall to the nurse's station. When they stopped Edwards slapped a stiff hand on the counter like he wanted to break it and the lady tapping keys on her computer almost leapt out of her skin.

"I want to send some flowers to 305. That guy looks like he could use a pick me up."

Banks held his chuckle back even though the woman in mint green scrubs didn't look amused. "Gift shop is downstairs on the ground floor," she muttered.

Edwards put on a smile. "Do they take MasterCard down there?"

"I'm sure they'll work with you."

"Geez, tough crowd."

"Welcome to the trauma ward, sir."

The nurse got up and walked away. After that there was no one left to play with. Everyone else in the hallway had a clipboard in hand that they were glued to like something on there could help them predict the future.

Banks cracked a grin. "That one's colder than my ex-wife."

"I seriously doubt that."

"You told her the truth. That guy looked like shit back there."

"Who cares? Let's get out of here."

Edwards tossed the plastic bag in a plant pot beside the elevators. Banks laughed again. He knew the trick, fake hair and a few splashes of Tabasco sauce, mix it up in a standard evidence bag and even the coldest son of a bitch will double back against himself. He stared at it for a second while they waited for the metal box to ding open and take them in.

"Get anything out of your boy back there? Any news we can use?"

"Sure, big news is he's a fucking liar. Says some girl shot him in a botched robbery."

"Did she get anything?"

"No."

"So, it's a robbery with nothing taken. How does that work?"

"It doesn't. You been up and down through that house just like I have. Ain't shit in there to steal." Edwards hooked a thumb over his shoulder. "That fat motherfucker is full of shit. He's covering up something. I just don't know what it is that's worth hiding and getting his teeth kicked in. Not yet anyway."

When the elevator came Banks walked on first. He claimed a spot in the corner, put his back against the cool, steel, safety rail. When the doors slid closed again revealing their two foggy reflections Edwards pulled a pack of Basic lights from his shirt pocket, not his usual brand but he was trying to cut back on the nicotine for personal reasons.

"Don't light that up in here."

Edwards cut his eyes towards Banks in open annoyance. "See this?" He tapped the cellophane around the pack. "These things suck. My wife wants me to cut down. She nags me day and night so now I choose this floor dust over my precious Marlboros just to shut her the hell up. Problem is I have to smoke two and a half of these just to get the same relaxation that I could have from just one of my cowboys."

Banks looked at him blandly. "If you light that up in here the smoke alarm will go off and this whole elevator will grind to a halt."

"Jesus, all that just for a fucking cigarette?"

"Yep, fire chief says that little gag is what keeps people obeying the rules."

Clyde tapped his cigarette box on the rail. "Rules, rules. So many goddamn rules. No wonder people are always getting in trouble."

Banks nodded slowly like a man deep in thought. "Yes sir, that's what keeps us in business."

CHAPTER 27

BABY INROADS

Now, this is my job, taking care of those who been taking care of me, making a new sun rise.

Redemption.

Chevy wore her new sundress on the ride through South Carolina. Her body missed me, all the curves and grooves made a tiny tune that I could feel underneath a palm that stayed stuck to her thigh for most of I-95. Of course we were already reacquainted like two adults are supposed to be. After Bandy left the other night we were coming down hard on those doctor prescribed painkillers and we realized life is too short. Plus, all our other feelings had been worked out anyway so...you know. There was a celebration on the bed with fireworks big enough to light up a Montana sky and we were into each other without even a thought about tomorrow or closing the blinds. Part two was in the shower the next morning and the saga continued right before we left to go chase this weekend of dreams.

One day when I have a son I'm going to have to reach him and teach him all the facts, about how superheroes make girls wet and superwomen make men hard but insane. When he's old enough to know all about why Chevy James is his mother then we can take a trip. He'll be on his last leg of innocence when the freedom of boyhood will be whittling down into the grittiness of what the world really has in store. Before real life cuts off the last slivers off his adolescence we'll take a long ride down to somewhere like Jacksonville or Tampa or maybe Myrtle Beach as long as bike week has passed because I know all those pretty strippers in thongs will turn my wife back into the old Chevy James.

As soon as we crossed the Talmudge bridge into the Peach State my grip changed on everything. In the back of Chevy's new Mercedes little Bandy had her head against the window, neck tilted back, eyes so far up they had to have hurt. That was me as a boy the exact same way. Riding up front in the Cutlass about to break my neck trying to find the top of those wide, white suspension cables that held the Talmudge up to the wide, blue sky.

Savannah used to be a place for fun, this city had more great spots to love than I had fingers and toes to count on. Aunt Denise used to bring me down here twice a year, once on the fourth of July and again come Labor Day. Those dates were the bookends to my summer vacation. But this wasn't nostalgia season and I wasn't her little boy, nephew anymore. There were a lot of hopes and dreams riding on me this weekend. Chevy, Bandy and Neesha weren't lonely hearts, they were just pleading ones out here trying to cast a net to snag a future. And then of course there was the money.

Always the money.

The boat on the river welcomed us with open arms. A redheaded college girl named Rebecca booked us in our cabin standing behind a small desk while a smattering of white folks swayed back and forth from the lobby to the bar just like the waves slapping against the deck. If Savannah was better known, if it had that same superstar, celebrity, allure as say, Atlanta, we would have never found a room. But this was the sleepy city by the ocean, a place that pushed back on the hype with as much invigoration as you pleased.

In my peripheral I could see Chevy sideeyeing me. She wanted to know if I was thinking about the appeal in something underneath the red head's black cotton blazer. But Rebecca was no Henna and Henna was never a thing like Seville. I knew she was somebody's type, just not mine. Sugar on the lips and ginger up top don't make me weak but Chevy never missed a chance to be jealous.

When I asked Rebecca told me she went to The Savannah School of Art and Design. She fired back a string of questions like we were showing off on a speed date. Where you from? What do you do? How's the weather up there? All standard inquiries. Stuff you could talk about to kill the mechanical noise of computer keys clacking and still easily remember if the police came back to do an investigation.

A bald man standing at the counter next to her said he was going on break in five and I told her we were just in town for a wedding and we'd heard about the boat from a friend of the groom. After rolling out all the lies Taneesha got uneasy, she stared at the ceiling and rocked on her heels a little. Bandy touched her arm like I touch on Chevy's every time we're about to check the results of her pregnancy test.

Rebecca handed me the key cards. "Here ya go. Suites 707 and 719."

She said, "seven one nine" and I said, "thanks." Then, I lowered my voice to just above a hum. "Tell me, Becky. Between you and me, what is there to get into around here?"

Her rosy cheeks brightened up for the spiel. "There's an on-board nightclub with dancing and drinks. But the boat departs at eight so make sure you get some half price because once we're really on the water everything is like, way more expensive. Of course there's gambling. Baccarat, dice and slots are all legal once we hit the ocean."

"When do the shows start?" asked Taneesha.

"First performance at ten," she replied.

The bald man left for his break and then Chevy leaned in. "What other lively activities can we get into out on the water?"

Now, Becky wasn't a square. Or maybe she was just a little, like her edges were round but still angled enough to stand out like young corners. I mean, she did buy my story about being in town for a Baptist wedding and everything.

But before Chevy could shake an answer out of her Bandy stepped up, flipped some hair back behind a shoulder to show off that new scar and said, "listen, honey. You knew we wasn't the port authority when we stepped on here, right?"

Becky from Design school nodded her head just enough and Bandy winked her eye. "Send us up a care package, then. Make it for Mrs. Bandanna flowers in the junior suite. Can you do that?"

"Yes ma'am," said redhead Becky. "I can definitely do that."

Savannah is a city right on the water so the coke rolls in fresh with the produce. A barge pulls through loaded with bananas and when customs turn their heads one rusty freight trailer winds up missing. At least that's what I heard, not from Rebecca though. She's just a little white girl who's sweeter than a Vidalia onion with a good pedigree and a penchant for uppers.

She sent the powder up through room service hidden in a tray that had crab meat spread on buttery crackers, compliments of the boat. "Dope and a snack," I said. Bandy laughed and then divvied it all up into perfectly straight lines. I took the longest one off the silver room service tray and passed the rest to my left. Chevy made the next white stripe disappear like witchcraft. After it vanished she held the tray up to her face like a mirror, touched both sides of her nose lightly and sniffed a little. Wild finger streaks zig zagging across the polished stainless steel showed where the powder residue had already been swiped away clean.

While Chevy checks herself Bandy jumps up from her spot next to Taneesha on the loveseat waving the TV remote around in her left hand. "Y'all wanna see my dress?"

Chevy sniffed again. "You mean the red one?"

"Huh-unh, no the green one. That's what I'm wearing to-night." She tossed the remote on the cushions and it bounced to the floor. "Stay right here. I'll go get it on."

The girlfriend's slid away hand in hand to find tonight's outfit. After the door shut behind them I turned to watched my baby who had moved on from her checking her face to brushing her hair. "Did she just say they were gonna go get it on?"

Chevy rolled her eyes. "You have issues."

"Did you ever stop to think about what if something happened to me? Who would you have to ask all the right questions?"

"Please don't tell me your on that philosopher shit again."

"Nah, it's just the drugs. Seriously though, did she say they were going to have sex?"

"Why don't you ask her when she gets back?"

"Or we could go over there and join in."

She flung her hairbrush at me but I weaved it, ducked down low to scoop the remote off the floor where Bandy dumped it and blew through thirty channels before landing on a baseball game. Wake Forest was playing Virginia at the home of the Demon Deacons. A pop fly sounded off going high enough for the runner on first to get halfway home before it came right back down into the web of an infield glove. I heard the ball smack leather through the TV speakers and folded my arms. Then, Chevy crossed her legs, one high heel over a knee creating a soft noise like paper rustling when the smooth skin of her toned thighs rubbed together ever so gently.

"You know, you never really did tell me what all you did that week you were gone."

I talked over my shoulder and kept my eyes on the game. "Come on, Chev, you still on that? Here we are in a different state, out on the river and we couldn't have more to do. Let it go already."

"It's that big of a secret, huh? Must have been something pretty wild if even LaDecerrio Lloyd won't talk about it."

"How about you break the ice first and tell me everything you did. Start with how you got that Mercedes."

"I worked for it. How'd you get that AR-15 I found laying around in your auntie's car? 'Cause I know it don't belong to her."

"Had a friend give it to me."

"Well, that's a damn good friend. Who was it, Socks? Did he give you that big ol' chopper to ride around with?"

"I'm not doing this."

She uncrossed her legs. "You ain't doing what? Be very specific, Cerrio."

"I'm not doing whatever this is."

Chevy made those eyes, the ones that demand a fight. I could feel them burning a hole in the back of my head. It was just a second before we went toe to toe on the water before Bandy burst back in swimming in the color of money, Taneesha right behind her.

She sashayed through the room, stopped by the mini bar and spun around on a heel then looked back at me. "What do you think?" I stared at two perfect handfuls of Bandanna tail poking through the fabric. She had the type of round, sculptured ass you only see on a garden statue.

"What do you think?" Neesha repeated.

"Tell them what you just told me," said Chevy.

"Wait, what did you tell her?"

"I told her Bandy was gorgeous. And she's going to be knocking'em out all weekend if stays dressed like that. I guarantees it."

The singer smiled all the way to her wisdom teeth. "I bought different dresses for all three nights," she said. "Different wigs too. All designer of course."

I nodded. "Of course."

She plopped down on the bed where she could see herself in a full length mirror, on an invisible cue Neesha pulled out a thick wad of cash and tossed it high and underhand to her girlfriend who caught it midair with a loud smack against an open palm. It was balling, ballplayer shit and absolutely the bossiest thing I ever saw Bandy do.

"Let's go over the plan."

"What plan?" I asked.

"She means the numbers," said Chevy.

"No, she means the money," said Neesha.

My head was swiveling when Chevy got up and kicked her heels off by dresser. In the beginning I thought it was part of her high and then I realized she just wanted to get better balance for when she picked our luggage up from where it all got casually dropped by the door and that was wrong too.

She plucked one bag off the floor, left the rest for me to handle later on once the room was less populated. All she brought over is the same backpack she used to bring a change of clothes in to the 43-Dimes club. When she unzipped the Jansport a strong wave of Chanel No. 5 bloomed in the air on an invisible cloud. A pair of sweatpants neatly rolled up right on top had the perfume ingrained deep in its thick fabric like sand in a clam. By the waistband is where it lived strongest, right where the stretchy elastic hugged her lotioned skin close like a mother gripping her two kids hands when they hurried across the street.

That was her decoy. Underneath the sweats was the little .32 she held up the liquor store with and underneath that was all our cash. She pulled it out and tossed the sixty thousand we stayed up late last night counting against a heap of fancy boat pillows. Bandanna followed suit with the wad Taneesha pitched and then just when I thought it was over they produced another loaf of hundreds to put on top of the pile like the last brick on a pyramid.

The room was quiet, the air full of reverence. A moment of silence while we stared at one of two things, could be our future or maybe our regrets. No matter what it was all on me.

"We're here for three days and just that many nights," said Chevy. "That's a little bit of time to make a lot of profit."

"It can be done," said Bandy.

"That's why we're here. Bandy checked the risks and the rewards so you don't just go down to the casino and play all loose."

"Don't talk to me crazy," I said, "I never play loose."

Chevy looked at me like her mind was tepid, jogging between different thoughts that couldn't mix much better than oil mixes with water. I never saw that look before. It was exasperation and love and a frustration that couldn't boil over into anger for fear that it would just create a misunderstanding when all she wanted to do was be selfless.

"I love you LaDecerrio, and you saying that's crazy talk. Is it crazy when I say that I want a life with you that's better than this? Something where we're not all fucked up in public housing? Because if it is then I'm exactly what called me. But if its not then I'm exactly what you need me to be."

I thought about one day when I have a son I'll give him the answers about what women really want. Until then I'm speechless.

Bandy returned to the conversation licking her lips. "Listen, we got three days to flip this into a hundred fifty thousand dollars. If I can show that money to the bank they'll loan me at least twice as much. That's enough to kick off Chevy's salon. She can lease a building, buy supplies, hire a couple of stylists. Whatever she needs."

"What about the rent?" I asked. "She needs that."

"Her rent is paid up for the next three months."

"Shit."

"Shit what, Cerrio?"

"You guys are flying on this."

"It's not some all the sudden thing," said Chevy. "Bandy's been in business school for a year before you met her."

"Another reason why they'll give her a loan" said Taneesha. "She's got the business plan already wrote up."

"This shit crazy. Where did you write it down at?"

"Remember that little black journal you always saw me with at the kitchen table?"

"Really? You hid the plan like that, right under my nose?"

"Mm-hm, I wrote right there while you ate your grits every morning. Then, I typed up the whole thing so when we go home with all that cash you can take me straight to the bank."

"I even picked her out a new pant suit," gushed Taneesha.

"And I got the loan officer on speed dial," said Bandy.

I nodded because what else could I do? The women had me, they came cocked and loaded. Then again maybe they always had me and I just thought it was the other way around.

We stopped for a moment. There was me, full of questions and getting my bearings as a player in this plan. There was them, full of momentum, unyielding, pitching forward through it all. Through the rises and falls and the hospital trips and my absences they made a coalition for the by-and-by.

When the subject changed it was still the same. "What are you singing tonight?" I asked.

Bandy twisted her mouth in thought until the pale spot crinkled. "Dunno. Either Kelly Price or Summer Walker."

"Can you do Billie Holiday?"

"Man," said Taneesha. "Why didn't we think of that?"

"Because, I don't know any Billie Holiday," replied her girlfriend.

"You never watched Lady Sings the Blues? Richard Pryor and Diana Ross in New York?"

"Bandy shook her head. "Never heard of them."

"Chevy you seen it?" I asked.

"Is it a Tyler Perry movie?" she shot back.

Want to see a man stunned? Then, you should have seen me on that boat. This was like Peter telling Paul he never heard of Mary. I looked at Taneesha who shrugged her shoulders like a shy, little schoolgirl standing in the principal's office. That's when I realized how I would tell my son his place as a bridge between two cultures. He'll have his daddy's nose and his mother's eyes so he can sense the future and always see his way through the darkness.

When my left hand itched I scratched it feeling each fingernail go over the grooves where his name was etched in my palm. Bringing people together is a full-time job and if my son is any good at it he won't ever get enough rest. Looking at Chevy I knew he wouldn't ever be the crossroads, our baby boy couldn't settle for that. He will be the inroad, the last part of the last part of a downhill journey right before you land waist deep in a pool of understanding.

CHAPTER 28

HONEY MOUTH

I knew if anybody on the boat smelled weed smoke they would have us kicked off before we even got away from shore but I was too tired to argue on the side of doing what's right. Diana Ross was in the middle of 1978 doing her best version of Billie Holiday on the cabin flat screen. Richard Pryor just got killed by two drug dealers behind a bag of heroin. Then, Billie's boyfriend came to take her back to New York while Taneesha was trying to finish a joint without a crumb of ash falling down her shirt.

As it all went down I fell asleep on my back inhaling different perfumes from all my favorite colors. By the time I stirred awake two of them were tiptoeing out like bandits to go get ready for the night while the first bruised hues of the evening crept through the vertical blinds and sliced all over an arctic white comforter. Pink sun rays climbed a hill of big G's riding on Chevy's thighs. Women change clothes in front of each other with no inhibitions. I like that piece of mystery about them but it still made me the only one who missed out on her long legs when she pulled on those Gucci sweats.

The capital letters followed the curve of her hips and above that led straight up to a clock behind her with red digits that said a quarter after eight. Bandy's debut act began at ten thirty and we still had things to do. Before I could ask Chevy what she was going to do her hair my jaw started aching like I'd been grinding my teeth.

She propped her elbow on the bed. "Bad dreams, boo?"

"No." I stretched my arms to the ceiling and my shoulders crackled like fireworks.

"Really? Because you were grunting like a pig."

"It's just a little anxiety." My arms came down. "Hey, you think that Rebecca is still downstairs?"

"Oh, you remember her name, huh?"

"I admit that."

"Well, I don't know where she is. But it doesn't matter anyway." She got up. "You don't need more drugs."

"Maybe I'm just hungry. Becky is our room service connection."

"Fine, I'll order us something. I already checked and jumbo shrimp and oysters are good and cheap."

"That's because nobody down here pays for that. You want to eat a shrimp, get a nylon net and you can catch a hundred of them in the river."

"Is he a fisherman now?"

"No, but if I was we'd be feasting instead of wasting money."

"Ew, I hate shellfish. Especially shrimp, they're like the rodents of the sea." She shuddered. "Nasty little things."

Why something that couldn't be good enough for her would do just fine for me didn't matter. That part of us never changed. Besides, it was useless. Chevy had had me in a corner and she knew it.

She walked across the carpet and threw the room service menu on the loveseat. "Socks called while you were sleeping." I reached for the room phone and she shook her head. "No, not on that, he called you on that phone in your pocket. Seems like there's something he really wants to tell you."

I touched my face without thinking about it. Chevy had never heard about me and Socks, about our trailer park shooting or what happened right after. Maybe that might change soon. Looking at her now I could she was in anticipation and that made my jaw ache worse.

"Are you going to call him back?"

"Nah, it probably ain't a big deal. He can wait."

"I think it's urgent. What did you two talk about the other night when we were at the club?"

I shook my head. "Nothing. We were just talking shit. You know how we do."

"Who were those other two guys? The ones who were kept staring at my tits?"

"I don't know. Some young boys from Happy Hill."

"Who the hell do you know from Happy Hill?"

"Nobody, damn. They're Socks friends."

She sat on the bed with her behind at the edge. "Want me to go downstairs and get a drink so you can talk to your friend alone?"

"You're being dramatic. It's not like that. I just got a lot on my mind and he ain't going anywhere anyway. Hell, the nigga barely leaves the house to get groceries. He'll see me when I get back."

"You mean on Monday?"

"Why, what happens Monday?"

"That's when the boat turns around and brings us back to Georgia."

"See that? How in the world can I afford to be distracted by Socks's bullshit when I can't even tell if we're coming or going?"

She made a noise. "Now, who's being dramatic?"

I eased up on an elbow and put my head in my hand while she emptied the cup we used as an ashtray. Chevy didn't want a fight right now. I was wondering what it was going take to get her up and started. The hairbrush incident was less than mild, we weren't even firing shots yet. Maybe she wanted to make a baby.

"Let me ask you something."

"Okay," she said. "Long as you don't start no shit."

"You forgive me for when I talked you into moving out of your parents house?"

"Wake up, boy. Back when I was in school and you decided to quit, that's when I forgave you."

"You know I wouldn't blame you if you didn't. I mean, you could have been anything and I was supposed to help you get there. But look at us now."

She wiped her fingers with a moist towel and sat down again. She was peaceful when she reached out to me from her heart. "The problem is, Cerrio, that you haven't forgiven yourself. And that's on you." She said, "I won't lie to you, I was in my feelings, I had to leave you alone for a little while and let you think about what happened. You pissed me off but then you came back. And whatever came before is what brought us here. We'll call that an introduction."

"To what?"

"To us. We'll say its part one of the story. And the beginning of part two is right now." Chevy tapped the bed with a finger. "Riding out to the ocean is perfect. That's why Bandy and I picked this trip, because there's no place like the water to clean things up. This weekend you can fix all the things you need to fix inside yourself and prove my daddy wrong."

"I know there's some kind of motivation in what your trying to tell me but I just don't feel it."

"And there he is, classic LaDecerrio. Only wants to hear what makes him feel better. I don't have much left to say, though. You want to make things right? Fine, then I'm with you. 'Cause I always been with you. This my dream and your time to shine. Whether you win or not we're still going home together. That's the gospel. The God's honest truth. But if your having problems inside yourself then you know what you need to do to get it right."

"Don't worry," I said. "I won't let you down."

She said, "no, you're not going to let yourself down. Remember that and you'll win all weekend."

Chevy knew when to quit talking and lean in and before our tongues met and a piece of iron tried breaking through my jeans I meant to thank her for her wisdom. Strange that even though she knew how to read my mind and ease it to rest she still never tried to go around solving me. But by now it made sense, it was instinct, and I knew to expect it right at the end like X,Y, and Z.

I ran both hands up her strong back, feeling muscles created once upon a time in a gym and honed on a pole ripple gently beneath my fingertips. Since she was a teenager the girl was all about healing, making things better. Sometimes the method was a little bit unconventional but it never, ever failed. Her pink bra was already on the floor before I touched the crevice of her spine. Then, it was shirt up, breasts out and a little bead of sweat moving down easy in between them while two bronze nipples called out for my tongue.

Skin on skin and a little whipped cream in the middle. Earlier she had ordered up a can from room service while I slept through the second half of Lady Sings the Blues. That's how she knew all about the menu and those would-be shrimp specials. Chevy sprayed a fat dollop on my mouth and licked it off before the aerosol coolness had a chance to make my lips tingle. I took the can from her, put a little topping on her left breast where she was inviting a tattoo of my name and cleaned it off with no hands.

We went back and forth like that, playing the game until everything ached and blushed all over. But pain wouldn't get in the way of pleasure, Seville wouldn't let that happen even if I might. I picked her up and dumped her back first on top of the cloud, soft pillows. She didn't waste a second slipping down the designer sweats, wriggling them over her wide hips in a funny little dance that could have made me laugh. But I didn't giggle, instead it was better to get involved.

Together we got the Gucci's off. I pulled from the legs, she pushed from the perfumed waistline. After that there was more cream on another set of lips with thighs on each side like an all Chevy sandwich. She called out my name in a voice so velvety soft it brought on a chill that made the flesh around my joints tighten. Before I could say yes or no or even let the shiver roll over my body she put a hand down to the only place I wanted to be and wiped everything else off that my tongue didn't clean up. Then, she licked her pretty palm all the way from the bottom by the wrist to the tippy top of her middle finger and smiled. "My turn."

The woman had power. Chevy took me slow a half inch at a time until my whole length disappeared between her cheeks. Her mouth was oily. She went gently as the ocean rolls going down easy and back fast so she could feel it jump inside her. Then, she tossed her hair behind her shoulders and blew the doors off. She worked overtime, brought me right to that part where you're about to shoot across the sky on a bolt of lightning and then quit just like that.

There I was, hanging in midair cold and alone watching her bare ass twist on the way to the bathroom. "Where the hell are you going?"

"Got to fix my hair," she replied. "We'll finish up later, I promise."

"What?!"

She yelled from the bathroom. "Cerrio, I don't need you all tired tonight while you're downstairs trying to gamble. If I suck the life out of you now you'll be no good later on when it counts."

"I'll take a nap."

"You already took a nap."

"So, I'll take another one. Come on, you're ruining our vacation."

She stuck her gorgeous head out and said, "I didn't cum either. And this is not our vacation. We have work to do."

And then the door slammed shut.

Out on the Atlantic ocean the boat screamed energy. Pure vigor emanates from all corners, winners shouting, spectators cheering, slot machines beeping, chips clacking, dealers calling, waitresses strutting. It was so much different, another world away from the gambling spots in Winston-Salem where I slipped cards from the Circle K in the deck and clapped back at the sore losers, and it was all part of the allure, exactly why casinos are where hard earned paychecks go to die.

Across the room somebody whistled. Chevy flared her nostrils but none of the girls fired back. Too much energy would sweat their perfectly done hair right out of place so instead we walked coolly across the plush carpet stepping heavy but feeling light.

Bandy swerved left with a roll of cash to go get the house money, fifteen thousand dollars in different colored chips. Taneesha considered the slot machines until a waitress in heels with a high slit up her skirt stepped right in our path holding a plate of blue point oysters up to the chandeliers. She was a looker and Neesha did a lot of looking but she only got away from us because of the shellfish. The next one wasn't so lucky.

A shorter girl cruised by smiling, holding up a plethora of drinks on a tray that was just higher than my shoulders. Chevy really couldn't help herself, she reached out and snatched a glass off so fast that I could feel the wind from her arm when she pulled it back. The waitress froze, didn't speak though. She had seen Chevy's type before, she already knew better. It would have been amusing except her shock was the type that makes people go pale and lose consciousness.

Chevy dropped the empty champagne flute back on her tray and helped herself to another. I guess the waitress saw a pattern. She left before getting robbed a third time, spinning off on a wobbly heel that almost laid her ankle flat on the floor.

Chevy shoved the champagne towards me. "Take this."

"Quit it. I ain't here to get drunk."

"One little one won't hurt you. Come on, you need it to loosen up."

I took the drink under protest. "Look, don't show your ass in here tonight. And quit torturing these waitresses before they start complaining."

"Listen to you all high and mighty giving people orders."

"I'm serious, Chevy. We're not at home where you can just do anything. These people will eighty-six us quick as shit."

"Jesus, you act like we come from the sewer."

She waved me off like a gnat and Bandy came back around the corner of a row of change machines holding three, neat stacks of chips. She looked vintage in a pillbox hat, bangs spiraling down on both sides of her face and that money, green dress fluttering by her ankles. I don't know if it was her own style or the inspiration of Billie Holiday come to life but either way she dripped and heads turned.

She stopped in front of me and put the house money in my hands. I examined it close while she took a minute to break everything down.

She put a finger on each stack when she mentioned it. "The green ones are small change, fifty dollars. White is a hundred. Red is five hundred."

Taneesha pointed. "What about those?"

In Bandy's other hand another cache was clutched like a diploma. Even in her tiny palm the size of the stack was a midget. Between that and its deeper color I knew they had to be more precious. She held them out shyly. "These here are a thousand dollars a piece."

"They don't look like a lot."

"That's because I only bought seven."

I put the champagne glass down so she could let them clatter in my hand. These ones had weight, like they were made somewhere else special and the ridges were trimmed in gold. Bandy looked hard to my face. "Promise me Cerrio, that you're not going to throw these away on nothing but a feeling."

"This is me, you know I know what I'm doing."

"Stop. This isn't a joke. Promise me you'll only throw them in the middle when you know you're going to win."

"Alright, I promise."

"And you're going stick to the plan?"

"Like dog shit on a boot."

"I'm serious!"

"I know. I know, you're serious. They're serious. Everyone's so serious it's nauseating, but who's more serious than me?"

I saw Chevy watching me with a look that was all vinegar and I knew we were a long way from good times in the suite right now. She cleared her throat, a sound meant to pave the way for the real truth which was that no one here was more serious than her. That had been a fact for a very long time, since before winning at cards was really a must and the future was unlimited because we could barely see past what was right there in front of us.

I passed the chips to her so my hands could be free to hold Bandy's waist. If the girl wasn't a friend and a confirmed lesbian my baby plucking drinks off trays would have killed me right there on the spot in front of God and the whole ship. But life is full of risks, so what are you going to do?

When I moved in to whisper in the little singer's ear she looked down at my shoes. For the first time ever her mascara didn't have glitter in it. Someone's growing up, I thought.

"Remember what I said to you in that yellow house?"

"How could I forget?" she whispered. "You know I love you too. I would have told you that day if I'd the strength to talk."

"Then there's nothing left to say. No promises. No contracts. If we love each other like we say we do, like we know we do, then that's more than enough, right?"

She nodded like the student she was and I turned and looked back at Chevy. "And you. I know you're in on this."

My baby was without charity. "In on what?"

"Worrying to death all the goddamn time. It's like a cold around here, everybody's catching it. Don't say you're just fine either because I know that's a lie."

"Please, confidence is my first name." She dabbed her champagne lips with a linen napkin and spoke to Bandy. "But if you keep sweating it you're going to blow your act tonight. Just focus on the music, girl. We got this."

Then, the little singer nodded and that was the final touch. It took a whole day but all the validation that could be settled in words was finally over. Bandanna and I swore our vows on the water suited up for the ball, her in that dress and me pulling off Scarface in a chalk white suit and a blood red tie. Chevy and I hashed ours out without a stitch of thread on our bodies, but don't believe for a minute that she was off the hook yet.

One of the hosts broke through our tight circle in a pair of polished smooth wingtips, the gold Figaro around his neck looked like it was snapping pictures every time it hit the light. When he walked up I let go of Bandy and she took a polite step back.

He was all swagger, medium height, a light beard with just a touch of gray on the sides. Ruddy complexioned, a hundred and sixty pounds. Probably not a day over fifty five. "Is this Miss Flowers?" he asked. "Tonight's blues girl from…?"

"Winston-Salem," she said proudly.

"It's Miss Bandanna Flowers," I said. "From North Carolina. And she was just looking for a place to get ready for her show tonight."

The host stole a glance at a foxy Movado wrapped around his wrist with a black, leather band. Goddamn, I hope I look that fly when I get old. He said, "by the looks of it Miss Flowers I'd say you're already ready already. But let me show you to a room where you can relax."

And just like that everything became natural. Bandy giggled with a small gloved hand held over her mouth. She liked the host's line, that triple play on the one same word did something to change the climate of her mood. She shed the girl and out came the woman. Watching her walk away was like watching the vision of music exit, almost like Diana did it in '78.

After the talent stole away like she was none of our business we got passed off to a gangly kid in a worn blazer. He had a demeanor better fit for a Dollar Store job. Maybe pushing carts in the parking lot or stocking detergent down the back aisle where people sneak off to steal shit. The way he was so painfully charmless made me think he'd even be bad at charity work. It wasn't the freckles and the wire rim glasses, it was the guilt free air of stupid. With a guy like that the Red Cross would never get a dime.

I felt much obliged when he left us alone by the bar. I scanned tables all around, everything shined, I mean, the glitter was endless. My eyes pulled up and stopped behind a dice game in front of a black jack table. Poker hung back like a pickpocket at the airport with a wide open spot on the felt that had my name written right down the middle.

I didn't waste any time pulling up the last empty seat, throwing my legs around the stool like I was stepping up in the saddle. Seven people sat around me, four on the left, three on the right. Two ducks on both sides were tossing away chips like peanut shells but a big dick in the middle with caps on his teeth was playing for keeps.

Every poker setup in America is just like this. A few cats are there just playing for fun without any real care. There's the born loser giving away his life savings and then there's the serious guy. The one who does this type of thing for a living.

Every third hand he went all in, whenever that happened Chevy's shoulders sagged and she said, "Jesus, Jesus, Jesus," three times in a row like she was calling on Beetlejuice. She clutched a pink drink smelling the same as her perfume and when the sound escaped her lips there was a double dose of peaches sweeping over the table. Thirty five hundred dollars went down in that persistent cloud of sweetness and the losses started having their own effects. It made me dizzy just like those painkillers did when we mixed them up with Hennessey.

I thought it was just my problem but the fog was so thick even the dealer was taking deep breaths. He shuffled the blue deck making the cards clap together like an audience. I didn't know if the fifty-two hopes in the middle were mocking me or calling out for a ride. A complex side of me felt a little bit partial to both. He passed the deck left and I let my hand hover over it just a second before lifting up and waving off my chance to slice the cards up the middle. That wasn't me, I never turn down the chance to cut but the essence creasing my brain pushed aside all the usual habits.

The dealer didn't make a face, he couldn't care less if I cut the deck or not so long as the house got paid. Over my shoulder I asked for the time. Chevy checked her wrist while the hands got dealt. "Twenty after ten," she said. I heard the numbers, breathed the peaches, nodded slow.

We had ten minutes before Bandy went on and I had to figure she'd probably be five to eight minutes late. Some sort of show business gimmick to keep the crowd waiting. Keep them on edge for the main event, I guess. I had no idea if any of that was a real thing but the numbers rang in my head like a catchy tune on the radio.

"Five to eight," I whispered.

The dealer whipped his neck around. "Come again, sir?"

"Just thinking out loud," I replied.

"Check, bet or fold," he said.

"Check."

"And your ante?"

I smiled like a idiot and pushed a green chip in the middle. "Check again, man."

It was checks all around until someone threw a hundred in the middle just to keep the hand alive. I went along in the blind, tossing in a blue chip before even looking at what I had in front. Something invisible kept me patient. I didn't even bother to see what cards came to me on the deal until the first three on the table were all turned over. When two clubs showed up around an ace of hearts all the sudden the will to wait evaporated.

I had the sort of hand that needed a lot of luck and a long prayer. The clubs were poised to kill, a black five and a fucking eight, they wore an evil smile like a cloud casting over the dream. The big better in the middle did his signature move and shoved all his chips straight to the dealer. This time Chevy didn't make any noise, she knew what was coming just like I did. It wasn't a wave of deja vu washing over us, more like voodoo, root magic, or some other prescription my aunt told me to stay away from a long time ago. She said she didn't believe in that kind of stuff only I knew better. Where I'm from everybody believes in magic.

Chevy's breath was as hot and ragged as the best sex we ever had on the back of my neck. The tart smell of fruity alcohol wafted all around me in a vapor that ran goosebumps up my arm. The big better with the capped fangs watched close. He heard me whispering numbers a second ago and thought I was calling on two pair. I scratched my face slow for effect, anything in his hand beat mine but the last two cards could change all that, and one more three toed club could kill it.

Decisions.

I shrugged coolly like somebody just told me the gift shop ran out of chewing gum and called his all in. Since there were no more chips to toss in the dealer scooped the last two cards on the table and flipped them over together and my stomach dropped.

There was good news and there was bad news. Bad news is I had no more money to put up because part of Bandy's plan was to keep me at fifteen bands a session. If I lost all that then we would regroup. If I won we'd party like...well, like we were on a fucking boat. How else?

The big better threw his hand down with a look on his face like he was the brightest star in the universe. "Three aces," called the dealer. I laid mine out in a two card fan. The dealer glanced over quick to my side. "Jack, seven," he called. "Big straight."

Gambling is just like a beautiful woman, very elusive and never in the same mood long enough for you to get used to her habits. One minute you're down then the next it's all to the moon. That's the player's leap and there's a thrill in jumping off that goes hand in hand with a nasty curse and a little sneaky, snatch of stardom too. That's why the pretty, tan thing sitting under the dealer winked my way over the rim of her wine glass. I watched a few bubbles pop up and dive happily down her cleavage. Native American, I thought. Looking like the lottery. High cheekbones and a slim figure. Fine hair so black it was midnight blue. While I wondered about her tribe all the chips came to my end of the felt and that's when Chevy finally caught on that we had won.

She yelped like an auctioneer making the final call on a bid and the guy in the suit and tie beside her must have seen what was coming next. This fine, excited, tipsy woman balancing herself against the fifth glass she killed in an hour meant to step forward and throw her arms around me but the Rosé took her a half turn left. She tilted sideways in a pair of new Gucci slingbacks bought only yesterday and put on about an hour ago. I tried to run interference grabbing her by the waist mid stumble and pink wine sloshed all over my crisp lapel.

The stain was instant, spreading greedily through the white fabric like a hungry disease in the perfect shape of an hourglass. Chevy cooed like an angel with that potion on her breath. "Oh baby, I'm so sorry. I got excited." I was flinging stray drops off my hand when she snatched a silk napkin from another long legged waitress just trying to carry somebody's order across the floor and dabbed at the suit.

I took the napkin and crinkled it in my palm. "Come on, enough. This thing is ruined already."

"My fault, baby." She swayed a little. "You forgive me?"

"Sure, just as long as you land in a chair so I don't have to kick anyone's ass."

She smiled. "You won."

"We won."

She planted a wet kiss on me with her fully wine soaked lips. "Mmm, you smell wealthy. How about I make that suit up to you after Bandy does her song?"

"Is this how the rich do it? A little now and a little later?"

She winked. "Money talks."

CHAPTER 29

FRANKY'S BACK

I can only do complicated math to the sounds of music, any other time the figures just collide in a heap except for underneath the right melody when they mesh together perfect like cake ingredients. I crunched the numbers listening to a glowing woman play the grand piano on the boat's, broad, lit up stage. It started with what I won on the card table then I subtracted from how much was left to gain before we could finally hit a hundred and fifty racks.

Chevy sat next to me and next to her was Taneesha smirking like she had a sexy secret to tell. They were both waiting for Bandy to come on. Seeing them side by side like that reminded me that this trip wasn't a hundred percent all business. But while the glowing woman's musical fingers danced over the ivory keys I mixed every digit from one to ten back and forth in a soup of formulas that all died in the end with the same wicked variable.

That mean son of a bitch called time.

When the last note left the piano it hung in the air for a long rented second before hands came together. I joined in the applause for the blushing lady taking her long dreadlocks off the bench behind her. She took a careful, little bow before the host moved in to hook his arm around her waist. His hand up above her hips seemed greedy. Then, he ordered another round of clapping and we gave it generously until Chevy grabbed my arm.

"She's coming up next."

"I know. You excited?"

"Think I'm not," she replied.

I motioned across the table. "Look at Neesha over there."

We checked out the big singer's little lady. Taneesha looked like she was built out of wood, hands in her lap, back ramrod straight like a flagpole. All night she'd been keeping a ritual about her hair, never once touching it once for fear of a single strand being out of place on Bandy's debut.

Chevy reached over and put a finger up in her bun. Taneesha rolled her shoulders and tensed her neck. "Careful don't mess it up."

"Yeah, don't mess it up," I said.

I almost caught a smack on the wrist for my mouth but I moved away just in time and Chevy's fingers glanced off the cuff of the black Aramani jacket I'd just changed into. She flexed her hand, gave me those hate-you eyes and turned to scratch the itch Neesha had been fighting off all night before it turned into a full body tick.

Stuck beside these two what more could I want? We were in thick of it, living life on our own terms, keeping true our identities in the face of this overt magnificence. Sometimes when better things come the old you dies away but it felt like we were just beginning to live. I never knew what to anticipate on this trip, now I was suddenly envisioning my whole life. Me and Seville living in a big house, three or four kids bouncing around upstairs in the halls, two cars parked out front and a boat for when we want to take the brats down to the river. Money coming in faster than we can spend it. She's got a chain of salons and I'm doing whatever I do which is anyone's guess but I'm always staying faithful to my promises.

Chevy pushed a drink on Taneesha who told her she already had one to which my baby gave the classic response. "Well, come on, have another."

I had some other smart ass comment ready to fire off, something that would definitely get me smacked before the clapping kicked up again. Suddenly Chevy quit pushing alcohol to join in with the hands coming together and the three of us watched as Bandy strode on stage to a light tune shaking out from a violin. She came ready to serenade and all at once I felt nervous, that same feeling when the unexpected comes true, that strange fast and hard excitement that leads to agitation tried creeping up my sleeve. Because things had never gone this distance, not on land, not in the city, not anywhere ever.

I shook it off. I never had a worry in prison, never felt anxiety climbing up my back during any fistfights or shootouts. If I did I'd be extinct by now. After it melted away that's when I found out how much I really liked this side of Bandy. Watching her sit up on the back of the piano commanding the whole crowd's attention while blowing the likes of a young Mary J. Blige made her mature and worldly. And at the same time it wasn't excessive, she was still guileless like the sum of all things pure.

The way her voice hit every note just right in a perfect race to the end of the song made me suspicious. All of her practicing wasn't done waiting in a hot car or behind the door of the shower. She'd been rehearsing for this moment and the preparation paid off well. Every effort climbing out of her throat took the music to a place where I can only go on the edge of consciousness. Right on that border of genius that always sends me back with tears in my sleep.

Her song wound down easy leaving a team of warm hearts beating through the audience. While they put up more applause I thought about a way to tell her how she was so astonishingly good without saying it just like that. Stringing the right words together wasn't going to be easy, then again the list of things that got us here read out like a full-length struggle. I thought hard as she approached but nothing came to me until she lept up in my arms in front of the whole boat.

Her hand gripped the pillbox hat while I spun her around like a carousel. "That was beautiful," I said. She kissed my cheek all up one side. "But, I couldn't have done it without you."

Taneesha stood by patiently, hair still pristine just waiting for her turn. "Can I get some of that?" she asked politely. Clearly I'd been selfish, I stopped the spinning and put her baby down and they went right to each other like magnets. The audience was still clapping as they pressed their lips together. That extra applause could have easily been for the next performer coming up to the mic but no one asked because we liked to think it was all for us.

Chevy's benevolence was showing. She let it go until the time was just right. She allowed the passion to float but didn't let it get redundant and then broke the kissing women up by shaking a bag of quarters out of her purse. "Let's go play slots."

Taneesha squealed with delight. "Oh yes, I been waiting to all night."

Bandy looked back at me. "You coming?"

"Nah, I hate slots. You guys go ahead. I'ma go find a pool table."

"Fine, be like that," she teased.

"Oh, leave him alone," said Chevy. "Come on, we can have some girl's time. Plus, his pool game needs a lot of work anyway."

Bandy laughed and waggled her fingers goodbye as Taneesha tugged her arm to go find one of those shiny machines. I lingered by the stage like a memory watching the three amigas float away like bottles drifting out to sea. That last comment from Chevy about my pool game made me think about Henna and The Rose Petal. But that was neither here nor there and those thoughts didn't carry very far anyway because everything I needed was all right here beside me just like the lipsticked stained wine glasses still sitting on the table.

Doors opened on the boat lounge around eleven o' clock but good luck finding out what time it closed. Not that I cared. Everything in the place sparkled and what didn't sparkle gleamed and what didn't gleam was made of leather including a lot of tight, sexy, skirts wrapped around firmly toned thighs.

On the far wall a roped off area with one long couch in a curve held three men in dark suits trying not to look corrupt. It was definitely a party, bottles all around and more on the way. Hidden speakers pumping bass made the glasses on their VIP table tremble like they were shivering in the winter cold. Five women hung around them, each one supermodel gorgeous like she had been hand picked out of a magazine. From this distance the smiles on their faces looked like well done tattoos. Two waitresses carried in sparkles wearing more trained smiles on lips so glossy it looked like they were sweating from the mouth. They were an onslaught of seduction walking in like a troop one in front of the other all switching hips together. The boys drank it in while I nursed a beer on the other side thinking about how much I would bet that those dressed up suits had left their wives home alone with a story about how this was all nothing but a work trip.

I sat alone feeling good, just me and my drink. The solitude felt cushy because for once things were going okay. The last time I remember my life going smooth for a whole entire day I was eleven, now I was twenty something and it was night and we were on the ship and things couldn't be better but the best was still over the horizon. I know somewhere Chevy had a seat in front of a slot machine pulling a lever with one hand, snatching drinks from some low paid girl carrying a full set of glasses. In an hour she'll be swimming in the warm energy of all that white champagne. That's when she'll text me with a line like, "where you?" Two words going straight to the heart of the matter but that's all I needed.

She means come quick because these are the nights she dances for me. The Dimes club and Sugar Bares, those are just gigs. When she works at home it's more like a sport. Chevy becomes Seville, not a stripper but a sophisticated specimen, a grand athlete turning up into a storm when she moves her whole body straight from the hips. She can wind it up good and then throw it all back in a circle. We play this little game, it's all emotional. If I reach out and touch then she wins but sometimes she might forget herself and look back and then the victory belongs to me.

I was thinking about who would come out on top tonight when a cheer went up from the party squad. The business suits and their girls had something new to drink to over in the roped off section. I would have joined them but when the beer touched my lips someone behind me up and said, "well at least their having fun."

I could tell that voice anywhere. The words came out like a waterfall spilling on a harp, skulking in like a hunter rising up from the grass. In a thicket full of strangers or the hollows of the mind when you hear those vocals a gasp catches in your throat. A couple out of their element paused mid conversation, flabbergasted by the panther, black woman oozing so much sexuality. Chocolate ignored the looks and smiled at me like the crescent moon. Her grin flashed different from the other girls in the lounge because hers was for real. I knew because my natural surprise made her so happy she giggled.

"How the hell did you get here?"

"You didn't think I'd miss out on Bandy's big show did you?"

"You knew about that?"

"Chevy told me. You know that mouth of hers does more than just make you feel good."

"I didn't see you in the audience clapping."

"And you didn't see me come in here either. Nonetheless here I am, baby." She winked and pointed to the bottle in my hand. "Just one?"

I said, "for now."

A long time ago somebody told me that one is never enough. Then, someone else repeated it which just proves the point because they couldn't let a single person have such a good saying like that all to themselves. Now I'm living it so I know the whole thing must be true.

Chocolate bought us three rounds and we drank together nice and slow on the boat's deep leather couch. Before I get drunk I get honest but being too sincere felt a little villainous like maybe I was tickling the feet of betrayal. That's why I asked if Chevy talked about what we did in south Winston, because I didn't want to tell Chocolate how Bandy got her gold tooth in case the devil's duchess hadn't seen it just yet.

The Panther looked at me with the jungle in her eyes and said, "the short answer is yes."

"Yeah, and what about the long one?" I asked.

"The long version is you should run for mayor just as soon as we get back home."

I had to laugh. "That's a good one. And uh, how drunk would you have to be to give me your vote?"

"Drinking ain't got nothing to do with it. I got the tea, the down and dirty details about the gunplay. And I've seen you in action before. Remember us in High Point?"

"Interesting. But you can't transcend from common criminal to big office like a caterpillar to a butterfly."

"Why the hell not? Real politicians do it all the time. I'd campaign for you." She squeezed my knee. "Just promise me immunity, Mr. Mayor."

"You're drunk."

She took her hand back. "Probably not."

"Look, I'm just a man. Truth is Chevy is the one who got us out of there."

"Is that right?" Chocolate drug her words out. "Did the princess shoot a way out of there with that little .32 she keeps tucked down in her purse?"

I squinted at her, there was something else dripping with that sarcasm. Maybe a little tinge of vitriol crowding in. Or maybe it was just the gin.

I killed my shot and put the glass upside down on top of two more creating a little pyramid on the table in front of us. "I thought you said Chevy gave you all the details?"

"There's two sides to every story. You know what they say."

"Actually, they say there's three sides. Mine. Yours. And the truth."

"So what's the truth?"

"I can't believe you're coming to me asking that. You really are drunk."

Chocolate could see she had hit a wall. "Fine, I'll ask Chevy later. In the meantime, what happened to that pretty pearl blazer you had on at the casino earlier?"

I coughed. "Damn, woman. Spy much?"

"Well, I got on the boat late. Barely made it actually. But I don't have to be on time to know exactly where to find you."

"Good eye. Chevy got excited after I won a big hand and spilled her drink all on me. I can't walk around with a stain on my lapel so I put on this." I pulled on the Aramani fabric.

"It's not too shabby. The color looks good on you."

I almost gave her the punchline. Almost said "the color is black" and made an ass of myself because that was the whole meaning of her remark. She was perched on the edge of the cushion just waiting for it.

"Very slick," I said. "You got anymore questions?"

"Yeah, just one. Were you mad when she spilled the drink?"

"I don't know. Should I have been?"

"I don't know. It was a nice blazer."

"Yeah, you never lied. I'd get buried in that thing if it had a tire mark up the back."

Chocolate sucked her teeth. "Wow, Cerrio. You sound thrifty."

If tongues are sharp then hers must have been a box cutter. I walked right into that blender, though. The woman let her sting of words settle and looked away to the other side of the lounge. I don't know what was on the other end of that stare, it could have been a big pot of gold but my mouth didn't ask because my eyes were lost too. The Panther had on a yellow dress with no shoulders and no neckline and I was staring deep into the fabric like it held my heart's deepest desire when suddenly she switched right back and caught me looking.

"Want to play some pool?"

"Think you can beat me?"

"I heard you're not very good."

I blinked and she studied hard on the tables that were nothing like the kind Socks helped me break in back home at The Rose Petal. A lot of marble on the frame made them unmovable which would really mean something if the boat started swaying. Pretty good engineering, but it was the black felt on top that said padded luxury. That little touch set off another burnt orange couch where a soul from Augusta watched the pair of us stroll right up.

He was half debonair in a charcoal gray suit with a purple pocket square. His other half still had her legs crossed on the sofa washing down something clear with a Sprite soda when I forgot to chalk the stick and scratched in the corner pocket. Somewhere else they might have laughed but Augusta was too esteemed for all that silliness. After I paid him what we bet on the game he shook my hand like a gentleman and they went to walk off, him and his top heavy lady, but Chocolate wasn't giving up so easy.

"That's it?" she chirped. The competition had his back turned a little, he twisted his neck around so slow that he managed to make it look like a big production, like the muscles up there hurt. Another woman might have been shaken. In all fairness he was massive, big as a kitchen with a barrel chest and gargoyle eyes. But you already know nothing shakes Sugar Bares finest. She stood there with the stick in her hand, one brow up, head cocked to the side. "I don't know about out here in Georgia," she said. "But where I'm from gentlemen always gives a rematch."

Big Augusta shrugged his bowling ball shoulders, his girl sat back in her spot. I guess they do this type of thing all the time. He put down four solids in a row before banking one too soft off the right buffer. After that his shot dried up. Chocolate drained four back to back to match him. She swaggered around the table chalking up the stick, humming a little tune while she lined up her next play, and then missed on the fifth. She put the cue ball in a cluster where there was no way out. That wasn't a mistake, as usual it was strategy. When Augusta's woman stepped up she got caught in the trap. Her options were none. All she could do was hit the eight ball and close the game or hit the rail and give up a turn and somehow she managed to do both.

The black ball sailed away and then the couple did too right back to the bar. Of course they paid me first, I waited for Chocolate to demand her cut but she's the type who likes to stack up favors to keep a debtor down until she thinks she needs him.

I put the money away and a vibration went off in my pocket like a baby explosion. It was Chevy texting me with a pair of simple words. "Where you?" Chocolate leaned in with the shade trying to read it upside down. She saw the message but not the source and pretended like she just wanted to look at the clock.

"What time is it?"

"About one thirty."

"Ah, goddamnit."

"Uh-oh, you got a date waiting?"

When she swept her bangs over to the side with a finger the lounge lights reflected blue curves off her cheekbones. "Those suits behind the velvet rope are all my dates. See the one in the pinstripe tie?"

I looked to the velvet rope. "Yeah."

"He's a heart surgeon. See the one beside him?"

"Yeah."

"A loan processor, works at a bank in Atlanta. But they're not what I'm late for. It's little Franky."

"The dog?"

"Yep, I snuck him on in my luggage. And now he's all alone in the cabin waiting to be fed." She slung her purse over a bare shoulder. "Come on, I got something up there for you too."

I hesitated. "Wait, what is it?"

"A roll of cash on my nightstand."

"Really. For me you say?"

"Oh yes, Cerrio. I don't want you forgetting I'm still in on this thing."

God help me keep my sanity. On the way to her room I found it easy to get hypnotized. Her movements in the hall, the cherry body lotion wafting off the coasts of her curves as we passed by other people. Even the big triangle earrings swinging back and forth but never quite kissing the satin, flesh on either side of her neck made things complicated.

But nothing happened, the big triangles swung like a pair of pendulums but they never made it to the goal. They swung slower, slower, slower, spending some more of that eternal energy emanating from the tower they hung off while Chocolate stayed beside me all the way to the elevator. Inside the metal box her perfume closed in on me. At first I fought it and won but the battle changed like a subject when she leaned over to press the right button for her floor.

I wonder if really tall guys have this problem. Can they stick their head above the clouds of fragrance and gulp fresh air or does the essence rise up to pull them in like a hand reaching for a grip on a cliff. Through the vapors Chocolate spoke.

"So, I guess Chevy's not fighting with you anymore. I bet that's got to feel good.

"Yeah, nothing like a crisis to bring a relationship right back together again. "

"Reminds me of a saying. Me and my brother against our cousin. We and my cousin against our enemy."

"That's not a saying."

"Well, then why do people say it?"

"Because it's an Arabian proverb. Nobody says that unless they look like me."

She put her hands up like I had a gun in my pocket. "Excuse me, I just thought it was something old folks used to say on the porch. I didn't know you had it trademarked."

And I didn't know I overreacted until the elevator dinged open. Chocolate had her hands back down by then and we stepped off on the fifth floor, walked past an army of black doors down to the one marked 22 where her card fit perfectly. It slid right down making the light on the lock flash from red to green. She pushed the handle and the door popped back with a shick-shack sort of noise. I imagined the roll of money calling out to me from beside the bed, dancing like a Moroccan burlesque, but instead there was that heady flavor from the elevator flooding out to make my acquaintance.

Her spread looked like the smaller version of what me and Chevy had up above. A fake Victorian style chair sat in the corner by the bed instead of a love seat. Less throw pillows adorned the mattress. The rug was the color of a nectarine which made me feel more carefree about spills than that eggshell hue in 707 that couldn't take a smudge of anything.

Early in I saw the bedside table betrayed a lie. No cash. Just a coaster with the boat's logo beside an old looking telephone with a blinking light. "You got a message," I said. Chocolate yelled from the bathroom for me to check it and I pretended not to hear her. I'm not anyone's secretary.

It was all lavish in here, all pleasures and frills and extravagances. I smelled the air even more to get that cherry delight and got a little taste caught in my throat. The flavor was indulgent but it dissolved in an instant and I didn't smell any dogs. No wet fur or kibble. A bowl of food should have been around my feet. I looked for Franky's water dish next to the high heels beside the dresser but there was nothing. No signs of a pet being hidden from the room service staff, just the tells of a woman saturating the furniture.

"Where's the dog?" I asked.

"He's in here," she said.

I turned around and saw the bathroom door standing wide open. A rectangle of light stretched out across the floor with a shadow taking up the middle that had no sort of waist. When the pitch silhouette moved I moved to the side like we were two people dodging each other on a flight of steps.

"Man, I don't hear no barking."

"He's right here," she called.

I pulled on my collar, the shadow looked like it wasn't wearing a dress. "You sure he's in there?"

"Would I lie? Come on, Franky baby really wants to see you."

Maybe he does, I thought, and maybe he doesn't. Or maybe he's not even here and this is all about something else. Still, I couldn't leave this room without knowing for sure.

I went around the doorframe easy, crossed the threshold braced for anything. Under the red heat lamp Chocolate stood next to the shower with the hot water running, her dress off and hung on a hook. She had changed into a robe with the sash tied around her waist like a bow on a gift and in her arms the little terrier I met right after Judy was panting like a wild animal. In the way of explanations she said, "I have to keep him in here so he won't tear up the room."

I wiped my forehead and nodded like a real yes man. "Yeah. Yeah, that makes perfect sense."

Then she laughed because I said the words, "perfect sense" like I really knew what any of that meant.

CHAPTER 30

TY NOODLES

Police got a tip. Junior Investigator Michelle Heinrich slammed it down on Detective Sergeant Ryan Banks' desk in a clasped nine and a half by twelve file folder just like they did in all those R-rated cop movies. She always wanted to do a thing like that and once upon a time someone told her there's nothing better than getting exactly what you want, so why not?

Banks looked up from the news feed on his phone. "What's this?"

Michelle squared her shoulders. "New action on the Dominguez case sir."

"You mean, that shooting at the yellow house?"

"Yes sir, same one."

Banks put the phone down and wiped the aggravation off his face. "Let's have a look."

Michelle smiled wide inside. She kept right on talking as the veteran detective reviewed a typed page of her latest findings. She knew she didn't have make a report but it was an added touch so the big boys and the brass would see her as a serious cop.

She said, "an old woman who runs a candy house across the street from the scene made a statement. She said, 'she was looking through her window blinds and saw a strange car parked out front by the curb that she didn't recognize as belonging to anyone in the neighborhood'. Two people got out of it, a man and a woman, but three people got back in after the shots were over."

"Did she say one of them was Barney?"

"Sorry sir?"

"Did the old lady see Dominguez get in or out of that car?"

"No, I showed her a picture of him before the beating he took and she just shook her head."

"A head shake means nothing. My grandmother shakes all over if she forgets to take her pills."

Heinrich cringed. Her first mistake on the case, not being thorough enough. She was supposed to rattle out a real yes or no from her witness. She recovered quickly.

"I asked the woman pointedly, sir. She said, 'it was a man and two females who got back in the car'. One woman was barefoot, no shoes."

"I know what barefoot means."

"Yes sir. The male was slender built. Shoulder length black hair. Wearing red, suede shoes."

Banks rolled his hand. "And the second female? The one who had shoes on?"

"The witness said, 'she seemed fine'."

"I don't understand."

Second mistake. She hadn't mentioned the finer points of her investigation.

"The uh, barefoot woman had to be helped out of the house. According to the witness the slender man had to carry her out because the girl didn't look like she could walk anywhere on her own."

"Why didn't you lead with that nugget, Heinrich?"

She fidgeted. Banks sighed.

"That might explain who's blood is caked up in the tub," said the veteran detective. He waved the folder in the air. "Does Edwards know about this?"

Michelle fumbled for words, she had no clue what to say here. Edwards did a bang up job of acting like he had charge of everything but it wasn't a state secret that Banks was the real brains of the operation. Clyde was more of a mercenary, solving crimes via force while his partner finessed the puzzle pieces around to make the big picture.

One couldn't get the job done without the other, they didn't function solo, that's why they were a team. Right now the big question wasn't brains or brawn, it was all about who really served as the face. Who led the cases? Who was the go to? Michelle didn't want to get shouted out of the room for heading up the wrong detective before she approached the right one.

Third mistake, never appear to show favoritism, especially on an incredible assignment.

While she debated an answer Banks plucked his office phone from it's cradle. "Does Edwards know about this? Tell me before I get him up here." Michelle cleared her throat, she pointed to the folder resting at an angle on the desk. "There are photos in there too, sir."

Banks paused for a moment. "The candy lady took pictures?"

"No, she described the strange car and an agent from gang task force thought it matched a vehicle around the scene of the Palmetto Homes trailer park shooting last month."

Banks blinked. "So, gang task took pictures?"

"No sir, stoplight camera. The car was speeding at an intersection and ran a red. I showed the traffic cam picture to the neighbor and she said without a doubt that was the car parked outside her window that day."

Michelle Heinrich wriggled off the hook, after the photo came out no one cared anymore about who got to see things first in a junior investigator's file folder. Banks kept her there in his office for a minute while his partner broke away from his own desk to come breath up the action. She felt proud explaining her fresh find all over again to a new set of ears. These types of succulent breakthroughs were exactly the sort of thing that would earn her another promotion soon.

When the explanations were over both cops eyed her astutely. She put her hands behind her back and held them together out of sight while their stares burned into her like acid. From the other side of the office window someone might have thought she was standing to receive a reprimand. But that was much better than wringing her palms nervously in front of two seniors on the force.

Banks thanked her, Edwards didn't say a word, just watched her leave and close the door as soon as she crossed back over into the main area where a clutter of anonymous metal desks stacked with equally anonymous looking paperwork barely fit a person in between them.

The two men sat on either side of Banks' office examining the black and white picture trading thoughts. The traffic camera only caught the car's front end. It was an old sedan. Good condition. Boxy around the hood and headlights. Something you might see at a Barrett Jackson auction on an all classics weekend charity drive. Edwards knew only three sorts of people drove something like this, drug dealers, car collectors and elderly folks. And collectors and elderly folks were more careful than to blaze through red lights in the early afternoon.

The North Carolina sun glazed the windshield with a glare that reflected back as a stupid white stripe. Why couldn't a hurricane be on the coast? One rain heavy cloud in the sky that day and Edwards could be looking at a face instead of a useless, blank streak catching ultraviolet rays on the road. Suddenly he craved a cigarette. Banks noticed it when he tapped his shirt pocket. "Smoke later," he said. Clyde took his hand away from the box of Basics and shifted his weight in the chair.

"So, what did gang task say?"

"I don't know. Want me to bring Heinrich back in and ask her?"

Edwards waved him off. "Forget it. They probably know squat." He tapped the picture. "Only Mexicans live in that trailer park. That guy we tried grilling at the hospital, LaDecerrio. He's the only outsider. And he fits the old lady's description all the way down to the haircut."

Banks scratched his chin. "And?"

"And Dominguez is Mexican too. So, maybe there's a connection."

"Dominguez is from El Salvador."

"Well excuse the fuck out of me. All I'm saying is maybe the brown savages are out fighting with each other to lay stake on some open territories."

The other detective sat back and steepled his fingers. "That sounds a lot like gang unit work."

Edwards put his elbow up on the desk. "What about that little, old bitch at the pawn shop? She knows something I bet. Her and LaDecerrio look like they could be mother and son. If there's a turf war in the city then she's probably knee deep in it."

"That's a no go, Clyde. We been watching Bibi for years. Chief says he won't make a move on her unless the proof is absolutely solid."

"The old fart is waiting on something solid, huh? Well, that's good to know. Meanwhile the whole city is getting shot to shit."

"Hard to blame the man. Bibi is smart. Ten times out of nine the woman already heard about what happened at the trailer park and has her house and store all cleaned up by now. If the Tac team goes in for a raid, I guarantee they come back out holding nothing but their dicks in their hands. Then, the city has to settle another lawsuit."

Edwards looked away, pretending to be absorbed by the plaques on the wall commemorating his partner's service and dedication to WSPD. Upstairs Clyde had his own display of acknowledgements nailed up to the wall in an office with his name on the door but none of the accolades meant much right now when some rookie kid found a lead on what was currently their biggest case.

For Heinrich it was a good day but for Edwards it was woeful. He should have been the one to put those pieces together, they were almost too simple to miss. Problem is he did things old school, like shaking up perverts for information while they were laid up half dead in the hospital. Maybe that was a sign that it was time to retire, his style was outdated. He'd had a good run. Dodging bullets in Cleveland Park, interrupting full scale bank robberies by both universities, knocking around wannabe thugs in a holding cell downtown. Yes, there was plenty to reminisce about. Edwards could leave now proud and standing on his own two feet, mind and body intact with a plethora of memories to linger on.

Banks pointed to the folder. "If we find this car then I think we can get some answers."

"Think it's gonna be that easy? Gang unit has got to be looking out for the same thing."

"Then that should make it all go quicker. There's not too many Oldsmobile's left like this riding around the city. Chances are the one they find is the one we want too. Who knows? We might even get lucky, catch one sitting at a stoplight."

Edwards laughed humorlessly. "Personally, I think you're dreaming. But that's all the excuse I need to grab some fresh air." His partner reached in a drawer, pulled out a lighter, slid it across the desk. "Who needs fresh air when all you want to do is smoke?"

Detective Ryan Banks believed in police work and he believed it was all pretty basic, but of course he had it in his blood. His father who was a lifelong state trooper gave him a simple tip. "If things don't make sense, then you know something's off." Banks added his own proverb, "if things do make sense then don't over think it." He knew Edwards felt worried. He saw him rubbing his moustache, anxious about being outshined by a spry, young woman or some other stud with a loaded gun and a shiny badge. The curse of old age was a nasty part of the game. It strangled the mind, choking off sound reasoning like a dying animal breathing up smoke in a raging forest fire.

But just like Edwards predicted there weren't any Oldsmobile's out on the street. From the passenger's side of an unmarked Dodge he blew three Basic Lights in a row, hanging his hand out the window so the ash would fly off down the road. Country music played low inside the car. At thirty five miles an hour the twangy melodies were barely audible over the draft of wind roaring through like a stadium crowd.

They drove by what looked like a Blockbuster video in a sad looking shopping center with a Chinese Garden takeout nestled right against a Dollar Tree. A slinky neighborhood boy hustled CD's in the sparsely populated parking lot without much success. Kid needs new territory, thought Edwards. He flicked ash as the cruiser moved down the block. Five parking spaces away from the front entrance of a thrift store sat a maroon colored Honda. He squinted in the sun, through thin eye slits he could make out the wheels, black rims with faux chrome lugs. "Pull in there."

Banks had no hesitation. He swung the steering wheel all the way right, using the sidewalk to bounce the Charger up into the shopping center. All the women noticed immediately, one in a blouse threw her lit cigarette on the ground and turned right back into the second hand store. The other simply quit walking, then that's when the fellas caught on.

First it was the kid with the CD's dropping his product and bolting towards the bus stop leaving a trail of broken cases littering the asphalt in jagged, plastic, triangles. Another man fled around the corner of a Big Lots holding up his jeans. Edwards would bet a hundred dollars and his firstborn grandchild there was a warm pistol tossed away right there in the bushes behind the concrete building.

He didn't care about any of that, they weren't out here chasing down crack dealers and random knuckleheads. That sort of thing was for gang task or beat cops or somebody the hell else who had the time and needed the stripes. He had eyes for only one, the man coming from the Chinese restaurant talking into his phone with two white takeout bags dangling from his fingers. The detective and the hood were acquaintances in all the wrong ways. When their eyes locked the takeout bags dropped to the ground.

When he turned to flee Edwards didn't budge. He pulled hard on another Basic and watched the runner pick up speed going in the same direction as the last goon holding his pants while noodle grease slid down the curb towards a steel drain. Back in the day, about twenty five years ago, he would have chased him down like a lion does a gazelle. But times have changed.

Before the grease made it halfway to the sewer grate Banks cut him off with the Dodge. People standing at the shop windows were glued to the action, iphones already out, cameras on. No matter, let them record. Edwards wasn't foolish enough to beat a guy in the middle of the day in front of an audience. That had nothing to do with being old school, that type of unforced error was just plain stupid.

He walked up casually while Banks put the cuffs on with a signature click. Edwards shook his head in a big display of disappointment. "Geez, Ty you used to be a lot faster than that. What happened? All that weed slowing you down?

The man bent over the hood breathed hard fogging up the silver paint job. "What the fuck is this? Why you chasing me? I didn't do shit!"

"Well, I just saw your car out here and thought I'd come say, hello. Why you running away?"

"Because you're the police!"

Banks chuckled like a fool. "Looks like you dropped your lunch, pal."

Ty glanced at his takeout order still steaming on the sidewalk. "Hey, I smell a lawsuit. A big one too. My lawyer knows all the shit. Illegal arrest. Fourth amendment. Search and seizure. He's the fucking best!"

Edwards looked at his partner, they stared at each other for a brief moment of silence before breaking out in hysterical laughter. Ty whipped his head around side to side like he could catch the joke somewhere behind his back.

"What the fuck is so funny?"

The cop leaned down close enough for the snitch to smell the cheap tobacco all over his breath. "You don't have a lawyer, stupid. What you do have is the right to remain silent. Oh, wait... you don't even have that because we own your ass, remember?"

Ty blinked. "The fuck are you talking about?"

"I'm talking about last Halloween and all that dope we pulled out of your pocket tied off in a condom."

Banks whistled low. "Shit, I remember. That sack was worth ten years at least."

Edwards grinned down like a sick executioner. "Trick or treat, bitch."

CHAPTER 31

TWO FACED

The boat cruised slowly up the coast towards a spot of land that everyone said was Hilton Head Island. In passing conversations they mentioned the place had golf. I never golfed in my life, didn't have a lot of reasons to now. But the wider that slice of earth on the horizon got the more Chevy talked about how many fancy places there were on shore to drink good wine. So, I guess we just might have to see where this goes.

The future was on her mind. She could see it forming around the edges like the beginnings of a jigsaw puzzle. Last night when the charm of the ship got stale we dreamed about the rest of our lives with eyes wide open in the bed of our suite. It was the subject of much pillow talk, the best part is everything sounded doable. We weren't spouting fantasies like two kids laying back in a tree hammock on summer break. The aspirations were real and touchable like budding baby hairs on the back of your neck.

It wasn't just our future either. Bandy's was coming to the light blazing a hot trail of excitement. The girl was burgeoning on this trip, blooming like a big, fat, sunflower in the yard. A month ago we were going nuclear, fighting about her reluctance to sing like Tom and Jerry. Now, Chevy couldn't wait for us to get back home so she could become a local star and then a major one. Since it was hard to disagree with fame I didn't argue.

On the top deck they served us dinner out in the open air. With the sun long gone I ate comfortably across from her by soft candlelight. Little flames burned bright on the table illuminating our faces in a bath of butterscotch yellow. The flames bent gently in the breeze but never blew out thanks to the glass circles that bordered each tiny tongue of fire on all sides.

"Look at us" she said. "If we were at home right now I'd be telling you to pick your clothes up off the floor and you'd be trying to walk out the front door on me."

I worked a knife through a pink piece of fish. "You know, I was just thinking that same thing. Maybe we should do stuff like this more often."

"Maybe, you're right. Seems the way we grind so hard all the time makes us hate more than love. We could afford to escape a little bit."

"You mean so we don't kill each other?"

"Please, like you're going to do anything."

"I'm talking about you killing me."

She dabbed her mouth with a napkin. "Baby, that's just a risk you have to take."

I laughed. "Timewise, this boat has taught me that life is too short and the world is too big. We got to dig in while we're still here. In the morning it could all be over."

She raised her chardonnay high. "To many more cruises."

We tinked our glasses at the rim. She drank a small sip and stared away at the water. I watched the fire on the table dance in her eyes while she got lost in the endless field of waves. "Hearing that ocean almost makes me forget the money we came here for," she said.

"It's beautiful. I mean, the reflection of the moon and everything."

"I can feel my mother out there. She's watching. Looking down from somewhere with a big smile because we're finally on the right path."

I tried measuring my words to give them the right effect. "I thought hard about what you said when we first got on this cruise. All that talk about wanting to live better. It got to me."

"Oh, did I create an epiphany?"

I watched the flat shape of the Atlantic. "An epiphany? I don't know. Maybe, we just understand each other perfectly for the first time."

That bought me a lazy smile. She tried to cover it up fast with a quick drink of wine but I saw that lipsticked mouth curve behind the glass. In the breach of conversation I took us a step further, moved my plate to the side to take her hands in mine across the table. A waiter came by to check on us but whipped around quick on a heel after he saw how we were in the moment.

Smart man, I thought, but it didn't take a genius. Maybe he saw it all the time on his job, the love manifesting between two people. Who knows? A boat like this, on an ocean like that, with an island on the skyline and the stars hung high was the perfect recipe for an epiphany. Maybe even a new religion. We already had an angel on our side, Chitara James. Even your favorite romance can't brag about that.

"Everyone talks about potential," I said. "What I could be if I just applied myself. Man, I been hearing that for so long it feels like I was born hearing it. But now I finally see it."

"Well it's about time. Twenty-two years old I didn't know how much longer you we're going to wait."

"Hey, you know I'm stubborn that way."

"Wrong. Not stubborn. Foolish."

A searing truth. I didn't know if I was ready to go that far and admit to having no sense and then Chevy kept right on pushing. "But your my fool," she said. "That's why we're here. I know what you want, Cerrio."

"Speak to me, baby."

"You want to be more than a number. More than the toughest inmate walking the yard bragging about the things you did to get there because none of that is the real definition of LaDecerrio Lloyd. Everyone who knows you knows that. I knew it a long time ago. Maybe you just figured it out since coming to the ship but that's okay because I'm still the same as I always was. And I couldn't think of a better place for you to see the truth than when it's just us. Together. Right here on top of the world."

We survived off that romance for a day and a half. Not all of it was laying down. In fact most of it isn't even what you think. Chevy wanted to invest quality time, she wanted to see the shows on the boat lounge and watch the stars on the deck and absorb the salty sea air with her hair down. We did all those things, experiencing life instead of just surviving it, never hurrying through the moment. But by Sunday we were way off lover's lane.

In the casino our money was fleeing fast like the last hostages left in a crisis. That first night when Chevy spilled wine on my lapel was a one off, after that the plan started going downhill on skis. Saturday, I sat at the same table in the same spot where I tossed different dollar chips looking for the same victory I had on my debut. And before my house money could even stop spinning and settle down on the green felt it was that same dealer sweeping it all away to the other side.

Chevy stood by watching a cool nine thousand dollars go up the first hour, ten the second, twelve the third. She sucked her teeth until her top lip went dry. I got out of there before the bottom half of her mouth chapped and now she was standing in the middle of our room, five inches away, drunk on sass with one hand on a hip and the other snapping like a backup singer.

"You suck, Cerrio! They're fucking laughing at us downstairs!"

"Shut up. Sit down. What are you all worked up about? I thought you said, 'win or lose none of that mattered'."

"Get real. I never said that."

"And here I thought we were having a good time."

"No, we have a serious problem. We bypassed the plan and blew a ton of money without ever regrouping." She sighed. "Bandy doesn't even know it yet."

"Well, maybe I can change my routine before she finds out. Lemme try shooting dice and see how that goes."

"Cut the shit, Cerrio! This isn't funny. We're getting closer and closer to leaving and you haven't won a thing."

I stopped in my tracks to the mini bar. "Who's joking? You know, I never fuck around about money."

"Well, you been fucking mine around. Isn't that enough?"

"And you? Always standing there me making little noises. I can't concentrate with you hovering around like a helicopter all the time. And what about those big dinners and fancy wine? You're drinking champagne around here like its malt liquor. You think that don't add up?"

"That's different. I'm enjoying myself. Or did you think I would just sit around watching the water everyday while everyone else is having fun?"

I popped the top on an eight dollar can of soda. "Fun isn't something you ever mentioned before. That was never part of the plan. At least not the one that got pitched to me."

Officially I was right, she told me we weren't on vacation. And if I took that seriously it would have been offensive to my logic. This was the unlicensed break, the breather, the honeymoon. We weren't even engaged and yet we fought toe to toe like a couple ten years deep in a marriage.

Bandy emerged from the bathroom with her hair wrapped in a towel. I don't know why she came down to our room to get ready for her shows the same way I could never figure out why she did her college homework in Chevy's kitchen when she had her own apartment to study in. Seems like no matter where we go some things just never change.

She had her head to the side trying to get water out of her ear. "What's with all the noise? You guys are louder than the frigging band downstairs."

"It's just an argument," I replied.

"Wrong," snapped Chevy. "I'm trying to figure out why we're going to leave here pretty soon with less money than what we brought to start with."

"She's blaming me for everything. As usual."

"So, who's fault is it then?"

"Relax Chev, it'll happen."

She shot a look at Bandy that could have cut a diamond. "Are you on his side?"

"No, I'm on our side. Cerrio had some bad hands that's all. There's still some time left to get what we came for."

The singer disappeared back into the bathroom. Chevy stayed where I left her for a sixteen ounce can of cola a minute ago and breathed in deep through her nose. "Cerrio, can you...just make better decisions? Please."

"It's called gambling for a reason. No one means to lose. Yeah, I could have made better decisions. None of which you could ever understand because you don't play cards. That's why I never explained anything to you."

"Don't dare act like you're smarter than me. I know how to play cards. It's not rocket science."

"All you know is what I tell you."

"Do you think bleeding out all my money, everything that I worked for, makes more sense when you put it that way?"

"Guys!"

Bandy tore away from the bathroom to come wedge herself between us. The look on her face was rife with annoyance.

"You two stop it. Come on. We're all going home together. Don't let the boat split us up before then."

"Well," said Chevy. "Then, he needs to make something happen. I want to see some adjustments."

"Cerrio promised he'd win before this trip was over and he's going to deliver."

"And when does that start?"

Bandy took her towel down and a wave of sleek hair fell out on her shoulders. "Later."

"No, that's too broad. Later could be any time including after we get back home and the car note is due."

"Chev, relax, everything's going to be okay." Bandy looked at her and then looked at me. She said, "don't worry. It'll all work out." And then she kissed me.

For several reasons I felt my heart freeze. Her mouth tastes like papayas and it's somehow cool as cream. I thought it was a mistake, maybe she forgot herself, or maybe we were just closer than ever now. Chevy seems to take it well, she's just standing there like she sort of doesn't know what to do which isn't like her at all. Bandy touches her shoulder and repeats part of her last line. "Don't worry, it'll be alright." Then, she kisses her too.

Except this isn't a quick smooch. I mean, it started out that way but things sped up fast. My baby pulls Bandy in by the waist, the little singer responds kindly by wrapping her arms around Chevy's neck to show her that this is no error. She's shorter than my girl so she tilts her head back to make sure their mouths meet more comfortably. I stand by, admittedly dumbfounded as the passion grows deeper and little, light, moans lift up in the air while soft lips swim back and forth over and over one another. Chevy catches Bandy's tongue gently between her teeth and sucks it like a long finger of ice until the pink muscle stretches unbelievably far out of her mouth. When it snaps back she slips her hands inside Bandy's robe and pushes it right off of her petite shoulders.

She has white spots in the sexiest places. One by her nipple, another on the collarbone, a pair riding high on both sides above the curled hairs at the top of her womanhood. She has shallow breasts that are still a little damp underneath from the shower with tan lines slanting down in the phantom shape of her summer bathing suit. Chevy kisses her exposed neck and then steps back like she just remembered I was present in the room.

But I don't get acknowledged, not officially, nobody says anything clumsy like, "oh, sorry didn't see you there." Instead, Bandy comes over to me with no hesitation, takes my hands and puts one over each side of her chest and stares longingly in my eyes.

There's no question I'm hard and while I massage the cocoa nipples easily she takes care of my pants. In an instant they're gone, incidentally so are Chevy's. She undressed while I took over her role as Bandy's French kissing partner.

I was the last one with any clothes on, just a shirt, but that was okay because this isn't a race. They beat me to the bed and kneel on the covers kissing again, breasts smashed together with the flesh ballooned at the top because there's no where else for it all to go. Chevy's are heavier so she sits a little lower and it looks like she's giving Bandanna's perky B-cups a Wonderbra lift. I stand up on the bed and stick myself in between them, Chevy flicks her tongue out, Bandy wants to go full steam ahead and suck right away but I don't want that. I want to feel what all that precious, succulent flesh feels like pressing in on me from both sides.

They're good girls, they love each other and they love me too, so they oblige. Rising up a little each with a stack of pillows under their knees so I'm jammed right between two layers of silk and then get they creative, kissing again but this time with my shaft in the middle like a barrier. Bandy giggles when her tongue can't meet Chevy's because the dick in between is too big. Then, my girl takes me in her mouth and sucks from the side. She shows Bandy how to do it, going faster and faster and then letting it pop out and wag like a wet pig tail. When the singer takes over she's better than I thought, surprisingly good with a mouth soft as cashmere. She managed to put on a smile and let it pop out and before it wagged two times Chevy had me again.

They played like that, popping and sucking, kissing and touching and somewhere in between Chevy goes under to give all her attention to the double pale spots between Bandy's thighs. The little singer kept working me over on her knees. She cheeked it and held me there with my cock straining against her lips until it stretched the white spot out on her mouth like a piece of gum and when she looked up I almost lost my mind.

We weren't going to fuck. I knew that much right away. These things are progressive, Chevy and Bandy might be familiar but the trio was just getting started. You have to crawl before you walk, doggie paddle before you swim, count before you add. Next time, when we all get back home and there's a ton of cash everywhere, then we'll go the full nine with it. In the meantime I was going to try really hard to be satisfied. Trying not to be selfish because I was still trying to hang on to my destiny somehow.

After we were dressed again the singer kept getting herself ready in our room. I embraced the ritual, appreciated her presence without even thinking about it anymore. After a few years sharing iron houses with random men I was reminded that a ship full of women was like dipping the toes in paradise. Then, Chocolate showed up and instantly things got much harder.

CHAPTER 32

SHADE SYMPTOMS

Bandy let her in with Neesha and Franky who took off like a jet trying to sniff up every inch of carpet looking for something fresh to chew on. Chevy thought fast and jammed her heels down in a suitcase so he wouldn't maul them once he got hooked on her scent. After inhaling everything in a fever that's when I realized his owner was here for no reason. Arriving was Chocolate's cause, she just came down to be down. I didn't mind, the more the merrier.

They talked a million miles a minute. My woman had the gossip, Chocolate brought the propaganda. She had a video on her phone showing Chevy's replacement at Sugar Bares reaching down to touch her toes. I got a glimpse. God love her, the girl tried. The new talent gave it her absolute best but the real experts still laughed heinously. From where I sat it looked like the rookie had an ordinary problem. She danced with no goals. Limp and unincorporated with the thing that told her to come be a dancer in the first place. I remember when my card game was just like that, a little earlier at the table when I was playing not to lose like an ordinary sucker and got my pockets turned up.

After Franky got tired of racing through new territory he curled up by Chocolate's feet while she did Bandy's makeup on the loveseat. Taneesha looked like a surgeon's assistant passing her brushes and pads. Tweezers came out and I knew things were serious but my focus was much closer to the remote in my hand.

The home team Wake Forest had Virginia Cavaliers on the ropes. The guests were standing in the outfield chewing gum and donning dark Ray Bans while the Deacons stood on every corner of the diamond. They were leaning off the bases watching the batter twist the stick in the vice grip of his hands at home plate. The kid's name was Fenalda, he was probably going to get a major league contract after this. The scouts were getting sunburned in the stands right now and he didn't look like he was going to let them down either. I held my breath and watched him cut at an elevator fastball that dropped six inches right before his swing. When he swiped at air the whole crowd fell silent.

Behind me a door opened, the palm oil scent rolling out from behind it bombing the air made the room smell exactly like home. Meanwhile on TV the Fenalda kid was going through his motions, touch the helmet, adjust the gloves, golf swing the bat. When he finished and came back to the plate the pitcher nodded. He built the suspense, wound up, went back on one leg, turned his head, fired. By the time he let the ball go I was on the edge of the bed. Fenalda had two strikes and I had the volume up to fifty trying to ignore the female chatter going on in the background. At that all or nothing moment my whole body braced for the crack of the bat. Fenalda swung for the fences but the rest is just a mystery.

Chevy walked right in front of me, a thick full-length towel wrapped around her chest, another one on her head. Gucci slippers padding the carpet drowned out the game until commercials blared over them with that extra loud enthusiasm.

I looked up at her with my hands held out. "Hey! You serious?"

She halted. "Now, what's the matter with you?"

"I'm sitting here watching a game and you walked right in front like I'm invisible."

"So what? It was only a second. Now, I'm out of your way."

"Remember that when I throw all your makeup in the trash. I'll say, 'Chevy, it's out of your way now.'"

"Don't you dare touch my shit, Cerrio. I mean it."

"Stay out of way of the TV then. You got the whole room, you got to walk in front here too?"

"This bitch will walk wherever she wants. And you ain't gonna do nothing about it."

"Don't push me."

"Shut up."

From the loveseat Chocolate broke in. "You two. Over there. Make peace."

"This man don't want no peace." Chevy shook her head. "Trust me I tried."

"You're right, I wanted a shower. But nobody can take one after you used up all the towels."

Chocolate stood up. "Come on, y'all need to separate before you kill each other and I have throw your bodies overboard. Cerrio, give her a little space to unwind."

"Hey, she's got all the space in the world." I gestured to the area that the women had control of, clothes and shoes laid out everywhere showed a literal no man's land. "You guys got your own planet over there. I just want the TV."

Chocolate put on her performer's smile. "I heard there's a bigger one playing downstairs. Somewhere around the lobby by the bar. Come on, why don't you help me find it."

"What about Bandanna's makeup? You're not done yet."

"Neesha can finish."

"I can't do it all now anyway," said the star. "I need to meditate first."

"Bandy, I didn't know you meditated."

"Yeah, well, there's a lot of things you never knew about me."

Chevy made a noise like a tire losing air. "Definitely no shortage of ignorant on the bed over here."

When I finally heard the bat crack it was Virginia hitting a line drive down center field. The sunburned people sitting high in the stands validated the good hit with party noises. That's the last part of baseball season I remember because for the rest of my summer too many things made it impossible to focus on watching television anymore.

Don't think I was fooled. I knew damn well Chocolate knew where the bar was in the lobby and she knew the TV was set up behind it like a pair of posters. We left the room without any deep discussion about where to go and ended up in exactly the right place on a wood slab with a man wiping down glasses considering us carefully like we had a deal to offer him. On her order he poured us up double shots of tequila and she paid him from a stack of twenty dollar bills pulled out of a white envelope with a little logo in the corner.

That was another part of her intrigue. Perhaps her best feature was that wherever Chocolate went dollars were never far behind. Franky eyed our liquor over the brass snap on her purse that had nothing but Cover Girl and a dog inside. When he sneezed on the back of her hand I had to laugh.

"Damn it, all that Clive Christian is giving him a bad reaction."

"Ah, he's just being fussy. Probably wants a bone like somebody else I know."

"I told you once, I'm good. Me and Chevy argue plenty but we make up even better."

"I'm talking about the other thing. The being fussy part."

"No, that ain't me mama. Never fussed a day in my life."

"Fine. Agitated then."

I shrugged. "Okay, maybe a little bit."

She said, "that's it. Dog's get fussy. Men get agitated."

I drained my tequila. "This sounds a lot like a conversation we could have had up in the room. You should have joined team Chevy when she was riding me like a rocket to the moon. You could have earned your NASA wings."

"You calling me an astronaut? Funny." She put a hand under her chin. "And what if the moon just won't take us?"

"Then at least you'll have a helmet on so it doesn't make a mess when I blow your mind."

Chocolate didn't come back with anything. The bartender poured us a second round in fresh shot glasses and she accepted my line. Her envelope sat on the wood bar with a banknote hanging out of its open mouth like Franky's dangling, paper thin, tongue. Both of them just waiting for their master's touch.

I picked up the conversation before my time expired. "I got to tell you, I'm really glad we came out on this cruise. Even with the war in up the suite it still feels good to get away. Right now the city has too much heat in too many of the wrong places. The sort of places we be at. Times like this, man, you don't know what people are all about."

She fanned more bills in a arc between our glasses for the bartender to see. When he brought drinks again she said, "I'm glad too. This is the month when all the bodies start popping up. Who knows? Somebody might have come out and got me too."

"Sounds like this is just what the doctor ordered for both of us, then.

"Doctors. Lawyers. They're all here. Enough about them, though. How about you? How's the boat treating Cerrio?"

"Good. Then. Not good."

"Everything turning on you, huh?"

"I wouldn't say that. More like it's trying to strike a balance somewhere."

"A man of substance. I like that. Most people would have agreed with me so they could go on and rant about how everything's going all wrong. How it's all so unfair. Like that noise upstairs. You know, the girls are up there talking about you right now. They're saying all the usual stuff about how Cerrio doesn't listen and he's so selfish. Common complaints about every man. All of them true, though.

But before you come back they'll circle around to talk about how good you are. Especially that Bandy, she really adores you.

She'll start the redemption and then what else can Chevy do but follow? Hell, thinking about it right now almost makes me sick."

Chocolate cut her eyes to show me she was being playful.

I said, "Bandy's a gem. Have you seen her on stage, yet?"

"Yeah, she's good."

"Shit, give the girl some credit. She's a lot better than good."

"Okay then, she's a star."

"Now you're saying it like I picked an opinion for you."

She took a drink and smacked her lips. "Cerrio, do you want to pick a fight with me too?"

"Never that. Wouldn't even dream of it."

"That's good. Because I don't like to reconcile much. And that would have made things difficult since there's something I forgot to do when you were in my room last night."

She slid the envelope over. In the corner I saw an embossed blue shield smaller than a postage stamp trimmed in gold so thin it could barely catch the light. Underneath the shield was a street address to a bank in Atlanta.

"I am a woman of my word, Cerrio. Remember when you came up to my room and I told you there was cash on the nightstand?"

"Of course I do."

She touched my shirt collar right at the corner. "I'm sorry I forgot it then. That's my bad. A little slip, it happens sometimes."

"Don't I know it."

"For sure, we all do. Anyway you take this," she patted the stuffed envelope, "and go win something big tonight before our girl Bandy goes out on stage."

I weighed the package in my hand. "Something tells me the boat has been good to you even if it's turned around on me."

She shrugged coolly. "It pays."

"Would you say a little or a lot?"

"Doesn't really matter. Let's just say it keeps the dog fed."

I never told Chocolate about what me and Chevy were actually arguing over before she came in our room. About how fast I had lost on the table and that's the reason things were tense and getting tenser. I gave it to her in generalities and pluralities with no actualities. I let her think it was cabin fever or baseball or whatever she could deduce on her own and in turn she never told me why she didn't give her money directly to my baby like she had always done before.

The envelope was swollen with rectangle greenbacks sporting Andrew Jackson's long face in the center. Alone in the bathroom of me and Chevy's suite I counted thirty-nine, hundred dollars in twenties across the sink while she was sunning on the deck. That was the first sign of distrust. The second came when I kept the money a secret and slipped downstairs to gamble pretending like I had a lot less. Those were just minor things, itty bitty symptoms of greed like that last small toe on your foot. But in a while they would be able to stand on their own.

CHAPTER 33

DIVA MUCH

Ilost again, like all fatal moments it happened fast. One card got flipped over, someone hollered Jesus Christ, and that, as they say, is all she wrote. The little luck I had leftover from Friday night had been fully used up on the dice table. I threw like a boss, three sevens in a row. But nobody saw those rolls leading up to victory so all of that hardly existed. On the other hand plenty of witnesses came around the poker table to watch my downfall like a public execution. If I would have charged a cover fee maybe I could have broke even on my losses.

Tonight the girls serving drinks had on different outfits, black camisole and silver sequin skirts with no slits up the thigh. Every one of them knew Chevy, they even had a nickname for her. "Diva Much." Bandy told me she overheard it once when she was back in the dressing room getting ready for her segment. Personally, I'm used to other females aiming their hostilities at my baby. Sometimes they're practical, other times they're unplanned but never understated. Back in high school the other cheerleaders used to spin loose webs of gossip about her that only got worse when we moved in together. That sort of thing was just a natural jealous phenomenon, but this name they gave her on the boat was patently clever and it smacked of something like real disdain.

I found her playing nickel slots two at a time. When I walked down the aisle lined with beeping machines an old woman smiled at me from behind a pair of bifocals. Her being right here made sense because this was an old lady's game. Just press the button and wait for your moment. I smiled back at her just to make things even.

Chevy didn't see me until I came close enough to touch her and even then she still kept her face glued to the machine watching two lemons line up while praying for a third. I jammed both hands in my pockets and saw the third panel wind down slow to a cherry as a skirted waitress made a detour around the other side of us.

I leaned an arm on the slot machine. "How's it going over here?"

Another nickel went down and she pressed the play button again. "Not bad. I won two hundred dollars an hour ago."

"Nice work, mama."

"Yeah, then I spent it all on the five dollar machine. The rest is right here." She shook a tall cup of silver coins like a tambourine.

Before I could make a case for her to give up the old lady's machine started bleeping a chorus of happy notes down the aisle. Chevy looked over just in time to see a waterfall of coins dumping in the trough at her knees. "Goddamnit," my baby said. "And I was just over there too."

The fast rain of money drew a curious crowd. In a minute a houseman showed up followed by a train of women trailing nine feet behind him. He put fifteen hundred dollars in the old lady's craggy, white palm while she stood there blushing like a fever. He asked for her name and she said, "Jeanine." She said, "she'd never won anything in her whole life." The houseman took a picture with Jeanine smiling right beside him and Chevy shook her head. "I can't believe it, the rich just get richer."

While the houseman shook hands a tall waitress with a string of islands tattooed on her shoulder came by holding a tray of wine and mixed drinks. She had a flawless complexion and a sheen in her hair that caught every streak of light. Hawaiian, I thought and a long way from home on a whole other ocean. Being that far away maybe that's how come she didn't know any better. Poor island girl didn't see the cataclysm waiting for her at the dead machine. And the other girls must not have told her about "Diva Much." Otherwise she would have never brought herself down that aisle.

Chevy snatched a merlot off the Hawaiian girl's tray and killed half of it. I saw the islander step back, she had never seen this before. The snatching completely shocked her, so violent and out of nowhere and her loaded expression looked like it might be permanent. Chevy caught the look too and dropped her half empty glass right back on the serving tray where it fell at a crazy angle before rolling out to the edge.

Jeanine's celebration died when wasted alcohol bullied its way into the air. It wasn't just that one spilled merlot, everything came down. I mean, it rained and poured. The waitress did her best to catch the runaway wine glass. But she listed a little too far and those stilettos on her feet were way unforgiving for so much imbalance.

She walked the tightrope, tilting a little bit left and then back right before falling sideways into a slot machine and slamming her shoulder with rhino force against a ledge most people use as an armrest. Immediately her camisole was ruined. Turned into a rag when different color drinks splashed up and across her and the four legged stool right next to her ankles. I looked at Chevy who looked sapped dry of remorse.

I would say I couldn't believe it but what other choice did I have? Laying on the floor the Hawaiian girl was a long sculpture of pain. Mouth held open, eyes squeezed shut, face twisted up with a hand clutching the opposite arm right at the elbow. Seeing her like that it all became clear. They say revelations are a manifestation of everything that already was and here's where it all came together. The way Chevy snatched glasses with such a raw sense of entitlement. Watching her drop a half empty one back on the fallen girl's tray with no more regard than flipping a coin in a wishing well. She earned her handle. Because around here "Diva Much" meant "what a bitch" in plain English.

She didn't know about the name and I didn't tell her because that would gave us one more thing to fight about. I grabbed her arm while the houseman was caught up tending to the heap of pain writhing on the casino carpet. "Come on, we gotta go."

"No, I'm staying. I'm about to hit on this machine and get my payout."

"Are you blind? Did you not just see what happened?"

"Where we gonna go, Cerrio? Huh? You can't run away from everything all the time."

I bent down and got right in her face. "Grab your cup of fucking nickels and let's get out of here. Now."

Sugar Bares finest checked her watch, little hand on the ten, big hand pointed straight up north. That meant Bandy was due up to the stage any minute now for the opening act, the one everyone else would be following tonight. What a dream come true for the college girl. Chocolate wasn't sure but she suspected there might be a sneaking sense of pride fomenting inside of her for this big comeback that the little flower had pulled off. Bandy had so many things to sink her teeth into, a business prospect, a musical journey, a degree in effect. None of that was tainted by all the messes unfurling on the water right beneath her nose.

If she knew things would have turned out so good Chocolate might have introduced her to Barney months ago. Sure, she lost a tooth but the gold in her mouth went well with the new edge she had adopted. Plus, it complimented the white spot on her face. Loose a tooth, gain the world. Not a bad trade for a girl. Better than the cause Cerrio contributed to where he gave his life in small increments while the cause fled away fast into insanity. One day he would be grieving on it. On some lonely afternoon just like that one when she found him sulking in Sally's bar he would have to come face to face with regret and that's where Chocolate always came in. Swooping down like a hungry pelican to soothe the pain left behind by a failed commitment.

Hands came together as a circle of spotlight shined bright on the curtains. Bandy wasted no time emerging in a white dress with a pink lace pattern that curved from her shoulders down to the seductive crease of her cleavage. Her performance was like an explosion. Not like that backfiring Honda but like the Big Bang that created the whole charismatic universe. First there was murmuring in the crowd and light sounds of anticipation then she came out in a burst of raw power like a new revival.

She performed strong to separate herself from the mundane and the average. Both hands in the air and fingers up to the ceiling with the high note on her lips like a worshipper singing high from a mountaintop. The crowd was in love, she manipulated their emotions exactly like they wanted and they never stopped applauding her for it. These weren't tiny golf claps either, it was hard, championship applause that bordered on something next to furious.

Chocolate did her part, putting the light side by of her palms together. Because after all she couldn't hate it. She shot a quick look around but didn't see any sign of Cerrio. His absence brought on the strangest sense of anger and a touch of concern that she fought to suppress. Where was he? Usually the grin spreading across his face after the show was contagious, Chocolate caught it too when the muscles in her cheeks began pulling a little more taut because she knew he felt that same sense of pride that she did for the little singer. Only different.

Before Bandy's show I took Chevy back up to our cabin suite. She wanted to protest and I could see the complaints riding on the tip of her tongue in the elevator but none passed through the apricot gloss on her lips. Down the hall the nickels in her purse jangled like a belt buckle. I twisted around to give her a look and she tried keeping the noise down but that just ended up making us walk slower so I told her forget it.

When we got there she showered and then got dressed in her usual nighttime pajamas because the Gucci sweats smelled like weed. I hardly paid attention to her naked right in front of me, dripping wet like fresh lobster. The Hawaiian girl was still on my mind. Ordinarily the spill she took would be something to laugh about but being so close to her humiliation stole all the humor away.

Her arm would be okay but what about the rest? I kept seeing that moment when she crumpled into the metal slot machine and those islands on her shoulder went horizontal. That fall marked a change in realization when a person stops believing that all people are good and starts watching out for the mean ones. I witnessed that unfolding in that Hawaiian girl's face on the ground, saw the instant the tides changed inside her and knew she would never be the same. A piece of her innocence had been pressure washed off like a thin layer of paint.

Chevy went to sleep on the bed next to me in her bra and panties. I put a sheet over her, pulled it up to the shoulders. When the light snoring began then I thought about the stuffed white envelope hidden underneath my clothes in the duffle bag. So many moral dilemmas but never enough time to reconcile. That's what makes us different from the animals, morals and the ability to put a price tag on anything.

Downstairs the houseman who paid out earlier strutted around the tables with a new pair of girls at his left and right. His eyes were peeled looking for the honey skinned woman playing slots with a tendency to snatch drinks and raise hell. When he came close I stared hard at his face and saw just another trick in a suit. He probably paid good to sleep with all the sequined skirts gliding around here. Now, he was angry that the pretty Hawaiian got decommissioned before her time. Just to be malicious I'd like to introduce him to Chocolate.

The tables were filling up faster than a long list of wishes. Legions of gamblers came from across the boat to infiltrate the house's budget. By now we had come to a point where there weren't many more mysteries. Every better knew what served his palate, maybe baccarat on the sides, blackjack as the main course. The dice lovers crusaded even sided cubes all over red felt while the roulette wheel spun out half and half promises.

Every chair had a body in it, seemed like the only person who didn't know their place around the house was yours truly. My spot for two nights straight at the poker table had been filled by a wide man in narrow suspenders. I put my hands in my pockets feeling like a stray dog in Babylon until a pretty Janet Jackson looking type came by carrying drinks and a conspiracy in her eyes.

She was tall and slender and coming through killing it with the muscles in her legs tensing on every single stride. Her waist was tight but going up the breadth of her shoulders told me she was strong as rebar. The bangles on her wrist sang happily together when she handed me a rum.

"What's the matter?" she cooed. "No more dice?"

I realized she had been watching me since earlier. "Nah, turns out dice aren't so much my thing."

"I see. And so what is your thing?"

"Well, I guess it's rum right now." I shook the ice cubes around.

She giggled and it sounded like a crackling fire. "You're funny."

"Sometimes. Say, what is that over there?"

She followed my finger pointing to a blue table where a dealer stood tall in front of a woman swimming in chinchilla fur. He carefully passed out cards to the players all around her who were decked out lavishly in subtle sort of ways. I saw cowboy hats on top, silk ties in the middle, red bottom shoes below.

The waitress whistled low. "Oh, that there's big money. A thousand dollar buy in, two hundred dollar antes every time. I think somebody won ten grand over there earlier."

"No shit, ten grand? Man, that's like a ransom."

"Yep, all in one hand too."

I swished the rum around and nodded slowly. "You know, you just made me feel a lot better."

She laughed again and glanced at me to share a quick look of amusement but I stared straight ahead. I wasn't joking anymore.

Chevy woke up alone pitying herself. She got out of bed thinking about how everyone had become her adversary as of lately. There was Bandy taking Cerrio's side and Cerrio taking the boat waitress's side and no one ever stopped to think about what would actually make her feel better. She wished she had a Klonopin so she could have slept even longer. Maybe nap away all these people who lived in glass houses. Chevy knew they had good intentions but so did she and they weren't fucking righteous enough to be pointing fingers in her face at the slightest offense or when some drink carrying waitress took a fall in her line of vision.

She looked at the clock, 11:13 p.m. and too early to call it a night anyway. She had been out long enough to let the effects of the wine seep away and so sober as a nun she crept out on the deck to watch the waves, waiting for her mother to say something inspiring to her from the ocean like she used to years ago when life was all about high school. In those days they lived in the middle of Polo road in a brick house with a big backyard and no fence. On moonlit nights when he couldn't snipe his aunt's car Cerrio would catch a ride to the top of her street and cut his way through every neighbor's back lawn just to sneak into her bedroom. Chevy remembered watching him scramble through the grass, she used to adore his effort.

That was the epitome of LaDecerrio Lloyd, wild and uncomplicated. Before the ugliness of drugs and jail had invaded their affair she used to stand way back while him and Socks made their teenage ruckus. Those were the days of loud reefer and rookie sex with a cool gulp of young freedom riding down the highway in that long Oldsmobile. When Chevy laughed out loud at her old memories someone spoke up beside her.

"Having a good time?"

Her golden eyes shifted to a tall figure half hidden in the shadows.

"Just thinking," she said.

"Well, it must have been a nice thought. Care to share?"

"What makes you think it was good enough to share?"

The figure stepped forward to reveal himself. "Do you like putting people on the spot?"

"Do you like accosting women on boats?"

"Touche," he replied. "I don't know. I could be wrong, maybe it wasn't a very good thought after all. Maybe it was naughty. Or maybe you just always smile pretty like that all the time. It is your best face by far."

The boat's top deck was never empty, never starved for people. But somehow the man slinging compliments made Seville feel like it was just him and her with the sea salt air swirling around them like juice in a blender. He got closer and put a hand on the rail poising himself like a gate to get through. She was scared to take serious notice of him the same way an old fiend is scared to taste new drugs because maybe they might find something better and never go back.

"My name is Ferris," he said. "Everyone on the boat calls me Mr. Pinckney."

"You like being called mister?"

"I hate it. Titles always make people seem pretentious."

"Then, nice to meet you Ferris. They call me, Chevy."

"You mean like the car?"

"Or the truck. They make those too you know."

"Why?"

"Why do they make trucks?"

He laughed richly. "No, why do they call you Chevy?"

"Because my real name is Seville James."

His green eyes smiled in the moonlight. "That's a beautiful name. So, what do I call you?

Chevy shrugged her bare shoulders in a deep brown dress she had bothered to put on just for her very own glamour. "It doesn't matter. Just don't call me ma'am whatever you do."

"Easy enough. You don't look like a ma'am anyway. Too spirited and not stuffy like you come from privilege. Misses and ma'ams are mostly slanted in that direction. In fact, if I had to guess I'd say you're not from Georgia at all."

"I'm not sure if I want to be. The way you make it sound Georgia women are more trouble than what they're worth."

"My apologies. That wasn't on purpose."

"It never is. So, what do you do Ferris? Besides accost women on boats?"

"Well, boats are my business. I own a dockyard on the port of Savannah." He reached in his blazer for something to hand over. "Here, my card."

Chevy took the thick paper between her fingers and read it in the dark. "I thought you were going to say you're a store manager or something. Like at Target."

"Good guess. I did work there once back in college. Now Target depends on me to get merchandise on their shelves."

"That's a nice switch."

"Uh-huh, can I make another?"

She blinked. "Something tells me you don't take no for an answer."

Ferris came all the way forward putting his features on full display in a saturation of light. Chevy stiffened. He was ruggedly handsome double dipped in luminescence, a little more than half coming from the boat and the rest from the sky. Standing in the glow his face was alarmingly stronger than the voice from where it came. With a jaw chiseled out of stone, a broad nose and hooded eyes he was a statue of a man molded from the finest dark clay.

"That guy you been with at the shows. What's the situation?"

"It's difficult to explain." She caught herself wringing her hands.

"I believe you. He has that aura as if things are very complicated."

"Well, you know that's life. Complex. Hard to describe."

"Except it doesn't have to be that way."

Chevy didn't have to ask, she already knew. Right from the moment he approached she never had to guess where this conversation was going. Now here they were at the crossroads of casual, silly, flirty talk and full on adult rated cross fire. She flipped Ferris Pinckney's business card over and over in her hand watching the name go away and then come back again like a dolphin slipping through the waves.

He stood smiling in front of her, perfectly straight teeth, thick lips below an impossibly neat moustache. Except nothing was funny. Ferris was too gorgeous to laugh at so Chevy stayed somber. She wondered if this was how Cerrio felt all the time, like life was just one big game all in the cards. That seemed so lasse faire, so flippant and annoyingly carefree. But he was absolutely right about one thing, Chevy wasn't much of a gambler. Cerrio had that part figured out even if he had the rest of the world upside down.

Her mother whispered to her through the wind saying exactly the right thing at exactly the right time the same way she always did. "Life is too short." And after that Chevy knew what to do, what direction to take from here. She didn't need any more advice or another draft of cool air blowing in her ear. She tucked the business card down in her bra with no straps, on the opposite side of her heart, way outside of her lover's jurisdiction, and smiled.

CHAPTER 34

MUHAMMAD'S JERSEY

Never let a case afoul of the evidence. I heard that in a courtroom once and it almost made up for all the bullshit every cheap suited lawyer splashed around without any second thoughts. Plenty of things don't make sense between the halls of justice but that one short sentence had perfect harmony. I wrote it down when I got back to my cell, right on the wall above the sink so I could read it every morning when I brushed my teeth. There was no way to own those words so I did the next best thing and memorized them until the meaning got married to my own piece of mind.

The plump lady in the chinchilla showed me the evidence, she held her cards above the high rollers table at just the right angle to give me a little glimpse of her luck. A very dangerous pair of sevens winked back at me just north of her lacquered nails. But I wasn't worried, all the rest of the case was in my hand, a king of spades with his blushing red brother in diamonds stood posted for a verdict that was just bursting to have a nasty ending.

She bet her sevens immediately, it didn't have a thing to do with luck or being rich or poor. Any gambler here who was worth

✦ 321 ✦

the flavor in their drink would have played her hand the exact same way. I watched our dealer scrape the two grand towards the middle out of fur coated lady's reach before she got any second thoughts.

I touched my own house money sitting cold right in front of me. Those seven black chips Bandy made me swear to be careful with called out in a voice to tell me this is the time. For the better part of three days they had slept peacefully inside my pocket, through the good, the bad, the sloppy arguments and even the the sex. Chevy liked the way I took care of them, she laughed and said I babied those chips and of course she never lied. I pulled them out at the end of every night, carefully brushing away dust, fear, and weed crumbs from between their little ridge toothed edges. It was my last end of the day ritual before folding up my pants and laying down beside her.

The dealer waited patiently, he was a heavy man with a slushy gut. I could hear the creases in his vest flattening out every time he took a breath. When I pushed a little more than half of my big chips in the middle the people who were around didn't even bat an eye. They weren't from the projects. In their world a few thousand dollars gone was a forgotten afternoon, small money that dried up like broth in an oven. For me it was a moment leading up to the rest of my life.

Nobody hesitated to join in the risk, around the table it was anybody's hand to win. They were all thinking like me but not praying the same. I prayed I wasn't forcing anything, I prayed this would be over soon, I prayed that the cloud was lifting. I prayed to God and Seville James and the silhouette on the flag knowing that these are the types of games that you always remember and no matter what God, whoever she is, will never forget.

When it came back to the chinchilla coat she flipped more of her money in the middle and I felt my heart race even faster. Let the fools rush in, I thought. A half dozen of us around the table meant I was about to be twenty thousand dollars richer, twenty five after the house threw in their big winner bonus. Already I could see the glee in Chevy's face. All of her dreams coming true and her mother smiling down on me in a vision fit to be painted in oil.

Once he had it all in the middle the heavy dealer did his job, flipping up the first three cards to show two low diamonds and a six of hearts. A brown man across the table who could be me in twenty years doubled the wager. Two people folded and the dealer shifted to the cow rustler in the wide brimmed Stetson hat. He was doing a thing with his lips like he was thinking hard, everyone waited for his decision and listened to his chips clack as he slung them forward to join the mountain of money.

I followed suit shoving the last of mine up front, the fur coated woman saw no reason not to chuck hers right behind it. Splashing house bread on the pile like dirty silverware going down a stained sink. There was no music playing but I didn't need any melodies to add up that we were in the fifty thousand dollar range and that's a good payday. I don't give a fuck who you are.

Mr. Brown skin was chasing a diamond flush but five of a kind wasn't coming. I knew because after a while you can just feel these types of things even if you can't feel anything else. Our dealer turned the fourth card over, a nine of spades popped up and I smiled inside. I had the hand won but brown skin who was me in twenty years kept on raising taking the other two with him. By now the dealer was sweating from raking up so much money, he scooped with two thick paws until every unloving cent was piled up all in his reach and then he gave it to us, the very last card. A jack of hearts holding a hatchet next to his head.

On the other side of the casino Chocolate stood in the middle of the floor by a dice table between two fools throwing away their mortgage. She kept on a smile like one of the real spectators while the bright lights flashed all around them. She even gave a little cheer when someone hit their point but all the time this was how she waited. Almost the whole trip had seen her hanging out on the fringes ready to move in whenever the chance came. Any moment now her opportunity would rise up faster than a space shuttle and she was going to be right there to catch it on the way up.

A thin man in a polyester vest rolled a seven for his ump-teenth time in a row. The crowd exploded in fresh excitement but she didn't celebrate with them this time. While they went banan-as Chocolate stayed stoic as a gravestone just watching, waiting. Despite her calmness on the outside feral anticipation raged right beneath the flesh, it felt like an organism trying to break through the skin. It knew things, sensed things and right now it was telling her the same thing that the monkey said right after he cut off his tail. "It won't be long now."

Around the high rollers table there wasn't any liquor house bullshit. No one hung on to their cards for dear life in case what-ever the person next to them had beat them out. No hands slid to the waist with itchy fingers looking for a trigger to squeeze. And I didn't slide anything extra in the deck, better than that I didn't think I really had to.

All of our hands were laid out, exposed for the tired dealer to see so he could do his job right when it counted most and call the winner. The chinchilla woman died with her sevens, mister brown-skin-gonna-be-me-in-twenty-years was bluffing, he didn't even have a pair. My kings looked prominent laying face up on the felt, like they could incite a new beginning. And I was ready for a fresh start but when the sweaty slug in the vest called a full house all those wistful dreams got stabbed through the heart.

"Jacks over sixes," said the dealer. The man in the cowboy hat smiled like an idiot. "Meet me at the river," he said in thick Ten-nessee accent. I could have killed him right after that. His crested lips hidden underneath a salt and pepper moustache made me wish we were back in Winston-Salem where I could do some real damage instead of out here on the Atlantic where the Coast Guard would draw down on me quick as instant soup.

Watching him pull all the chips away that should have been mine made my eyelids twitch. While the dream burned down fury was quickly taking it's place like a Phoenix rising from the ashes.

I left the table in a hurry, bumping into a waitress on my way to anywhere that wasn't pregnant with defeat. The room swirled, glitter, noise and people swimming around together until nothing was precise anymore, just a mesh of colors like a child's finger painting. I had to get out of there. It took the rest of my energy to find a place to escape the madness and in the end I landed on a stool in the exact same place where the Hawaiian girl went down like a plane crash.

This time the slots were vacant. No old women pressing buttons or silver nickels dropping down slender coin chutes. The solitude was priceless. Strange that didn't seem strange. I hardly thought about how unusual it must be sitting all alone while everyone else in my orbit indulged without planning, free of grievances. Or maybe they were really the strange ones and the payoff of this tiny seclusion for me was a rare moment of clarity.

Difference didn't matter, though. How could it after losing like that?

I sat facing away from the bleeping machine with my elbows on my knees, head in my hands, thinking about how I would break the news to a small circle of doe-eyed women who had so much undeserved faith in me. They would, eventually, say money was replaceable and all that meant anything is how we stuck together through thick and thin. They would forgive me, but how could I forgive myself? That had always been the question, even long before this boat.

The real truth is I have no answer. Somewhere inside there was a hole in me where the solution should have been. I needed a blunt, a line, or a woman to fill it up. All three would be nice but in my experience one usually leads to another, sometimes directly, and when I took my hands off my head to think about where to find any of it there was Chocolate who had whipped up in front of me clutching a drink close to her chest the same way Chevy used to hold her schoolbooks back in the day.

The satisfaction on her face was clear as a window. "Tell me you're not a slot slut now. Has it really gotten that bad?"

I twisted my finger around in a small circle. "What, you mean all this? No, I'm just here because this is a good place to get in touch with my botched aura."

"Aw, poor thing. How much did they get you for tonight?"

"Who said I lost?"

"Oh, well in that case how much did we win?"

"Now, it's a we thing."

"Don't go changing up on me, Cerrio. We're together on this boat just like we were in High Point. In fact, we've been a team for a long time now."

"You're comparing apples to oranges. High Point was nothing like this."

She scratched my back with five, long claws. "But even if it was you still took my money yesterday."

The crisp white envelope stuffed with bills still laid untouched in my duffle bag like the last pair of clean socks. I wanted to steal away, grab it, come back down and try again. No Tennessean or anybody else sailing the wide, blue ocean would beat me with a full house twice in one night. It just wasn't going to happen. But when Chocolate parked herself on the stool right next to me suddenly my feet anchored down to the floor.

She looked hard at my eyes, directly in where she could see her reflection looking right back. Suddenly she had gone from smug to sympathy like changing TV channels. "Blaming yourself like always, huh?"

"Look around, there's no one else here to share it with."

"So, you lose a little. Who gives a shit, right? Money comes and money goes. The secret is you just got to keep more coming than going."

"It's a lot more than that and I lost more than a little. Think about it. You know me better. I don't ever bet small."

She scratched my back a little more. "Cerrio," she said softly. "I know you blame yourself for all of Chevy's problems. But that's a lot to carry on your shoulders and it's just not fair."

I shook my head. "You have the luxury of saying that because you just don't understand."

"I understand a grown woman makes her own decisions. I understand that you didn't get beside yourself and make that waitress fall down earlier. Did you?"

I narrowed my eyes. "How do you know about that?"

She tsked. "Cerrio, when they say Diva Much did something around here everyone knows who that is. Do you know that Hawaiian girl fractured her wrist?"

"Jesus, it's like the more this boat stays out on the water the more everything just gets worse and worse. My best suit is ruined. Chevy's drunk all the time. Some girl is walking around with a brace on her hand. This trip was supposed to put us on track. Instead it's been one, long, floating, fucking headache. I'm over it."

"Sounds like it's a lot worse than you thought."

I jumped up off the stool full of piss and vinegar. "You want your money back? Is that what this is? You don't got to waste energy trying to be likeable, Chocolate. Come on up to the room so I can give it to you now and you'll have plenty of time to stay the fuck out my face."

"Easy tiger, that's not what I want at all. I'm just here to help. Honestly, I thought you would have figured that out by now. After all, I don't ever come around empty handed now do I?"

"Then, why are you here?" I growled.

She stood up, face creased with a plot "I have a proposition for you."

"What?"

"Getting some of your money back, that's what. There's a different kind of poker game going on around here with much better odds for you."

"How much better?"

"A lot better. And no stresses like down here on the floor."

Here I was, about to go down the rabbit hole. Funny how you got to call for help, call your mama, call on your conscience and just hope for an answer. But call on the something sinister and bam, the wait time is instant.

"Where's the game?" I asked.

She tossed some Chinese weave back over a shoulder. "It's not here. The game is private. Kind of an invite only thing. I can get us in, don't worry about that, the rest is up to you."

I stared at her with a look so full of malice it couldn't be separated. "I'm not in the mood, woman. If this is bullshit I promise you won't like me."

"Name a time I've been on bullshit, Cerrio. Just one. You call it and I'll give you whatever you want. Pussy. Money. My dog. Anything. All you got to do is come up with something."

When I couldn't answer she said, "I thought so."

The evidence didn't lie, Chocolate's case was solid. She was her true self and she never, ever played games and she hadn't once come up to me with her palm open.

She set her full drink down for a waitress to pick up on their next stroll. "Do you remember the signals we used to use at Chucky's?"

"Of course I do."

"Alright then. The money's guaranteed."

"Oh yeah, like that?"

"Goddamn right. Just like that."

"Well, are you going to lead the way or just stand there and talk me to death?"

"Now, that's the Cerrio I know." She smiled and I swear to God a chill went up my spine.

Turns out we didn't need any signals. Sugar Bares finest took us to a suite that looked a lot like mine where the gambling was casual not professional and losing big was just a way to get along. A white bobbysoxer answered the door showing the sides of her breasts in a tank top barely big enough for an American Girl doll. She had the same face my aunt always wears when Socks comes around, some razor-sharp look of deep seated suspicion.

Chocolate pulled a fat envelope from her purse that looked just like the one hidden up in duffel with the small shield in the top corner. Call that our passkey. When the white girl saw it she slid to the side with a toothy grin like we were all old friends.

Inside was dark, like back alley in the city and bloody horror movies type of dark. A lamp in the corner threw barely enough light to reach the ceiling. Squeezing my eyes into thin slits I could see this suite was a step above the one Chevy sprang for. It was in the background and foreground, a bigger television and a couch instead of a loveseat, a kitchenette where no one made dinner. The whole spread was a status symbol, all of it was extra like a top snap on a winter coat that zipped to the neck.

The white girl brought out a wide bottom bottle that said Chianti across the label. I watched her chest bounce underneath the ribbed tank top as she carried it over to two men sitting at a table clenching cigars between their teeth. I recognized them through the piss poor light, the surgeon and the banker who made a splash behind the velvet rope in the lounge last night. As smoke lifted up to a fire alarm with wires hanging down telling about the time when they stood on a chair and tore the batteries out Chocolate made introductions.

"Y'all, this is my friend. The one I talked about before. You remember?"

The heaviest man took the wet end of his cigar out and blew a cloud. "Is he going to be joining us?"

"Just for the game," she replied.

"Good to meet ya, I'm Phil." He pointed to the one who had to be a surgeon because his fingers were like talons. "And this is Jared."

Money echoed behind their names and when I moved in to shake hands I saw figures running up.

Jared nodded towards Chocolate. "So, uh, Rita. Does your friend have a name too?"

She shrugged. "Ask him yourself."

The white girl lit up. "Oh, I bet it's something exotic."

Phil wiped his face with a thick palm. "Show some respect, Tabitha. This guy's not a fucking exhibit."

"Relax, nobody's treating him wrong. I just think that if I had to guess his name it would have to be somethin' unique."

"You're acting like he's a side show."

I sat down in the empty chair already pulled up. "It's cool. Go ahead, take a guess what my name is."

Tabitha leaned in until her chest was resting on the table. She was a wilting flower, still attractive these days but in a year or three she would wake up with the power to dazzle in her rearview. She looked at me close like I was a gem and her the appraiser. "Is it Muhammad?"

I blinked at her. "Wow, on the very first try? You're good."

She pumped her fist. "I knew it. I used to date a Muhammad. Oh, he was such an angel too."

"I bet he said the same thing about you."

Chocolate made a noise like spit on a grill. Tabitha ignored it and smiled at her memories. "What didn't that man say? He adored me."

Phil snickered. "If he loved you so much then how come you're here with us instead of wherever the hell he's at?"

The wilting flower leaned back with a cigarette between two fingers. "For your information we were very much in love. He just couldn't bring me home because his family is Muslim. But I would have converted if the price was right."

Something sincere rang out about her story. Not just the confession of a price on her faith but the love she knew once upon a time in a past life. It made me wonder how everything fell so far apart. How did she get here? Would she even speak the truth about it if I asked because I know there are some things you just have to lie about. Not for appearances but because the truth is exactly what you want to forget.

I passed the cards around. Tabitha took a hand too. Chocolate walked around the table behind me to find a place to sit. For the once it seemed like she was okay to play the background and let this white girl with the Jersey accent suck up all the attention. She might have wanted less focus but I still knew who to keep my eyes on.

She was right on one point, all the anxiety that was so extra thick in the casino didn't exist right here. Things were more than casual, they were phenomenally easy, child's play. No stresses in the least, not even a ghost of pressure. Not even a small phantom. I bet on bad hands and good hands with cash from the envelope Chocolate flashed at the door and won every single time. It felt like a miracle with no controversy and if we'd played all night I could have won Chevy a new house.

Things were pretty. I pulled the sleeve back on my wrist to see how much time I had to work and when I looked back up Jared had Tabitha's nipple between his teeth. The white girl held a freshly lit cigarette, with her other hand she pushed the party boy's head deeper into her chest. Phil wasn't playing odd man out. He had his nonsmoking hand down her jeans brushing over the short hairs on her pussy. Her head went back and she blew smoke to the ceiling when he slipped a finger in. I watched him smoke the cigar while he played with her, then he did the Bill Clinton thing and wiped it between her lips before taking another deep drag. Phil wasn't talking about the damp Cuban when he asked if I wanted some.

Tabitha wasn't my type, too pale and too thin. But even with just the little light in the corner I could still see tan lines running north to south on those alabaster C-cups. The girl from Jersey snapped her eyes across the table and gave me the most pleading look and I knew she was seeing me as her old lover, Muhammad. In the darkness it was hard to measure how much she could really see our differences. You know they say we all look alike. I couldn't read her thoughts but I admit being on the verge, about to break my own rules and forget myself and my types and affinities maybe just to have a good time when Chocolate suddenly stood up and said, "Muhammad just came to play cards."

The whole room snapped out of it and Philip cleared his throat. "Sorry, Rita. Guess I must have forgot what you said before."

"It's okay. I'll help you remember."

Tabitha stayed unfazed. She let her titties hang out and sucked on the menthol some more. "Come on, let's go to the room. We'll be a lot more comfortable with the bed in there."

She shot one more look on the way back. A last chance glance over her shoulder that might haunt me in my sleep. It didn't linger long before the tricks had her crowded in one of the suites bedrooms with a train of tobacco smoke rolling right behind them.

Chocolate stepped up and got in my face. Hands on hips. Nose so close to mine we were almost Eskimo kissing. "Don't do anything," she hissed.

I heard a little music drifting out of the bedroom. "And just what do you think I'm going to do with everybody sweating naked behind that door?"

"I mean it, Cerrio. Don't eat nothing. Don't drink nothing. If you get hungry find something in the mini bar. The key is right there on top." She took one hand off her hip and touched my collar. "Be back in just a bit, okay?"

"Is it really gonna be that fast?"

"This is me we're talking about. I'm here for a good time, not a long time."

Do me a favor when I die. Don't prop me up in a eulogy with all that flowery talk about how I was a good son or a great nephew. That canned shit is really disgusting. Tell the truth and talk about the time when I went on a cruise, chaperoned an aggressive fly girl to a very private party and drank a bunch of pocket-size bottles of expensive hot shot Perrier while she made a living because it was all free and I could. And maybe leave out the part about how I lost my old lady's fortune forty minutes before all that. People can read that in the fine print.

CHAPTER 35

FEVER WATER

Chocolate came back out of the bedroom looking pristine, not a hair out of place or a smudge in her makeup. The best make it look easy but somehow she made it look like nothing ever happened. A shadow moved over to the door and closed it behind her with a soft click. That sound had something final to it like the latch was saying this evening was really over.

She swung her wide hips all the way to the coffee table before halting in front of my line up of empty designer water bottles. "You ready?"

"Ready as I'm gonna get," I told her.

She made a noise halfway between a grunt and a three ring pool losing air. "I swear you are so stupid sometimes."

"I think late as it is, I can be as stupid as I want. Where's your protégé, Tabitha?"

"Shutup, that's not my protégé."

"Whoa, take it easy. I'm just making sure there's no loose ends we got to worry about."

"So, you're worried about her now?"

"Well, what if I was?"

"Then, you're really an idiot because I can guarantee she damn sure ain't worried about you."

I rose up off the sofa. An irritated Chocolate stopped me with a finger held out to the collection of bottles and club cracker wrappers strewn across the glass coffee table. "Are you going to clean up your mess?" I shook my head and she shrugged her shoulders like none of it mattered anyway because she already got paid for the time.

On a last look back I saw the bedroom door crack open again. I didn't need to ask who was spying. A sense of intuition told me the truth. Tabitha had her eyes on me on the way out which made my hostess Chocolate all wrong about the Jersey girl's position of concern. I almost told her so out in the hall just to get a rise but the blinding rush of light stunned me into forgetting.

"Man, it's bright out here."

She snickered cruelly. "You act like you just jumped out of a coffin."

"Shit, maybe I did. I feel like a vampire at dawn."

"Quit being like that."

"Like what?"

"Soft," she spat.

I opened my eyes letting the bulbs dilate my pupils into periods. "Are you okay? Seriously. I'm asking for real."

"What is that supposed to mean?"

"It means you're acting like I did something to you except I know for sure I didn't. So, maybe somebody..." I nodded to the suite where we just came out of. "Maybe somebody in there really did do something. And you know me, I'll handle it any way you want. So, tell me now or forever hold your peace."

She stopped walking. "Is that all it takes to get you in your feelings? A little four letter word most people use to describe pillows. Wow, usually I can't get a man riled up like that unless I cut a minute off his lap dance."

"You know what? Fuck you. It's too late for this shit. I'm going back down to my room."

She reached out and put a hand on my arm. "Now, hold on. Is that really how you gon' treat a girl who's given you an envelope of cash for a second time today?"

"Looks that way don't it?"

"Don't get brittle, Cerrio. For your information nothing happened in there."

"That's got to be a lie."

"See, now you hurt my feelings. We been through this before. Mama don't play games." She glared at me. "I want you to tell the truth. Did you eat or drink anything out in the open while I was working?"

"Why are you worried about what I do?"

"Because Tabitha has herpes. That's why."

I stepped back. "And you-?"

"Never touched her. I was just in the bedroom working the camera while the other three played their parts."

"How come you didn't say anything to those suit and tie tricks? Let'em know what they were getting into at least?"

"Well, honestly I would have but there's this thing about me. I like to get paid. And I wouldn't have made a dime if they knew. Do you feel a little sorry for them?"

I looked back at the room like a good answer would rush out any minute. "I don't know."

"Don't know what?"

"No one ever felt sorry for me. If the shoe was on the other foot they probably wouldn't care. They'd probably laugh about it."

"But look at you," said Chocolate. "You're not laughing because you're not the same. If you were then I'd have to treat you just like I treat them. See, you thought I was being pushy when I told you not to do anything. Don't drink and don't eat was like giving you an ultimatum. You hated me and that's okay because now here we are. Paid and clean as virgins." She took my elbow. "Now come on, treat a girl solid and walk me back up to my cabin."

What else could I do? In the end my choices were slimmer than a broke ho's coin purse because it's not everyday someone saves me from a disease without a cure. Imagine bringing herpes back to Chevy. She drinks a beer after me or puts the coke straw up her nose and next morning her face bubbles up like a cauldron. No more three ways. I could say goodbye to Bandy cheeking me at the breakfast table while my baby bounces around making topless grits.

That's a nuclear meltdown. Not like the arguments we have on the regular. Those spicy disputes complimented the craziness our home got built on. They would always be with us and we could always recover but this, no this was born and bred murder. And who could ever blame her?

Unless Chocolate was lying. Since I first met her she had led me on just once in the club about a fake two for one and that was all by Chevy's motivation. Of course, that didn't mean much. The capabilities to defraud were living right there under the surface like a catfish in a pond. I saw it in her side profile while we stood still in front of the elevators. The universe in those eyes, the hollow of her throat begging for a taste, the curve of her bottom lip bending down in a perfect horseshoe shape.

She was cold as November nights. The type to freeze your heart and then shatter it with a hammer. But her room on the boat was like an oven. When she cracked the entrance open a thick heat wave billowed out like we were playing by a Brazilian blast furnace.

"Want to come in?"

I checked my watch, the little hand pointing northeast meant it was a quarter to two. "Nah, it's late. Everybody has to get up early tomorrow. Plus, you got it cooking in there."

"Says the man who makes his living at all hours of the night in the North Carolina heat."

"Are you trying to guilt trip me to come inside?"

"Never. I just want to know what it is I'm supposed to tell Franky. You know he loves seeing you."

"Franky, is a dog. And by the way you got it cooking in there probably a sautéed one by now."

"He likes it like that. Franky's anemic. Poor baby can't stand the cold. His thing shrivels up like this." She held her fingers up a hair apart. "And then he curls in a little ball right beside me on the bed."

"An anemic dog and a friend with warts. Damn, woman you know how to pick up the misfits running around."

"Uh-huh, and what does that say about you?"

Chocolate was smarmy and I like that about a woman. If the skin is dark then the tongue is silver but the game is free. All you have to do is soak it up like a sponge. But when the game is too good, too pure, too resonant, too rhapsodizing and the riddles are too hard to figure out then that's when the hating sets in. That's where we were. She was so clever that the innovation made me sick. I wanted to hate her but that ugly feeling just couldn't be reached. I couldn't despise the way she smashed my average intelligence so poetically because I'm a sucker for sass.

I ended up stepping into her lair with that paradox dangling like a crucifix hanging at the end of a rosary. Soon as the door was closed sweat started brewing underneath my collar. Franky came racing out of his bathroom prison like a wild stallion. For a short dog he was impressive, perfect stride, all four legs slicing through the air at once as he hit the corner. I watched him reach full speed and then skid at my feet and jump up on my legs.

His paws scraped me, wet nose inhaling everything. I liked Franky. He was pure and even if he was anemic then that was okay with me because at least he kept it honest. The dog liked what he liked and rolled up in a ball when he didn't like it because he had no idea of how to hide anything.

I scratched him behind the ears until his eyes shut. "You know, I think maybe this dog really likes me. He ain't bit me or nothing yet."

"I told you!" Chocolate shouted from the bathroom.

"I never had a dog. Chevy did. When we were kids her daddy bought this doberman with a pointy head that hated me. All he ate was chicken scraps and bones and shit. I think that's what made him mean. Wrong diet."

"I give Franky baby a little piece of bologna when he's good sometimes."

"How much is a little piece?"

"Oh, I don't know. Like a slice. Bring him here I'll show you."

I scooped the terrier up in my arms. When we started walking to the bathroom he gave me that look like the man in the mirror in solitary confinement.

"No, I don't think I can do it. Franky looks like he's going to cry."

Chocolate laughed. "I thought you said 'he was just a dog'."

"Yeah, but...this ain't right. I feel like a guard taking him back to his cell. You should see him. His eyes are begging me for mercy."

"Just bring him here. He'll be fine once he eats."

I apologized to the dog staring up at me and made a promise that if he did get locked in the bathroom again, I'd let him out ASAP. Franky licked my hand to make our deal official while Chocolate kept on rushing us. "Bring him in here!" she yelled. I turned around to go back to her and when I rounded the corner still hot from fresh canine tracks the dog flopped to the floor.

Somewhere during our conversation the woman had lost all her clothes. The only thing that stayed on were the heels and the effect was enthralling just like it was supposed to be. In the strip club under dim lights and deep in the trick's basement in her bra I saw a body that never quit. Looking back now I realized those were demonstrations, fantasy field trips. Maybe those moments might have even been a little bit cruel but now here was the feature presentation.

She had her hair up, breasts out, legs spread shoulder width apart in a pyramid. At the top of it was a glistening wet spot like a triangle and right above that were two wide strips of neat black hair trimmed in the perfect shape of a V. You could build a nation between those thighs or maybe destroy one.

Chocolate did that thing again where she put a hand on each hip, then she arched her back and inhaled deep pushing two heavy D-cups up and out. Every crease, every fold, every line underneath both girls smoothed away like magic as they lifted a little higher. I didn't ask what she was doing. That type of question was just flat out stupid. Call it all out seduction. Overt type. No restraints. I knew I was supposed to take charge here but everything I thought to do felt wrong one way or the other. She let me soak her up, just standing there showing off watching my adrenaline rise while those two chocolate chip nipples hardened into pure hedonism.

She cocked her head to the side and started talking like this was all normal. Like we had been together for years and being naked in front of each other was something we did everyday.

"Remember, Judy? That girl I took back home to Tennessee? Her grandma was so happy to see her she baked me a cake."

I cleared my throat. "Lemme guess. Red velvet?"

"Mm-hmm, with cream cheese icing on top. I still got a little back at the house for you."

"Sounds like a long journey. You get the cake, bring it back. Then, I get all the leftovers. Maybe it's all just bullshit. Maybe you went straight to Myrtle Beach and left Judy at the shelter."

"Don't get ahead of yourself. I never said you get all of the leftovers. Maybe just a slice like how I give Franky his bologna treats."

I had forgotten all about the dog. Now, I just hoped his stubby legs weren't broken from being dropped to the floor.

"Anyway, I never thanked you for saving her."

"True, but I don't know why we're talking about Judy right now."

She moved in to close the gap between us. "We're not. I'm talking about gratitude. I never actually said 'thank you Cerrio for rescuing the little girl'. Or getting Bandy out of that house I sent her to. It's not that I forgot. Those things you just can't put into words and you know I know better than anyone that talk is cheap."

"And everything else costs."

She moved again, this time so close I could feel the tips of her nipples rubbing against my shirt.

"You pay bitches more than anybody and I don't really think that's fair."

"Are you an agent of fairness?" I asked.

"Maybe not," she replied. "But I do know how to show my appreciation."

Her room had a shower, the kind with a sliding glass door but no bathtub. That's where we sinned. With the idea being that when it was all done and over with the scalding water would wash away our transgressions.

In the beginning I went fast. Fueled by the hot steam and making her wet ass cheeks ripple I thrusted hard. Chocolate is such a pro she never even took the heels off. That extra height put the bottom of her wet sex right under my manhood and when she slid back a brand-new sensation came to life.

Nerves I didn't know about rejoiced, some screamed some sang, some were warm, a few were liquid. None of them were choosy, though. We all just wanted more and Chocolate gave. She threw back with fury, smacking over and over again with some insane, violent energy. Bucking those wide hips so that every new collision was more powerful than the last. I put both hands behind me on the shower rail, gripped hard and stayed rigid. Do your worst I told her, and the girl didn't hate me for it. She had no pause, zero retreat, no reset. Chocolate was built for this, back flexing, shoulders rolling, little beads of hydration mixed with sweat cruising off both sides of her body until they careened off her pole lats and died happily in the drain.

For her this wasn't just fucking. This was competition. She wanted to know what I was made of. Whether I could take everything she had to give or if I was just another flash in the night with a hard dick and no stamina. She didn't want a quick finish, she wanted war. She fought with her body, hammering relentlessly with that swift, lethal weapon at the bottom of her back like a demon was being worked out under the long boat's shower.

I held on tight and watched the show. Every tendon in my body straining from the ones in my knuckles to the arches of my feet. One moment I was completely swallowed up inside her and then the next my manhood reappeared like he was pulling out of a garage. My shaft swelled until it hurt and somehow we were still greedy. We wanted more, we wanted to dig and show off and prove something important.

I took my hands off the safety rail and put them on the body assaulting me, spread the cheeks of my female assailant wide enough so that tiny bubbles came through the middle to stream down around her lips and plunged in deep. Chocolate gasped. This was no professional act, I really hurt her that good. She liked me driving hard, splashing burning hot water up her naked back, smacking flesh against flesh in this twisted, forbidden pleasure.

It was sinister chemistry that put me and the baddest of the night in sync this way. All those trips to Chucky's, throwing signals and cheating people and robbing them blind had built up a fire between us that was half force, half anger and all the way out of control. It would never matter that it really hadn't happened on purpose, no one would care that it shouldn't have went down like this in the first place. All that mattered was that she knew what I wanted and I, unlike other men, understood what made a real dancer's blood run hot.

The mirror brought it home. I looked up and saw the reflection of her Hershey kiss nipples pressed impossibly flat against the shower glass and everything around them fogged in a circle like they were panting with us in the throes of lust and I couldn't last a second after that. Nobody could. Chocolate caught my drift coming back one more time and clenched around me for the photo finish. Nothing got left behind, all I had went in her piping hot like tea from a fresh kettle. A little backfired and I watched it drip down her thigh. She laughed, swiped it away, then rinsed her fine fingers under the shower that had grown tepid in our sins and asked me to pass the soap.

C H A P T E R **36**

LONELY VALIDATION

Life is too short. So, don't go killing yourself with needless regrets. That's something Chitara James used to say in life every week if not every day. Even though her husband wasn't always right or good to her or even what you might call loveable she still never stepped out with another man. Of course all that was a long time ago, before marital drama became people's entertainment. Back when lovers and others kept their dirty laundry much closer to the sheets. But in this era of shade strife is the stuff of good prime time TV and these days Chitara James brand of loyalty is what the new generation calls old school.

Ferris was a winner in every category. Chevy didn't think Cerrio was completely the opposite like forward to reverse but a smart girl knows good potential when it's smiling down right in her face. He had the fundamentals, the looks, the money, the charisma. If she wanted to do a web search of the perfect man a picture of Mr. Ferris Pinckney out of Savannah, Georgia would probably pop up on her phone.

But what about the rest? A handsome face on an open deck at midnight is the sweet stuff filling up the pages in a romance novel. But when it was all over there was still only going to be one LaDecerrio Lloyd. Chevy knew Ferris's hands couldn't navigate her body the way Cerrio's did. He wouldn't kiss her feet spontaneously on the bed or buy her the right lotions that mixed perfectly with her body scent. Clothed in a slice of moonlight the slick talking businessman had all right stuff but he simply hadn't put the time in.

Cerrio wasn't just her man, not just the line she was stuck to or the shade she couldn't get out from under. He was the validation of her wonder years like the rings inside a tree trunk. It had taken a long time for him to get to live inside her like that and she wasn't ready to throw all of it away in one hot night.

Horny didn't have a damn thing to do with it. She was ready, sex was everywhere, men were a dime a dozen. Even the good looking ones. Then, when the fun was over all that slick rap on the deck would devolve into something less sentimental. Unless Chevy got real lucky and Ferris left right after he blew the pillow talk would decline into some unspirited chatter about all the business down at the docks.

She ached for her longtime lover, just thinking about Cerrio made her warm inside. She liked his game, his foreplay. When they were naked he manipulated her hormones good when he drew himself so close that the head was just a whisper away from her southern lips. Then, he would brush the mushroom tip over her and make her whole body shiver like it was cold inside.

Cerrio didn't always play fair but Chevy liked that too. She recalled plenty of nights getting dizzy from being flipped over so fast. He liked to spread her wide from behind, sometimes running his tongue south to north up the middle before dipping in her pudding and then plunging to the hilt. She touched herself while imaging hanging on to the comforter, face buried in a pillow, clutching the mattress for dear life as he broke her in half. She could almost taste the bedsheets and the stars behind her eyelids were clashing together like supernovas.

Right before the end she quit. It wasn't a strain on the will, her fingers came off automatically because Chevy knew she didn't want to be alone in the moment. She had flew solo before but these times were too special. She would wait all night to share the best part of herself with the only one who had really earned it.

✦ 344 ✦

CHAPTER 37

TWO DEATHS

For the first time in her whole life Bandy felt like a giant. On stage at The Rose Petal singing in front of all those strangers she grew into the new her. Reinventing yourself isn't easy. The old Bandanna had to die in a dilapidated yellow house on a sizzling afternoon with her face torn half apart. After that there was a vacuum that needed to be filled with something big that got found in the audience every time they shouted their love up to her.

Bandanna Flowers was signature, the bronze-skinned girl with the gold in her mouth donning luxurious evening dresses didn't have any parallels running beside her. Being one in a million is why the crowd couldn't get enough. No how much she gave, even when she thought she was stale, they still wanted more.

Tonight, she had put on an act with another small time singer from Mobile, Alabama named Lacey. They danced a few high leg kicks on the boat's stage with a song on their lips like a couple of real showgirls from Vegas. It wasn't anything complicated but together they were brilliant. Bandy and Lacey dazzled a full house in front of a curtain swimming with every color from violet to aqua blue like a hologram. The music still made the show but their chemistry was the match that lit the fire. Lacey had a little height on Bandy, three or four inches which somehow made them a perfect match when they danced. After it was over the two women hugged breathlessly in front of a raging audience throwing roses and the Lacey's manager approached Bandy with an offer to do a show on land.

It meant so much to be singing and dancing and living this dream. Bandy had arrived and she was exactly where she wanted to be, on that steep ascent to becoming premiere. But Taneesha had fear in her heart. "Things change," she said. "People change and ideas change. So why wouldn't you?"

At the end of the night, when the show had ended and the lights weren't shining anymore. After Bandy had peeled off her dress and scrubbed all the makeup away they held each other tight in their cozy cabin. The little singer put her arms around Taneesha's waist and explained why her loyalty could never waiver. Because the people in this world who had seen her go from casual to classy, from stripper to a star, were the only ones she had who ever meant anything because she knew she really meant something to them. Without them Bandanna Flowers was just a barefoot lesbian from the North Carolina backwoods. That was especially true for Cerrio, without him there would be no singing Bandy, quite possibly no Bandy at all.

Chevy waited up for me like she wanted to make love. A slow paced romance movie played on the big screen. I watched it for a minute picking out the actors who were all big shit in the nineties and had fallen off years ago. A lucky few moved on from screen careers to go bury their head in the sand somewhere out in Hollywood. I was thinking about how easy it must be to get lost forever in the rolling landscape of Beverly Hills when she asked how much I had won downstairs.

I shrugged. "Couple hundred. Nothing major."

"You want to buy a bag? Those waiters are still up on the fourth floor."

"Not tonight. I'm too tired to jam." I threw the key card on the dresser. "You know that waitress girl fractured her wrist?"

Chevy stayed still next to a makeshift table she had built out of pillows. If I seem colder than the meat and cheese platter she ordered up from room service it's not because she found me this way. I talked myself into it coming back down from Chocolate's room. My girl never told me how she got that Mercedes, that was her secret and now I had mine. I sat at the foot of the bed unbuttoning my shirt cuffs with a somber attitude, felt fingers running up my back and heard the mattress springs groan as she got to her knees behind me. Next those hands were on my shoulders pulling away the shirt. Chevy kissed my neck with lips just barely brushing the skin like a stone skipping water. I held her in abeyance until the sweet breath landed in my ear, until that first wave of testosterone washed over me but then I couldn't take it any further.

I gave her a little stiff arm and she looked at me strange. This was something new. Never before in my life have I been able to resist Chevy James, not when we were kids, not at Sugar Bares, not even when her daddy told me he had a .22 shotgun with red shells that had my name written up and down the sides. Since forever she has always been the woman of charms but now the charmer stared down wondering if her spell had worn off.

"My bad," I said. "It's been a long night, baby. Shit, what am I saying? It's been a long weekend. Long as kitchen ingredients."

"Yeah, I guess it really must have been if you're turning me down." She sat back.

"Come on, it's like three in the morning. I'm a man not a robot."

"Fine, nobody's pushing you. Wouldn't want to shave a minute off your sleep." She kicked her pillow table apart. "Anyway, Socks called again."

I slid my eyes over to her. "What'd he tell you?"

"That's a strange way to ask about a phone call. All he said is that he stills needs you. I don't know what that means, though."

"Neither do I."

She set the meat and cheese platter down on the floor. "I know you're lying but I still think it's amazing the way people cling to you. Somehow everybody seems to find a path in your footsteps."

"Your mama told me that I'm like a tour guide in a corn maze."

"I believe it. Because I'm the one who told her first."

I didn't hide my surprise. "And you never told me?"

"Honestly, there's a lot of things I never told you. Some stuff you're just not always ready for. You know, wrong place, wrong time. All that sort of thing."

"What about now?"

She laid her head down next to me. "Well, now you're all I've got."

I tried to swallow down my guilt but it just wouldn't go. The more I forced everything roiling inside to settle the more all of it fought back. The battle lasted all the way into my sleep. Past the border of consciousness clear on to the other side where dreams build up so you can climb back down them again and hopefully make it home with something half pleasant to measure real life against.

The man who lost everything came back again. He stood closer to me this time, almost near enough to touch but there were too many levels of pain to make out his face. Only the scarcest hint of a person came through the fog of my dream, barely enough to know who I had in sight. Any features like a nose or a chin I would have given my life to see. I don't know why it was so important to know him just like I don't know why sometimes these visions are so real that I can feel the panic. Still, everything I could see amounted to nothing, just a man on the moon peeking at me behind dusky storm clouds.

❖ ❖ ❖

Late one afternoon when Cerrio was using Taneesha's phone to sell twenties either Judy or her grandmother called just to tell him thank you. Taneesha was usually wary of drugs and giving her phone number out like a business card. When people asked she had the word no in her mouth like a sour capsule, ready to bite down and spit it out at any given request but this situation was frail. Saving her beau had given Cerrio an advantage if not a right to make her cancel that acquired habit of inhibition.

He needed the phone for everything because his got destroyed in the same shootout that saved Bandy's life. And what other answer do you give a man fresh off rescuing the key to your tender, loving heart? In a slick reversal Taneesha always told Cerrio yes. Now here she was slam in the middle of the teen girl's story like a bookmark.

Judy's grandma called Taneesha at four o' clock in the morning. The girl had run away again and of course no one could find her. Even if there was some chance of tracking down a runaway foxy enough to cross state lines the boat hadn't come in yet so there was nothing she could do, and even after it did the old lady would still be on her own because Neesha did not know how to rescue people the same way LaDecerrio did.

She had never even seen Judy's face but she had heard the story and absorbed the details and knew right away that grandma's baby wasn't built for this life. No body for the pole, not enough brutality for the streets. That's half the reason Taneesha hung up, she didn't want to think about the nasty business of Judy either sinking or swimming. The other half was she just didn't have the energy to explain the longer truth. Judy was never going to give up her baby, not to a foster home or a brick clinic on the corner. Without ever seeing her it was clear to Neesha that the girl needed love the way fire needs air and that tall order of motherhood was going to be her saving grace.

She rolled over trying to kill any second thoughts and left the phone off the hook. For a million reasons written down in the gospel no one could tell grandma a thing. It was a sin to be with child just like it was a sin to get rid of one. Still, everybody has to have faith in something. For Judy it was going to have to be all in herself, for Taneesha everything she believed was already scribed deep in the walls of her own intrepidness. That young girl's pregnancy was a sign, one that Neesha herself had once been a part of before.

Even as the sun began to creep over the ocean she flipped on her back still chasing sleep. Trying focus on a tiredness already sabotaged just to blank out the memories of a time before when she had a roommate that wasn't also a lover. She rolled over on the mattress wide awake thinking about a girl who had a son named Jermaine. He was a beautiful boy, alive and crying with so much energy and completely the opposite of the stillborn some masked doctor pulled out of Taneesha's body at the hospital just a few months later like a chopped off tumor.

In the beginning the roommate felt sorry for her and then she felt awkward right before she left to go raise that tiny boy of hers with two large aunts up in New York. Those days hurt, every morning waking up to a fresh refill of agony. The pain slipped from that dogged crush of loneliness punctuated by an empty house to the stabbing feeling that maybe her womb had somehow gone rotten. Neesha had done everything not to relive anymore of that grief even just for a moment and now here it was jumping out of the darkness like a mugger with a switchblade.

Even in a half perfect universe she would have gone back to sleep before the recollections crippled all chances. Except perfection is a concept made up only after the world became broken. Taneesha laid there staring up at the ceiling while Bandy snored softly beneath the covers. She blinked and thought about what it would be like to be pregnant again. Hard to do without the touch of a man but there was somebody out there who's child was about to be lost real soon just like hers was.

That wicked understanding made a gateway for more bitter thoughts. She tried to shake them off but they stuck fast like windblown ashes on a roof. Eventually the afflictions would build a pyramid stretching across her chest with enough square footage to suffocate her in slow motion. That hadn't happened in a real long time and right now wasn't going to be a brand-new episode.

Taneesha got out of bed wrapped tight in a casino boat robe that was going home with her after the trip. Tiptoeing lightly to the window where the waves extended out for endless miles she anticipated the outline of the ocean. On the way there she caught the feeling of stone butterflies clamoring around in her stomach. She braced to see someone struggling on the water. A son, a daughter, a nephew or a niece, battling for a last suck of air, fighting with everything for a simple breath. This wasn't some sick, angry desire to witness a fleeting death, she just wanted to be there in time to save the child.

Her feet shuffled faster now, hurrying with less concern about making too much noise she closed in on the glass facing out to the water. When she got there no young, dying swimmer waved a hand above his head like lifeguards might save him. Nobody's daughter or son fought hard against the mighty Atlantic in a desperate attempt to fight for his or her life. In fact, the ocean was east now because they were back on the Savannah river and all of it was laid out like normal. Undisturbed with millions of glittering ripples rising to collapse again just like they always did in the first hours of the day.

CHAPTER 38

RENEGADE PLAN

Sleep was rushed, when I woke up thick storm clouds had gathered outside and Chevy was standing right over the top of me holding the cordless telephone. "Socks wants to talk you." I wiped both eyes with the heels of my hands and said, "tell him to call back." Before I could roll over she chucked the receiver on top of my chest and marched off to the bathroom in a long shirt brushing the skin right above the backs of her knees. She never looked back, just locked the door and cut the shower on. I heard the water hiss like cold bacon laying down on a skillet.

I wonder if she knew already. The day had barely begun. Nobody had a chance to break the news yet even if they really wanted to. Chevy wasn't stupid, though. The girl made it further in school than I ever did. Maybe she was in there working on her payback already. I imagined that trim naked body standing there reaching over the wall of the tub to adjust the faucet knobs and a master plan brewing up in that big brain. For a minute I forgot about the phone and worked to think up an alibi. The cabin's cordless laid there right above my lungs just like the fog that wouldn't lift in my dream. I felt no pressure to move it, the thing could hang with me all day and I never would have noticed if Socks hadn't opened his mouth and said, "cut the bullshit and get that ass out of bed already."

I almost fired back with a better curse. Except it's bad to wake up and waste energy right out the gate. So, instead I grabbed the phone and sat up with my feet on the floor.

"What's the big emergency that you been blowing me up all weekend?"

"Easy brother, I just been worried. Chevy tells me you're mister high society down there on the water."

In the bathroom the shower cut off. The sudden hush blew up across the suite and when I looked at the bottom of the door two dark shadows showed where a pair of feet were blocking out the light. I knew on instinct that a nosy ear was being pushed up right against the crack listening for disclosure so I talked a little louder in the phone.

"Actually we're on the river, brother. And right now the old lady is fishing."

"I see," said Socks. "And is she catching anything?"

"No, the tide keeps going in and out and the water's too shallow right now."

"Too shallow or too rich?"

"What do you think?"

"I think you're shoveling shit. So, what about you? How's my brother doing? You still ill with me?"

"Oh, you mean because you knocked me out?"

"Man, don't put that on me. I mighta popped you one but I didn't knock you out. That's the drugs messing with your brain."

"Fuck you."

In one smooth motion I switched phone ears. At the same time Chevy perked up on her tippy toes inside the bathroom.

"Where you at right now?"

"Dez's house. I'm here watching my nephew until noon."

"She still working on that tattoo?"

"No, but she could be if you need some time to break away from the ol' ball and chain."

"Take another session and tell her I said 'hello' while the gun is hot."

He cleared his throat. "What are we talking about, brother? An hour?"

I checked the clock on the nightstand. "Sure, that works."

"Fine, be ready to cooperate when you call back."

I said, "fuck you again." Then, Socks turned it around and told me to go fuck myself because I could get more pussy that way. Hateful as that was we weren't malevolent. It wasn't an issue to be incensed about, nothing to hold a grudge over. Sometimes brothers just fight each other. It's almost a must and from time to time when the powder is in her Chevy puts her hands on me too. It's less of a malicious thing and more of habit decreed from within like something hereditary. I mean, we're simply fighters because that's what's keeps us alive and fighting isn't tidy but it's in our nature. You can't cancel it so I saved myself the labor and hung up the phone and a minute later the shower came back to life.

Socks knew I wouldn't call back in an hour. My signature attribute is being chronically late. It's the reason I've never done well at all those nine-to-five jobs. The work ethic is great, it comes straight from Uncle Daya pouring molten hot metal at a foundry twelve hours a day. The clock hates me, though. Maybe you think a good supervisor would know how to give some and take some but most bosses really just want it all. They want you to be there on time, on the dot, so they can go hide in their office. I told the last one up at Costco to make me a promotion and then he could have the full package. Just pay me a little more and he could be invisible all goddamn day. Now I don't work anywhere anymore.

My brother picked up on the second ring and shot straight to the point. "I need you, man. I need you on this like a motherfucker."

"Calm down." I leaned back on the top deck railing. "Take it easy. You already got Chevy looking at me cross-eyed. She knows something's cooking. If I tell her it's a bank job she'll flash on me."

"True enough. So, don't tell her then."

"Small problem with that. Chevy ain't stupid. What am I gonna tell her when that big bag of money shows up in our kitchen?"

Socks grunted. "I never known you to to be the scary type. This is a hundred G's we're talking about. That kind of bread can buy you a lot of explanations."

"And if we get caught they won't take it easy on me. No first time felony breaks. My record is already too bad."

"Do you think the D.A. is going to see me as the lightweight? The one most likely to contribute to society?"

"No. I mean, I hope so but who knows?"

"What is it then? Tell me Cerrio, what does that stripper broad have to make you move on a heist that I don't?"

"You mean besides the T and A?"

"I thought you said she had a plan? What's obvious don't need to be asked."

I took my back off the rail and turned around to see barges floating on the river. "Besides the obvious thing she has, what's killing the vibe for me on this job is your crew. I don't know them from fucking Adam. And I can't take the kind of risk you're asking for with perfect strangers."

Socks thought about it silently. "So, you think they can't be trusted?"

"I think they're high risk. One of them is going to get nervous and shoot a teller for no reason. Some old lady behind the counter can't put the money in the bag fast enough and then, bam, they blow her head off. That's the death penalty for us, Socks."

"Fine then, they're out."

I almost dropped the phone. It should never have been that easy to make Socks flip. Sure, I'd made a good case but kicking two goons out of a six figure play isn't the same as dumping leftovers. Before I could get over the shock he was back in my ear. "Now, what's wrong?"

"To tell you the truth," I said. "It's a lot of things. And they don't all got to do with you either."

"Talk to me, brother."

I watched a seagull land on a trash barge and peck out his breakfast. "Look, I know Chevy told you a lot about our trip but she didn't tell you that I haven't paid for much of anything. Even the clothes I'm wearing. And believe me they're nice."

My shitty little problems didn't resonate. I could tell when Socks started heckling. "Goddamn, you sound just like one of those rich people bitching about bad caviar on their ten million dollar yachts. You wanna trade places with me? I got some real problems you can have."

"Let me finish. It ain't just me and Chevy cruising up the coast on a honeymoon. She brought her friends." I thought about Chocolate and stopped. "Actually, she only brought some of her friends. They put this whole trip together thinking I could win them a fortune on a boat with my card game."

"And let me guess. You been fucking up all their money and it didn't take long so you been spending most of your time lying about it."

"Gambling ain't the same on the water," I growled.

"It's got nothing to do with the water, brother. You just can't cheat your ass off in a real casino like you usually do it at home."

I sighed. "There's cameras everywhere. People watching me all the time. I can't get away with anything."

"Did it occur to you to maybe tell them the real truth about how you actually play before y'all packed your bags and took off down to Georgia?"

"Right now that's neither here nor there."

"True, it's way too late for honesty to save your ass now. Like or not brother that means you need a good payday soon as you get home."

"I don't know. It's pretty bad. Maybe not bad, though."

"Put a face on it."

I did a quick tally in my head. Counting everything including hair appointments, fancy alcohol and Chevy's room service receipts the number grew up fast.

"It's, uh, hard to say exactly what the damage is. Call it a rough forty bands."

Socks spit out his morning orange juice. "Did you say forty thousand dollars? Fuck Cerrio, how'd you let your feet slip off the fence like that?"

"I don't know. And Chevy don't know either. Her and the other girls think I been winning more than losing."

"Brother, this shit is fixin' to blow up in your face real soon."

"Faster than you think. We're coming home today. At eleven o' clock we're off this boat back on dry land and out to the interstate. If I can make it home tonight I think might be alright."

Socks sounded doubtful. "Probably not, but my couch is always open if you need it, brother. Whatever happens you won't be out on the street."

"It's all good. Aunt Denise still has my old room fixed up for me."

He was about to tell me something else but he barely got half a word out before a hard shove from behind made me drop the phone. I watched it tumble over and over again on a long drop down the side of the deck. When it splashed in the water there was a tiny sound that didn't even reach me.

I turned around to choke somebody but standing there with arms crossed and a look that dared me to do something was Chevy James, herself.

"You fucking liar," she hissed. "I heard everything. Forty thousand dollars! When were you going to tell me, Cerrio? Or did you really think you'd make it home with me before anybody noticed?"

I shook my head. "How can I tell you anything? Look at how you're acting right now. I only got that phone three days ago and I now I have to buy a new one because you're up here going crazy just like I told you not to when we first got on this boat."

She put a finger in my face. "Don't even try to turn this around on me! We been on the water all this weekend and you been fucking up the whole ride!"

"It wasn't on purpose. Cards are unpredictable. I told you that already. Ain't you been listening?"

"I listened good, Cerrio. To all of your lies. You're so full of shit it's disgusting. I don't even want to see you right now."

"Get lost, then."

"Is that how you talk to me after all the faith I've had in you?" She shoved me again. "Fuck you."

Before I could react a third little voice interrupted our madness. "Now, what's going on with you two?"

Both of us, Chevy first, then me, looked over to see Bandy standing there in a nightgown that swayed gently with the breeze. Together, we were all spaced apart in a perfect triangle The singing girl reminded me of a phantom with the satiny fabric billowing up and out like a ghost tail underneath the stone gray sky. Me, Neesha and Seville had all quit dressing up our second afternoon on the ocean but the star had her own way. She was still dipped in designer all the way down to her house slippers. Probably had something to do with performing. I mean, a top stage act can't just walk around like common folk do looking any old way even if it is first thing in the morning.

The hem went down to her ankles and whispered in the breeze. The rest of the gown was intricately decorated with a gold leaf pattern that looked busy wrapped up and down her slender figure. The whole thing screamed Dior but I didn't know for sure. If Chocolate were here right now she could call it out with no hesitation, that woman could eyeball fashion at a glance from fifty yards away.

"What is this?" she asked. "I thought y'all were good. We even made up proper. Instead, people are looking at you two through their windows while you scream at each other like animals."

I shook my head. "Don't take much guessing. You know who's out here raising hell."

Chevy smacked a fist inside her open palm. "He's been using us. Using us girl! Working me and you like we're his marks!"

"Don't even listen to her. She's putting a lot on a little."

"A little huh? Is that what you think about forty thousand dollars that I had to pick up off the floor? That it's just a drop in a bucket?"

Bandy blinked. "Forty thousand dollars?" She looked at me. "Cerrio, what's going on?"

I sighed. "Look, the simple version is I lost. The game got away from me and the truth is I didn't know how tell anybody. It's not easy to break your heart."

Chevy laughed humorlessly. "Now, he wants to talk about the truth."

Bandy touched a string of pearls hanging from her neck. "Maybe he just needs more time, Chev. He can figure it out if we stay a little longer."

The other woman almost fell over. "You want to stay so he can give away more of our money?! Huh-unh, enough. I thought we were going home to start a business. Now, I'm just hoping to pick up some extra shifts at the club to keep the lights on."

Bandy kept her fingers on the pearls when she looked at me. "We still love you, Cerrio."

"Yes, we still love him," said Chevy. "But what makes you think another day or two is going to make a difference? If he ain't won nothing yet that's a good sign he ain't got a win in him."

My eyes filled with pure hatred. "Fuck you, Chevy."

"Fuck yourself," she barked. "You came here with no plan. No strategy. Not even decent amount of common sense. And now it's costed us something major."

"I thought you two had the plan."

"No, we had a budget that was our life savings. We brought everything to our names down here thinking you could be effective and instead you been donating it to these people like they're you're family."

I was going to turn up, a dense web of scathing abuse rose inside me until my ears started ringing. I forgot that I had no real rights to be brittle. I forgot about the things that got us here, the daily deceits when I took gas station cards to the liquor house and put the rest down the sink and the signals across the table and even my infidelity.

But before I snapped back the real phantom showed up in the corner of my eye like a wayward tear. None of us knew how long she had been there or what all she heard. Not that it was so important, all that meant anything is when she parted her lips to say, "calm down." And that's exactly what we did.

Me, Bandy and Chevy stood still on each corner of our square. Half our faces painted by the gloomy dawn while the other half showed jawlines rippled with agitation. People with lesser problems kept watching, enjoying the show we were putting on. Conversations blended, a woman laughed, I felt like we were props in a drama feature all made up by the boat as a last gasp of entertainment.

Chocolate took a long pull off a short cigarette, embers crackled backward in a staccato burst that made the tip glow super orange. When her lungs were full then the cherry died down to a much tamer fever, hot red.

"Shit," I said. "I never knew you smoked."

"That's because I don't. But the way everybody's been stressing out around here lately I had to go find one just to ease my nerves."

"Glad to see you're so concerned," said Chevy.

Chocolate flicked the butt over the rail with the tips of her fingernails There was another moment of silence while we listened to the waves lapping in the morning mist. "The problems not in the cards," she said. "Or the player. Or any sort of lack of planning."

"Then, what else could it be?" Bandy stepped right up waiting for an answer.

"It's the boat."

"The boat. What does that mean?"

"It means I know Cerrio can win just like you do. But he just can't do it here. The same way we can't dance here. Because the game isn't the same everywhere you go."

Chevy waved her hand around like it was deep mosquito season. "How do you know all of this? I haven't seen you around the tables once since we've been here."

"Yes, but I've seen you're face every night when it's over. You forget this is my money too. And you must not be able to see that I know Cerrio the same way you do. If I didn't then we wouldn't be here because you couldn't have made it this far without me. And I damn sure wouldn't have let him bet on my dime."

"I'm right here. If you want to run your mouth about my game at least look me in the face while you do it."

A smirk played at the corners of her mouth. "You're not listening. Sharks don't hunt in the desert."

I shot back. "That's a good one. But riddles don't pay the bills."

"It's not a riddle and you're still not listening. True, you are the best neighborhood gambler any one of us know. That's at least some of the reason we're all here. The problem is none of that matters because right now you're so far out of your element that you can't even see which way to go."

"And what is his element?" asked Chevy mockingly. "Say it so we all can know."

Chocolate spoke in measured tones. "The liquor house on Emerald street. That dice game underneath the steps of your building. Not in a real casino where's actual rules and chips and a dealer who has to show you his hands. He didn't learn the ropes in a place like this. Cerrio, can gamble anywhere but he can only win in the street."

And there it went, my ego was filleted. It's actually very painful to hear your shortcomings broadcasted so easily as if someone were talking about the weather. Standing in that square with the river behind us I felt small as a fucking raison. All that reasoning coming from the phantom wasn't just theory, it was truth, every word. I realized my ceiling had been touched, I had reached the highest peak of gambling that I would ever see on my very first night here.

"But I have a remedy," said Chocolate. "Anyone interested?"

"I'm listening," Chevy replied with a hand on her hip.

"Me too," chimed Bandy.

"In the city there's a spot by the Greyhound station. A liquor house where all the dope boys go and play spades. And the good news is it's just like everything else you're used to in Winston-Salem."

"You saying I can go in there and sit down and nobody's going to look at me funny?

"Only if I'm with you. Otherwise you're going to be doing a whole lot of explaining about who you are and how you got there. Probably to some people thinking you're twelve."

"Do I look like the police?"

"A lot of police don't look like police. Sometimes that's the point."

Bandy arched an eyebrow. "So, Cerrio can win all of our money back tonight?"

Chocolate pursed her glassy lips like a woman deep in thought. "I don't know. Maybe some right now. Then, ten or eight more tomorrow. Give or take."

"Who the hell said we're all going to be here tomorrow?" asked Chevy.

"Stay or leave, it doesn't matter. If I can win tonight then that's a lot better than us waking up to another loss first thing in the morning."

"He's absolutely right," said Bandy.

Chevy wasn't trying to give an inch. "If he was right then we would be having another sort of discussion right now. We'd be talking to the bank on the phone instead out here arguing on the deck."

The little singer finally let go of her pearls and took control. "Chev, it's not a bad plan. Look, I didn't want to say anything before because this was supposed to be a surprise but last night I got an offer to do a show."

"So? You can do a show anywhere."

"This one's different. It's a paying gig. When the night is over the house will break down with me instead of us paying them for the time on stage. We can use the money to rent rooms and buy food."

Chevy screwed her face up in a scowl. "Well, look at you all full of charity. Thanks, Mother Teresa but were not destitute just yet."

"I'm just offering, Chev."

"And I'm just telling you, Bandanna. A couple of shows on a boat is okay. But don't let it go to your head."

I could see things were getting emotional again. We were turning on each other and we had to move fast like nomads under a siege before we collapsed. Another mass of ignorant language was about to snap off like the smallest bone in my body if someone didn't clutch and go quick so I stepped forward to the middle of the square and took the spotlight.

"Nobody's going home yet. Bandy's got another show booked and Chocolate is exactly right. There's money out there but I'm just in the wrong place trying to get it." I looked at Chevy. "Right now I need to go in the trap and win. We can get a room somewhere. We got plenty of cash left and later on when we're off the boat then we can figure out when to go or stay. It'll be your call. Just gimme until tomorrow and I promise whatever you say we'll do."

She swayed her hips, bit her bottom lip, kept the arms crossed. It was that indecisive dance I always see whenever there's a debate about how long she wants to stay mad. Finally, she tells the rest of the square that we need a minute. Bandy spins away on a heel. "I'm going to go rehearse and pack." Chocolate takes the cue her own way and finds somewhere else to be on the ship's deck.

A long time ago someone told me the definition of love. They said, "it's when someone forgives you no matter how many reasons you give them to hold on to anger." That's being loved but loving another is really much simpler, it just means surrendering. It can't be a partial thing because a half surrender is an unjust wavering that lets you hold the other person's heart hostage.

When the other girl's were far away and there was no chance they were coming back Chevy took her eyes off the water. I put my hands out and she took them just like she knew exactly what I wanted.

"You must be really mad at me, huh? Going off like that."

She said, "I'm just like, trying really hard not to lose my mind."

"I think I'd rather have you pissed and bitchy. Is it all about the money?"

"No!" She snatched her fingers away. "There's going to be plenty of chances to get money. It's about you. And me. Don't you see that? Don't you know that this is how we lost each other last time? You dive head first into the paper chase and you never come back."

"But I do it all for you."

"Oh my God, please. It doesn't have anything to do with me."

"How's that?"

"How's that? Several times I tried to tell you my love is not an item on the shelf. You can't buy my happiness like it's a bag or a watch. That's not it works, Cerrio. That's not how any of this works."

"So eliminate the money. Alright, but who just roasted me in front of her friends?"

Chevy was prudent. "Fair enough. But listen, what I said has nothing to do with how I really feel deep inside." She took my hands back. "I gave you all of me and nobody can purchase that. Now, if it makes you feel better then go to the gambling spot and win. Win like a motherfucker. I know that'll make me feel a little better. But if you don't then I want you come back to me all in one piece. That's more important than anything."

They told me about love but nobody teaches you about chemistry, that's a lesson you got to find out on your own. So, I can't explain why I knew what to do next but when we pressed our lips together the boat applauded. Maybe they thought the hard part was behind us, a good guess but completely wrong. I think they just like seeing a happy ending.

Chevy blushed deep, cheeks turning pink like a beach sky sunset. I felt the pulse quicken in her fingers and smelled the fresh wave of perfume coming off her skin as her body heat

turned way up. When our mouths release more palms come together like the gallery of clappers called more friends to come
celebrate with us and then the clouds unlock to let a few stray
drops come down on our shoulders. The soft rain reminds me
that we're only guests of love.

CHAPTER 39

TOW BITCHES

Turns out Ty didn't know much of anything. Edwards threatened him with jail time and the snitch knew he wouldn't renege on that promise but he still had no useful information. When his partner Banks waved the black and white traffic photo around in his face all he said was, "he'd seen the car before." The rest was very basic like those cheap cigarettes the detective kept on smoking.

He told them it was a Cutlass or a Caprice. Ty didn't know the driver because he never saw anyone get in or out of it. But he did remember seeing the same car parked outside his mother's cousin's card house down in the Simmons street cul-de-sac on a night three weeks ago when he came by to pick something up.

Edwards could have roughed the snitch up and got the names of everybody who came in and out of that south side den. He could round up a whole crew of underground gamblers teeming through the city and hamstring the whole operation in just one night but he knew better. Aside from modern police protocol strictly forbidding shakedowns and perp beatings it was just a bad play. Because the only thing worse than a rat is a scared rat with his tail pinned down in a trap. Push him hard enough and Ty would give up phony information simply to get out of a jam. Then, Edwards and Banks would be running around chasing bad leads and criminal ghosts while the young studs over in Gang Task Force laughed their asses off.

So, their investigation hit a wall. Then, it a corner. Literally. If it hadn't been for the Chevron by his house running out of premium coffee he would have never even laid eyes on the Cutlass. Edwards was just driving by looking for a place to fill up his Thermos, passed by a gas station where an old junkie out front held the door open for strangers and there she was, sitting alone in the parking lot like a spaceship on a lost planet.

It was before the first crack of dawn but even in the weak light the paint shined like a trophy. He stopped in the middle of the street, whipped the cruiser around with one hand on the wheel while shoving the other in the glovebox to pull out the crumpled stoplight picture. When he got close enough to the Cutlass to read its license plate then he flattened the sheet of paper across the dashboard. Edwards went over the numbers carefully, flicking his eyes back and forth from the figures on the plate to the same black and white photo that failed to yield a thing from Ty. That's what had always made him a good detective, attention to detail, double checking all the finer points. But then again he never really had a doubt.

The judge signed their search warrant without ever reading any of the printed words. It could have been Clyde Edwards power bill from Duke Energy Company and the Honourable Leroy Marcus would have still approved. Him and Edwards went so far back they were on a first name basis. In the courtroom it was, "good morning, Leroy," and "morning, Clyde."

Detective Banks hung around the halls of justice like a third wheel on a date. He sensed that a round of beers were in order between the other two men, maybe even a Sunday barbeque at Your Honor's house. It wasn't a game so much as a fraternity. Police, judges and the prosecution were all on the same side. If they bent the rules then that was okay because they made them too and when they didn't work out so well then they merely made adjustments.

Of course he had his own connections in this courthouse. A magistrate here, a bailiff there, handy people who could pull strings like a puppeteer. Banks didn't need them this time. Fact is the two detectives could have walked in anywhere, slapped the warrant on the bench and got a signature right away. It was easy as taking a stroll down the main street because crime in this city was an epidemic.

He crossed his legs in a thin cushioned chair in the jury box usually reserved for triers of fact while Edwards talked up the judge. They did a little good ol' boy backslapping until some lowly court clerk came in toting a load of papers thick as three phone books. Banks knew grunt work when he saw it. Poor kid, he thought. She came down the aisle slow like a bride on the way to the alter giving the men plenty of time to finish up. All that was really missing was the wedding music.

Before cutting out Edwards and the judge made arrangements for a drinking date on the weekend. The Demon Deacons were starting their basketball season and Your Honor said "his son would be on the court starting for the home team." The detective just laughed and shook his head. Leroy Marcus's son majored in sociology. Everybody knew he'd be riding pine on game night.

Until then they had a car to go tow. Banks stood up and Edwards took the cue. They walked out into the hall with the court clerk's voice echoing behind their backs and met a white janitor slinging his mop east to west with little notice. Just missing their loafers by a breath the old man in coveralls made Edwards jump back and swear. "Jesus fucking Christ, watch it!"

There was a short staring match. The miniature tantrum didn't elicit more than that, not even a carefree shrug. Because this guy had seen it all, pissed off lawyers disbarred, murder defendants attacked, sloppy drunk judges still donning the robe. Nothing ever fazed the janitor. He pulled a handkerchief from his back pocket like he was going to blow his nose. Banks waited for the paisley cloth to catch snot but when the old man stooped down to wipe his partner's shoes he almost couldn't believe it. After he finished then he stood back up and tucked the cloth away. "There ya go, sir. All better now."

Neither cop said a thing and the mop went to east to west again while they tried to figure it out. Eventually the janitor made his way to the water fountain. "Should I tip him?" asked Edwards. Bank shook his head. "Gotta be honest with ya Clyde. That's your call."

Outside in the heat Edwards lit up a cigarette by the unmarked police cruiser. He was back to full flavor, at least on the job and any other time his wife wasn't looking. He was without question a chronic smoker but a handsome faced, well groomed one, at least. A cloud went up while he checked his moustache in the side mirror. Banks settled in behind the wheel. "Got a little silver coming through on the sides there, hass."

Edwards turned his face to check the shade of gray by his temple. "Comes with the territory like a shootout."

"Old age is worse than getting shot. Given a choice I think I'd rather take a hot one."

Edwards opened the door and eased in the car. He put the search warrant on the dashboard where it slid down by the windshield.

"Speaking of choices who are we going to get to tow that Cutlass?"

Banks reversed out of the parking space at a patient speed. "I know a new outfit working out on twenty fifth. They're Bulgarians."

"Yeah, what's that?"

"It means they're central European. Strong people. Good rates too. They do alignments dirt cheap."

"I can do alignments myself." Edwards spat. "Nah, I don't trust new people. New people are always the first ones to try something stupid. Who knows? They might pull over somewhere and strip the rims. Let's call your brother in-law. We'll pay him fifty bucks and bill the city two hundred. I need new shoes anyway."

Banks chuckled and turned on Foster avenue. "You get new loafers and what about me? A buck fifty ain't what it used to be."

"Shit Ryan, you sound like my wife. Remind me to pick you up a dozen roses after work."

"I don't want'em unless they're long stemmed."

They both laughed. Skimming money was just regular police work. Edwards knew all about how Banks cleaned up on maintenance fees for their cruiser. Three hundred extra for a new set of tires, a half grand on an alternator. The Dodge had been on tour to every garage in town for one reason or another. Banks called it all hazard pay.

On the other hand, Edwards supplement came almost exclusively from the streets. If he arrested a drug dealer their dope money never made it into evidence, same for a working girl's service fees. Once he found a diamond bracelet on a dead hooker under the Broad street overpass that appraised for over three thousand. Christmas was good that year.

When they arrived at the apartment complex sixteen minutes later things were quiet but the subtleties were loud. Project busybodies watched the two cops close. The hair braiders, grandmas and little sisters wanted to see who the police had come to take away this time. They went inside, shut their doors and peeked through the blinds. Later, when the orange tow truck hauled the Oldsmobile off to the impound lot and everything was clear somebody's Aunt Mabel in hair curlers would come out and say she knew this would happen. Of course she would be right, confiscation was just business as usual in a place like this.

Banks stood in the sun while his brother in-law connected a chain to the big car's back bumper. Turns out he didn't have to pay him a dime for this job. His sister's husband came through knowing exactly what he wanted, first dibs on the Oldsmobile as soon as it went to auction. They shook on the deal while Edwards stood back in the shade thinking about how many more phony miles he would have to add on to his report to pay for a new pair of Steve Maddens.

The tow hook went on politely so as not to mark up the chrome, then Banks brother in-law went all cliché. "They don't make them like this anymore," he said. Both detectives nodded dutifully. What an idiot, thought Edwards. His partner's wife was such a beautiful, intelligent thing. So fine, a real catch by anyone's standards. Her sibling on the other hand had the brain of a flea and all the charm of a brown recluse. One of these days when they were too drunk to care Clyde was going to have to ask if Dallas had been adopted into his family.

The truck beeped while Banks squinted into the sun. "Whaddya say we fit Heinrich in on this one? We do owe her a little bit ya know."

"No, we don't. I just happened up on this on my way to work."

"Come on, at least let her dust the doors and steering wheel for prints. She might hit on something."

Edwards furrowed his brow. "And if she don't? If the whole thing's clean?"

"Then, at least she'll feel useful. She'll look at you like her mentor. Plus, bonus you don't have to mess around with that black dust."

"You're right. I hate that stuff."

"I bet Heinrich loves it. She has a thing for doing grunt work." Banks jammed his hands down in his pockets. "She's one of those who dreamed about working in law enforcement since childhood. They say she was a star in the academy."

"Shit, Ryan if I didn't know better I'd think you were sweet on that woman."

Banks shook his head like the thought of laying with Michelle Heinrich was too pitiful to consider. "All I'm saying is use your rank. She's a junior investigator, bright eyed and bushy tailed just waiting for orders. Giving her a few will make your life seem a lot easier."

The tow engine whirred in front of them. Dallas worked the levers on the back of his truck with his tongue hanging out like something complicated was going on. If he wasn't already irritated Edwards might have found the whole thing pretty funny. The rear end of the Cutlass inched up off the ground slowly and a ray of daylight shone underneath the back tires, after a minute it grew into a full shadow of the trunk.

"So what's the call?" asked Banks. "You want her in on this or not?"

The other detective in the shade pretended to mull it over. In a top floor window he caught sight of plastic blinds snapping back in place. Whatever Heinrich contributed to this case didn't mean nothing because she wasn't out here getting spied on like a deer in a rifle scope on a crisp morning at the peak of hunting season. Before Clyde could say "fuck her" in the nastiest tone possible the tow engine cut off.

Dallas spit a thick stream of tobacco juice across the next parking space that splattered like oil. "Almost done here. But y'all got to sign something first." He pulled out a piece of paper from folder that looked freshly bought at an office supply store and waved them over. Both detectives stepped off at the same time but the in-law got there first.

Banks pointed to the sheet. "What is that?"

Dallas put another dip in his jaw. "New protocol. Something that tracks towing fees and transportation and things like that."

"When did it start?"

"Beginning of summer. Look, if y'all don't sign it then I can't tow the car."

Banks skimmed the document and whistled low. "Say goodbye to your new loafers, Clyde. They got the seal from the Mayor's office on this one."

"Fuck the mayor." Edwards immediately went for his shirt pocket. "Goddamnit, now I need a cigarette."

The other detective finished reading the paper and signed his name on Dallas' shoulder. When he passed it Edwards blew smoke and wiped a thick coat of sweat from his lip. The only thing he hated more than crooks was bureaucracy and the only thing he hated more than that was budget cuts. After every sentence he muttered a low curse. Finally, he got to the end and held his hand out for a pen. Dallas passed over one full of blue ink after clicking it first and Edwards snatched it away before going on a rant.

"Maybe it is time for me to retire. Everybody's all full of shit nowadays. The Chief. The Mayor. They don't care about things getting worse out here every day and you know why? Because they got pensions growing fatter every year and thirty foot Bayliners hiding out in their garage. Meanwhile cops on the ground can't get credit for anything. You know, when I started out they used to give a deputy the keys to the city for making a good bust. Now, you can't even make an arrest without Internal Affairs crawling up your ass asking if you've been profiling people."

Dallas shuffled his feet nervously waiting for the paper back. Banks took off his sunglasses and chewed on the left arm. "I remember all that. Except the keys to the city part. You had to be a real hero to get those."

"Point is things have changed."

Edwards walked to the Cutlass and put the paper on the glass, held it steady and scribbled his signature in ink. When he snatched the document off the back window to hand it over something caught his eye. In the back of the car a rumpled blanket laid across the floor. It was a big piece, nice too, not like that junk they sold down at the flea market on weekends. No, this looked genuine. He cupped both hands around his eyes to cancel out the glare of the sun while Banks pulled his glasses out of his teeth. "What do you see, Clyde?"

Edwards didn't answer. Instead, he kept looking through at the floor. It was obvious what he saw, polycarbon grip, black stock, wide magazine hanging out like a best friend on a sunny Sunday afternoon. Most of the assault rifle was hidden, maybe if the blanket covered up a little more it could have stayed that way. He took his face away from the window and smiled. "We don't need Heinrich. Come here Ryan, you're gonna love this."

CHAPTER 40

SINGER'S BLUES

Downtown Savannah. The rain kept up, never got heavier and refused to fall any lighter on the roof of Chevy's Mercedes that still had that new car smell. I dropped her and Bandy off at the lounge where the little singer was supposed to perform tonight and now I was sitting at the curb so Chocolate could go in a 7-11, grab some cards and maybe an airport bottle of Crown Royal. The radio hummed while I contemplated how to tell her that our weekend rendezvous was at its expiration. She wouldn't just let it die. Even if I can be naive I still knew better than to believe we were just going to shake hands and walk away. She would roll her eyes like, "who you kidding?" Then, show off one of those inky, black thighs to make my mouth water. But I had to deny the flesh, even if it was luxurious with an ending fit for paradise I still had to grit my teeth and turn away.

For a long time I sat all by myself, head back on the leather seat listening to drops pitter patter on the roof. The spot where Bandy was singing tonight would be less busy on account of this weather. Plus, it was Monday and normal people had to work in the morning. For those two reasons her last show in Georgia would be in front of a thin audience. For me the leaking sky meant I couldn't drive the purple Jeep with no doors, good news because that glittering truck was a rolling basket of trouble.

Mercedes hazard lights blinked off the damp street. Every time they pulsed falling rain drops lit up bright yellow with brand-new energy. Chocolate emerged from the store holding onto a small, brown, paper bag swinging those hips west to east like an all night flight to London. Both turn signals flashed on her picking that tall, supple, figure out from the night, separating woman from world and quietly reminding me of everything I would be missing pretty soon. I savored the view because in a minute this whole messy entanglement was going to end.

She hopped in the car, set the bag in her lap. I watched her take out all the contents one at a time, chewing gum, a pint of E and J, rolling papers. When there was nothing left then she folded up the empty sack and put it in the door pocket.

I looked at her like her wrists were slit. "Where are the cards?"

She looked back at me like the faithless look at a tattooed Psalm on your arm. "What?"

"The stuff I told you to get. The cards, I need those."

For a second there was nothing. Then, she snapped her fingers. "Oh yeah, the cards. Right."

"You remember now, huh?"

"Of course, you asked me to get some decks of cards. Three right?"

"Four," I replied.

"Three, four, five, whatever. Don't worry about it."

"The fuck are you talking about? I need those to win!"

She folded a piece of red, cinnamon gum in her mouth and changed the subject. "Chevy ain't happy. What all did she say after I left?"

"Fall back, that's none of your business."

"You're my business and business is good. So, what did she say?"

"Keep asking me that and you'll be walking in the rain like Mary Poppins."

"Does she know about us?"

I gave that last question a lot of thought. "No, she hasn't figured it out yet. And I don't want her to either."

"You scared of her?"

"No, I just want to get serious. We're building a future. Trying to anyway. I don't know. All I know is shit's not going to work as long as me and you are creeping around in strange cities together."

Chocolate touched my arm. "You and Seville really are in love, huh?"

I looked at her hand like I wanted to wipe it off. "Yeah, tough as that is to believe."

"Aw, so beautiful."

"Most of the time."

"Do you know I never came?"

I blinked. "Say what?"

She laughed. "I said, 'I never came'. You got me real close in the shower but I had to finish up all by myself after you were gone."

From her purse Chocolate pulled out a bag of reefer, something to soothe the burn she had just put on my manhood. She tossed it in my lap the same way she always did Chevy's cocaine. I knew what she wanted and she knew what I needed but this was no time for games. I held my hand out like she owed me money and she popped her gum.

"What is it?"

"I need the papers."

"Go ahead. Grab them."

The Zig Zags sat high on her thigh. When I reached for them she didn't flinch.

"Don't worry it's not just you. Most men have trouble making me cum. In fact, it's pretty much all of them. Guess I'm sort of complicated that way."

"Complicated, huh?" I nodded like I was absorbing her meaning. "So, does that make me simple?"

She shrugged. "That depends."

"On what?"

"If you really think there's a gambling house four blocks from the Greyhound station."

"Come again?"

"Come on Cerrio, you're a smart guy. You got your GED in prison. Think about it."

Uncle Daya came to mind again. I rubbed the bridge of my nose slowly and recalled his theory about how one day women would take over the whole world. Maybe there really was a gambling house behind the bus station but I'll never know. Instead, we went back to the Savannah Marriott overlooking the river where me and Chevy bought a room and started from behind. Then, it was me on top driving forcefully, burning up the mattress springs all over fresh, cream linen put down for me and my baby to hold each other on. That should have been the worst part but truth is dirty sheets were trivial. I already had a plan to call the night clerk downstairs reading magazines behind the desk with a lie about how I spilled ranch and needed a new spread.

Chocolate plotted this caper in such fine detail, even better than that thing in High Point. The confrontation between me and Chevy on the boat had made the perfect opportunity for her to step right in and call an audible so she could get hers and since hers was my responsibility that made us accomplices. I smoked plenty and arrived on my own sweet schedule. She knew good reefer was going to make me cum late. Late as melted ice cream and a while after her which was all that actually mattered

The woman was nuclear, though. She egged me on and arched her back and sweated bullets all over the pillowcase until heavy, damp spots blended together to make one fat blotch of our blended salt water. When I got to the finish she could feel me grow another inch pushing deeper up her back. She whined as I flexed and touched her bottom, clenched her teeth and spread her legs wider with a look on her face that sent me pouring over the edge until nothing was left.

When it's over Chocolate stays naked on the bed, arms above her head, chest swelling with every deep breath. If someone took a picture of her right now they might have thought she had just woke up and was going through a morning stretch. She was Cleopatra and I was Mark Anthony. Too bad they both killed themselves in exile but right now we were both sitting pretty on top of Rome.

"Damn it, I'm supposed to be out winning right now."

"Uh-huh," she said. "Well, aren't you?"

I looked over a shoulder. "Breaking even doesn't count. It's going to be hard trying to explain why I was gone all night and brought home nothing."

"Poor baby," she sighed.

She got up, a wrinkled indentation showed where her body had been pressed down hard in the bed. Looking at it made me remember that we were supposed to break up. So much for denying the flesh, I thought.

I pulled my pants on thinking about how to dress down a story for room service so they could bring those new sheets in a hurry. When I looked up at the French door windows leading out to the balcony Chocolate's whole backside was reflecting to me in the glass like a watery dream. The way she was bent over I thought she had to be getting dressed, but when she stood tall it was all ass and thighs glaring back like facts.

For a moment the reflection disappeared, then a second later the real thing came into view. That tight body swooped in right in front of me stark naked, holding out a knot of cash strapped in a rubber band just like it came to me on that first night in the club.

"There's three thousand right there. Give it to Chevy when you see her. Make sure you put on an act like you finally got your shit together and maybe we can all go home and live happily ever after."

I looked at the money like it might bite my lip off. "How the fuck are you still throwing bread around when everybody else is trippin'?"

She leaned in close so we were eye level, those big bountiful tits hanging down like lush fruit still glistening wet with perspiration.

"Because this is me, baby. That's why. And I ain't worried a bit because I know when we get back home you and me are going to get back every single dime and a whole lot more."

Then, she winked an evil, sly, wink and I knew she had something else cooked up. A robbery or a heist in another town or maybe a job right here. I said, "maybe we'll get the money back. And maybe we won't. Who the hell knows? But for a woman on edge you sound real sure."

"Because I know you, Cerrio. And there's two things you can't turn down, pussy and a payday."

I was arrested right then, very briefly and not long enough for us both to recognize a change. So, I retreated, bounced out of the subject like a tennis ball on springs and circled back around.

"Did you cum yet?"

"I don't know," she replied. "Maybe."

"What does that mean? Either you did or you didn't. Can't be any in between."

"Well then, let's just act like I didn't."

Chocolate was too smart to argue. Facts are I don't think she ever had to contend a day in her life. When you look that good you never fix your mouth to bicker. Besides, who would challenge her anyway?

She put her hand gently on my neck, traced her fingers down and across in straight line until a smooth palm landed lightly on my shoulder. I sensed the slightest pressure, not a push though, not even close because force doesn't work better than persuasions. In a second my jeans were gone again and she was up on top in the spot where she had all the control. Even if I really wanted to I couldn't stop what got started. No more zero orgasms, a woman gets what she wants and this one was adamant.

Right there on my back looking up I decided my favorite part of her. There was plenty to choose from, a flood of options at least but those scandalous D-cups had to take first place. They were raven and rolling in the lamplight, nipples stiff like it was chilly. Bouncing and raining salty droplets down that were meant to be tasted. In the past it was always Chevy's body that drove me crazy. She was the one I thought about when I was alone, the one I used to think about in a cell by myself. It had been that way for a lot of years but in just one weekend the vision changed. Now, here we were on the corner of a revolution. From this point on it would be Chocolate's body running through my mind on those solo moments.

I watched her rise and fall like a wave, letting the image burn in my brain knowing she would make the next appearance whenever me and Chevy were together by ourselves. Maybe I was just too high to care, her body was like a narcotic after all, warm and comfortable, and somehow nothing else mattered but all these empirical feelings. The pleasure of her riding me rough and easy, her slippery moisture painting my manhood, the aggravation of short pubic stubble rubbing hot against my skin when she grinded down to the hilt. That's just like home, though. Our town was a source of pain and pleasure. What wonder is it that a girl from the underbelly of Winston-Salem would be all about that same sort of paradox?

She was ready now. Chocolate spread her thighs wide, knees dug in the comforter as she leaned forward and put her hands on my chest. She worked me all the way up, spine arched in, ass lifted high. Then back down again, skin slapping skin in a vertical dance like she was trying to press me all the way through the box spring. A lesser man would have coughed up his soul. No more infant hairs rubbing, now it was just Chocolate gliding herself fast and furious slamming on my shaft straight to the mound before lifting right back up again. She rocked hard making the mattress springs cry out like a hurt animal. The noise was ridiculous. That's why we didn't hear the key card sliding in the door, or the latch moving back, or Bandy stepping in on her light dancing feet.

It took another five seconds before she abandoned her pinnacle. I knew for a fact this wasn't the first time Chocolate had ever been caught. More than once I'd overheard salacious stories colored with filth coming from the back bedroom of Chevy's apartment. They always got good reviews, lots of four letter words and howling laughter with never an ounce of shame. This one would be at the top, the final piece to nail home her infamous legacy.

Bandy stood frozen, feet nailed to the floor, mouth open, eyes wide and white like paper plates. My face was blotched with so much raw shame that my cheeks felt like they were melting. Like if you killed me right now I would barely feel the flames of hell on my face. I snatched a sheet off the bed to use as a cover around my waist like it mattered while the woman beside me stayed naked and defiant.

"Bandy this ain't what it looks like. We just got a little high and carried away." Chocolate made a noise like she wanted to dissent. When I shot her a hard look, she kindly put a hand on both hips and held her peace.

"You shouldn't be here," said Bandanna. "I came to get my other wig to match this outfit tonight. But y-y-you shouldn't be here. And you," Bandy pointed a finger. "Backstabbing slut!"

Chocolate clicked her tongue. "Poor, little baby. Still so pure even after all they done to you. Tell me something girl, do you like the way your mouth looks now? Personally, I think the gold really pops against your spots."

"Wow," she breathed. "That's the nicest thing you've said to me since we met. It's a shame it took so long for you to cough up a compliment. Guess you're just a bitch like that."

"Guess so," responded Chocolate.

The little singer reached in her purse. She dug down deep inside and when her hand came back out I saw that pearl handled pistol Chevy waved around after we smashed a bottle of liquor at the ABC store.

"No, Bandy don't do this." I swallowed. "I know I hurt you but we can talk about it."

She swung the gun away from Chocolate and pointed it straight at my heart. The way she handled the steel showed me she had never shot a thing in her life. Doesn't matter, though. A new killer is born every day and that look in her eye said she was ready to come out of the womb right about now.

"Bandanna, listen to me. I know I made a mistake. But I promise, I promise I love you and I love Chevy. Just put the gun away and we can talk about it."

"I never trusted a man because I always knew better," she said. "I saw how my mama's boyfriend treated her before she killed him. She had to do it. Anybody would have, goddamnit I would have even done it for her. But Chevy said you were different. And I believed her."

"Relax, baby. It's still me. I'm still the same."

A hot tear flowed down her cheek. She swiped it away fast leaving behind a scratch mark that curved from her eye down to her mouth where the white spot grew rose red. "I trusted you. You were my family. I didn't come down here to sing for these people. I did it because I knew you wanted me to. All because you said you loved my voice."

"And that ain't changed. Nothing right here will ever change your gift. Now come on, no violence."

I reached out for the gun. When she looked like she was going to hand it over she snatched away and pulled the slide back. "But I trusted you."

"Bandy..."

"I trusted you."

"Just let me explain."

"Shoot him!" yelled Chocolate.

"Shut up!" I screamed back.

"I fucking trusted you!"

The little singer's body was shaking hard with sobs. I could hear the pistol barrel rattling like metal teeth chattering in the brisk wind. She clutched the weapon two handed to aim it better and the muzzle went up, up, up until I could see right into the black hole where the bullets would rush out before I could see them in a searing, hot flash I would never remember. I prayed there would be no regrets when I left and then the girl with the gun screamed one, long note like every oppressed woman had just woken up to die inside her.

Bandy threw the pistol straight, before it bounced off my chest and tumbled harmlessly to the floor she was already backing out of the room. Thrown a little lower it would have cracked my rib but if she would have pulled the trigger then a freshly blemished Cerrio would have been blown away to the other side. Don't know where I would have went. But that didn't matter because right now here I was, born in the sand, raised in the sun, living in the heat. And how in the world could it get any hotter than this?

There was a sincere plea in my voice when I told her to wait, I was scared for her fresh off that kidnapping barely two weeks ago. But Bandy went one foot behind the other backing away from us until she reached the door. Just beyond the threshold she gave her final words, just three of them but without the gun in her hand I could actually focus on their sting. When she bit her bottom lip to hold back a round of tears that single gold tooth gleamed in the cozy hallway light.

"I trusted you," she whispered.

CHAPTER 41

BEAUTIFUL SUSPECTS

Crazy little bitch."

Chocolate celebrated her comment with a scathing laugh. For a veteran dancer at a hole in the wall strip club like Sugar Bares this was just another day at the office.

She reached down to scoop the semiautomatic off the floor. When she checked the clip it slid out easy. A noise escaped her throat that was something between a soft hum and a low purr because the magazine was just the way it was supposed to be, clean as soap and filled to the top with shiny, new bullets. I felt a bittersweet sense of pride. Chevy knew a gun with an empty belly was just a liability and after I told her as much she always kept it loaded.

The clip went back in its place with a frigid, snapping noise. Chocolate held the .32 up in the air like a Bond girl, she pointed at me and made cartoon sounds like a wild west gunfight. I blinked and she giggled until her stomach muscles rippled like a puddle.

"Man, what the fuck is wrong with you?"

She frowned. "Jesus, Cerrio lighten up. If we're going to keep hanging out then you have to know how to let stuff go sometimes."

"We almost got killed," I said. "All about some goddamn pussy."

"Please, even this gun right here knew Bandy wasn't going to shoot it. And by the way, this ain't just some pussy. Remember that."

"No one gives a shit about your bragging. This whole trip is a disaster. Ever since we got here everything has been upside the fuck down."

I stared at the window again by my side of the bed, not looking for a naked reflection, just trying to figure things out. For sure I had just put out whatever flame got ignited on the boat a day ago but this was about more than that. More than the menages and the escapades and the big soup of sex were the women themselves and the betrayal laid on them. In some way I couldn't help it and I sort of wished we really would have died in that house so I wouldn't have caused their pain. But that thought was crazy and when I was on the way back from that place of loathing insanity suddenly I stopped.

I looked across the bed at Chocolate still nude as fuck admiring Chevy's piece. "You planned all this didn't you?"

She didn't even lift her eyes to me when she said, "I don't know what you're talking about."

I shook my head no when I meant to say, yes. "Yeah, I see it now. All the time you were acting like you wanted to come and watch Bandy sing. That was your cover. The friendly act." I stood up. "But the whole time you had a sword behind your back. You didn't come for the shows. You don't a give a shit about any of that. You're here strictly for sabotage."

She shrugged. "Well, if that's what you think."

"No, that's what I know."

"Fine then, let's say you're right." She tossed the pistol on the bed with the handle facing my way and stared with no feeling, no dilution. Only a simple plainness.

Our eyes were raised to each other without any layers of titillation over them to disguise real motivations. No more swords behind the back. Just two pieces on a chessboard. The body and the dog and the pressure was all on the dog. She kept her plain stare on me until it changed into something smug. If Chocolate was anything she was economic, the woman wouldn't waste an emotion even if it was really no emotion at all. She only stared long enough to make a point. Once it was clear she turned her back and slipped into her panties.

"Don't go trying to get ahead of this, Cerrio. Just wait and see what happens. Maybe Bandy won't say anything."

"And if she does?"

"Then, deny it. Tell Chevy the little girl is out of her mind and she pointed a gun at you."

"In case you forgot. I just saved that little girl's life this month. Now, I have to throw her under the bus?"

Chocolate buttoned her jeans. "Listen to me, I know Chevy. She's going to believe your story no matter what because your relationship is like gold to her. God, if you only knew."

"What does that mean?"

"It means you have power. The power to manipulate. She already handed you her life savings. You fucked that up and she still keeps hanging on. So just say what you need to say and say it right with no hesitation."

"Fuck, I really been dancing naked with the devil the whole weekend."

The black dancer shook herself into her bra. "Want me to suck your dick?"

"No."

"You're lying."

"How's that going to help anything?"

"Because you need to relax. This is not a big deal."

"Man, you been doing this shit too long. This hoing game got you jaded. This ain't a little coke and a robbery. I can't shake all this off in the morning like a long piss."

"Okay, tell her the truth then. Take the moral high ground and tell Chevy everything we been doing and after you do make sure she returns the honesty. But, just make sure you buy her a bigger closet first."

"What are you talking about?"

"I'm talking about more space to hide all your bae's skeletons. You can call me the devil if that makes you feel better but she ain't no angel to compare neither." Chocolate breathed in deep with a fresh stick of cinnamon gum hot on her tongue. "That week you were gone. What do you think she was doing? Sitting by the fire knitting sweaters? Your baby runs back and forth from the club to the streets. Dancing. Fucking. Getting high. Getting money. And you know how bae gets money. But all the time what are you doing for her? Shooting it out in the street and risking your life every night at whatever liquor house we drive past all for a dream while she puts her tips up her nose?"

"She does what she does. I do what I do. It's all just temporary."

"So is life. It's all just temporary."

This is the stuff of shadows, screwbaby's dying in secret and withering flowers ground down into dust. A mix of unspoken truths growing in the dark like a mushroom until they breed vexatious notions. Use a half dose of minor honesty, a little truth like your name or your age, split it with illusion and stir it all up until nothing makes sense anymore. When two wrongs seem like they make a right then you know it's already over.

I was hoping Chocolate would go, just step out and leave me to wonder all on my own about the finer details. But that would have been too simple and politics doesn't work that way and if nothing else this woman should have definitely been a politician. She knew how to impose her will, worm people out of their last dime, disrupt loyalty and push a scandal. I guarantee if she threw her hat in the ring those hips and thighs would own the whole country in just one campaign.

She reached out to touch my chin, lifting it slightly with a finger, tracing the nail so lightly that it felt like a hallucination.

"Don't worry," she said. "Mama ain't ever going to let you starve. You can always come home to me if Chevy won't have you anymore."

After we got our clothes back on I drove her to a hotel by the convention center. I think it was the Holiday Inn but honestly I wasn't paying much attention to signs anymore. When the Mercedes stopped Chocolate opened her door, swung her tall heels out onto the parking lot asphalt and looked over a shoulder. "Sure you don't want me to suck your dick?" When I kicked the radio up she just shrugged like whatever, and got out.

There was no walk of shame. She strutted away never once looking back straight up to the hotel entrance where the double doors yawned open like they were glad to have her. I lingered right there in the handicapped spot until they closed again. The whole time wondering what it was I stayed there waiting for.

I figured, in all seriousness, that this woman must have toured with the devil himself. Her decadence went far past the streets. A long way beyond the small offenses of petty thieves hooked on a drug and the difficult murders caused by the ones making a living off the trade. There was something philosophical about her corruption. A bold touch of genius that you could casually hate but still admire at the same time and people would just understand.

The rain dried up and passed over the city like a hustler moving on from tired territory. After a half hour of wrong turns I took Chevy's new Benz down River street on the seedy side of town, right near the docks where you could find trouble and get lost. Maybe killed. Broken bottles on the curb crunched under the feet of hunched figures darting into shadows that swallowed them whole. In the deepest layers of darkness random flares shot up from over fueled lighters showing trap ghosts with hollow, sunken faces. Most people would have turned the car right back around and got out of there, but not me, I felt right at home in the valley of the lost.

There was a brown, brick building with a sign on the side all trimmed in rust. It had a red circle with a slanted line cutting the circle in half and inside that was a silhouette of a super sized cigarette. On the same corner a cold, crew of temptations mingled in tight skirts with enough skin showing on top to make me fiend for it. I watched them put on a show in the headlights. A lot of leg, a little bit of tail, still wet between the breasts from dodging all the rain. These were the best type of girls, shameless gifts to their craft, the heartbeat of all things pleasurable. True ladies of the night. The ones who fought for their spot on the block and used their bodies to pay rent to the landlord and buy formula for the baby or maybe just to get through the next day.

For a second I thought about the roll of cash Chocolate stuffed in my hand that was deep in my pocket but not too far down. Never before in my life have I bought a stitch of trim, it's against my religion. But sanctity seemed futile since in times before I've evolved so far into the darkness blind and clueless about where I was even going. On the way down I've been loved and used and laughed at and now it seems only right that I take this last leg of the journey to the shadow world with eyes wide open so I could at least see what I had coming.

None of the girls hesitated. When the window went down they all swarmed the car like angry wasps. First one off the curb was the tallest of the crew. She might have been a jumper, the assertive type who pulls opens the door and hops right in the ride before the wheels quit chopping. I've seen that at home right up on MLK boulevard by a gas station that gets robbed every single weekend on Fridays like a scheduled embarrassment.

This corner was the perfect place for an aggressive jumper but a smart girl never takes a blind chance like that. Maybe the car's dome light comes on and the trick says no while the competition left behind on the curb gets a sure thing pulling up to the sidewalk. Or maybe something worse might happen like being handcuffed to a bathtub in a sad, yellow house where pretty things go to die.

The hooker leaned forward, bending far enough down to get face level with the window. I could smell perfume mixed with rain when her blonde wig swung down inside the door. I smiled like an idiot only because I never bought pussy before. But when she tucked a lock of fake hair behind one ear I almost put the Mercedes into a telephone pole. She didn't have imperfections, she had a story to tell. A long, harrowing tale splintered with horror written right on her face.

I love a scar, a pale spot on the skin, even a blemish on the soul. Those are the purest parts of a person, the parts you don't have to find out because flaws find their own way out. But there's a border, juxtaposed in a place you don't see when the flaws quit looking like decorations and lurch forward into the savage. That's where she was, more like that's where her story was. With the blond wig out of the way I saw a crooked mark that traveled from the top of her brow down to her mouth. It wasn't a shallow scar like Bandy's, this was a trench dug deep with malice. Whoever gave it to her did a good job with the knife. It squiggled to the lips and divided the top one so her mouth couldn't close all the way and her eye was white from where she hadn't closed it in time to avoid the tip of the blade. That's all I saw when she smiled, that crevasse in the mouth pulling over her teeth and the cloudy eye that didn't know how to be dead or alive.

When I stomped the gas eight greased cylinders shot me straight through the intersection. The money hungry women hollered out the evening's specials to a set of German taillights. In the mirror I saw the tall monster picking up her purse off the street. She was red hot at me. Weren't they all, though. Still, I didn't know what to do about any of it. I was too scared to come to the light and look for rebirth and redemption but if that was the darkness calling out to me then this was Cerrio saying goodnight.

CHAPTER 42

MESSY REFLECTIONS

Bandy dashed away from the hotel without knowing much about where to go. She moved urgently, fleeing before Cerrio could come out on her heels and try to make his pleas. That's how these men did it. Lie. Cheat. Apologize. Repeat. She wasn't a particularly weak girl but LaDecerrio was a strong hitter in the art of seduction. She saw how Chevy folded so quick after he came home, how she gave him the middle drawer in her bedroom dresser for his clothes and let him run up the mileage on her car. Whatever game he spun in front of her cousin to get that admiration against her better judgements was probably more than just a line and more than Bandy could handle.

She didn't realize how much this was going to hurt. Walking in and seeing Chocolate's back arched over the top of Cerrio she felt the sting of betrayal about to buckle her knees, but walking away had taken the wind right out of her sails. She had given him so much but never enough and in the end plenty to be ashamed of. He had even seen her naked. They came close as two people could ever get just to get cut apart by some slut.

Wasn't that a man, though? Absorbed in fascinations, always benevolent until the house of cards came down. At least the charade was over now. And anyway she shouldn't hurt so bad seeing as how Chevy was going to have it much worse.

At night on foot this city was completely foreign to her. She walked in front of a smoky bar where laughter flowed freely out into the street. Right now she could use a glass of something good and strong. It would be nice to go inside, sit down and drink until her mind went numb. Maybe she could deal with all this tomorrow morning after she woke up. In the end that's exactly where she'd have to meet it because right now the show must go on.

She promised the talent agent she'd be back at the White Azaleas Lounge in half an hour. That's how long it took to race to the Marriott to get her wig and return but eighty minutes later Bandy was trekking in front of the Savannah nightlife scene with dreams of getting drunk. She needed a cab, fast. She pulled her phone out to call the club and make an excuse and then a ride to get there in time to save her blossoming entertainment career. The top of the screen said 2% battery but that was a lie. Soon as she fired up a search for the next thing smoking out to Center City her Android faded to black.

Stay calm. That's always the first rule in a crisis. All these people drinking out here had to find a way back home and by the rules of business that meant a savvy cab driver must be close. Bandy came to end of the street and stood on the corner where she could look all four ways. A group of people shoved by her reeking of rum, college types who probably smelled right now just what their frat house smelled like all the time. Without even turning around she could feel a pair of hungry eyes lingering on her ass. A lusty grunt sounded off above the noise of cars in the street and she snapped the frat boys a look sharp enough to cut their throats.

The group moved along, she crossed the road. On the other side Bandy checked her four ways again. No cabs in sight but they had to be close, around the corner parked in front of some establishment just waiting for a sloshy fare to stumble out. A Prius cruised by slow, the new model of modern taxi's because they were good enough on gas that a driver could make twenty runs to the airport before he hit half a tank. Bandy focused on the beetle backed sedan as it passed by, the middle aged couple up front were oblivious to her personal messes.

So much for evidence of relief. If this kept up she might be out here all night getting fooled by compacts and stared at like a slab of meat in a butcher shop window. There was an urge to go back to the Marriott just to ask for a ride until repulsiveness swept it right off the front steps of her needs.

After that one second of contemplating such a sellout move Bandy reloaded her sanity. She wasn't going to be an accessory to the degradation, her own or anyone else's. She was going to be sand in the gears of all this misogynistic bullshit, now and always.

A city bus rolled by with its engine groaning, before it banked a left turn Bandy saw herself in every one of its four foot windows. Looking back at her in a liquid reflection was an astonishing piece of work, hoop earrings, heart shaped lips painted rose, hair in ten straight back braids that Chevy had twisted in her head earlier that afternoon. She laughed at the contrast of ghetto fabulousness and regal style. She was the Z at the end of the alphabet. That crazy slash that told you it takes all kinds to make this biography of civilization work.

A car came behind the bus, close enough that only one headlight was clearly visible behind the gutteral engine chugging off. As she watched the last image of herself go away in the final window Bandy could hear it slow down at the light still lingering on green. She felt lighthearted and hopeful as it reversed to a stop beside her. A cab. But how did it know she even needed a ride? Well look at me, she thought. Walking alone around the bar scene with hair in cornrows and a fancy cocktail dress on a Monday night. She looked so far out of place that even the unborn cabdrivers of his universe could see she was meant to be somewhere else.

The brown face behind the wheel was an Ali or a Kumar or maybe she shouldn't be so into stereotypes in the first place. But he had Arab written on him like the headline on a Sunday paper. He flashed a smile that curved up to a pair of large eyes above a set of bearded cheeks. "Need a ride?"

Bandy cleared her throat, looked at the white Grand Marquis a decade and a half out of production. "Is that a cab?"

The driver reached a hand outside and smacked the door. "Yes. I take you anywhere you like."

She laughed at his brand of enthusiasm. "You sure you can handle me?"

"I can try," he replied.

This was a good time, already she was pulling back from the cloud of despair. No matter what came out of tonight for sure she was going to be alright.

Bandy stepped down off the curb to put her pain in a grave but she stopped between headstones. The dashboard on the Lincoln was ordinary. Doubt took a turn at her. "Where's your meter?"

The brown face changed into a look of confusion. "The meter?" he repeated.

"Yeah, to track your fares you need a meter. How else do you know what to charge people for a ride?"

The driver opened his mouth, just for a second he was twisting in the wind and then he said, "this cab is new to the fleet."

"New?" Bandy asked like a skeptic while she came even closer to the car.

"Yeah, yeah, bought three days ago but the meter hasn't been," he snapped his fingers, "ah what's the word?"

"Installed?" Bandy filled in the blank for him.

He beamed. "Yes, installed. The meter will be installed probably on tomorrow but I can still take you anywhere you like right now."

A Lexus honked its horn and bent around them. Bandy realized she was in the middle of the street and the night was getting later. "How much you charge to go to Center City?"

"Get in." He smacked his hand against the door again rapping a pinky ring off the Grand Marquis sheet metal. "We can work out the price on the way."

CHAPTER 43

DRAMA SPITTERS

No clocks on the wall. Chevy looked in every high place but the lounge didn't keep track of time. She took out her phone to check the minutes, exactly three had gone by since she last took out her phone and did the same thing. Frustration wasn't the word for this, a little emotion like that was far too small for the moment. Almost like squeezing a wide pair of feet into a narrow set of heels.

On the same stage where Bandy was due to perform a gospel singer was giving it her everything. The audience listened comfortably in their seats while each note untangled a little more heart and soul. Strange place for gospel, thought Chevy. Blasphemous even since the White Azaleas Club had drinks in the front, reefer in the air, and gangsters in the crowd. Savannah was a strange place, though. Sort of like the devil all dressed up in a business suit.

From the back of the audience Taneesha materialized. She hustled through tables muttering polite pardons to people trying to enjoy the show. They looked up at her and nodded like it was all okay before going back to the lady in the light laying down her vocals. As she came closer Chevy could feel her heart grow cold.

The signs of stress were louder than the singing on stage. Taneesha was a wreck, puffy eyes and dark circles underneath, rings of nervous sweat in the armpits of her lightweight black blouse. That strong anxiety was contagious. Chevy could feel her own symptoms start up when her mouth suddenly went dry. She had to take a fast drink of sparkling water before her voice arrived. "Anything?"

Neesha shook her head. "I looked everywhere. The dressing rooms. Bathroom. All over."

"What about the hotel?"

"I went there too. All I saw was her wig laying right there on top of your suitcases."

"Shit."

Taneesha wrung her hands. "You think maybe she's backstage? We could have walked right by her. Maybe she was too busy getting ready and didn't see us."

"No, if she was this lady wouldn't be taking up her stage time doing an extra number right now."

"This ain't right. She should have been back by now. Bandy wouldn't miss a thing like this."

That was the setup for the ugly truth. Chevy knew it too. The little singer wouldn't just skip out on her dream at the eleventh hour and that had to mean something was wrong. Perhaps just a small mishap like too much traffic on the highway or the cabdriver got lost. If Cerrio would have been here he would be the strong one holding it all together right now. He was a well of broken promises but at least he knew how to be the calm in the storm. Always there to catch Chevy when she fell. Except he wasn't here and the panic in Taneesha's face was building.

Chevy sipped more water. "You know what? I bet it's the roads holding her up. They're all wet from the rain. I bet traffic has to be a bitch right now."

Neesha wanted to believe. "You think so?"

"Yeah, you know it's always something simple. Like when Cerrio picks me up late from the club. Some nights I sit in the dressing room thinking all types of crazy thoughts and then he shows up out of nowhere like, 'sorry baby, the police are out there everywhere'. Which just means he had to drive slow and take the back roads because he doesn't have a license and the cops will run his ass straight to jail."

"Well, then why don't he just get a license?"

"I don't know. He's a shithead. That's how men are." She pulled a chair out from the table. "Come on, sit down before you fall down. Bandy will be here any second."

Taneesha listened and took the chair. Side by side they both looked up at the woman in the spotlight, watching with interest mostly because she was a beautiful break from worrying. She had talent. Her voice could go from gravelly to soft to sad depending on what part of the spirit she wanted to touch. What Chevy knew about gospel wasn't enough to spread across a cracker but under the drifting smoke this soothing woman seemed like the perfect fit.

Her song was coming to an end when Lacey's manager approached the table. Taneesha almost jumped to the ceiling when he cleared his throat.

"Sorry to startle you. But, uh, has Miss Flowers showed up yet?"

"Not yet." Chevy growled out her answer like a threat.

"Well, I can't hold this up forever. The woman on now, she'll keep the crowd for another song, maybe two. But after that the house is going to have to move on."

"We'll figure it out," said Taneesha, a little intensity coming through in her voice.

"I hope so. Bandanna needs to figure it out very soon because no shows never make it in this business."

It must have been the shallowness that made Chevy snap. The counterfeit formality coming out in a willowy voice when he said "Miss" in a drawn out way before Bandy's last name. The talent manager had a greasiness under all that polish that shined through when he told them that this little lounge with the leaning roof wouldn't want to let its fans down with a no show. A low level agent acting like he had a major reputation to uphold, like he was handling mega stars on Broadway instead of scooping up acts in obscure places where nobody else had time to look. He didn't care if Bandy was alive or dead. The show must go on.

She leapt out of her chair and threw all the sparkling water she never drank into his carefully groomed beard. Some landed in his mouth and splashed in his eyes. The way he shrieked people must have thought it was battery acid. But the greasy agent got away lucky, if her mouth wasn't dry all over again she would spit right in his face.

A few tables paused to watch the scene. The drama was all bang, bang, wide open and animated like a real train wreck is supposed to be. Gangsters laughed and their girls gasped while security rushed over in baggy black suits to wedge themselves in between the crazy woman throwing drinks and the frail man drowning to death on dry land. All the time the gospel singer never missed a beat, she went straight into the next number hitting all the notes even harder than before.

Chevy half cried, half screamed while sparkling water dripped off the talent manager's chin. Taneesha tugged her sleeve, trying her best to get them safely to the door before the men in cheap suits could reach out and catch them. They lumbered a little like they weren't sure where to step, came in arms reach just brushing their fingertips against the black blouse damp with sweat. There was a turning point when things slowed down and both women reversed easy to the exit like the last phase of a robbery, almost tripping over the club's greeter standing by like a roadblock clutching a handful of half price drink coupons in her hand.

That's when her mouth got moist. The spit gushed forward from beneath her tongue and was still fresh when she let it fly from her lips. Security got hit in the middle off his black tie with a juicy glob of saliva that splattered and dripped down in a droopy stream of bubbles. "Keep the change," said Chevy. Then, she wiped her mouth like a barbarian. Back of the hand swiping a dribble off her bottom lip and her and her cousin's girlfriend were gone off the river for the very last time.

✦ 400 ✦

CHAPTER 44

86 STREET

Alone in the bathtub all over again because she wanted to fill a void for a bunch of wrong reasons. Actually, there had been a lot of baths this weekend and each one seemed like it was hotter than the last. The air on her bare skin was too chilly for an exit but the water had grown tepid a half hour ago. To solve her problem she sank down deeper into the whipped bubbles until they tickled her chin. Ordinarily, she would cum in the shower and be done with it but for some reason right now that same old routine seemed like a waste of an orgasm. And who knows how many of those your going to get in this life.

Chocolate finished what Cerrio started back at the Marriott. Even though for the most part he wasn't really her type she still couldn't deny him. He was pathetic, just a simple sucker for love who would always fall for the head games. The only thing worse than his thirst for that honey-eyed woman who baited him was the way they both died a little without each other, and then with each other. Chocolate didn't get any part of that and she didn't want to either. Love made her sick. Still in a way he really wasn't so bad. A man more Chocolate's speed would have shot her right through the head when he had the chance.

And truth be told faint feelings had grown, not love but a dose of affection, a mere pinch in the soup. She tried hard to cancel it and failed so miserably that now real chaos had broken loose. All of this went completely against Chocolate's code which was money first and everything else came second. Including her pretty, pink vagina. It's just Cerrio had that thing inside him. A primitive, juggernaut force that these prima donna boys who caught her between shifts at Sugar Bares or borrowed her ear in a dark club couldn't act out even with a gun to their head. He was a wilderness, a zoocat too feral to know how many screws he had loose. Chocolate hated herself for breaking the rules every time they got together and yet she still wanted more. When that fiery Arabian anger rained down it flooded the Nile between her legs. The part about never cumming only made it so much worse. When he got her so close that she could feel her thighs tingle that didn't do a thing but make the twisted affection grow stronger.

On the edge of the tub Chevy's gun rested at an angle. Just a tap would have made it clatter to the floor but Chocolate was so very careful. She grabbed it with a wet hand ignoring the cold air and the cold grip and instead relished the goosebumps that had all at once become apparent on her skin. She held the weapon just barely above water of her bubble bath closing in on room temp, admiring how the reddish, pink heat lamp in the bathroom played off the metal while a crowd of white foam slid down her arm.

What a nice piece, she thought. A girl pistol if there ever was such a type, pink pearl handle, chrome all over. A lady's best friend. Chocolate teased the trigger with a slippery finger wondering where it came from. Maybe Cerrio saw it one night in a liquor house, part of some bet that he cheated to win so he could arm his precious woman. In a rare flash of humor that amused Chocolate almost enough to coax out a real laugh.

Wherever it came from one thing was for sure. If any gun was going to be pointed at her then it should definitely be the one she was holding. Thinking like that made Chocolate want to keep the sassy thing all for herself. She could tuck it in her dresser drawer, tote it to work for those too handsy tricks who thought her services were for free. Then again maybe she would give it back just to have fun.

Chocolate could lay it down somewhere in that cluttered, junked up apartment Chevy drank herself to death in. Hide it behind the couch when she was high as a kite and watch the dizzy dancer spin in circles asking fruitless questions to that flock of yuppies from 43-Dimes who made up her carpool about where the thing had gone. That would definitely earn a laugh. Only Chocolate didn't play games unless they were very dangerous.

She popped the pistol's clip out and dropped over the side of the tub. It slapped on the bathroom floor. Whap! The weight of a full jacket hitting linoleum sounded off like an angry surprise. Chocolate slipped deeper in the bath until the bubbles kissed her lashes, spread wide and braced her feet against the tub. The gun disappeared underwater, new bubbles gargling to the surface as the .32 burped air from its barrel and filled up with soapy liquid slick enough to be lubricant. The steel was still cold when it tickled her lips. Barely a degree above a coffin lid when she slid it up inside her. She pushed all the way to the trigger guard and pulled back, clenching around the metal, gripping the handle harder and harder. Panting happily through the bubbles every time she clicked Chevy's weapon on empty.

Eight miles away in Center City Taneesha looked up at the sky, she held her breath while lightning flashed and counted seconds until the thunder rolled in. Then, blew it all out when mother's nature clap didn't reach her ears. No big boom, the storm noise stayed across the horizon and another silent flash struck up the night. In the light she could see clouds moving on their journey to the islands off the coast and then eventually out to the vast Atlantic.

"Goddamnit," said Chevy. "The last thing we need is more rain."

"It ain't gonna rain." Neesha made her prediction with confidence.

"You're crazy. Didn't you just see that lightning flash?"

"Yeah, I saw. I got eyes. But that don't mean rain is coming."

Chevy put her knuckles on her hip. Ever since they left the Azaleas Lounge she had been even more brassy than usual.

"How you know it won't rain?

Taneesha pointed her finger up to a bright star in the sky. "That's Jupiter. All the clouds running away from it to the right tell me the wind is blowing east carrying the storm away from us out to the ocean."

Chevy kept on being surly. To her it all sounded like a mystical fairy tale, planets and stars and invisible winds. She made a rude noise to fully illustrate her disgust, a dramatic racket from her mouth that begged for a fade. That was the point. After being eighty-sixed from the club they had walked a long, hard mile on the road and now she was ready to fight.

For a girl in heels the asphalt shoulder was no kind place. Her ankles were ready to fold into the grass, the only thing still keeping her walking tall were the weeds scratching against her bare skin like little roach feet. Chevy was scared of this long winding back road in a town she didn't know, with the tall brush on either side lit up only by the occasional strike of lightning it felt like a perfect spot to go missing. She marched on out of necessity, every step a struggle to fight fatigue and every third step a dandelion scratching against her leg snapping right her back to attention with a nagging itch.

The women walked straight, toes aching, calves on fire, eyes focused on the distance at the glowing lights coming from the all night Waffle House that was still too far away to offset their misery. Much as Chevy didn't want to get soaked while they were out here stranded she would confess that a downpour sounded like a big dose of heaven right now. The thought of soothing rain seemed like a blessing in disguise, something to wash away the pain while she kept trying to dial up a ride. She tried Cerrio, Chocolate, The Yellow Cab Company. The first two wouldn't answer and the last one couldn't help because Chevy had no idea where she was at. At the end of every call Chevy hung up her phone and cussed into the night.

Taneesha listened to the stream of swears and embraced the storm running off to somewhere else. They were a good distraction, both too intense to let her mind get tied up with worry because Bandy was going to be okay. In fact, she was going to be just fine. They all were. Bandy was college educated, she was smart enough to look out for any trouble that might be looming. Plus, worse come to worse she had a gun if any real danger sprung up. Just point and squeeze the way Chevy taught them back at the hotel room.

The incessant aching in her body was another good distraction. Not a welcome one but definitely the best. More effective than harsh words and noiseless lighting strikes going off under the dim stars. With every step a fresh wave of pain rearranged her thoughts into agony until finally her heels went numb.

A warm breeze blew through bowing long strands of grass into the road like humble servants. Taneesha looked down at her toes, no reason, just to see them because she was tired of seeing the dark landscape spread out in front of her. A plant stem caught between two on the right stuck out like a straw. She tried manifesting different thoughts to the ends of both feet where the shoes opened up stylishly to show off her painted nails. She tried the sensation of pain, nothing. Ticklish, nothing. Even irritation but nothing came because Neesha couldn't feel any better than a shadow could speak.

Chevy kept going around in the same pattern. A three step ritual she had adopted not long after they were thrown out of the Azaleas Lounge. Step one, stop walking. Step two she hangs up her phone with a touch of the red circle at the bottom of the screen because nobody answered her call. Step three, redial. Taneesha didn't think much about it. She knew this was Chevy's own brand of relief, a way to keep from losing control on the side of the road where there wasn't a talent manager to act out her frustrations on.

She was at step three, tapping buttons with numbers inside them to call the Cerrio again when Taneesha bent down to undo the straps on her heels. She came back up all natural from the ankles down with the night air licking her arches. Probably the best moment of the whole evening is when she was flat on the ground and could feel her toes again. Perhaps not a miracle but enough to make her head tilt back for a deep sigh of relief as another white bolt cut across the starry Georgia sky.

"What are you doing?"

Taneesha kept her eyes closed. "Just giving my feet a break."

"Put your shoes back on."

"Come on, Chevy. We been out here more than hour, almost two. My toes are cramped and I know yours are too." Neesha opened her eyes and held up her shoes. "I'm just going to carry these in my hand while we keep on walking."

Chevy swept forward, four inches taller than Taneesha made her seem like a mountain in heels. She put a finger so close to the girl's face that the tip almost got tangled in a wisp of loose hair. "This is not an option. When you slice your foot on a broken piece of glass in the dark no ambulance is gonna come because I ain't calling 'em. Now, put your goddamn shoes back on and let's go."

Neesha looked confused. She couldn't help it because that woman standing behind a rigid finger scolding to her face wasn't someone familiar at all. This new fuming stranger held on to her temper while a truck cruised by spilling a halogen glare all over the cracked blacktop. In the basin of light it was easy to tell Chevy never lied. This road out of sight was a field of waste where debris got tossed away like rice at a wedding. It looked like a battlefield of trash where litter and napalm met up for war. No doubt a broken light bulb or a needle was laying out ready to dig in the sole of some soft, tender, foot.

But she wasn't going back in those heels. Huh-unh, no way. Just like she wouldn't go on another moment with this woman she had never seen before. Taneesha sat down on the side of the road, put her shoes right next to her left thigh and crossed both arms over her knees. One of the open toes fell over on its side like a lame horse.

Chevy looked down, all the pent up cruelness in her ready to spring loose like a coiled cottonmouth jumping out from the grass. "You gonna pout now, Neesha? Is that how you deal with life? Things get tough and you just sit down wherever you're at and throw a tantrum?"

"I'm just resting."

"Get up!"

"No!"

"I said, 'get up'!"

Taneesha snapped her head around and looked up with defiance. "And I said 'my fucking feet hurt.' You want to keep walking go right ahead. But I'm not moving. If you want you can come back and pick me up in the morning. Until then," she slapped her palm on the road, "right here is where I'll be."

The night, just like the whole weekend had suddenly gotten very complicated. Normal roles begun twisting over each other like weaves in a basket. Who was who wasn't such a given anymore. No matter what one thing was for sure, both Neesha and Chevy were far from two broken mistresses cast away with the garbage on a busted night. The next car going by probably saw it that way but, no. They were two lovers with lost lovers trying to do something, anything, everything not to capitulate to their very worst fears.

Now, the pattern of diversions was broken. No more cars came to bathe them in light, no more calls going out unanswered. Things were tense and terse but the absence of petty interruptions felt right. More pure than going down the road like nothing really mattered except a ride and the rain. In the vacuum of distractions a chorus of southern crickets gladly sang their country anthem. Another shot of lightning ran up the dark strobing across Chevy's features. Ten seconds later the east winds changed, reversing course to bring mother nature right back into town.

Thunder finally arrived like better late than never, but Taneesha didn't care about the storm anymore. She didn't turn to see the clouds come back like someone with regrets, just slid her eyes over cautiously to watch the bottle glass figure standing close at her shoulder. There was no worry, no fear pumping in her heart. She didn't weigh much more than a hundred and ten pounds but if Chevy wanted turbulence then she would be unpleasantly surprised. Taneesha could fight just as good as any east Winston scrapper from any project lining any block. Anyway, she had given her word. There was no getting up off the ground to walk again. Not another step, she had sworn it.

Seville James eased gently to the ground right next to her, scraping jagged road rocks with the pointy heels she had worn just for Bandy's final show tonight. She picked them up in Savannah as a little retail therapy to get over the deep, catastrophic, losses on the boat. She scooted over close so that their knees were touching.

"I'm sorry, mama." She put an arm around Taneesha's waist and pulled her close. "Look at us, out here together in the storm trying to get somebody to pick us up. We're sisters, baby. It's just this worry that I been trying to walk off all night won't let me go."

Neesha stared off at something in the distance. "You think I'm not worried too after what's already happened? I'm terrified." She turned to look at Chevy. "You think one of us should have went with Bandy back to the hotel?"

"Don't start blaming yourself. We can't crack now before we even know what's going on."

"You're right. I shouldn't be living in fear. It's just that this doesn't make any sense. Bandy isn't the type to just up and disappear, ya know?"

"I know." Chevy held up her phone to show her last call that went unanswered. "None of this makes sense. A trip that was supposed to be a good thing makes me wish I'd just stayed home. Last time I felt this overwhelmed was when Cerrio went to jail. Back then I almost lost my mind."

"What got you through it?" asked Taneesha.

Chevy sniffed. "Cocaine."

CHAPTER 45

COFFIN NAIL

Chocolate laid on the bed. Hand in one pocket, pistol in the other as she twisted the sash of her hotel bathrobe between two, fine fingers thinking about her decision to keep the gun. Not for playing hide and seek games around Chevy's apartment, there would never time for that amongst all the fast business in Winston. Fact is Chevy's little .32 simply deserved better. The same way Judy had gone back to grandma's house where she belonged this sexy piece of steel had found a way to come home all on its own.

Cerrio would be on board with the choice. His girlfriend's gun had a fatal attractiveness that fit right in with Chocolate's ill-starred darkness like a key in a lock, fingers in a glove, bullets down a barrel. Even if he didn't already owe her for all the cash she gave him over the weekend the man still wouldn't protest. The way he turned down a blowjob but took her money showed a savvy style of survival that would always, always, always elect for Chocolate to have the right protection just in case things went wrong on their next caper.

The phone rang on the table, another one of Chevy's calls went straight to voicemail. Bandy must have rushed back with the news of what she saw falling off her lips like all those bluesy notes she blew for the crowd on the casino boat. A big mouth with a pretty voice, thought Chocolate. A diamond in the rough nearly crushed then pulled back like a deep sea anchor. Her tragedy was necessary, it brought balance to those serious mistakes Cerrio had made in past times before. When she touched his head that night they had brought Judy in from the street Chocolate saw scales of fate leaning towards something nasty and then felt them tip back days ago when she answered her phone for him down in Myrtle Beach. Bandy's melody had washed his ugly sins away. She was the yin to his yang when the yang stood for flaws and Chocolate knew some of Cerrio's flaws were colored in blood.

Taneesha kept looking to the sky. "This is Bandy's weather. She hates the rain, loves the lightning though. I think the school did it to her. Last semester she had a class about Greek mythology. It wasn't nothing serious. Just something she took for the easy credits. But you know Bandy, she's a hundred and twenty percent when it comes to everything. So, she aced the class and then fell in love with it. Now every time lighting jumps out of the sky she says, 'there goes Zeus showing off again.' And I never miss a storm anymore. Whenever one comes to town, she pulls me over to the couch with a bottle of Rosé so we can drink and watch it out the window together."

Chevy swallowed the lump rising up in her throat. Big girls don't cry, at least not on the side of the road like hopeless, little tramps. She touched on Taneesha's hair, petting it softly where it flared out at the shoulders. "Don't worry. Come tomorrow afternoon you two will be right next to each other on the couch sipping wine again."

Before another shaky promise fell out of her mouth a set of brakes squealed out in the dark like a blind bat. Both women looked up as a two-toned Caprice that lived its past life as a cop car slowed down to a stop. Chevy nodded, "there's our ride."

Neesha picked her heels up off the street. Contention was gone now, blown away with the clouds that had changed their minds yet again. They had sat down together on the asphalt long enough for all the anger to melt away just like the pain in their shins. Now the women were sisters, brushing dirt from the back of each other's jeans and sliding in side by side through same rear door of the cab.

In the backseat Chevy blinked at the face looking so familiar, like he could have been Cerrio's little brother or big cousin or any deep, brown leaf in his family tree. Same thick eyebrows, same pronounced nose passed down from generations who lived and loved hard way in another land. He even had a wild name that made a hard purchase on your tongue when you said it out loud. Chevy saw it on the driver's license stuck to the dashboard for company reasons, a four or five syllable handle. A straight import.

The driver put his eyes on the new fare in the mirror. "Where to?" he asked. He watched the women carefully, admiring them some before asking the standard question again. Taneesha spoke up before Chevy could even remember herself. "Downtown Marriott," she replied and the cab rolled forward with rocks and storm blown twigs crunching beneath the back tires as they put faster distance between them and the White Azaleas Lounge.

In a mile Chevy shook off her astonishment. If it had been the other way around, if Cerrio accidentally mistook some other honey complexioned woman on the street for her would judgement be certain? All black women don't look alike. She could forgive him that little error but what if he reached out and touched her? What if Cerrio offered the other woman a ride home, or worse yet a rose?

While Chevy pondered on the bright line separating honest mistakes from aggravated flaws that begged off a cure Taneesha stared out the window. She kept her eyes on the street watching the broken spaces between palm trees lining medians down the long Savannah roads. She was hoping for a miracle, to see her bae going the opposite way. Maybe looking for them just like they were looking for her right now.

Between round tree trunks were short glimpses of regal homes, random strangers, but no Bandy. Neesha was ready to bounce up and down in her seat and point out the window like a happy kid when she caught sight of her. The driver with the long name would think she had lost her shit but she couldn't care less. Except that didn't happen. No lucky sightings of the woman who had the keys to her heart followed by a blast of excitement. Instead, all she saw were more flashes of the same storm they were missing out on together.

Somewhere down the road the driver changed the music. He let go of the woman signing a Pakistani lullaby for a local station singing '90's R and B. Much more American thought Chevy and exactly the type of thing Cerrio might do if he was giving a lift to two sisters and liked what he saw.

She was humming along to In Vogue, drifting away from her vast world of memories and worrying about if she would be able to make new ones when she suddenly looked up and caught him staring in the mirror. They locked eyes in the reflection, the cab driver's irises glittered some when a streetlight saturated the windshield. Chevy tried so hard not to smile at him but she couldn't help herself. He was just too much like Cerrio, one glance and her stomach flooded with steel butterflies. He smiled back and asked if she liked the new music. Chevy nodded and grinned some more with her palms flat down on the seat. The resemblance was so uncanny she had to sit on her hands just to fight off the urge to reach out and touch him.

Chocolate didn't notice the tapping at the door. At first it was too light to be heard over her own thoughts and the TV weather girl going on about all that lightning creasing the sky outside.

Then, like a scalpel on a cheek the knuckles came down hard to slice through the crowd of noise. She knew it wasn't Chevy. Even that last leaden knock was fly weight for a woman scorned by failed friendship. That is if she already found out and if she had then that meant it must be Cerrio looking for a place to get out of the storm.

She was off the bed tightening the robe around her waist. On her way to the door Chocolate stopped to smooth her hair and turned to the side to check her reflection in the glass of a picture frame. Tough break for a fella all alone in this weather. She licked her lips to say as much and whatever else might seem clever then slid back the short chain above the lock without even looking through the peephole.

Names escaped her. The man standing in the hallway seeking company wasn't Cerrio. He wasn't even close. Just a forgettable joker wandering desperate and alone in the night as the sky over the city flashed like a photoshoot. Round eyes much too big even for the paunch under his shirt and the flab in his jaws. Meaty lips that were unusually soggy. Sweat in places Chocolate thought he should have had amputated. He paid well, though. With a body and a face like that he had to.

Chocolate remembered him from the boat and once in this same room earlier when he humped her like a frog. She forgot his name but remembered the lie he told his wife who sat solo in a church meeting. Probably a select falsehood picked out from a myriad of dishonest excuses he mixed up and fed her here and there when he needed to with practiced ease. On the phone he told her that he had to work late. Whatever that meant for a paper factory employee in the middle of a Monday Chocolate didn't know but all the same she still hated him for it. If the fabrication was crafty instead of cliché, sharp and not careless, if it had spirit or style or even a hint of flavor she could maybe get on board. But it didn't and she despised him for the way he barely tried because it showed how cheaply he regarded his wife. This fat fucker smacking his lips, slogging through the weather for a nut, regarded the only one who would have him for free as much as a broken shoelace.

He put a hand on the wall and leaned on it with his weight. "Hey, sweetness. How's it going?"

Chocolate couldn't even pretend at romance. "It's late. What are you doing here?"

"Yeah, yeah, I know it's late. But hey you're up. Got time for a quickie?"

He wiggled his eyebrows and Chocolate almost puked.

"Go home." She tried to shut the door but the man who's name she didn't remember stopped it with a size fourteen boot. He put his foot in the way to keep himself from being left out in the hall.

"I just can't stop thinking about you." He huffed. "You drive me crazy. Those legs and those fucking tits. I was eating dinner with my wife tonight and she was going on and on about some stupid thing from her book club and the whole time I was thinking about your body. I need it, baby."

Chocolate knew his hand had moved off the wall and was now on the other side of the door. She wished Cerrio were here. Sitting on the bed right now the sweat box would guess him for another thirsty trick and she could play it off like they were just getting started.

"Where does your wife think you're at right now?" she asked.

He giggled and wheezed at the same time. "She thinks my brother's truck got stuck in a ditch. I told towing him out might take all night."

"That was good. But I'm really tired baby. Why don't you come around after work tomorrow?"

"That's too long to wait. I wanna fuck you now."

Suddenly it came to her, Gary was his name. Bigger than Barney who could choke the life out of a woman easy as squeezing a lemon dry he had a body like cold oatmeal sliding off the wall. Chocolate's heart slammed inside her chest. She took a step back to open the door and Gary's soggy lips pulled themselves back into a slimy smile.

"Alright, that's what I'm talking about. Hey sweetness you got a nice spread here. Whoring must pay pretty damn good, huh?"

She paused. "Hold on did you hear that?"

"Aw, don't worry baby. It's probably just the thunder outside."

"No, I know what thunder sounds like. This is something else."

Chocolate stuck her head out in the hall, checked left, then right. Gary did the same thing with a puzzled look on his face until something hard pressed deep into his groin. When he looked down the muzzle of Chevy's gun was buried deep in the crotch of his work jeans.

"What the...?"

"Shut up," she hissed. "I'll blow your dick off right in the hallway."

Gary eased back a half step. "Hold on, baby."

"I'm not your fucking baby."

She pushed the pistol hard into the spongy flesh of his limp manhood until he went obediently back. Gary took his air in quivering, shaky breaths as she put a free hand in every pants pocket to take anything she wanted, her fee in fifty dollar bills, his leather wallet bloated with credit cards and random paper trash, a cell phone housed in a case with a Braves logo. The would-be trick stood there until his jeans got turned out to show the cloth lining stained brown from leaky cans of chewing tobacco. Car keys and and an aged pocketknife fell to the floor but he didn't dare look down. Then, Chocolate took the gun away and kicked him where the end used to be.

First his face blushed red, then the neck and eyes. She stifled a laugh while he held himself like everything might fall off. "Now, get the fuck out of here." Chocolate pulled the slide back on the gun. "Come back again and I'll shoot you for real." She kicked his knife hard until it bounced off the back wall. "And take all your shit with you. I don't want to see none of this when I wake up tomorrow."

❖　❖　❖

Back at the Marriott the room seemed strange, untouched and bothered all at the same time. Bandy's forgotten wig laid out on top of the suitcases just like Taneesha said. The money they had left still locked up tight in the safe by the door. But standing arm's length from the French windows with her head cocked to the side Chevy thought the bed looked rumpled.

She really wished her mother were here. Chitara James could call out a mess in a minute. No small upset ever got past her. Chevy had to admit that since mama died her love of powder had changed a lot of important things. These days she was more easygoing about cleaning up, some might even call it lazy. Cerrio left dishes in the sink and she never complained, ditto for Bandy whenever she skipped drying the tub out after she took a bath and no one had vacuumed under the couch in a month.

Bad habits beget bad habits, that's something her daddy used to say in life. But just like him none of that was here or there. Chevy stood sober as a priest, full concentration on the bed with her head straight to get a different point of view. Near the headboard the edges of the blanket seemed crooked, uneven with the corners hanging slack around the pillows. In every hotel housekeeping always folds the top comforter back a foot or so but Chevy couldn't feel the maids touch in here. Somehow they just did it better, they kept the linen edges sharp and tucked the corners in with precision. Someone else tried to pull off the same thing and missed the mark. It was amateur hour in here.

Taneesha cleaned up her face in the bathroom. The last bit of mascara surrendered to a moist towelette that brought all of her features right back to a glowing, pecan color. She thought a moment about crying, not so much as an urge but more like a menu choice to ease the anxiety running through her like the water in the sink.

In the end she never had to, if she had no hope and no hero perhaps tears would flow. Weeping might be appropriate then but not now. Neesha had confidence because she knew Cerrio would level this town if something happened to Bandy. He wouldn't leave Savannah without her, he wouldn't leave and go home without any of them. Her eyes stayed dry because Tanee-sha had learned during their time together under one roof that the list of people Chevy's lover loved was shorter than a note in a fortune cookie but deadly serious. Everybody on it walked with confidence knowing he would pluck them out of the closed palm of death or get crushed inside right along with them.

She threw the wipe away in the toilet without thinking. The water converged like a hungry beast on prey and sent up a party of makeup swirls spreading across the porcelain bowl. It wasn't supposed to go down there. Taneesha knew it would clog the pipes but if it was the worse thing that happened to her all week-end then she promised to be better and never do it again. No last look in the mirror before she cut the light out. She flipped the switch and bounced before any second thoughts could put down seeds to grow up into a tree of doubt. Then, paused soon as her feet hit the carpet.

Chevy had a knee on the bed, the other leg out at an angle so her high heel was hanging right by the bedside table in front of the hotel telephone. Both hands were on the mattress, Taneesha watched carefully as she picked up one and grazed it slowly along a pillow like a child petting a horse. When the pillowcase ran out then her hand stopped at its corner and Chevy's long, lean, body stretched out almost flat next to the headboard, stomach six inches off the mattress, butt in the air, both legs behind her with two feet floating off the edge. From where Taneesha stood it was easy to see what Cerrio liked, a beautiful dancer down in a crawl like that did a lot to strike up all the right feelings in all the wrong places.

Chevy caught her looking. "What happened?" she asked. "Did you find something good?"

Neesha shook her head and said, "no."

"Well, why are you grinning like that?"

"I don't know. Just something to do I guess."

Chevy looked around. "I think something's shady in here. Look at this bed. Does look like we left it last time?"

"It's hard to tell with you spread out all over it like that."

After the dancer got up then Taneesha took a second to examine. She pointed. "I think, maybe right there looks a little messed up." Chevy put a hand down in the spot where the finger was aimed and a scent lifted up in the air.

She paused to judge the aroma. It was sweet, pushy, intoxicating, poisonous. Female. She leveled her eyes at Neesha. "Smell that?"

"No."

"Then, come a little closer."

Taneesha came in range, close enough to get the thrill of the fragrance. "Smells like lavender."

"It's familiar. Reminds me of when Cerrio walked into Sugar Bares VIP room that first night and I popped him a good one and made him fall right back in love with me all over again."

Chevy smacked the comforter to get another whiff. When she hit it lightly something jumped off and fell on the floor. Taneesha peeked around her leg to get a glimpse.

"What is that?" she asked.

Chevy narrowed her eyes. "I don't know. But I know it ain't mine."

In Latin they say, dux famina facti. Chocolate remembered those words from her own few days of college. Literally it meant a woman was a leader of the exploit. And after two semesters she left campus to go make that line come true. Not like she wasn't making it happen at school anyway, but a part-time student could never really be a full-time hustler.

One day she'll go back, not soon like next year because the pressure to get an education isn't severe as getting money and paying bills. In a while, though. Definitely by the time she turns twenty-eight, before thirty at the latest. In futuro, thought Chocolate, which was another Latin phrase that translated easily. It simply meant in the future, which is exactly where she'll be whenever the time came.

For right now she was in the thick of it and today was so good it only made her crave tomorrow. After an all night storm Tuesday morning promised to come around bright as high beams. Chocolate could already feel the cancer of the sun biting at her heels. In a few hours the sky would turn velvety purple, then Caribbean blue and not long after that it would be time to blow this town. Between then and now there was still a chance to get a little sleep. Chocolate just needed an hour or two so she could recharge her batteries.

She twisted a hair tie around Gary's stack of credit cards and planned her dreams. She could do that, of course she could. She was the master of puppets, the wizard behind a curtain calling fools down a winding, yellow, brick road. So, controlling the thoughts she had when she wasn't awake was very basic. Every beginner's volume to manipulation says you have to get a hold of yourself before you can play master of fools.

Gary was the last in a series. Even though her toes hurt from kicking him in the nuts the money she took from his jeans almost made her partial to the pain. In fact everything, dare she say, felt good. How could it not with a new gun full of shells and a pocket full of cash? Tomorrow it was a long trip back home but tonight in her sleep she wanted to cover the epic distance from here to the future. Who knows? Maybe Cerrio would be there clapping his hands at her college graduation.

CHAPTER 46

NEVER HERS

Chevy thought that this had to be wrong. Not just a mistake but wrong on top of wrong capping off a night of error to finish up a weekend decidedly tipped away from joy by so many errors. The part of her that didn't want to understand pacified so much of her that purely didn't want to know. Denial was a life raft saving her from the truth but here came the high tide of reality rolling in.

On the nightstand Cerrio's gold chain sat slightly twisted, a few links hung off the edge like an ivy vine. He never talked about the way he got it or where it came from. He returned off that one week hiatus dipped in new clothes and fresh secrets swimming in a mist of concealment. Whenever pressed about the things he'd done while gone he just gave a wink and a smile, sometimes just a shrug and a walk off.

The pain of realization was sharp, it arrived suddenly to wash away confusion for the clean birth of anger. Cerrio would never leave without his Cuban links. No one knew how he got them, nonetheless Chevy knew how precious they were. That piece that went around his neck held pride. She remembered the night on the boat's deck when they ate over candles, how the small light adorning only half their faces splashed off the jewelry he wore and how when they came together to press lips it kissed so cold against the skin right up above her cleavage. Staring at the yellow gold now she could feel the thin flesh tightening around each knuckle in her hand. There was no good explanation, only the truth. He had came and gone in a rush, made the bed in the hurry to cover up another layer of secrets. While the rest of the world fell down all around him the dog was shopping a new strange lover with an old, familiar, fragrance.

But who?

Chocolate sat straight up in the bed. Those dreams about tomorrow didn't wither away, they died all once. Flatlined.

Outside the storm carried on with every white flash exposing the landscape like a snap of deja vu. Before the Gary came knocking with his dick in his hand the weather girl on TV said, "it would be like that all night."

She began to wonder about Cerrio. Was he back at the Marriott or had Chevy put him out to the curb like Tuesday's garbage? That spark of curiosity grew up into worry until Chocolate felt full blown concern calling out from somewhere between her legs. Shit, she hated this fucking feeling. She went to kill it with a text, a jazzy message loaded with a hint of aggravation so he couldn't see it and just leave it alone. That was her way to check on him, with a cool joke and a tease. At least that's what she told herself to make it okay.

She was deep in it, smiling at her own joke about how changing the sheets wouldn't do a thing about the mess Cerrio splashed across the carpet. Everything was going so good, she was still the wizard, still in total control until she blinked and noticed her typing thumb was short. Chocolate checked her hand again to make sure it wasn't a quick spell of blindness, some trick of the light that made her lose focus because those things tend to happen after a long day. In the end they all still looked the same, five at full height on the left, four on the right with the fifth missing that last quarter inch. "Fuck," she muttered. That little Korean nail could be anywhere. Best place to look was the last place she saw it but since that was her hand she checked out in the hallway instead.

Maybe it came off in Gary's pocket while she was running through them. If so then it was evidence. He could show it to the cops and they would have her dead to rights. Chocolate wasn't a jail bitch, she had bond money and a lawyer standing by who already owed her a few favors. His number was down in the first page of her little, black book. She wouldn't need to use him, though. Not unless Gary wanted to explain in open court how a woman at a hotel robbed him at one or two in the morning when he was supposed to be working late. And once his wife got a load of Chocolate's rich, dark skin Gary would be paying alimony forever. For ever, ever.

No, a trial in front of the whole world was not what the fat man wanted. He might be a first-class moron but stupid still has its limits. Losing a wallet and a swift kick to the nuts was a small price to keep a secret.

But her nail wasn't in the hallway, or lost in the bedspread, or face up in the bathtub. It wasn't in any of the places Chocolate last touched. She even went outside, took the cover off the Jeep and checked the mats using the flashlight on her phone. The night manager got off shift and walked by her without even stopping to offer any help. She might say that was unusual but right now that was the pot calling the kettle black. Maybe a woman in a bathrobe rifling through a truck in the middle of a lightning storm is just all in a day's work around here.

Now, you know me, and if you know me then you know by now had I found a game. Not inside some card house or down in the basement of anybody's trap spot. This match was wide open on a side street behind a real anonymous looking building that could have been a strip club just as easy as it might have been the post office. The players were three random locals all dressed down in mall clothes and of course me, Lacoste shirt, Gucci slacks, boat shoes on my feet that Chocolate picked up when she went shopping this afternoon for a new pair of jeans. We were grouped around a burgundy Brougham, slapping cards off the hood, trying hard not to bang our knuckles on the paint job or drop ashes from the purple we were smoking.

This was spades, the game I love to hate. There were hangers on calling backseat plays in between drags off the reefer and teams who already got beat waiting for their chance to break even against me and a partner who were currently running the show. An extra measure of excitement came via a few wide-eyed neighborhood boys placing wagers on the side and making stealthy moves out of sight whenever the croaky voice of money called from down the alley.

This was my scene, the genuine rawness of it. No singing, no dancing, no pit bosses in polyester vests, no river boat with all the frills and upper class eye candy. Just a deck of 52 under a lonely streetlamp and may the best man win.

My partner's name was Clover, he was a surgeon at spades. I don't know if his name came from the streets or if it was the real original one his parents gave him at birth. Some things you just don't ask a man. I knew he'd done time, probably a stretch at the Georgia state penitentiary starting in his twenties. He was old now and his body was built strong from endless pushups on a concrete floor. But the luck he had made me believe he had sold his soul to the devil on the yard. We won back to back games but the victory here didn't open up an abscess like it always did in Winston-Salem. Nobody complained or reached for a gun when they lost, they just tossed their twenties and fifties on the Cadillac hood and got back in line for another chance to try it again.

Chocolate knew that in the end none of this truly mattered. The weekend was so far past saving nothing short of a miracle could ever bring it back and a fake fingernail gone in the wind wouldn't make the slightest bit of change. If she hadn't shot her mouth off already Bandy would do it soon, she'd run straight to Chevy spilling all that got witnessed and before the first light of dawn reached over the Savannah river both of them would be up in a rage. Cerrio could hit the Powerball tonight, but if he didn't then his love and his gambling career in Georgia were both sacked.

So, in the end everyone was going home with their head in their hands. The good, the bad, and now even the beautiful. Nothing could stop it, nobody could halt the wheels in motion and that's why it didn't make sense to pursue. Except there were feelings, a fatal sense of pride enfolded in her ego that had Chocolate's good sense strung up like Christmas lights in March. During her whole career she had never left a thing behind, not a pair of lacy under-wear, not a chain or an earring, not a tube of mascara or a designer clutch. Nothing. If a man slept with her and got caught it was be-cause of his own negligence. Attribute it to male sloppiness, they were all animals anyway. Whether it was bad timing or a lame excuse or the kids walking in on them the error was always his, not hers. Never hers.

Chevy opened her hand, the painted nail that bounced off the bed laid dead in the middle. She still hadn't figured it out. Who did this fake body part belong to? Sweat from her palm, oil from her skin, rage from her heart had all worked together to curl it up into a tiny taco shell. She examined it like a specimen beside the indents pressed down right into her life line. The color scheme was bold but not one she herself would ever try to pull off. Burnt Sienna tipped with blue didn't mesh with her skin at all. It would have clashed with Taneesha, screaming project chick, making her look like a ghetto mama out trolling or tramping and Bandy always stayed tidy with a clear gloss and French tips.

It was foreign, that much had been decided. Or was it really? Because the one, true, detail in life is that nothing is really quite for certain. Maybe they had it in their luggage and it fell out accidentally when they were counting money and changing clothes. A house-keeper could have lost it putting a complimentary mint down on the pillow. Any maid might be walking around downstairs right now with nine nails and a bare finger just praying to slide in the tardy girl's slot at the salon in the morning.

Chevy focused on her palm. "Call Cerrio."

Taneesha looked up. "But you already tried that, like a hundred times."

"I tried a hundred times from my phone. Try from the hotel line and let's see what happens."

"You think he's avoiding you? Like he knows he's in trouble?"

"Maybe, maybe not. Doesn't matter 'cause he's got to come home some time. I just don't want to leave any stone unturned. If he knows where Bandy is then it's at least worth a try." She sniffs and stares away at something on the wall. "I'll play his game. I can act like we're okay until he tells me whatever we need to know."

"You...you sure?"

Chevy snapped out of it. "Yeah, I'm sure. Pick up the phone."

Neesha knew not to argue. She plucked the phone out of its cradle and dialed the area code back home. She had the whole number almost to the last digit when the lock on the door clicked over and like a last witness to a crime in walked the end of the mystery.

Chocolate froze in place as the door slammed shut like a gate on a hyena's cage. Chevy stared, considering her like a painting in a museum as her hand closed over something tiny inside. No one moved while she gave the stone face to her ex-coworker. It felt like a lifetime ago when they both set Cerrio up in the room with the red, leather couches. Now here they were, seeing each other for the very first time, falling down slowly into the wrinkles of fate.

Taneesha stayed on the edge of the bed flicking her wide, brown eyes from one woman to the other without any sort of idea about what to expect. If the tension in the room was thick enough to stir then it was hot enough to serve on a plate. She clutched the phone in midair until the dial tone cut through the silence.

Chevy tilted her head. "It's pretty late to be dropping by unan-nounced. Everything good with you, girl?"

Chocolate staved off the murderous glare. "It's all good, baby. I just misplaced my phone. Thought maybe you mighta seen it somewhere around here."

"Nope, ain't seen no phone around here. You seen a phone, Neesha?"

The other woman held up the plastic receiver in her hand still making noise. "Just this one. And mine. And yours."

Chevy tsked. "Sorry, no phones."

"Damn," said Chocolate. "You know how bad I need that thing too."

"Oh, I do. A phone is very important to a girl like you. You know, it might be somewhere around here, though. Maybe we just missed it. Thing is me and Neesha spent most of the night out looking for Bandy."

Chocolate kept her face straight, lips tight. "What do you mean looking for her? Weren't y'all at the club together? Me and Cerrio dropped you guys off."

"Yeah, and then she had a wardrobe thing. She called a cab to bring her here so she could get her wig. Girl thinks she's a fashion icon now." Chevy shrugged like, what are you going to do? Then, she turned around and looked at Taneesha. "That was what, about ten-thirty when she left White Azaleas?"

"Yeah, about ten-ish."

"Uh-huh, and ain't seen her since."

Chocolate almost laughed. "So, the sweet thing is missing again, huh?"

Chevy nodded. "Gone, like a thief in the night. If she keeps this up and I'ma have to change her name to Vanish."

"Any clues?"

Out of nowhere Taneesha dropped the phone on the nightstand. The sudden explosion of noise ratcheted up nerves already stretched tight. "She mumbled a soft apology and put the thing back on the hook.

Chevy turned back to face her prey. "What about, Cerrio? Where's he at?"

Chocolate hooked a thumb over her shoulder like he was waiting right outside in the hall. "Still at the spot downtown. Gambling like crazy, winning too. He probably thinks I'm out handling a little bit of business."

"Makes sense, you are a woman of business."

"Not tonight. I been putting all my energy into keeping an eye on your boy, tonight.

"Good looking out," said Chevy. "Lord knows he needs eyes on him. So, did he just lose his phone too?"

Chocolate could see the trap opening. The mechanical jaws pulling back, yawning wide like a wolf so the bait could sit down comfortably on the tongue in the middle. It was devilish too, genius as fuck. Because she must answer. Feigning ignorance would only spawn another question, and another then another in a nonstop barrage. Chevy would hop across inquiries like a frog on lily pads until she painted Chocolate in a tight corner.

She looked at Neesha like maybe there was an answer in the girl's long face. No help. Just like usual Chocolate was all on her own. She licked her lips and sat down comfortably in an armchair with buttons on the back.

"When's the last time you called him?"

Chevy did the shrug again. "Shit, I don't know. I been trying to call him all night. I tried calling you too."

"Really? Well, then my phone really is lost 'cause I ain't heard a ringtone all night." Chocolate crossed her legs. "You know, it's that place. Card houses in Winston-Salem are loud but here it's something different."

"Different like how?"

"Baby, it's turned up. People hollering. Music playing. It's sweat and money wall to wall till sunrise. Somebody could shoot a gun in there and you wouldn't hear it. Ain't no way you can hear a phone ringing."

Chocolate smiled for her audience. The trap hadn't closed on her. Before Chevy could think it through all the way she reached inside her purse and pulled out a bag of white powder. "Want a line?"

"Now's a bad time for that," said Taneesha.

"I wasn't asking you," snapped Chocolate.

"But I'm telling you. Nobody's looking to get high right now. In fact, from the way you tell it the party is on the other side of that door. Why don't you turn around and get back to it?"

Sugar Bares finest nodded genuinely impressed. "Wow, Chevy. I never took this one for a rider. You must have shown these girls some things when I wasn't looking."

"Call me Seville. And actually that sounds like a good idea. I don't want Cerrio on the table anymore. It's almost two a.m."

"But he's winning."

"I don't care. He can win more as soon as we get back home. Right after I figure out what's going on with Bandy."

Taneesha stood up ready to launch. "Let's go."

Chocolate stared daggers at the haughty, lesbian housewife. All domestic and dewy eyed, mopping floors and cooking dinner for her partner. No one held a thing against a girl loving another girl. On occasion Sugar Bares finest had even shared that affection herself.

No, she could never blame Taneesha. Truth is Chocolate would love to taste that singing mouth one day, someday, maybe sooner than later. Sure, Bandy was a prize but Taneesha was useless. She didn't strip, didn't hustle, didn't sell ass or dope. When her girlfriend got beat like a drum in some freak's bathtub she stayed locked up tight in her tiny apartment and let the hood have its way.

Pathetic.

Before anyone could start trouble Chevy rose to her feet and sneezed without a warning. Chocolate cringed. Neesha said, "bless you." Chevy didn't give a shit either way. She came right back out of it directing traffic.

"Neesha, we need a ride. Pick up that phone again and call our cab driver from earlier. Tell him to slide back over to the hotel. Chocolate can give him directions to the card house. " She sniffed. "Right now, I'm going to the bathroom. Soon as I come back out y'all two be ready to skate."

CHAPTER 47

MIRROR CROSS

The trap shut it's jaws in the elevator, and like all real bait Chocolate never even saw it coming. She was focused on the lie. What the fuck was she going to tell Chevy when it turned out there was no card house by the Greyhound station? On the ceiling six mirrors separated by thread thin lines reflected the prelude to hate. Whoever had the chore of keeping them polished must hate this life. Such a thankless job but it took a lot of pride. The same sort of pride Chocolate usually took in being extra careful about her own work.

Pride and fidelity. Was it all just a fantasy? Chevy stared up to heaven hoping Cerrio wasn't corrupt. At least not completely, at least not tonight. She saw herself right above looking back like she was praying to a twin. Each piece of glass on the ceiling was completely spotless, free of water drops, wiped clean of dust, zero streaks. She promised to fill out a compliment card before they all went back home. Good work deserved recognition, that's something her daddy used to say. She squinted at the ceiling like a coded message was scrawled up there. That's when Chocolate looked up herself and they locked eyes.

It happened just like it did in the back of the cab. But instead of Cerrio's look alike all Chevy saw was the pink, pearl handle of a little pistol tilted sideways an inch below the top of a purse. Deep in there enough to be considered tucked, but just like all secrets it wasn't buried enough.

Now, it could be that this was all just a crazy misunderstanding. And it could be that no funny smell came walking through the door of her room ten minutes ago. And it could just be that the scent didn't stink anything like lavender. It could have been some other strange odor that had Chevy sneezing like a fox sniffing black pepper off a skunk's back. Maybe the fingernail still clutched in her hand really did belong to the last housekeeper that fluffed the plush, bed pillows. Chevy liked all those ideas, every one seemed warm and inviting and she would embrace them all despite what it cost her dignity. That was the sick, side effect of love. So much helplessness and the fatal will to hold on tight to it. Best part is she could get plenty of help with her denial. Cerrio would lie. Chocolate would always lie. But the mirror never lied.

She reached past Taneesha to mash the emergency button at the bottom of the panel. When the elevator jerked to a halt the lights went pink and alarm bells shrilled their high notes. Chocolate didn't have to ask because she already knew. Her purse closed quick but Chevy's hand was faster. She had it in and out of the Prada bag with the .32 gripped tight and once the gun was pointed at a pair of moist lips coated with gloss then the interrogation commenced.

"Where is Bandy?"

"How should I know?"

"I know you know because this is the gun I gave her to keep her safe. And this fake nail in my other hand looks like the tenth one missing from your set."

"Let me see it." Chocolate couldn't resist a chance to make things fun.

"Play stupid with someone else."

"Why? What are you gonna do, Chevy? Shoot me in the fucking elevator?"

She raised the gun to her right eye. "Are you going to tell me what I want to know? Or you trying make those your final words?"

"Bitch, be for real"

"You go first."

"Come on Chevy, girl. I might know something about Bandy and I might not, but both of us know good and well you're never going to pull that trigger."

She pulled the .32's slide and let it rack back. "You're talking like a slut with a bulletproof forehead. Guess you're ready to die all full of courage."

"Don't be dramatic. You're not a killer. I know you got something to prove to this little girl behind me but it just ain't the truth. You got heart. I admit it. You got to be a tough old bitch to put up all that shit you do. But a killer?" Chocolate clucked her tongue. "Huh-unh, no way baby."

"I'm not asking again. Where is Bandy?"

Chocolate moved closer. "I know you're scared," she whispered. "All of this is a lot. Just put the gun away and go find your boyfriend while there's still innocence left in you. Before shit gets real."

"Shoot her," Taneesha growled.

"No, see she can't. You know wanna know what these white folks down in Georgia do to trigger happy ho's? They hide 'em. Lock 'em up somewhere in a concrete chamber with a number until you forget you ever had a name. I ain't talking about a cozy cell with a cute girl to hold on to after lights out. This is chain gang country. You and a bunch of redneck bitches lined up side by side with pick axes breaking rocks until your back gives out."

"I'll fucking shoot her," said Neesha.

"Shut up!" Chevy yelled.

"Gimme the gun."

"No."

"She's right! You're too scared. Just let me do it and you go on."

"I need you to settle down and shut up, Taneesha!"

"Then, shoot or pass the pistol. She knows what happened to Bandy. We're wasting time!"

One more chance to talk before the shots rang out. Neesha was either hot or cold. A lover and a fighter with no places of uncertainty to hide her feelings. Chocolate hated it but she knew there wasn't a chance she could talk Bandy's girlfriend out of this killing. If that little Barbie pistol changed hands her murder would be selling newspapers tomorrow.

"She dropped it on the floor."

Chevy blinked. "What?"

"Bandy dropped your gun. I picked it up. Pretty fucking simple, baby."

"Where?"

Chocolate looked up without moving her head. "Happened earlier in your room."

"Bullshit," hissed Taneesha. "Shoot this bitch already."

"For what? I have no reason to lie."

"You got plenty of reasons to lie. We just don't know them all. Yet."

"Shoot me and you'll be thinking about what I told you for the rest of your life, wondering if it was actually the truth."

Taneesha held her palm out. "Give it."

Chevy could have taken the offer, passed the weapon and kept her hands clean. There was a lot of power at the end of her arm. Enough to end two lives, or maybe what it took to save only one. She changed gears.

"Give me your purse."

Chocolate laughed. "What, you a jacker now?"

No answer. Instead, the dancer got her shoulder jerked like a necktie caught in a blender. There was a cry of shock that fell out of her mouth and then her bag got turned upside down. Chevy shook it hard, lipstick, compact, iPhone, matching clutch dumped out all over the elevator floor.

When nothing else shook loose then she tossed the empty Prada in a corner and reset the alarm. The lights flicked back to margarine yellow and the noise hit a wall. Next second the trio of women were back on the way to the top floor to unravel the mystery of Bandy all the way from its sputtering start. When they stopped Chocolate was the first one off, rubbing her arm, stepping gingerly at gunpoint, careful not to look back per strict instructions. Chevy kept the .32 steady when she reached to the floor and plucked the little, white baggie out of the mess. Everything else got left behind for the maids to clean up.

CHAPTER 48

<h1 style="text-align:center">LAST KISS</h1>

Me and Clover slapped cards off the hood of his car. The Brougham reminded me of the Cutlass which made think of Chevy until I drank a little more from the glass bottle being passed around. The wind began to kick and money flapped under a card box from a collection of bets we had won playing a dozen games. In the beginning the bets were small, twenty dollars, twenty and a ten if someone thought they could bench us. Just a little scratch to make things interesting.

An hour later there were nothing but big faces tucked underneath the box on the stretched out luxury hood. We were at fifty bucks a player and a hundred dollars for me and Clover to clean up in three quick hands, four if the boys on the other side got lucky. When the bets got figured out then my partner shuffled on his side of the Caddy. In the tangle of smoke I could see him stacking the deck like firewood which was just business as usual until a pair of high beams washed over the late night huddle.

Everyone put a hand over their eyes as the car drove by slow and all the neighborhood boys slinked back to hug the alley. Perched on a milk crate a man who looked like he had seen it all blew a cloud of Swisher Sweet smoke out of his mouth like an exhaust pipe. "Wonder who that be?"

"Maybe police," I said.

"No, police don't ride like that all slow in just one car. Maybe in Carolina they might do. Gotta uncle lives in Durham. I'll ask him 'bout it next time he calls."

Since the conversation had nowhere to go it died. Clover went back to dealing, distributing the whole deck with a sleight of hand that sometimes flicked a low card off the bottom. I hit the bottle again when it came back, felt my beard grow with the sting of cheap gin in my cheeks and then the headlights came back. The car crawled along slow, I could see checker blocks on the fenders like a chess board traveling through the bricks alone.

Even though it was that time of night and this was just that sort of place where anything could happen my back didn't stiffen like that night coming from the cul-de-sac with a dog and shooter siccing their worst on me. But I underestimate, real trouble was here. When the sedan brakes squealed a few wise men reached for something out of sight on their waists. Didn't matter that it was just a taxi, best way to do dirt is in a car that's not your own.

My own hand was wrapped around Taneesha's gift to me from the very bottom of her deep heart. Lightning broke up the shadows with a double strike that made it look like the first woman jumping out of the cab's backseat had shot through different worlds to find me. As I started to pull the steel from my belt she charged a beeline straight towards the burgundy coupe, Neesha right behind her like two bulls closing fast through early spring wildflowers. I was baffled. No actually I was a fool and because foolishness hates to fold I held out hope for the best right up until she got in arms reach and slapped me sober again.

The pop noise carried a ripe, rift of midnight mayhem down the block. It was a break in the standing crookedness that knotted together everything with an 'er. Every hooker, every shooter, every chaser, every dealer, every loner bored with the same old, same old got a shot of fresh vile going down with a sudden burn. Someone whooped like a jackal in the alley. Clover swore out loud and chuckled. In the humidity I could feel Chevy's angry palm print burning on my face before another stab of lightning showed the abandonment in her eyes.

There were oohs and ahs and then Taneesha screamed like she was tussling with torment. Not a yell of pain or hurt feelings, the battle cry of hate riding on a warbird aimed straight for a flaming ditch. She shoved me back against the car and swung up at my face. The first fist missed, the second crashed into my chin with a cracking noise that must have been her tender hand fracturing. No one could hear the bones shaking up through her hysterical tirade. She was passionate with her hate. "Son of a bitch! Fuckin' liar! Fuckin' pig!" She brought another left while pivoting off her back foot. I dodged opposite direction just in time for Chevy to catch my cheek with another hot slap that drug a fingernail fast across my eyelid.

Our audience thickened. We were ghetto fab, a hot fucking mess and then the camera phones came out. I pushed both women off me before anybody got off a flash and then tried to focus on the one most dangerous. I couldn't be completely sure who that was but Chevy took a half step forward like her name had been called. "I know about you and Chocolate."

I rubbed my stinging eye. "What are you talking about?"

"I'm talking about you fucking the Ice Queen! Why Cerrio? Why did you have to do it? Haven't I given you everything?!"

No one laughed anymore, her pain was too real. The city's most wanted crowded around in waiting silence. There was a gravity in the hush, something that pulled them in into us like the relentless tug of the cosmos.

"Alright," I sighed. "Fine, I messed up. But look at me." I pointed to the Brougham with the money and the cards laid around on the hood. "Out here in the middle of the street in the middle of the night trying to make it work. This ain't me. This ain't us. We're all way out of our element down here."

Chevy came closer. "Save the mind games for your aunt stuck in a fucking wheelchair, Cerrio. 'Cause it ain't going to work with me. I know you. I know you so good and everything about this is all you."

"Leave my aunt out of it," I warned.

"For what? You drug my family in when this whole thing got started. Right from that very first day you got shot."

I shook my head in pure confusion. "What the hell are you talking about?"

"I'm talking about my cousin, Bandy. She's gone."

"Gone where? Wait, you're... you two are cousins?"

"Oooh, you thought she was just some dizzy broad hanging around my apartment everyday, huh? Thought she was like my pity case. Or did you even get that far? Have you ever stopped once to think about anybody but yourself this summer?"

"Where is she?"

"Gone. Didn't you hear me? She saw you and Chocolate in bed and got so disgusted she never even came back to the lounge where she was supposed to perform."

My eyes flicked over to Clover standing by a big, blue mailbox. We exchanged wary glances. Everywhere was scintillating with hate for yours truly. From here on out I knew I was in exile but that was less important.

"Did you try calling? I'll bet a hundred to one she's sitting at the Waffle House right now looking at her phone."

"You think I'm stupid? Of course I called her. I called you too."

Her words cut off like a faucet. She was so close to me that I could smell the sweat layered over her anger laid on top of nervous fear. I could see the trail of salty tears dried on her cheek. She cleared her throat, ran a tongue across her chapped lips, spit more venom.

"This is my fault. I should have seen this coming. You and Chocolate. How long has it been going on, Cerrio? How many times did you hit it in our bed while I was out working at that club you sent me to?"

"It only happened once. And we only did it down here, never at the crib. I wouldn't violate you like that."

"Liar!" She shoved me hard. "That bitch told me everything! The time you guys did it on the boat! All the trips to High Point! I know it all, Cerrio!"

"Fine, it is what it is. But I promise it ends tonight. No more. I'm done with her."

Chevy cackled. She tossed her head back and howled with mindless laughter. "You really think I give a shit what you do now? No, you go ahead and enjoy her baby. The slut is all yours. You deserve each other. But you two better team up and find my cousin."

"How come you never told me? How come neither of you said you were related to each other?"

"Like I said Cerrio, 'there's a lot of things I don't tell you'." She came closer and whispered in my ear. "You're such a piece of shit. We were going to bring Taneesha in. Get her naked for you on your birthday as a surprise when we got home but you blew it. I bet you thought you had a chance with her all on your own, huh?"

"You know I never thought of her like that. She's just like a sister to me."

"Who knows what you thought? I used to fantasize that I did but that was just a dream."

Chevy backed away. "All I know is this. If you dare come home without my baby cousin on your arm I swear to God I'll kill you. Then, I'm going to find Chocolate and hang her from a lamppost. The one outside Sugar Bares." She kissed two fingers and put them on my lips. "Promise."

Never did I think it would come to this, where the woman who loved me best was muttering death threats in the dead of night on a street lined with shadows. From the first time when I took Chocolate in the shower I knew I was asking for trouble but we were much farther down to the bottom from when I previously looked up.

Chevy stepped away to go reclaim her Mercedes from where I parked it. Taneesha flew away in front of her, I never even saw her slide in on the other side of the Benz. And then they were gone, up the block, around the corner with the engine roaring on a clear path that didn't have to unfold. No more woes and disillusions. Nothing else to divulge so the street came back to life. The neighborhood boys went back to selling crack, weed sparking up again, someone smashed the liquor bottle that had given me comfort.

In my grip I still clutched cards. They were damp and curled from sweat on my palm. When I fanned them out the scene fit perfect. A pair of aces, a few kings, plenty of trump. No Queens.

But nothing really changed because bad things, usually you don't feel them right away. You carry on like nothing can break you until you're slumped in a corner, terse with no words, failing to understand even if its clear.

I won my thirteenth spades game in a row and bought another stolen bottle of gin from underneath a fiend's jacket. He spun off in a pair of high top Nikes that had seen better days to go get his last high of the evening, or maybe his first one of the day. Clover kept cups in the back of the Brougham for occasions just like this. We drank together leaning against the trunk, officially off duty while the lesser players took our spots in a match up front.

The lighting had slowed down, the night dwindled along into its final hour and the sky flashed less and less like a broken bulb in an attic. I had nowhere to go and no means to get there. Chevy would kick me out again, this time for good. I had to find my way home, she wasn't going to ride me back to Winston again in her luxury whip.

For a while I let hindsight eat me up. What I should have done better, shouldn't have done at all, or at least been slicker about made a train of thoughts that were never going to be realized. Maybe something in there would have saved me from being on my knuckles a few hundred miles from home but all that mattered still wasn't going to change.

I thought about Bandy. Her voice played in my head like that alphabet song you learn when you're young and never forget. I'd never forget her songs either. But she wasn't really gone, I thought. And what if she is? the other half asked. Both sides of me argued their point of the case, one towing the other along like a wagon while I tapped my finger against the side of the plastic cup.

"Was she fine?" asked Clover.

No interpretation. I didn't have to think about what he meant. "They're all fine," I replied. "In their own way."

"Yeah, that's women. Pretty creatures. I had one who was thick as a forest, top and bottom. Fucking incredible. Deadly though just like a rattlesnake."

"What can I say? They're my weakness."

"Not just you. They're every man's weakness. Remember Adam?"

I sipped from my cup. "You mean the one from the Bible?"

"Yeah, same. He ate that fruit because Eve made him do it."

"I don't know about that. Maybe he could have chose better. Shit, I could have chosen better."

Clover shifted his eyes towards me. "You really believe that?"

"What, the Bible? Or, I could have chose better?"

"You serious? You think Adam actually had a choice? Imagine this, you the only man on earth with the only woman and she never gives you a stitch of pussy. What are you gonna do?" Clover took a drink. "I tell you what I would of done. I woulda have bit down on that fruit and apologized to God later."

"I guess."

Clover stared off and thought about the forest while Chocolate haunted me. Alone and nude in the Garden of Eden no man stood a chance against her. If Eve looked like that, covetous black body burnishing like a wet trophy, I would've bitten the goddamn snake if she asked me to.

CHAPTER 49

FOUR PLAITS

As the first gold bar of dawn snuck up over the trees I found out what it was like to be an island. No one wanted LaDecerrio Lloyd anymore. He was too Machiavellian for your love, too malformed to be admired, too clumsy to even be seriously maligned. Just a mass of sand in the water watching ships turn east in the sea. My role simple, keep the wayward travelers from drowning until they can a find a way to move on. If anyone lands on my beaches it's only because they have nowhere left to go.

Clover snuck off after the gin dried up. He took his silver luck and his red car and whisked off. We would never see each other again and that was okay, I had no affinities. But once he left it was like the hem snagged on one of Aunt Denise's old sweaters pulling the rest of the crew apart. The crowd dissipated, at first one by one, then the rest trickled off to go sleep late into the afternoon.

I think, but I don't know, that that's when reality really set in. My schemes panned out and then circled back, that much was evident. The rest of the fall out couldn't be told yet this far away from home.

I wanted to tell Chevy the truth. That I'm a just a man and women like Chocolate are the Achilles heel of my whole species. Real truths didn't matter though, especially not mine. Especially not right now when Bandy had come up missing again and no one even knew where to look. I had a theory, very simple because I didn't want to have to go through this all over again, the little singer got lost in Savannah and wound up on the other side of town. She found her own way back to the Marriott right after Chevy pulled up on me breathing threats. Now, she was right there chilling on the bed, patient as a puppy when my woman, ex-woman, came back in jangling her Mercedes keys.

I let the simple theory roll across my mind as I marched on from the docks going nowhere fast. Every little neighborhood has its own corner store. Except the docks wasn't a hood so I had to walk my way into one. I walked with the ebbs and flows of morning traffic from corner to corner. Cars spitting smoke, crawling between red lights spaced out on every block. When an empty school bus rumbled by and bent a left up ahead I did the same thing with both hands in my pockets.

Three kids saddled with bookbags saw me coming. The little girl with four plaits in her hair looked up first, skin like cookie bread, tall like a growth spurt was on, high cheekbones like her daddy was enrolled. She watched me close like I was going to do a magic trick before the other two stopped kicking weeds back down into the sidewalk cracks. I guess that bus blowing by the other way wasn't their ride. I thought she might get scared. Maybe grab her brothers and run back in the house yelling for mama. Instead, she gripped the straps of her pink Jansport and glared missiles at me.

"Who you?" She made the question short and pointed like an accusation. Like if she was a grown woman who didn't think her mother would actually find out what she said she might call me something out of pocket because she knew I didn't belong in her neighborhood.

"Is that how you talk to anybody walking by?"

"No, just you. 'Cause I never seen you before and you look dirty."

Little four plaits never lied. My pants were wrinkled, my hair looked like shit, the top button on my shirt had gone missing somehow. I tried making adjustments in the window of a parked car. One of the boys squinted behind my back. "Hey, are you Mexican?"

"No," I replied.

"Well, what are you then? Mixed?"

"I'm lost, that's what I am." I turned around. "Where's the store at around here?"

Four plaits pointed north towards the railroad tracks and the noise of a train going past. "That way. But they don't sell no hangover pills."

"Who said I had a hangover?"

She twisted her hair. "I dunno. But an orange will do the same thing to make you feel better. I got one if you want it."

I wasn't hungover. Not yet. But my stomach was growling hard enough to rival the train engine in the distance. I held my hand out. "Give it to me."

"Five dollars," she chirped.

"For what?"

"The orange you want to buy."

"I ain't paying a dime."

Four plaits shrugged. "Okay. Starve."

"I'll give you two now. Three later."

"Yeah right, and I'm Janet Jackson. Five dollars right now. Cash."

"Three."

"Five," she repeated.

Her little brothers started marching around in a circle chanting like they were on a picket line. "Five. Five. Five dollars." The girl pulled the straps on her bookbag again. "Better hurry up," she said. "Here comes the bus."

The big, yellow, monster burning diesel at the red light stared back pressuring a decision. The light went green, a miniature stop sign folded out of the yellow beast's side like a wing and then the heavy duty engine kicked up to a low growl.

Only in Savannah could my good sense disintegrate all the way down into my stomach. The bus left me and the five dollar orange on the sidewalk. At least the little girl gave me directions to the store after I paid her. I followed where her finger pointed and secretly wished for a daughter like that with matching plaits pulled tight over a head full of brains.

When I got to the fruit's brine the store came into view and when I bit down it was just in time to get a mouthful of sweet exhaust as a truck cruised by to my left. It raced on in a hurry ignoring the school zone sign leaning by a fire hydrant. Before it beat me to the end of the block the brake lights flared. Tires squealed and the back end went up like a short kid standing on his toes to reach the triple X tapes stashed high in his parent's closet.

I need a wingman, somebody to pick up wherever I leave off. That's what I was thinking when the purple Jeep reversed to a stop right beside me because it is way, way too early for this shit. Per the usual Chocolate was dressed to kill. Black shorts cut off an inch above the cheeks and a plunging V neck with teeny sleeves that showed her feminine shoulder muscles. I wondered if she ever took a day off. From the bus stop across the street junior high boys stretched their necks to get a better view. But they were too green to know that the best perspective was looking down not up.

She cast me a glance down from the bucket seat like a judge on a bench. "Are you drunk?"

I sucked an orange slice. "Not anymore. How'd you even know I was here?"

" 'Cause is the part of town where the shit pops off."

"So, I'm shit now?"

She shrugged. "If you are then at least your popping. Come on, we gotta go. And throw that fucking thing away. I'll buy you some breakfast."

I made pssh sound and said, "fuck no. Why would I go anywhere with you when you ratted me out? I had a good thing going and you stabbed it in the heart. Ain't no egg sandwich and a hash brown gonna fix that."

Those words stung her, manta ray not bumblebee. I had hit a nerve. It was easy to tell when she swung the Jeep up on the curb so close to my feet Goodyear radials almost crushed my toes. The young'uns at the bus stop quit slap boxing just to see her hop out. Dropping down from the truck like a pile of bricks, five foot and ten inches of femme fatale clacking a pair of open toe Jimmy Choos so hard on the sidewalk they sounded like fireworks.

She was right in my face, close enough to kiss. "I need you to listen. You listening?"

I sucked another orange slice. "All ears."

"Last night your little girlfriend put a gun in my face."

"What gun?"

"The one Bandy threw at you."

"Shit, Chevy got it back?"

"Yeah, and I looked hard in those soft, candy eyes while she held it and told her to cut the shit. Chevy ain't a killer. Bitch ain't got what it takes and I told her as much. But Taneesha, that's another thing. That one has no cut card."

"She held you hostage? That's what you raced up the block to tell me."

"I'm trying to tell you there were two choices. Either tell why Bandy ran off or get killed by her wife. Do the math."

"I know math. Two options, death or dishonor and you said 'fuck honor'."

"And he still don't listen. After she shot me, Neesha would have came out here and blew your face off next." Chocolate made her hand like a gun and put up to my temple. "Bam, some longshoremen would have found you laid out this morning with the cargo."

"You're talking like the girl is crazy. Taneesha's upset. It'll pass."

"No, crazy ain't a threat. I see crazy girlfriends all the time. Wives on the loose. It's all part of the business. Crazy people just want to get even with somebody. But Neesha is passionate. Passionate people have goals, Cerrio. And a girl with goals ain't nothing to fuck with."

I spit out a seed. "You underestimated her didn't you? That's the part you're trying cover up. Chocolate's embarrassed because she never thought a flower like Neesha had it in her. Sucks when you're wrong don't it?"

I don't need her, I don't want her. Both of those were lies but they sounded real good because yesterday it was all the truth. I wanted her body and I needed a ride home but the other side of the coin is why she needed me.

"You're scared aren't you?"

She snapped her head up. "Of who?"

"Who, she says. Neesha, that's the who. She's thundering through your mind right now."

The dancer smiled. "Nice try, baby. But it takes a lot more than a little girl to put the ghost of fear in me."

"Then, why are you here? Just came out to find me and buy breakfast? Come on Chocolate, tell the truth, shame the devil."

She paused. Not a frequent thing for a woman with agile wit. Her face was bland as the Moroccan desert, as fragile as I'd ever seen it. You hate to say when your feasting on another's misery but what's another crime to me? And then she reached deep into that bag of tricks she had for a mind and came back with the answer.

"What about your destiny? How are you going to put the scales back right?"

Sleeping in smugness, suddenly I woke up and almost fell out of my skin. "How do you know anything about that?"

"Is it really important how I know? Is that how you're going to fix the problem? By trying to figure me out?"

True, a dog barking up the wrong tree never chased down his purpose. Listening to the whispers of the business of fate now I was all turned around.

Bandy wasn't lost. I knew it from the moment Chevy smacked me and started screaming in my face by the curb. Did I spend enough energy trying to keep a lid screwed down tight on all my worst fears? Didn't matter. In true Chocolate style she came and blew the top off of everything. The threats she tried to relay felt like a tease. I wish I had it in me to worry about a little thing like getting shot, at least then I'd know my conscious was more closer to normal. Murder wasn't the problem, wasn't even the principle. It was the aftermath and like I said, 'I knew math'. There were two options, find Bandy or be destined for ruin.

Chocolate told me she knew this town. She said, "the little singer wouldn't last longer than a tube of ChapStick around Jay-Z." Since I thought so too we took off in her purple Jeep, driving fast trying to find an answer. A sign. A footprint. Any goddamned thing. No GPS, she didn't need directions, just a quick once over in the rearview for her makeup and one stop for gas before we hit downtown.

A couple of times we caught each other's eye. Once at a red light, again behind a slow delivery truck. That's the lock of a really good vice, the draw of delicious poison, when the thing most deadly is the face of your desire.

She adjusted her sunglasses and grinned. She knew I was looking and I didn't even care that she hadn't shaved her legs since Sunday.

"Want to hear a story?" she asked.

"I'm down."

"When I first met you Chevy was in the back of the club peeking through the curtains about to lose her ever-loving mind. I never saw her get that way. I said 'girl, what is your problem?' She points and says, 'see that guy? The one drinking slow? That's my ex.' I looked at you sitting alone, not getting no dances and thought, cheapskate. Then, I brought you in that back room and got a surprise."

"How? You there only there five seconds before I saw your ass twisting back out the door."

"Five seconds and your dick was so hard I could have stood up on it. Very impressive."

"You mean in the VIP room?"

She tsked. "Ain't you learned nothing yet? Two couches and a bottle of cheap champagne isn't VIP. That's just where the girl's go to fuck between stage time." Chocolate hooked a right on a one way. "You were in the quickie room."

Chocolate doesn't do well with silences, she can't last in the staleness for an hour like Chevy. For her the quiet is a trap. She couldn't even make it a quarter mile in the city. Just when I thought our conversation was over she gave up something close to the chest. "That girl Judy. She reminds me of me at that age. You know, except for the pregnancy and the Jesus loving grandmother. And the running from one town to the next. I knew enough to at least keep it local until my money was right. After that I escaped.

This is where I started out at. While you and Chevy were dry humping in the back of your aunt's old car I was doing my business down by the docks. Yeah, she told me. Back in those days you could see the perverts coming. Now, there's a lot more of them. Fuckers are crawling everywhere like maggots. So many that a few people got together and made a racket out of it. They snatch girls off the street and send them out all over. Vegas. Sacramento. I know a New York girl who got sent down to Tijuana. It's all a business. Fucked up but still a business. They never got me, though." She shook her head. "Huh-unh, no way. Too many johns got stabbed when I'm around you know what I'm saying?"

I did know and I smiled thinking of Chocolate pushing a steel blade in the soft belly of some old, gray, pervert. "I think I get it."

"We're here." She pulled to the curb and cut the Jeep's engine. Looking around I saw a part of town where the loud truck with no doors and her too short shorts didn't blend in at all with the fabric.

Chocolate sprayed perfume on her wrists. "This is the Starland District. Pretty nice, right?"

It was nice. The Starland District of Savannah was exactly what you thought the deep south looked like right after a storm. Rustic storefronts with broad windows, trees with moss swaying in a breeze, just enough pecans blown around on the sidewalk to look sexy for the postcard. All that upscale feel of privilege was vivid right here in a Town and Country painting.

I shifted around in the seat. "What are we doing here?"

"Going to a meeting." Chocolate nodded to a restaurant standing across the street. "Somebody's in there waiting for us right now. He knows what to do about Bandy." She opened up the Jeep's center console and pointed inside.

"What?"

"Come on, give me your gun."

I snickered. "Fuck you."

"This ain't Winston-Salem, Cerrio. You're not at home, you don't know these guys. You don't even know where to get a bag of white. If I let you go in there with that cowboy, drama shit we will never see Bandy again."

How did a face smooth as marble get folded up into all this tragedy? How did lips soft as felt cut like a butcher? How did she even know to be here in the first place? I swallowed my questions because answers were spare. When the harvest seemed bountiful then I'd pull out the plow. Until then lips were sealed.

I looked across the seat, the moodless eyes on the other side were a vault. Nothing coming out of them but calculated precision. I had to cuss on instinct when I reached behind my back. When my hand came around again it was holding on to the only thing I trusted in this whole, soul sucking world. Chocolate held the center console open until I pushed the Remington all the way inside. She covered it up with a dogeared owner's manual from the Jeep dealership then slammed the lid shut. I listened to the latch click hard in place and breathed deep as the ache of loneliness washed over me but didn't cleanse.

CHAPTER 50

CHASING DANCERS

She melted right into the aristocratic swagger on the other side of town like a popsicle in a pan. Two cars stop on each side of the road to let her pass right through in front of them even without the help of a crosswalk. One of them is a cop.

I didn't fit in, on the other hand Chocolate was a chameleon, meshing right into Starland seamlessly. She was an elegant mess minus the mess and I was plain short on elegance. Somehow it worked though, moving together around all those polished Georgians pooled together enjoying brunch on the sidewalk we set off just the right amount of shock like a plug in a socket.

The restaurant was a good place to hide in plain sight if you were dipping your knuckles in crime. The same dignity carbon copied from outside and the sense of raw privilege made Sorry Charlie's Oyster House the last place anybody would think to look for real Machiavelli's. Nonetheless, here I was. A maítre d in standard black and white uniform pulled out chairs for us with a rich deference and a little bow. He gave Chocolate a wine menu with a list of vineyard names. Most were in other languages. She ordered a glass of red and a piece of cake. I took a bowl of clam chowder to ease the hangover that the girl kicking grass at the bus stop knew would happen.

Our waiter listens intently like he's truly got an interest. He nods at all the right moments to let us know he gets it. Never mentions a special of the day but that's okay. We're not really here to eat. When his little pencil quits moving then he takes back the menus. It's a sad sight watching him leave. The subtle presence of an average person working his normal job on a Tuesday was the antidote to this misadventure some people just called business.

The anti-drama, I kept thinking about it after the waiter went back to the kitchen. How he was so much the opposite of us like red is the opposite of blue. I tapped my fingers on the table while Chocolate twisted a silk napkin. Both of us killing time. My thoughts went long, from considering how colors really don't have antonyms to how badly I need to call Aunt Denise and make up.

I scanned the restaurant while my new crime partner played with her silk some more. Searching the house for the right face screwed up suspiciously. I thought I'd find him, I thought it would be imminent, but I didn't even know what I was looking for. A family by the window were all deep into their phones. In the corner a wife cut her husband's panini sandwich in half letting mustard bleed out on the plate. Past that it was dead. If anyone was here looking ominous and out of place like they were struggling with a fraud it was me and Chocolate sitting across from each other with our silverware still untouched.

"Where's this guy at?"

"He's coming." Indulging in a little impatience she looked out the window.

"I'm growing old here. Thought you said, 'he was already waiting to meet us'."

Chocolate bunched up the napkin in her hand. "Don't get tied up in the details, Cerrio."

"Why not? Ain't that where the devil lives."

She answered with contempt like a big sister babysitting, like she was the clearheaded realist and I was naive dummy reaching for a long shot. "Petty details are bad for business. Things ain't gonna go as planned. So, get used to it."

"That's a funny way to frame this. A business trip. Like we came here to sign contracts for a roofing job."

Chocolate caught her bottom lip between her teeth. I looked at her, she opened her mouth to say something else but changed her mind and looked away. "What's on your mind?" I asked. "Nothing," she said. "I just hope the wine comes soon."

But it didn't. When the waiter came back I could hear his slacks swishing behind me, pssh, pssh, pssh. Short strides so he could chop his legs quicker without looking hurried. Since I'm the last one to figure things out, always, it took me a second to realize his hands were empty. No wine or cake, no clam chowder or a pencil to write down anything else. He nodded to Chocolate like they had a code, an implied understanding. No speaking, she doesn't even nod back.

What happened next made realize I had trudged deep into the belly of the beast. The waiter handed Chocolate a slip of paper like a receipt and spun off before she even had a chance to read it. He never asked her name, never thought she might be the wrong person to give the message to. Looking back in my mind I saw how anonymous he was, black slacks, white shirt, short hair. No real way to pick him out if the message fell in the wrong hands. That sort of nobody and everybody thing is what made him useful.

The best way to look if you were going abduct somebody.

Chocolate stood up, her napkin fell to the floor. "We got to go."

"Go where? You said, 'the meeting was here'."

"Change of plans. Remember when I told you not to worry about petty details? Here's the why." She held up the note with writing on it that I definitely couldn't see. "Our connection called. He wants to link up somewhere else."

"What the fuck is this? Are we on tour?"

"You know for somebody in a crisis you sure do ask a lot of questions." She threw her keys on the table. "Come on, you drive."

"Drive where?"

"Again with the questions. Let's go already, this dude ain't going to wait all day."

She beat me outside. The long legs and the shorts that didn't make a stitch of friction carried her back across the street on her own crosswalk before I even came off the curb. Saying she was fast is like saying blood is bloody. But keeping up with Chevy had me seasoned in the game of chasing dancers.

I caught her on the other side of the street, right when she stepped her first heel up on the sidewalk cement I grabbed her shoulder and spun her back around. "Talk now. What the fuck is going on?"

She seemed less surprised at the interruption, like she expected more than this little spat by the curb to start off the day. "What do you think is going on, Cerrio? We're in the shit now."

"That doesn't mean anything."

"Then let me give it to you uncut. Bandy is in real trouble and you been having strange dreams."

I snatched her by the V neck collar and slammed her back against the Jeep. "Don't play games with me. I swear to God that if you're a part of this Chocolate, I will kill you."

"I'm all you've got," she hissed.

A couple walked by holding hands. We separated and let them go until we were knew our voices were drowned out by the sounds coming off the street.

"You're too familiar. How do you know these people if you never dealt with them?"

She took a minute to smooth her shirt until it looked untouched. "It's hard to explain. How did you used to know who wanted a shot of dope before you went to jail?"

"I went to prison."

"Petty details."

I shook my head. "Is this a real question?"

"Well, I'm a real woman."

"I don't know. I mean, at first it just happened. After a while I caught on to who's who and then the junkies started coming to me."

"Uh-huh." She crossed her arms. "And after?"

"After what?"

"You don't need to do that. I know you still sell it when Chevy ain't looking. How do you know who's who after all that time in a cell?"

"Shit, it's my game."

She let her arms drop. "Exactly, and this is mine. Last night after I left your girlfriend at the Marriott I went to a little bar where they serve shrimp macaroni and called some old numbers. It took a while but eventually I got someone on the line. A rich guy. One of the only one's I'd much rather kill than sleep with. He offered me a job. I let him down easy with a simple, no thanks. You know instead of a straight up, fuck you. Then, I let him know I had a friend who had a friend come up missing." Chocolate pointed at me. "You're the friend."

She lies all the time, to be fair so do I. Lies make people happy and lies drag on like the years, except years keep going and eventually a lie crashes and then the sadness ensues. It made sense that we were running together, birds of a feather and all that. Chocolate told the truth when it was critical, though. She was all I had left.

She didn't want me whipping her Jeep around tired so before we pulled off she gave me a quick bump, a little taste of powder from a sack stashed deep in her bra. Chocolate can be a doll when she wants, she even made up a line for me on top of her license. I snorted cocaine off a picture of her face and a second later fatigue was just a memory.

It wasn't all about me, though. Much as I'd love to make that claim, much as it would soothe my ego like aloe on a burn I couldn't stretch my imagination that far. Not even when I'm high. Chocolate might be a lot of things, stripper, liar. She might even be scared for her life the same way I was scared of the afterlife. There's always something out there that makes the next beast tremble. But she was still a human, heart beating warm blood, and her soul wherever it might wind up, was not so cold as she tried to make other people believe. She really wanted to find Bandy just like me, like Chevy, like Neesha. We were in different camps now but we were still bonded for a while longer by that girl with the white spot next to her mouth. None of us had ever thought about going back over the bridge one woman down.

I made a bunch of turns that meant nothing, lefts and rights on one ways, riding melodiously with the traffic like the visitors we were. Driving by shops, an art college, circling around an army field surrounded by a chain link fence. Since we had no destination on the road it was impossible to get lost.

Chocolate had an outburst. "I need new shoes," she said. "Something glammy for the Fall. A pair of boots maybe."

"I'm not making any donations." I snapped.

"Okay," she smiled. "I know. I know you don't want anything to do with me. But you still owe me."

"Owe you for what?"

"For what?" she mocked. "Did you forget about all that damn money I gave you?"

I ran a hand through my hair. "Look, I'll pay you back. I just need some time after we get home to-"

She touched my leg. "I'm joking."

"So I don't owe you?"

"No, you're in debt. I just wanted to get your mind off the stress. You been grinding your teeth all over town."

"My mouth is numb."

"Well, you're welcome. That's some of the best coke in Savannah."

"Must be if it's still keeping me up."

She switched subjects. "So, what happens after this?"

"I don't know. Chevy moves on, I guess."

"What about, Cerrio?"

"Back to the drawing board." I stared straight ahead and kept talking. "I didn't mean to put my hands on you back there. It was the heat of the moment."

She took her hand away. "Don't apologize. It makes you look weak."

"That's how I know you'll never understand me."

Her phone started ringing. It was a shitty flip, I didn't ask what happened to the Apple she usually carried in her purse, or what happened to the purse she usually carried on her arm. She fished the phone out of her pocket and the call went quick. I tried eavesdropping while I steered but all I caught were partial answers. Uh-huh. Yeah. I know where that's at. We're on the way.

After Chocolate hung up I knew better than to ask. Just followed her directions that took the Jeep right up to a tan building made out of old bricks that had been drying in the sun since 1800 and God knows when. I saw high windows and a steeple on top and willed myself to be sober. In Starland we looked out of place but now we were just off the wall.

"This is a church."

Chocolate finished the last line off her driver's license. "I know. The last place anybody would think to look."

"That's genius."

"No, that's part of the game. A way to assassinate your purity so it melts away easier."

"I don't have any purity." I looked at the crucifix posted above the heavy wooden doors. "That, uh, ship sailed a long time ago."

"I ain't talking about you. I'm talking about Bandy. She's got more purity inside her than me, you and Chevy all put together." She sniffed. "Come on, maybe we can get some prayers in while there's still time."

We had come to the holy ground. The First African Baptist Church is history and faith and protection all braided together, configured in a vine of precious souls to help the living limp through this life. Built by slaves, part of the underground railroad, this was more than a house of worship. It was a documented artifact like the bone filled catacombs of Paris or the

The Declaration of Proclamation. And I know God isn't just a simple human being because a mere person would have lit me up at the door and burned me down like a forest fire. After all I'd done a man wouldn't hesitate to show his vengeance and shed his virtues. A thing like that would have been reasonable in his eyes, seen as only proper. The same way it's only proper for animals to eat the little things they pounce on and kill.

For twelve dollars a guide walked us around pointing out all the things to remember. The brass chandeliers hanging down, the high vaulted ceilings trying to steal your breath away, a giant organ ready to bleed and smash eardrums. I paid the fee but skipped the details. My focus was just the same as it was at the oyster house, all on trying to find the odd man out. Sure, he walked right in front of me last time but now I knew to look for the one blending instead of the one standing out.

Chocolate stayed close hacking a piece of gum, strutting in her shorts that were not church appropriate. The tour guide could barely keep the group focused with her thighs out like that. On the floor a dark, murky, shape shifted. Dipping in and out of the holes someone put into the lacquered wood beneath our feet before church tours were occasions. That was my shadow down there, the dark side moving like a ghost over swamp water. Once again I was the one here who didn't belong.

"That's so they could breathe," said a male voice beside me. When I looked up one of the tour guides was pointing back down at my feet. "The holes," he said. "They made them so the runaway slaves could breathe when they hid under the floor during raids."

I looked deep in a brown face maybe one shade darker than mine courtesy of the Georgia July. Fine lines were coming in around the eyes, another decade in the sun would turn him into a California raison. He had on a long sleeve polo, the real kind, teal with a little pink horse on the chest. It was an awful color that disagreed with his skin and a reminder to me to never wear anything that goddamn ugly.

At the end of his sleeve was a hand reaching out all glittered in gold. I saw a yellow pinky ring, yellow watch, yellow bracelet and a manicure. I was supposed to shake it. Problem is I'm not a business man and so my instincts were different. Instead of wrapping five fingers around and giving two pumps, maybe three, like we were just some white-collar boys on a round of golf I reached for what I knew. Of course my hand came up empty. The .45 Taneesha bought for me was still on hiatus, still in that center console, baking helplessly like a batch of muffins.

"It's okay," he rasped. "There's no disrespect here. We can be friends."

"Fuck your manners," I spat. "Just tell me where the girl is."

"Trust me, I know how you feel. I have daughters. But there are rules. You don't know my name. You don't even shake my hand. Right now I can't tell you anything."

Chocolate slid up on my right. "Shake his hand."

If I didn't shake that probably meant Bandy wasn't ever coming home again. I pumped his hand once strictly out of politics

"Now what?" I asked.

The teal sleeve made a gesture towards Chocolate. "This one told me that your name is Cerrio."

I snapped my head around to Chocolate. "You told him my name?"

The man went on. "She said, 'you come from somewhere else three or four hours away with some friends'."

"And one of my friends is missing."

"Well, all the same I like your company. You should be proud, Cerrio. Not many men have the nice things that you do."

He was talking about the women. He was referring to Bandy like a new pair of gloves.

Chocolate cleared her throat. "The tour is moving. We should follow them."

"Yes, we shouldn't be awkward. You can walk behind me and Mr. Cerrio while we get to know each other."

The woman beside me smiled coldly at the man who demanded handshakes. "No, see I can't do that. He's my friend and I have to keep him safe."

Teal shirt looked stunned. "You don't trust me?"

"Nothing to do with trust. I just don't want him getting hurt. You boys can still talk. Trust me, you won't say anything I haven't heard before."

"I never come to church to make violence. Even if I don't believe what it represents. You should know me better."

The hand trimmed in gold reached out to touch Chocolate's arm. She snatched away fast and laid down the rules. "This is how it's going to go. We're all going to walk right beside each other. You two can talk about whatever you want and I'll take in the sights."

"No," I said. "I did the handshake. So, nobody moves until I get some answers."

The brown face in front of me shaped into a crooked smile. "But my friend, you haven't asked any questions."

First African Baptist stayed still, I guess so the spirits could break free. Pitter patters sprang forward from a small boy escaping his mother, the sounds echoed up to those high ceilings but no one noticed him until he found the organ. Tiny fingers banging black and white keys but not making real music. His parents got riled up while the rest of the tour laughed.

Mama cut to him like a shark on a minnow. He tries to get away but six steps on the run he slipped on nothing. That's life in a moment. You're running smooth, dodging every big stone in your path and then the pebble you never see trips you up on your face. It was a hard crash, chin first right on the wood floor. Pain registered and then a volcano of noise erupted. Mama screams, daddy swears, baby cries, the rest of us watched. It was a nasty refreshment but still enough to ease the weight off of the holes in the floor and the messy weekend and the lost money and the kidnap shit.

I had my attention invested in the chaos until a hand dipped in my shirt. Bandy's kidnapper moved smooth like a poem. His fingers went down and came back out all in one fluid motion. When my head swiveled away from the boy getting picked up off his stomach I saw a yellow piece of paper in my pocket and that teal polo beelining straight for the heavy doors. Chocolate grabbed my arm. I tried to jerk away and take off on a chase but her nails dug in deep like a boa on his dinner. "Save your energy. He's got a car waiting outside. You'll never catch him and even if you do he won't give you answers."

I shook her off. "We could have kept driving around in the Jeep and got farther than this. I'm a firm believer that something is better than nothing. But this..." I gestured around the church. "This is the exception to my rule. We didn't get answer one coming here."

She ignored my rant and reached for the yellow slip. Yanked it from my pocket and picked at each folded corner with a polished nail. I noticed one was missing from the first finger on her right hand but deviations like that were minimal. At least to me.

"What is that?"

"These are the answers you keep bitching about."

I looked at the scrawled handwriting without actually reading it. "Does it say where Bandanna is?"

"Get real. Bandy's worth a fortune. Never in a lifetime would anybody in this racket just up and tell us where to find her. That's against the rules."

"More rules, huh? Just like the handshake thing you cosigned." I pointed. "What about that number?"

"That's not a number it's a price."

I blinked and thousands more questions paraded through my mind. Not all at once, they sort of trickled out slow like a coffee maker dripping fluid in the morning. Some came after we left church, more arrived later as I walked through Chocolate's hotel room reeking of lavender.

She was patient, never once blaming me for what I had to ask because she knew I had to know. Because it was just us now. We were a team, nothing like Chevy and me had been and that would never be replaced. I wasn't trying to plagiarise what I'd lost. I just had to be ready. We couldn't go out there having each other's back with one of us wise and the other ignorant as a moron.

Answers were food. Answers were medicine. They were half of everything we needed to look ourselves in the face without the permanent stain of what happened to the little singer haunting us forever. First thing I learned about was the train. On Wednesday night Bandy was going to be put in the back of an all white van with a catering magnet on the side and driven south. Where they stopped nobody knew. Chocolate said "probably Miami, Florida." She imagined the train pulling up somewhere with orange groves and blistering sunshine and homes built with hurricane windows. A city down in the panhandle where fine women made somebody a killing. She said "Bandy would have a bag over her head for the whole five and a half hour drive." Or maybe a real entrepreneur would put her on a boat down to Cuba. Then, how would I look at myself in the mirror?

Second thing I learned is the price on the paper. Fifty thousand dollars by Wednesday or Bandy took the train. Wednesday. AKA tomorrow.

CHAPTER 51

JADED PLANET

All night in the street took it's toll. Last time I slept was before the storm but if I could have a choice I never would have laid down in bed again. Chevy's mother stood over the top of me with a handful of fire. She made me swallow it down in my stomach where it burned like an iron. Falling head first in my dreams I vomited heat until I crashed awake in Chocolate's hotel room.

She shook me back to earth like I was a kid who missed the bus and laid a brand-new outfit down beside me on the comforter with an extra light touch. We didn't talk about how loud my teeth were grinding in my dreams. Unusual because she's always been known to gut a soft spot. But this Chocolate was merciful to me, almost caring like I was her chosen one. It would have been easy to lose myself in that, if she had a hot meal ready I might be telling a different story. But I was hungry and far from being charmed and besides, even a skull wears a grin on their face.

"You were sleeping like the dead," she said. "I got you some new clothes. The one's you got on smell like ass."

"Thanks for noticing. What time is it?"

"Getting late, boo. It's almost five and Chevy's been calling since noon."

I wiped my face, the slick moisture of sweat greased my palm. Things were getting too generous, now. "Did you just call me, boo? Is that where we're at?"

She turned around from feeding Franky. "Excuse the fuck out of me for being a little nice. What do I call you from now on?"

"I don't know. Guess it doesn't matter."

"Exactly."

I held the shirt up to see if it would fit. "What did Chevy say when she called?"

Franky crunched a dog treat. Chocolate said, "I don't know. She don't want to talk to me."

"How'd she get your number on that shitty, little phone you been toting?"

"It's an insurance phone so my number is the same. Apple store let me use it until I go home and get me a replacement. And I called her first."

"Why?"

"Checking to see if she went home. I wanted to know how much this really meant to her."

"You think she'd leave Bandy stranded out here?"

Chocolate gave me a maybe, maybe not look. "Stranger things have happened."

"Why she call you if she don't want to talk?"

"Let's see, before you and me were together she wasn't blowing up my phone at all. Now, she's sitting in her room at the Marriott waiting for you to walk in with Bandy. And you don't have a phone on you because she made you drop yours off the boat. Chevy don't want me, she wants the person I'm with. And far as I'm concerned any woman who wants Cerrio can get exactly what she's looking for."

"Funny, that's the same thing she said about you."

She watched while I stood up and stepped to the bathroom. Kept her eyes glued to my back when I closed the door. The walls were thin in here, like a fort made out of boxes, and it was easy to hear her flicking a lighter on the other side. I heard the wheel spin twice and then a pause as the little controlled burn touched the brown end of a Newport.

She shouted. "Nobody cares about your shame, Cerrio!"

I looked in the mirror and talked through the door. "Yeah, you're telling me."

"So, be a man and serve her the facts. Tell Chevy we need the rest of that money she brought to get Bandy back. We got to buy her like meat by the pound. Otherwise her little cousin ain't never coming home again."

"Beautiful, I'll tell her just like that. Matter of fact why don't you come with me? Both of us can knock on the door and we can count the money out together like one, big, happy, family."

"Oh I'd love too, boo. Except she ain't going to believe a damn thing I got to say."

I washed my hands and walked back out to the scent of tobacco. "But you knew that already," said the dancer.

She was sitting at a table looking noir in the corner with the phone and the dog treats. Elbow on the back of the chair, arm with the cigarette hand held up in the air. Menthol smoke curled all around her face like fingers groping for something solid.

"Damn," I said. "You're really serious about them cigarettes."

A clear cup was by the phone, she ashed her square in an inch of dirty water. "How come men..." She took a pull. "How come men are all the same? You'd think with two ears and one dick you'd be trying to listen more than fuck but most of you can barely do either."

"Shut up, that's not how you really feel. If it was we wouldn't be in this at all."

"So, you got my number. But you still don't listen because I already told you on the boat these cigarettes are for the stress. First it was the money you lost and now Bandy's disappeared. We're sledding downhill, boo."

"And you running around blaming me for being nervous? After this trip I swear to God I'm ready to burn Savannah down to the ground."

She blew a cloud. "So what? You need some more powder?"

"Save it. I don't want to see Chevy while I'm numb. Then, she won't believe me either."

Behind the cloud a smirk pulled on both sides of Chocolate's mouth. She's the bride of wickedness behind the veil of smoke. "They say sex relieves a lot of stress, ya know. All those hormones just melt the pressure away."

I walked over to the bed. "Yeah, I heard of that too. How did you know Bandy is Chevy's cousin?"

"She told me."

It had to have shown that I didn't buy it. Or maybe it was the disappointment of yet another thing I'd come to find out last showing when I turned my face away.

"When did she tell you?" asked Chocolate.

I ignored the question and spit back one of my own. "What side of the family are they related on?"

"Mama's side. Third cousins from an aunt named Wanda who died in Texas. She never told you?"

No, she never told me. Guess I wasn't worth knowing. Guess it was just another one of those things she felt she had to keep hidden for reasons untold. I picked the new clothes up off the bed and slung them over a shoulder. "I need to shower. Before you smoke the whole pack pick up the phone and order us some food. I'm fucking starving."

When I was a kid in school they taught us about the planets. Mercury and Mars and Jupiter and Neptune. The teacher said those worlds a million miles away from us had different atmospheres, some were just pure gas, others were thin and couldn't hold back the power of the sun. That was Chocolate and Chevy, two planets with different atmospheres, and planets do not give a shit that you can't help yourself.

The atmosphere at the Marriott was different. When I came into the orbit of Chevy moons rearranged because even though she had feelings they weren't for me anymore. It must have started in the hallway on the floor of her room where the Saints pattern on the walls seemed to run up and on forever. I slipped around a housekeeping cart in front of a wide open door. A maid stepped out bringing old towels to wash and hauled back in the fresh replacements. Needless to say I came to this galaxy all on my own. I left Chocolate in the other hotel, on her own planet to go where my failures had never truly gone before.

Chevy acted bored when she answered the door, she didn't make a comment about the new clothes, True Religion jeans and an old Gibeau shirt. This is business not flattery. I heard the TV mumbling and smelled the familiar body lotion leaning out. She had her hair in a long braid down one shoulder like her mama used to do it. She had absolutely no problems letting me stand there forever. She didn't make a move until I pressed.

"Can I come in?"

"You're fine in the hall. Where's my cousin?"

"I'm working on it."

"I told you not to come around without her. Think I was playing about that?"

I shook my head. "This ain't no drive-thru, Chevy. I can't just order her up and pull off with a bag."

She paused to read between the lines. "It's that bad, huh?"

"Yeah."

"Worse than last time? Worse than when we went to go get her on the south side?"

"Hard to tell. I don't think it could ever be that bad, though. That was fucked up."

It was a truth and a half and half a lie. Things were maybe okay now but by tomorrow's rise that could all be upside down.

Taneesha slid past me out the door. No words. She was too broken to talk. For a week and then some she had every reason to trust in me and then suddenly no reason at all. Chevy watched her go down the hotel hallway before turning towards the elevators. Her face darkened.

"Well, at least you brought some good news," she said with sarcastic malice. Then, stepped right back into the guts of her lair. I barely got a foot in the door before she tried to slam it on my nose.

"Chevy, just listen."

"Fuck you. You're full of shit. Every time I trust in you something bad happens. Not little bad. Big bad. Devastating."

I gave her the dead face, no soul in my eyes. Just a flat stare through the space in the door. It wasn't easy facing those gold, candy, drops staring right back.

"Move your foot. Now."

"You don't have to believe me for the rest of your life. Hate the shit out of me, Chevy. But trust me on one thing. You're going to want to hear what I got to say. I love Bandy. And I'm going to bring her home."

"Come back when you do."

"Think if it was that easy I'd be standing here all by myself?" I pushed against the door to save my toes from getting ruined. "I need you. Bad. Think about it, last time she was in trouble you were mad at me then too. We worked together and brought her home because we put all our feelings aside. It's the same right now. I'm not asking you to squash anything, just put it on the back burner. Hate me later. 'Cause right now all she's got is us."

That was it, my hail Mary in the last seconds of the game. Not pretty, barely clever, but it did the job. She eased up on the door, looked at the carpet, shot her glare up at me and then as far as she could see down the hall. "Is that skank here?"

I shook my head. "Just me. No chaperones."

The door opened wide. I got silent permission to step through. She tossed her head hard to the side so the braid wiggled like a banner and then stood back out of my path.

The room smelled like the female brand of upset nervousness, like dry rose petals left in a old book and sugar coated perspiration. There were rolled up dollar bills and little baggies on the bedside table. The hotel flat screen was on the local news, a weather girl talking about today's sunny sky's and the shrimp tide going out. She isn't the regular forecaster, I could tell by the way she over explained everything with those long technical terms so dummies like me couldn't understand.

But Chevy didn't give a shit if the sky was falling. She had been watching news waiting for Bandy's picture to pop up. I watched her stand perfectly still by the mini bar, no sense of time or space or that she was no longer alone. And since none of us had called in a missing person the only way the little singer would show up on the news is if they found her body.

"How do you know she's in trouble?" I asked.

"Because you just told me." She talked without looking away from the TV screen.

"I mean before that."

"Neesha knew. She felt it. Sort of like how I felt it when you were headed to jail and tried to stop you. That's all over with now, though."

I rubbed a hand over my head. "I'm sorry, baby."

"Fuck you. I'm not your baby anymore."

"Still, I'm sorry."

"You said that already."

"I mean for everything. All the way from the beginning."

"Apology not accepted. And it never will be. I'm not taking your sorry's anymore. So, save your breath and just let it go."

"Shit, I was only saying-"

"No, don't say anything." She whipped around. "Why her, Cerrio? You never told me why it had to be that bitch. Me and Bandy weren't enough you had to go and do that?"

"What do you want me to say, Chevy?"

"Nothing. Nothing makes sense anymore. I thought a lot today and you know what I realize? I realized that the only person who's a bigger fuck up than you is me. Because I keep on believing in you. No matter how far you drag me down I always think things are going to get better like a stupid little high school girl hanging on to a fantasy.

My daddy told me before I left home that you'd always be a weight around my neck. He was wrong, though. Because I'm not doing it anymore. After this you stay away from me. You and that bitch and whatever other sluts you keep on the side. Or maybe I'm the one on the side." She laughed like a creep. "Wow, I never thought of that before."

"Come on Chev, it don't have to be like that. Think about the history we have together. We can at least be friends."

"Friends?" She scoffed. "Are you serious? With a friend like you I might as well write out a suicide note. God, my daddy was so right. I just wish I could see him one more time so I can tell him I'm sorry for not listening."

Repercussions were expected. Delivered they were death sent. She had dwelled on this moment, lived in it, dyed herself in the color of hate. Chevy's words were violent. They stabbed me clean through like a dull knife and twisted deep into the bone.

I cleared my throat. "Is Neesha coming back?"

"Don't count on it. She wants to be somewhere you're not."

We were getting nowhere. Even changing directions drove me down a dead end.

"Let me get something to drink."

"There's tap water in the bathroom. Cups are on the sink."

"Alright, Chevy. Its over, you win. I admit your daddy had a point. And after this I'll leave you alone. Forever, if that's what you like." I sat down in a plush armchair. "Now that that's taken care of let's get down to business."

"I'm listening."

"Somebody reached out to me. Actually, they got to Chocolate first and then she got to me."

"Shit. You two must be the luckiest backstabbers ever."

"Luck isn't my forte. Chocolate grew up in Savannah. She knows where to look when a pretty girl comes up missing."

Chevy came off the wall she was leaning against. "Chocolate knows where Bandy is?"

"Take it easy. She just knows the players in town who deal in the shade."

"Were you with her after midnight?"

"That's a dumbass question. You know where I was. Out by the docks playing spades."

"Then, how did you two link up this morning?"

"I don't know." I paused. "She just rolled up and found me."

"So, let me try and understand this. The bitch disappears in the middle of the night. Nobody knows where she went or who she was with. Then, out of nowhere she materializes at dawn with the sunrise. Somehow finds you all by yourself. And, wait here's the best part, she tells you she knows something about where Bandy might be? Tells you she knows somebody who can put you on the right track."

"Yeah, I know how that sounds."

"Do you? Is the pussy so good that you just believe whatever she says just like that." She snapped her fingers. "No questions asked?"

"I asked a lot of questions. Aggressively."

"Is it magical down there? Is it like Disneyland?"

"Will you stop it! I saw how she acted when we met one of those goons. Chocolate hates these people. Trust me, you can't fake that kind of disgust."

"But you faked love."

Chevy's nostrils flared. She came straight towards me with new energy. Stopped in front of the chair right in front of my knees.

"Get up."

I allowed myself a moment of shock. "Why? You want to fight?"

"Just get up. I want to see something."

I rose carefully off the cushion and let her pat me down. She went cautiously around the waist of the new jeans like the cops do it when they run my tags.

"Where is it?"

"Tell me what you're looking for."

She sniffed. "You're gun. Lemme guess, Chocolate got it. You let her take it away from you and now you're out here running around naked."

"Cause we had to go to church."

"I see. To pray, right? For a miracle, right? Because you're a godly man now, right? Well, you better be because if ever a sucker deserves to die screaming it's you."

I pulled the yellow note out of my pocket. "I went there for this. If I could have I would have shot the guy who handed it to me. Who knows? Maybe I'll still get a chance. In the meantime, this is the best news you're gonna get."

Chevy is smart but I know when she's out of ideas because something drains her face. It hits in the gut and wipes her down like a squeegee. She unwrinkled the paper, read it once, then again and again. After a dozen times the yellow slip went back in a wadded up ball. "I get it," she said. "They want ransom. Fifty thousand dollars. And you came here to ask for the rest of the money I brought to pay it, right? You want the part of my life savings that you didn't fuck off to buy Bandy back off the market?"

Like I said, smart girl.

Chevy twisted her pretty mouth up while she waited for more. I told her plain and simple, that was it. What she said was everything. Fifty thousand dollars dropped to the place on the bottom of the note brings her baby cousin home. She relaxed her lips and blew out some air. Her breath smelled like orange juice.

The news had gone off. Now it was talk show banter playing to the tension in the room. She put a finger on her chin like she was drumming up a thought while Maury grilled somebody's maybe, maybe not dad. The thought never came. I guess it got jammed in a place between mind and matter. She turned her back on me and went over to the bedside table, pulled a baggie out of the drawer that looked a lot like the one Chocolate was carrying around in her bra.

"Want a line?"

"Nah, I'm good," I lied.

A small mound got tapped out on a coaster. Chevy used the Marriott key card to split it up. She raked a little left and little right until two equal rails formed even like identical twins. The first one went quick like the years do. A straw cut off with vanity nail trimmers touched down and the dope vanished immediately. I waited for the ritual. She sniffed, touched her nose, threw her head back.

"Last chance," she teased. "Sure, you don't want in on this?"

"I'm straight. Trying to cut down."

"Yeah, right."

She touched the straw down and cleaned the coaster. Once it was clear then the audience on TV clapped their hands. Tremendous applause as Chevy licked her key card and threw it back in the drawer.

"Man, you don't know what you're missing. That's good shit right there."

"I'll have to take your word for it. Now, focus. What are you going to do about Bandy?"

"What can I do but what you told me? You got me over a barrel, Cerrio. I'm going to pay for my cousin and you're going to bring her back."

"You think I got all the power?"

She smiled. "Yes, definitely. Now, turn around so I can get the money."

I almost perished from the sting. "You gotta be kidding. It's like that?"

"A thousand percent it's like that," she replied. "Turn around."

"Get real."

"I am. And I'm not asking a third time."

Commercial break. Maury promised to be back in a few minutes with DNA results. That's all the fans wanted anyway, that's the whole show right there. Everything else, the back and forth, the finger pointing, name calling. That's all preliminary. Soon the goods would be produced, right after these messages.

The way they do it these days advertisements run on forever. By the time the show comes back you forgot what you were even watching. Who's that guy with the blond dreads? Is that the baby's dad? I heard someone selling used cars, fast food for a dollar, cheap insurance, and a gun clicking behind my head.

She sniffed again. "Do not fucking move."

"Don't be stupid, Chevy. Kill me and Bandy is gone forever."

The barrel pressed hard against my skull, deep into the hair until I could hear it scrape inside my ears. "You're losing me right now. I'm high and I got a gun and you piss me off. All that put together means you should really shut up. Why do I have to tell you that, Cerrio? Huh? Why?"

"Don't know. But if you're going to pull the trigger do it quick while you got the courage."

"Smartass, huh? See, that's your problem. You think you're so much smarter than everybody else. But in the end what do you really know?" She shoved the pistol into my scalp. "Come on, Cerrio give me your knowledge."

"I got nothing."

"Damn right. You're stupid. Chocolate ain't from Georgia. She grew up out in Oakland in the projects by the freeway. She came to Winston-Salem to go to college. Got kicked out second semester for sleeping with her professors."

"This is a real funny way to tell me she was lying."

She spun me around by the shoulder. That little .32 we jumped the liquor store with aimed straight at my chin. Four slender fingers gripped the pink pearl handle and one was on the trigger when she hit me in the chest. With a brown paper bag.

I juggled a little and caught it. "What's this?"

"That's fifty," she replied. "Spend it however you want. Gamble. Get high. Go on a cruise. Go on a goddamn spaceship, I don't care. But know this. Bandy better come back all in one piece or you and your new best friend are going to the bottom of the Savannah river."

The were was no laughter in my eyes when I said, "I thought you were going to hang her from a lamppost."

"Changed my mind. But I bought a rope anyway."

"If you don't believe me why would you pay?"

"Because Cerrio. Even though you're a no good, side winding piece of shit I still know you won't let anyone touch a hair on Bandy's head. And there's no way you wrote that ransom note, either. I know your handwriting, it's absolutely beautiful. Maybe sacred. Remember all those love letters we used to pass back in high school?"

"Yeah."

"Back when your cursive made me wet?"

"I remember. Good times back then."

"Yeah, those were the days. Too bad they're gone now."

"Not yet."

"Cerrio?" She wiped her eye.

"Yeah?"

"Get the fuck out of my room."

CHAPTER 52

ONE DOWN

What's a bunch of money between two friends? Everything really. I remember all the tellers at the credit union overflowing with politeness until Aunt Denise's savings melted down. Then, they tore away the red carpet right in front of her wheelchair like a piece of duct tape. No more courteous names like miss and ma'am unless it was condescending because bank people don't waste good manners on poor folks. No one does. They looked down on her. Literally peering over the counter aiming loaded stares at the little wheelchaired woman rubbing two quarters together inside their big marble lobby. That was about the same time I started really running the streets.

But what's money between family? Now that I don't know. There's never been any money in my family. Coming back from the Marriott with a fat ass sack of cash was a big hint, though. Chevy handed over fifty stacks for her cousin like it was spare change buried down in between the couch cushions. All the loose bills swimming around the bottom of the bag proved she never even counted out the money. Just crammed the bread in and served me her ultimatum.

Chocolate went straight to work after she saw it. Soon as I walked in the room she was on the phone putting together another rendezvous like we had at the church but not at the restaurant. I don't know if she was the architect of this job. I don't know if her attitude counted as much of a clue. I knew Chevy smelled a rat but that's always the scent for a person standing knee deep in betrayal. Anyway, that wasn't the only thing going up her nose.

Then, there was the bigger problem. What else did we have? Chocolate could be lying through her teeth. The girl might really be from Montana. Fifty thousand dollars could go up in smoke and Bandy's kidnapping could be a zero sum game but the only alternative to figure this out wore a shiny badge and nobody, not even the little singer herself, would want to call the police.

All I really knew is that we were a mistake. In the beginning it seemed classic. The type of match people talk about as legendary. Her the Jezebel dancer, and me, the card hustler with the steel married to his waist. Two tarnished gems riding on a tidal wave taking whatever they wanted. She comes for your wallet, I put a bead on your forehead. Then, we spend up your money and dance all over your grave hand in hand. Together, me and the Panther had plenty of potential to be the type of outlaw couple no one could ever forget. That twisted chemistry shimmered with so much allure that sometimes I squinted in our own light.

I prayed some while Chocolate got her face together in the Holiday Inn's bathroom mirror. Not the out loud hymns, more like mental pleas that no matter what happens things won't go so far sideways that they can't tilt back. Counting money helped. Shuffling bills gave my anxious hands something to do while I tried making contact with God. And eventually we settled on nothing, no promises, no contract, no commitment for either side. Then, the bottom of the bag came and I found one of my last prayers shattered underneath a few loose bills, the stragglers Chevy hadn't organized.

Chocolate is mechanical, she's what happens when feelings crawl inside a woman's body and die. She's sex, money and greed wrapped up in scraping thorns. All of it felt like a wet dream come true until I woke up missing the greatest part. Chevy had something her used to be coworker left behind in the hoods of Oakland or the docks of Savannah or at some point in between. She had that warmth that got passed down from her mother like the arch in her top lip. Seville James was that little square of sunshine melting ice at high noon on a winter Monday, the tiny light you try to arrest so the dark doesn't swallow your hopes.

I needed that light and that warmth. I needed and I wanted a blowout fight with my day one baby so we could make up between the sheets like mature adults. We weren't getting back together. At least that's what she said but a mouth will say anything when the heart is suffering. Although, the gun was a pretty convincing touch. Everyone knows actions speak louder than words. That's why it hurt in the soul to see the herringbone I gave her coiled around the bottom of the empty money sack like a lizard.

The gold lady head charm I dreamed of grinned in the bag like she had a joke to tell. Or maybe she just liked being part of this little death inside me. Bibi's chain was just scrap metal now. Vacant spaces where links had popped out were an effrontery to Chevy's anger, it told the story of when she was high on rage and ripped the gift off her neck like she was freeing herself from the hold of LaDecerrio Lloyd.

I tilted the bag sideways, watched was left of the necklace spill out on the table. More links came away, they shook free and tinkled all over in different directions like loose teeth. Chocolate heard the noise of gold raining down and emerged from the bathroom exploding with questions. I swept them all away like I swept the small pieces of gold into one of her empty cellophane cigarette wrappers. She stood rock still by the hotel dresser while I gathered the last of my affections into a plastic piece of trash and shoved it deep into my pocket. That's about the time she really got the message.

There was no meeting place, just live directions out on the road like we did it earlier. Whoever had Bandy wanted to make absolutely sure we came alone, no help, no backup following us into a hole where there was one way in and no way out. Leaving the state made it federal, back across the Talmudge bridge into South Carolina felt wrong and eerie. In the Jeep with no doors the bridge's suspension cables seemed near enough to write your name on and that rotten odor from the paper plant was close enough to touch. It got on my clothes and stuck like Velcro. Chocolate thought she had a trick, she held her breath for almost a minute and when she finally let it go she gagged so loud I couldn't hear the radio. That was the funniest thing from the whole weekend besides when I saw a rich girl on the casino boat with a Pomeranian shitting in her purse.

Three miles after the bridge they called with more directions. Chocolate talked low. I didn't listen. Any hint of bullshit, real or imagined, would have dissolved the last small bit of sanity I still had left. All I heard was her snapping the flip phone shut after the chat.

In the last Carolina midnight looked different. A pitch black sheet hung low and imposing over strong cypress trees. Branches curled over the road like thick talons of a falcon, moss dripping off them in gray clumps falling down like eternal slaves to gravity. These were the hanging trees where poor souls got put up not that far back in the yesteryears of human suffering. Tortured spirits blew through me fast on that winding stretch of blacktop. A faint wind whispered through shuddering the leaves until we got to the marshland. That's where the air quit talking so the crickets could perform their chorus. If souls ran through trees then the bodies were buried down here in the mud. It was the perfect place to go missing, a wide open field of cold cases. Crabs skittered on the slippery shore, birds fought beak to beak for the most blood bloated mosquitoes and when I closed my eyes the shellfish smelled just the same as an open tomb.

Criminal minds think alike. I know because Chocolate saw it all the same way. She knew this area like the back of her hand because it's the place where we always have the most fun. Right at the crossroads of bad decisions and sabotage. And she was so loaded up on her own excitement that she started packing her bags to take a trip to a memorial of us. Recalling how we slid around our old friends so dispassionately she parted her lips to get out that first virile thought but all I heard was more engine noise.

Another car on the road moving fast on all cylinders like a horse at the derby. From twenty yards back it was just a lonely dark shape in the Jeep's sideview mirror but he caught up in a hurry. That's the sort of energy cash missions provide, because pure and free stamina rides hard on every payday.

High beams flicked as he narrowed the distance, edging closer and closer and just before he tapped the back bumper the '69 Charger broke over the solid yellow line and hit fifth gear. Looking through the door that wasn't there I saw glossy paint hauling ass under the stars and chrome glaring back like wet silver. It was old enough to be a collector, quick enough to outrun time. The driver tapped the horn with one short note and then the Hemi ate up the last five feet to pull in front of us.

We went slow, downshifting but not crawling, easing along the road like light Sunday traffic. Chocolate didn't have to tell me to stay close just like no one had ever told me how to live in the heat. Our little convoy rode tight for a mile and a half until the 553 out front lit up his turn signal. No point asking where we were going. If the woman beside me knew then I guess that was all bad and if she had no idea then what was the use. Or she might play dumb and then I could play crazy, because in the end lunacy beats ignorance every time.

I cut down the radio on a dirt packed road. In the sudden hush a hundred pitted stones crunching underneath four, fat tires sounded loud as wedding bells. We pulled up on a partially done building that looked like it was doomed never to get finished. A tumbleweed of construction worker trash bounced in front of a black Suburban four yards away blending in with the night. I parked the loud Jeep caddy-corner under a pecan tree and the fast Dodge eased around to put itself beside the other truck. Headlights went dark, after that there was stillness. Insects kept their peace and the waves lapping up on riverside shores were too far back to hear. Another car came and I thought it had to be more bad news, maybe an ambush or a state trooper. The new set of headlights grew brighter and stronger against the trees before fading down the road harmlessly.

In the seat beside me Chocolate was trying to cannibalize her nerves, trying to chase away the poison of torment with her own brand of venom. The SUV flashed its lights and I saw her jaw clench but the teeth didn't grind. I never asked about it, didn't even ask if she was good. Details like that didn't mean anything. All that mattered was my own anxiety and my pistol. I tore the keys out of the Jeep's ignition and jammed one down in the center console lock.

"What are you doing?" she hissed.

"What the fuck it looks like. Getting my gun."

She pushed my hand back. "And I told you that's not how this goes."

"Yeah, before we went on tour in a church. Not at midnight in the fucking swamp."

I wiggled the key but it wouldn't turn. Like the little fucking thing was against me too.

"Here we go with the saucy shit again. Why don't men ever listen?"

I said, "maybe you haven't figured out how to speak our language yet."

I went to the next key in the ring and pushed it in, I got a fit but it would not turn. Chocolate hated the effort. It was such a raw affront to her standing doctrine. She grabbed my wrist and dug a full set of nails deep in the flesh until the nerves in my arm burned like a black widow bite. The girl was strong just like Chevy was smart, just like Bandy could sing, just like I was filled up with lots of good soul but not a lot of common sense.

She squeezed down to the bone, I took the pain and then shoved her. It should have been a little push to get off me before

I really flashed but the fire shooting up my elbow spiked adrenaline and roughed up the touch. Chocolate stumbled sideways out of the Jeep. There was a tangle of long legs and a heel dragging the floorboards like an anchor over a seabed before she crashed to the dirt. I promise I tried catching her. My fingers reached out for those same claws that sank down in me like golf tees on a green when she thudded to the ground. A tiny noise came up with the impact. Some ashamed, pathetic whimper that didn't go at all with the vixen who derived erotica from pain. In a second all the danger sprang away like scared rabbits in the fox's shadow. The edge faded and suddenly Sugar Bares finest was just like a small hurt child getting bullied off the playground swings. My guilt soared past the moon. I was hopping out on the passenger's side of her purple J-truck apologizing on a loop while she got up on hands and knees.

Another fingernail got broken off, it laid curve up by the front tire. The one on her naked ring finger was bent backwards like the top of a tent. The Suburban flashed us again like it was enjoying the show but getting impatient. I bent down to scoop her off the ground and she pushed me away while holding her shoulder with a jagged manicure.

"Just get your precious fucking gun!"

"Look, I didn't mean it. This shit is just driving me crazy."

She made her words sound like a slit up vinyl. "Well, it's almost over. Now, grab your shit and let's go."

CHAPTER 53

SHOOTER'S DISPOSITION

When I think it's complex is always when it turns out simple. Exhaust from both vehicles licked up off a plastic tarp holding down a load of bricks or a body or maybe both. White plumes of smoke rose high and mixed together in the air like liberated spirits dancing down to Georgia. I expected the cartel, twenty gangsters in the Suburban, six more in the Hemi. Instead, it was just two men, brown skin, pits for eyes, close cut beards. One short and one a little taller than Chocolate. I know they saw every bit of action between me and her because they came out smiling like fools. They didn't see the gun, though.

There was no meeting in the middle. We went to them as a soft reminder of who held the power. The short one I recognized from church that afternoon. He had on less gold now and his hair was pulled back in a loose ponytail that let renegade strands blow free in the breeze. The taller goon looked a lot like my older brother, except I have no brothers. We did the handshaking again. Both of them looked at Chocolate with a mix of scorn and lust. She didn't get a hello, didn't give one either. Fair is fair.

The tallest produced a pack of Marlboros and a lighter. He lit up cuffing his hand around the flame to shield it from the wind before stuffing the squares back in his pocket. I don't know about morals but these dudes are tight on manners. The short one jabbed a finger at his partner and they started arguing in a language I understand, but only a little.

In foreign languages you don't need to know every single fucking word, just the fundamentals. So, if less is more than I had the most. When I got enough to cover the basics then I jumped in and swam.

"Don't worry," I said. "I don't smoke anyway."

The short one didn't care. "That I know. But, he's still supposed to offer."

"Smoking don't turn me on. That's not what I'm here for."

"Smart." He drew the word out and rolled the R long. "I like that. You went to college?"

"No, I went to prison."

The smoker breathed out a dense cloud. "Me too. Seven years."

"Nice." I said it deadpan to shit on his suffering.

"No, not nice."

"He didn't do the time in America" said the short one. "He's here to, uh, get over it."

"Sounds rough."

"What that got to do with us?" snapped Chocolate.

The short one ignored her. "You want to know where he went to prison?" he asked.

"I think you want me to know a lot more than I want to find out."

Both of them laughed. Hearty chuckles floating over the car engines idling. The smoker mumbled something I didn't understand and stole an extra laugh after his own remark.

"What did he say?" I asked.

"Salaam, said you should be a comedian. Do shows and make people laugh. He says you're good at it."

I reached for my waist to show him what I was really good at but Chocolate cut in with before my hand touched gunmetal. "Where's our friend?" she growled.

"Where's the money?" he snapped back.

The Panther held firm. "Prove you got her. I ain't heard a scream, a grunt, nothing."

"Strange. Would you pay more if we tortured her?"

"Simon says stop." I looked at Chocolate, now it was me calming her down. She dialed back a fraction. Just enough for me to play the good guy.

I looked at the ponytail swinging like a bait line. "Fifty thousand is a lot of bread. We just want a little something."

Shorty nodded, when he snapped his fingers the smoker moved like he heard an order. I watched him walk around the Suburban to the left side, pop the door just enough to reach in. He dug around, I heard a knock like someone was kicking the back of the front seat and then he pulled something out and slammed the back shut. I was openly curious. Couldn't even hide it if I tried. The tall goon shuffled his feet and tossed the thing he took from the back of the truck on the ground. A white string of pearls with a snapped clasp hit the dirt.

Salaam ashed his Marlboro in the breeze. "Seen enough?"

I had seen enough and if I never saw any of it all again it would be too soon. I tossed the bag of money to the one who didn't smoke. He caught the sack like a football. "Okay, we have a deal. Just give me a minute to look at this."

"Trust me it's all there." It wasn't. We were short by a lot, I mean a whole lot. I only counted it up in Chocolate's room to know how many one's I had to slip in the middle to make the rubber banded stacks seem legit. If the cash got tallied then I was going to have to shoot somebody for real. Not a bad thing but I was starting to learn that gunfights are like garlic, most of the time less really is more.

Salaam waved his cigarette. "Sure, we trust you. We just have to make sure there's no marks."

"Marks?"

"Goddamnit," said Chocolate.

"What do you mean marks?" I spat.

Ponytail tried cleaning up for his partner. "He don't mean nothing. Just let me take a look." He held up a finger. "One minute and you can have your friend back."

"You think I'm a sucker? You think this money is marked? Tell me the truth. You two fuckboys got me down for a rat?"

"Not me. It's our boss. He never takes any chances."

"I gives no fucks what you boss takes. Rats get killed and I ain't dead yet so now give me the girl."

"Hey, relax."

"I'll relax in a minute. As soon as I get what I came for."

Slow motion. Salaam flicks his Marlboro away. The ember burning at the tip falls out and rolls to a stop and the rest of the square dies in the Georgia clay. That little glowing cherry was the only thing that made me comfortable. Without it his hands are invisible against the dark. My hearing tells the rest of the story. There's a rustling, a sound of fabric on fabric too rapidly haphazard to be anything casual.

I go for my waist and this time Chocolate doesn't stop to interrupt. One day I'm going to leave this life but whenever it comes I promise it won't be because I let the next man get his shots in first. I squeeze the .45 trigger. Boom, thunder claps and the Suburban's headlight bursts like a water balloon. The short goon clutches the money bag close to his chest like a mother with her newborn and tears open the driver's side door while Salaam stands tall so his bullets can land in my forehead. I duck right on time, another second and I'd be history, and a hot one breezes through my hair like a comb racing at the speed of Saturn.

For a moment Salaam seems dumb. The type of wild eyed, fearless barbarian you just know is going to die young and proud like a Crusader. I can see the coroner slicing through him with his tools and pure adrenaline pouring out on the table. But he isn't stupid, in fact Salaam is just the kind of useful crazy needed in a cash only enterprise.

After his bullets bury themselves in a stack of wood beams laid by a tractor he figures me out. He knows where my loyalty is centered which is genius because I don't even know how to explain it that well. To me it's just instinct to push Chocolate out of the way when he shoots at her and not me. I let go of the Remington, dive left and pin her on the ground. Salaam is a crack shot. Even with the mask of the dark making things harder he's accurate. Bullets rip open the back of my shirt. The third or fourth one hits my shoulder right in the same spot where Bandanna stitched me up like a battlefield nurse.

My new gun slides to a groove in the earth, stops on a dime dead in the middle of twin tread marks made by heavy equipment. The ponytail is swinging hard now, lashing like a whip as he screams for his partner to come on while Chocolate squirms under me like a wet eel. She's got the strength of a lynx and with my shoulder broiling like a hamburger it's impossible to hold her down.

She gets to the gun before his yelling can echo off the lonely woods watching down on us impassively and she lights up the night like New Year's Eve. Sparks fly off the Suburban, she pops the grill and the radiator whistles like a steam pipe. The way she shoots is all American action hero. Rambo. Terminator. Gangster. Plenty of shells hit the ground with lots of bullets streaking nowhere but that last one makes up for anything. When the Panther squeezes one final time I saw Salaam take it high in the leg. From where he clutches I know this is it. Maybe ten minutes to find a hospital and then he would be in paradise with eighty virgins.

The boys didn't waste any precious seconds trying to shoot back. I hear fabric rip as Salaam makes a tourniquet for himself out of his shirt sleeve and then the Hemi roars into action as they evacuate. Those big custom wheels come flying in fast. I knew they were sick, getting beat by a girl and all, they want to get even about it by running my face over in the dirt. They only miss by stupid luck, three more inches would have left burning rubber on my cheeks. Instead, gravel sprays in my teeth as the vintage muscle car gets lost in a dizzy trace of taillights.

I thought we'd won. The minions were gone to the hospital, we slid without paying them the whole fiddy bands and the grand prize was sitting in the shot up SUV left behind with the building materials. Chocolate sat down on a slab of concrete and wiped the pistol with her shirt while I drug myself off the ground. Nothing seemed off about her couldn't-give-a-shit less attitude. Cold Chocolate is the only kind I ever knew.

She didn't look up to ask about me getting shot, just sat there content, humming a sweet love song while getting rid of her fingerprints. I got to my feet, shoulder searing like a New York ribeye. Some noise came out of me like an animal sound that even made my own skin crawl. Still, she never looked up. Not when I spit blood and rocks out of my mouth, not when I stumble to the Suburban and open up the back door, not when I blinked twice at an empty truck with no Bandy tied up inside. "She ain't here," I said. I screamed it. "She ain't here! She ain't here. She ain't fucking in here! Bandy ain't in here! Where the fuck is she?!"

Nobody answered my question. It went up and out and then dropped back down into another round of solo quiet. I heard little bugs chirping again, looking around I saw it was simply me and nature. Chocolate vanished. She left the gun down on the cement and pulled the Jeep away in stealth mode. I knew better than to call for her. In the end it's always just me, a little more hurt, a little more broken, a little more tired just trying to save a few breaths for a good explanation. I plucked the Marlboro off the ground that Salaam tossed off and lit it with the Suburban's dashboard lighter. One good drag had me coughing, when the hacking ceased the next pull had me leaning against the truck blinking up at Wednesday's sunrise.

CHAPTER 54

YHAY YUDA

Chevy put a hand on her chest where Cerrio's solid gold charm used to hang. She must have touched that spot seven hundred times unconsciously since leaving the Marriott for a little fresh air. Her and Neesha had to get out of there because waiting for Bandy in that little hotel room with the white towels and the white sheets and the white people coming down the hallway was like death by a thousand cuts. They went out to find a distraction, reroute their worried minds until the magical phone call came saying their girl was good, that she was back like the band and on the way. Then, the three of them were going to go home and watch a movie on the sofa just like sisters.

Sitting across from each other in a cold diner was not where they were supposed to land. Instead of running through Savannah on a good time mission for fun Chevy sat in an almost empty Denny's while her little cousin's girlfriend worked hard to hold down her anxiety. Here they were, watching the locals plod in one by one to get the special of the day.

The waitress came by to pour more coffee. Taneesha forced a little smile and then went right back to staring out the window.

After the girl in the apron laid down some peppermints and their bill Chevy asked who had the tip. That question brought down a layer of awkwardness approaching something contentious.

Chevy rebraided her hair at the table. "Oh, it's just a joke honey. Don't worry I got this."

Taneesha protested. "No, it's on me. You already gave your life savings away. I can't ask you to spend anything else."

"It was a joke. That was me trying to lighten the mood. I guess I didn't do a real good job."

Taneesha dug in her jeans for something to give the Denny's waitress. "We don't have to keep apologizing to each other. You're good, Chev. If I had to go through this with anyone it would always be you."

"That's the best thing I've heard all weekend."

"It's only the truth."

Chevy sipped hot coffee even though her stomach was already acidic. "Girl, if it wasn't for you I'd be checking my phone every two minutes waiting on somebody to call who actually gives a damn." She laughed. "You know what I'm saying?"

"Somebody?"

"Okay, anybody. Man, woman or child just as long as they got some news I can use."

"I don't believe you."

"It's true, Neesha. You soothe me."

"No, I mean you're lying about who you really want to hear from." Taneesha leaned in. "You don't have to hide your feelings, at least not from me. Because I know exactly how it feels."

"Sounds sweet. But I don't quite understand."

"I think you do. That's why we're sitting here together. Because we both love someone. Love is like a scar, Chevy. And scars don't fade."

"Scars fade. A little cocoa butter and some Ambi-"

"Stop." Neesha turned her mouth up in a tumultuous smile. "Everybody who gets hurt badly really wishes that were true."

Four fingers went back to the spot in her chest, it was meant to hold the heavy charm, without it Chevy felt underclothed.

This was the most honest thing she never wanted to hear. Love can't be killed, it doesn't die passively like wheat in the winter. Roses are red and violets are blue but those shrivel up as the spring wears on to the end. Love is not like that, not trapped in mortality. That's what her mother said a long time ago in the days of fancy cornrows and pink velour.

"Why did it have be Chocolate," she sighed. "I could accept a mistake but not like this. Not when it's with the most heartless bitch in the city. It's just cruel, you know?"

"Cerrio didn't mean it like that. I'm mad at him too but he's just a man." Taneesha shifted in her booth seat. "Men are born with something inside that makes them stupid and reckless. That's why they don't live long as we do. Trust me Chevy, no matter what he did your name is still written all over his heart. That week he stayed with me he ate, breathed, and slept on a way to get over whatever what you two were fighting about."

"Yeah, then he up and does some shit like this."

"Chocolate chose him. She saw something she wanted and took it."

"He gave in to her and humiliated me! And why she did have to take what's mine anyway? She can have any man she wants!"

"Because, the rest of them are tired. Look around Chevy. Half the men out here are gay."

"You're gay."

"Yeah, but I don't try to hide mine. Look, the point is Cerrio is the opposite of what you can get out here. Whatever pathetic dick comes through the club is too soft to handle a real woman. It's not money and clothes. Nothing fancy because he's above that and beneath it all at the same time. I can't explain it good but you know what I mean."

Now, it was Chevy's turn to stare at the window. She saw the movements in diner behind her, cooks plating up eggs, ketchup bottles marrying on the counter, somebody fanning themselves off with a laminated menu. She sighed because she had nothing else to do.

"He was born that way. Back in school Cerrio was just an unusual occurrence. He was an odd kid until I made him special. Gave him his first piece, and he was my first too. But nobody would be talking about him like you are if it wasn't for me. I turned him from a little schoolboy to a...a fine, fucking exotic man. Now, I regret it all."

Taneesha smacked her tiny fist on the table drawing some looks. "Damn it Chevy this is not your fault! There's no punishment for doing a good job!"

"Of course, but what am I going to tell my kid?"

"I don't know. Wait, what?"

Chevy caught her bottom lip between her teeth. She hadn't meant to say what she said but it was too late now. You can't put the toothpaste back in the tube.

"I'm late this month. I've been throwing up in the mornings too. Cerrio doesn't know. I haven't told him yet."

Taneesha was floored. "Why haven't you said anything?"

"I wanted to give him the news after we got home. It was going to be perfect. A big bag of money and a whole brand-new life. What else could a girl ask for?"

"Well, I guess nothing. But should you be, you know." Neesha touched her nose.

Chevy shrugged. "It doesn't matter. It's just another situation far as I'm concerned."

I went to the hospital and lied. When you come in with a bullet hole people ask lots of questions you do not want to answer, then they run away to call the police. I hid my ID in my shoe, gave the nurse a fake name. My story was I got shot in a robbery and that's why I didn't have any cash or a wallet. I told it to a Gullah woman in purple scrubs, a big boned, dark-skinned, super no nonsense type. She probably had a brother or cousin waist deep in the streets and that's probably how come she knew I was lying.

Soon as the doctor had the bullet out I headed for the exit with a bandage on my arm. Chatham county sheriffs posted up in the lobby so I took the side exit down a closed corridor. It was one of my more foggier escapes. Between staying up all night again and being high as fuck on pain killers that made Bandy's seem like a pack of Nerds I spent a lot of energy handling side effects. Fighting off vertigo, wading through thin air like gravity had a big brother with something to prove.

When I got outside I breathed deep breaths of morning sunshine to make sure I wasn't hallucinating. Yellow beams bathed a parked ambulance, the paramedics moved back and forth in no particular hurry. I had stepped into the calm before the next storm, the eye of the hurricane. Moving left or right meant getting blown away but staying still didn't guarantee safety.

A police cruiser rolled past me with the front windows down. I put a hand up like I was scratching my face until he got far enough away that I could cross the street. A blue BMW came screeching to a stop in front of my feet. Another near miss, when the driver rolled his window down and told me to get in I took a slow step back. My plan was real simple, keep reversing until something else stopped me like maybe another car.

I drug my feet until another cop came bursting out of the hospital screaming for me to freeze. More were behind him, spilling out of the side exit like jokers jumping out of a clown car. That's how cops work, where there's one there's a million. Choices were slim, go or stay, jail or the unknown. I chose the devil I didn't know, hopped in the Bimmer with a perfect stranger just like he asked and sped off down the ambulance lane, cut a left, another left and we were ghosts.

Inside the car I could see his face perfectly. Without any shadows to help me resist it was easy to tell that me and the man behind the wheel were the same almost exactly, like two shingles on a roof. I could have been looking in a mirror, same hair, jet black and not dull like pepper flakes, brown eyes and a heavy strong nose that always got clipped in a fight. And it wasn't that comforting. Because he looked just like Salaam and more or less just like the goon from First African Baptist church who was stirring in the backseat.

One look back had me cussing like a rapper. The driver cut me off mid tempo. "Relax," he said. "Abdullah is angry but he won't do anything."

Next second a string of protests went off in the backseat, ringing out fast in the same foreign language I half understood from the construction site set back in the pecan trees. The anger wasn't true, though. Real emotions were strained through the filter of fear. Flip the coin and on the other side there was no holding back. My driver returned fire without hesitation, yelling uncontrollably until little flecks of spit speckled the windshield. Abdullah cringed in the backseat like a scared puppy.

I know that there's no power struggle here. All the force is right beside me driving straight down the boulevard into the sun drenched city. What went down last night had shaken out the top order of the racket and if he was going to kill me, well then that's what I had coming. In the meantime I had a mission.

"Where is Bandy?"

The driver calmly lit a cigarette even though he was still huffing from his outburst and kept his eyes straight forward. After a soft drag he spoke awkward English buttered in a thick Arab accent.

"Don't worry. Your friend is safe. Nothing happens to her." he held the pack out. "Smoke?"

"I don't want to smoke. I want my girl. Where is she?"

"I told you. She's safe. But my cousin. Him, not so much."

The BMW slowed down for a yellow light draining down to red. If he was nothing else my driver was careful about traffic. "Last night you killed him," he said referring to Salaam. "He wasn't my only cousin. He was not even the best. But, I took care of him. Like I take care of Abdullah. I take care of all my people. I even take care of you."

"The fuck are you talking about? You don't even know me."

"Oh, I know. You came to town to play cards. And you," he smoked, "you love your girls and I respect that."

"Is that all you got?"

He pulled hard on his square. I was getting to him, digging down on his nerves and maybe digging a hole for myself all at the same time. He said, "we're the same. I know you know this. That's why I give you a good deal to get your friend back."

"I paid fifty thousand dollars to get fucked. And your cousin is the one who started all this shit in the first place. I gave him the money and he treated me like-"

"Shameful, yes, Abdullah told me." He glared in his mirror at the ponytail in the backseat. "But then your girl, the one with the dark skin and long hair. She shot him dead. See, I know that too."

"You think that shit matters? Think it makes us the same? We just look alike. That's all. We're two sand niggas in a small margin. Welcome to America. I don't even know your fucking name."

"My name, is Yhay Yuda."

I paused to digest. The first part sound like yes I, but without the S. It was slick and sexy but I didn't want to admit it so I said, "shit, that's a crazy name."

He laughs and blows smoke out of his prominent nose. "See, I told you LaDecerrio. We are the same."

Taneesha asked the million dollar question at a park beside the hotel. "Are you going to keep it?"

Chevy really didn't know how to answer. Being honest she had to admit that there never was much thought about what to do with this life inside of her. It was an important decision but there were just no chances to think about it. All the time and money gone to waste had systematically ate up her concentration like little dots in a Pac Man game.

"I don't know," she admitted. "I'm not even sure I'll ever tell Cerrio. Some part of me thinks he just shouldn't know. Maybe it's better that way."

Taneesha winced. "That's kinda cruel, Chev. Don't you think you're being a little hard on him?"

"You think I'm wrong? If I don't tell him you think that makes me the bad guy in all of this?"

"That's not what I meant."

Chevy quit walking and turned to face Neesha nose to nose. "Well, what it is then? Because everything we been through in the last few days is just a sample of my life. It's how things have been since the first time I met him. Back when he was a boy. And he's still a little boy."

Neesha talked low. "Calm down. People are staring."

A jogger went by unconcerned. Chevy tossed her braid back with a tinge of violence. "Fuck calming down. They want to stare, fine. Let them eat. I'm always the bitch anyway. The one everyone loves to hate. It started at home with my father and it's not ever going to end. Not as long as I'm with him."

"So, what are you saying?"

"I guess I'm saying I can't keep it. You think it's cruel for me not to tell Cerrio? No, it's crueller to start a family with a man you know is going to fail until somebody kills him. I'm moving on, Neesha. I got to get out while I still got a chance. I can't be tied to a man forever who can't stay out of prison for even a year all because of a baby. Huh-unh, not me. You'll never see Seville James fucked up like that."

Nobody called him Yhay Yuda, a name like that is just too unique. If he held on to it police would have already had him by now. They would have picked him up years ago and buried him under the prison for life. Maybe they wouldn't even do that. When your brown like us sometimes they hunt you down like a deer and take smiling pictures with your deceased body. Ask Escobar.

So, he took the handle Ahmet to stay anonymous. Because there's a thousand Ahmets out there blending in on the sidewalk, driving taxis and mowing lawns, behind the counter at the corner store. A random one snatching girls off the street is like trying to find a needle in a haystack of needles and trying not to get pricked. I guess Doorman wasn't just telling stories out of school. I thought the old man was spinning loose tales on dope but turns out he really knew his business. Ahmet is a real pimp with a real stable and vicious tactics and now a real ho had killed his cousin.

"Somebody has to pay for the funeral," he said. I looked over at two fingers pointing towards me with a lit cigarette hung in the middle and I didn't have to kick any confusion.

"Lemme guess, that means me."

He beamed. "Yes, Abdullah said you were smart. I don't always believe him but this time I have to." He swirled his smoking hand like this was just all regular conversation. "Did you make college?"

"Why do you guys keep asking me that?"

Yuda let my annoyance go like it didn't matter. I watched in the sideview mirror as a minivan crawled behind us at single digit miles an hour. Abdullah was inside Burger King, waiting in line to get croissants while me and his boss sat parked across the street at a bustling coffee house talking business. Chocolate had made a mess, now I had to clean it up. She was right about one thing, though. I couldn't shoot my way out of this one. A cousin was dead and the big dog already had the other one running errands like his secretary. No feelings here, no sadness, or anger, or grieving. Only greenbacks. Money talked and walked and everything else just brought it home.

Yuda flicked his cigarette out the window. "These streets. They're too messy. A life for savages." He turned to me and asked, "what do you think?"

I shrugged.

He went on. "You should be my cousin too. You're smarter than Salaam. Braver than Abdullah. I can teach you everything. Then, you would live clean."

"What can I say? Guess I'm one of the savages."

"No, but you're not. That's my point. Getting shot and stealing crumbs, that's no life for you. No life for us. I know because I used to do all the same things. I was in America, the richest country in the world and living like a thief. Then, one day I met a nice girl." He patted the steering wheel. "Now, I live nice. You want to live nice, right?"

"Yeah, maybe. Or maybe I get killed by a hooker like your cousin did last night. Bang, bang, no more Cerrio. Who knows?"

"Salaam wasn't going to live long anyway. He was too crazy. Prison made him that way. Not you though. You have dinesse."

"You mean finesse."

He snapped his fingers. "Yes, that's it. Finesse, like an artist."

"Is this like the type of shit you tell all your girls? Are you trying to pimp me right now?"

He laughed. "Maybe if you were my cousin then you would know."

I looked at him for a long time, it was like looking at myself painted in macabre. He had a gaze like a wood doll, like nothing was really in there and you had to use your imagination to bring him to life.

"Do you know where Chocolate is?"

He frowned. "No, I don't know. Why?"

I opened my mouth to talk, closed it without a word. Opened it again for a two word sentence. "Just asking."

Yhay Yuda didn't believe it. "You want to pay for Salaam's funeral with her?" he asked.

He had read my mind. Maybe we are alike after all, unlikely siblings brought together by forces that can get you rich or get you killed in action.

The gears in my head turned fast. This is the evolution of evil. The reverse epiphany when life beats you down and then all the things you fought to avoid suddenly walk up and present themselves like great ideas. I didn't know where Chocolate was but I knew where she'd been. The key card for her room at the Holiday Inn was still in my pocket swimming around with Chevy's chain. And if she wasn't there then I could go to her ground floor apartment back in Winston-Salem, slip in through the window and wait for her come home. She wouldn't go quietly, I could handle her, though. The woman was strong but she wasn't Hercules.

I could bring Chocolate in like a bounty. Trade her for cash just like the brown bag that got lost last night. That's what Yuda wanted for "his cousin's" funeral. Money. Except I wouldn't make any payments. We would just be even, an eye for an eye as they say. He could have the dark dancer and then Chevy's money would go back to it's original purpose which was bringing Bandy home.

Yeah, I'd feed her to the wolves. And there was no thunderstorm in my conscious telling me how far over the edge I had gone. An even swap made perfect sense. Practical as rinsing your plate to keep food pulp out of the dishwater. Anyway, Chocolate had started this problem. She was the alpha, why not let her be the omega to round things out? And who knew if she had put this whole thing together from the start? Maybe she had a hand in the shit right from the beginning, right from the boat and the whole plan backfired. Or maybe she switched alliances at the very last minute. Maybe under the hard shell she was weak like that and maybe I should exploit that weakness for all it's worth and after that a little more.

Chapter 55

LATE REMINISCENCE

Fifty thousand dollars for Bandy was a bargain and we hadn't even paid the whole thing. A girl like that can go for two hundred easy, at least that's what they told me, and somehow that made Chocolate worth more. Yhay Yuda said, "he could get half a ticket for a prize like that."

Still, I did no kidnaps. I didn't even go back to the Holiday Inn to see if she had checked out already because that would have been too tempting. A real fast and easy way to throw out whatever I had left in my shallow bag of goodness.

Of course, Yuda was disappointed but I was still his people and on those purposes he gave me another option. A cool hundred and fifty thousand, if I could make the triple up he promised Bandy's safe return and he would keep her off the train until Friday. "That's still a very good deal for your friend," he said. Shit, I don't know. Could have been a bargain or a scam but like I said, that's what he told me.

There were a million uncertainties. Things so far up in the air they might shoot over the rainbow, break into little pieces and crash down on one side or the other. Plenty of mystery but one thing was for sure, the girls didn't love me anymore. Those warm, beautiful feelings that always sustained me before were laying cold in the gutter right now. Craziest part is Chevy's hate still had lots of space to grow.

Her and Taneesha were sitting side by side at the hotel bar when I walked in about an hour before noon. They didn't care about the rules that forbid alcohol before the day sees twelve. The Savannah Marriott didn't make any unnecessary fuss either. When I came up on Taneesha's side the bartender was emptying out his cocktail shaker pouring up two white Russians.

She felt me there before she ever saw my face. We didn't talk, tensions were so strong now that words were just clutter. She peeked around my shoulder and saw no one in my company and all the somberness in those bloodshot eyes flipped over into despair. I knew better than to reach for explanations. Nothing would have been more pointless.

Neesha took a long pull off her new drink before sliding off the barstool. She hugged Chevy for a long time before walking away without ever looking back.

Small music played by the bar. Alicia Keys on a piano singing that famous "Some People Want It All." A fascinating tune for this moment but the notes fell on deaf ears that didn't want to hear anything coming out of my mouth. To Chevy it all sounded like clutch excuses. Damage control, a load of crisis management shit sold for cheap relief when it hits the fan.

She said, "I don't care if you got shot again. You come in here all damp and dour with no fucking Bandy like you're the victim. I should shoot you my goddamn self since I promised I would. That was my word. And unlike you I don't break promises."

"Shut up a second. I got a plan."

She lifted her eyebrows. "Oh, do ya now?"

"Yeah, and please don't say it like that."

"What is it, then?"

"I can't tell you. I don't want you involved."

"More secrets, huh? You told me to shut up for that? Fine, you wanna play games Cerrio?" She dug around in her purse. "I'll blow your ass away right now."

I took a swig of the drink Taneesha left behind. "You want to shoot me? Will that make you feel better?" I set the glass down hard and spread my arms wide. "Go ahead, baby. I give you permission. Fuck it, I'm a ghost anyway. Minus well be dead."

I thought she was going to do it. Just blast me full of holes right there by the bar like we were in a Hollywood Western. The bartender stepped backwards into the bottles lined up on the shelf behind him. He was more timid than me and more wide eyed than Chevy. Her hand came back up clutching green. She slapped a pair of twenties on the wood and the guy on the other side eased his back off the bottles just far enough to snatch them away.

She came off her stool and got in my face so close that I could smell the liquor and milk still drying on her lips from the White Russian. We were so near each other I could see the small chunks of mascara in the folds of her eyelids. Different pieces of me started to remember her, pieces that would make it embarrassing to have to stand up. And that was it.

The last thing we ever shared was what we grew in best. Silence. She spun away on a heel and left me sitting there alone right in front of the scariest barkeep in all of daytime liquor. I finished the drinks because they were already paid for while he made a slow show of wiping down glasses that weren't dirty at all.

Then, I took the Greyhound home. Socks bought a ticket over the phone because I didn't have a cent to my name. The trip was long, the same way the days are long but the year always finishes before you run out to buy a new calendar. On the open road there was space to think about future and past and everyone who hated me until I fell asleep with my head against the window. Eight hours later I woke up in Winston-Salem again poor and destroyed with Wednesday fading faster than savings on a shopping spree.

I was barely above slain when Socks met me at the bus station downtown. He came in a Mazda rented for a few rocks. The car was decent, I guess these days even the fiends are living better than I am. When I stepped down off the bus his face blushed from the color ebony to a deep shade of purple. I was a man worn down. Shot, bruised, dejected, penniless. Even the rages of Satan would be jealous of the job Savannah, Georgia did on me.

My brother didn't see a man, what he saw looked more like a struck match blowing towards him through an open parking lot.

"Goddamn brother, what the hell happened? I thought you went on a vacation."

"Yeah, that was only on the first day."

His face sagged and his chin jutted out. "Where's Chevy?"

I leaned against the Mazda fender and sighed like a stabbed blimp.

"Comes a time when everybody makes deals. I'll tell you all the things you want to know if you get me loaded tonight."

"I was going to do that anyway. I mean, look at you. Shit, I seen people come back from Iraq in better shape. Come on, I'ma take you home so you can change."

"Huh-unh, can't go home. It's not like that anymore."

"Well, you ain't going nowhere with me like that."

Socks dug in his pocket and pulled out a sack. He tossed it high over the car's roof like a pack of peanuts and I snatched it out of the air. "Come on," he said. "Let's get out of here already."

We hit a drive thru for chicken sandwiches, kept it all American via fries and a soda. After that it was straight up to the North side on 27th street where a white house sat on the corner with a chain link fence around the back. Socks told me to give the sack to Linda who answered the door barefoot in a pastel nightgown with lace at the bottom.

My memory isn't so good, there's holes all the way through like an orchestra flute. But I cannot forget Mrs. Linda. Before the drugs and the violence took us under on the deep end she passed out books to me and Socks in a remedial English class back in elementary school. She taught me how to write paragraphs and what synonyms are. Then, after class we would catch the city bus up to this big white house. Fall afternoons we got off at the stop right on the corner of Boston avenue so we could cut through the alley and run fast as our legs would pump to the fenced in backyard just so we could jump on the trampoline with her son, Bobby.

Linda smoked the stones in the baggie Socks gave me and washed my clothes for free. Never in a million years did I have her on the rock. Guess you never know who people really are, huh? She didn't know about me either. How I lived off cheating at cards or how lost my girl's money or how Chevy's cousin got jammed in a faceoff with me and the reflection of myself in Lucifer's mirror down in The Hostess City of The South. AKA Savannah, Georgia.

Sometimes I see Linda around town running errands, getting the milk and eggs from Food Lion, pumping gas at the Citgo. She's the nicest woman, pretty too like the ageing and the drugs haven't found a way to box with the likes of something so dis- armingly elegant. We never speak in passing, we don't even do the friendly head nod. I guess we should be better but being who I am turns small gestures like that into a gateway for questions that have no good answers.

Drugs don't make a person bad. The whole world is just mad- ness and everybody deals with their difficulties different. Mrs. Linda had a smooth high. She wanted to make lemonade iced tea and talk about her son while cleaning up the den. She said Bobby was up in Kentucky working a student labor program at the university and earning his degree in economics. After the ar- moire got dusted with a whole can of Pledge then her talk turned a corner.

"What did I do?" she asked. "What became of me after school?" It was strange because no one had stopped to care late- ly. If it wasn't about life or death or money then no one turned around and asked about how the weight of the world felt on my shoulders. She said she always saw me and Socks, said Socks talked to her and she waited for me to notice her at Food Lion and Citgo but I never stopped to say anything. She wondered if she had done something to make me not like her and I told her the truth because lying was part of the load on my back. Told her that I'm up to no good and it's been that way for a while now. Mrs. Linda gave me a warm smile that took me back to days when I sat at a desk and realized words like love and passion mean mostly the same thing. She said "don't worry, Cerrio. We all get a chance to redeem ourselves."

When Socks came back I had my feet up on her ottoman, a beer warming in my hand, the pink robe around my shoulders tied the whole picture together. Mrs. Linda offered ice cream. He shook his head and she went on talking about how much we'd both grown up. I could have died right there happy as a gnat in the streetlights but you know fate always hates on a man whenever he's comfortable.

My brother took me back to the beginning. Underneath the stars at Sugar Bares where the mouth of the maze swallowed me whole all over again. Tonight's crowd was thin. The girls still danced though, they dance no matter what because no matter what somebody is always there to throw a few dollars around in the air. The one on stage glitters like a watch bezel. Five foot five, blonde streaks in her hair, tattooed on the back and the ass, wearing a Gypsy's anklet to catch the heart of a fetish.

"Want a dance?"

I touched my pockets. "No money, mama."

She slid upside down on the pole. "On the house, then."

She came down off stage to give me the privilege, carrying the smell of a tropical breeze on her curves. The club was hot and the stripper was steamy, waving raw sex around like a wizard wand. The club music changed from Lil Baby to rock, loud guitars bursting over the speakers like the DJ wanted to incite a frenzy. She jumped right in, threw her hair back and got down on me, grinding her hips in a circle until we were basically fucking through my jeans. I'm getting more into thighs now, started noticing them a lot down in Georgia where the thick women in shorts where out everywhere in droves. But the heat in my lap made me lose track of all that. Just for a second I forgot about Savannah and Yuda when she slowly slid her hand down from below her neck to the soft rise above her left nipple and then rubbed in a circle.

"Touch'em," she growled.

When I hesitate she grabs my hands and plants one on each side. In this light you can't tell what's real or what's fake, but at the touch I deem that she's all woman. Comfortable in my palm but it's killing me everywhere else. She knows, she can feel it, she leans down in my ear as the guitars in the speakers go apeshit. "Let's go to VIP."

Why? Why did she have to say that? If she'd just took my hand and yanked me back to there to that room it wouldn't have made a difference but she had to say it.

"There's no VIP. It's just a sad room with two couches and cheap champagne."

She kept grinding until it ached. "Who told you that?"

"I just know. And when you know you know."

"Well, we can drink champagne out here if you don't like couches. But I want to have a private party. With my mouth."

"You like to party?"

"What kind of man asks that? I just told you."

"Maybe it's the kind who's not looking for any new friends."

She balked like I'd just slapped her, hopped off my lap where the heat cooled down immediately. "Whatever. You ain't no star. I ain't going to sit on your dick and beg to blow you."

I watched her prance back to center stage, tattooed ass cheeks moving in time with the bass of the next song. Back to thinking about thighs again. Except I didn't want to remember, except I couldn't forget. Fuck.

Socks slid up on me, he's sneaky for a big man, a heavyweight ninja. He sat down at my table in front of center stage. "Hey, what the fuck is going on?"

At the sudden sound of his voice I jerked up. "Huh?"

"What do you mean, huh? I paid Jada good money to give you the full tour. You're supposed to be in VIP right now having those drawers."

"That's lit. But I can't go back there. I can't face the memories in there."

Socks reached in his pocket, pulled out a cigarello. I watched him split it up the side perfectly with his fingernail and dump the guts out on the table. "You told me you wanted to get loaded. Now, here we are and you're running away from it." He licked the cigarello. "Brother just sabotaged a free blowjob. Never seen a man do that."

"First time for everything."

"I don't know."

"I'ma go get your bread back." I started to stand up but that didn't go very far.

"Sit down," said Socks. "Jada ain't going nowhere. I don't give a shit about that anyway."

"Then, why you tripping?"

"I'm not tripping. We had a deal. I held up my end of the bargain, now it's on you." He pulled out a sack of reefer that smelled like oranges. "What the hell happened down in Georgia, brother? Why you home all banged up. And where's Chevy?"

I took a deep breath before breaking it all down. "It ain't Chevy. It's her cousin. We all went down there on that boat and she did some shows. She was good too. They bought me a bunch of clothes before we left but I don't have them anymore since we fell out. The one who I used to take to Chucky's, she showed up too doing what she does, tricking. We started something. I don't even know how it happened. It was like a tree falling, you know once it gets going it don't stop until it crashes to the ground."

Socks loaded weed in the hollow tobacco paper. "You slept with her?"

It wasn't truly a question, anybody who heard what I said could have easily figured out the rest. I answered anyway. "I had to. You should have seen the body on her."

"I did see it, in here. And I already told you I don't blame you, brother."

"Chevy does."

We smoked. A new dancer came to the stage in pink lingerie. A welcome distraction besides blowing oranges while I figured out how I should tell the rest. What about Chevy and Bandy and the three way on the boat? Should I embellish? Do I have to mention that they're both cousins? And then there were the important things, the parts I really fucked up that I wanted to be extra careful with. Wanted to make it look like I hadn't blown it a hundred and fifty percent which wasn't even vaguely true.

But if you can't be real with your brother then who else deserves the truth? Brothers lie to their parents together. Me and Socks told Aunt Denise a few, like that time we got caught with a girl named Courtney in my room. We said we were studying for a test and the eighth grader had come to tutor us. Didn't think that one through. Aunt Denise is a substitute, she knows every kid in the county school system from filling in over the last twenty three years and she never ever saw Courtney in any of our classes.

In the end I told everything. Though I fumbled through the hard part about the little singer walking in on me and Chocolate the weed kept me going. Socks watched the blunt turn to ashes. After the thing where Bandy got snatched off the streets of Savannah he was ready to take off.

"So, what are we doing still sitting here, brother? Let's go get her."

"Look at me, you think it's that easy? I'm shot in the arm and the whole world is my enemy." I shook my head. "This one ain't going to go away with a war. I don't need guns. I need a hundred and fifty thousand by Friday or this Yhay Yuda fucker is taking her down to Florida."

Now, the switchback. I dazzled with the story, now here I came with the agenda. "That offer you made once upon a time on the napkin. Is that still good?"

He took a minute to consider. Every relationship has it's gives and takes. Even brotherhood. "It might be," he replied.

"Might be or it is? I need to know."

"Is that what this is? You want to get in on the back end of the bank job now after you stuck your nose up at me?"

I thought about it, shrugged, nodded. "Yeah, I'm pretty much here to beg for a spot on the team. It ain't about the money. This whole thing is my fault. Me and Chevy," I paused. "I don't know. But even if I can't fix it I can't just leave her cousin down there in the swamp."

I held my hands out in a genuine plea for understanding and Socks nodded. "You love'em, huh?"

"Yeah, I love'em. Stupid, right?"

"No. I love'em too, brother."

CHAPTER 56

LAST LAUGHING

The women in my dreams didn't want to hear me anymore. They came on a train, not that white van to Florida but a real locomotive. It started with my aunt's, Denise and Bibi, and ended with the nearly forgotten Mrs. Linda. In the middle was Chevy's mother. None of them wore makeup and accessories. No fake eyelashes or whipped up hair, no painted nails on hands or feet but still the greatest creatures ever put together in life or a vision. When I fixed my mouth to say so the train cars all flew away in a flash of murky steel.

I woke up in Socks' living room, sweat on my palms, the sun still hours out of town. His deep sofa was my bed until the noise outside tore through the darkness like lights in the fog.

I stayed up separating opinions like they were the rarest of leaves. The talking heads on cable news were giving theirs out like Mardi Gras beads when he came in handling a bottle of Jack Daniels.

"Sup, you nervous?"

I shook my head. "The train woke me up."

"Oh, yeah. That's 'cause we're right by the tracks. This ain't the Westside, brother."

"This ain't Grand Central either. You live two miles away from the tracks."

He took a drink. "Yeah, but this time of night there ain't no street noise. Motherfucker minus well be in the backyard."

"You don't have a backyard."

"What I tell you about being a smartass?"

"Same thing I told you about being a dumbass."

He huffed and stomped off to the kitchen. Came back a second later chewing on one of those hot sausages that come in a huge jar from Sam's Club. He threw me a sandwich dripping with mayonnaise, literally tossed it up and let it land on my leg.

"Man, are you serious!?"

"My bad, brother. Did I get ya?"

"Looks like I had a wet dream over here." I looked at him. "Have you been to sleep at all?"

He took a pull of Jack Daniels. "I'll sleep when I'm dead. In the meantime eat some breakfast and try to calm yourself. You won't be no good if you're hungry and anxious."

"I'm not anxious."

He ignored me. "I know what your thinking brother. But don't worry. The girls are gonna be okay. They got you on their side. You just got to trust yourself. " He pointed at the sandwich. "And eat something."

"I can't help thinking about Bandy locked in a closet somewhere. Want to hear something fucked up?"

"Shoot it."

I bit the sandwich, ham and brick cheese with hot mustard. "If we pull this off..." I chewed, "I mean, if we get away clean. Then, that makes me the answer to her prayers."

"Yeah, you're a miracle worker. That's why I asked you to ride with me on this."

"No, that ain't the fucked up part. If we get away then I'm the answer but I'm blasphemous. No way around it. But if not then Bandy goes to hell. Period."

"Eye for an eye, brother. You from the mud. You know the rest."

"But is that the best we can do?"

"Unless a nigga from the mud got a better answer."

I stared at the television. "Guess I don't."

Socks passed me the bottle. I washed down bread and meat with two pulls of sour mash whiskey. The sting went good with hot mustard the same way gasoline goes good on a tire fire.

"You wanted me to help you, brother. I'm helping. But don't try weighing your guilt because that ain't going to help neither one of us. If there's a hole in you fill it up with drink. Hurry up, though. We gotta move soon."

"It's fucking four o' clock. The bank doesn't open until nine."

"You nervous?"

"I'm tired of you asking me that."

"Reason I'm asking is 'cause we got a lot to do. So, if you're feeling nervous let me know right now so I can just cut my losses and pull you off the team right now."

I drank a little, weighed my guilt. Drank some more and it weighed less. There was a pattern here that was starting to pick up. "Alright," I said.

"Ready?" asked Socks.

"Ready as I'm gonna get."

He told me bring a light jacket. Autumn was creeping in slowly. The leaves weren't changing yet but the early morning wind had a whistle and a soft chill. This is the time when every single year Aunt Denise predicts it's going to be a nasty winter. She says it's in the Farmer's Almanac. I don't even know what the hell a Farmer's Almanac is but seems like every year her predictions come true when the snow gets deeper and the cold bites harder. Soon, the October fair would be in town, then Christmas trees go up. The fair I do, Christmas not so much. Not since I read the book of Isaiah during my second year in prison.

Traffic lights flashed yellow up MLK avenue. I watched them blink caution at every intersection. This time of day no one had to be in a hurry and the signals were going to keep it that way.

After sunrise then the blinking would end and the lights would get back to their real work. When the streets were full of people treading back and forth over the ladder of crosswalks the town would come out again to find order restored.

Cruising underneath a set swinging on a power line I thought about what would happen if the lights weren't there. If some loose cannon came around and cut them all down in the night as a practical joke would people still be cautious on their own? Even if they were traffic isn't so much like life. In life there are no rules, only consequences rolling in one after another like waves crashing on a rocky shore.

We passed a cop on the corner. The roller wasn't hiding, his marked chariot sat right up front in a CVS parking lot like it was hot on the auction block.

"That's something new. Police sit at the pharmacy all night, now?"

"Don't worry," said Socks. "They just pull in over there so they can nod off on their shift."

"Wish I had a government job. I'd love to sleep and get a check."

"You don't need a job, brother. You need a payday."

He swung into the grocery store across the street, when the Firebird scraped on a dip in the asphalt my stomach dropped. The Winn-Dixie was closed for a few more hours. A sprinkle of abandoned shopping carts out front looked like spooky remnants of the purge.

Behind the store a blue Isuzu slept next to a dumpster and bales of crushed boxes. Socks had the guns inside the stolen ride plus a change of clothes for both of us. We eased in on the other side of the dumpster, Firebird brakes squealing just a bit before the transmission went in park. Socks brought the bottle with him, he hit the Jack Daniels and nodded to me. "Let's do it."

I sat on the trunk with the whiskey and loaded clips. Shoving nine millimeter bullets down a magazine felt therapeutic, like the medicine I never knew I needed. My rubber gloves made the shells slip a little in the morning dew but somehow I always knew just how to hang on. Socks was sitting up front changing stations on the radio, gloves on his fat hands so he didn't get prints all over the knobs of the stolen car. After a love ballad he said, "I wish you would have won some money down there in Georgia."

"Me too, probably wouldn't be here right now."

"Nah, you'd still be here. The money was calling you home. I just don't ever want you thinking I'm happy about all the shit that happened."

I paused on loading. "Are you drunk?"

"Maybe. But do I need to be drunk to tell the truth? You know how this shit is."

"The streets? Yeah, it's a bitch out here. A cold bitch at that."

He shook his head. "I'm talking about life. And all these people who get excited about your failures. Not yours personally I'm talking about in general. Remember when we were in school? You were always the smart one and the other kids would cheat off your tests and homework. Then you'd lose in a fight and everybody who copied your answers would laugh at your black eye."

"People always laughed. We were a bunch of kids back then. All full of shit just showing out when mom and dad weren't around to whip that ass."

He got out of the car and stood up. "Are you kidding? I know people that got through the whole seventh grade copying off your work. How many of us would have failed middle school without you?"

"Is that how you passed? By stealing my answers?"

"Sometimes, on the hard stuff. But I busted heads for you too."

"So, you earned the right?"

"Are you listening, brother? I hated those kids. Wasn't a day that I came home feeling good about school."

I slapped a full jacket up inside a matte black Glock. "I don't know. Everybody always loved you. The girls went to all your football games. Boys were scared to death. I was just the crazy motherfucker hanging in the hallway."

Socks was pissed, he pulled his gloves off and threw them down. "Fuck football!" he roared. "We never won shit! You know how many days I woke up in pain? Body hurting? And those were just the junior varsity days but my knees still ache when it gets cold.

And when we did win it was all the other players who got the props. The offense. Linebackers are just scapegoats." He pointed to the store. "I see'em in there sometimes. Those kids all grown up now still talking about high school ball. They remember me behind the losses. Never the wins or that time I broke my leg. Just defeat."

"I still got a few pills left from the hospital if your knees really hurt."

"Keep it." He looked at the back of the Winn-Dixie like someone was calling him from the loading dock. "This bank job is all the medicine I need."

Nothing was there but he focused on the wall. Eyes tattooed on the red bricks as if a living ghost would step through time to heal his knees and the deeper pains that I never heard about until now.

I slid off the trunk. "School's over, man. We made it."

"Yeah, we made it."

"And we're still here."

He tore away from lingering at that brick wall and gave me a crazy smile. "Still here, brother." Then, he grabbed me, snatched me up like a rag doll and squeezed me until my back cracked. We hugged hard for a minute. His skin smelling like whiskey and the red spices from those Sam's Club sausages. I didn't breath because I couldn't. I hugged him back and when we let go things were suddenly alright.

"So, how we doing this?" I asked.

Socks picked up a pistol and checked the slide. "Real simple. Every third Thursday of the month the Wells Fargo truck pulls up with a big bag of cash. Enough for thirty days worth of small withdrawals. They take the bag inside and pass it over the counter to the lead teller. Then, the teller puts it on the floor under the counter until the bank manager comes to do the next step.”

“What’s the next step?”

“Who knows? It ain’t important because they’re not even going to make it that far. The bank manager has a lot to do so there’s a window in between when the cash gets dropped off and the time it gets put away. Enough time for the Wells Fargo to pull off and us to go inside and get that bag. Then, we come back here, switch rides and count up somewhere else.”

“I don’t get it.”

“What’s there to get, brother? We’re stealing a sack of money with pistols. It’s straight up robbery.”

“Sounds classic. But why do we need four men on a move this easy?”

“Ain’t no more team. It’s just us, now. Just like you wanted.”

Now it was my turn to glance at the back of Winn-Dixie. “Those Happy Hill boys really going to let you cross them out on this?”

“They ain’t got a choice. Thing is I just can’t trust them. They might turn around and rob me, shoot me in the back and take my cut. I know you’re better than that, though. We family.”

“Family always does you the worst. Isn’t that something you used to say?”

Socks shook his head. “Not the family you choose.”

Whiskey and guns. People cheating off your schoolwork. The smell of armed robbery first thing in the morning.

If this is the bottom then at least the nostalgia is good. But the Pinnacle Bank didn’t look like any type of bank at all. It looked like a plantation house with the big white columns and huge windows set in the face of a beige brick front. Underneath my mask I took it all in, the green shrubs by the handicap parking ramp, white fascia on the overhanging roof, all the way down to the azalea bushes catching dew in the parking lot median.

There’s an expression, throwing rocks at the penitentiary. Aunt Denise was going to be livid if I went back to jail again. I think she might sympathize with the circumstance but she would never understand my resolutions. She knew Socks. Growing up he was to me what I was to Chevy according to her daddy. Back then I had all the great reasons about why she was wrong and now I couldn't think of one. Here we are all grown up hurling a handful rocks at every eight by ten cell built by a bitch called justice.

I could hear her cussing and talking about how she always knew this would happen. I could hear heavy duty pistons lifting and falling in a diesel engine coasting to a stop. The armored truck didn't say Wells Fargo on the side. In fact I don't really remember what it said. When the canvas bag came out Socks tapped my arm. "Here it is."

Immediately, I saw why he didn't want to take the bag before it entered the bank. A lanky guard with veiny hands and a crooked lip had the money handcuffed to his wrist. Out here by the azaleas we'd either have to chop his arm off or get shot trying. A little breeze blew the guards comb over out of place when he looked at the traffic moving on the street behind us.

Beside me I heard the shick-shack noise of an oiled gun cocking. "Ready brother?"

"Ready as I'm going to get."

Soon as the truck guttered out around the corner we were running through the parking lot. I went in the bank half blind. When the armored truck guard scanned traffic I slid down so low in the Isuzu's front seat that the morning sun hit me straight in the face and made fat, salty tears stream down both cheeks. Now, I was blinking away red and white spots and pointing my gun around. We definitely didn't need more goons. The bank staff was listless, drinking coffee and munching bagels when we burst in like cowboys.

Socks came in charging like a bull. He barked out orders to a frightened group of first shift tellers who threw their hands to the sky. One was pregnant, crying like...well, like she was being robbed. I told her to sit down and take it easy. I mean, it wasn't like she was going to go vigilante on us. One had a move, real subtle like it was her assignment every time the shit went down.

The name on her acetate tag said Jenny. Not Jennifer, or Jen, but Jenny, like this was the real housewives of Winston-Salem. She was a miserable looking woman with dry lips and a weak chin. She slid a hand under her cash drawer and hit the silent alarm. Then she looked in my eyes still flashing red and pale blotches and pointed up at the ceiling. "You're on camera."

"What the fuck does that matter?"

Jenny shrugged, both hands still up. "I guess it doesn't if you need three hots and a cot."

I almost shot her. The whiskey was talking that same violent language that left Chocolate's High Point trick twitching on the floor. All that stopped me were Socks words running through my head. You were always the smartest kid in class.

I knew we were on camera just like she knew I saw her reach for that silent alarm. The banter was bogus, more fucking worthless than every flat penny weighing down her cash drawer. While Jenny worked to incense me security was putting a gun on Socks, he almost had him right between the sights. Another two, three inches and my brother would have been in an ambulance. He was an old guard, white Colonel Sanders moustache, bald with hair by the ears, potbelly on thin legs that made him look like a cartoon dad. He could have been a hero, instead I kicked him deep in the soft spot between his legs and his pistol went off.

That bullet meant for my brother's back spun straight into the wall behind the teller trying to match me in wits. Jenny stumbled sideways on a broken heel. Her ankle twisted with a sickening crack and she screamed herself into redfaced agony.

Socks whipped around. "The fuck was that?!"

"Nada, just grab the bag."

"Don't fuck with me. I heard a shot."

"Fuck a shot. We're down to twenty seconds. Where's the bag?"

He pointed. I followed. Straight over the counter to the canvas sack like an animal with a stomach full of Gideon Bibles. The money was heavy but I had all kinds of help, adrenaline and alcohol and a friend with a tortured future down in Georgia waiting to be shipped off like fresh avocados gave me more than enough strength to do anything.

The tellers on the floor squirmed. The pregnant one had found a Kleenex and was sniffling while Jenny with the broken heel was down on the tile, hand on her back, grimace on her face. She thrashed in pain, flailing on the ground like a slaughterhouse pig.

"You look good down there." I said it with thankfulness. "Does it hurt? The embarrassment I mean."

She got up on elbows and spit on my coveralls. "Fuck you."

That's what they always used to say in school when I lost a fight. Jenny sounded like one of them, maybe she was. Maybe she's one of the one's who cheated off my tests and made it to the next grade on rubbernecking. I might have asked except I was too busy laughing inside my mask.

CHAPTER 57

COUNTING SHEEP

Desirée walked to the end of the yard where her mailbox leaned a little like that big tower Italy. Inside it was empty. At a quarter past nine it was too early for mailman to have dropped anything off. In fact, the morning mist had barely lifted off her lawn about twenty minutes ago. She pulled the lid down, slid a Publishers Clearing House envelope with no return address in, closed it back and checked the street casually. A utility truck with hardhats swinging in the rear window rolled by doing the speed limit on the way to the stop sign at the end of the block. After it bent left, she turned around to come back up the driveway.

Socks' cousin looked like she had done this type of thing before. That wasn't so much of a surprise considering who was her fam. I watched through the window without touching the blinds until an orange cat got in my way. Too porky to be a stray the little fatback fucker looked like he ate the rest of the small house pets that came up MIA around the neighborhood. When he sat down to lick himself both hind legs spilled over the porch railing making the wood look like it had fur upholstery. I thumped the glass and he put his paw down just to stare. When I did it again he got the message. After fat cat scrammed there was Desirée again turning around towards the mailbox. She put the red flag up, checked the street again. Then, began a final trek to the house.

Socks sat at the same table where he got tattooed last time I was here. The canvas bank bag laid on the floor beside his chair, the cash itself spread out before him in small stacks. Our jumpsuits were double bagged in the bottom of Desirée's neighbor's garbage can and we left the Isuzu parked behind the Winn-Dixie dripping wet with bleach and ammonia. If forensics wanted any clues off the truck they were going to have to figure out a way to breathe around it first.

Desirée still had acid in her tone when we talked but after the bank job she tossed half a pack of cigarettes in my lap with a whole book of matches to help ease the nerves. I guess that meant we were okay. When she came back up the porch I could hear footfalls thudding on the wood boards. She walked through the door straight into a plume of menthol fresh out of my lungs. I waved a hand, wiping the air down but most of the smoke escaped outside before she could cough or complain or maybe do both.

Socks looked up from the little hill of dead presidents. "How's it looking out there?"

"All good." His cousin wrapped her dreadlocks up in a bun and used the scrunchy on her wrist to keep them held high. "The power company rode by, I think they're checking meters today. Don't worry, they won't come inside the house unless it's a problem."

I sucked the cigarette because that last line made me antsy. The power company could be just the Trojan horse for the police to get a good look inside before they surrounded the house. That's how Chocolate scoped her victims out, front unassumingly and assault unexpectedly.

Dez cut the ceiling fan on in the living room while I rubbed my face and smoked some more. In seconds the phony oak wood blades picked up speed creating a small noise that was enough to drown out any telltale sounds like a cruiser rolling up the driveway or a tank creeping on the lawn. I thought about saying something but what was the point? Having one of us paranoid in the house was too many people already.

Socks put a hundred dollar bill on the edge of the table. Desirée picked it up and stuffed it in her bra. She knew there would be more for her when the count ended. "You want me to go buy a money counter?" she asked. "I can get one cheap from the flea market and be back in an hour."

"No," I snapped. "Cops will be on it in a minute. Anybody in the city who needs a money counter right now is a person of interest."

Socks agrees. "Yeah, bet the robbery made the news already. Probably got surveillance footage rolling on a loop."

"Think they're offering a reward?"

When Desirée asked the question we both looked at her the same way, like two Great Danes would have been eyeing that fat cat lazing on the porch.

"That's not what I meant." Her eyes flew from me to her cousin and back again. "I was just curious. Socks, tell him that's not what I meant."

He slid another big face to the edge of her kitchen table. "Why don't you chef us up some breakfast, Dez? Cerrio, put down those squares and come help me count this."

I crushed the Newport out in a green glass ashtray. After it died with a sizzle and a long tail of smoke that rose up like a genie I grabbed a spot at the money table. Up until now I had never been around so much of the stuff. We weren't rich by any real standards. Probably little more than kings for a day. Socks' cut might last longer if he paced his spending right. Of course that was just a fantasy. He had too big of a heart, too many friends and too many habits. I mean, he was already giving away hundreds before we even knew what we had. It made me sweat because I couldn't come up short again and still get Bandy back. But that's just how he was and really who could blame him? Nobody robs a bank to be frugal.

As far as my half it was already spent. I prayed while we counted, not to God but to Chevy's mama who had the same omniscience. She was probably dipping her hand in a lake of fire to cut me a swimming pool right now. I asked her to take a break from digging that trench and please, please, please let this money from the flat cash bag laying on the floor like a gutted sheep be enough to take back across the long Talmudge bridge.

Desirée brought us a pack of hair ties from a junk drawer in her dresser. Tiny black ones she put at the end of her son's hair whenever she twisted him in braids. A hundred of them were stuffed in a bag for a dollar. Asinine almost at how something so laughably cheap could hold together all these riches just as good as that plantation house bank out by the highway.

But I didn't have time to enjoy these silly, little paradoxes. I couldn't be amused while I was still praying, pleading with whatever deity still wanted do me a favor that we'd make it through the pack of ties. Me and Socks were strapping up the stolen bread by the grand and a hundred small bands meant a hundred thousand dollars counted. Then, I had to pray that Desirée saw enough reasons left over to bring us out another bag of ties.

Instead, she threw down a hot plate of grits, the green peppers and bacon crumbles made me halt. She brought it close to home, right at the beginning of summer when things were actually happy. A half stack of bills locked in my hand as a whole three months flashed before me like a slide show of the good times. It was me and Chevy in the woods after the liquor store, enjoying each other in the YMCA parking lot after the club. We had touched every corner of this town together and now I was back here all by myself.

The man who lost everything becomes a whisper in my ear, telling me a secret pressed into a question. "What would a man give in exchange for his soul?" I answered with a simple "nothing." Because my soul is clear, not sparkling like crystal but empty like that mailbox outside before the envelope to nowhere went in it's mouth.

Socks stared. "You good, brother?"

"Yeah, just tired that's all. Been a long couple of days. Thanks for the breakfast, Dez."

She stood with hands on hips. "You act like you ate it already."

"No, I will. I will. I just need to use the bathroom first."

"It's the door by Parker's room. Put the seat down when you're done."

Though I smiled it was completely fake because I knew we weren't going to make it. Even if Socks gave me his half, took back the hundreds from Desirée and stole another canvas bag full of cash we weren't even about to get close. A hundred and fifty thousand dollars was a mountain of money and all we had in the kitchen was a hill.

The bathroom was easy to find because Parker left his room door open, I could see his short football gear left out after a practice. I wonder how Socks felt about his nephew in the game he raged over. I trudged deeper down the hall and found what I was looking for. Inside Desirée had a seashell theme working. All four walls were painted with fist sized conk shells running in a row above white molding that could have been used as a baseboard. I liked the setup, very anesthetic for a moment like this. Even the towels swinging from a hook behind the door were embroidered with baby blue clams.

Leaning against the coral pink sink I wondered if Socks already knew. Did he see we were going to be short? He didn't act like it but how is a friend with a friend with a problem like mine supposed to act? Maybe he does it like everybody when they don't want anything to be wrong. The same as when you drop your keys in the street and even after you know they're long gone you're still checking your coat pocket like an ass. It's that drawn out denial that still keeps hope alive. Unless your me, because me I just run.

I stood there for who knows how long. Until the shells on the wall started giving up little details. A hint of yellow at their tops showed where beach sunshine was splashing off them in a Caribbean afternoon. Before I got really lost in the colors Desirée came banging on the door. "What the hell you doing in there?"

I jerked out of my trance and cut on the faucet. "Washing my hands. Be out in a second, girl!"

"Hurry up, I got to pee."

"Calm down."

I ran my hands under the water for looks. Flung the drops off my fingertips and put a wet hand on the knob. It took two tries to twist it open and on the third one she was standing there with her dreads down again and her chubby face painted with indignation. Sort of like how Aunt Denise's used to be when the school called her to say I forged another report card.

"It's all yours." I meant the bathroom but Dez didn't budge.

"I want know what's going on." She said it with implications that were clear. And I said, "trust me, you don't. Maybe there's an idea floating around in your head but the finer points," I shook my head, "that's nobody's business."

"Your business is town business," she snapped.

"Ha, that's cute. You're cute. But the town ain't helping this time so business is closed right now."

I went to leave but she broadened her stance in the doorway. When those two hips went out like brackets on parentheses there was nowhere to go.

"Read my lips. There can't be anymore secrets. You're in my house hiding out with the Pinnacle Bank's money on the same table where my son takes his dinner. Police come in here right now I'm going to jail for harboring fugitives. Then, they'll take Parker to a group home where he'll be scarred for life."

"Then, why did you let us in?"

"I'm helping Socks. And he promised me some of the money."

"That's it then. Whatever I got going on is separate from your deal with him."

"Indulge me, Cerrio. Or find another place to post up and he can bring your cut later on a time you two decide."

Well, I was fucked. No way around it. If a man knows how to fight then he has to know when he's beat. I sat down on the edge of the tub and stretched my legs out. "Fair enough. What you want to know?"

Seeing she had conquered me Desirée visibly cooled down. She leaned her shoulder against the doorframe and crossed both arms. "There was a lot of money in that bag."

"Indeed. That's the whole point of robbing a bank. You ever seen that much at once?"

She shook her head. "Never. Except on TV."

"I don't play a gangster on TV."

"Neither do I. So, what are you going to buy?"

I shrugged. "Nothing, I'm just going to blow it all at Sugar Bares."

"Don't lie to me. If you whatever you need costs so much that even robbing Wells Fargo can't afford it then that's saying something."

I looked at her, raised my eyebrows, nodded with genuine admiration at her investigative skills. "How'd you find out?"

"Socks. After he snapped a hair tie around the last stack at the table I heard him moan and say, 'this ain't enough'. I cornered him by the stove until he gave up some answers."

"Kind of like you're doing me right now?" I interlaced my fingers and flexed them palms out until the knuckles cracked. "I'm in between a rock and a real hard place and it don't feel good at all."

"Then, how come you didn't say anything before? I don't like you Cerrio, but like you or not you're still in deep with my cousin. Just in light of that you have the privilege to divulge and I have the obligation to help."

I had to laugh. "You kidding me? Last time I was here you wanted to cut off my balls."

She shrugged. "You know how Jamaicans be. We don't take no shit off anyone."

"You sound like Socks. Where's he at anyway?"

"Out in the backyard burying y'alls guns."

"Aww, goddamnit!"

"What?"

"I just got that pistol. It was a gift from…from a friend."

Desirée waved a hand. "There's plenty of guns out there. Trust me you'll have another one before the weekend. I'm sure Bandy won't mind buying it for you after what you did for her. Saving her life like that and all."

I blinked. "You know about that too?"

"Told you, Cerrio. Your business is town business. It took a week to hear about her down at The Rose Petal but only a day before somebody called and told me about what happened to the poor thing in the yellow house." She shook her head. "Poor thing," she repeated.

"Why don't that surprise me? Bad news always travels quick. If I was bad news I'd never be late."

Dez parted her mouth for another round of questions. I had wide open ears but instead of her voice crashing into them it was a heavy pair of footsteps coming down from the other end of hall. Socks hit the corner skidding in his boots with a shovel full of dirt crumbs clutched tight in his hand. His breathing was hard and jagged and instantly I stood up to meet the emergency.

"Rollers," he said between breaths. "I saw them pull around the house. They at the front door right now."

On cue a thunderous knock shook the drywall. Winston-Salem sheriffs dramatically announced their presence above the fan still spinning up front in the living room. Desirée snatched the shovel out of her cousin's hand and lashed out orders. "My room. The closet. Big enough to hide both of you. Now."

Me and Socks raced to vanish. Behind our backs Desirée used toilet paper to mop up mud off the floor so there wouldn't be a trail of dirt leading up to us when deputies walked through her house. More knocking sounded off, harder this time with a twinge of annoyance and a loud, white man calling out his name and rank as Sergeant.

While he yelled for the whole block to hear I slid the closet door open on its metal track. The walk-in was tight, moving boxes in the back, shelves on the top, shoes on the floor. Desirée screams back at the cop that she's just woken up and still in her bra while we cram in shoulder to shoulder, brushing sleeves with the Fall coats she had ready to go for the season. By the time the door is slid back shut on the track she's got the mud cleaned up and her volume tapered down to meet the cops on the porch.

It got hot in there quick. Agitation built up from me and Socks cooking in suspense made the unseen beast of heat build up into a snarling inferno. Through a thin sliver of light slashing a line between the closet door and the wall I could see a solo bead of sweat rolling down Socks' temple.

Throat dry as ashes he asked me in rasp. "How you think they found us?"

"Ain't no telling. It could have been that utility truck was really just the feds prowling."

"What do you want to do, brother? If they come for us do we takes'em?"

"It ain't going to be no one-on-one fistfight. They got guns and ours are buried out in the yard like fucking turnips."

"Better out there than laying around in plain sight on the table."

"Doesn't matter. If we hurt the cops then they'll come for Desirée too. Shit will be relentless. They'll put her in jail and take her son to live in a foster home. He'll be lost in the system before she even gets arraigned."

I don't know what the sergeant said out on the porch. His normal, resting voice didn't float down the long hallway like all the overambitious yelling. On a educated guess I figured the words must have been arresting because soon four boots were plodding through the house. I could hear their leather creaking past the seashell bathroom, turning left in front of Parker's scattered sports gear. It was more than one coming straight towards us. I was trying not to become illy. But the closer they got the louder my heart beat in my ears, shut my eyes and I could smell them like sulfur drifting from an open pit.

On my side Socks was fighting to hold down his own panic. His labored breathing in the dark told me his heart was crashing just as loudly in his own ears. He swiped a sheen of sweat off his forehead.

"What did she say to you?"

"What?"

"Dez, what she say to you?"

"We'll talk about it later," I whispered. "Now ain't the time."

"There might be no other time. Tell me what she said."

Looking in the narrow stream of illumination, even with the restricted light and the weight of the deputies sniffing us out I could see the chance to ease my brother's antagonism shifting in the dark like deadly quicksand.

"Your little cousin didn't like how I kept the whole thing in Savannah a secret. She wanted me to tell her what happened to Bandy in Georgia before you did."

"She don't know."

I almost shaped into a pretzel trying to snap my head around. "What?"

Socks shook his head next to a jacket sleeve. "I never told her what you did in Savannah. I never told her anything. Desirée doesn't even know you been out of town."

CHAPTER 58

MARSEILLE CLEVELAND

Parker's daddy was in jail again for child support. The whole thing was a fucked off error started by a lazy social worker who didn't like men anymore than her job and must have thought painfully little about single mothers too. Dez's old desire swore he mailed the checks out every month on time like clockwork but court records disagreed. For all my loathing of the system I admit that court records are just about the best universally.

Except for this time. This time they got it wrong and Parker's daddy really did pay his child support and now his lawyer had sent two deputies over here straight after my last crime with a paperwork subpoena for Desirée's document files. If it sounds like a complicated web of nonsensical legal jargon that's because it is. I mean, if the man paid what else did they need? Child Support can check the books anytime. In fact the government has a whole agency just for checking books. It's called the IRS.

The long and the short of it is that the records in Desirée's bedroom were better than what the wise men up at the Department of Social Services kept. But of course me and Socks didn't know all that standing up rigid in the closet.

Behind the sliding door anticipation was murder. I could hear the rollers coming closer, caught a whiff of kevlar coming through the door crack on Socks' side and the knocking of stainless steel cuffs closing the distance. There was a slit on my end of the closet just like Socks had and through it I could see one in the hall with the other following close behind. Both sheriff's deputies wore pleated tan shirts and black pants with a stripe down the leg that distinguished them from ordinary dress slacks. Badges on the chest, a spiraled radio cord slung over the right shoulder. They were sizable men but still smaller than Socks although not by much. The largest was naturally bald on top and shaved the rest of his scalp clean with a razor. He did a good job, very cop-like, no phantom fuzz showing down around the ears where a little stubble was expected and could be forgiven. The other had a high and tight fade close enough to the skin that I could see the moles standing out on his scalp like acorns.

My throat was so tight when I swallowed I swore they could hear it by the dresser where they both stopped cold. Desirée dug around in the drawers. Pawing through all the light summer clothes that weren't surrounding us in the closet while she hid part of the frenzy donning over each one of us like a gown. With my eyeball an inch from the crack I had this idea of us all going to war. Maybe she was digging for own pistol, the only one not buried out back by the shrubs. It was a wild idea but those are the best kind. Not like the safe thoughts that live a hard existence just to gutter out face down in regret.

I watched close. I'm not adulatory about a war, not a disciple of violence, but if Dez clutched and pulled I was going to be right behind her. Killer instincts were running through every one of my veins head to toe. I couldn't feel my face and I was sober. I tapped Socks on the arm, when he looked I curled my fist in a ball and smacked it soundlessly against my palm. He pointed to boys in tan and I nodded. That's all it took. No words but we were still on the same page like a name and an address.

One of the sheriffs, the one with the tight fade came up to the closet. He stood and stared straight at the crack in the door on my side. Socks saw him too and when he took down Desirée's jacket real easy so as not to bang the sturdy hanger against anything I knew his plan. Something we used to do in school, throw a coat over a kid's face and hit him as many times as you can before he claws it off. But it's like I told him, we're not in school anymore.

I silently pulled a sweater down from a wire hanger on my side. This time I wasn't going for hits to the face, it was all about that fat .40 on the cop's hip. Whoever reached it first would ultimately prevail. Watching close I saw him turn sideways in front of the closet then suck in his gut underneath his vest. I paused. What the hell was going on? Socks didn't know either. He just held his breath while the white man petted both sides of his head where his hair was shortest. Before he blew out and let his gut expand Desirée yelled. The sound of her cracking the air made the cop twirl on a heel.

I remembered the scriptures, thou shalt have no fear. Staring through the slit, clenching the woman's sweater in my hands, I felt a burgeoning sense of optimism growing like the sound of music. We were supposed to be getting arrested right now. Except from where I was standing it looked like the manhunt was moving back on its tracks. I saw the bald cop take a manila envelope from Desirée that had that loopy, lady style sort of handwriting in the top right hand corner and after that all three of them left like a crowd exiting the movie theater when the lights came on. Socks didn't try to expand on it, when he finally let his breath go there wasn't even an attempt. Instead, he came up for air looking to finish the whispered conversation that had got started before.

"Dez thinks you need money for your Aunt Denise in the hospital."

I wiped off my face with the sweater. "Why does she think my aunt's in the hospital?"

"Because your business is town business."

"That's getting to be a popular line. Desiree said it once and it was cute. I'm not so sure what it means, though."

Socks kept his eyes glued to the crack on his side ready for anything. He licked his lips. "I'm a firm believer that people who mind their own business get to live a lot longer. But I had to tell her something. She had to be convinced. Some lame excuse," he shook his head, "she would sniffed it out before I even got done talking. Little cuz is far from stupid."

"I been watching her in action ever since we walked in here. I know that she ain't stupid.

"So, you see why I had to come with a good lie. I'm just sorry it was so personal, brother."

"What did you say?"

He licked his dry lips like he was preparing a major confession. "I told her that we had to rob a bank to pay for your aunt's surgery." He half shrugged. "Like I said, 'it had to be something extremely convincing'. The upside is your business about what happened in Georgia is still your business. Desirée don't know and she's sympathetic instead of just pissed off like she would have been if she'd found out the truth. You know she already thought you was a pimp anyway."

I disagreed with the phenomenon but my eyes weren't open yet. "I never told you to do that. You fucked everything up."

"And you think it was good before?"

"You don't get it. While you were outside digging we were talking alone in the bathroom. We were finally getting on level playing field."

He laughed. "Must feel good to be so ignorant."

"You lost me."

"No, you're just lost. This is Trey-Four. All your old ladies know Desirée. They're friends. They talk to each other. Right now she can help you and trust me you need a lot of help because that bag was way short. But in a day or two, when the real story comes out, she isn't going to want have nothing to do with you. I did you a favor lying to her."

Things were getting contentious but still I had to know. "How much did we get?"

"Seventy bands. Minus three to Desirée for helping us."

"Are you kidding me? That's not even close to what you wrote on that goddamn napkin."

"Bank drops aren't always the same. Things change," he snapped his fingers, "like that. A hundred thousand a man is the top of what we coulda got."

"If we'd have brought those dicks from Happy Hill on the lick we'd have less than ten for each of us."

"Why you think I didn't bring them on? Just in case the bag wasn't loaded much as I'd like."

"Thought you said it was all because you trusted me."

He made a sputtering noise. "Yeah, that part too."

"Fuck me," I muttered.

"Look, it doesn't matter. Desirée knows somebody who can help. But she already thinks you were using Chevy. What do you think she'll do if she finds out Bandy followed you around somewhere and got snatched? We wouldn't even be in here right now."

He was right. Lies beget lies but sometimes there isn't any real choice if you're looking down the barrel at your only option.

I heard the rollers leaving, leather boots creaking farther up the hall past Parker's messy lair out to the living room. Desirée played nice with them at the front door, giving thanks for their concern out on the porch. When she came back it was just her, the cops were dismissed. They got what they needed and we're on to the next errand. Goodbye law.

Me and Socks spilled out of the closet like we were jumping off the train. Desirée slid the door back with a pssh sound and snatched her cotton sweater right out of my hands because I was stretching the collar out into a lasso. I looked back at the mirror on the other side of the door. All three of our various reflections stood there in a row like a collage of characters. Her, plump and curious. Socks, big and abrasive. Me, slim and harried because the truth was eating at me like a home baked pie. Even looking close it still took a second to realize that's where the deputy was checking himself out when he sucked in his gut as we held our breath and considered killing cops. His vanity was like a teenage girl, holding his stomach, petting his hair. Fucking diva.

I would have laughed about it but there were more reasons not to than could fit in a day. Socks was absolutely right. When Chevy came home my sins were going to spread through every nail shop, hair salon and mimosa soaked girl's night out until the whole female persuasion of Winston-Salem was ready to break your boy in half like a sugar cookie.

I didn't want to get ahead of the story, that would be as if I was righteous and I'm wasn't ready for anything new. Maybe that's the reason I'm not dead just yet, because the tainted side of me just won't let the rest rot in condemnation. As compositions of life go I need new philosophies. The disaffections in me work overtime. Deep down though I knew this one was truly simple, no upsets in a battle of right or wrong, moral strife, or a voice of a conscience echoing in my brain. It was just that I couldn't lie anymore. I mean physically I couldn't do it. Because if another girl from the city I love gets entangled in this web of treasons just to meet disaster I know I'll really die. From the inside out.

After I told Desirée the real story Socks held his head in his huge hands like his brain was wracked. She looked at him, back at me, then at her cousin like she was trying to figure out who to slap first. In the end no one did anything. She lit a cigarette in front of us, after a fat drag that drew the paper back half an inch she seemed to adapt to the new reality.

She pointed with her square. "You know, I was just starting to like you. Well, thank God you put a stop to that because otherwise I might be just another one of your silly, little bitches jumping through hoops in my skirt."

"Stop it," said Socks. "Are you going to help him or not?"

"I shouldn't. And I ordinarily I wouldn't, but I have to because Bandy doesn't deserve to suffer."

It was a startling answer, even from her. Real help when I needed it the most. Desirée paced the floor, thoughts running through her head, dreads swaying on every footfall. "That girl is worth more than your life," she said. "And that means we're going to need more money than what I just hid under the kitchen sink to get her back."

"A hundred and fifty thousand dollars," I pointed out.

She stopped. "And I know who can you put you on the right track to find it."

"Who?"

"Who, he says. Like a fucking owl."

"Fine, you want to play games have a ball. But do me a favor first."

She smoked, every word came out in a cloud like a dragon. "Listen at him cuz, still asking for favors. Unbelievable. Okay, what is it?"

"Call Chevy. Make sure she's okay."

"Call her yourself. Phone's right there on the table. Just pick it up and dial."

"She won't answer if she knows it's me."

"Good for her. Girl is finally waking up."

History gets taught and then it gets repeated. After dumping my uneaten grits in the trash Desirée did a good job play acting like she didn't want her cut of the bank cash. She made Socks beg to give to give it to her. For a minute I thought he was going to have to tie the woman down and pour the money over her like maple syrup. That little game lasted all afternoon. In between rounds she made a quick call to Chevy. It was hard finding out her and Taneesha had moved from the Marriott down to the Super 8 motel by the bridge exit. That was history repeating itself, me making the woman I love poorer and poorer. The next step was desperation and after that, well, then it was pretty much anything. History taught me that part right at the beginning of summer.

After the sun went down we had work to do. Desirée took Parker over to a neighbor's house while I dug our pistols back out of the ground. Where we were going you'd rather be caught with them than without. The hole was shallow, I struck metal before the shovel handle burned my hands and bent down to scoop the Remington out of its grave. After I shook off cold clay I took Socks gun out too. He had a Glock .40 with a thirty round clip hanging down like a dog dick. I tucked them both in my waist and threw the canvas money bag back in the hole like a body, put a foot in to pack it deeper and splashed white lightning all over like champagne after a championship. Dez kept a jar of the stuff hidden in the top shelf of her cup cabinet like we were still living in 20's Prohibition. Her connection had to be good, though. Because when I tossed a lit match down the bag went up like it was soaked in gas.

The orange and yellow flames were hypnotizing. Their image stuck with me in the car while we rode across town. Desirée drove us through the city streets in her dark colored Equinox with a white spoiler on the trunk. We travelled in silence listening to shock springs squeak over all the divots laced in the road. She was still the only one with any idea about who we were going to see, hanging on to that secret like the last can of beans in a famine. Socks tried to press her earlier while I took a nap on the couch but the woman was a wall. She wouldn't even hint if we were seeing a man or a woman.

Personally, I could care less about clues. I had seen so much and felt so little in the past few days that now the whole underbelly of this world seemed like one, long, unbroken fissure derived off anguish. And even though the power of having a mystery under her lid turned out to be good punishment for lying I still wouldn't give Desirée anything from me that rang out like worry. See, after those jokers down in Savannah I thought that whoever we had to meet couldn't faze me anyway. I catch on slow though.

Cleveland projects is what the old hustlers call a hole, a one way in, one way out trap with buildings all around so you can't flee too easy when the police drop in for a raid. These projects aren't high in the clouds like in those massive cities up north or in LA somewhere but what the hood lacks in volume it makes up in sheer danger. Down the loop of decadence outsiders are picked out immediately. Only the lucky ones get flipped and sent back to where they came from all in one piece.

When Desirée's dark Ford pulled up a flock of kids ambushed the car offering all types of product from their hoody pockets. She tried to shoo them away, thought because she was a mother she could turn on the sternness and they would just fly off like geese. But these weren't Parker's football brothers, they didn't take no for an answer without a heavy hand behind it.

A man big enough to be in Socks weight class shoved them to the side. The little drug dealers squawked until they saw the the giant making his way through the ranks. He got to the driver's side barely impeded and leaned down to get eye level with Desirée. At first sight she drew back a little like a snail trying to get in his shell. I couldn't blame her, the huge man breathing onion vapor all over her cheeks was so saturated in ugliness he didn't even look real. His face was strange like a Hollywood makeup job, like he woke up everyday and sat in a chair at Warner Brothers studios for a Halloween revenge flick. He had sagging hound dog cheeks hideously pockmarked with burns and a nose probably smashed at least three times. He reminded me of a shaved bear who ran through a field of thorns only to crash into a bed of nails.

I nodded to him, he nodded back. Socks did the same thing and then introductions were over. "Y'all here for Marseille?"

"Yeah," squeaked Desirée. "This here's my cousin Socks. He came to make sure everything's alright."

"Cool. Who's that in the back?"

"I'm Cerrio. From Greenway Ave."

The ogre eyed me for a second through the driver's side window. "You know Bonny?"

"Green eyed Bonny Frasier from Natty Hill? Yeah, I know her."

"That's my sister," he said.

Hearing that made me glad I didn't tell him how I knew her. "Damn, small world."

"Ain't it, though? Say, y'all want any loud?"

Dez cleared her throat to get us on track. "We ain't here for that."

"You sure? This ain't like that other shit. What I got comes from California."

"Everybody says that," responded Desirée. "We're just here to see Marseille."

"Alright, but y'all can't bring your guns."

"What if something pops off?" she asked. "This ain't Disneyland."

He grunted. "Nobody gonna do nothing to do you when here you're with me."

We put our pistols under the seats, Bonny's brother watched closely like we might pull some shit and slip them back in our pants. After they were out of sight he yanked Desiree's door open. I thought he was going to pat her down and double check. That might have been a problem but instead he said, "come on" and led us through the projects that smelled like everything.

From must to reefer smoke to pickled pig's feet and stale beer Cleveland projects had a different essence standing outside every apartment door. Underneath a flight of black iron steps a dice game was going full swing, the players circled up betting on a point paused when they saw us coming. I wished for my Remy, I know Socks wanted his Glock. We had ten beady eyes on us while we took the stairs one by one to the second level where somebody's baby was crying by an open window with a box fan in it.

The steps ended on a cracked wooden plank rotting at the edges. By the rail I saw spiders scramble in all different directions. One stayed frozen in a web, curling his spindly legs to his body as a breeze swept through. Bonny's brother kept leading the way like everything was normal and I mean maybe it was, after all we were the outsiders. Three strangers from the east side of the city looking for a friend had no room to speak on what were natural matters.

We stopped in front of a door, beige paint chipping around the peephole made it look like somebody had tried to shoot through it with an elephant gun. Our guide stuck a key in the deadbolt, before turning it he looked back at us. "My name's Giggy by the way."

"Good to know," replied Socks. "But we still don't want any weed."

Giggy turned the key. "Fuck it. You guys stand out here for a minute. I'll get Marseille."

"Whoa." Desirée stomped her foot. "I didn't come all the way down here just to get left outside like the dog. She knows we're coming. I called an hour ago."

"Chill, ma. Marsielle paid me to watch her back and that's I'm doing. Y'all stay right here. I'll be back."

Giggy put his foot down. I didn't know any Marsielle but I could tell she was a suspicious type of girl. I bet she picked this spot just for the way door squeaked on its hinges. When it opened all three of them stabbed my ears like a knife. There's no way anybody could sneak in on her with an entrance talking back like that.

Ninety seconds ticked off before Bonny's brother came back out jangling his keys. Desirée thought she was going to walk straight inside but he pulled the door shut and her feet halted. Giggy had that look in his face that crossed between knowing something and not wanting to spill any revelations.

Socks squared his bowling ball shoulders. "What's the business?"

Giggy pointed at me. "Marsielle says she only wants to see him."

Desirée sucked her teeth. "This is bullshit."

I looked her up and down like a new suit I was thinking about trying on. "You're the one that brought us here."

"Fuck you," she spat.

"Save your energy," said Socks. "We can't turn on each other out here." He looked at Giggy. "So, what we supposed to do?"

"Y'all can wait at Bonny's. Her apartment's at the end."

Socks looked at me. "You going to be good, brother?"

I looked at the door with the chipped paint and a big dose of uncertainty swept in. Anything could happen to me in there and I didn't have a gun or even so much as a friend to help me out if shit got thick. But what choice did I have? Options and time were not luxuries right now, Socks knew it too. When I looked at him and said, "yeah" that was just my disclaimer. A way to tell him that if something went bad or even if everything went all bad he wouldn't have to blame himself for leaving me alone. Then,

Bonny's brother turned the doorknob again and I walked right on through into the next turn.

✦ 540 ✦

CHAPTER 59

THE INESCAPABLE

When the door clicked behind me everything else was left on the other side. Even Giggy didn't chaperone me in the apartment. This place was markedly different from the rest of the projects. It was quiet with a warmth and a smell intentionally removed and purposely divorced from every, single feature chasing away hope outside. I couldn't place the scent but it seemed familiar, like a childhood toy found in the back of an attic. In the front room a tall lamp stood high in the corner, the kind that blasts light up and out like a torch and then let's it fall down around you. It had three settings on the side, I didn't adjust it. A brown corduroy couch begging to be touched sat next to the lamp. I could see that piece of furniture being special in the seventies, maybe the eighties, now it hung around in the slums like forgotten aspirations.

After the front room the rest of the place was lit like a cave. Down the hallway I couldn't see a thing. There were no voices, no people, no sounds, no lights, not even the shape of a door or the glint of its knob. The only thing like a presence was that same aroma filtering in from some unseen source that seemed to be everywhere colliding in every empty space. After standing perfectly still by the window for a minute or maybe an eternity a figure shifted in the shadows.

I knew it was a woman. The snakey body told me so and I knew it was Marseille even though I still don't think I had ever met her. She stepped casually but purposefully, bare feet padding the carpet in no real hurry because we had all night.

Her movements were ginger and a slight limp touched her walk like her knees were stiff. At the end of the hall the living room light just barely touched her face but that's all I needed to recognize what that smell was making waves. Cocoa butter and Clive Christian perfume mixing around together in a reminder of a dangerous paradise.

I nodded like it all made sense now, shadows throw shade, circles come around. The world is just a lot of the same packaged like a brilliant surprise and every time you rip the bow off you get a little more savvy.

I licked my teeth. "What is your real name? I mean, the one actually on your driver's license."

Chocolate put on her fishhook grin, the kind that slays tricks like treacherous pigs. "All my friends call me, bad."

"So, what do I call you then?"

"Whatever you like. You know me a lot better than they do."

"Uh-huh." I walked across the carpet deeper into the living room. "That makes a big difference."

"Well, you earned it. Congratulations."

"Thank you. But it also makes things more complicated."

"You got to be ready for change," she said. "You know what they say, evolve or die."

I nodded. "Yeah, and you've evolved."

Women like having the last word but for her that just wasn't enough. To her words were futile, hollow things that you can sleep off and forget all about the next day. She figured if a man could sleep with her and forget her name in the morning then who remembers a sentence or a line or a paragraph or a confession. She wanted a whole lot more, she wanted a place in your mental space to live for all time like an obscene trauma. I crept closer to her wearing my own smile that made both cheeks cramp enough to bring on hints of a migraine and asked what happened to her leg. She bit her lip like a coy virgin. "They got me down in Savannah."

"Got you?" I cocked my head. "Got you like how?"

"That shootout. I got hit in the thigh. Just missed the vein by a teeny bit. I drove all night back to Winston right afterwards and had somebody patch me up."

"I got one too." I hiked up my sleeve and circled my finger around the new bullet hole. "Can you see it?"

She squinted in the dim light. "Did you get hit again in the same spot?"

"Minus well be a bull's eye right there." I rolled my sleeve down. "I went to the hospital. Had to run out of the ER at the crack of fucking dawn. Come on, lemme see yours."

She liked this morbid twist on an old classic, a little show and tell from our fast times dipping in and out of the jaws of death. Chocolate couldn't wait to let me leer at the going away present Salaam gave to her on vacation down in Georgia. I moved a few inches closer while she bent down to roll up the leg of her Calvin Klein sweats, the cheapest thing I think I ever saw her wear. When she had the cuff almost right above the knee then I snatched her by the shirt patterned with lotus flowers and pinned her shoulders flat against the wall.

"I should kill you right now! You leave me down in Savannah and then call me back for this shit? What the fuck type of games are you playing?!"

"There he is," she rasped with perverted joy. "Cerrio, the hooligan. The hood, nigga. I was beginning to wonder when he was going to come back."

"You're lucky I don't choke you right now. You're lucky you're still breathing."

"If that's all you wanted then you should have just called, boo. I ain't like Chevy. I'd've answered the phone. Maybe you could have come over and had a drink."

I pulled her off the wall and then slammed her back against it hard enough to make her teeth clack. Our faces were an inch apart but that wasn't nearly enough. Chocolate used her pink tongue to close the distance, flicking it out and licking my lips seductively in one swipe like a popsicle. She smiled deliciously, took a ragged breath. I could smell cinnamon gum rolling off the back of her throat because she just swallowed a piece whole.

"You gonna hurt me Cerrio?" she cooed. "Do I need to suffer for what you think I did to your precious little Diana Ross with the gold in her mouth?"

"Shut the fuck up and tell me what happened to Bandy."

"Well, I can't do both."

"Then, you better chose wisely."

She giggled. "You wouldn't hurt me."

"I wish everybody thought that way. You're the only one who imagines that I'm weak."

"Oh no, I could never lie like that. I know you, Cerrio. I seen a lot of men in my day. Some got cheating in their blood. Some got tricking, gambling, all kinds of vices. But you got the gift of assassination. You're a killer and that's what I love about you. It's in your veins" She put both hands on my chest. "But you could never live with yourself after hurting a girl like me. It's against your religion."

I stood by the corduroy sofa trapped in confusion. Chocolate's touch was so gentle like she wanted affection when it should have been firm to shove me away. None of that mattered though, because somehow it worked. When I released her the hands didn't stop at all, she rubbed me up to my shoulders and cuffed the skin down at the base of my neck.

"Was that you at the bank this morning? I saw your work on the news."

"You're worried about the wrong thing. What did Yhay Yuda do with Chevy's cousin?"

"So it was you," she said, a note of hilarity in her voice. "I knew you were smart. They said, 'since the tellers didn't have time to put the money in their system it isn't even traceable'."

I ignored the long winded compliment and the complicated touching. "I won't ask you again."

"Cerrio, what are you doing? I just said how smart you are a now this." She gripped my shoulders, the look in her eyes anxious and firm, shaken but strong. "Think with that same head that made you rich before lunch. I killed Yuda's cousin. Do you think I could really be that close to this, that deep on the move to steal the girl and still be alive? How would I get my money and live to spend it?"

"Unless it's all a big lie."

She dropped her hands and pushed me off. Chocolate had strength from all that pole work and almost knocked me off balance. She pulled her pants down around the knees then spread her legs far as the elastic waist would allow. I saw her right thigh hit the light at an angle. On top of it a fat pad of gauze stained red in the middle contrasted hard against the smooth, black skin. She ripped it off like a sticker and underneath a hole gaped open like a shocked mouth in her body had woken up to cry.

I cringed inside. Where Salaam's bullet went in it looked like a cigar had been put out against her silky flesh. Compared to Chocolate the thing on my arm was a needle prick. She grabbed my wrist, pressed my finger on the rough scab and rubbed it around the sides. I knew it hurt. Damaged nerves jumped and twitched and I could see leg muscles tensing all around her green panties while she kept forcing my touch on her.

"Is that real enough for you?" She threw my hand off and pulled her sweats up again. "Or do you think I shot myself when I came back home? Maybe you want to see the blood stain on my Jeep seats."

"Shut up. Don't get fucking dramatic."

She trampled my suspicions but not quite fully. Then again, nobody could put them down all the way in the middle of a crisis. She settled her plump behind on the couch armrest until the corduroy looked like it might fold in half.

"Why you looking at me like that?" I asked.

"What? We fuck and get shot together and now I can't even look at you?"

"Is this what I came here for?"

"Well, you can leave."

So I stayed.

"So, how's the Misses?"

"Chevy is still down in Georgia. She won't come home without Bandy."

"Then it's been a few days since you had a woman. Shit, you're going on five days already."

"I been dry a lot longer than that."

"Well, difference is you're not in prison anymore."

She leaned back and rolled her neck. I watched the movement travel south down her shoulders and across her collarbone into her chest.

"My back hurts." She drew out the last S like a diamondback in the dirt.

"That's the side effects of extra duty."

"One of them. Can you fix it?"

"No, we got other things to work out right now."

"We got all night for that."

"I'm not here for sex."

"God, who said anything about sex? Dick is everywhere around here. If I wanted some I'd be ass up in the back bedroom right now. I want a massage. And I want you to give it to me."

I shook my head. "Ain't no time for that. I got people waiting."

"Are these the same people who stood by you in a shootout two nights ago? Or some new friends who just dropped in so you can help them get rich?" She rose up off the armrest steady on her hurt leg, cupped my chin with a cool palm. It was a rhetorical question and she gave the answer. "Come on, I got oils in the bedroom. We can talk about everything while you rub me down."

That's when all my crooked stars slowed down to a pedestrian pace. I couldn't hurt her, I couldn't hurt any of them, and then again that's all I did was hurt. If Chocolate would have came hurtling out the back room like debris in a storm then maybe things would have gone different. If she wouldn't have led me by the hand down the hall and gotten undressed on the bed and laid face down so those plump breasts pushed out underneath her weight I would have still been on a cliff ready to jump off at the sound of the bell. Instead, my vengeance was emaciated at the scene of her thigh. She told her story about getting shot without a twitch of an eyelid and enough proof to donate to any minor deception. So, I guess it was time for me to heal.

She pinned her hair up to clear the path and set the oils down to pave the road the road for my fingers to savor the journey between the breadth of her shoulders like a voyager in love with a naked continent. I felt relaxed with her, up there straddling her waist it seemed like I was falling forward into her universe right where I belonged. Some of it was her reasoning about loyalty and some of it was my inadequacy in reasoning. But that was less than most of it, most of it came from how in all the world Chocolate had to be the only one who held me close. She didn't just tolerate me, didn't glance away at my flaws and pretend not to notice, she embraced them as a gifts.

She moaned pleasingly when my thumb hit a knot next to her spine. "Put some more oil right there," she told me. I tipped the bottle filled with something that smelled like Moroccan argon and spilled enough to wet the natural crevasse running up the middle of her back. She writhed as I increased the pressure to make the soreness evaporate. When the short discomfort was over I saw a smile on her cheek. "You're pretty good at this."

I had a reply, something slick. Before I could get it off the television broke us up.

Giggy must have shopped at Goodwill because the set had to be twenty years old. Boxy with thick bubble glass and a row of buttons on the bottom it looked like a stone slab. When the ten o' clock news came on screen Chocolate turned the volume up with a remote she had warmed under her body. Pinnacle Bank still held the headlines. The anchors drummed up the story and then cut to the surveillance video of me kicking the security guard on a loop. She watched close, when they showed it the third time she burst out laughing. Between ha-ha's she said, "that guy's never gonna have kids."

"What could I do? He was aiming a gun at my brother. A few more inches and I'd be carrying his casket."

Chocolate froze with the remote in her hand. "You have a brother?"

"Sort of," I replied.

"Did he thank you?"

I shrugged. "Doesn't matter. Family don't count favors."

"How much did you get?"

"Seventy bands."

Chocolate did the math. "That's thirty five a piece."

"Minus three for a little extra help."

"Oh, a getaway driver?"

"More like a fee for diversion."

"Diversion, huh? Well, give three, take three, that still don't add up to one fifty. And if you want diversions you could've paid me. This girl right here could use a new bag."

I worked my way down her sides, when my slippery fingers brush the bottoms of her D-cups Chocolate wiggles on the mattress. "What's done is done," I said. "And right now, what I need is a new plan."

Instead of answering right away she let the last sentence hang in the air. She went quietly into the massage, absorbing the touch like the oil seeping in on her back. When I worked out to her arms columns of muscle relaxed as the news went on to another story. She exhaled into the bedsheets and said, "I got another mark. Better than that last lick we did in High Point by a landslide."

"Oh yeah? Then, how come we didn't hit his place that night instead of the whale?"

"Had to get all the facts," she said sleepily. "Sometimes people play rich when all they have is credit cards. If we went in his house and found silverware you'd call me sloppy."

"You're right." I got off her back, wiped my hands on a towel. "I don't want to be up in nobody's house taking forks and knives. So, where does your friend live?"

"Asheville," she responded.

"By the zoo?"

"This trick could buy the zoo."

"Like that, huh? Who is he?"

She turned to face me, elbow on the bed, head perched in a hand, heavy breasts ruffling the linen. "Jimmy Watson," she chirped.

"You want to rob the mayor's house? You know what that takes? He's got armed guards around the clock. Nobody's getting in there and if they do then they damn sure ain't getting back out." I spiked the oily towel in a bin that was supposed to look like woven bamboo. "I ain't going on a suicide mission."

She got off her stomach and pulled the lotus flower shirt on. Part of me was disappointed. She would have stayed topless but with her nothing is ever free. She picked a new phone up off the TV, held the power button down until the device woke up. It was a burner, forty bucks and a SIM card and everything she did on it was anonymous. While her fingers danced all over the touchscreen I watched intently over her shoulder. Showing on the glass was a pic of Asheville's Mayor shirtless and sweaty, features contorted in a screwed up face of forbidden pleasure.

"Jesus, what was you doing to him right there?"

"Whipping him," replied Chocolate. "He gets off on that. A lot of big men in power do."

There I was, looking into the unseen world. And all I could say was, "dig it" like a dumbass.

"A lot of white collars have a dominance fetish. Some of them like getting whipped, spanked, burned."

"Burned? You do that?"

Chocolate shrugged. "Hey, they like it I love it."

"So, what's the point of all this?"

She tapped one more button on the screen and tossed the phone on the bed. "I just sent Mrs. Edith Watson a picture of her husband's infidelity. She gets them a lot."

"From you?"

"No, that was my first. Usually, it's a girl from the escort service or some pro from Atlantic City."

I rubbed my chin. "So, Mayor Jimmy Watson is a gambler."

"Don't get any ideas, Cerrio. He's not going to sit down at some east side card table with you over a blunt. This man is very rich and very careful. He owns a chain of cash machines in Asheville. Some in Winston-Salem too. After his wife gets that flick of him sweating she'll raise some hell, kick him out the mansion maybe. Threaten divorce."

"I understand. It all sounds like the usual."

"Uh-huh, except this is election year and he don't want the scandal."

"When do they ever want the scandal? You say that like it might've been all good a week ago."

"You in a rush to hear the handy part?" she asked.

"It wouldn't hurt to keep me interested."

"First Jimmy Watson will deny it which is typical, not just for him but for any man. Then, he'll concede. And Edith Watson is an old broad but not a stupid one. She knows if she airs her dirty laundry out all over town Jimmy's career is over and he'll be worthless. So, instead the smart old bitch will extort him. Corner her husband with the picture I just sent and demand something. A diamond bracelet, a new Audi, a girl's trip to France. And Mayor Jimmy's gonna pay because he knows what's good for him."

"An old lady gets her way. So much for the patriarchy, I guess. But I still ain't heard how we're going to make out."

She went on like daylight pushes on into the evening. "All the money used to buy cars and jewelry comes from those ATM's he owns. Jimmy moves it around to cover up the lavish gifts he has to keep giving Edith so no trace of the scandal gets out."

I dialed in on her looking for the wolf in the story. The part buried down deep enough inside to jump up and bite you while you were busy being fascinated. "How do you know all this?"

"This girl from the club named Keena sent his wife a video on a Friday. By Monday the Porsche dealer was out front dropping off convertible keys at the mayor's door."

"Chevy used to talk about a girl named Keena when she was at Sugar Bares. She said, 'the girl just quit showing up one day.' When they cut the lock off her locker she had a black trash bag in there with all her clothes inside like when she was moving but didn't have a suitcase."

"Maybe she got enough money out of him to quit dancing."

"Or maybe Jimmy got tired of Keena's shit and got rid of her."

"You playin' detective now?"

"I'm just sayin'. Why doesn't he buy his wife gifts outright like a normal person? It's not a crime to have nice things."

"Because he's a public servant and if some tax preparer or somebody sees big expenses like that popping up all the time then they're going to start thinking. And then they're going to start looking. And that's when things start to unravel. This ain't slipping on a banana peel. It's big shit, Cerrio. After the exposés Jimmy is going to end up washing dishes down at the country club."

I turned around to look out the window. Through the horizontal blinds I could see the little crack dealers swarm a hatchback that had pulled up in the projects.

"So you want to blackmail the Mayor of Asheville? That it?"

"Think bigger." Chocolate said, before coming closer. "It takes forty thousand dollars to fill up one freestanding ATM machine. The mayor owns eight of them. Every Monday morning, scandal or not, he sends out a white van full of money to stock each and every one for the week. Except this Monday he's going to load a little extra in the van so that when it reaches the last machine by his house he can just slide over after work and pick up the bread to get his wife whatever she wants to keep their marriage looking right."

"That's three hundred thousand. No, wait it's more."

"A chunk more," she added. "I know what the van looks like. I know the plate numbers, who drives it. And there's a map in my apartment showing where each money machine owned by the mayor is located."

"You want to hit the van?"

"Now, you catching on. It's easy. I'll drive you right up to it if you want. We take them before they fill up the first ATM and get everything. I mean everything. Then, Bandy comes home and you still got enough to make Chevy happy again. You can buy her that salon she's been dreaming of."

I thought for a minute while the news kept going. This plan, if it was real, sounded wilder but better than anything I had ever heard before. It almost made me sour that she hadn't brought it to me a long time ago on a day before Savannah and High Point were under my belt.

Except no one goes around in a van stocked with cash all alone and that meant Socks would have to be with me and even then it was still a dangerous mission. We'd be heisting in broad daylight, probably right by the road because most ATM machines are in plain sight to make sure there's plenty of witnesses around. Plus, we had the hard part and all Chocolate had to do was sit in the car and keep the motor running. If things got out of hand she could just pull off in a cloud of smoke. Then, we were fucked.

When I turned around she was standing so close I could taste the massage oil wafting off her skin. "What do you think you gonna get out of all this?"

"Simple." She licked her lips. "I want half."

"No fucking way. Me and mine are not going to do all the heavy lifting and then split fifty-fifty."

She looked at me sympathetically. "Am I pushing it? Do you think I'm going too far, Cerrio?"

"Goddamn right. You lost your mind. And you can say whatever you want because I know you don't have anyone else who'll do it. And they damn sure won't do it and give you whole half just to sit back and look pretty in the car."

She paced in front of the bed. "Uh-huh, and was I out of my goddamn mind giving you all those envelopes of cash on the boat while you were losing every night? Was I going too far when I threw all those back porch poker games at your pretend uncle's house?" She pauses and looks hard at me. "I ain't Chevy. You can't take and take from me with no return."

"How do I know this job is even real?" I asked. "You could be selling me a dream."

"Do I ever come to you with empty hands?"

That same argument again from the boat. That's the trouble with never trusting anyone, eventually the landscape of suspicions skids into a wall. We stared in each other's eyes for a long beat. I counted a lot of things that didn't make sense and for each and every one she had a move. The next one better than the last, like sequels on sequels, line after line going up like a story written backwards on a notebook paper.

"Okay, I'm in. But you only get thirty percent."

"Forty," she fired back.

"Fine, and we need guns. Something to put a horse down."

"So, we have a deal." Chocolate smiled, always zealous at the scent of fresh chaos.

"But Monday is too late. Yhay Yuda only gave me until Friday to get the money. After that Bandy's going south to Florida."

"Wasn't it supposed to be Wednesday?"

"Yeah, at first. But you know that didn't work out."

"Why did he give you longer?"

"Are you try to fuck with me?"

"Just answer. Why did he give you more time?"

"Because I'm his people," I replied. "Because I'm middle eastern and we look the same."

"And you still look the same." Chocolate picked up the phone off the bed and slapped it in my hand. "Now, make a bargain like the girl's life depends on it."

You'd think a man like a Yhay Yuda would be hard to talk into a favor. And you'd be wrong. Favors are like that though, uncomfortable most of the time you ask and especially when they cost something. He wasn't so bad. I've had more problems changing my order at IHOP than convincing the pimp to give me a little longer to come back to Savannah. Keeping it one hundred, some of those waitresses at the pancake house can be brutal. Anyway, we spoke the same language. I don't mean Arabic, I mean money. I expected a little push back and I got it when Bandy's price tag went up another fifty thousand. I did the math on the back of my hand with an ink pen. When it was done I felt stupid. Desirée had it right, the girl really was more valuable than my life.

Yuda wanted a show of good faith. That meant nine thousand dollars wired to Georgia before the clock struck midnight. He was smart, if he'd made it an even ten the government would have had a reason to investigate. In the meantime Chocolate wanted to make our deal official. She laid back in Giggy's bed, parted her thighs and showed me the oasis in the middle. The dancer couldn't do the things she used to with a bullet hole in her, fact is she would never be the same again. When I pushed hard I saw her wince, just a pinch in her mouth and a flutter of the eyes. Of course she had too much pride to complain out loud but I don't get off on agony, so we made love instead.

The whole time we did it I knew this was me making the same mistakes all over again. Maybe that makes me insane or something, but it felt so much better than losing my mind. Chocolate had a smell. Nothing offensive, just the airy redolence of feminine sweat and project sex blending together in an association of aphrodisiacs. Her breasts were big enough that she could touch them with the tip of her tongue. She did that once or twice to make me grow longer inside her and when I was throbbing so hard it hurt then she twisted her hips and brought on the finish.

Midnight was still forty minutes away when we pulled out of Cleveland projects. Desirée wanted to know what took so long but Socks already knew. From the backseat I filled in all the details that were safe to discuss. By the time I was done we had twenty minutes left.

I never worried about making the time. If I had to I would have ran on foot to Desirée's house and got Yhay Yuda's nine grand myself before both hands on the clock went north. Socks wants to pitch in half but I tell him no and his cousin does too. She stood in the kitchen, dreads hanging, swinging every time she makes the heated point that this is all my responsibility. That must have been the first thing we ever agreed on. We found common ground and then I left to go find an all-night corner store with a Western Union sticker in the window. The gun back on my waist again made things feel at least halfway right.

CHAPTER 60

HARVEST WEEKEND

E dwards hated working weekends. Saturday and Sunday were supposed to be for drinking beer and mowing the lawn, not putting extra hours in like some shitheel still looking to make his stripes. That was the conventional wisdom but after his wife found that box of full flavored cancer sticks hidden in the garage it was a relief to be somewhere other than home. Detective Clyde Edwards loved his old lady. He had been together with her twenty-seven years going on eternity but still in all that time she never understood the pressure that came with this job.

If Cecilia Edwards spent all day seeing what other people do to each other instead of just hearing about it on the news she wouldn't be in his face going on and on about making better choices. Her nagging had been nonstop. She yelled and cried and waved emphysema pamphlets from the doctor's office around like a parade flag until Clyde signed himself up for extra duty.

Now, suddenly retirement didn't seem like such a nice, little reprieve anymore. Not while the home front was wallowing in deceit and the case with the Cutlass had just caught fire. In reality a pestering woman couldn't bring Edwards down at all. Finding that assault rifle with a clip half full of bullets was red meat for a guy like him. It made his day, his week, maybe even his career.

He was looking at a color picture of the gun, thinking about how he owed Judge Leroy Marcus a beer and trying to decide where to go from here. The long Cutlass that Banks brother-in-law towed to the impound yard was registered to an old woman living out on Greenway Avenue. That was in a decent part of town and the detective knew he couldn't ask her any questions but all of that hardly mattered. This wasn't some television drama where every single person orbiting the case got subpoenaed and drug down for an interview in a room on the other side of tinted glass.

The old car wasn't reported stolen but the owner Denise Lloyd had the same last name as Edwards most wanted man. The infamous, blasphemous, one and fucking only LaDecerrio. Finding that part out was detective work. The rest was just common sense like sidestepping a nail sticking up through the floor. All of it together meant he had enough to put his man away for an extra long while. Edwards might even figure out a serious motive along the way. Maybe he could happen up on a good one to pin Cerrio down before the prosecutor sewed the pieces together to make up her own story to walk in front of the jury. If not then oh well, things like that were all extra credit anyway.

Michelle Heinrich had something to prove, if not to the cops at the station than at least to herself. She grew up with a focus on determination. In junior high school she joined the girl's softball team. When her father found out about it he made her do wind sprints at the park with aerobic weights around both ankles. When the teachers said she wasn't proficient in math he made Michelle study fractions all summer break until she came back to class in Autumn impressing the same teachers when she could multiply eighths and fifths all in her head without pencil or paper. "Don't ever give up," her daddy said. "Don't ever give up and don't ever show fatigue." For those two reasons she worked every single weekend.

She found the old lady across the street from the yellow house watering plants on her porch. A pot of petunias hung down, baby sunflowers were by the railing, aloe cactus sat in the window sill catching the sun. The first words out of her mouth were that she had already told the other sheriffs everything she knew. Michelle gave her a weak smile and a nod that was supposed to be easygoing. "Just one more question, Mrs. Tracey."

The old woman tipped her water pot over a young lavender bush and clear liquid splashed the soil around the flowers. "That's what they told me last time. And even the time before that. But now you're here."

"I know this must be frustrating, Mrs. Tracey."

"No, you don't. And stop saying Mrs. Tracey after every sentence. I know my own name."

"Yes ma'am. I just wanted to know if you'd take a look at something."

Tracey looked visibly shaken. "Is it a picture if a dead body?"

Michelle reached inside a pocket of her cargo pants. "No Miss...um, no. It's a photo of a man."

"What man? Is it the one who did all those...things to that poor girl?"

"Uh, no ma'am."

The old lady quit watering plants. "Well, now you've got me wondering."

Cedric Addison worked every weekend so he could to have Tuesdays and Fridays off. He needed those days because that's the only time he got to see his four year old daughter up in Garden City. Her mother moved there right after their chaotic break up. She said, "she needed time away around other people who would actually listen to her." Cedric didn't know if that meant she wanted to be around family or another one of her boyfriends with a bigger house and a heavier wallet. Either way he wasn't stupid enough to believe it.

He knew the real reason for Rebecca's move to the invisible town just north of Savannah was to make things harder. She wanted him to be a no-show dad, and what would be easier than having a built in excuse about too many miles between work and his kid? Every Monday and Thursday night like a ritual she waited on him to call and cancel his visit. She was going to be waiting for a long time, a dozen plus two more years at least. Because Cedric Addison wasn't losing out on the opportunity to be the dad he never knew. He would walk barefoot to Garden City over a bridge of hot coals just to see his curly haired baby girl.

All things considered this weekend wasn't so bad, though. Most of the hotshot veterans with stripes up their arms were piling on the sick days to squeeze out the last few drops of summer before the leaves changed. It had been a hot one too. A lot of killings in the city of Savannah which equated to a lot of dots that needed connecting. Addison liked trying. Dabbling in the major crimes gave him an excuse to play with all that facial recognition stuff usually reserved for the shirt and tie detectives who cuffed their sleeves and wore their badges clipped to the belt instead of high on the chest.

The computer did the work. Addison loaded a piece of surveillance video from the hospital into the system then sat back while the program shot through thousands of wild-eyed criminals who were probably high on something or at least wishing they had a way to get there. Cedric thought about the case as the magic happened. It was still fresh, two or three days old, which meant it was actually solvable unlike so many others hopelessly collecting dust in a file cabinet.

Tuesday morning in the small hours just before dawn a man got pushed out of a car in front of the hospital with a .45 round in him. Whoever dumped him there didn't hang, they screeched off in a loud cloud of tire smoke because they'd rather not talk about it. The gunshot had hit the artery in the thigh and the poor bastard was ninety percent dead even before the first nurse got to him.

A little while later another guy comes in hit high in the arm. This one showed up to the ER on his own and survived. Investigators wanted to ask him questions but somehow he slipped out of the hospital side exit before anybody got to him effectively.

Every cop that breathed on the case agreed both shootings were related, connected like links on a chain that dropped down into a swamp where an unseen anchor held everything beneath the surface. By all accounts it looked like two goons trading fire, one got hit and made it, the other not so much. The dead man and the survivor looked identical, same brown skin, black hair, thick eyebrows. Any policeman worth his uniform knew the only people like that who shot up the city belong to the nasty pimp, Yhay Yuda. Because all the rest of them worked at 7-11.

Of course none of it was provable. It was all just a fat hunch set in stereotypes and every single court in Georgia would brush it off like lint on a wool sweater. The intuition was invisible like wind blowing through a gorge or the rising temperatures arriving on the heels of the afternoon. So here he was, Officer Addison with a kid in Garden City trying to make a cop's theory more than just a figment of the imagination while everybody else played outside in the sun.

When the computer stopped he saw the programmer's perfect genius manifested on the screen. Facial recognition worked. Nineteen points from the hospital footage lined up with a Department of Corrections photo taken in harsh, unforgiving, white light. Cedric scooted his rolling chair closer to the monitor, one of the casters stuck and he had to hop it the last six inches to the desk. Somewhere he had heard that prison is like a freezer in that it preserves you. For all the intended downsides incarceration has the benefits of zero pollution and no wear and tear from the everyday rat race of normal everyday life. Missing out on all that stress made a good argument for the theory that men who get locked up often defy their age and right now Cedric was starting to believe it. Because the man staring back in his mugshot hadn't gained a year at all.

❖ ❖ ❖

Edwards had a funny expertise. That's one of the things this job gave you, a good sense of discernment with a lining of something ugly and stilted. The detective knew all about injuries. After so many years on the force he'd seen enough cuts, gashes, and holes that now they flashed back in his dreams. He learned them, became a student to the gore, it wasn't a conscious education, more like a force if habit. He understood severities of pain the same way mechanics know the size of a motor just by listening to the car.

One look, even if it was just a photo and he could immediately tell if there would be permanent damage or if it was only a playground scrape. With Patrick Dominguez there was no question. Edwards knew the damage was permanent leaning towards life changing. The man called Barney would never chew anything on the left side if his mouth again. His eye socket needed a few more surgeries to reconstruct and that whistling from his nose coming every time he breathed guaranteed he'd be a long time investor in handkerchiefs. Another blow to the head in this life would probably kill him, his nostril was going to drip like a broken faucet and cold weather was going to make his jawbone ache in the winter.

Yes, Barney would be a patient at Baptist Medical Center ICU for a while yet. He had no balloons in his room wishing a get well soon but with that coalescence of major injuries he might be there long enough to start getting mail. Living like that made him easy to find when the time came for Edwards to shake him up or down. Only problem is his mother was there too pretty much every day.

Every time they came around to ask her son more questions she stared a hole through the detectives behind a pair of drugstore reading glasses. All those indignant eye games made Edwards purely sick. He stared right back at Barney's mother hoping she would get it in her head to be mouthy so he could ask if she knew what Patrick was all about. Do you know what he's capable of? Do you what your little boy has done? Then, instead of an answer he would pull out a picture of a young girl with a mangled face. That one from Wilmington beach Barney left for dead, he'd hold it up to his mother's face right at the end of those reading glasses so she could get a grip on reality. Much better than talking or arguing because truth is mamas don't ever want to believe bad things about their babies. That's another reason he was happy about not having to talk to Denise Lloyd in the wheelchair.

Maybe it was all a sign of the times they were living in. The battered women and the willfully ignorant parents turning their heads. Maybe it was the new progressive style of raising kids. Things change, they always changed. After a while everything and everybody might just go back to being the same again. But Edwards still stayed static no matter what. He did things the old way which wasn't always so simple but somehow it worked. More often than not that meant keeping your eyes peeled. That's how he found out what Mrs. Dominguez did on weekends. In her world Saturdays were for grocery shopping and Sundays she went to Our Lady of Trinidad Church in Walkertown about ten minutes outside Winston.

Edwards zoomed to the hospital while Barney's mother picked out this week's dinner items. Riding next to him in the passenger's seat was a manila envelope full of pictures. He patted it like he would a good puppy. Everything was in there, close ups of the gun, the house shot to shit, the Cutlass, the prime suspect. Mrs. Dominguez was a coupon clipper. Something the detective found out by lucky accident when she dropped her purse in the grocery store parking lot and little rectangles of paper spilled out underneath her car. That notoriously time consuming habit gave him a long window of opportunity to corner Barney. All he needed was to scare him into picking out Cerrio's picture like a fresh head of lettuce and Leroy Marcus would sign the arrest warrant without even blinking.

At the hospital Edwards put his badge down on the nurse's station next to a sign in clipboard. He slid it across the ledge with a blood curling scrape made on purpose. The heavyset blonde on the other side wearing a leopard print headband took it between her painted fingers, turned her mouth down in a frown, passed the shield back.

"What can I help you with, sir?" she asked blandly.

"I'm here to see a patient in ICU. Patrick Dominguez." He pantomimed a writing motion through the air. "Got a pen I can use to sign in?"

"Mr. Dominguez checked out yesterday."

Edwards blinked. "Are you serious?"

"Why? Do you I think I'm making jokes?"

"He's eating through a straw. Drinking Ensure. What doctor would let him leave like that?"

"His mother wanted him home. She hired around the clock nurses from an agency so the doctors, that's more than one, decided to let him go. We needed his bed anyway." The big nurse clicked a ballpoint and threw it up on the counter. "But you can still sign in if you want."

Michelle didn't know what to do. The woman she called Mrs. Tracey hadn't figured out all that went down in the yellow house but she had a grasp on the basics. And to her LaDecerrio Lloyd was a hero. He had been there when the police weren't and carried the broken girl to a place of safety in his arms. Now, Winston PD looked like drivers of petulance, running through the neighborhood asking questions then taking down notes like thirsty newspaper journalists hot on a headline.

The junior investigator fingered Cerrio's picture in her pocket. Michelle could feel the edge of the paper threatening to give her a slice that would sting viciously when it hit the air. After seeing his photo she could tell the man was handsome in that rugged sort of way that makes young girls feel free and old ladies feel young.

Those unsophisticated types always made the best lovers too. Without any filter to strain out raw emotions they were much more passionate, unimpeded by social norms they fucked like wild animals. Michelle understood that fact firsthand, don't ask.

Anyway, all of it was more reason to be hesitant. She didn't know what Mrs. Tracey would do if she saw the image and realized this square jawed Arab was the person of interest. She might think the police were on the wrong side of things. Even worse she might see LaDecerrio Lloyd as flat out misunderstood. An attitude like that would make things harder for anybody coming back around here with a badge. Instead of doing some light gardening on the porch she might just slam the door in a cop's face from right inside the house.

The woman stood with the water pot in her hand. "Well, aren't you going to show me what you got?"

Michelle kept silent. Somewhere inside she struggled with the foggy line separating good guys from bad. A rapist got top notch care in a public hospital while the man who thought they put him there was getting ran down like a fugitive. Wherever Cerrio was he had a pair of handcuffs waiting for him downtown. Was that right? Heinrich knew which side she was on but sometimes it was like the law couldn't come to a decision.

Mrs. Tracey asked her question again. Instead of answering Michelle backed away from the old woman slowly. One step at a time, cautiously off the painted porch until the heel of her right boot hit the first stone on the walk. Then, she turned around and double timed it back to the cruiser while crime scene tape flapped in a breeze across the street.

Addison did a little research. He found out the man in the surveillance video wasn't a local. He came from another state, maybe another country but Cedric wasn't ready to presume a thing like that just yet. His own family came from Haiti. He was a first generation American but the difference between him and these goons getting shot up like purple heart vets was all about choices. His mother always kept him in school. Away from those neighborhood boys who liked to joyride in stolen cars and smoked too much weed. Maybe these guys, the one who died on the hospital curb and the other sliding out the side door never had any mothers. Or maybe theirs were just like Rebecca.

CHAPTER 61

HEAD COLLECTER

Chocolate had worked hard to make herself the big joker in the deck. She toured with me around the city through every slum, trap, and basement card game in Winston-Salem that ever held cash. We came up easy off a defiled trick's pathetic lust to take a few days off. Even pulled a little move out of town on the ocean with a white girl spreading her legs and a mean infection. Looking back it was hard to know how all that would fall into place, which time was going to be more memorable, more fun, most exhausting. Ah, but they were all just truck stops, places to lay over a while before reaching this, our final destination.

The guns she brought just like promised were a black Draco with a scarred wood grip and a sawed off shotty that smelled slightly used. I knew it was Chocolate's theme to argue. Nonetheless, we still went at it about the 12 gauge.

Sawed offs are trouble in general because you don't even have to use them to be in some shit, I'm talking ten years for the bust, another five for pulling the trigger. She smiled about the risk in Socks living room while the weapon laid on his couch like a throw pillow. I hated that smirk, seems it always showed up when my back was pressed against the wall. She knew she had game too. That was her sixth sense, maybe seventh or eighth. I opened my mouth to level a threat at her, closed and gave up before I even got started. What was the point? Chocolate knew I wasn't going to do anything, at least not to her, to her my wrath was embargoed.

In the end Socks took the chopped Mossberg. He saw the same bad chances as I did but after the last blowout with Desirée he couldn't taking the bickering anymore. It was all ridiculous anyway. Me standing by the wall between a poster of Tut Ankh Amon and a portrait of Jesus Christ. Chocolate hanging next to the sofa in shorts with gauze taped above her knee. Me, being judgmental about a tampered gun when we were going on the most decisive heist of our criminal careers on Monday morning like an office job. Her, cheesing like a fucking idiot counting up her share of the cash in that scandalous mind.

My brother had a bad case of the nerves but he hid his well, the only reason I sensed his anxiety is because it takes one to know one. The thing at the bank had been a wild success, Socks planned it well. In two days the lick blew over like tall cattails in the wind. By the end of the weekend the news latched on to a story about mail fraud and we were so tight with the money that I didn't even tip the pizza boy when he dropped off dinner. But this was not like the bank, this was a blind job. We were going to have to trust a woman who's morals changed flavors like a bag of Halloween candy.

Trust issues were everywhere pollinating my tiny circle that grew slower than a fir tree. To soothe the jumpiness me and my brother did what we always do, a little bit of drugs that would have turned into a lot if somebody hadn't been right there to watch over us. Sunday night we went to The Rose Petal with Desirée chaperoning like it was a middle school dance. She was there to play big sister, checking her watch a lot, making sure we didn't drink too much, and when me or her cousin caught another girl's eye she pitched the shade like a Yankee fastball.

I did lines in the bathroom, the drought was still on in the city and the coke was cut twentyfold so you had to stuff your nose just to feel the rush. Socks took bumps off the web of his hand between finger and thumb. It felt good for a moment and after the moment passed like a twinkle in your eye then the singing started. Bandy was on The Rose Petal stage hitting the high note in a Dior dress with a string of pearls slung around her delicate neck. Even listening close the voice didn't clutch my ghost like that first time when we were in the parking lot supposedly getting Chevy's battery. I saw the gold in her mouth flash off the light. Then, I blinked once and she was gone, vanished like a pack of sugar in hot oatmeal. The place got took up by another girl chasing that same dream, the flash in my retina came from her wristwatch when the lamp bounced off its cheap metal.

My mind was playing tricks on me like a symptom of guilt. Blaming it on cocaine helped me feel halfway sane so I lied to myself like those delusions of seeing my little singer were all just part of the high. It was easier to digest than facing facts. Bandy wasn't just out of sight, she was hanging at the end of a rope and my hand was caught at her neck trying to pull it free because my other hand had put her there.

Chocolate left before the night became long. She walked out of the club alone for the first time in a thousand trips. Somebody should have taken a picture to capture the moment because after this we would never be able to prove a thing.

The night passed as it always does, the weekend bridged into Monday and at eight thirty before the dew dried on the ground she came back in a long bed truck with a toolbox bolted down across the back. This time there wasn't going to be any naked tricks flailing on the carpet by a king size bed. No defiant bank tellers going in with their spitting and bad humor from a cold spot on the floor. The plan was flagrant two-eleven, real robbery the way robbery was supposed to be without all the extras.

The Silverado she brought wasn't anything special, tan cloth seats, digital radio, old coffee stains caked on the floormats. I don't know where she got it from, not my job to inquire. But I knew when we were done she was going to dump the truck off in the water like a jet ski. Chocolate brought another gun too, a compact nine millimeter with a green sight that stayed tucked under her thigh while she steered the 4×4 through morning traffic. She drove better than expected, though I truly didn't know what to expect. Pretty stupid to think a woman couldn't whip a man's truck effectively when she'd been driving a Jeep since day one when I'd first met her. But that was something to work on later because right now funny, little biases were way down on my list of things to fix.

Socks checked the sawed off while we turned at a light. I did the same with the Draco as Chocolate rolled up some cute, chic avenue with quaint offices and Wi-Fi cafes lined up on both sides. We were on the nicer side of town, Asheville's version of the Starland district in Savannah. The people posted at crosswalks clutching lattes in their tender palms never saw real trouble. Everything they knew about crime came from prime time drama just like all I knew about life came from low in the trenches.

While my heart raced like a thoroughbred up the track Socks hummed a song in the backseat, Dreamlover by Mrs. Mariah Carey. He was doing what he had to do to get ready but when Chocolate drove up on the first teller machine marked by her map no one was around it. Fog hung over shopping center parking lot like it didn't know whether to fade away and evaporate or drop down to blanket the smattering of vehicles resting between the white lines.

"Where are they?" I asked.

She did a quick check in her sideview mirror. "Relax, they'll be here any minute."

Socks glanced at the clock on the dash. "We're late."

Our driver snapped her head around. "What?"

"Look at the clock. It past nine already. They done came and gone and we missed them."

She checked the time right as the seven changed to eight minutes past. My heart was dropping, before it fell out of my chest into my lap we were swerving in the parking lot. Chocolate leaned to the right as she pulled the steering wheel all the way and flipped a bitch, tires snatching a piece of curb as some early bird jogger dove to safety by a trash can. She gave up good driving for raw speed and had the Chevrolet weaving around nine a.m. commuters down a four lane street with the tires screaming on every lane change. Me and Socks rocked back and forth in the cloth seats like shutters in a storm.

"Buckle it up!" she yelled. "We gotta get to the second money drop before they fill the machine and leave!"

The truck hopped up on the concrete median barely missing a wrong way sign as Chocolate used the left side of the road to bank around a line of cars waiting for a green light. Nobody had time to be shocked and I'd be lying if I said panic didn't exist in me right then as we closed in on the intersection. Heavy diesel trucks streamed east to west like a row of ants marching to a picnic. There was no break, no clear way, no window for us to squeeze through. Beside me the dancer stayed cool as a ripe tomato on the vine, she shot her eyes left once to gauge the flow of traffic. Then, she hit the brakes and the truck shocks shrieked.

I almost cracked my forehead against the windshield glass and Socks burst into a stream of curses as the Silverado bumper made contact with a solid object that dented the hood up front like a check mark. It was a yield sign, Chocolate had hit it on purpose but she had her reasons. I watched the triangle rise and twist in the air before coming back down on a Camaro painted azure. The blue coupe screeched to a halt hoping to stop short but the hatchback behind it never could cease in time. It slammed into the I-Roc's custom spoiler as metal cried out in a sharp transformation. The sound made me cringe and just after I'd thought I had seen it all a four car pileup spirited itself to block the flow of traffic and make a clean path for us.

Chocolate mashed the gas pedal down to the carpet and the street got swallowed up in a cloud of smoke as the back tires brutalized tar. When the truck lurched forward the tools in the toolbox clanged like they were trying break through the cab.

After launch I remembered skipping breakfast this morning, my stomach had knots in it where the food should have been and there was a bad feeling like even those weren't going to stay down. Acrid bile stung my throat as she jerked the steering wheel left to angle in front of a bus coming in hot, upshifting in the opposite direction of the ruined Camaro. I was ready though, for thorns or roses or riches or ruin. Before I just thought I had come prepared but when the stripper shot up the median on full tilt her speed turned me on like cocaine never could.

Chocolate whipped the 4×4, snapping the big truck in a tight half circle until it leaned hard as she sailed us up into another shopping center where a sandwich shop and a nail salon were connected on both sides of a sprawled out pharmacy. The ATM sat near the edge of the blacktop next to the street behind a clustered row of baby trees on the curb protecting it. The van was there, all white, blacked out back windows, no markings on either side and a license plate with all the numbers crammed together and no spaces in between them. It could have been a maintenance truck coming to make repairs but the bald man shoving money down the back of the machine told me don't be a fool.

Admittedly I'm not always right, my pencil ain't the sharpest, my crayon isn't the brightest, my motor doesn't run quickest. Maybe it's because of the drugs. Still, I know what I know and I knew Chocolate had done this before when she pulled off the perfect slingshot. That's when a driver rips the emergency brake and jerks the car in a 180 so whoever's riding shotgun can spring out like he's jumping from an airplane. I've seen it done in movies, never once in real life, but when she skidded the truck sideways all the sudden I got the full effect.

Before my shoes landed the bald man looked up. He knew what he knew just like I did and he didn't need to see a watch to know what time it was. He went for the magnum on his waist until I pointed the Draco straight at his nose. "Huh-unh, don't do it. Now, you be cool and all this is gonna go smooth."

His fleshy hand hovered low over the dirty Harry. He had ex-cop written all over him, complete with a potbelly and a Monopoly man moustache. "You're making a big mistake son. You know who's money this is?"

"Quit talking. Lay on the ground."

He stayed still. "You know who I am. I'm a fucking depu-"

He was talking too much, I turned the Draco around and swung it like a baseball bat. When the wood connected ex-cops teeth cracked and that's when Cerrio arrived. I didn't hear him creep in, he wasn't high on anything, just fixed on destiny. He wasn't nice, not the type who said "you go first" while time was running out. He came to get this money either by force or something that could get him a little more notoriety. And he knew Chocolate was behind him watching in a big way with two lips smiling and the other pair sweating.

Ex-cop spat and a white nugget trailed with blood hopped on the ground. The Draco was still turned around, my grip was choked up on the barrel to swing again until both doors on the money van swung open. The kid jumping out was a lion. Six foot six, high and tight haircut, steel bands of muscle bulging everywhere. Twice as young as his partner holding an MK-5 that could spit rounds like sunflower seeds. He had me and I couldn't do a thing about it with my gun turned around the wrong way. The bald dick on the ground smiled wickedly, all his life he had waited for a day like this when a robber went down in a spray of gunfire. Coming on the heels of my own violence I guess fair is fair.

Spectators glued to the pharmacy windows and ducking behind shopping carts peering through the metal like rats in a cage waited to see me die. I tensed while the eyes studied me hungrily. An explosion sounded like a cannon boom and in the corner of my vision a bright ball of orange fire roared right about the same time a shower of pink mist sprayed the Monopoly man's cheek.

Inside my ski mask breathing came fast and ragged with a little bit of spittle clinging to the fabric. I was still alive and the shopping center parking lot reeked of charred skin. The scene was like a crash, tragic and delicious and horrible all at once. Socks stood close to the truck pointing the Mossberg that no one really wanted. The lion was gone. A second ago that muscled chest in front of me could have bench pressed a tractor, now it was blown open and steaming in the cool morning air. The MK-5 clattered on the ground because you can't hold a gun without a shoulder and then the back of the crew cut banged hard against the money van's rear bumper as he went down gurgling by a tire.

Ex-cop changed his tune and threw his hands high, "take it, take it. Take the shit. Take everything."

His arms were above his head while the wider eyed faces in the windows scrambled for cover. I felt something warm between my fingers. Looking down I saw the dead man's blood seeping through my glove, drying quick on my hand to make the skin beneath smell like pennies. More back spray was on my shirt and some splattered across the white van mixed with bits of blood and tissue like a textured paint job.

Socks reached down to pull the revolver off the bald man's hip and tucked it in his belt. Past the fallen body I saw more boxes like the one the ex-cop brought to fill up the ATM with. Seven more were crowded in on the left wall side by side. The right had a one plank bench with a thin cushion where the dead lion once sat waiting for his moment.

There's no time to move it all to the stolen truck. The sirens were already in range, a dozen of them wailing in earshot while I'm trying to hold down the panic. The cavalry was riding in, firefighters, ambulance, SWAT. Socks pressed the hot sawed off barrel against the aging man's cheek. "Keys!" he ordered. Yesteryear's finest twisted his scabby mouth downward in a last protest. But when the 12 gauge cocked his bravery withered and died right next to his partner.

Me and the brother I chose may not have might not have made it all the way through school, well I didn't anyway, but both of us were smart enough to know who's life meant more than ours. Ex-cop was white and we were not. He had a badge once upon a time and right now we were robbers for the second occasion this week. So, we left Chocolate behind like an old problem and took him with us in the van. All the shoppers watched the white Dodge peel rubber as we screeched away. In a jam the

Monopoly man would be a hostage, a pawn in this new phase of the game. And in a real fucked up situation he would become my shield.

Chocolate stared on in disbelief as Socks whipped the van around a sharp turn and tore out of the shopping center. I kept my balance in the back trying to hold the Draco steady to the bald forehead on the bench cushion. He hated me, this fucking old cop, the feeling seethed in his black eyes like tears of joy or the heartbreak of depression. With us was his partner's assault rifle sliding around on the floor. The only reason I brought the MK-5 is because I thought she was too pretty to wind up in some precinct evidence locker.

Socks blew a red light and the cop flicked a glance as the weapon skittered towards the door. "Don't try it," I growled.

He shifted his weight on the small bench. "You really think you're gonna get away with this? There's a shitload of money in here. Powers that be ain't just gonna shrug it off like nothing."

"Free health advice. Shut the fuck up and you can live longer."

His split lips curled a little, if it wasn't for the pain in his face they might have actually formed into a fully blown smile. "I'm an important man. You know that? They're gonna give me a medal and give you two assholes the chair."

Up front Socks swerved. Behind us a black and white cruiser with two uniforms inside came just close enough to see the wind dried blood splatter painting the van's back door. They hit the lights and the sounds and the bald man howled with pleasure. Socks tried to gun it but the money and the metal boxes and the big, slow, van mocked us. We had a full load and not enough horsepower to flee a supercharger on an open stretch of road.

He took a hard right to get away then an extra hard left that almost put the Dodge on two wheels. All the wild steering made me topple backwards against the cash boxes. I lost the gun and hit my shoulder against a sharp steel corner. Ex-cop saw his chance and leapt off the bench to pin my right hand down with a knee while the Draco spun next to us like a top. He had me down raining hits, clocking me with no real distance to miss. He got the nose, mouth, and chin. His hands were big but every knuckle was buried under a thick layer of fat. Maybe the cushion kept his fingers warm in December but it tickled in a fight.

Socks takes the van off road for a second and the bald cop stops to wring his hands. Stupid. You never stop when you're fighting for your life. I smile under my mask. "You hit like a bitch." He punches me again and winces with brand-new pain. "Fucking punk!" he screams.

Another sharp turn put the van on the sidewalk. When it jumped the pedestrian concrete ex-cop's knee barely lifted up a half inch off my hand but that was still too much. I slipped my arm free and stretched out for the lost Draco. It was an odd angle. I felt the tip of my pinky nail just scratching the metal of the barrel before the money van slammed down off the sidewalk so hard my teeth clacked.

The rifle popped up high, when it came back down the handle landed dead center of my palm. In one smooth motion I clutched and swung. The Monopoly man's eyes rolled back in his head, on the second hit he went down sideways and I hopped up like a running back getting off the turf. Socks jerked left, I went down again on the fat cop's body. He wasn't dead. I could hear him snoring through his nose but the sirens were so close now that my ears felt like they were bleeding.

I turned around and grabbed a piece of wall to stay steady. "Socks, get us home!"

"I'm trying, brother! They're too fucking fast!" he screamed.

"Just get us out to the highway!"

He changed lanes, side swiped a Miata and sped the wrong way up an interstate off ramp. The sirens were still ripping the morning but at least they'd lost a little intensity. I wobbled to the front and clung to the grill separating the money van's cargo space from the seats up front.

"How we doing?"

Socks checked the mirror, shook his head. "I lost one but there's still a pair of 'em on us. Those goddamn Hemis they ridin' ain't no joke. And we're in this fucking box." He smacked the steering wheel. "Faster you stupid bitch!"

Now, this part is for Bandy. So, when they talk about me like I'm an animal make sure it's known how I did my best to bring her home.

On the floor ex-cop was coming to more and more. He touched his jaw gingerly with a bruised hand trying to reassemble the events from seconds ago to manifest the reason about why it is he couldn't talk. Before he had it figured out I pulled him to his feet and had him dreamwalking. He was sluggish, a side effect of the abuse, but he moved like I wanted straight to the back doors. When I kicked them open brisk morning air and exhaust fumes rushed through the van all the way to the driver's seat. Socks stole a quick glance over his shoulder, he couldn't read my mind but he recognized the wasteland in my eyes.

Outside a pair of Crown Victorias were hot on us, lights and sirens still going like we might give a shit and pull over. One floated in the other lane putting them side by side and Socks set the Dodge van over the yellow line to play defense driving dead center of the road. Up ahead a semi slowed down, airbrakes hissing like a serpent bitch. In his sideview mirror a uniform barked into his radio for help. Behind him the Draco ratcheted back.

When I screamed "no more turns!" he didn't ask why. Just held the money van steady and raced straight towards the eighteen wheeler. We were fucked anyway. So, I shot the Monopoly man in the right leg behind the knee. Bone fragments sprayed through the air like angry skunk piss and he was screaming over the sirens as I stood by dispassionately. Slow motion as he went down, legs folding in and his spine going the other way. Before he hit the deck I put a boot in his back and shoved.

The body twisted in the air over the road like a figure skater on ice. I watched him spin in the wind in some elegant death dance until he crashed bald head first into the cop car windshield glass like a rock smashing pottery. The Crown Vic braked, skidding and sucking the broken body underneath the front tires and then halting over the top of it and then there was just one left.

Socks swung over and committed to the left lane just in time to miss the truck laying down on his air horn. The last cruiser filling the empty spot on our bumper rolled hard with us as we blew by slack jawed drivers terrified at the edges of the road. I upped the weapon one more time and went Rambo, squeezing the Draco until it had nothing left and was just a hollow piece of metal. I yelled when I opened up, yelled off the top of the mountain as I swung in the van like a rodeo cowboy and flamed the police. I don't know where the bullets went, didn't think to count them, didn't watch where the holes perforated. The cop car veered left and plowed through a speed limit sign straight into guardrail and I beat my chest like King Kong.

Then, the helicopter came.

CHAPTER 62

TOWN IMAGE

Edwards sat in his office blowing smoke through a desk fan. Soon as he came back through the precincts front door on Saturday afternoon the detective slammed his manila envelope full of Cerrio's mugshot pictures face down in the trash can. Now, it was Monday. The weekend had ended but the idea of retirement had come back with a fierce resurrection after what happened at the hospital.

How an old woman clipping grocery store coupons could possibly afford a private nurse is something he wondered about for a day and a half. During one of his wife's rants he realized those little rectangular slips of paper Barney's mother spilled out of her purse were exactly how she made the cost fit into her budget. That should have been rookie knowledge. Any zero experience, day one out of the academy, no name douchebag kid would have added it up immediately. But there he was blowing the dust off the crevasses of his old brain on what should have been a fishing weekend just to gain control of the obvious.

Only problem was the cigarettes. He couldn't retire and stay at home all day with a wife who hated smoking. Hell, he wasn't even supposed to smoke here with his feet up on the desk. Nobody would say anything to him at the precinct, though. Edwards had been here since forever and he was old enough to remember when these little cancer sticks were romanticized. Especially in this town where tobacco had practically built everything. Now, it was all so much more complicated and his kind of relaxation was almost as criminal as bank robbery.

He pulled on the filter and held his breath. Before the tar and nicotine could spill over his lungs like a mud avalanche Edwards office door flew open with sonic force. Fingers of smoke whipped around the ceiling as the draft of wind met his habit. The old detective dropped his full flavored in a cold cup of coffee and it died with a sizzle. He took his shoes off the desk and sat up straight so fast the casters on his rolling chair almost cracked in half. Michelle Heinrich in the door gripped the knob as aromatic grey wisps dissipated into thin air.

Edwards coughed in his fist. "Shit, Heinrich don't you knock? What's going on that you just barge into my office?"

"I got something I think you're going to want to hear, sir."

"It better be important. I'm busy right now."

Michelle nodded politely. "Yes, I see."

Edwards pointed to a chair. "Take a seat."

"If you don't mind I think I'll stand, sir."

"Fine, get on with it."

"I just got a call from Chatham County sheriff's office."

"Where the hell is that?"

"Savannah, Georgia. On the river, sir. They say they're investigating two shootings. One a homicide. The other isn't. Unofficially they're both related."

"Every crime is done in a vacuum, Heinrich. Unofficially it's all related."

"Yes sir."

"So, what does all this have to do with us up here in North Carolina?"

"The victim that lived is the one we're looking for, LaDecerrio Lloyd. Deputies down in Georgia say he came to the hospital with no ID and an nonfatal wound in the arm. The detective's there wanted to ask him questions only he snuck out before anybody could talk to him."

Clyde Edwards thought about it. "Or slap some cuffs on him. If LaDecerrio didn't have any ID how do the they know it's really him?"

"Emergency room surveillance video."

Heinrich pulled a slip of paper from her pocket that had letters and numbers scrawled all in pencil. She never had what you called good handwriting. All that chicken scratch she put down was the Chatham County cop's information who told her about the facial recognition software that matched the hospital footage with the Department of Corrections mugshot. His name, badge number, desk phone digits for the lead officer in Winston to contact him on the follow up. Unofficially the Savannah cop had also offered to buy Heinrich a drink but she left that part out.

She held the paper to her senior. "A deputy named Addison compared the footage with Lloyd's mugshot from prison. He put it through facial recognition and all points came back a perfect match."

Edwards took the paper with the two fingers he used to smoke. Heinrich backed away a step. She held both arms behind her back from a habit practiced in cadet training.

"Are you going to call him?" she asked timidly.

Edwards shook his head. "No."

"Why?"

"Because it's too late to call."

She blinked. "Well, what are you going to do? I mean, we've been looking for this guy all over the place and they say he was last seen in Savannah."

"Exactly." The detective stood up and snatched the pack of Marlboros off his desk. "So, that's where we're gonna go."

CHAPTER 63

BITTER EXTRAS

In the valley of crack decadents expect the unexpected. A knife in the back is not unusual. I should know, unusual is my middle name. After we had all the cash I asked Socks if he planned on double crossing Chocolate right from the beginning. That question came out of pure curiosity. Not like if he'd told me yes I would have held it against him. From the driver's side of the van he looked at me long and strange. It was tough to tell if those hooded eyes were glimmering with shock or just plain out disbelief at what we had done but driving back to Georgia gave me an opportunity to sort it all out in the front of my mind.

Bobby's mama let me use the Buick that used to belong to her husband. The Cutlass had vanished, best guess is Aunt Denise had come and gotten it back. I could see her riding away from Chevy's vacant apartment ill because her car had been rode hard and put away with no gas. So Socks borrowed the old LeSabre from Mrs. Linda and said, "he needed it for something really important." At least he never lied but when he tried to pay her with rocks I wouldn't let him. That earned me another strange look,

✦ 580 ✦

maybe he thought I was going soft. He could be right, or maybe I'm just growing up.

Where I was weakest my brother was strong because he never had faith in a woman. A definite coldness came with that kind of strength that I couldn't comprehend no matter how hard I tried. Part of me envied his attitude, the shunning of a species so charming must be a special sort of freedom. But the other side of me thought my brother might be a droid. Of course, I knew he had feelings, sometimes he doubled down on them like a few weeks ago when he punched me in the street. But feelings and whatnot didn't mean much because the way he was is what got us through the jam.

He assured me that everything extra was just in case Chocolate got crafty. Like say, if she would have took us off course to get killed by Yhay Yuda and his "cousins," or some other wild shit like that. I nodded. I believed him because he was my brother and he was all I had, no more women around me in the struggle anymore. Plus, when it came to the dancer with the deep skin nothing was unimaginable, just like me kicking a man out into morning traffic wasn't a pretend hallucination.

When the news chopper spotted us over the highway it should have been over. Socks aimed the Dodge into a thick patch of fog like that one hanging over the first ATM where we waited for the marks who had already came and went. The van doors hung open in the back swinging on their hinges like butterfly wings. I had hands braced against both sides while the road wind whipped my black hoodie like a state flag. The helicopter camera-man angled his lens down with one eye shut so his other could focus on a good shot of my face. A close up was the dream. All that saved me from it was that sweaty ski mask soaked with blood and saliva.

We plunged deeper into the cloud doing eighty and Socks screamed at me to "close the goddamn doors!" I slammed the van shut as he skirted sideways on a half donut and whipped up on the interstate off ramp that cut us straight to the Asheville Zoo. We hit that exit at light speed with the money van backsliding and the wheels spinning hot. I was falling all over cash boxes dizzy as hell with a queasy gut and a hand groping out trying to cling on to anything. My stomach hated it but at least we lost the bird stalking over us. I guess Channel 8 thought we would speed down the highway forever going the wrong direction. Nobody in media imagined these two niggas might just be smart enough to turn around.

I flashed my eyes in the Buick's mirror. A Ford riding behind me through the first hints of dusk had its parking lights on. I remember Bobby getting picked up from in front of our red brick elementary school in this same vintage whip. His father loved this car, treated it like a baby, bragged to Bobby's uncles about the soft leather like he was talking up a woman. But he was dead now and here I was steering it all alone. Socks wanted to make the trip down to Georgia with me, damn near begged to come, but I couldn't risk anyone else getting hurt. No more pain, at least of that variety.

Up ahead I-95 curved, just enough daylight hung in the sky to see the road bending in the distance before it faded around a crowd of trees that reached up like the Statue of Liberty. Behind the wheel it looked like the most direct path to nowhere. When I checked the LeSabre's dashboard the gas needle leaned hard left, the way this car swallowed unleaded at least I knew I wasn't going nowhere fast.

Socks had a muddy Windstar hidden in the lot at the Asheville Zoo, a soccer mom ride. He parked it far from the entrance where you come in, hid it good against a wall of pines that were growing up into a jungle and put the red streaked Dodge right in the next spot over so the vans were backed up side by side. We moved the money fast. Standing in the brush high on our homicides, heaving cash boxes like movers do sofas. I felt overgrown weeds scratching my shins and wild vines snagging my boots like some mischievous kid in the leaves was tugging my laces.

One of the boxes sliced down in my palm between the knuckle crease. I didn't feel a thing. Later on when the rush of murder and money died away like a day old fruit fly it started to itch. By that time I was crashing so hard with so many thoughts blowing up in my mind there was no room left for the pain to break through. I was thinking about everything, this mess and what came after it finally ended when four bent fingernails pulled off a half dried scab. It stung but didn't hurt and I smelled that same copper scent of pennies that pervaded the air after Socks blew the Mossberg. Smelling more made me wonder about my own viciousness that had come wide awake.

When I pulled into a gas station Yhay Yuda called. The Buick wasn't off yet before my new burner phone made vibrating chatter in the middle console. He blew a slew of different inquiries that all meant the same thing. Was I on the way? Where was I at now? What exactly did I have? I listened to the fundamentals shoot off gummed up in his thick accent while pulling money from a Nike duffel loaded with essentials. I had a Mack-11 and pounds of blue Benjamins. I slipped one out to feed the Buick's massive tank, any change I'd use on food and Newports. Probably just Newports.

Drowning in cash should never feel this way but really what else should suffocation be like? This hapless style of living, jumping off from one zero-hour moment to the next could be called a life of adventure. It was fun at first, everything new is, now it turned into this thing where I felt like I was swimming vigorously through the rapids. My arms were tired. I couldn't kick my feet anymore. I wish I could give up and drown. Just die for a little while until the emergencies blew over.

Yhay Yuda didn't want me to forget about his big favor. He reminded me that the train to Florida, or Chicago, or Saun-Juan-the-fuck-somewhere-else was being held up all for me and my priorities. I knew what I was hearing was pimp talk, a sneaky way of trying to trick my conscious into feeling an obligation for something. And even if I don't particularly like the man I couldn't discriminate against his wits. He had a savage, cold style and a hidden aggressiveness veiled under good manners. Pay attention and I could learn a lot from him even though I still had that one weakness. Femme's. My brother on the other hand had none, no vulnerabilities, no Achilles heel, no soft spot for a woman. I don't know if Yuda would take him, though. Socks wasn't his people but he was definitely mine.

All those cash boxes we strong armed had locks on them. They were married to the steel casing in two places on the sides like briefcase clips. Deep in the woods where the sound of metal crashing on metal couldn't find its way out Socks and I took turns knocking a sledgehammer over each one. It was labor, the little money safes were built for punishment and they tested the will of every back and arm muscle in my anatomy. In the end they were weak against my will. I hit from every angle, top, bottom, lefts and rights until the wooden hammer handle blistered my palms.

The sky broke open and Socks took his turn as the downpour came. Heavy drops pattered the thirsty earth turning bone dry dust into muck that looked like cake frosting. Every time he brought the tool up high his boots slid backwards digging a deeper trench. It looked like torture, sluicing through the earth's wet porridge, wielding a heavy hammer that cramped your knuckles, but sitting on the Windstar's front bumper it all felt incredible to me.

That fucking soccer mom van meant everything. It was the plain dash of simple genius that changed our heist from virtually destroyed to absolute certainty. When I asked why he brought it to the zoo Socks wiped rainwater off his forehead and said, "he knew to do it after Desirée told him all about Chocolate's plan."

On a night that couldn't have been too long ago Winston-Salem's most salacious daughter got drunk trying to kill the gunshot pain in her thigh. No one knew why she picked up the phone after that fourth cup of vodka and dialed Desirée to spill it all. Maybe she thought she was ordering Domino's but personally I think it was the painkillers. Mix those in your alcohol and you might wake up anywhere the next morning. Anyway, she was in rare form, and while Chocolate ran her mouth on one end of the line Socks' baby cousin grabbed a pen and took down the finer points of her plan on a yellow pad used to make lists for the grocery store. All of this went down before we ever robbed the bank.

Desirée was a master note taker. I mean, you couldn't ask for better. She had everything crucial laid out on that yellow pad, from the distance between each cash machine located around Asheville to the third and fourth escape routes. With that and a little help from the internet she cooked up her own heist route for us and gave it to Socks before we all took it to The Rose Petal on Sunday night. The whole time we were robbing and shooting he had that banana colored slip in his pocket like a credit card. When he pulled it out to show me I stopped and stared. That's when I saw his weakness, the same time when I saw that he really did have faith in woman. Otherwise how could he trust this perfume soaked map as our final guide?

Seventy miles out of Savannah my thoughts changed from one woman to the other. The way they stayed in my mind I should have charged double for the rent space. Chocolate had the corrupt gift on naked exploitation but that was so exhausting. What I really need is a woman like Desirée. Someone strategic and saucy with those everyday good looks and baby making curves. Thinking back that sort of defined Chocolate in a nutshell. Big difference is Dez would actually look out for a man, she had proved that in writing.

Chocolate was wrong about one thing, though. I don't mean the locks on the boxes or even being late to the first stop. Her numbers were off, she quoted forty thousand to fill every ATM but it was more like forty-two. Sometimes the boxes we destroyed had more but never less. There was even one with fifty thousand in it, must have been Jimmy Watson's juice money to kill any potential buzz about his fetishes. Me and Socks agreed to keep the extras secret but I told him if the dancer ever came back he had to give her what's fair, minus what it cost for being tardy to the first stop. Errors have consequences.

That extra money didn't mean a lot. I only thought about it inside the gas station looking up at a Western Union sign put right beside the register. I bought a full tank of premium 93, a box of long Newports, a sandwich that the clerk had to heat up in a quick cook microwave. While American cheese melted over roast beef I made up a money order. A quiet debate kicked off in my head to find a nice, easy number. When the timer rang I settled on an even thousand. I put the figure down right over the name Seville James and a one sentence message with a dotted i at the bottom.

Get back to the Marriott.

CHAPTER 64

GHOST TRAIN

Istepped out of the Exxon into the full-blown evening. The cool air was dirty, tainted by fumes and crisp from the Atlantic Ocean. Confused by the rules of reasoning because I know only hot breezes carry odors. Swamps, garbage, and dead bodies murdered yesterday blow through in the heat but Autumn winds always pass by pure. Unless a lowly man sticks his fingers in nature, then it's anything goes.

It was a puzzling enigma shaming common understanding down into corner and while I stood there finishing my disbelief the weather bit in like a hungry bear. The air blowing on my face was striped with pollution, a fresh cigarette dangling from my lips added flavor to it like kitchen seasoning. Before I took a second drag on the filter twin orbs of stark halogen white cut through the early night like back teeth on celery and then died fast in a split second.

A car reversed easy trying to fade in with shadows, I could hear four wheels whining backwards. The sedan tried hard to camouflage with the evening but high street lamps gleaming off the sheet metal like a full moon on the river snitched on its presence.

I watched close while suspicion rode in on a fresh breeze and the whip across the street waited for a break in traffic. Painted dark, somewhere between a midnight blue and the hue of middle space beyond the stars just like that Ford riding behind me with the yellow parking lights on. I counted up the seconds until the motor eased off in a slow sayonara. Twenty-one passed, at twenty-one and a half it sailed by upshifting at the end of first gear before the headlights cut on again.

After that I rode the last leg of the trip high on paranoia, burning menthols back-to-back down the interstate on a nicotine marathon. Mrs. Linda didn't want me to smoke in here but she was at home and she'd never know. I blew the clouds up to a slim crack in the top of window and stalked the mirrors watching the road behind me much more than the road stretched out in front. Family sedans reflected back much closer than they appeared. Although none rode with the lights off they all looked suspicious. In fact, the whole road was made up of suspicious vehicles that had men and women drivers and child passengers petting dogs and random people riding in peace.

No music drifted out of the Buick back windows, just ashes flying back into history across the Talmudge bridge. A tall sign on the other side flashes the time, a quarter past ten when Mrs. Linda's LeSabre crossed into Savannah and here I was, back to where the future hung only by a thread. I could hear it dying, breath gasping for air over the broad river just like Chevy once told me she heard her mother's voice calling to her on the boat. But all that was over with now, archived in another era like a year ago's news.

I thought about Bandy and how if all these dead presidents riding beside me didn't get her back I'd burn Georgia down. Me and this pack of Newports and this Mack-11 all by my goddamn self just the same way I was born. That wasn't going to happen, though. Because she was coming home. I was going to bring her back to Chevy and reunite the cousins like they do in all those daytime talk shows. Maybe take home an Emmy while I'm at it.

If anybody asked I'd tell them that's why I wanted her to go back to the Marriott in the first place. Because the nice hotel on the river would be so much easier to find after I found Bandanna. Not true, if I could track a kidnapped girl twice in a month then I could find a shitty motel just by smelling. Truth is some stubborn part of me just couldn't let go of Seville. She was still mine, my woman, my rib, my responsibility, and I just hated to think about anything of mine being in some doghouse riddled with danger. I know, I know, I know she was way past money and far over my apologies like a runner over the hurdles. But seeing how fast prices went up in this town a thousand bucks to keep a girl out the trap was a good bargain.

My arrival back in Georgia didn't stay secret for long. Yhay Yuda called again, he timed me coming down from South Carolina like a fucking track coach. When his stopwatch clocked four zeroes then he picked up the phone to clap off another round of questions. I got to realize that's how he started conversations, by using common inquiries that spun into useful information. I found that ah-ha moment, a silver lining carved out of this game of quizzes, but it would still be another year or two before it sunk in that that's the same way he maintained power too.

He gave simple directions, go to Truman Parkway, drive to Highway 80, wait for another call. I gave him some back. Yhay Yuda didn't know Bobby's mama from a mall Santa Claus but I told him no matter what happened tonight make sure Mrs. Linda gets her husband's car back. He swore to Allah on his manhood that he'd grant me that one thing. So, if he breaks his word then I guess we'll both be in hell together.

I never been to east, Savannah. Just another thing not considered until careful consideration didn't mean much anymore. Driving on the Parkway is when reality seeped in and the storm kicked up.

See, I had run a hard distance and that was by anyone's standard. But I did not want me and Socks laughing out loud about the bodies left in our wake while they secretly haunted us in our dreams. All that feigned humor would just gloss over the pain until somebody up and asked, "what about the girl?" All those best laid plans and spur of the moment murders meant nothing if Bandy got on that train going down to Florida. If she didn't come home then all of this was pointless.

And what about destiny? What about good and bad weighed on the scales with no more help and no more seasons left to make things more even? This is my destiny, if Bandy doesn't make it back than neither do I. It was clear as that. Because loyalty is the only thing that's not a menace if it never swerves, it's not fashionable, not if it's real. It's that nagging woman in your ear and she's loud because she knows you know she's right. So, it was either Chevy's cousin, or me, or the whole three of us. We were links in a chain, pull one and rest go down like the crew with its ship.

A Georgia Trooper blew by in the passing lane. His tan on white cruiser was a needed distraction from the truths coming down on me like the fat drops splattering all over the windshield. I left the parkway, found Highway 80 running right by a marsh, the stench of rotten mud went in my mouth and sat on my tongue trying to make it down my throat. I shook out another long 100 and pulled the cigarette free using my teeth. When I lit up that's when the G-wagon came up to hover on my side.

The boxy SUV drove close, edging towards the car like it was trying to shove me off the shoulder. I didn't waver when it crossed the solid white line like it wanted more road, the Buick was a ship, anything that hit me would pull off looking for a body shop. I held the Newport in my teeth and rode parallel with the Benz truck around a curve for a flat twenty yards before it sped up and cut me off. The brake lights flared and we dropped speed before my burner phone clattered in Mrs. Linda's center console again.

Yuda was on speaker. He echoed another easy instruction while I blew a smoke plume off the windshield. Two words, "follow us."

"How did you know what car I was in?"

"How?" he asked with smile in his voice.

"Yeah, how you know?"

The guerilla pimp laughed. "Because you told me to bring it back when were done."

Fuck.

East Savannah is gangland. Personally, I've never been in a gang. I always told people it's because I'm too independent but truth is the cliques in my city just never liked me. I'm too different to be the same. I wondered if Yhay Yuda ever had that same problem because we were so much alike. Not that it mattered now, I had this bag of cash and a Mack-11 and a bunch of cops hunting me like a duck so there wasn't much missing from the life of a gangster. The coroner wouldn't know the difference anyway. My uncle used to say the cemetery isn't sorted by colors and sets, only sets of numbers. The year you come and the year you go and if you're lucky they might not be exactly the same.

The Mercedes truck hit its turn signal and took the cut down West Anderson street. The neighborhood changes from good looking family homes to trap after trap, plywood for shutters, local boys posted on the porches wearing the hoods colors. They stare intently at the black Benz as its wheels go over damp asphalt with a noise like a zipper being yanked. After the third lot it speeds up and flees around a corner leaving me alone in front of a burnt out brick house sporting dead grass in the yard.

Before I could feel setup my phone rang again. This time Yuda told me to stay. A minute went by with the Buick's engine clicking under the hood and the neighborhood cats trying to stay dry in the weeds and gangsters stirring behind me up the block. Without taking my eyes off the windows I reached deep in the Nike bag, shook out the gun, laid it across my lap. Funny how when the last thing you want to do is hurt anybody is always when it has to be the first thing on your mind.

This would be the time for that seedy dark Ford to come around with its lights turned down and pick me off. It could all be so easy, just pull up on the side and unload. No one would even care until tomorrow morning when the first fiend came to smash the Buick's glass and steal the radio. A perfect expectation but waiting on it I realized that a ending like that would make too much sense.

Minutes went by, enough to almost get complacent as if that might happen. After four of them slipped away a whip too fancy for the neighborhood bent the corner up the street. An Audi, I could tell by the rings interlocked across the grill. It crept the block at a crawl, hugging the curb with the side mirror floating dangerously close to a row of mailboxes built on rotting posts. It didn't feel right, but then how could it? I was waist deep in the game with no rules, parlaying with the villains on the board who didn't pay a sentimental tax on anything.

When the Audi braked I saw Salaam's brother alone up front. He looks at me, emerges from the car and stands full height on the cracked sidewalk dotted with dusty gum spots that have been stamped down and smoothed over by every heel in the hood. The living brother's face is another link in the chain of quiet things that don't feel right.

I hopped out of the American ride. "Where's the girl?"

A smirk pulled on the corners of his mouth. "She's here."

"I don't see her."

"She's here. Where's the money?"

I licked my lips with a tongue blistered from too many cigarettes. "If she ain't with you then what the fuck is this?"

"It's the exchange," he replied calmly.

"So where's your half?" I asked.

"You ask many questions. Too many without thinking. If it was up to me your friend would be gone already. She could be making somebody very happy right now. Yhay Yuda thinks that's not right, though. You're a lucky man, LaDecerrio. I never seen him do a favor big as this."

"I'm fucking flattered. Now, where's the woman?"

"Another question, huh?" He sniffed, nodded, pointed. "Fine, she's in the house over there."

Across the street from the burnt out place with the dead lawn was a squat house with trash bags over the windows. They blew in the wind, growing belly's that burped out as air swept through every room and a blue tarp stapled to the roof helped the rain go somewhere else other than straight down to the kitchen. It was funny in a sad way, like a short man who wants to play basketball or when my aunt forgets she can't get to the box of cereal on the top shelf in the grocery store.

Salaam's brother could be lying, it could be just another broken down house on the street. But he was right about one thing, I was a lucky son of a bitch even if I didn't know my own mother. Because if it wasn't for Yhay Yuda and his weird sense of mercy I wouldn't have even made it this far.

I showed him the cash me and Socks had stolen just for this moment. Salaam's brother watched me hold the duffel bag straight up and pull it open at the zipper like Superman ripping his shirt away. He blinked once while taking in the blue notes crammed in like shoes in a suitcase. Then, he stepped back when I threw the bag on the ground in front if his boss's mirror waxed Audi.

"Take me to Bandy before the money gets drenched," I said.

He hoisted the duffel from the wet ground. "Go on, you lead the way."

"Just give me the keys. I'll leave them in the mailbox when I know everything's good. You got my word."

He shook his head. "It's not that simple. There's more in the house than just the thing that belongs to you."

The thing, he said. Like Bandy was just a hollow object and not a flesh and bone woman. We stared at each other with something livid in our eyes. His seasoned with hate, mine wilting from a cluster of frustrations wearing me down like a dull knife. A perfect recipe for a meltdown because there was no reason to believe and everything to lose.

After this I need a vacation. Not like last weekend with the endless pressures and flagrant temptations spinning me like bike spokes in every different direction as I spiral out of control. I'm talking a real holiday somewhere far off where I can gather myself. Put Cerrio back together again like Humpty Dumpty's glue.

I stepped swift, behind me I could hear Salaam's brother plodding his shoes through the grass. Somewhere in the overgrown yard I actually realized I had forgotten his name. To me he was just the brother who's brother hadn't made it after tangling with that flashy girl and my barking pistol. I missed my Remington, the Mack was good but it wasn't gifted, it was simply all I could get on a last minute's notice. Yhay Yuda mentioned his name a few times in the BMW that day we all rode together after I escaped the hospital but that seems like a lifetime ago. That little piece of forgetfulness ate at me up the lawn like a termite in a tree until I turned around to ask him and that's when the gun cracked my skull.

I heard bells ringing, thought somebody needs to answer that phone. I never been pistol whipped before, hurts like hell though. The ringing in my head came with an echo that sang out musical agony all the way down the spine. When I hit ground the Mack-11 jumped out of my hand and rattled on the chipped sidewalk too far out of reach. How do I remember his name now? Abdullah, it came back to me like a lost dog running back to his daddy while he jerked on my shoulder to roll me over.

"You came back," he hissed. "You and that bitch killed my brother. But you the stupid one who returned."

I shook my head as I laid in a puddle. "I didn't kill him."

"But you were there, and she was yours. And that's good enough for me."

He meant that Chocolate was mine. Part of his indoctrination was that I was supposed to control her in front of other men and I had failed. So, in the end even my own people hated me. Abdullah spit in my face, I could feel his warm saliva mixing with the cold rain down my cheek. I tried getting up to do something about about it until he put a foot in my side. He pushed down hard bouncing my head off my the ground.

"What's Yuda gonna do when he finds out about this?" I asked.

Abdullah grinned coldly. "He's never going to find out. After I kill you and your little girlfriend with the spots he'll have all his money and then all of this will be forgotten."

"Just like your brother."

He wanted to kick me again. Salaam's brother pulled his leg back and brought it forward fast right into my open hand. I caught the cuff of his pants right where the fabric was stitched. He didn't realize his angry mistake, how he'd reacted just like I wanted him to without thinking until I pulled and his back thumped the ground in a mud splash. Splatter erupted six different ways as I scrambled to get on top of him but I froze when he pointed his gun.

I could see the barrel winking at me in the light of the only street lamp that the delinquents had decided to spare with their driveway rocks. He squeezed the trigger so full of confidence but nothing happened. No loud bang or the flash of a muzzle because his hard fall had shaken the clip loose. It laid harmlessly on the last slab of concrete going up to the sagging porch like a dead branch.

Abdullah didn't rush, he rose off his back in a smooth motion like he had done this all before. I moved quick, pivoted off my back foot and crashed a fist into his chin. He stumbled sideways towards a bush and I tried catching him with another but Salaam's brother weaved and sliced the gun right into the same rib where he had kicked me before. It hurt like someone was trying to stitch up my side with a nail gun.

When you're fighting toe to toe always remember to breath and don't do it through your mouth, take the air in your nose and keep on working. I inhaled and the pain was scathing. Swung wide and Abdullah caught my arm and pulled me close. There was a quick moment where I got to reflect on my own mistake but everything else happened much faster. He put a foot behind my leg then pushed me back and watched me tip off balance and thud on the ground again in a splash of scum water. This time the stars around my head had grown into asteroids. They came in a deluge across my vision like an unleashing and I understood that these were the last moments.

Being paralyzed with everything happening all around you is something I never imagined much. Aunt Denise couldn't express the feeling well enough to do it justice. Now I knew what she lived through every single day. Laying helpless in the sopping grass I could hear him pick up the clip and slide it back in the handle. I willed myself to rise again and fight, for Bandy and Chevy's mama sitting somewhere in a redone bar shaking her head back and forth because it was never supposed to be like this. Nothing moved. I was too tired from running too hard for so long. All the robbing and shooting, smoking and fucking, lying and craftiness had finally caught up at just the wrong time.

Salaam's brother stood over me, looked down and spit again. He pulled the slide back on his pistol, aimed it, frowned and pulled the trigger. Over the pattering rain I heard the muzzle explode in the last clap of death that mingled nicely with the stars swimming on my horizon. Then, I went to sleep.

When my eyes closed a light broke through the darkness like a kiss of sun in the mist. It began as a blur, just a shadow on another shadow melting into each other like blots of wet ink drying on a canvas. Then, I focused hard and saw Bandy sitting on top of a piano singing the blues.

Her legs were crossed under a silk dress. The white spot on her mouth had vanished and the gold inside burst with the energy of a scream but her voice fell like a waterfall. That grand piano underneath was just for show, an instrument to remind me of the time when we were all so proud of one another. A harp played to her song, lilting notes that glowed all around her emanating some eternal passion for the sound of music that had set up shop deep in her heart when she was just a little girl singing to herself in a mirror with a hairbrush.

I felt proud again listening to girl from Winston-Salem. And we flashed through all kinds of luxurious places that weren't built for us while she sang better than before, through Madison Square Garden and Carnegie Hall and the ball rooms overseas donning clothes of silk. Her song was more candid than I'd ever known, dripping with harmony and a sweetness like honey poured over the dreamiest lies.

And the number ended and I turned to the audience expecting them to be in the fullest throes of applause. But when have things ever been as I expect them? There was a woman behind me with a face so pure it shined down like a beacon and cleansed my soul. She had prophesies in her eyes, sons and daughters in her smile, and I feared her as all man fears everything unknown on the other side.

Finally I blinked and when I looked again there was Judy sitting in her chair, motherhood unimpeded. She'd had her baby without being ashamed. I looked up trying to find the roof of her home and felt my neck crack. The glass house she lived in bounced light in all corners and when I rubbed my eyes they became watery. After the cloudy tears cleared the woman with the shining face who smiled down on me before reached a hand out. She touched my forehead and called my name. "Cerrio. Cerrio."

I tried pushing her finger away, she just tapped my skull harder and cried my name louder.

I avoided her. All I wanted to do was hear Bandy sing one more time but the voice rang in every empty space in the house of glass louder and louder. "Cerrio! Cerrio, get up!" I tried making my pleas. Just leave me alone, I thought. But today wasn't the day. Maybe tomorrow.

The light faded and when I open my eyes Desirée is kneeling in the grass screaming me back to earth. Her dreads draped over my face like pasta, water dripping off them down on my neck from the storm. She grabbed my cheeks with both hands and squeezed. "Can you hear me, boy! Come on, we gotta find Bandy!"

I struggled for words. I wanted to ask why the hell was she talking to me like a dog. Except my brain hadn't reloaded yet and through the downpour and woozy circuits in my head all I could do was lay there inhaling her body lotion. She smelled like limes.

"Up, Cerrio! Come on, get up goddamnit! Let's go!"

"Fuck you," I croaked.

She tilted her head sideways. "What did you just say?"

I told you I needed a woman like this, one who can rile me up, talk a little shit, come save me in a jam. In my peripheral I could see a little nine millimeter in her hand. Looking further I noticed a midnight blue Ford parked behind Mrs. Linda's LeSabre. It was her Equinox, the same car that rode me out to Cleveland projects to meet Chocolate and followed me over the bridge with its parking lights on.

Salaam's brother laid dead in the grass, his feet tangled up with mine in the same mud puddle. Deep crimson leaked from his neck and streamed out to feed the Georgia clay back his soul. The pounding rain kept the wound clean as his life poured off into the earth, ashes to ashes, dust to dust. He was a fairweather prostitute, here for the money, gone when I came back empty handed. Both of his eyes stared up in shock. I stared back like a fool knowing that look would reach me again in a nightmare coming soon.

"It was either him or you," said Desirée.

"Thanks, you saved my life."

"You owe me, motherfucker."

"Undeniably. The proof's right there." I turned to face her on my feet. "Where's Socks? He didn't come with you?"

"He's at home. He don't know I followed you."

"Shhhit, do you know what he'll do if somebody clips you out here? There's a reason I came by myself."

"Doesn't matter," she said. "I had to come. Your business is town business."

A drenched cat came up to sniff Abdullah's groin, trying to see what parts were good for food. Desirée tossed her hair back making the locks slap off the shoulders of her water heavy T-shirt.

"Did he tell you where Bandy was before you hit the ground?"

I nodded to the house. "Supposed to be in there."

"Then, why are we out here?"

She turned up the stoop and I plucked my Mack-11 back off the ground where it came to a halt before kicking in the door. We could have came in through a trash bagged window but you know me, I'm a kicker at heart. Desirée stayed behind me for a second until her vision adjusted. I was still fuzzy from getting hit in the head and the living room listed left as we walked through carefully on damp carpet that squished beneath our heels. There was rat shit in the corner and bird feathers on a mattress ripped open at the side. The whole place smelled like mildew.

Through the dank odor I treaded down a hallway that led into the kitchen. Down both sides were closed doors with deadbolts on the sides that locked from the hall. That was a good sign, it meant Abdullah hadn't lied because nobody puts in locks like that unless they're keeping prisoners. But this is not what I wanted, to be in a dungeon with all signs of death and torture looming across the threshold. Desirée turned to the front while I eased closer to the first knob. She whispered to me to hurry as the clouds fell down outside. I could hear the fat drops slapping the roof tarp while I reached a hand out for the faux brass handle. I twisted slowly, the door opened creaking wide on its hinges while I tried not to crawl out of my skin. Behind it could be anything, a man with a gun, a dead girl, a living one wishing she'd just pass on already.

When it yawned all the way I peeked my head around the scarred wood frame. Finally, I exhaled. A bare room with a blood stained office chair taking on water from a hole in the roof was completely free of danger.

"She in there?" rasped Desirée.

I shook my head and crept further into the house, deeper into hell before she could tell me to hurry up again. The next knob had a dent in it like somebody had tried to crumple the metal. As soon as I laid a hand down on it a squeal pierces the air. This time Desirée didn't have to ask so I didn't have to waste any precious seconds with a smartass answer. I used my foot again, kicking the door hard enough to make the wood around the deadbolt splinter like matchsticks. The squealing amped into muffled screams, between the rain on the roof and crashing in the hard way the extra noise was falsely gentle.

The door flew open smashing into a rubber stop down on the baseboard. Everything was still listing to the left but none of that mattered now. Dizzy or not I still knew who that was on the floor with her wrist chained to the radiator. She had her eyes covered with a paisley scarf double knotted in the back and another one stuffed in her mouth as a gag. Yuda's boys weren't stupid, they knew better than to mess up her face. Bandy didn't have any bruises or cuts because nobody wants a good time with a manhandled hooker.

Desirée ran to her and fell on both knees. She pulled the rags off her face and out of her throat and clutched the singer to her chest in a hug so tight it made the little singer wheeze. She looked her over. "Are you good? You okay?" Bandy nodded and cried. Then, she looked up at me and I had to turn my face away. By all accounts I wasn't ever going to see this woman again and now that I had it was all too much.

For a second I thought we might be taking too long. I expected to hear sirens whining up the block at any moment until I remembered what type of place this was, the type of place where cops don't come when the shots ring out. Why waste the gas when it's just people like us killing other people like us?

Desirée ran back out to the yard to get the key to Bandy's chains out of Abdullah's pocket. He's lucky he didn't swallow it, she would have cut his throat out on the lawn just to get to that thing. The girl in Bandy was all grown up now and she didn't need me to carry her out in my arms like I did on the south side. Another reason to be proud like when I saw her singing in my dreams. Her legs wobbled and I caught her underneath the arms to straighten up. The little singer was going to leave Georgia just the way she came, standing on her own two feet.

We were almost back out in the rain again when she froze in place. I looked at Desirée who didn't know what to think either. Here we were six inches away from freedom and the girl between us stopped moving like she wasn't ready to go yet. "Wait," she said. I spoke back softly, "what is it mama?" Bandanna didn't answer, instead she slipped away from me to walk a crooked line in the direction of another door on the side of the house. Without question I followed her with Socks' cousin following behind me, both of us holding on to the same blind faith that there was a good reason for the detour.

Our leader put her delicate hand on the knob but it wouldn't turn. Another locked entrance in the house of misery. Desirée handed me the keyring she pulled off Salaam's brother and after three tries I found the one that fit. There was no light on the other side when the door opened like a mouth into the sort of pitch blackness that makes your flesh cry. I brushed my hand against the wall groping for the switch. Sticky webs and a spindly insect touched my fingertips before I found the little plastic nub that kicked on a lonely bulb hanging down from the ceiling.

I looked around the garage, drab concrete floor with oil spills, massive rolling door, the smell of sweat and a long white van parked in the middle with no windows. I looked at Bandy who spoke with no words, just the simple sliding of both eyes from east to west. I followed her silent gesture and walked in carefully, clutching the wet automatic with my trigger finger ready and my heart slamming against my bruised rib.

My steps were slow, methodic, measured out in small paces across of the front end of the long Econoline with my back pressed hard against the bumper. Right at the corner I could hear the blue tarp on the roof slapping in the wind. The plastic flapped angrily against the shingles while I spun out with the Mack-11 pointed. I had it aimed straight. Finger tickling the trigger ready to let loose right into the faces of six lost women chained together for the long train ride to nowhere.

EPILOGUE

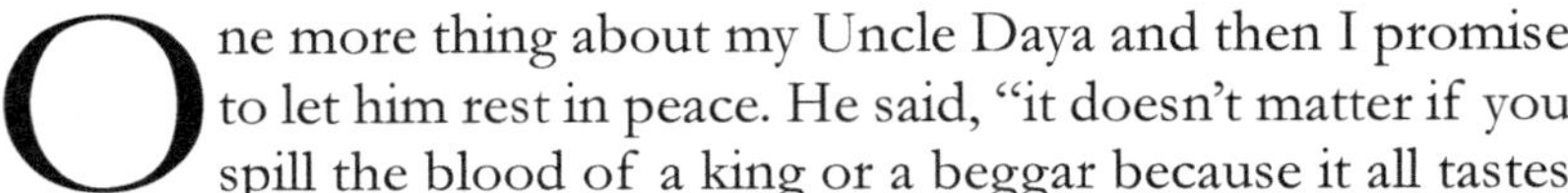

One more thing about my Uncle Daya and then I promise to let him rest in peace. He said, "it doesn't matter if you spill the blood of a king or a beggar because it all tastes the same when the dogs lick it up."

I thought about that on the ride back to prison. Staring at the metal cuffs in front of me I wondered who came up with something so vividly true. Was it the winner of a conflict or the one who got decommissioned? Words of victory sung from a balcony or a last testament before finally blowing this world? In the seat right next to me an old man wearing a Muslim kufi sneezed like he had a cold. His face looked penitentiary weathered like he had taken this ride a hundred times before. As the bus shifted gears down the highway I wondered more and more if my own features were starting to catch that same demeanor.

Me, Bandy and Socks little cousin were all long gone before they ever found the dead Arabian laid out in the front yard down in Georgia. By the time they got to Abdullah's rain bloated body, stray cats had eaten off the fleshy part of his cheeks. No one could prove I had anything to do with it. Not the lead detective, or his female minion, or even the Savannah cops who actually couldn't care less because they just wanted to take credit for the kidnapped girls found cold and starving in the garage.

Lucky me, but I couldn't ignore that everywhere I went people around me wound up in a bad way. Lying awake later looking up at the cell ceiling filled with nonsense scribbles born of idle and simple minds I thought about how that sort of thing was a testament to my life. Aunt Denise had passed too, she died that first night Bandy sang on the boat. Socks tried telling me while we were at Desirée's house hiding after the bank job but there was too much going on for me to listen. That's how it always is. I'm forever in the fast lane and it's just a matter of time before I spin out.

They held her funeral on the day I saw that boy split his chin in First African Baptist Church. Then, the detective who grilled me in the hospital towed the Cutlass away from Chevy's building with all the memories we left behind. After that he rode down to Savannah just to find yours truly. He had a hard on for me since that first time I wouldn't sign that folded Miranda paper living in his back pocket and now I'm fucked. He blazed into town with a hunch and a woman destined to make police captain and together they built a case against me that stuck like leeches.

They pinned me down after Detective Edwards flashed my photo around to the half dozen women chained up like slaves. He showed them my face on a glossy 8×5 in a tiny room over hot tea and warm blankets, soft touched their hands like he really gave a shit about their fate and they all nodded immediately. I couldn't blame them, it wasn't like they knew that the cop was taking advantage of a broken crowd. Every one of those girls on their way to Miami, or Dallas, or Juarez thought they were nominating me up for a medal when they said, "I was the one they saw in the garage. I was the one holding up the bronze-skinned girl with the gold tooth. And I was the one who saved them when no one else was even looking."

Edwards tried to bully the Chatham county prosecutor to hit me with a homicide. He was drooling to lock me up on murder in the first. The suits mulled it over in their ivory tower for a day before they let him down easy, shook their heads and told him the proof just wasn't there. That's when Winston started throwing it all at me. It started with the guy I thought Chevy killed in that yellow house on the south side. Next the trailer park shooting and then they rounded me off with the beat up trick from High Point. Every other week I was sweating out a new motion hearing for different charges, each one stepped up from the last like I was climbing up a legal ladder with a life sentence at the top.

They drug me in front of the same good ol' boy judge for what had to be ninth time in a row when Desirée finally showed up with a real lawyer. Not some public defender off the pile paid by the state to lose cases. She paid for the mouthpiece from all that ATM cash me and her heavy cousin hijacked. The attorneys name was John or Joseph, maybe it was Jerry. Fuck, I don't know. All I remember is how he kept poking holes in the government's cases until they were whittled down to the very bottom of their deck. When they pulled out that last charge for the illegal AR-15 hidden under a blanket in Aunt Denise's Cutlass then Jerry, John, Joe advised me not to call their bluff.

I signed for eight years on the dotted line, breathed a long sigh of relief and thanked my brother's lady cousin at a visit through the riot proof plexiglass. Except she didn't want any of my gratitude. Desirée never hired the attorney for me, she only did it because she thought I was a liability. Understandable, if the detectives ever found out everything I did this summer they'd be letting me out of prison in a pine box. She was shaky about how much pressure I could handle but I'd never tell about all the things me and her and Socks had gone through. Not ever. And it wasn't from some obligation born out of a woman saving my life in the rain. Snitching just isn't me, I'm a dog not a rat.

The chain bus stopped in Charlotte to pick up more men in jumpsuits headed for the penitentiary. We were on the way to Atlanta to an ancient federal prison famous for mice and roaches and staff infection. The new passengers filed on clanging leg shackles against the metal floor. Tired from being woken up too early for the longest ride they spent the smallest amount of effort possible hunting an open seat. It was a terrible comfort that I knew how the misery on their faces was just the beginning.

Last time I went up like this Chevy wrote to me for a little while. She sprayed perfume on her letters and dotted the i's with loopy hearts like we were still passing notes by the hallway lockers between class. I had this crazy idea that Chocolate would take her place with the pen on this bid. After six weeks in county jail I finally woke up and realized that hope was just me being stupid again. The dark strutting woman fell completely off the map. She cleaned out her apartment and her locker at Sugar Bares and skipped town without giving somebody so much as a callback number. Nobody told me but I knew she got her share of the cash just the same way when you know what month your birthday is on.

So, I was alone. Bumping along the interstate in chains watching people pass by on the road to do whatever they wanted today. If they got fired from work or wound up with no money it wouldn't matter because come tomorrow they would all wake up undefeated again. Seville James was among them now, at last she had enough and I couldn't be mad because God knows she deserved to go. I wished her well, her and the rest of the world out there looking forward to this coming weekend when they could get a break. And I was thinking about eight calendars from now when I could join them all again.

Eight years sounds like a long stretch. I wonder if Bandy will forgive me when the time is up. She was the last woman to escape Cerrio before the exit slammed shut. Every now and again I can still hear a song she sang on the boat playing back in my head. Funny how she left me but can't seem to find a way to put her voice in the past.

After ten more hours we came to the last stop. It snows in Atlanta and it was December, the week before New Years. Everybody got off with a hunch in their back trying to brace against the bitter chill whipping on a breeze. I could tell winter was going to be long around here.

Prison is the sort of place where wasting time is perfected. If the situation wasn't so sad it might have actually been kind of funny. Everybody from the bus sat in a big cell waiting for the next step in a sequence of something that would add up ultimately to an incredible amount of nothing. After the chains were off we took turns using the loud toilet in the corner while a flashlight cop went back and forth outside the bars calling us out one by one to ask if we were suicidal. Yet. If you answered no they gave you a new jumpsuit and whoever said yes went bye-bye for a while.

The question was worth less than the trays of slop we ate. I mean, if somebody really wanted to kill themselves why tell it? Through the grapevine I heard Taneesha hung herself at the King's Inn where I hid out for a while. I think that's just a rumor. The person who told me didn't give a single detail but that little piece of gossip still stayed with me even after I got my new jumpsuit on. It followed me back to a much smaller cell where me and the old man with the kufi didn't say one word to each other. I wanted to kill the thought of her body dangling, legs kicking, lungs wheezing, neck cracking, before it grew a life of its own and toured down the halls of my narrow mind. I tried calling Socks once to ask him to ask Desirée if she had heard anything from Bandy's girlfriend but these days his number was disconnected.

Eventually she came around in my dreams, that's where all the women in my life live now. Except Taneesha didn't have the animation that I saw in that cozy apartment where she made me try her sauces off a long wooden spoon. Instead, she swings limp from a noose. I tried waking myself up, all I needed was an opening but I was trapped in every way a man could be. Above my head white dots perforated the sky like stars. That's where the help was, in heaven where Chevy's mother watched over me like a newborn in the cradle.

But when I reach for her the constellation reforms into an evil face framed by blood and smoke. I squint and see Yhay Yuda smiling down on me with vengeance. He swings the end of Taneesha's rope from a finger and blows on her kicking legs. I had killed two of his and now he had one of mine. That still didn't make us even and I knew someday he'd be back because my people just don't know how to forget.

In the Atlanta federal penitentiary when the lights cut off hungry roaches crawl out from the cracks in the walls. The halogens stayed on all night to keep the vermin away and when my eyes popped open they buzzed on the ceiling like broken beard trimmers. I hopped off the bed, jumpsuit drenched in sweat, jaw aching, heart fluttering. The old man with the kufi watched me close. He asked if I'd had a bad dream. I said, "yes." He told me I was grinding my teeth. I said, "that happens." He told me there's pills for shit like that and I told him to watch it and then he turned over on his side to face the wall.

At the stainless steel sink I splashed water on my face. The cold liquid felt refreshing but it tasted filthy. It was oily with a hint of dirt like someone had washed their hair in the pipes. After trying for the fourth time I got tired of expecting a better flavor and looked up in the mirror. Staring back at me with bloodshot eyes was the one my aunt had told me about months ago. He was raw and flustered and full of agony. He was me, the man who lost everything.

www.ingramcontent.com/pod-product-compliance
Lightning Source LLC
Chambersburg PA
CBHW060256100726
47907CB00002B/180